THE COSMIC FOLLIES

By the same author:

Fiction:

A MOMENT OF SILENCE
THE THERAPY OF AVRAM BLOK
CITY OF BLOK
THE LAST TRUMP OF AVRAM BLOK
THE DEATH OF MOISHE-GANEF
THE SILENCER
YOUR MONKEY'S SHMUCK
RESURRECTIONS FROM THE DUSTBIN OF HISTORY
WHAT'S UP, GOD?
THE DAYS OF MIRACLES AND WONDERS

Non-Fiction:

IT'S A GIFT
MAN ON THE FLYING TRAPEZE: THE LIFE AND TIMES OF W.C.FIELDS
MONKEY BUSINESS: THE LIVES AND LEGENDS OF THE MARX BROTHERS
STAN AND OLLIE, THE ROOTS OF COMEDY: THE DOUBLE LIFE OF LAUREL AND HARDY
KEYSTONE: THE LIFE AND CLOWNS OF MACK SENNETT

Simon Louvish

THE COSMIC FOLLIES

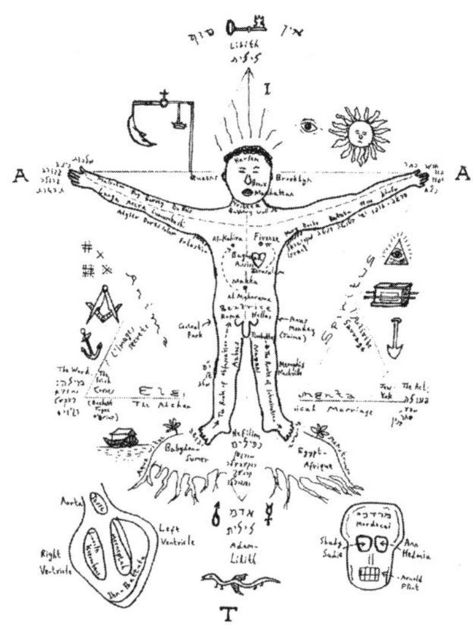

ICA & BlokBooks

THE COSMIC FOLLIES

First published in the UK in 2004 by
Institute of Contemporary Arts
The Mall, London SW1Y 5AH
in co-operation with
BlokBooks
7 Lysia Street
London SW6 6NF

Cataloguing-in-Publication Data
A catalogue record for this title is available upon request from the British Library.

ISBN 1900300419

This novel is a work of fiction. Any resemblance to persons living, dead, or in intermediate states in the currently recognised time-stream is entirely coincidental and incredible.

Cover art by Roger Brown: *Liberty Inviting Artists To Take Part in an Exhibition Against International Leftist Terrorism (IRA PLO FALN Red Brigade Sandinistas Bulgarians)*, 1983, © The School of the Art Institute of Chicago and the Brown family. Image courtesy of Phyllis Kind Gallery, New York.

Cover design by www.researchstudios.com

Printed & bound in the UK by Alden Press
Osney Mead Oxford OX2 OEF

DANGER!
KEEP OFF

Book 1:

Wind -
Hurricane Hilda

Fall 1992

ADAM.

He crawled out of the sea
at the Battery,
pulling himself up over the railings of the Promenade
to mingle and fade
with the tourists disembarking from the ferry ship Miss Ellis Island,
carrying their souvenir brochures
and gilded effigies of the Statue of Liberty
with her outstretched torch
and spiked crown
looking out over the tarnished town.
Other figures, in the shadowy rush
up the shoreline crush towards the Castle Garden
clutching their immigration papers and their hopes of a pardon
from the long life of misery and degradation.
The hopes of a new nation: Women in long black smocks and aprons and socks,
carrying bundles of clothes, children and babes.
Men in ankle length coats, kaftans, capes and grey beards under squashed cloth hats,
young boys carrying mats,
old men bent under their load,
old women with raisin eyes darting out the wrinkles of their doughy faces framed by black headscarves and shawls and laces
young women with white chemises buttoned up to the chin
children in ragged jackets held together with bits of string

young men in torn trousers and busting waistcoats
manhandling immense packing cases
onto carts already loaded to the aces
crates and boxes, piles of bedding
shedding pots and pans and a few family keepsakes of the Old Country,
some token sticks of furniture, a chair, a mirror, a framed portrait of grandpas, grandmas, uncles, aunts, brothers and sisters,
all their family members left behind,
to follow on at some future double blind.
The tourists, passing through them,
draining their Diet Colas and licking their ice creams,
pausing for a Hot Dog Shish Kebob Italian Sausage Knish or Beef Burger at the stall by the War Memorial, listening to the Jamaican street band -

"Ooo I'm bound too saay, I'm going awaay,
Won't be baack for many a daay..."

No one wants you to stay. The loudspeaker bawled out the last call to the next Islands ferry tour. But Mo moved away from the milling crowds, up around the Immigrants' Memorial along the benches of the Battery Park, pausing to relieve himself at the public urinal and luxuriating in the rare pleasure of hot tap water in a clean sink. Noting the nooks and crannies and cubbyholes and corners where a man could settle for a night's sleep, given a good hack a solid whack with a chisel on the padlock, or some fancy work with a bent pin. Moving on out the Park to the traffic din of Battery Place and State Street, across the road with a wave at the passing cars yellow cabs vans trucks buses prison transports rolling up to The Tombs. Crossing the street to Number 1 Broadway, by the Colonial Coffee House and Restaurant and the Post Office building along the railings of the Bowling Green. Its fountain's soft sheen, trickling away quietly, its olde iron benches basking in the autumn sun. The massive black bronze bull on the traffic island at the tip of the Green gazing blindly up Broadway. No way. Its big round haunch and hanging black balls thrust in his face. Can't take the pace. The solid paws pawing at the ornamental paving. The tail waving towards Wall Street and the financial center. Do not enter. He stopped to place his palm at the triangle of the smooth black anus, between the tail and the great round cheeks, but the giant animal stayed rooted in place, with nothing but the low rumble of the subways to express its paralysed shame.

"Fuck you ass, baby."

Another time maybe. But no one passing paid much attention to the ungainly tramp rubbing his black calloused hand upon the rump of the stone bull of Broadway, tickling its balls, running his fingers to the great stone horn in its belly pointing down to the pavement. "Only one teat, Goddamit." His stubble scratching against the bronze abdomen, his parched tongue receiving no nourishment. The golden horns of the beast pointing uptown.

"One hell of a tight assed mother."

The man lurched on up the road. His baggy camouflaged pants, his army surplus shirt and jacket, leopard spot hat and old army boots, the recognisable roots of the intransigent homeless, the multiple pockets sagging with trash bin salvage, the plastic bags draped around his wrist ravaged with scavenged loot. Bits of cardboard, plastic bottles, rusty forks, discarded cans, old straws, paper cups, half eaten fruit. He turned down the narrow canyon of Morris Street, emerging at the open swathe facing the multi-laned traffic rushing in and out of the Battery Tunnel, the modest sign along the gunnel proclaiming: Manhattan Plaza: Longest Underwater Vehicular Tunnel in North America - 9,117 feet in length. Opened May 25th 1950.

In and out. Those long gloomy days, and dark roomy nights. Primeval creatures, rooting in junk before the dawn. The beaming Gods, standing over the freshly laid foundation stone, scraping wet clay with their gloating trowels stamped with the sign of the Social Welfare Office. The Moon and the Sun, the bull and the lioness. The Cave Bear, gnawing at his skulls and thigh-bones. Long before the stars were born...

"And was it lonely and cold up there, mother?"

He looked up, but there was nothing but the glint of the sun off the twin towers of the World Trade Center. Do not enter. He walked on, towards the light, into Trinity Place, past the Blarney Stone and the Pig and Whistle Maryland Crab House, Smiler's China Chalet and the Exchange Italian Gourmet Deli, crossing Edgar Street past Volk's Taproom (Established 1882) and the blank facade of Sym's Department Store, with its sole legend:

AN EDUCATED CUSTOMER IS OUR BEST CUSTOMER.

Past Illusions Hair Design and My Daddy's Pizza: Calzone, Jo Jos, Roast Beef, Ham, Sausage, Eggplant, Coffee, Donuts. Blessed are those that can provide for themselves. McAnn's Bar, Best Burger in Town, Karaoke Contests, prizes, Surprises, Buy Any Drink, 2nd Free. Across Rector Street past the maw of the subway, the BMT Line, N and R. Netsach and Ruach, Eternity and Spirit. To our left, the American Stock Exchange building. To our right, the raised wall and railings of the Trinity Churchyard. Oldest burial ground in town. The parish created by Royal Charter in 1698 - destroyed by fire once, rebuilt twice, its steeple used to guide ships into the busy city harbour. And now the high towers of the commercial district hemmed it in from all four corners - North south west east. The janitor sometimes let him sleep here: An old Irishman named O'Connell. O'Connell, who had seen the city grow up around him, from the lush hills of the Algonquin Indians to the wood huts of the Stuyvesant Dutch and the baroque houses of the English colonials, the pirates, the slavers and the revolutionists, bearing these truths which are self evident, through fire and flood and the epidemics of typhus and cholera and the civil war, and the reconstruction, as the great towers of babble grew around him, O'Connell tended the graves, hoeing and weeding and marking out the trails from fountain to monument to sarcophagus, brushing off the mud and bird shit, till his face was as hard and worn as the stones, but his soft heart led him to break the rules, unlocking the gate at night to allow the city's wandering shadows to cohabit until dawn with its corpses, spreading their beds of old mail bags along the church railings and loosening their makeshift belts and braces. Taking off those Marine issue boots, kept tied by a shoelace round the big toe to guard against the lowest thieves and brigands.

"Are you all right there, brother? Do ye need a band-aid?"

The heavy shaking of the head. It was on just such a night, in a shrivelling winter, with frost tickling the ancient inscriptions, and the wind whistling round the spires and belfries and buttresses, and the darkness of shut down lights in the towers, so that the crucified stone man high on the Webster Memorial seemed to be shrieking in the pain and anguish of it all, that Mo Smith began to endure the chain of convulsions that culminated in The Creation -

- At first he thought it was only a burp, emanating from the gases of a recycled Macburger dragged half consumed from the litter bin on the corner of Trinity Place and Exchange Alley. The decomposite of relish, pickle and meat patty forcing its way up from the ileum, through the jejunum and on into the duodenum. The pain, exploding in the intestines, splintering from one scorching nodal point in one instant into a thousand ulcers, each budding into a thousand tumours, each bursting into a hundred blackened petals, peeling off into the boiling blood. A thousand blacksmiths pounding the blood vessels with molten brass hammers, piledrivers and drills. Jabadab. Jabadab. The great bull, thrusting behind him, forced its immense tumescent horn between his cheeks into his sore black ass, its black hooves clamped firmly round his groin, the fetid breath of its nostrils scalding his neck as its bronze tongue licked at his left ear. The great balls swinging at his calves like cannon shells, his sphincter muscles tearing like snapped cables. With a final grunt, the bull shot its seed wide and deep. Blinded blacksmiths scattering, all four intestinal coats withering away like burnt leaves in the fiery shower of sparks. The calcified tumours howling and screaming in the agonised ecstasy of their insemination, their tiny hands and feet and heads and eyeballs popping out like ripe corn of the nation. Mewling and pewling and clutching with their fetal fingers they swam, tadpole tails forming and breaking off, riding the bucking red cells, kicking off the marauding whites, ripping down the walls of the veins, sheering off in every direction like a shoal of piranha, screeching their embryonic defiance, biting through the skin and bone, bursting out from every orifice, oozing out between the follicles, squeezing through the pores and sweat glands, falling off the surface of the skin, cast out in his mighty eruptions and belches. Fire, water, and wind. Many perished in the frost gripping the graveyard, but many survived, invigorated by the icy crystals, cooling down as they melted the drops, scampering off in all directions to fill and replenish the earth. He saw them, and felt the pitter patter of their tiny feet, as they squeezed from his tear ducts, climbed out of the muddy wax of his ears, flowed out of his snot caked nostrils - the good, the bad, the beautiful and the ugly, the tall and the short, the fat and the lean, the pale and the dark, the quick and the slow, male and female and those who could not make up their mind, the hunters and nurturers, peasants and nomads, the city slickers, of all the nations and sects and creeds and skins of the earth: the Sudanese, the Egyptians, the Syrians and Assyrians, the Babylonians, Sumerians, Han and Nihon, the Aboriginals crossing the sky on their dreams, the Hebrews wracked through the heart and skull with their promises, the Persians with their twin Gods of fire and night, the Medes, the Greeks, the Myceans, the Phoenicians and the Philistines, the Vedic tribes, the Wei, the Chou, the Celts, the Mongols and all the tribes of the hills and plains of all five once united continents, which now cracked and buckled and fled apart, nursing their separations and their fears. AND I WILL CONFOUND THEIR SPEECH, AND SCATTER THEM TO THE FOUR CORNERS OF THE WORLD. Out! Out! And still they poured, leaping from the corners of his eyes, a band of Turks hacking their way out of the cracks in his small toenail, shinning down to the ground on rope ladders, crews of garlanded Samoans sculling down the torrent of his tears, Innuit in canoes shooting the rapids of his involuntary piss, disgruntled Angles, Visigoths and Huns struggling out of the droppings of his stool, while Somalis and Mocambiquans and other navigators shouted instructions from the folds of his forehead, broadcasting their advice down his nerves and ganglia, stirring up the sluggish politicians still stuck stubbornly to the folds of his gut. Out! Out! Out! His torn anal glands relapsed completely, releasing greater and lesser mounds, in which the base clay writhed and fermented, wriggling free and multiplying, putting flesh on their gristle, growing moustaches, beards and side burns, great thickets of bushy hair, afros, mohicans, helmets, top knots and top hats, skullcaps, fezzes, spats, galoshes, sneakers, creepers, moccasins, clodhoppers, stilettos, sandals, thongs. Tap dancing on the cold hard earth, gobbling up the after-birth, oblivious to his body jerking and twisting in his interminable birthing pangs, his arms flailing, his legs kicking at the frosty ground, his eyes bulging out with the effort, releasing several thousand more from burst blood vessels, washed in the blood of his limbs.

"Goddam! Shit! Motherfucker!"

And was there the wisp of a smile from on high? He lay there, rocked in the sea of his own piss and sweat and excrement, the foam and blood from his split lips and bitten tongue, while the janitor O'Connell wiped his face with a wet towel and washed the fetid pools away with Dash. Dragging him by the scruff of his old army greatcoat into the shelter of his room under the churchyard stairs, he lay him down on his bunk bed and released the soaked boots, dipping the calloused feet in hot water.

"You O.K., Mister Smith? You O.K.?"

"Goddamn the little fucking bastards!"

"You want me to call a doctor?"

"No, it's done. They've all got away by now."

"Who was it? Was it someone attacked you? Who were the bastards?"

No. Mo waved him away. "The ones inside. The ones that's still in there. Gimme that bucket."

He tried to vomit them out. He could still feel them, restlessly turning behind his tongue, in his armpits and elbows, chest, stomach, groin, knees and feet. But only a thin fleck of green spittle emerged from his depleted gut.

"They's still in there." A few bedraggled Methodists dripped from his eyes into the pail. He watched them drown, impassively. "Goddamn the motherfuckers." The reluctant midwife sat exhausted before him, with a kindly look on his old hatchet features.

"I'll brew up a coffee." And he took, from a shelf in his leaning, broken cupboard, a half empty bottle of Irish Whisky to pick up the flattened spirits. A couple of drops swirling in the black sluggish liquid. While outside the wind still howled...

"I really ought to book you in to a shelter, Mo."

"No thanks man. I gotta keep going."

But Adam fell asleep, that first night, after his exhaustion of naming the foul of the air and the beasts of the field. And in the night SHE came and stood over him, gazing at the sprawled figure, noting his rags and his bones, the lumps on his face, the shit on his thighs, the mud in his hair, the dirty grey beard that half covered the mottled blackness of his face. And he awoke, startled to find this alluring ebony black woman gazing down at him, with eyes in which deep fires glowed, and a shimmering robe which reflected every hue of the sunrise at that primal dawn. The gold, the red, the amber, the rose, the purple, the amaranth, tourquoise, aquamarine. The spectrum trembled about her, uncertain of its response to her sable beauty. For a brief moment which might have lasted all of time he paused, struck dumb, but rapidly recovered, pulling the squashed paper cup from under his blossoming shreds and patches and thrusting it under her nose:

"Spare a few pennies, sister? I don't rob and I don't steal but I ain't got nothin to eat. Thank you very much. Have a nice day."

And he awoke the next day in the graveyard, with his head propped against a tombstone. A fresh autumn morning, the sky a deep cloudless blue, the city's towers gleaming in the cold sun, birds trilling in the trees shading the churchyard, and sightseers, escaping the Broadway traffic, already ambling through the cemetery, stopping to marvel at the worn carvings of skulls and crossbones, winged cherubs and masonic signs. The stone that dug into the back of his head bore the inscription:

here lies jos. walrond son of mr henry leconte of
france and grace his wife,
being the only child of his parents he was born the
30th of july 1691 and god was pleased to take him unto
himself the 3rd of august 1692,
being the very day 6 years of their marriage.

Easy come, easy go. Two tiny graves, side by side:

anne, daughter of thos. & anne western,
who departed this life february 20 1796
aged 4 years 18 months.
anne western ball, daughter of flamen and ann ball
who died 22 august 1805, aged 20 days.

There is never enough time. He rose, joining the tourists following their guidebooks around the yard, seeking out the old monuments to the more prominent citizens of the town:

ALEXANDER HAMILTON, WHO DIED JULY 12 1804 AGED 47 -
THE PATRIOT OF INCORRUPTIBLE INTEGRITY. THE
SOLDIER OF APPROVED VALOUR.
THE STATESMAN OF CONSUMMATE WISDOM.
WHOSE TALENTS AND VIRTUES WILL BE ADMIRED BY A
GRATEFUL POSTERITY LONG AFTER THIS MARBLE SHALL
HAVE CRUMBLED INTO DUST.

ALBERT GALLANTIN. Born in Geneva in Europe 29th January 1761, landed in America 14th July 1780, died at Astoria New York 12 August 1840. Deeply imbued with the bold and liberal spirit of the times he came to AMERICA amidst the scenes of her REVOLUTION, and after many years of public service in Congress and in executive offices of the highest trust, at an advanced age, he withdrew to private life and passed the remainder of his days in philosophic studies and literary pursuits and went down to his grave universally honoured.

Motherfuckers. The tourists floating by, clicking and rustling. At the center of the maze, the mock-gothic column raised by Caroline Astor Wilson for her mother, Caroline Webster Astor, hoisting a grim stone crucified Saviour to the level of the third floor of the adjacent Trinity Building, the four corners of the stela marked by four matching sets of Pat-and- Matriarchs:

DAVID, JACOB and NOAH.
JUDAH, SHEM, ADAM and EVE.
RUTH, ABRAHAM and SETH.
JESSE, ISAAC and ENOCH.

For As In Adam All Die,
Even So in Christ Shall All Be Made Alive.

KEEP OFF THE GRASS!

But he sprawled splayed upon it, listening for the murmur of the extinct. Trying to extract the dribble of ghosts from the rumble of the Municipal Subways. To his left the IRT, the 4, 5, and 6. To his right, the BMT, N & R Local. But no signals yet of any meaning. Just the sad sack face of O'Connell the janitor, looking reproachfully at him from the Trinity Place entrance, above the stairs, holding his pail of fresh water. O'Connell who knew all the inhabitants of the graves and the ups and downs of their stories. O'Connell who claimed to know all the children who had died of the early epidemics which ravaged the city and sent her citizens northward, to the valley of 14th Street and beyond. He knew all about Caroline Webster Astor, society grand dame who kept a list of the Four Hundred citizens who were acceptable socially. She had a diamond belt which had belonged to Marie Antoinette, the beheaded Queen of France. "They cut off her head, Mo, along with the King. Can you beat that?"

"Sure beats shooting the Presidents, Mr O'Connell."

"Grist to the mill, Mo, grist to the mill."

He had known Robert Fulton, who had invented the steamboat and the submarine, which he had named the Nautilus and tried to sell to Napoleon. But it did not come up to scratch. O'Connell knew Alexander Hamilton, Secretary of the Treasury, who was challenged to a duel by Aaron Burr, the Vice President of the United States. They had met on July the 11th, 1804, at Weehawken, New Jersey, at a secluded cliffside niche. The seconds handed the duelling pistols to the principals and stood aside. The shots rang out, and Hamilton slumped to the ground. "I carried the wounded gentleman down the footpath to the boat, in which we rowed him back to the island," O'Connell told Mo, "but it was all over for the pore bastard. Still, he has such a fine shrine."

"Any brothers in this ground, Paddy?" Mo asked him.

None, O'Connell said, who were acknowledged. But rumour had it that some of the dead of the slave rebellion of 1712 had been hurriedly ploughed into one corner. On April 7th that year twenty three negro slaves had escaped from the slave market on the east side of Wall Street, armed with axes, knives and muskets. They set fire in the dead of night to a house and killed nine white men and women who ran into the streets. The fear of a general slave insurrection spread as far as the white bourgeoisie of Harlem. When day broke hundreds of soldiers and colonials beat every bush and searched every cranny. Twenty one slaves were captured alive, tried for murder and tortured to death. Some were burned alive over slow fires. Others tied to the wheel and their limbs broken one by one with large mallets, which then crushed their heads like ripe melons. One slave who had killed his master was suspended alive in chains until he died. Another was dragged through the streets, from Maiden Lane to Beaver Street, and lashed with bullwhips at each street corner. Their bloody remains were disposed of in the small hours.

"It was a terrible sight to see, Moses. My hair turned white on the spot. You can see the spot, here," he inclined his piebald skull to be admired. And there were other stories O'Connell told, of the pirates who infested the city in those days, and Captain Kidd, who had a house with his newlywed widow Sarah Oort Cox on Hanover Square just off the Old Slip, within sight of the great piers and the sea. All the great frigates and sloops and schooners and cutters and barques that plied the oceans, bringing the goods, the slaves, the spices, and later on all the wretched of the earth. Your poor, your huddled masses yearning to be free.

"It was out of the frying pan and into the fire, my boy. What goes round comes round. In the winter we would sleep huddled up by the steam gratings of the houses. The poor have simply changed colour, Mo, though in all the soot and muck we were as black as you. We lived in shacks in a stinking valley to the north until they chased us out and built the great park there, with its ornamental rocks and skating pools. People picked rags off the garbage dumps and sold them in Mulberry Street, the `rag-picker's court.' Bottle Alley, I remember it well. They wanted to stamp us out, the Wide Awakes and the Know-Nothings. We had to organise ourselves in the gangs. The Bowery Boys and the Plug Uglies. I ran with them first, then I joined the Slaughterhousers. We wore copper wedges on our fingers, to gouge out an opponent's eyes, you know. It was a rough time. The poor killing the poor."

"It's a wonder we are still around."

"There's plenty more where those came from."

Eventually, O'Connell related, he had obtained an honest job in the construction of the Brooklyn Bridge. The great caissons sunk below the water, the navvies working like deep sea divers on the massive foundations. Perching like eagles on the tall arched piers, slinging the cables from shore to shore. Once the piers were up the men had to walk along the slender wooden slat footbridge to reach the cradles far over the water. In winter the footpath rocked in the biting wind like a cotton thread in a storm. Rain soaked the slats into slippery death traps.

"Crazy people paid us to walk them across. It was the great dare of the day. Later on the thing was to jump off the Bridge. You would hold your nose and go down, five hundred and ninety five and a half feet down into the East River. Few men lived to tell the tale. But still they lined up to evade the cops who lay in ambush for them with handcuffs and novocaine syringes. They was a different type of people in them days. Full of Dutch courage, Irish pluck, black guts, pep and vigour."

THE NEFILIM, aye. The colossi, who, with Adam's daughters, begat the heroes of the world. Captain Kidd and J.P. Morgan and Astor and Vanderbilt and George Washington and the great Eye in the dollar. The Pyramid and the New Secular Order. In God We Trust. And Mo, too, walked among them, gliding down the narrow gorge of Wall Street, from the Bank of New York past the New York Stock Exchange and the Federal Hall, past Nassau and William Street and Hanover and Pearl and Water and Front to the East River Drive. Captain Kidd replaced by the New York Health and Racquet Club and the tour buses lined up by the Seaport Museum, Evergreen Lines, Pine Hill Trailways, Academy Tours and the American Way, unloading the trippers to gawp at the Peking, the four masted bark giving off its whiff of days gone by, so many months on the open wave with hard tack, sodomy and the lash, until the glorious epiphany of that first glimpse of land, high up from the crow's nest, now becalmed and at anchor, reaching merely to the ninth floor of the 110 storey World Trade Center on the other side of the bay -

Land ahoy!

Wandering up past the Fulton Fishmarket and the Burling Slip and Schermerhorn Row, with its upmarket seafood restaurants and reconstructions of the good old days, when fish was fish, its entrails torn out by rows of men and women with calloused hands plunged in ice and salt; past the tourists now flocking to the Pizzeria Uno and the Seaport Pleasure Arcade. Threading through the packed car park, past the Danger Keep Off signs on the wharf and the row of wooden poles crowned by African masks placed there by some anonymous hand, perhaps to scare the car thieves away -

The torn wire fence, the rubbish strangled waves washing in to the abandoned concrete stump underneath the bridge, but no foolhardy jocks leaping off the edge to oblivion, just the steady hum of traffic crossing the dull grey water. No Styx to be crossed by Dante's gaunt boatman. No flow of eternal life for Gilgamesh. No four rivers of paradise streaming from the tree of life. No wonder one is told not to eat the fruit thereof, shining with the glut of new toxins.

Here, under the bridge, Mo joins the night bivouac of the bums and panhandlers who work the Seaport and the Financial District, down to the Battery Park, the flotsam armies of the city, with their supermarket trolleys full of empty cans, discarded bottles, scavenged trash, yesteday's newspapers, dead bones of the consummate society. Annointing themselves with the droppings of the enfranchised, preparing their cardboard displays of out of date world atlases, tattered calendars of bygone centuries, gaudy posters of the saints of all creeds and cultures, the Buddha, Vishnu, Ganesha, Jesus, Mary Mother of God and the Bleeding Sacred Heart, Zervan Akarama of "the Boundless Time", Nelson Mandela and Malcolm X, along with used Hannukkah candles, blunt pencils and frayed Baseball Cards and copies of The Koran, The Truth, The Prophet Muhammad, the Book of Judgement 2000. Pushing these with all the patience of Job and all the persistence of Sisyphus, back up the canyons of the mighty glaring down at them with their basilisk stares, through the skin of the serpents, bulls and bears:

"Any spare change for a cup o' coffee boss?"

"I'm sick man I really need the money..."

"Hey man I'm sick I have AIDS I don't have long to live I hurt real bad you have to help me out..."

"Just a few coins man help out a brother who has lost his way..."

"You look like a kind hearted gentleman you wouldn't turn down a man who's down on his luck you have a house a wife and three wonderful children now all I have is this old street right here I know it's not a burden to you sir I'm sure you'll spare a dollar or two to help out a fellow human being who's fallen on hard times..."

"Please help me I just come out of the hospital..."

"I need money for an operation..."

"HELP ME GODDAMIT
HELP...!"

A most favoured pitch, Wall Street, the crowd ebbing and flowing from the catafalques of Bankers Trust and Manufacturers Hanover and Citibank and Morgan Guaranty Trust Company and Barclays and the Equitable Building and Chase and Brown Bros Harriman, eager to sacrifice and be sacrificed in the light of the full moolah, the street's trashbins glittering with an abundance of fresh scampi cocktail sandwiches, bagel and lox shreds, slivers of burger king escargot flambee, almost full cigarette packs and individual massive butts, diet champagne, mcdonald vinaigrette, poulet kentucky au whisky et basilic, creme de pantalon, condom de foie gras et souffle chaud, stuffed crocodile tears...

"A billion dollars for the love of Christ..."

"Thank you very much have a nice day..."

He paused by Wall Street Nails, ogling the rows of well dressed women sat in front of glass counters shimmering with the instruments of beauty, their fingers buffed by personal attendants, a stern determination etched in their smooth white faces. Even the black women in the row appeared pale. Next door, he examined the titles in the window of the Nassau Bookshop:

Business Opportunities in the United States.
The Psychology of Smart Investing.
The Disciplined Trader.
Getting Started in Options.
The Mergers and Acquisitions Manual.
The Making of a Stockbroker.
Selling to the Affluent.
Getting Started in Futures.
Understanding the Dead Sea Scrolls.
Culture Wars - the Struggle to Define America.
Prayers, Praises and Thanksgivings.
Knock 'em Dead - Great Answers to Tough Interview Questions.
Al Quran, a Contemporary Translation by Ahmed Ali.

For he that receives the gift of wisdom is rich indeed (sura 2; 269): Yet none except men of sense bear this in mind... to be charitable in public is good, but to give alms to the poor in private is better and will atone for at least some of your sins, as we trudge on, up Church, towards the City of New York's Department of Human Resources and Social Security...

"What is your name?"

"Mohammad Ndabaninghi Smith."

"What is your age?"

"I really can't say, ma'm."

"Where were you born?"

"I'm afraid I can't remember."

"Are your parents alive?"

"Is that a trick question?"

"Do you have a family anywhere? Have you ever been married? Do you have any children?"

"They are all my children."

"Do you profess any creed or religion?"

"I had them all, lady."

"Have you ever had a job? Do you have a social security card and number? Are you registered with any municipal or state or federal program? Are you registered with any medical facility or clinic? Do you have an attorney or a legal advisor?"

"I just have these here clothes I stand up in, ma'm. I'm just as you see me, there ain't nothing else but what I am in front of you now."

"Can you spell out your name again for me?"

"Moses Nelson Samooha."

"Now that is not what you told me before."

"I'm real sorry about that, ma'am."

"Now Mister, uhm, Samooha, do you want me to help you or not? Are you applying for assistance?"

"I really need a pair of new shoes."

"Do you wish to be housed? If you wish to be housed I can fill out a form now for the Housing Department and they can find you a place on an Emergency Program, which may be short or long term."

"I am already on an emergency program, ma'm."

"Is that so? Is that in another city?"

"That's in every other city, yes, ma'm."

"You're not making it easy for me to help you, Mister, ah, Smith. I cannot put you on an Emergency Program in this city if you are already registered in another."

"No ma'm. I ain't registered nowhere."

"Well, let's begin again from the beginning, shall we. Let's try and agree on a name. I would like your natural born name, if you please. The name you were born with."

"Adam Kadmon."

"All right. Adam. Cadman - how do you spell that? C - A - D - ?"

"Mitra. Mitra Noah Saidi."

"Are you putting me on, sir? Is this your idea of a joke?"

"No ma'm. I'm just trying to help."

"Well I can only put one name down here. Or I can put down an alias. Is that what you want me to do?"

"N. Elias. Sure, that should do fine."

"Can we get back perhaps to your parents. You must have had folks, who came from somewhere. A home town. Where do you come from?"

"I was a hidden treasure and I wanted to be known. So I created the world."

"Excuse me?"

"Man is the highest manifestation of God. So man is God. They were all born of me. Except those who still remain inside. They too are a powerful trouble, a living canker in the soul."

"Are you all right, sir? Do you want a glass of water?"

"I found the world complete on my arrival. And yet it was full of ruins."

"I'm afraid I'm not following your drift. I have a suggestion to make, sir. I would like to book you in for an emergency session with our therapist in residence. We have a very good lady in attendance today. Doctor Caroline Dexter. Would you like to have a word with her? Would you like me to fix you an appointment? She may be able to see you within the hour."

"Well ma'm, the problem is with these shoes. You see I have a long way to go."

"Do you have an appointment elsewhere? Is this at another office?"

"No, I just have a long way to go."

"I see, and you need the shoes."

"Yes ma'm."

"But you have to understand, Mister, uh, Smith, that I cannot provide an emergency discretionary grant unless I can properly fill in the form. It's not a complicated procedure. We can do it. But I need some straight answers and I also have to be satisfied that I'm not allowing you to neglect your other needs. You have to appreciate my obligation in this office. I can't help you if I can't understand what you're saying. Do you understand what I'm saying?"

"Oh ah yes ma'm."

"I'm not convinced that you do. Now if you just wait over in those seats there I will call you as soon as I have made the arrangement. There is a free water dispenser over there by the wall and there are soft drinks and sandwiches just by that counter over there. I don't want you to leave now or to think that we are turning down your request. You have to appreciate that I do need to establish an identity for you before I can sign over money for you to obtain the appropriate clothing, or anything else."

"I understand ma'm, you have to know who I am."

"Exactly."

"Well, maybe I ought to talk to the lady then. I really need those shoes."

"Absolutely, sir. Just hold on there for a little while. Mildred, can you put me through to Doctor Caroline on three six six I don't seem to be getting an answer. Yes thank you I'll hold. Excuse me Miss can't you see I'm on the telephone, if you will only sit down and wait your turn I'll call your name, what is your name? Harris? Miss Harris I'll call you over in a short while. Is that Doctor Caroline? I have a male walk-in, aged maybe mid-forties to mid- fifties, wearing a U.S. Army surplus jacket, pants and hat, with khaki overcoat, you know the whole gear, apparently he is applying for a discretionary emergency grant for new shoes, but he can't seem to be able to give me a name. First he tells me his name is Mo-hammad Daba-gingi Smith, then the next moment it's something else, then he said it was Adam Cadman. He doesn't seem to be able to produce any documentation whatsoever, I just have these torn pieces of paper in front of me, there seem to be all sorts of disconnected words and phrases, some of it not even in English, I have stuff here that looks like Arabic or even Hindu or something, and some words in Hebrew even, I think I recognise them, but it doesn't look like the Hebrew on my courses, you know the stuff I took two years ago, with the Learning Annex, you know all those courses, How to Turn Your Walls into Works of Art, Learn to Play the Piano in Two Weeks, Design Your Own Jewellery, How to

Turn Your Man into Putty in Your Hands... I would really've gone for that one, but you can't do everything you want. At any rate I can't make this out at all. There are all sorts of diagrams, five pointed stars, what do you call them, pentagrams, triangles, all sorts of I suppose mystic symbols. Then there are some newspaper cuttings: Brooklyn Butchers, Cocaine Deal Goes Awry, One Hundred Million Dollar Army Offer on E-Systems, Tiffany Blames Japan For Slump. It makes no sense, he's talking some kind of religious stuff, I think he is definitely one for you to see, at least so we can establish some identification to put on the form so that I can give him a check for these shoes. His other clothing seems to be in reasonable shape but the shoes really are in a pretty shabby state we cannot let him walk out of here without at least addressing that issue. Uh-huh. Uh-huh. Uuuh-huh. Well, he may be putting on an act you never know with these people but he certainly doesn't seem stupid he knows he only has to give me a name and I will sign a form for this item of apparel as a discretionary grant but I have to keep some kind of record or else we will just be buried down here. And I think he is willing to be helped and I think he does need help. He certainly looks like someone who has lived on the streets for some time we probably have him in our records if only we can pin him down to that name and then we'll have a better idea of how to assist. Uuh-huh. Uh-huuuh. Uuuuh-huh. O.K., that's eleven-forty, twenty minutes from now that's very kind of you, Caroline, I appreciate your making this window. Thank you very much. Excuse me Miss I'll be calling you in just one moment please take a seat sir I do have your number with me and I will be with you as soon as I can. Excuse me, sir, Mister Mo-hammad? Er, not you sir, the other gentleman, sir, about the shoes: I have an appointment for you with Doctor Caroline Dexter for eleven-forty, that's only twenty minutes from now, she has a fifteen minute window, that may be a short time but you can establish a later time for a more extensive session if that is appropriate, I think she can straighten you out. Now listen, you take this paper here, don't lose the paper, and the identification form, and don't forget your cuttings, take the whole lot, down that corridor there, to the right, then you go through the glass doors and turn left, for a little while, then you turn right again, O.K., that's right, through the doors. Then you go left then right again, till you get to the lift or the stairs to the third floor. I think only one lift is working so you might want to take the stairs if there's too much delay, if you do that you have to go through the glass doors again at the third floor, that's another set of glass doors, right, not the first, that's on the third floor, then you turn right down the corridor until the corner then take a left. If you get lost or have any doubts there are attendants and there is a policeman on every floor. He is there to help you so don't hesitate to ask for assistance. After you speak to the Doctor she will fill in this form and you have to bring it back here to me so that I can make out your check in order that you can get your shoes. Now just in case you have any problems getting back here from there here is a ball of thread. If you attach the end of the thread to that faucet over there and just unravel it as you go you will be able to find your way back down here when your appointment is over. But of course you will not be able to use the thread if you take the lift so I would advise you in any case to use the stairway at the second turning after the doors. And make sure you don't lose this piece of paper because you will not be admitted to the Doctor's office without it, and if you return here before being admitted I'm afraid the regulations specify quite clearly that I cannot issue a second ball of thread. Do you understand what I'm saying?"

"Yes mama."

"Off you go then."

I will give you the end of a golden string,
Only wind it into a ball -
It will lead you in to Heaven's Gate,
Built in Jerusalem's Wall...

A tall, wide policeman bars his way, laden down with his badge and his ire and his nightstick and his handcuffs and cans of mace and tiny shrunken skulls hung on silver chains on his belt.

"Uh, looking for the stairway, man."

"Straight ahead, sir. Have a nice day."

He ascends, the ball unwinding as he proceeds. The chorus, as he climbs the steps, not of angels, but of all the supplicants kept from their due. The benefits stopped, the unemployment unpaid, the soft manna of promissory notices. Client's name, reference number, abode.

David, Jacob, Noah, Jesse... Judah, Shem and Adam and Eve... KEEP OFF THE GRASS! Jesse, Isaac and Enoch... Shadrach, Meshach and Abednego...

Mo climbed on up the stairs. His toes bent out of the frayed caps of his boots. Tiny crawling creatures in the unmopped dust scrambling to get out of his way. Go forth and multiply and replenish the earth. But how can one with only half of the leaf? The old tree with its bulging red fruit. He felt the old rumble from his insides. Is this another purge? But the voices only rustled along his nerve ends, their tiny fingers plucking at his ganglia. The selfish ones who were not willing to be born yet clawing at his joints and innards.

"Are you all there?" He rested at the top of the second flight of stairs. Another policeman stood in the haze ahead of him, by another set of frosted glass doors, his great feathered wings unfolding from his shoulder blades and the golden sword of office bulging in his pants. The cop smiled benignly at him with O'Connell's face.

"Are you ol roit sir? Can I get yez anything?"

Mo shook his head, looking down the pit of the stairway towards the clearing far below. The bowed heads of the supplicants massing and moving towards the high mud walls of a city crowned with turrets, battlements and lofty minarets. The battlements bristling with gibbets upon which condemned thieves had been hung, their hands and feet cut off and nailed to the crossbeams above their grinning skulls.

"In the Name of God, the Compassionate, the Merciful...!"

"Are you all right sir? Are you awake? Can you hear me?"

He looked up, into a face like a black moon with perfect ivory teeth, compassionate eyes and a short haircut, a firm hand and thin but strong forearm at his shoulder, a plastic cup of clear water held in the other, swimming before him. A small round pill dissolving with a gentle fizz in the center of the cup.

"Drink this down, you'll feel a lot better."

He took the cup, his trembling calloused fingers touching hers for a brief instant.

"Excuse me, mam," he said, "I'm afraid I lost the fucking string."

"Don't worry about it," she said. "Can you stand up? Let's go talk all about it in my office."

And so he rose, and followed her into the chamber...

BENJAMIN.

I'm always amazed at the way Americans use the word "history". You're history, man! A total obliteration. No one needs the past. Everything starts from right now. Who needs memory?

At the northern end of Cooper Square, in the Village, where Saint Marks Place, Astor Place, Lafayette, 8th and Stuyvesant cross Fourth and Third Avenues, there is a giant cube, placed diagonally so that it seems to rest on a point. If you put your shoulder to the cube and push with all your strength, you can rotate it, very slowly, and uselessly. A lever to fail to move the world. Interactive art. It's no longer enough to think. You have to touch and feel.

A blustery day, the wind against me as I cross Broadway, past Washington Square. The skateboarders practically windsurfing and the chess players driven away by the spattering rain. Storm warnings up and down the coast. Hurricane Hilda. Why are they always named for the ladies?

On my way to Caroline. Battering past the signposts. UNNECESSARY NOISE PROHIBITED. That one always gets to me in this city. I've read my Barthes, I know we are a society of signs, chasing the invisible signifier. NO STANDING! ONE WAY! LOCAL TRAFFIC! YO FAGGOT! MEAT, TECHNO-TRIBAL, HEART-BREAK! There can be a career, a mystery, in anything.

Descending into the West 4th subway. The maze of corridors, peeling walls, vomit flecked stairs, multi-level platforms. The arrows Uptown and Down. The uptown A train has just drawn up, so I dash inside, find a seat between a tiny Chinese old woman with twelve string bags bulging with what appear to be raw roots of some kind and a vast beer bellied African-American local with paint spattered overalls and a baseball cap with YSG in red letters on faded blue. Gazing up, as the train judders out of the station, past the strobing beams, at yet more supplications, pasted above the swaying passengers:

> CALL US WHEN YOU'RE PREPARED TO RETURN FROM THE LIVING DEAD: Users of drugs and alcohol lose their friends, their families, their jobs and their lives.
>
> LASER TECHNOLOGY - Stop the Agony of Hemorrhoids, Hernias, Warts, Quickly and Painlessly...
>
> TORN EARLOBE? Call 212-665-EARS.
> Also specializing in nose surgery and breast enlargement -
> Board certified plastic surgeons.
>
> YOU TOO CAN HAVE BEAUTIFULLY CLEAR SKIN -
> Custom designed skin care regimens:
> Dermatological facial cleansing -
> Acne treatment / complexion problems -
> Skin - hair - nails -
> Removal of moles - chemical peels - scar correction -
> Jonathan Zizmor M.D.
> Board certified dermatologist.
>
> DID YOUR PROBLEMS START BEFORE YOU WERE BORN?

Tell me about it. I often wonder, what is this Board, sitting in ethical judgement over these prophets of pure skin and straight teeth? A youngish man, carrying the stigmata of the street, the rags, the ravaged face, the chapped lips, the toeless boots, the paper cup, the calloused hands, moves down the carriage, moving in on his captive, deaf audience:

"Good afternoon ladies an gennelmen. Ah don want you to feel upset or intimidated in any way but ah wanto interduce myself an explain my predicament. I was born in Noo York City but I have been severely disadvantaged from the year of my birth. My father died a violent death an my mother was left to bring myself an my six brothers an sisters up on her own. Two of my brothers were also killed on the streets an my older sister had to become a prositute in order to support the rest of us when my mother fell ill with a terminal disease which was the result of the poor an unhygienic conditions in which we were brought up. When she died at the age of thirty two she looked like an old woman. I have been permanently unemployed an I have suffered from a variety of diseases includin tubercolosis, chronic bronchitis an uremia. I have recently contracted the HIV virus but I have not yet developed the full symptoms of AIDS. Owin to this I have not been able to receive the full disability payments which my status and condition should allow. I am livin on the streets an do not have sufficient clothin to survive the comin winter. I have applied for accomodation at several shelters but have been told there are no places for me at the present time. Please give generously and do not be afraid to contribute notes as well as coins because I am in a bad way an your contribution will help me to survive. I hope you all have a pleasant trip, thank you very much have a good day."

Hardly enriched by my dollar bill, he passes on down the carriage, past the seeing blind, rattling the door to the next compartment, making way for the next supplicant climbing through the door from the other end - "Good afternoon, ladzangennelman, ah know you just wanna geton with your journey..."

I never asked to be taken on their journeys. I've travelled enough on my own. From the moment I landed here, mooning about the streets like the Invisible Man whose bandages even were invisible, having endured the eleven hours of non-stop flight from Tel Aviv, and survived the pitiless gaze of the Immigration official who couldn't find my name in the databank of national enemies, undesirables, malcontents, agents of the Evil Empire of the month, members of organisations hostile to the United States, its constitution, its government and its people. It used to be a book, I am told, a great Bible of subversion. I remember feeling, in my bones, as the officer's fingers flew over his keyboard, that I was sure to be found out. Not because I had any hostility to the people of the United States, their government, which I thought was no worse than any other group of national or international criminals, or their constitution, which seemed to me a fine dream, but because I seemed by definition to be a suitable case for exclusion...

"You're history man!" I tried to live by that once. For a long time I refused to remember anything, and tried to just merge with the mass. I decided, at one point, to redefine everything as if I had been born the day before. I would wake up each day on an alien planet, and every sound, vision, gesture would be mysterious and unique. I would rediscover my own limbs, objects, furniture, the pristine wonder of the world beyond the windows. But my brain refused to co-operate. As soon as I woke up, it crammed my head with memories like an angry swarm of bees.

The next obsession was a recurring urge that had first grabbed me, I remembered, when I was about twelve, back in the Unholy Land: I would try and understand everything, what motivated not only the people I thought I knew, but people I had never met, whose actions I read about in the newspapers or history books, or even the people who just passed on the pavement. I would try and grasp the universe, in its human entirety. The more impossible the dream, the better. Even passing by U.S. Immigration, with my seditious thoughts engraved on my forehead like the mark of Cain.

But the man, who was a short, friendly Hispanic type with spectacles, just waved me through. Three years have passed, and now I have practically melted in the pot: The city that grips, rattles, rolls and shakes me, bloating my skin and eyes in summer, freezing me stiff in winter, soaking me in its sudden downpours, allowing me those few precious moments of crisp sunlight in the spring and fall. Settled, as far as settling goes, at this point of time - if time has a point - in my dilapidated cage in the city's human zoo, East 4th between First and Second, an as yet ungentrified block of four flights of rough stone stairs, with the cracked plasterwork blowing out in the corridors and rooms as if past tenants who've been buried there are straining to break through and get out. An absentee landlord who lives in Spanish Harlem and a super, Esteban, who keeps the whole gimcrack show going with his old brown bag of monkey wrenches and magical spare parts. No elevator of course. A mythical eldest resident, Mrs Yugo of apartment 2c, whom Esteban feeds through a cat flap in the reinforced door.

But it suits me fine. I am not upwardly mobile. Just travelling sideways, on as even a keel as possible, shuttling between my self-furnished four walls, and Caroline, Doctor Caroline Dexter's Sanctuary on Amsterdam and 93rd...

At 59th Street, I have to change trains, or I will be carried Express to 125th Street, gateway to Harlem. Follow all the white folk rushing out. Threading the tunnels towards the Uptown Number One or Nine. Stupid questions: Why the merger between One and Nine? One of my "students", at the East 4th Film-makers Co-op, is obsessed with this kind of number mania. She would tell me that nine are the Kabbalist sephirot without the One, and the One stands above the Nine. It all means that hidden hands are manipulating the New York subway system. The gnarled tentacles of endless conspiracies. The high and the low. The deep and the wide...

But I believe that chaos has no meaning. I'm always ready, in this city, for surprises. My life here has flowed, from point to point, by chance, by random meetings. The chain of strange connections that led from Frances to Salim, Salim to Darwish, and from Darwish, to Caroline...

Cat's-cradle memories... My second week in the City, lost in Babel but still attached by an umbilical cord to my host, fellow Israeli ex-army comrade "Mad" Nathanel, who was kindly sharing with me his cluttered and stifling hotel-apartment room on West 73rd. Chaotic New York Apartments I Have Known... It all comes flooding back, between 14th Street and Times Square... How, to escape the heat, Mad Nathanel dragged me off to the back room of a synagogue, a venue I hadn't been seen dead in since my Bar Mitsvah, to join a group of Progressive Rabbis, cocooned in a Talmud lined but airconditioned library, basking in the thrill of being harangued by three bona fide Palestinians from the occupied West Bank about our collective sins. "Don't think you've escaped your quota of crazy Jews, Benjamin, just because you've left the Promised Land," whispers Nathanel, "after all, this is the mother lode." And there, among the congregants, in a queenly slouch, she sat, or rather, reposed, a commanding young woman with an enormous crown of orange hair, clad in a sea blue jalabiya and mediating the two camps with the authority of an ordnance corps Major. Embraced by Nathanel, who introduces us:

"Benjamin - Frances."

"Hi." At first sight, that familiar hazard, a woman who wants to Do Good. But then we escaped, after two bone-crushing hours, from the Rabbis, Frances, Mad Nathanel the three Palestinians and I, to a Middle Eastern Broadway cafe called the Shall Va, serving the usual microwaved falafel, to gossip languidly about all the usual woes and dreams. The warring peace movements and wavering hopes of change, before Desert Storm, the Gulf War, Peace Conferences and the New World Order. The three Palestinians soon departing to roll their Sisyphean stone up yet another hill, Progressive Catholics, Primeval Protestants or whatever, Crazy Nathanel splitting to his shift security checking for El Al, Israel Airlines (the things we have to do to earn a living in this town), leaving me with Frances' invitation for a further schmooze and "real" coffee at her apartment. 86th Street between Amsterdam and Columbus. And entering the door, I am face to face with a baby faced Arab youth, with black curly hair, lounging in a matching jalabiya on a sagging sofa, leaning forward to shake my hand as Frances makes that second connection -

"Benjamin, this is Salim. You ought to hear his story. He used to be a bodyguard for Yassir Arafat."

"You don't say?"

That dreamy boyish smile: "I am not in politics any more. I am just a student."

"That sounds a lot safer."

"Not in this city."

The safety of her crazy apartment: The cardboard boxes of unpacked books, after three years of her occupancy, jumbles of magazines, pamphlets and catalogues of exhibitions and art shows, wax candle souvenirs from Jerusalem, the obligatory "bedouin" saddlebag, kefiyas chequered red and black, lampless lampshades, upended cookie jars and little plants in cans, Russian nested dolls scattered all over the place on tables, chairs and over the thick pink rug, strange coloured cushions everywhere, with Salim just another piece of wreckage fetched up on the couch -

"Salim's doing a course at Flatbush College with a friend of mine. Do you know Professor Allan Darwish? He teaches a course in Middle East History. It's Adult Education, anyone can enrol."

Give me your boors, your muddled masses, yearning to be free... Exiting the 96th Street station, gusts of wind foreshadowing Hurricane Hilda blowing discarded newspapers out of the trash bins all over the pavements, wrapping the front page of the New York Times round my feet: CLINTON LEADS IN LIVE DEBATE. Kicking it away as I turn down and then left towards the old four-storey brownstone house hiding between the Amsterdam Gourmet Deli and the Kwae Dee Cleaners Co-op, a rare survival among the apartment blocks. Knocking and entering through the old glazed glass doors, which can be opened, more often than not, by a complete stranger, with that immense black mutt of hers barking and leaping up to maul your face with its huge rasping tongue.

Down boy down. Choose somebody your own size. Like, the Hound of the Baskervilles. Fluppy Puppy. What a name. But past the dog it's anybody's guess. You never know what you might see, in Caroline's Sanctuary... You just have to be prepared for the three ring circus. The Big Show of all and any nations and creeds. Jetlagged political jugglers, misfortune tellers, economic escape artists, highly wired mental acrobats, remorselessly unhappy clowns. In the morning it might be Caroline's local mental health group, from the "Department of Human Resources." At lunchtime it might be the Haitian exiles, meeting secretly with their immigration lawyer. In the afternoon, a posse of people's pyschiatrists from the African National Congress of South Africa, straight off the plane from Jan Smuts Airport and eager for tips on psychotherapy among traumatised populations. Or Sri Lankans, lost between civil wars, gaunt Timorese survivors, or terminally sad Cambodians with skulls shimmering in their eyes.

But now the cavernous front room is empty, behind Caroline, as she holds back the giant hound straining to get at my crotch.

"Hi, Ben. Just come through. Allan's in the kitchen. Frances and Salim should be here soon."

"No lost souls to be saved tonight?"

"The word is out. I'm on a Caribbean cruise."

Only the echoes, as I walk through, the dog wheezing at my pants, of all the voices raised and passions flared in the four storeys of immense old New York rooms, filled with the litter of a thousand and one visitors who rested their bones for a day, a night, a week, an age, amid the debris of two abandoned marriages, not to speak of the scattered belongings of Karim, the estranged son, who departed four years ago at the ripe age of fourteen to join the Nation of Islam in Pittsburgh. His abandoned flags of disavowed football heroes and Michael Jackson preserved against his return in the loft, above the "doss house", one gargantuan room comprising the entire storey, a junkpile of blankets over broken floorboards always about to be fixed, creaking above the second floor bedroom and bathroom. Every nook and cranny of the entire house filled with endless piles of professional medical magazines,

American Analyst, The American Journal of Orthopsychiatry, The American Journal of Marital and Family Therapy, The Pharmaceutical Review, the Caribbean Times, Foreign Policy, Central American Report, Lies of Our Times, Z, The Nation, and of course the books, lining every wall down to the basement. Since Caroline is the custodian, apart from her own library, of the overspill archive of Professor Allan Darwish, mentor, advisor and brother-in-arms, including his total stock of African and Asian anthropology, world history, studies of a hundred and one religions and cultures from the Abbasids to Zoroaster, as well as his collection of paranoia and conspiracy theories down the ages, old faded volumes of sources in cracked bindings and folders of decaying documents in Arabic, French, English, Italian, German, Hebrew and Dutch, Russian, Polish and Urdu. A massive life support machine for the Professor, since he had moved from his great barn in Brooklyn to a tiny box high on the eleventh floor of a tower block on Riverside Drive, with three interlocked roomlets, a tiny kitchenette and bathroom and a series of guest beds which fold up into the walls like props in a Laurel and Hardy movie...

Climbing down the wooden stairs to the basement-kitchen, Allan Darwish is raiding the icebox. Raising his eagle head with its white thatch and Mediterranean beak under those piercing grey eyes -

"Somebody hasn't been shopping, Caroline."

"The Zimbabweans cleaned me out last week."

"Looks like another night for the Gourmet Szechuan."

"The usual tea, Ben, till the others turn up?"

"It's getting windy out there. Hurricane Hilda."

"Good, it'll scare the yuppies away. We can have our table by the window."

For a man of politics, Darwish has turned into a real foodie. Is this the man who was arrested in 1969 for allegedly plotting to kidnap the then Secretary of State, Henry Kissinger? A plot dreamed up to fool an FBI informer, who was fooled only too well. What was it like, I asked him once, to share a jail cell with Noam Chomsky, Norman Mailer, Abbie Hoffman and the Berrigan Brothers?

"Very noisy, Benjamin. No one could get a moment's sleep."

Another hybrid mongrel like the rest of us, only more so, this son of an Egyptian-born father and Italian mother who met and mated in Tuscany courtesy of the U.S. Army in World War Two, born, as he always tells us, between Hiroshima and Nagasaki, growing up through Truman, McCarthy and Eisenhower to blossom as a natural cultural freak in the brief American Spring... Not the kind of American professor I expected at Frances and Salim's recommended adult course on Middle East History at far-off Flatbush College - the latter day Wizard of Oz, stomping up and down in the crowded lecture hall, waving his hands and haranguing his audience of mature and decayed students of all the usual shapes, colours and sizes: "You have to learn to throw out your garbage! Clean out your head before you can put in anything fresh. There's nothing more putrid than rotting ideas." The students, wide eyed, writing it all down carefully: R-O-T-T-I-N-G I-D-E-A-S...

Days and nights, in the cafes and then crushed up in his own tiny apartment, joined, some times, by his alter ego, the cryptic Armenian Professor of Egyptology and other Easternisms - Aram Djerdjekian. Two old birds scanning a familiar landscape, primed for the intellectual battlefield... And from Allan Darwish and Aram, the final link in the chain of random, fateful, strange connections - on a night when I visited him on my own, to unpick a typically knotted strain of Middle Eastern revision - something to do with the liberal thoughts of Vladimir Jabotinsky -

"Why don't you come with me, Benjamin, I have to see a friend who lives nearby. She's just across Broadway, 93rd and Amsterdam. You'll like Caroline, she's quite a character. She's a clinical psychiatrist. Lets see what she can make of your angst."

Random chance. Accidental meetings. And Allan's amused dismay, a year later: "Oh God, Benjamin, I just wanted to introduce you to a friend. I didn't bargain for Tristan and Isolde..."

You shouldn't carry all those love potions about then, my friend... My mother would certainly have disapproved: My Benjamin has fallen in love with a black woman?! Chayim, explain to me, what is the boy talking about? But my mother, in her Alzheimerian fog, back in the Homeland, is beyond knowing what anything around her means... Now there's a chain of connections: My poor mother, who came with my father thirty years earlier to rebuild Zion, she from ruined Poland, he from accursed Germany, propelled by that powerful repulsive thrust - Come let us leave this Europe where the fires are burning, where they spit out the heretic and stranger, where they glory in the murder of their fathers, mothers, siblings, daughters, sons... And they saw a new life and a new nation rising from the ashes of a scorched world... And so they fought, loved, toiled, sacrificed and made a new generation in their own image, or so they hoped, to give us dominion over their proud works, but things did not work out quite as they had imagined. So now my father writes plaintive opinion pieces in his Party newspaper urging his new Labour government to fulfill its pledges of Peace and Prosperity, while my mother lives out her mysterious twilight in the geriatric ward of the Light of the Eyes sanatorium, the remnants of her memory slowly flicking out like lost quarks in a failing centrifuge.

Like Nietzsche's eternal recurrence, it's deja vu all over again... When I last visited my mother, crossing half the world to mitigate some portion at least of my guilt, she completely failed to recognise me. My father pressed her in vain: "It's little Benny, your son. You remember Benny?"

"Go away," she told both of us. My father was delighted. "A response! It's a good sign, Benjamin." Down, Dad, it's only terror interspersed with farce. But an old woman beside my mother, whom I did not know from Eve, recognised me falsely as her own long dead son, and took my hand and jabbered to me in Arabic for at least twenty minutes, until the nurses came to coax her gently away...

The dog barks, and the caravan gathers... It leaps up the stairs, scrabbling at the door. The voices of Frances and Salim, trying to calm him down, waft through. I go up to open the door. Frances is wrapped up as if ready for the Flood, and Salim's yellow cab is parked down the steps. "I found a parking space, Benjamin, can you believe it?"

Allan hurries up the basement stairs, putting his coat on. "Don't settle down," he says, "we're off to the Szechuan Gourmet."

"I got the cab," Salim offers, "we could do Chinatown. Sixteen Mott Street. Or the Shee King." The exiled Palestinian exhibiting boundless pride in his new status as a registered Medallion driver, a bona fide knight of the grid. But Allan waves his offer away.

"I'm hungry. Lets just stick to the neighborhood, if you don't mind."

Reality triumphs. Trailing back to Broadway, in our group of five. The wind picking up again. Garbage round our ankles. The styrofoam cup nation at every step. One veteran is already curled up asleep in a mail basket at the corner of 95th. Caroline stops to murmur briefly with a young woman she knows, slumped in the doorway of Fowad's clothing store. A bill of some sort changes hands. But at the Chinese restaurant we are greeted by a gauntlet of friendly voices ushering us in to our favourite table, by the large front window looking onto the street. Pots of tea and glasses of iced water. The many-sheaved menu. Darwish taking charge as usual -

"Let's begin with the Crystal Shrimp Dumplings. Note, tout l'monde, that Asparagus is Out of Season."

Darwish has been in the dumps the last few days, when I spoke to him, two or three times, on the phone. A phase he is apt to fall into, when bad news comes through from some strand of his many networks abroad: The arrest of some old colleague in Algiers, a family problem in Cairo, a sinister silence from an old contact in some Human Rights office in San Salvador or Port au Prince. But now he's back in form, ready to debate the election. In Clinton versus Bush, Slick Willie against the Wimp, Darwish is rooting for Bill: "We have to get those bastards out, Benjamin. He's useless on the Middle East, sure, but who isn't? You have to get rid of your illusions..."

Clean out your head! If it were up to Allan Darwish we would collect all our dreams in a grand bonfire and dance round the flames. Like the other doomsayers of this country, the Noam Chomskys and Edward Saids, he wants us to see things as they are: "We live in the most open society on earth, Benjamin, but our minds are totally closed. We have to make such an enormous effort just to see what's really going on, let alone to hear all the people who are being killed and robbed and maimed in our name..."

Vietnam, Chicago, the Armies of the Night, the Freedom Riders, Birmingham, Selma and Montgomery...

Darwish: "Just place your orders, mes enfants."

Caroline: "I'll go for the Prawns and Scallops."

Frances: "Empire Ginger Chicken."

Myself, I am going for the Lamb with Szechuan Ma La Sauce, I have a large hole to fill.

"Four main dishes between the five of us should be enough," declares Darwish, "and two vegetables. Or do you want to go for broke, Salim?"

"I'm still searching." Salim is always slow to make a move. Brought up in scarcity he never ceases to marvel at the west's abundant choices. "What is a Creaky Chicken? This menu doesn't make sense."

Darwish: "Forget the sense, Salim, go for the flavour. It's a hot and fiery dish. Smoke will come out your ears."

"I'm used to that."

Frances throwing us both one of her old glances. The sieve of memory. The magic potion of forgetfulness. The golden slipper and the pumpkin carriage, bumping and grinding through the Queens-Midtown Tunnel with Darwish as my fairy god-mother -

CLEAN OUT YOUR HEAD! CLEAN OUT YOUR HEAD! I should have stuck with the rejection of memory... I should have paid the rent on time. I shouldn't have abandoned my mother. The day I began eating pork...

"The scallops!" Caroline applauds the Gourmet orders steaming into view, the eager waitresses standing by with more iced water and fresh pots of jasmine tea.

"Watch out, very hot, very hot!" Hardly has the plate touched the table when Caroline's chopsticks go into action. I suppose it's the buzz of medical practice that brings on this speedy gobble. I've never seen anyone as small as Caroline shovel in so much so fast. All that burning energy.

"Well, what's the agenda this time?"

Our regular feasts of babble: Clinton Bush Perot Palestine the latest CIA scams Iran-Contragate, the degradation of health care in the City, the creeping gentrification of Amsterdam Avenue, which is the best Chinese restaurant in town 16 or 20 Mott Street or the Silver Palace, rumours of crisis at Zabars, Salim on taxicab driving, Frances on the crisis in "conceptual art" and the latest ripoff in the art gallery business, or her most recent exploit, joining a class action in San Francisco against the Zionist Anti-Slander League alleging a lifetime of damaging blacklists revealed by recent shenanigans and discoveries in the downtown Frisco Greyhound bus station. Pause for the choice of further dishes, Paradise Chicken or Prawns in Kong-pau sauce...? And from Caroline, the latest bulletin in her war against the city's mental plagues:

"Listen up, my friends, I have a tale to tell you. A homeless man came into the office two days ago, looking for money for a pair of shoes. The reception couldn't make head or tail of him. He gave them several different names. Turns out I have a classic case on my hands. MPS. Multiple Personality Syndrome. Or else he's the best faker I've come across. I want to do some detective work on this one. You can't believe who's out there nowadays. One minute the man talks like the village idiot and the next he's spouting Dante and the Koran. I'm going to need help from you all. I want to try to map the world inside his brain. I simply don't have the background to analyse what's going on inside there. Medieval history, the Pharaohs, Islam, Renaissance Italy, God knows what else. We'll have to pool our resources. And to cap it all, there's a Jehovah Complex. It seems that he created the world, and we are all his children. Which means that all of us are inside his head. This man is really something else. If the psychoanalytic establishment got hold of him they'd put him in a cage the rest of his life. I'm going to need a think-tank on this one. See if we can somehow break through."

"Sure, Caroline, no problem. When are you seeing him next?"

"I gave him an appointment for Wednesday, but I can't be sure he'll turn up. This might be your department, Salim."

"What do they call it? A needle in haystack! No problem. You want to join me in the cab tomorrow? How about you, Benjamin?"

"Anything for the cause."

"It's a deal. Tomorrow at ten?"

The steam from the crystal prawn dumplings still rising like a genie from the plate - *All dishes are free from salt, sugar, corn starch or MSG...* A hand raps against the plate glass separating our table from the pavement of Broadway. Thin smudged fingers splayed against the window. A pale, acned face with lanky black hair. The girl points to her mouth and works her jaws up and down. A bent black man slides up beside her, shaking a small paper cup. The soft jingle of a couple of coins. She turns and examines his haul. They move off, together, like ghosts, towards the kerb. Motorists are stuck at the traffic lights on the corner of 96th. The girl walks jerkily towards their windshields. Side windows are swiftly rolled up. She raps against the glass. The drivers look ahead, up, praying for the lights to change. The red lights turns abruptly green. The flow brushes her off like a fly. She moves on with her companion, uptown.

SALIM.

Driving a cab in this City. Tell me about it. Ploughing backwards and forwards in the grid of Manhattan, navigating around the potholes like a canoe dodging the undertows. Trying to figure out whether the next guy flinging his arm out at you is the psychopath who will blow you away for fifty bucks and small change.

They used to have these cabs built like a prison. You had a grille between yourself and the passenger, who put the money in a metal flap. You put the money in a sealed box which you couldn't open till you got back to the depot. But the psychos would just shoot the drivers anyway. Now they tell me these are new, more friendly times, my cab is open like any other vehicle, but the passengers don't talk much any more. A lot of cab drivers don't speak much English, so I suppose the clients are happy to just get where they're going, and not be dumped in the South Bronx.

I was only held up once. A white man with a pony tail clapped a Saturday Night Special to my head, and asked me for fifteen dollars. I had given away my last ten in change, so I said: "I can only give you twenty-five, man."

"I want fifteen," he said, "give me fifteen dollars or I'll blow your head off." I gave him a twenty, and he rapped the side of my head with his gun. "Foreign asshole," he said, "gimme another five!" I gave him what I'd already offered and he ran out of the cab, slamming the door.

This is the nature of the West as I have observed it: People talk at each other and not with each other. Nobody listens, a web of monologues. Where everybody is an individual, everybody is a closed world. Where everybody has to be a winner, the loser forfeits every right. I was grateful the mugger only took twenty five dollars and spared my life. In this City he was an angel of mercy.

The Medallion driver cruises the City like a Samurai without weapons or armour. He is like a priest who does not speak unless spoken to. He touches people briefly, at random, listening to little snatches of lives. Collapsing marriages, itching romances, twitching business deals, rising and falling friendships, overflowing resentments, confused desires, unexplained memories. I had a girl who wept her eyes out so much I thought I would drown in the flood. I didn't know what to say, how to console her. She wouldn't pause to say what was wrong, and only stopped for a moment to tell me snappily to shut up and get where I was told. Then she tipped me five dollars for an eight dollar fare and vanished, bawling, into the entrance to a ritzy building on East Seventy-seventh. "It can't be as bad as it looks," I shouted after her, but she didn't stop and the doorman waved me irritably on my way.

Another time I had a yuppie looking businessman in a good suit and a shiny black briefcase, who talked to himself loudly all the way from City Hall to West 83rd. He was accusing himself of various crimes of self-harassment, of denouncing himself to the Internal Revenue and masturbating over pictures of footballers, who were choking his dreams. The entire team of the Chicago Bears was plotting to rape him at Easter, in the Church of Saint John the Divine. "You gotta be ready," he told himself, over and over again. Then he got out at his door and paid me calmly, saying "thank you very much," and walked away.

I had a fare who told me he was the King of Cambodia, and later I saw his picture in the paper, and it was true. And I had a young man who looked completely normal but said he was Jesus Christ, and that he had an account with the company. I let him go. Life is too short for all that.

People fuck in the cab, oh yes, and jerk off. Men and women. Just like in Martin Scorsese's "Taxi Driver", with Robert de Niro. Only I never got hung up on prostitutes, teenage or old raddled crones. I had a wisp of a girl with a little whip who offered to pay me in trade. I told her: Some other time, honey, I get hit enough in real life. The whores are always so tired. They fall asleep in the cab, and I cruise around with them, cradling them in my big yellow crib, thinking in my mind, fantisizing. But in this day and age, there's too much contagion. You know what I'm saying. It's just too sad.

Sometimes I imagine the City is singing to me, chanting its own requiem. The tall buildings are leaning towards me, their windows winking, their fire escape ladders rusted in their wait for Jacobs to climb up and wrestle angels on the roofs. They are crying out in their loneliness, calling to the smoke that curls up from the subway vents and maintenance chutes. The houses are wrinkled old men, weighed down by their bloated appetites, the smoke is all that remains of long lost lovers, dancing to forgotten tunes. Below falls the echo of the subway, drumming signals in a dismal code. Kadum kadum, kadum kadum. The street bucks and writhes beneath me. My cab is grating on the City's skin, which is sensitive as a one thousand year old baby. In the rain, it hisses in self-pity, whispering and letting out its breath like a sighing and despairing mother. Mother and child, with me the Holy Ghost. Except I can create no Messiahs.

Kadum kadum. And in this windy autumn, the added shrieking of the storm, buffeting the vehicle, jerking the steering wheel, threatening to pick me up and dash me against the houses. Pretty soon we'll be into the winter, which is far worse - the blizzards sweeping in from the north, icy roads, frost setting in the bones. I have seen too many of those, too, by now, my fourth year in the City. A far cry from the snows of Lebanon... The white canopy, crisp and clean, blanketing the mountains above the bloated city. Beirut. The deadly labyrinth, where every street corner and alleyway was a lethal trap. Once it was a place of laughter and singing, but not when I was there. That was another another kind of killing. They killed you there because they knew who you were. They kill you here because they don't.

One period I picked up fares from JFK. I would make a point of meeting the incoming El Al flight, the jetlagged Israelis piling into my back seat, jabbering among themselves in their own rough tongue, which sounds like a file on sandpaper. They regard New York as a suburb of Tel Aviv, as well they might, since their daily Hebrew papers are sold in all the kiosks here a few minutes after they appear over there. I used to ache to tell them: I am a Palestinian and how are you enjoying my country? But they don't care who's driving as long as he takes them where they want. They can see my name on the dashboard: SALIM HALIMI. But it just confirms to them that they have not travelled far.

Benjamin keeps telling me that I am living in the past. Nobody cares now, everyone is bored with the war, if only they knew how to end it.

"It's not that they don't want to give you your rights, Salim. It's that they don't care about rights, period. It's dog eat dog, nobody bothers to chase cats. It's the zeitgeist, honey."

My friend Benjamin. The Bible tells me that he was the youngest son of the Patriarch Yakub, and the only one who was born in Palestine. The thirteenth son. His patrimony stretched from Jericho to Ajlun, in a rainbow curve north of Jerusalem. What else does the Old Testament tell me? He was born on the road between Bethel and Bethlehem, and his mother Rachel died in childbirth, calling him Ben Oni - son of my sorrow. So what's in a name? Nothing much, as Shakespeare said, it has the same smell. My mother was a stickler for the Old Testament. It is our irony that Benny's mother, poor soul, remembers virtually nothing, so he tells me, in her geriatric state, whereas my mother remembers everything, from the least tenets of her religion to the tiniest tics of our national sorrow, every pinprick ripped away since by our gaping gushing wound. She remembers every moan I made in my cradle, and every whisper of my father's litany of woes.

Which are of course our speciality. We are the Moaning Minnies of civilization. I remember that phrase from Margaret Thatcher's Britain. In this, as in much else, we have replaced the Jews. The Jews still moan, but people pay less and less heed. Today, even our justified lamentations have to struggle for attention with the cries of so many other oppressed peoples: Bosnians, Serbs, Croats, Armenians, Azeris, Ossetians, Somalis, Kashmiris, Afghans, desperate for help and salvation. The magic wand of the United Nations. The U.S. Marines. The I.M.F.. Stretching out our hands to all our tormentors, asking them to change their spots. Perhaps the blows will change into caresses. You never know until you try.

I tried to leave all that baggage behind me but of course it followed me as it always does, to New York City, alive with its own disunited nations... I take things as they come, though I appreciate my friends, who are so eager to pin down the world... Against Professor Darwish's advice on priorities, I have been reading Marx. Just when everybody has thrown the old Jew in the trashcan of history I developed this curiosity. I borrowed Das Kapital volume one from Caroline's shelves. The Professor warned me: "Your brain will swell up, your eyes will bulge, your tongue will dry, your arse will push through your teeth." But I wanted to understand how a great man who changed the world thinks, even if the world changed back again. You never know how the wheel will turn. I opened the book at random to the following passage: "In the hardware manufactures of Birmingham and the neighborhood, there are employed, mostly in very heavy work, 30,000 children and young persons, besides 10,000 women. They are to be found in a range of unhealthy jobs: In brass foundries, button factories, and enamelling, galvanizing and lacquering works[73]. Owing to the excessive labour performed by their workers, both adult and non-adult, certain London firms where newspapers and books are printed have gained for themselves the honourable name of `slaughter-houses.'

> (73) "...One of the most shameful, dirtiest and worst paid jobs, a kind of labour on which women and young girls are by preference employed, is the sorting of rags. It is well known that Great Britain, apart from its own immense store of rags, is the emporium for the rag trade of the whole world. The rags flow in from Japan, from the most remote countries of South America, and from the Canary Islands..." *
> (* And now children are employed at file-grinding in Sheffield!)

Sometimes one has to go to the trash to rediscover lost wisdom. Only another thousand pages to go! And then I have volumes two and three! Not to speak of all the other mileage of Allan Darwish's shelves... I have no time even to begin to start to climb this mountain. But at least I can graze on the slopes...

Das Kapital. Law and Order... Let us tell the tale of Benjamin, the thirteenth son, since I'm sure he won't confess it himself. He has this problem of a false modesty. Or perhaps just memory gaps. Benjamin, a loyal son of his people, completed his army service in 1982. The year of the Lebanon war. My people fighting his people as usual. Benjamin joined the infantry corps, to test his mettle and better serve his country which claims to be fated to be at war. He sees action on the outskirts of Beirut. Let me explain what this means. It means that our people, the Palestinian fighters, and their families, and several hundred thousand citizens of Lebanon's capital, are trapped in the city without electricity or water while the Israel Air Force planes bomb and strafe "terrorist targets" wherever their maps show them such an animal is. The young man is wracked with doubt and loathing for the task he is asked to perform. But his conscience is rescued by a senior tank commander, a Colonel of the Armoured Corps, who decides to resign from the army rather than take his tanks into the heart of the city to finish off our Palestinian fighters and the shreds of his country's reputation at the same time. The Americans move in and impose a cease fire. Benjamin is moved out to the rear. Thus he misses out on the greatest shame of his country, the massacre at Sabra and Shatilla. One thousand dead, and so many blind eyes and deaf ears turned to the slaughter... All this is a matter of record.

We leap forward in time six years. Our maturing Benjamin is now a veteran of protests and demonstrations against invasions and wars. But still the Good Patriot, reporting dutifully for his annual reserve service. Still the thirteenth son. But time has moved on. The Israeli army has been forced out of most of Lebanon by the popular resistance of Hizbollah. Their readiness to die for their religion has proven a potent weapon. But we, too, have found our own. Our popular insurrection, *intifada*. Benjamin's infantry unit has a new task now, chasing the children who throw pebbles and stones. An ignoble combat for soldiers trained to fight armies. You loathed that too, Benjamin? But you were the Good Patriot. So when did it come to an end?

- Why should you understand, Salim? It's just an arbitrary border. I never asked you to accept my dilemma. It was just the way I was. And then I wasn't the way I was any more.

You saw your best friend beat up this Palestinian boy, what was his age? Eleven? Ten?

- He wasn't my best friend, Salim, he was just another shmuck.

But you pushed him into a corner in front of all your unit, and pushed your Uzzi up against his neck, and threatened to shoot him dead if he went on beating the Palestinian?

- It wasn't an Uzzi, it was an FN Carbine.

But still it was a very nice gesture.

- Fuck your arse through your nose, Salim.

And then they packed you off out of there, and put you on a court martial, and then they cancelled it, and instead discharged you from further duty as a psychiatric case. Wasn't that the way it was?

- Allahu akbar, Salim.

Would you have fired the shot, Benjamin? Would you have killed your best friend?

- I told you he was just another shmuck, Salim. There were thousands more like him. They didn't need me to do their dirty work.

Would you have fired the gun?

- God only knows, Salim.

He is indeed all knowing. My mother was quite sure of that. He waits and watches, noting everything down for the Day of Judgement, after the Messiah's Second Coming. The Revelations, the Apocalypse of Saint John. When the great city of Babylon shall be thrown down and will be no more. And a horseman, who will be called Faithful and True (or were there two of them?) will cast the Beast into the bottomless pit. There will be a great chain, to bind Satan for a thousand years. What happens after that is anyone's guess. But by then the only place to be will be the New Jerusalem, where only the purest souls will live. I am sure I would not qualify. But Benjamin? I still find your story very moving.

- It certainly was for me. I moved to New York.

The meeting place of the ages, Benny. Do you realise, there are people in this city who are Ba'athists? Loyalists of Hafez el-Assad? Not to speak of the loyalists of Saddam Hussein. Occasionally they invite me to their soirees. Raising the ghost of the Arab Revolution. Socialism and Unity. It's Scheherezade all over again. But I prefer to hobnob with the Enemy. After all, we share the same anxieties, the same indecision, skepticism and mistrust. Isn't that so, Benjamin?

- Absolutely, Salim. So get on with it. Tell your story you're aching to unload. The famous crash, manna in the desert, the staff beating against the dry rock...

Don't expect me to speak with your voice, Benjamin.

- I wouldn't dream of it, Salim.

My friend, the conscience stricken Israeli. Well, at least there is a conscience to strike. We should be grateful for small mercies. I know, they were so hard to come by in the past. Those pilots, shrieking over my head in their Phantoms, dropping liquid fire and bombs... I imagined, as a child, their faces. They had bulging foreheads and red, fiery eyes. Their blonde hair was plastered to their skulls. Smoke came out of their nostrils. They went home to nests of writhing vermin and dined on human flesh. Then a man came to our school, in Bourj, south of

Beirut. He was a famous commander of the Revolutionary Forces. Abu Hamid. He told us that the enemy was as human as you or I, but was following an evil ideology. I was ten years old and I could not accept that. I said that a man with evil ideas was an evil man, and could not change that. He commended me for my boldness and told me to grow up determined, but not to become twisted by bitterness.

A year later I joined the *ashbal*. The lion cubs. We dressed in uniforms and marched about with rifles whose pins had been removed. We swore blood oaths on playgrounds. We were determined to die for our country, that had been stolen from us. We had another commander, Abu Shahid, who told us to nourish our hate. He took us onto the field and hung several sacks on wooden poles. Then he took some cats out of a box and put one in each sack. We were given bayonets and told to kill the cats. I was the only one to do so blindly and without hesitation. Most of the other boys needed two or more tries, and some broke down in tears and refused. The cat stuck on my bayonet writhed and shrieked and tore the lining of the sack. I saw its claws rip through the bag. Then it stiffened and died. I pulled my bayonet out proudly. Abu Shahid hugged my thin shoulders. "Next time you do it to a Jew," he said.

I repeated this line, to Benjamin, so many years later. He said: "It's understandable." There is nothing as infuriating as an understanding enemy.

As things turned out, I never did bayonet or slaughter any enemy, Jew or otherwise, though I did fire some shots in anger, as they say, or I should say in fear, at phantom shadows running through rubble. Ein el-Hilwe, 1982. The red-eyed demons came and bombed the refugee camp to ruins. Then they came, on foot and in armoured cars and tanks, to conquer the remains.

That cat did haunt me. I remember it struggling in Abu Shahid's hand. It was a thick, almost furry hand, attached to a muscular and hairy arm, which held the poor beast aloft like a trophy. It was a skinny, ginger coloured thing. It followed me, to Brighton Beach, clawing at the window whenever the Atlantic Ocean hits the shore. It was certainly not my first corpse, for there were many, left behind in smoking huddles when the demon pilots had gone. Later I watched them floating in masses, off Ras Beirut. There were piles, on the rotting beach, blackened shreds of limbs pecked by birds. Then even the birds got disgusted and just wheeled above, keening and cawing.

I am fascinated by American teenagers, who pass their time in cars and diners, preening in mock battles, guzzling pills to forget the pain of their prosperity. Toys'R'Us. But we were the Mutant Ninja Turtles, reared in the sewers. What we wouldn't have done for a pizza. On my fifteenth birthday, to the day, I was evacuated with the fighters from Beirut, in accordance with an agreement hammered out between the American envoy, Mister Philip Habib, himself, by the way, a Lebanese, and the Israelis. An agreement that was torn up only three weeks later, with the Sabra and Chatilla massacre. We left the women, the children and the old men behind to be slaughtered, on an American guarantee. "Well," Darwish once told me, "you didn't learn the lesson." And still we suck America's ass. It's a sad reflection, but then, so is everything else. Nobody seems to learn from experience. Have you noticed this flaw, Benjamin, in the human race?

- And are we excluded from this, companero?

Yes, that was a truly mad day, as we celebrated our defeat. Riding, in our kefiyas and guns and wrapped in ammunition belts, in our jeeps wreathed in flags and banners, down the Rue de France towards the port. The great white Greek ferry boats waiting to take us to exile, to our Mediterranean cruise. The civilian women wept and wailed and embraced us. We fired round after round into the air. I saw Abu Hamid again, riding in beside our leader, Abu Amar. He was trying to stop this crazy habit of firing straight up as if the wasted bullets would somehow be swallowed by the air. As it was, I think there were only five fatalities from all that joy, a miracle of a kind. If we had fired so much at our enemies we might have made some impact. I remember glowing with pride at our showing on that day. Our eyes conspired to almost ignore the soldiers of the "multi-national force", the Americans, positioned all about us on the warehouse roofs of the port. We hugged our personal weapons to our breasts as if they were the guarantees of our return. Not to that city which had collapsed about us, but to the usurped homeland. It was only later, as the joyful hoots on the ferry's horns abated and we faced the August calm of the sea lapping at every side, that we realised how far we were sailing away.

Later, in Tunis, in the long hours of waiting for something that would never happen, I read Kanafani's Men in the Sun, which tells of three Palestinians in Jordan who pay a driver to smuggle them across the desert to Kuwait hidden in the drum of a truck. There is a line there: "*The lorry, a small world, black as night, made its way across the desert like a heavy drop of oil on a burning sheet of tin.*" But the driver is delayed at the desert border post and by the time he returns to release the three men from their hole they have suffocated in the heat.

We were not alone in our hole, and surrounded by water. But I remember the suffocation of despair. Singing patriotic songs only increased the feeling of a floating funeral barge. Abu Hamid took me under his wing, in Tunis. He brought me the books, and made me take the advanced English classes, and set me to reading the enemy's press and preparing digests for him and for the command. He had already fingered me for a fast learner, and I began to be aware of the power of words. Not the self deceptive power of rhetoric and its blinding repetition of vain wishes, but the real way in which words shape opinions. He astonished me by bringing me translated books by the enemy, works by Amos Oz and A.B. Yehoshua. Zionist writers. He also had a subscription for the Jerusalem Post, which was supplied to him indirectly from Jerusalem through an agency in Marseille. What do you think of that, Benjamin?

- A wise man we would do well to talk to, Salim.

You will have to fetch out your ouija board. The Israeli commandos came, one Friday morning, out of the sea. They came ashore in the first glimmerings of dawn from rubber dinghies, and climbed into cars which were waiting on the lido at Sidi Bu Said and promptly whisked them to our villa. I was sleeping in the annexe at the time. The commandos knew exactly where to go, rushing up the stairs towards Abu Hamid's bedroom. They shot down the bodyguard and fired twelve bullets into Abu Hamid as he struggled from the bedclothes. His wife, Soraya, was away in Cairo at the time. Before we knew it the assassins had piled back into their cars and driven off down the coastal road, where they were picked up by two helicopters. The Tunisian army was no use at all. Later we were told the assassins had tactical support from American AWACS in the air. So you see, reading Amos Oz and the Jerusalem Post are no defence at all.

- They always go for the pragmatists, Salim. The fanatics are never such a threat.

Of course. When I first came to America, and I'll tell you about my experiences in the Great Hall of Immigration later, I was invited by a Tunisian friend to the home of the Islamic exile leader, Sheikh Jedid, in

Queens. This friend had been kind to me in Tunis so I could not refuse. I just kept quiet about being a Christian. Aren't we all of the same wretched flesh? We took the N train to the end of the line and walked down, underneath the maze of freeways leading to the Triboro Bridge. Have you been to that part of the City, Benjamin? It's mostly Greeks, but the Arabs have put down a few markers there too. An old tenement with the faded signs of long closed garages and billiard halls turned out to be the Sheikh's mosque. Two fat men in faded overalls slouching in a van outside were, I was told, the FBI, keeping an eye on this barely tolerated guest. The Sheikh held court in a barren room covered with a threadbare carpet, with a few portraits of some clerics who were unknown to me pasted on the brick walls, and behind him, through the window, the traffic to and from La Guardia grinding by like an endless metal serpent.

The Sheikh was blind since birth. The crumbs of his lunch were still nesting in his white beard. I was introduced to him as a *fiday* who had fought in Lebanon for Palestine and had come to this country to gain specialised knowledge so I could return to fight again. I did not tell him I had undergone my Transformation by then. Nothing was required of me except to be an audience for his divine sermon. There were about twenty other people in the room, some of them young men in casual clothes or t-shirts, some older businessmen in suits, and a couple of elders, minor mullahs. The Sheikh told us that the material kingdoms of the west were doomed, that Godless Communism would be followed by Godless Capitalism into the dustbin of history. The Islamic revival was gaining strength throughout the world and nothing would stand in its path. A young man beside the Sheikh was recording every word for posterity on a Radio Shack cassette portable. The freeway snake rattled the walls. My friend, Kamal, took me aside while the great man was still droning on to offer me a job in one of the video shops which the Sheikh's family owned in all five boroughs of the city. There was a vacancy in one of the outlets in Flatbush Avenue, in Brooklyn, near Prospect Park.

That was my first job in America, for which I was duly grateful, but not enough to embrace the Faith. The Sheikh never visited my branch, which was filled with the abominations he condemned. Cary Grant made love to Katharine Hepburn, Student Nurses put out to all comers and Arnie Schwartzenegger blew off legs, arms and scalps in defence of the American way. I moved from the dormitory I was sharing with ten other refugees in Queens to a slightly less crowded one in Prospect, with only five room-mates, probably owned by another of the Sheikh's many relatives feasting off the flesh pots of sin.

Money from Tunis, from the Old Man himself, came to pay for my studies, in Allan Darwish's evening class: The Middle East in the Twentieth Century. I can't tell you how much it opened my eyes. The students were a bizarre mix. Half were Black Muslims and the other half Jewish fascists of the Kahanist tendency, who believed all Arabs should be expelled from the Holy Land of Israel. They sat there with their skullcaps and Stars of David snorting and stamping like young elephants in a cage. I was a kind of prize exhibition piece to Darwish, a "real live Palestinian" to show to these people who thought the only good Palestinian was a dead one. "Don't tell them what you were doing out there," he told me cheerfully, "I'm just telling them you're a bona fide refugee." But they became aware that I had spent the last few years in Tunis and guessed. They came up to me and asked, politely, if it was true Chairman Arafat was a faggot. I told them no, he was the whole tree. They let me alone after that. I never pick a fight with unfortunates. Particularly if it is a case of fifty to one. And I did not want to make Darwish's class a microcosm of the Jewish-Black war that was already happening out in the streets.

I loved the course. Darwish would make the crazies read documents that would upset their world of myths. The Land Without People For the People Without Land. He flourished land registers, researches, translated newspaper clippings of the time. He went through the whole history without pity for the prejudices of either side. We did the Ottoman Empire, the First World War, Sykes-Picot, Balfour, the Palestine Mandate, Syria, Egypt, Iraq. He gave us a wider view of Imperialism, and of the counter currents in European thought. He gave us the history of our own nationalisms, our disappointed hopes. As he approached the Second World War, the Holocaust, the forming of the State of Israel, the lecture hall began to shake and rattle with fractured delusions and cherished bigotries squeezed dry. At one point the Jewish zealots rebelled and began singing the Israeli National Anthem, *hatikva* - hope. Darwish, humming the stirring tune with them, moved among them, scattering photocopies of copious sections from Israeli revisionist writing, books by Benny Morris and Simha Flapan which punctured all the official mythologies. Sometimes they tore up the notes. But like real gluttons for punishment, they kept coming back for more. It was difficult to tell, in that bearpit, who was the baiter and who was the bear, as Darwish pranced and gesticulated, flinging his arms in the air to dispel the noxious fumes of denial. "Throw out your garbage. Throw out your garbage! You have to start to think in new ways!"

I never went back to the Sheikh in his warehouse. I could never explain to those people the changes I had gone through, or long conceal my faded Nazarene origins. Perhaps if the ghost of Abu Hamid had been there he could have formed a bridge between us...

- Tell the story, Salim. Unload the burden of your essential absurdity. You're no different than the rest of us.

A Palestinian is always more different. Wasn't this the way it was with the Jews?

- I'm blubbering already Salim.

Eventually I told my tale to Darwish, one day at his cubbyhole on Riverside Drive, up there on the twelfth floor, with the wind rattling the double glazed windows like a bad stage ghost, and Aram Djerdjekian nodding sympathetically by his side. Both were people whom nothing could surprise. If I entered their house with my head sticking out of my arse, waving three arms, they would only hand me three glasses, with an orange juice, a Miller Lite and a Scotch. Always options. Later, it made it easier to tell the tale to Frances, to you, Benjamin, to Caroline. The collector of medical curiosities. Perhaps I was her favourite freak, until this new guy we're looking for, what's his name, Mo Smith?

- Get on with it, Salim, quit stalling.

After the murder of Abu Hamid, the Chairman took me personally under his arm. I was living in the crook of his elbow, grazing in the shadow of his kefiyah... I quickly became one of his scribes, travelling with him wherever he went. I had become used to a world in which there was no certainty. I had become used to a world in which you were always uprooted, at the mercy of some faceless omnipotent power. But now I became like a leaf plucked in the ceaseless flutter of the Chairman's wings. We flew, from Tunis to Cairo, from Cairo to Kinshasa, from Kinshasa to Bombay, from Bombay to Beijing, from Beijing to Budapest, from Budapest to Kuala Lumpur, from Kuala Lumpur back to Cairo, then Dakar, then Dar es- Salaam. It was like that joke, if it's Tuesday it must be Bucharest. The endless protocol, embraces at the airport, national anthems, state banquets, red carpets and blather. Endless blather, promises, condemnations, soporific solidarity. The Chairman embraced them all, he gave them all the same earnest attention and smiles. Often he told me he could never tell whether he was kissing a baby or a head of state who had executed thousands of his opponents. "We take our friends where we find them. Our enemies don't care who they kiss, so why should our lips burn with shame?"

I was the one who carried his bulging bag of papers, my arm clipped to it like a handcuffed prisoner to his jailor. A prisoner happy to be serving the cause at the highest level. Although I was always left outside, in the anterooms, when the Chairman and his host had done with their videotaped blatherings and adjourned with their translators and heads of security into the private, protected rooms. The Chairman told me it was in my interests. "So you won't be a target, come what may." I knew almost nothing that wasn't public, though the Chairman was convinced most of what was said to him in private was taped and kept by all sides. "Never say anything that has only one interpretation," was one of his chief pieces of advice. "Prefer at least three or four different meanings. Always assume you are broadcasting, even in the toilet. Especially in the toilet," he laughed. He was always ready for anything. The more unexpected the more he expected it. Which played its part in saving our lives...

We travelled round the globe in the small private jet which the Chairman had been given ten years earlier by the King of Saudi Arabia. It had been swept so often for bugs a gnat would find it hard to climb on board. It was piloted and maintained, as far as humanly possible, by our own security people and engineers. We often carried our own small ground crew with us, to smell out any local sabotage. But one cannot control Mother Nature. The earth, the sky, the sea, the winds. On a routine flight from Khartoum to Tripoli we ran into a severe turbulence. A sandstorm, whipped up in the depths of the Sahara Desert, just over the border from Sudan. Coming up towards the Tropic of Cancer. And not the one from Henry Miller. There was nothing below us, above us, around us, but sand. The plane bucked like a stricken chariot. I was sitting opposite the Chairman, going through some papers, when they flew up, escaping from us like autumn leaves. Cups of coffee shattered against the ceiling of the plane. Abu Talal, the Chairman's chief bodyguard, staggered up the aisle like a drunken bull. "The instruments are not responding," he shouted, "we should prepare for a crash."

He unlocked his personal communication set, which would transmit our location directly to Tunis, as well as to any other electronic ear that happened to be tuned in. We asked the pilot for his estimate of our situation. He said sand had blasted into both engines and severed his control of the tail. He was doing what he could to regain power, but he had already lost the right. "All we need now is to lose the left as well," the Chairman quipped, "and we can be right where we started in the fifties." His eyes gleaming with the excitement of a crisis, the adrenalin rush of the trap. There was nothing he loved better than having his back against the wall, with all the forces of Satan and Man pitted against him in one great swoop. We sped on through the sand. It was as if we had been tipped into a hole in the ground and torn into the ranges of hell. It was sure we were going down. The bodyguards, all three of them, tucked themselves about the Chairman like a defensive cushion. I joined my poor body to the shield. We cocooned him like bees about their Queen. He put his arms around us and began to pray. In the Name of God, the Compassionate, the Merciful...

The desert swallowed us but saved us as well. Had we gone down on rocks or a mountain we would have been scattered like the Bible's dry bones. As it was the dunes parted like the Red Sea to let us through. The sands must have smothered the fires, because we simply hit the ground and snapped into three jagged pieces. I seemed to have missed out the moment of impact. All I remember is one moment the terror of the descent, the next the deep blue of the sky poking through a choking cloud of sand, with the pilot's cabin a compressed pile of metal on the other side of the hole.

Our sweaty bodies rolled off the Chairman with eerie sucking sounds. I realised the sudden silence was not punctured eardrums but the indifference of the desert after our long, loud fall. One of the bodyguards, Abu Tewfiq, was dead, his back skewered by a shard of broken window. The other two, Abu Talal and Ghaseem, were alive, though Ghaseem's left leg was broken. The Chairman rolled to his feet like one of those weighted dolls that cannot be knocked over. "I'm all right. How is everybody?" I staggered up, all in one piece, looking around towards the other seats: There had been two more comrades, and four crew, on the plane, apart from the bodyguards, the Chairman and myself. The comrades, Faisal el-Tlas and our deputy Chief- of-Staff, Jadid, were bruised but safe. The pilot, co-pilot and first ground engineer had died in the cabin. So there were seven of us crawling out of the wreckage into the Sahara desert.

This is the world of hi-technology, the global village, where every voice cackles to another across the electronic threads. Where every tug in Tokyo causes a jerk in New York. Where we can see death by starvation live over our creaky chicken. Nevertheless, for all this you need the magic box. And ours was dangled forlornly by Abu Talal, smashed in the crash, its wires hanging out like a gutted chicken. And all the cabin backups gone, including the emergency pack of medicines, water and food. We were as cut off from the world as any medieval pilgrim who lost his way in the sand.

But the Chairman took personal command. There was only one unbroken canteen, in his special survival pack, which included a Sony Walkman radio, several bars of chocolate and boiled sweets for sucking, a spare shirt, a pair of spare socks, and Belgian rash lotion. But the canteen was only one quarter full, and would probably last us in the most modest of sips for the first four or five hours. We ended up after the division with a Hershey Bar and three boiled sweets each. The Chairman used the socks, together with strips of the shirt, to bind Ghaseem's broken leg to a detached arm rest from one of the passenger chairs.

The Chairman's plan was this: It would be certain death for us to wander off from the wreck, into the depths of what we were certain was the Libyan portion of the wasteland. The closest habitation would be the As-Sarra air base, close to the border with Chad, at least one hundred and fifty kilometers distant. Their radar should have registered our plane's disappearance and trigger an aerial search. But the Chairman was not misplacing any optimistic trust in the Libyan Jamahariya's reliability. For he revealed now that he was carrying a special device, a tracer, much like an ordinary "bleeper", whose perpetual signal could be accessed by American satellites orbiting the Earth several hundred kilometers above, in the stratosphere. This had been, apparently, a gift from the outgoing Secretary of State, Mr George Schultz, at the brief period when the United States was engaged in an official dialogue with our movement, which was terminated due to an unauthorised attack on an Israeli beach by one of the Chairman's bitterest rivals. Mr Schultz told the Chairman: Whenever you're in trouble, the Eye in the Sky will see all.

We have only to wait, said the Chairman, for the two possible outcomes: Either the armed forces of our allies will find us, or, if they manifest their usual inefficiency, the Eye in the Sky will pinpoint our position and alert those who need to be alerted. We did not debate out loud the obvious drawback that they might inform our enemies so they might finish the job the sandstorm began.

So we remained by the wreck, and waited, taking shelter in the shade of the broken fuselage which thrust out of the sand like the ribs of a gigantic dead beast. Most of the canteen water preserved from the crash went on easing the wounded man's thirst. By six in the evening there was not one drop left. During the day, though, several of us wanted to relieve ourselves in the sand. But the Chairman stopped us, pointing out that once the canteen was dry our own urine would be the only liquid available. He made us pee into the small styrofoam cups which had survived the wreck scattered among the seats, and when the canteen was completely empty he filled it with his own water. We closed the cups with the little caps thoughtfully provided by a Swedish catering firm.

The night soon came, shielding us at least from the heat, but deepening our sense of seclusion and abandonment. The Chairman tried to keep our spirits up by reciting the number of times he had been pronounced dead by the world press. At this very moment, he promised us, the New York Herald Tribune was publishing an editorial about his likely successor. TV crews were probably combing the desert. In fact, we would be much more likely to be rescued by a rapacious team from CNN or CBS than by anyone else. We looked up into the sky, which was clear and glorious, and tried to make out the surveillance satellite. But the Eye in the Sky remained invisible, hoarding its dispassionate dreams.

We fell asleep, exhausted, despite the moans of Ghaseem, and woke to the renewed assault of the sun. Our throats were dry as the sand itself. We could not hold out any longer, uncapping the grisly cuplets of waste. Each man crawled off into whatever privacy he could manufacture by his hunched body and forced down the warm pungent grunge. The Chairman handed me his canteen, after taking the first sips himself. "Look on it as a metaphor for our fate," he said.

The day crawled by in slow agony. By the afternoon stomach cramps forced most of us to vomit in the sand. A thin, pitiful spew. But three hours later there was no option but to return to our vital fluids. The Chairman refilled his canteen, a task the rest of us were far too arid to achieve. But the Chairman's canteen, like some miraculous gourd, kept emptying and replenishing from the same boundless source.

The day seemed to last forever. The sun was stuck in its station, a burning, pitiless eye. Out of it swirled shapes and visions. Ancient horsemen galloped across the sands. Strange serpents crawled sideways across the dunes and shrivelled, leaving glowing parchments inscribed with letters of gold which burned up too fast for us to read. Giant skeletons reared out of the sands in undulating dance. As night fell, the shimmering stars gasped in and out of black holes. The taste of our urine stuck in my mouth like an infusion from hell. Wracked with spasms, I lay in the Chairman's arms as he hummed old lullabies.

During the night Ghaseem died. We tried to wake him with a touch of the Chairman's piss at his lips but he persisted in his pained rigor. I was already completely delirious, and saw dancing girls gyrating on the mounds. They told me later that when the Libyan jeeps crested the dunes they found us prancing like wild beasts. Only the Chairman remained sitting under the wreck like an ancient God surveying his nymphs. They told me that when the Libyan officer took hold of my arm I went down on my knees and asked him for his hand in marriage. I called him Layla and said I was her lover Majnun, the madman who would have no other desire. Apparently I had to be restrained. I spent the journey to the Libyan base babbling about moonlight, illegitimate kings and swords. The drugs they jabbed into me only increased my hallucinations. I was walking on the surface of the moon, holding a spray of hyacinths and roses, whose thorns drew rivulets of blood down my arms. The king of the moon, a bearded deity in a dirty white coat, clamped an anaesthetic mask on my face. I slid into a timeless world of wanderings, revisiting the bombed refugee camps, wading through the bones of my childhood friends and running after the ghost of my father, who kept floating off the closer I got. He was moving his lips but I was much too far away to hear what he was saying, and after a while he gave up trying and turned away, disappearing down an open well. I peered over its edge, into the darkness...

When I awoke I was in a crisp clean bed, in a room overlooking the sea. Green palm trees waved over clear white sand. It was a nursing home for government officials and army officers near Tripoli, staffed by charming Italian nurses who led me about the grounds like a new born babe. I learned to walk, and taste, and speak. The Chairman contacted me by telephone, but his voice seemed to represent a distant world. I walked on the beach, watching the waves for hours on end. I felt drained of thought, though I could remember my life until then as if it were the tale of someone else which I had just read in a book. I remembered Abu Shahid and the bayoneted cats, Philip Habib's broken truce and the festive retreat from Beirut, the Greek ferry to exile, Abu Hamid, the Chairman's shaggy bag. All the rhetoric of combat and struggle. It was all remote and unconnected to anything I perceived as my self. The Chairman came to Tripoli and whisked up to the sanatorium. "Can I stay here for a month?" he quipped.

As my surrogate father, he could see I was particularly troubled, and asked me what the problem was. I told him I was not the same person, that despite my continued feeling for the struggle and the cause I could no longer be of any use for any act which harmed my fellow man, even my worst enemy. He looked at me with those welling eyes of bottomless shrewd compassion. "You drank my piss and turned into a pacifist," he said. "One should not question the decrees of God. We will find you a way to serve with a clean soul." Two weeks later Faisal el-Tlas called with the answer: I was being offerred a visa to America to further my studies in English, and attend certain courses, by arrangement with well-wishers and friends. I would have enough time to straighten my thinking and absorb the world of our enemies, who would some day have to become our friends...

- A touching tale, Salim. From dog to dove in one big step.

A Transformation in more ways than one, Benjamin. When I arrived by Trans World Airlines they held me in Immigration for three hours. Locked in a small room together with a distraught and weeping Nigerian woman who had lost her passport, a huge bearded and turbanned Kashmiri man who couldn't speak a word of English and another Palestinian, who had been evicted from Kuwait because his name was Saddam Hussein. He regarded himself lucky to escape with his life, a luck fortified by his foresighted salting aways of funds in several other Gulf States, none of which would accept him either. The only place where he could safely find a sanctuary, it seemed, was Germany, no longer either East or West, before it too closed its doors to the multitude and vomitted its leaden guilt. He too was looking for a better Transformation, trying his luck as a piece of huddled mass. But the computer which keeps the list of banned souls at Kennedy raised the alarm, assuming that his namesake, the Iraqi dictator, had really turned up, seeking asylum.

- An honest mistake, Salim. But at least you passed muster.

Yes. The gateway opened, and let me through. They clipped the visa stamp to my Lebanese passport and then Darwish drove me off into the city shining under a steel grey sky. The melting pot in which I am still dissolving. You must forgive me, I am only an ignorant non-American from the furthest regions of the Earth, but it is nice to walk on my days off along the Brighton Beach boardwalk, just a short walk from my nice little apartment, among the Russian Jews from old decaying cities with Walkmans blasting old songs into their ears. Georgian kebabs and Ukrainian Tearooms. I remember my father and mother taking me by the hand along the Beirut beach. A hot, Mediterranean shore, with white waves in the deepest blue and suntanned young men and women splashing on coloured plastic rafts. A holiday from the lion cubs, the pinless rifles and the murdered cats. And I remember when I came back next the boys and girls were still cavorting, though the corpses drifted to the shore.

- People get used to anything, Salim.

My father never got used to exile. His misery followed him like a shadow wherever he went, and in the end it just drooped by him in the grit and dust of the camp. He was one of those people who always carried a key of the house he had left behind in Palestine. Though he came from a small village near Lyd, Al Haditha, whose houses never had to have keys. Others used to carry little buckets of earth from the soil of the homeland, you know all the stories, Benjamin, old tales of woe become so stale. But it was true, my father lived that day of 12th July, 1948, when your commandos came to our village. Commander Rabin, who is now your Prime Minister, and he was then much younger than you are now. It is all recorded in Benny Morris.

- What can I tell you, Salim? Here, take this piece from my arm.

Who wants your flesh? It's only my own... So can a man cry all his life? My father did, and died, like Moses, without entering his promised land. Unlike Moses, he didn't even get a last glimpse. But we are all shaking with the fever of history. Life goes on. A man is carried forward by hope. Always hope, we hope, but even without that - curiosity... To live to see what happens next, in the streets of our new diaspora. The dice rattled, and thrown down in the clutter of ten million other dice -

- Don't you think, Benjamin?

I think, therefore I think, Salim -

And now, about this Mo Smith...

THE STREETS OF EXILE, OH YES. The violins, the flutes, the low wail of saxophone and horn. The fire and brimstone of the preachers. The promise of salvation and revenge. Sweet Daddy Grace and Father Divine, the Living God of Harlem. The Lord in striped shirt and tie and black felt hat, passing out manna to the paupers, the vagrants, the tetchy of the earth. The slaves offloading the milk and honey from the great liners of state. Free at last! Free at last! The rag-pickers' cold feet at dawn. Unbearable summers. Tramp tramp tramp, up from Trinity Churchyard. Sacred to the Memory: *Sydney Breese 1797, Made by Himself - I here hye, all Time is flown.* Keep off the grass! Up, up, past Steve's Pizza, Burger King, burnt offerings. And Cain slew Abel. Am I my brother's keeper? Fugitive and vagabond upon the earth. 45 dollars and sixty cents, sir, them shoes will last you for some time. Nike, the Goddess of Victory. Zeus, King of all the Gods.

Tramp tramp tramp, up to the corner of Church and Liberty, the plaza of the World Trade Center, the crowds in the concourse between the Commodities Exchange and the South and North Towers. Can you spare a few cents for a cupocoffee, thank you very much, have a good day. PLEASE HELP ME I AM SICK / DISABLED / MENTALLY UNFIT / A WAR VETERAN... TRYING TO RAISE $1,000,000.50 cents FOR WINE RESEARCH. Smartass. The twin towers glitter in the sun. Look on my works, ye puny, and despair. Goddamm Mo, where you get those shoes? The kind lady doctor in the labyrinth dispensed them unto me from taxpayers' dolours. Well you lucky motherfucker.

I have a long way to go. The burning bush. Mo says. I am that I am. The bull rushes. Merrill Lynch and East River Savings. The Millenium Hotel. A nickel, sir? God fuck your ass. Onwards, onwards. Past the Northeast Plaza Building across Vesey Street. The shadow of the Federal

Office Building and Post Office. Graciano Constructions, Improving Your City. Saint Peter's Roman Catholic Church. New York's Oldest: *"Knowledge of the Past is a Precondition for Understanding the Present - Thomas Merton, 1915- 1968."* Allahu akbar, padre. CNA Insurance Company. Con Edison. The Emigrant's Savings Bank: "There hasn't been a Home Equity Rate like this in 20 years - 5.99%!" Deli Salad Bar and Grocery Cold Cuts. Hot Bagel Hot Croissant. Charlie Bow Roast Pork Bun - steam mix veg. $1.80 General Tsao chicken $2.00 shrimp with lobster sauce $2.50 fried fish fillet $1.00. Linda's Gourmet Deli. Shabnum Ladies Boutique. Sweta Mode. Facial, waxing, nail centre. Abdul Kareem videos and gifts. Jewellery. Joe Lot's Trading. Save 30 to 70% - candy, food, snacks, artificial flowers, party goods, luggage, accessories, HBA, pet supplies, household chemicals, hardware, toys, paint, bed, bath, rugs, cookware, bakeware, glassware, framed art. A Bargain is our Business. City Wigs Beauty: Jumbo, Superslinky, Golden Braid. Jesse Jackson and the Golden Fleece. The voyage of the argue-nots. Zaro's Bread Basket, J & J News, Mashugana Ike, Mizrachi Kosher Pizza and Falafel, All American Foods, yoghourt, ice cream, papaya, hot dogs, burgers, chicken, beer, soda, heros. Creep by, Nike and Zeus. Y.E.S. International Nuts: "WE ARE NUTS ABOUT NUTS!" Wholesaler, retailer, direct imports, gourmet coffee beans, cashews, almonds, pecans, groudnuts, brazils. NO TURKISH PISTACHIOS UNTIL NEW CROP COMES IN.

So what's wrong with the Turkish Pistachio Crop??? The rampaging, nutcracking hordes... He slumped his face against the cold shop window, his hot breath steaming up the pane, veiling the myriad jars of kernels from around the globe, the gathered seed. The cries of woe of indentured Ottoman growers, knouted off their lands by blight and frost. Led by chains round their necks to the waiting three masted square riggers, bolted in the holds for the voyage. Land ahoy! The bayous of Louisiana, echoing with the rustle of cotton buds...

"What have you got to say? Speak up!"

"Are you hearing voices, Mister Smith?"

"I could hardly not hear 'em, lady. They tend to shout if they're not paid attention."

"How many voices, Mister Smith?"

"Plenty o' them, madam Doctor."

"Just call me Caroline. Just take it easy. Coffee? Dekaff or Regular?"

"I'll take what I can get I guess."
"These voices, are they male or female?"
"Is this goin' to affect my getting the shoes?"
"You'll get the shoes, Mister Smith. Don't worry about that."
"Only I have a long way to go."

From the beginning. The old Adam. Trespassers will be prosecuted. In the morning, we all have to leave the garden. O'Connell, the gate-keeper, hustles us out, under the Leonard H. Stern School of Business. And where's Eve? Naked we go out into the world, hurrying to the five and dime. Tickets to the ark: $500 dollars. Gazing through the pane at the canned manna...

Preliminary Draft Report, by Caroline Dexter, M.D.:
Mohammad Ndabaninghi Smith,
An Authentic Case of Multiple Personality Syndrome?

Freud wrote (1933) that the ego stands for "reason and good sense while the id stands for untamed passions." He was considering a norm, a standard against which to set aberrations, disorders and pathologies. In practice, these categories could never be more than a rough guide to the complex terrain of the self. How less so than in a self which has apparently splintered into a series of interlocking but dissociative states.

Multiple personality has been historically described as a "hysterical" disorder of the self, in which the subject/patient manifests, in a consistent form, one or more additional personalities, either concurrently or in series, which seem clearly separated from the subject's apparent nature. All these elements appear highly subjective, and imply an observation by an outside person, the "doctor", who makes a judgement based wholly on the behavioural patterns of the subject. The terms autoscopy, doppelganger, dual personality, phantom personality and mirror image have been used. The basic loss of association with one's self is regarded as central to these syndromes. The subject will view his own self in an objective and observational manner (Lukianowicz, 1958). Setting aside disorders of self and affect arising from organic brain damage such as disorders of the parietal lobe, the most common states recorded are those in which a "phantom" personality is manifested in a condition of "one-way amnesia" (Abse, 1982), where one personality is aware of and can comment on the other while the alternate is unaware of the first. The two personalities are most often inverse aspects of each other, such as ebullient and gloomy,

obedient and rebellious, naive and cynical, even young and old, ignorant and wise (Scheinbaum, 1976). Disorders involving more than two aspects are not uncommon in cases of simultaneous partial personalities (Jerrold, 1967) and clustered multiple partial personalities (Chatterjee, 1969). But cases involving simultaneous well-defined personalities (Griggs and Klein, 1965) were considered rare, and often thought to be apocryphal rather than substantive. Often these were classified as fictitious or malicious constructs. It has only been recent work by Coons (1984), Bliss and Ross which has highlighted the growing incidence of MPD diagnosis and its origin in early sexual trauma and child abuse. The latter growth in the diagnosis of MPD has concentrated overwhelmingly on female patients. The majority of diagnoses of male MPD has been made in the context of criminal cases (Schwartz, 1981: The Hillside Strangler; Keyes, 1981: The Minds of Billy Milligan), but allegations of fakery and malingering have been especially marked in these instances.

The onus remains, in my view, on the analyst, to validate a multiple, simultaneous syndrome. In the case of Mo Smith, a homeless, vagrant African-American aged in his late forties or early fifties (the lack of documentation and any clinical history constitutes a chronic hindrance to formulating an aetiology), a man in apparently robust health notwithstanding the rigours of his familiar predicament, presented himself to the Department of Social Services Human Resources Office in Lower Manhattan (Tribeca), requesting a cash grant for the purchase of new shoes. Referred to an interview with the above due to an apparent confusion of affect, he proved himself to be highly intelligent and aware of a range of cultural values which suggested a formidable education, although he claimed to have no such qualifications and to have lived his entire life "on the streets."

The initial syndrome appeared to be a delusional pattern of grandiose self-reference familiar in schizophrenic paranoia. The subject appeared to claim to be God, having created the entire human race in a purgative night in Trinity Churchyard, lower Manhattan. The inconsistency of creating all life where life was already apparent is dismissed with a shrug. Reference is made to a "guardian", who appears on investigation to be the keeper of the graveyard, an employee of the New York City Department of Cemeteries, who substantiates the subject's medical crisis, though no hospital treatment has been recorded. The subject's central claim, that all Mankind derived from his body, leaving behind a number of individuals who inhabit specific areas in his organs and limbs, constitutes the bedrock of his manifestation of multiple personality syndrome.

In subsequent sessions, held informally in the presence of a number of lay colleagues and friends, Mr Smith was more forthcoming about the identity of these "stay-behind" personalities. They seemed to manifest themselves in a unique pattern of cascading levels, much like a pack of playing cards which are revealed as they are fanned out. To follow the analogy, the various "cards" would change their order every time they were revealed, as if they had been "shuffled." It is difficult to speculate how many "cards" there are in the entire pack. But the "hand" that Mo Smith has allowed us to see so far appears to consist of the following "individuals":

Arnold - a successful WASP author and occasional columnist who writes for Newsweek and U.S. News and World Report from a point directly under the Adam's Apple.

Ann - a hermetic woman of no clear identity who is usually asleep behind the eyes.

The Pharaoh Merenptah - son of Rameses II and uncle of Rameses III, who lives in the spinal cord, between the shoulder blades.

Muhammad Ibn Battuta - medieval traveller and wanderer, who moves around the blood stream.

Jesse/Yishai - a first century Essene, living in the right lung.

Lincoln Korombane - an exiled Panafrican activist, domiciled in the left lung.

Mordecai - a medieval Jewish doctor and alchemist, whose position in the body is unclear, though Mo Smith is convinced he lives out the body during the night, at a secret location in New York City.

Beatrice - "Mistress of Pain," who lives in the pit of the stomach, and

Jaime Fernando - a youth who plays mariachi and nostalgic tunes in his colon, interspersed with bursts of Rap. (I have suggested an appointment for a general test for tumours or, more likely, duodenal ulcers...)

> Notes: We are touching only the tip of the iceberg. How many more separate personas or splinters could there be beneath the primary level? Or should we beware of encouraging further "revelations" by the suggestive power of the process of therapy? Might this be a narcissistic disassociation? Is Mo Smith simply a fabulist, spinning premeditated tall tales? And if so, where does he get his tales? Long months, even years in the public library, boning up on all his subjects, from Pharaonic Egypt to renascent Africa, from obscure Jewish cave sects of Qumran at the time of Jesus to fourteenth century Persia, not to speak of the latest gossip from Westchester County. And how might all that have been internalised?

Anything's possible, if you have the time, and Mo Smith has nothing but time... Who can look into a man's heart, even a shrink... Echoes here of the idiot savant syndrome? But that is usually associated with subnormal intelligence, and that is certainly not the case here. Witness the heavy-set, bear-like fumbling, as he settles down in Benjamin's apartment. East 4th is as far Uptown he'll agree to venture so far, after Ben and Salim tracked him down at the "bivouack" under the Brooklyn Bridge. He refers to me, they said, as "Lilith." Lilith was Adam's first wife, according to Jewish legends. She refused to obey him and ran off to a cave in the Red Sea to copulate with demons. It makes perfect sense to me...

Settling in Benjamin's fleamarket armchair, putting down his mug of Sanka Coffee, groping in the air after a question, as if trying to pluck the answer out of some unseen dimension. Then he drops his head, resting his chin on his breast, eyelids closing till you think he has fallen asleep, and you might need an industrial crane to move him out of the chair, and then he turns his head, slowly, from side to side, as a series of groans, murmurs, rasps and belches travel up from the deeps, gas escapes from the abdominal cavity, rumbling geysers aching to blow. And then the voices, moaning and grumbling, dipping and dithering, dribbling out the slack lips. The languid sighs of Ann Hedonia, reminiscing about lazy Sundays in what might be nineteenth century Harlem, with lace white picnics along the river as the steamboats chug by. Or the arrogant twang of Arnold Flint, pontificating about the state of the nation, or the fluent Arabic of Ibn Battuta, which astonished both Darwish and Salim, who vouched for its albeit archaic accuracy, or the Hispanic quavering of streetwise Jaime, or the tremulous bass of Lincoln Korombane, inveighing against the CIA. Salim and Benjamin, in a second meeting, at the Liberty Street Burger King, coaxed out the enigmatic Beatrice, and the distant calls of the deceased Pharaoh, trudging through the Halls of the Dead on his way to an ancient Paradise. And hiding behind all these, the bass tones of Mordecai, the "controller", who knows all the secrets...

But our third meeting, once again at Benjamin's, when I looked into his eyes, trying to fathom what lies deep down in those oceanic ridges, I could see my own fears and questions reflected back at me as in a distorted glass. My face twinned, drawn and miniaturised in his pitchblack pupils, my soul shrunk into one more of his multiple homunculi, sucked in like a crushed bone. And at that moment I felt that truth in his eye that we were all his creatures, swinging on the threads of his conviction, flesh of his flesh, blood of his blood...

We psychiatrists are so certain we know the truth. We have factored in ignorance only as a temporary obstacle. Give us an enigma and we solve it, with our Quick Reference Diagnostic Criteria, our DSM-IV tests, our flow charts of error and delusions. Overvalued ideas, delusions of persecution, paranoia, misidentification. You read all the literature, from Adler to Zigmond, from vitalism to voodoo, from Sachs to Sacks. Then you give up and adopt the old Freudian saw: All I want is to enable my patients to live with ordinary unhappiness... A very Unamerican Dream...

When we start out we are always going to change the world. That sickness out there, waiting to be cured. The needy, crying out for help. Years later, you still hear the cries, but you are already performing your triage: This one for immediate action, this one to wait in line, this one a lost case, return to sender. Back into the streets, carrying their world about in plastic bags, or in a supermarket trolley expropriated from Red Apple, as they draw the last ounces of power from the electric ground beneath their feet. Though they come in all shapes and sizes, from every walk of life, of every age and race and gender, they end up the same rough mass. So who's to tell this can't be reversed, that we're not all Mo Smith's creations, living in his outer shell?

My method is never to humour a patient. I usually tell 'em straight: You're off your head. This would normally be enough to get you struck off the rolls of the American Psychiatric Association, but nobody in their right mind in that outfit wants my job. I discovered that it's not always a good idea to listen. Sometimes you have to challenge a person at the source. I've met enough patients, at the higher or lower social scale, who have a more solid sense of their delusions than "normal" people have of their selves.

Once, during my first year at Human Resources, my supervisor, Elaine Dole (she of that serendipitous name), took me down the maw of Canal Street subway (Broadway & Lafayette) into a maze of disused tunnels that had been blocked off in the sixties but unblocked in the eighties, the Reagan years, God rest our soul, by a group of homeless people who, like the Children of Israel, went wandering in search of a home, and landed up beyond the R and the N lines, living like troglodytes in holes where the old brickwork had caved in, all twisted girders and piles of dessicated rubbish left over from abandoned repair work back in 1957. In 1957 Eisenhower put through the Civil Rights Bill to safeguard black votes, and look where we are now.

There were twenty five people living in the holes in the wall, seven men, eight women and ten children, ranging from three months old to fourteen. They had followed a charismatic ex-preacher from the Bronx, who had declared himself the Messenger of the Second Coming and told them Jesus would be tunneling from the center of the Earth towards the light. Only when Jesus came could they return above ground. They had been living for more than three years on leavings from passengers on the platforms. That's how I learned a McDonalds hamburger could be kept for six months. I was reminded of all those people scavenging off rubbish tips in the Third World. Brazil, India, the Philippines. Human interest, the sad clicking of tongues. Today we know a lot more about the underground "mole" people. (Did Mo Smith spend time among those "communities", under Grand Central or even up on Riverside Drive? Another stockpiled query...) Benjamin used to describe a trashcan opposite his house which is a Mecca for the Lower East Side. A tramp comes and rummages in it for half an hour, carrying off every possibly usable morsel. Then another comes along, and spends another half hour retrieving what the first man had inexplicably overlooked. Then a third wanderer comes along and spends another half hour in the trough. It is a cornucopia of waste, a bottomless box of American detritus, like the magical bag of the Arabian Nights, out of which the whole world could be pulled...

Elaine Dole thought I could convince the Messenger, whose name was, of course Elijah, Elijah Dubois, that he should allow his followers up to the Armory Shelter, despite the fact that Jesus had not yet completed his journey through the bowels of the Earth. Those were the peak days of my reputation as Caroline The Ear, the Listening Shrink. They thought I could charm a Cobra out of its lunch. But I got nowhere with Elijah Dubois. I patiently put my ear down on the filthy damp ground when he asked me to: "Listen sister, don't you hear the Man? He's on His way." I told him it was the Broadway Local. But he didn't flinch, he'd heard it all before. "Blessed are the meek," he said, "for they shall inherit the Earth." I said the Gospels didn't say the meek couldn't take a bath and a square meal now and then. He said his brethren were free to go, wherever and whenever they chose. But they all stayed down there, until a new Municipal Order which cleared them out by force while I was away one summer, in the Blue Mountains, lying on the banks of a shimmering lake watching the sail boats go by, while New York's finest cleared Elijah's disciples to various Hotels and Centers, from which they all trickled out back onto the streets or back down the tunnels. The Messenger was locked up for an assault on two policemen, in the Tombs, not more than three or four blocks away. There he got into an altercation with a cellmate who stabbed him seven times through the heart. But Jesus is still down there, I have been told by others, burrowing away in the dark...

I know how I would tackle Elijah Dubois today. I'd lock myself up with him and his people in that dark, dreary stinkhole, and tell him straight out that he had it all wrong. A battle of wills. I know I wouldn't have shaken him, but I might have shaken some of his acolytes enough to coax them, one by one, out of that hole. Wooing them to my pitifully few beds or places in rehab projects in or out of town.

The Outreach. Donna Quixote fights the windmills. At least in this case I have my twin Sanchos, Benjamin and Salim, who have adopted Mo Smith and are trying, at least, to draw him back into the circle of visible humanity, winding off the bandages and puffing air into the inert clay. At least a try, until he vanishes again into the maze of rubbish skips, cardboard boxes, emptied mailbags, abandoned subway sidings and old shoeshine stalls, crates, container wagons, supermarket trolleys, churchyards and holes left in the road by day workmen, warmed by gushes of subterranean steam. The hidden city, scratching away while I lie in bed, awake, more often than not, alone or not, listening to the creak of my old brownstone walls, and the shuffling of The Dog trying to decide whether the tapping outside is an innocent passer-by, an ex-husband or the Amsterdam Strangler...

Or my son Karim, disillusioned at last with the segregationist call of Islam in Saint Louis and yearning for the comforts of his mother's house? Dream on. At least they keep the boy's veins clean out there, stuffing his mind rather than his blood with guk. Be grateful for small mercies...

But a night like this when Benny is here I have my guaranteed quota of interruptions. Plagued by my ex-Israeli's insomnia, as he sweats and turns in the sheets, crawling out to bump down the stairs to the kitchen, opening and closing cupboard doors and opening the icebox, which always sets off a sound like jackhammers tearing up the floors. And when I stagger down there to see what's up he's sitting at the kitchen table with The Dog, the two of them gnawing at whatever bone they've found in store.

"What's up, baby?" I ask in a zombied slur.

"Vot iz ziss baby? Ze fuhrer never said zis baby." He's a real mother at two in the morning in this mood.

"Honeychile. Fuckface. What do I care."

"I couldn't sleep."

"So what else is new? Are we going to get a break sometime? I have five disturbed women on my plate tomorrow. Whereas you only have one, so count your blessings. Get down, Dog."

The one point of having a man in the house is so that he can control this brain damaged monster. As Benjamin has it, this cross between the Hound of the Baskervilles and Bugs Bunny. On reflection, I suppose it's the second point. But they can run a close race sometimes.

"Why can't you be a proper American and live on pills like everyone else?" I have already lunged to my own stash. Codeine uber alles.

"The problem is I know my problems are not chemical," he turns those hawkish green eyes to me.

"Listen honey, I have a doctor's appointment at the crack of dawn and then a session at ten with a woman who thinks her welfare checks have been coated with poison by her ex-lover, who disappeared on the orders of the White House. She knows where the next U.S. invasion will take place."

"Oh, where?"

"In Orlando, Florida."

"Too late. The Martians are already there."

"You would be a great help to my patient."

"So what do you do?"

"We have to write out the checks in front of her, with a ballpoint pen she supplies herself. Even then she thinks he's still got at the checkbooks. But she's still shrewd enough to know beyond a certain limit, no dinero."

"Even the most far gone have a logic. So why is it blood chaos everywhere? I demand an answer."

"It's two fifteen in the morning, Benjamin. Do you want to sleep with The Dog, or will you settle despite it all for my tired old black ass upstairs?"

"I'll be up in a minute."

"I didn't know it was such a difficult choice."

Finding a sane partner in this city. Tell me about it. So why have I taken on board a mad rationalist, who lies awake at night, grinding his teeth? A born pessimist. Now that's Unamerican. It's the same problem he has with those kids of his at the East Side Film Co-op, who wake up each morning and look at the day with fresh eyes. People like Benjamin can't understand this, coming from a culture which was already admonished for being too sassy by Jehovah in five thousand B.C..

Tell it all to the daughter of an ex-Methodist from Bethel Episcopal Church. Salim understands. He and my mother can sit for hours talking ten to the dozen about God, Redemption and Judgement Day. Then he told her about his own transfiguration after drinking his leader's piss in the desert. She came up to me afterwards and said: "That boy is more than a little strange, Caroline. But then, what else can I expect in this house?"

But then, my mother is proud of my profession. Healing the sick in mind and spirit. If only she knew how little healing gets done. The Listening Ear. Delegated to my Israeli-Palestinian double act, the Siamese twins, as Darwish calls them, joined at the hip. Inherited from Frances, who tried them both and cast them out pretty quick. But each of us found her own sanctuary, and have hunkered down, in our respective bunkers, with the open doors, the storm winds blowing through. Hurricane Hilda, gaining speed, clipping Delaware and New Jersey and sending first gusts to rattle the panes in my decrepit windows, setting The Dog off like a primeval alarm. Barf, barf, barf! Now shut your mouth, hound!

Where are you tonight, my Wandering Creator? In what doorway are you huddling now? As one of the Middle Eastern twins returns to infect me with his insomnia, while the other cruises about the streets in his taxicab, peering out for the invisible men and women and the gibbering shadows of their multiple ghosts...

NO TURKISH PISTACHIOS UNTIL NEW CROP COMES IN!

The glass jars, in the corner shop on Church Street and Reade, shimmered before the hungry eyes -

Nuts. Nuts. Nuts.

The jars are full of every variety. The seeds, imprisoned in their hard shells. Wasn't it the ancient Greeks who wouldn't eat em, as they might contain the souls of the dead en route to reincarnation? Or was that beans? Memory evaporates so easily. And a huge pile of Iranian cashews in a glass jug - There lies a potent political story, Mo.

Who said that? Was that you, Arnold?

Yo, homeboy. Don't you know anything? The wages of Irangate, stoopid. Every time our stoopid government sent over a shipment of TOW missiles and deep-sea Naval mines and chemical bomb casings in return for a hostage that never got released from Bayroot the cargo ships and planes came back loaded with Iranian nuts, so they shouldn't make the trip empty. Now there ain't no more hostages to be released you know we're still sending the bastards weapons whenever you see their pistachios or cashews in the shops. I'm writing an Op-Ed about this for the Times: GUNS FOR NUTS. We'll see if the bastards print it.

Well, thank you for that contribution, Arnold. Anyone else want to loosen their mouth? Annie? Link? Jesse? Jaime? Beatrice? Or anybody who's been silent so far?

The kernels in the window, all the little beans, each with its soul, fresh or dry roasted. If you consumed them all, how much of the essence of mankind would you be taking in? The valour of your enemies? Is all ingestion, at the root, cannibalism? Body of Christ, unleavened manna.

Dear Sir,

Having rejected my Op-Ed piece for the New York Times perhaps you might allow me another space to put an alternative point of view to that expressed ad-nauseam by your regular editors and correspondents. The truth is that the glut of cashew and pistachio nuts currently choking the market is not, as you so inaccurately suggest, the result of unequal tariffs imposed on our native American nuts and preserves by Japan and the Third World, but the deliberate and preplanned quid-pro-quo for the hidden agenda of our Middle East policy as enacted by the Pentagon. The secret 1985 trip by National Security Advisor Robert McFarlane, together with Oliver North and Israeli "anti-terrorism expert" Amiram Nir, to Teheran, bringing the Ayatollah Khomeini a chocolate cake in the shape of a key which had been baked by Mashiach's Patisserie in Jerusalem, was merely the first in many high level contacts which led to the Iran- Contra affair and the eventual discrediting of Ronald Reagan. But few realised that the very same visit resulted in a top secret contract signed with the Iranian National Groundnut Company (*il qizidbash fistukiyeh Iranieh*) for seventy-five tonnes of cashews and pistachios to be imported at discount rates into the United States. This was done to offset the fuel costs of the vessels and aircraft returning after arms deliveries to Teheran and the Port of Abadan-Khorammshah, and also to line the pockets of certain mullahs who are known to be the Groundnut Barons of Iran. Profits also went both to the CIA's covert Africa programmes and to the Israeli Mossad for its own covert activities in Central Africa, Ethiopia-Eritrea and Kurdistan, and to joint subversion in Afghanistan and Kashmir.

One can therefore appreciate that the threads of Pistachiogate stretch far into the corridors of state and the murky cabal of global Intelligence agencies. Pistachiogate joins Irangate, Iraqgate, Contragate and all the other Gates, as well as the Kennedy Assasssinations, the Bay of Pigs, Martin Luther King, Malcolm X and so on and so forth. The covert linkage between Western Secret Services and International Terrorists to maintain the flow of armaments to combatants on opposite sides of ideological, ethnic, national or religious divides should also be taken into account.

It is in this context that the sudden shortage of Turkish pistachios takes on a particularly ominous tinge. The profound rivalry between Turkey and Iran for hegemony in that region of the Middle East should be well known to your readers. Turkey, as a secular but mostly Sunni Muslim country, shares its borders in the East both with Iran, an Islamic Shi'a state, and what was in the past the Soviet Union but is now the independent Christian state of Armenia, which is at war with neighbouring Muslim Azerbaijan. Turkey, a NATO ally, assisted the United States in our aggression against Iraq, in the Gulf War. The Founder of modern Turkey, Kemal Ataturk, who overthrew the remnants of the old Ottoman Empire, was determined to establish a modern state, separated by law from religion, in which the Latin Alphabet replaced the Arabic script. Iran is determined to establish the Kingdom of God through his authorised spokesmen, the mullahs. These two great regional powers are embroiled in a momentous power struggle which echoes ancient historical feuds. The Turks are building a massive complex of dams across the Tigris River which will control the water supply to the entire aquifer of the Mesopotamian Basin. The Iranians are training assassins and saboteurs to cripple Turkey's nascent power. There is little doubt that the recent failure of Turkey's groundnut crop is part of this secret struggle. NO TURKISH PISTACHIOS might appear an innocent sign in a small specialist store in New York City, but the subterranean war of Gog and Magog which is hidden below the innocuous surface should be brought to public attention.

The formulation UNTIL NEW CROP COMES IN might also be fruitfully examined, to find out whether any coded meaning or message may be implied.

Yours sincerely,
Arnold Flint,
Pocahontas,
Westchester County.

Addendum: The Ground Nut Barons of Iran: - the Grand Ayatollah Mehdi Javad Hojeteslameh, of Meshhed. - the Ayatollah Ali Khalil Takbadidzadeh, of Yazd. - Hojatelislam Taher Moshtahdzadeh, of Isfahan. - the Ayatollah Habibullah Habibullateh, of Qom. - Dr Reza Ahmedzadeh, of Tabriz. - Archibald Acker Muntsenberger the IIIrd, of Tulsa Oklahoma.

The hot fetid breath against the glass. You're a complete asshole, Arnold. Suit yourself, I'm only looking out for your best interests. There should be an investigation of cake shops preparing condiments for despots. Pandering to the sweet tooths of tyrants. They are gobbling enough of us already. But anything for a quick buck. And what about those firms that make American flags to be sent to all our enemies in the Third World so they can be burnt en masse in demonstrations? Do you know they manufacture them for ten cents apiece and sell them for three dollars fifty?

The red white and blue. Yo, it's time to move on, you guys. Crossing Reade, on up Church Street, past Blimpie Sandwiches. On the other side, the S & K Deli...

The S & K, comrades. The coded meanings and messages. Seth & Kronos? Samizdat & Kalashnikov? Saratoga & Kentucky? Somalia & Kenya? Sindh & Kashmir? Rugs and baskets in the Oriental Handicraft. They are all fakes, ya shabab, stuck together by Palestinian exiles in Queens. Who's that speaking? Is that you, Bat? Muhammad Ibn Battuta, at your service. Do not be deceived, my friends. I know what I'm talking about. No one travelled in the Islamic world as I did. I covered it all, from soup to nuts, from Tangier to Tatar China. From Mali to the Ramparts of Gog and Magog, where infidels cook men and eat em. From the high civilization of Granada to the land of white skinned savages whose heads grow out of their groins, and have eyes where other men and women have nipples. I have climbed Sarandib, the highest mountain, upon which the Blessed Footprint of our Father Adam can be found sunk in the living rock. I have walked from Khurasan to Yazmir, and on into the Lands of Darkness. I have starved in the desert and frozen on the ice of the great Itil River. I've seen what I've seen and I've heard what I've heard. I have sat in the counsel of Kings and in the dens of spies, eating dog's flesh. I can tell you stuff about the Turks and the Persians that would make your hair stand on end.

Well, bully for you, towelhead... Yo! Let's keep it civilised and polite down there. God, all we need is another ignorant peasant... Fear not, God's spirit hovers over the meek... the Son of Man... the seventh calvary... the Righteous Teacher is coming... Not quick enough for me, honey! down, dog, and lick at my feet! crawl to my boot! stick out your dick! Mistress Sadie is ready to take you all under my rigorous control and teach you humility and submission... Ah! the bordellos of Addis... Tell us about it, Link! Africa... the Defiance Campaigns...bus boycotts... passlaw protests... *osagyefu... uhuru...* Enough of all this whining and loafing - now take this down, every one of you: slow gentile erotic teasing and complete fulfilment a speciality... toilet training, golden showers, enemas and posing... your best erotic fantasy awaits, call 970-FUCK... 24 hours personalised one on one conversation... total satisfaction... $3.50 per call, $2.50 after the first minute... cum and caress my milky white brown coffee silky velvet black skin... once I allow you to look into my cool blonde ravenhaired icelandic teutonic aryan eyes you will want nothing more than to submit to Mistress I-Am, the ding-am- zich of sex ex ex crik crak brek ekek kek...

How much longer must I drag you all along in my guts... Tramp tramp tramp, up Church, across Duane, past Angelica's Pizza, On Call Communications, Ketan's Grocery, Chemical Bank. There's a name for you, Mordecai: Water into wine, paper into gold, piss into silver... The "pure elements" and the magical elixir... salt, silver nitrate and gold chloride:

(Gold) 1 X (Fusion) 1/200ths X 1000 = (Elixir) 5.

The Alchemical Marriage. Men and women inserting their little plastic cards in the 24 hour security door. Beware malfunction. Abandon hope all ye who enter... Trapped within they desperately tap out their secret numbers on the wall console. Please Wait, We Are Processing Your Request... the hours, the days, the weeks pass. We Are Unable to Process Your Request At This Moment Due To... the enclosed booth is filled with drek and rubbish, dried vomit and expired accounts emitting their putrefaction. Skeletons propped up in the corners, the bones picked clean by the starving customers sealed in, reduced to coprophagy. I saw the same display in northern China: Millions reduced by drought and famine. Babies cooked and eaten whole. Only I survived to tell the tale, because I consumed my slaves and bearers, and when I was done with those I dug deep in the sand for beetles and the dried mummies of kings...

Oh, shut up, Battuta. Across Thomas Street. On the right, the A.T. & T. Building. A massive concrete excrescence, rising windowless into the sky, only a row of immense black ventilating holes running round the tower some twenty storeys up. Across the barren patio below staff and passers by walk briskly, or sit on the concrete fence, eating their sandwiches to go. Loose flyers trickle across the stone paving, to be picked up by the discerning scavenger:

> **BACK PAIN RELIEF! STOP SUFFERING NEEDLESSLY! Disc Problems, Shoulder Pain, Leg Pain, Headaches, Arthritis, Spasms, Numbness. Most Major Insurance Plans Accepted. Special Offer to New Patients: A complete chiropractic examination, including X-ray, for only $20...**
>
> **"The doctor of the future will give no medicine, but will educate his patients in the care of the human frame, in diet, and in the cause and prevention of disease." - *Thomas Alva Edison.***

Ah, Eddy-son! It is better to light one bulb in the dark than to trip over a dog's shit and break your fucking neck. Money out of light, who would have believed it. And another flyer:

OMEGA SHOE REPAIR.
GRAND OPENING SPECIALS:

Men's Full Soles	**Sales price $29.95**
Men's Half Soles	**Sales price $24.95**
Shoe Shine	**$1.00**
Lady's Spike Lifts	**$2.00**
Lady's Sole Guards	**$10.00**

But the welfare check's already spent motherfuckers. Nike and Zeus. A marriage made in Heaven. The men's half souls, the lady's soul guards. And Doctor Caroline. A fanciable piece, Moses. I wouldn't kick her out of bed. Fuck your ass, Arnold. FUCK YOU ALL!

Waiting below the A.T. & T.. Sharp eyes can spot a piece of salvage before it's snatched by others off the street. And there! Across the road by the Merchants Square Building. A discarded BLT! Bacon. Lettuce. And tomato! Blessed is the Lord God of Toast. The bastards held the mayonnaise. It takes away all the tang.

The autumn night falling in shreds of damp and frigid air. Across the road, what used to be Worth Street, but is now for some reason named for Justice John W. Barlan, slap underneath the New York Law School. Across Leonard to 250 Church, the Office of the Administrator of Human Resources, South Manhattan. And will she be exiting through those glazed doors this night? Or has she already called it a day???

The great swathe of Franklin. Mighty avenues converge. Church peters out at Canal Street. The Avenue of the Americas starts here, at an unprepossessing traffic island, with barbed wire surrounding the concrete station of the New York City Water Board. One Way. Don't Walk. It's Your Right: Vote in '92! On one corner, the All Star Harmony Theatre, Daily Burlesque. On the other, the Topless Go Go Girls, All Beers $3 on Wednesdays. It's a Friday. The neon sign is just beginning to flash. Only some letters light up. It's just "less - - Girls, - - $3 on end."

Through a gap in the barbed wire we can enter the refuge of the water station. The humming sound of machinery deep in the earth. The usual shaking of the ground, the lullaby of Broadway. Nuzzling up to the sheet metal flank of a shed, behind a packed pile of plasterboards. Hidden from the warp and weft of the traffic, pulling carboard sheets up to the chest. The mayonnaiseless BLT settling, the advertising section of the Thursday Times mashed into a pliable cushion - the Sales Section: Cellular phones, video camcorders, desktop computers, notebooks, fax, computer accessories, home audio, word processors, copiers, electronic organizers, Casio, Sharp, Aiwa, Brother. All major credit cards accepted. Come in Thursday between 12 noon and 4 pm, meet the Okidata Representatives and See the Latest in Computer Technology. Apply for Instant Credit with the Bank of Georgia, tick here: YES, I want Credit Life, Disability, Job Loss and Property Insurance. Not available in all States, please refer to Options.

An early night, as the lights come on all around us... Men's full souls... The deep dive, snores battling the pumping generators... Water of life, water of life... Down, boys and girls, give us a break now. But, ever present, below decks, the restless rumbling of all the world's sleep-walkers -

Creatures of the Night.

MY NAME IS MEREN-PTAH, KING OF KINGS! I AM THE MAN OF WHOM THE EARTH SINGS! SON OF RAMESES, FATHER OF SETI, THE WHOLE WORLD SHOWERS ME WITH CONFETTI. TREMBLE, ALL YE MIGHTY, AND DESPAIR! I AM THE LION, THE TIGER, THE BEAR! ALL THOSE WHO DARED TO OPPOSE ME PERISHED. I AM THE SCOURGE OF ALL MY ENEMIES CHERISHED. I SCATTERED THEIR BONES TO THE FOUR WINDS OF THE EARTH. I CUT OFF THEIR PRIDE AND KILLED THEIR OFFSPRING AT BIRTH! I FILLED ALL THE VALLEYS WITH THEIR SEVERED HANDS, THE CHOPPED OFF EARS AND TESTICLES OF THEIR ARMIES AND BANDS! I HUMBLED THEIR GODS AND MOTHERFUCKED THEIR DEITIES!

MY NAME IS MEREN-PTAH, KING OF KINGS! Son of Rameses, Father of all things. My lineage stretches back into the depths of time and forward into eternity's slime. My name will endure for millions of years and my descendants will still rule the earth when all the careers and the fleeting victories and puny triumphs of ordinary humble everyday men have crumbled!

MY NAME IS MEREN-PTAH, KING OF KINGS! Scion of Dzoser, Senofru and Khufu. Scion of Menkewre and Shepseskaf and Khafren. Scion of Userkaf, Uniss and Sehureh. Scion of Amenemhet and Sekhenyenreh. Scion of Khemose and Ahmose, Amenhoteps and

Tutmose. Enemy of the usurping Son-worshipper, may his name be erased forever. I spat on his grave and sent my slaves to copulate with his mummy in his dismal cave. I am the Scion of Smenkhkare and Tut-Ankh-Amun, of Haremhab, Ramses and Seti the One...

Oh yah. Many have asked me for the secret of the Wisdom of the Ages. But only one principle can guide a Pharaoh: Be On Your Guard! Be Wary! Mistrust Everyone - Suspect Your Brothers - Lock Up Your Sisters! Kill At Least Some of Your Sons, pour encourage les autres. Look out for Number One.

Never give a sucker an even break, that's the only way to be Pharaoh... But let no one say I didn't succour the sick, or feed the widow and her orphans, or house the afflicted, the poor and the evicted, or operate proper social security schemes, to the limits of financial prudence and visions and dreams... Yes, I was renowned for my generosity. King of the Just and the Just King. But now I am just the King, and too tired to sing. Carrying my bleeding heart in my hands, adrift like a blind man in the night...

My rap echoes and fades, and the passageways stretch endlessly forward, and I have mislaid the thread... Where is it all? Those funerary objects, the chests of gold, the alabaster cups, the jewels, the chariots and harness, the golden solar boat, the necklaces and sceptres of lapis lazuli, the gilded staffs, the copper trumpets, the papyrus hampers filled with loaves and fishes and beer for the long journey through the underworld to the Other Side? Where are the lamps, the perfume vases, the ceremonial fans, the sacred geese, the maces, scarabs and amulets of Isis and Thoth, the pottery and stone vessels and *shabti* boxes, everything that had been so carefully packed into the tomb...

I've been robbed! The tomb-thieves dug deep into the heart of the mountain, through the walls and the great granite slabs, leaving me nothing, not even the canopic jars with my internal organs, without which I haven't a hope in hell of becoming whole again in the Other World... They left me nothing but my skin and sores for my journey down these putrid corridors...

Tramp tramp tramp...

It was never easy being an interim Pharaoh, waiting to be a living God. Waiting, for forty seven years, while my father grew old and welded to power, holding on to the throne with his guts and his bones, while his sons fell away one by one, till only I, the thirteenth born, was left, to grab my inheritance by the skin of my teeth. All the bowing and the scraping, yes, Paw, no Paw, whatever you say, Paw. All those years of tired debaucheries, jockrot, seed spilled into the sand. Trudging on those endless barren campaigns. From the halls of Mutawwa-alis to the sands of Tripo-li! Burning the palate with those Hittite slops. And oh, that Nubian pussy! Dysentery, scurvy and heartburn...

And then, for a brief ten years, I had it all! The pomp, the ceremony, the power, the call. Down the length of the Nile, everyone sang my praises. The universe danced on my palm, the Nile rippled to the droop of my eyelids. The sacred crocodiles licked my feet with their rough, calloused tongues, and I could gaze, unblinking, into the Sun...

Then, in the wink of an eye, it was over. Can you believe it? That even a Pharaoh is unprepared to leave it? Can you believe that you can train for Death all your life and still be poleaxed when it comes, dragging its evil breath? One moment you are ruling the world, the next you're flat on your back in the embalming chamber, with the high priest, wearing the mask of Annubis, drawing out your brain through your nose...

- It's tough all round, Nep, blood's thicker than water, there's no escaping that...

Ever inhaled embalming fluid? I used to do the stuff, when I was a small boy, a little Princeling. They used to take us in to show us the blag. The ceremonies of the priests of Thoth. My tutor, Tutmoth. That vile old man with his dangling, slithering snake... I used to take the fluid from the jars when their backs were turned. There was a whole bunch of us royal ragamuffins. Crawled into corners to drink the shit. Natron, caustic ankh- imy leaves, with a dash of bitumen. Jesus, man, that hit, it was putrid. But we were high on rebellion. We all fantasized of joining the Great Escape of the Hebrew slaves. Man, were we cool!

- You're only young once, Nep, you better believe it...

But it was a good life, in the land of my Fathers. Along the great river that nourishes the world. The fields of grain, the threshing floors, the songs and dances of harvest. The nubile maidens, always ready to serve us –

All the birds of Arabia flutter over Egypt,
annointed with myrrh -
the one that comes first, seizes my worm -

The simple contentment of the straight and the righteous... But it was not good enough for the Hebrew slaves. Some people are simply never satisfied. So off they went, marching into the desert, in their long, stiffnecked column, led by the man with the stave...

- You can't fool all of the people all of the time...

Those ill born swine. Once the people were glad to labour for glory, to raise the Great Pyramids of our ancestors with the sweat of their brow and the ancient songs. But now it's all sour grapes. I was a child of ten when the trouble started. I remember being taken by Tutmoth to watch the flogging of a Hebrew slave who had refused to make bricks without straw. That old saw. My first lesson in economics. So what does the state do faced with a straw shortage? You don't just keel over and import, falling into a trade deficit with those very nations you require to go down and kiss your feet. You make do with available resources. Slave shit has natural fibre. Tutmoth brought some in to our study classes. It was very dry, light and flaky. "We should not shrink from reality!" That was my first maxim in politics.

Believe me. I was never Ramses' favourite. Luckily for me, as he had three of my older brothers poisoned and one thrown into a well. But I was so far down the line I was protected from all those fractricidal intrigues. I was the son of his second string wife, Inosfret. She was a quiet one, biding her time, while he fretted and bragged for Nefertari. We were not in a hurry. I only came on stream when my older brother, Khaemwaset, passed away, so much later in life... But all us young brats were at our father's side when That Man first came into the Great Hall at Memphis, with his matted hair and his rod of power and his epileptic elder brother and that glower in their rolling flecked eyes.

"Let my people go!"

And so? Ramses was not prepared to be addressed this way. You're the one who's going, peasant, he told the upstart. Don't come back. If I see you or any member of your mangy family again this side of the border I shall have you all flayed and your testicles fed to the crocodiles and your women's vaginas made into purses. Am I making myself clear?

But he just repeated his curses: "Thus saith the Lord my God: Let my people go!"

Nobody listens. By now I'm immune to it. But it was an education then. Nevertheless Ramses was kind to the madman and merely turned him out with his head shaved and his ear cropped on the right side. Lo and behold, the cat comes back the next day, challenging the court sorcerors to a duel. Unleashing a whole parcel of weird snakes and reptiles which had the harem girls climbing up the walls. In respect of this show, my Dad let him go again, untouched. Then the terrorist campaign started. Frogs, and lice, and fleas, and plague, and locusts, and rats. Filling the Nile with blood. And they claimed they couldn't make bricks without straw!

Good riddance to the whole damn bunch I say. Workshy loafers, with their fiery God who lives on a hill. In the dead of night I watched them as I crept into the alleyways with my brother, Khaem, who was fifteen at the time. We watched them pack their bags, saddle their mangy oxen and prepare to sneak off in the dark, daubing the sides of their doors with occult symbols, so their God would spare them as they struck the last blow. But we were suffering from a Plague of the First Born anyhow, and my father was immersed in his own woe, mourning Nefertari's eldest son and heir, Amen-Hir-Khopshef. Everyone was bereft. Weeping and wailing all over the city. Mummifying the son before his father. That has to be the greatest pity...

They went off at dawn, and a strange silence came over the streets, which shimmered in the baking haze of the spring. Stray dogs slunk through the rubbish left behind by the departing horde. I walked out onto the palace sward. The half built pylons and stelae of the temple they were supposed to be building stretched out before me. Abandoned awls and mallets everywhere. Massive obelisks hanging at crazy angles, still roped to their pulleys and wrangles. The inscriptions to the everlasting glory of my father suspended in mid-sentence:

HAIL TO R - -
JEWEL OF MEM - -
VANQ - - OF NUB - -
CONQ - - OF - - AS - -

King of Kings. Are we all alive then, having passed the Halls of the Dead? This long, arduous journey of dread. The preparation is hard enough. The priests standing by with the canopic jars while the Chief Embalmer cuts out the stomach, the liver, the spleen, the kidneys. Thank God they leave the bladder, if only a man had a pot to piss in. The

Embalmer, donning his white glove, pushes his arm right up to the armpit to get at the windpipe and lungs. The main thing is to leave the heart, abode of the ka. And then the embalming fluid. Oh Ma... Dehydrating the skin, oiling the body. And then the wrapping, with all the jewels, cartouches and charms of office, and the priests reciting from the Book of the Dead:

"Behold, I was guarded and watched, but now I am free... I have gained the mastery over my heart, I have gained the mastery over my two hands, I have gained the mastery over my two feet, I have gained the mastery over my mouth, I have gained the mastery over the waters, I have gained the mastery over the air, I have gained the mastery over the river and the land, I have gained the mastery over all the things that were ordered to be done for me upon the earth..."

But I have gained nothing, nada and zilch. Naked I wander these fleshy vaults, with none but commoners and dregs to keep me company...

- Up yours too, motherfucker...

Perhaps I should have gone with the Hebrew slaves after all... Following their great pillar of fire, singing on their road to freedom, led by a fanatic into the Wilderness of Sin... This Mo-says - with his wild piercing eyes and stutter... Did you hear that story they uttered? That his mother put him in a basket as a babe, into the Nile, to escape my Dad's gory decree that all male Hebrew children should be killed. Whoever heard of a slave owner destroying his property? Children, too, whom one doesn't even have to buy. But the truth is, I always loathed slavery. How can a great nation endure half slave and half free...?

The "Children of Israel." That squabbling rabble, ridden with halitosis, eczema and warts. Nevertheless, I have this lingering sympathy, with the wretched of the earth... Some-taams ah feel like a mo-therless chile, a long wa-hays from home...

The dark is all enveloping. *Behold, I have gained the mastery over my heart... I have gained the mastery over my mouth... In a clean place I shall sit on the ground beneath the foliage of the date palm of the Goddess Hathor, having the books of the divine words of the writings of the Great God Thoth...*

Deeper and darker. They have wrapped the mummy and left the chamber. Daddy, daddy! They have dropped the great stone plugs in place behind them as they withdraw, chamber after chamber, level after level, leaving me with only the Dead for company, and the draftsmen's brilliant carvings all dimmed. The meticulously drawn journey of the Sun-God Ra through the night invisible to even the unnaked eye. All light gone, as I wander the endless subterranean chambers, trying to recall all the old charms and prayers to ward off evil and decay...

For behold I come as a pure spirit... To raise up the ka and make the soul live in the Underworld... To escape the clutches of the serpent guardians of Seker, of Samenescu, and Ceauscescu, and Amsahu, Samensnuff, Rerek, and Sensek, and the Eight Crocodiles, and the Eater of the Ass, and the headsman of Osiris who cuts off the heads of the damned and throws them into the lakes of fire and boiling water at the gates of the Judgement Hall of Maat, and the Seven Eaters of the Heart, Netcheh-Netcheh, Aatketket, Anertanefbesfkhentikhef, Ak-Her-Ami, Teshenmaat, Ubeshraperemkhetket and Maamkerhanefemru, who slaughter sinners at the Lake of Fire, and the Splitter of Skulls, who rushes forth with his axe...

There are either ten or twenty-one Gates to the Underworld, the priests could not agree so they prepared for any option... At each gate a Watcher, a Gatekeeper, and a Herald who announces your Name. Then there are all the other heralds, boatkeepers or guards, who assist you or tear your head off. My tutor Tutmoth tried to beat it all into me, but it was in one ear and out the other. In return for all his catechisms, when I reached eighteen, I had him strangled and his testicles and penis thrown to the crocodiles. I can still feel the weals of his stick on my back and buttocks... But can one vanquish the Gods?...

In our sleep, say the priests, we are granted glimpses of the Underworld that lies behind our dreams. If we could understand our dreams, we could call up the powers of the Underworld in the waking universe. But we must beware not to mix the two. What else do I know about the Underworld? At least one section, if not three, is an eternal fire. Another is filled with raging waters. Various serpents live in three other sections and devour the souls of the Dead. In another section the invisible spirits feed upon the weak and the uncertain. In the deepest pit lives the Destroyer of Souls, who has many Names, but only one Nature...

The corridors are narrowing, and there are a series of doors. Is this the Fourth Division of the Tuat? The passage through the kingdom of Seker, "the great god with two wings opened", whose domain is a barren desert strewn with serpents. At its Gate, I should be able to summon the two-headed serpent which would convey me on its back through the corridors. Is that it, that slithering sound? I shall not stay to find out. I begin running, pounding along the passageway. And pause, to the sound of a strange echo of the pitter-patter of my feet... I stop short, but the echo continues.

"Who's there?"

My voice echoes back at me. But also another, a kind of choked off cry. There is no doubt, I am not alone in here. I can sense it now. The smell of fear. Another lost soul, human as I.

"Anybody there?"

A low thumping beat, somewhere in the depths. And ahead - is that the flicker of some kind of torch?

I shout again. Can you hear me, Mo-says? The spark of fire, if not a pillar... Oh, for someone to lead us out of this wilderness... They wandered, I am told, for forty years, in the Wilderness of Sin, until Mo-says could grow a new generation... My Father sent his commandos after them, but they were drowned in an unseasonable flash-flood. Weather forecasters, oh boy... tell me about it... Forty years, in search of the Promised Land... I know the feeling. A lo-ong wa—ays fro-om ho-ome...

"You there, with the light! Yoo-hoo!"

There are two of them. I glimpse them briefly, then they turn a corner. I race round the corner but I can't see them. Yet I hear there mumbling, somewhere nearby...

"Watch your step, man, that's a nasty drop there..."

"I definitely heard a voice calling out there, Mordecai..."

"Ghosts, Battuta. They're all around us. Just ignore them and they'll go away..."

And then another voice, speaking out of the darkness:

"For God's sake keep it down. People tryin' to sleep here..."

And other, ghostly voices answering:

"Is that you, Lincoln?"

"No, it's Arnold. Can't a man get some kip? It's three in the fucking morning fer Chrissakes!"

A chorus of sighs, groans and mutters. The disturbed slumber of the Gods... If only I knew a lullaby that could soothe them back to sleep. My wet nurse, Nut, who had the largest breasts in Lower Egypt, used to sing to me her favourite love songs:

The wild goose soars and dives,
Into the fowl-yard pool,
But I turn towards my love when I am alone,
I cannot be far from beauty...

The thumping in the depths is like the beat of savage drums. The light glimmers again. I turn another corner. But I am confronted with a yawning cave from which garish colours and sounds batter my senses. The thumping beat is unbearable and a booming voice ensues:

"COME WITHIN! DILDOS, ASS FUCKING, GOLDEN SHOWERS, ENEMAS, DISCIPLINE AND LATEX! ALL FETISHES CATERED FOR. SWEET RUBBER DREAMS. FIST FUCKING, GENITAL TORTURE, SLAVERY, BONDAGE, DOMINATION! PROLONGED TEASING, LEATHER, TRANSEXUAL SEX, BULLWHIPS AND CHAINS! TOILET TRAINING! EXCLUSIVE DUNGEONS!"

Is this the fearful Fifth Division of the Tuat? The door to Seker's hidden kingdom...? I can see the red light, the weeping heads bobbing on the curling steam... The eight Goddesses holding the measuring cord... I can hear the cries of the damned, calling for help... I can't help them... I turn back and run... I hear the murmur of the infernal cats, and the cries of the Divine Hawk of Horus... I see the owl headed Gods armed with spiked clubs, the Serpent Seba, the twelve inert mummies whom the God Afu Ra beckons to remove their windings, to collect their bones and their own flaking flesh in their hands and walk... The magic formulas to pass by safely are on the tip of my tongue...

Mo says: I am that I am... the burning bush... the bull rushes up Broadway... all the one night stands... Frankfurters, Hot Pretzels, Diet Pepsi, Seven Up, Sprite, Shlitz, Tango, Coke Original... Spare a few cents for a cupocoffee man... a nickel, sir? Bless your black heart, mother...

"Is that you, Nep?"

My lips tremble, but I can't remember the Words... Set, the Eternal Enemy of Osiris strides forward... He has coagulated with the Eater of the Ass - a great squat dwarf-giant, his skin a mass of writhing worms, his dragon head topped by a rusty brass colander, pots and pans hanging all over his limbs and clanging together with a hideous clatter, pushing before him a supermarket trolley filled with twisting, naked homunculi, tin cans, empty soda pop bottles and plastic plates and spoons... From his molten groin rears up the head of the Serpent Ankhi, God of Time, with his two faces set in opposite directions... Up ahead, the Gods that are born anew each day are waiting for me to complete my passage... The Light in front, the Darkness behind me... Maybe if I took this turning...

"Are you there, Nep?! Grab my hand, I'm right up on this ledge - "

"I can't make it, man!"

"You can make it! There, feel my fingers! Comrades, give us a hand here, for God's sake... Arnold! Battuta! Jesse! Are you there? Move your ass!"

Can I can feel the warmth of the Womb of the Morning...? The Beetle Khepher-Ankh, pushing the Great Egg of Life before him, out of the tunnel, into the Light...

"Come on, king of kings, you goddamn useless cadaver! Stretch down there, Arnold! Grab this man's hand! Up! Up!" - - - - - -

Jesse :

We stood on the ledge, breathing heavily after our exertions, clutching the portly sweating figure of the old Egyptian as we dragged him out of the dark. The Traveller Ibn Battuta and the white-haired scribe Flint massaged his arms and legs, remonstrating all the while.

I left them as soon as I saw he would recover from his ordeal. As ever. Repeated again and again. It's best to leave the shadows to squabble among themselves in the cave. That Greek Aplaton has a lot to answer for. It's difficult to remember now what the cave might have looked like from the outside. It was so long ago. I feel no strong desire any more to lead those people to the light...

But I remember the sun. The hammer of the Great Disk upon the red rock cutting down in jagged steps in the shimmering haze towards the deep blue of the Dead Sea. The total silence in that sanctuary of pitiless stone and shifting sand. An eagle, soaring high in that deepest blue of skies, above the cliff, dedicated to the stern task of spying out his prey in the wilderness.

In the beginning God created the heaven and the earth, the light and the sky. The first two days. Then he moved on to greener pastures. But only a few twigs and bones from the third, fourth and fifth days quickened this meagre landscape. Of the sixth day we had our own passing wraiths -

The Sons of Dawn. We few disciples, waiting at the foot of the Qumran cliffs for our Teacher to appear. The men of heart, who pursue righteousness, who will understand his Words, when they are eventually spoken. All that has been foreordained, but requires the tongue to speak, the lips to move, the utterance to be made...

I remember it well, the Copiers' tents. The Silent Weeks, when all attention was to be focussed on the Revelations soon to come. The rumours that the Teacher had finally appeared, on the Coastal Plain, and was about to make Himself known. It was nothing new. Aspiring Teachers had been declaring themselves as long as I had lived. But all their contentions to date proved to be false. There was a claimant from Nazareth, whose followers said he had been born under a Star, in Bethlehem, but fell prey to the Romans, who nailed him up in Jerusalem. His disciples were still wandering about the region, weeping and wailing and telling the most extravagant tales...

But I still believe my Redeemer liveth, and He shall blaze forth in due course, even in this Domain of Darkness. For His coming is prefigured, in the Secret Scrolls, and in the Hidden Apocalypses of Tobit, Yubit and Hadramauth. He who comes under many Names: Kohath, and Abiatar, and Uzziah, and Yehoniah, and Simeon, and others that are Well Guarded. He is the True Noah, whose Ark sailed on unto the Ends of the Earth and never rested on Mount Ararat. He is Job, who was vouchsafed a second vision which could not be written down. He is Daniel, who chose to remain in the lion's den, and the Three Men who were not consumed.

We ordained it our task, while Waiting, to write down the Secret Messages. We scribes sat in our tent, arranged in two rows on either side of a single long table, each with his parchment scroll held down by clay weights, while, beside us, the Original Message was spread out, to be returned to its Hidden Source when the copying was done. Today even the copies have been lost. And yet I seek them anew every day...

There could be no women in our desert community: The risk of contamination from the menstrual flow was considered by our Founders to be far too high. The Nazarene was surrounded by women and look what happened to him. The flesh is simply an itch, said the Founders. Scratch it and it becomes inflamed. Only those who are truly free of the body can be entrusted with the holy task.

But here, inside the cave, I am a different person. Wandering in the body, shining my lamp into the gloomy folds of the large intestine, climbing up the ascending flexure of the colon to the liver, skirting the gall bladder, and the pancreas and pressing on into the lungs - everything is contaminated. The body has never ceased abusing itself since time immemorial. Scattered everywhere are the tell tale signs of a life lived in dissipation, deprivation, flagrant vice, disease, depravity, moral turpitude. There are actual cesspools, rubbish tips and garbage depots. The sediment of high tar roll ups cobbled together from discarded butts of anything from Malboro to Gaulloise sans-filter coats the lining with black putrid muck. Tumours, buboes and cysts push their way through the tangled nerves and piles of congealed burger crumbs, and gristle blocks the arteries everywhere. The heart wheezes and thuds unevenly in the depths, like an ancient worn out beast trapped at the bottom of the sea. I have to tie a handkerchief over my nose and mouth to shut out the stench of decay, as I pick my way over the wattled lobes to climb into the trachea.

I am imbued, nevertheless, with a deep ambivalence towards the wretched prisoners of this body. These shadows, who dance and jerk about to unknown strings and cry out in their multiple languages of pain, misapprehension and affliction, repel and disgust, and yet move me to a bottomless pity. It is not, like the impaled Nazarene, a desire to don the mantle of their sins, dead or alive - and how can a dead man atone, for himself or for others? A theological nonsense. Only life can be the anvil of repentance. But I cannot bear watching these poor souls suffer. It is a deflection, I know, from the task. Someone has to leave a testament to connect the past to the future. To set down the eternal codes for the initiates of coming generations. Someone has to plan for the rebellion against Rome. And I'm not speaking of the stockpiling of weapons, though that too is important. The axes, bows, lances, poison tipped arrows, sealed naphtha jugs and chemical formulae that we concealed beneath the paper-pits were part of the Lord's work, too, for He is the Lord of Wrath, not just of the Word. But there are also softer compulsions...

Continuing from the trachea to the thyroid, into the larynx, up the nasal cavity and ducts towards the lachrymal canals. A warm dankness hangs in the air, as I slip and slide my way down the corridor towards Apartment 12A...

I knock on the door. There is a faint scrabble from inside. I know the woman, Ann, is there. Where else can she be? As long as I can remember she has been tied down to this room, marooned in her bed and bedlam, relying on takeaway deliveries and call-out services to keep her going, or rather staying in place. My sandalled feet are ankle deep in the tears which have clearly seeped underneath the door. My nostrils wrinkle at the usual stench of half-eaten cans of preserved food, spoiled beef, congealed jam and spaghetti sauce, rancid butter, decaying rinds of various fruits, rotted sardines and tunafish, discarded french fries and TV dinners piled unopened but putrid in their silver foil. How can anyone live in this squalor?

But before I could knock again, her voice wafted through the door, languid and melodious as ever:

"The door's open."

I stepped inside, sloshing through the overflowing bath water which has mingled with the lachrymose stream. Easing past the mounds of prised open tins with their jagged edges which I have learned to avoid the hard way. I still have the scars of cuts of rust and dirt which even arrowroot failed to heal. The nostrums and unguents of old Mordecai. But I managed to reach her bed unharmed this time.

"I've brought you some groceries. Sourmash, wheatgerm mix, Boar's Head ham, Swanson Pot Pies, Aunt Jemima's batter, buffalo wings, Shofar bologna, Mueller's noodles, Philadelphia cream cheese, English muffins, mini-ravioli, cereal, crackers."

"You didn't get to Zabars?"

"There was a sale at Red Apple."

"Well, put it down wherever. I'm bushed."

She was lying spread out like a starfish, her legs and arms widely splayed, her frayed blue and white striped pyjama top pulled up over her belly button. That great white mound. The pudgy paleness of her forearms, neck and face, her wild dark hair flopped like seaweed over the pile of dirty yellowing pillows. The great hillocks of her thighs bulging under the rolled down sheets.

"Time for a laundry service, Ann."

"They're far too pricey, Valet Vanguard. It's a dollar fifty for briefs. I'd take the lot down to the basement if I could make the run. But it's too tiring. It's been a really heavy day."

Her eyes were fixed on the flickering TV which was running the Wheel of Fortune. An elderly couple from North Platte Nebraska had already won six thousand dollars and were being egged on to bust or glory by an incensed studio audience. But the image kept warping and fragmenting, sustained only by a bent aerial one of whose rods had been snapped off at the base.

"I can't count how many application forms I've filled in for that program," Ann bemoaned, "but not one invitation."

I pulled open the bedside bureau and showed her the stack of unmailed forms. She waved a lacklustre hand. I rummaged on curiously in the drawer. Old pencil stubs, rusty pencil sharpeners, blackened erasers, can openers, bandaids, anatacid pills, minicards of White Sands National Monument, New Mexico, Desert Yucca, Picnic Ground Shelters, Sand Dunes and Trinity, Site of the World's First Nuclear Explosion, Northwest of Alamogordo. "Where a New World Order Was Born." I doubt whether she had ever been there. Ann Hedonia had probably never been anywhere. She had winked into being, sui generis, in this filthy, debris strewn, waterlogged room. Ass deep in amniotic fluid. Self birthed out of that tremendous gut. But my fingers closed on a pile of unopened letters, some local, and others air-mail envelopes, stamped and franked from various corners of the globe, a couple from Albuquerque, New Mexico, three from San Francisco, two from Dallas, Texas, one each from Totonicapan, Guatemala, Bogota, Colombia, Lima, Peru and Sao Paolo in Brazil, one from Bloemfontein, Orange Free State, South Africa, one from Dabra-Markos, Ethiopia, two from Samarkand, Uzbek S.S.R., one from Alma Ata in Kazakhstan, one from Mashhad, Iran, one from Srinagar, Kashmir, one from Kfar Sorek, Israel, one from Cairo, Egypt, three from Pago Pago, Samoa. I thought I sensed, for a brief moment, the beat of bongo drums and the skirl of pan pipes from the cheerfully coloured stamps. But it faded in the screech of joy from the TV set where the winnings had reached ten thousand.

"Don't you feel curious about any of these?" I asked Ann, shaking the mail in her face. But she just pouted in a resigned twitch. "I had a file for opening the envelopes," she murmured, "but I lost it."

"It's here." I pulled it from the inner depth of the drawer. I put it in her hand but she let it drop, vanishing with a barely discernable plop into the shallow salt water covering the floor. I tried to scrabble for it but she pushed me away. "Leave it," she said, "make me an omelette. Six eggs, onions, ham, grated boloney. I don't think I can get up at all today. Tell me what's going on outside."

Outside?!! The world creaking and bludgeoning on in its incessant subterfuge. The legions of the Empire marching to a glory which would soon be dust and dry bones. The triumph of all the wrong Messiahs. The inability to read the ancient runes. Legions of scribes bent over parchments labouring to transmit false pasts. Scientists discovering the future. Workmen mending holes in the road, at the corner of Canal Street and Church, with posters announcing that Braun & Stavros, Inc, intended to develop this site on behalf of the City of New York. The body, wracked with the tremors of its internal organs, the night traffic around the enclosed island and the incessant beat from the Go Go bar tweaking the tendrils of its dreamland. The rising wind rustling the New York Times Classified and flipping cardboard boxes across the busy roads, whooping through cables and rattling all the loose street signs: THIS WAY, THAT WAY, KEEP LEFT, KEEP RIGHT, NO PED CROSSING, NO PARKING, LOCAL TRAFFIC ONLY, BRIDGE DOWN, THIS ROAD CLOSED...

And God was angry at the Children of Israel and delivered them into the hands of Nebuchanezzar, King of Babylon, to lay waste their lands and cast them into exile to the four corners of the earth...

"What's the weather forecast, Jess?"

"Gathering clouds. Autumn storm warnings down the Florida coast and advancing up Georgia and the Carolinas. Hurricane Hilda."

"The killer dames. We get the blame every time. Rampant sexism."

"I wouldn't know, Ann. We're a celibate order. God, when was this cooker last cleaned?"

In the last great scouring... when the skies and earth were not yet named, and no gods were manifest, and no names given, and no destinies yet decreed, and when the apple had not yet ripened on the tree, and even the serpent had not yet grown his fangs. And all the beasts of the earth and the fish of the sea and the fowl of the air gambolled and trilled in innocent glee... What horrors might have gone on before? The congealed lumps of fat, the blackened gristle, the burnt oil sticking to the sides of the oven, the Good Lord down on her hands and knees, dressed in stained apron and head scarf, scrubbing out the bottom and back panels with a scouring pad and Ajax Multi-Purpose Cleaner. Let us make a Man or Woman in our image. Gingerbread kids. With blank groins and brown raisins for eyes. The usual ingredients:

200g brown sugar,
150g butter,
300g treacle or syrup,
400g flour,
1 teaspoon salt,
1 tablespoon ground ginger,
1 desert spoon manna,
250ml mother's milk,
100ml spilled seed,
150g Greek raisins,
Fickle finger of fate,
Divine breath...

"I can't get this thing to work, honey..."

"Forget it. Pass me that bag of Pepperidge Farm cookies. The Chocolate Chip Pecan, on the shelf."

"You gotta look after yourself, Ann. You can't live like this forever. You gotta get some exercise, some fresh air."

But she fell asleep, after wolfing down the biscuits. I pulled the shredded packet from her quivering lips. Looking round the apartment with an inconsoleable foreboding. The waterlogged floor, with tin cans floating like Lilliputian wrecks, their prised up lids raised to catch the wind from her irregular farts. Occasionally a cockroach, protruding from a sardine tin, lowered its mandibles into the water to propel itself along. Others tried to find a purchase on the grimy, greasy walls. Gnat corpses dried on the room's single lightbulb. On the TV set, the elderly couple, having gambled all their winnings, as well as the mortgage on their house and their entire savings on a wrong number, were carted off the studio stage, bankrupt and weeping, as the audience cheered and waved...

I gazed at her as she slept, the fat lady. Was she ever thus? Was there a time, back when, that she was slim and svelte and dressed in silk kaftans and turbans? Was her voice ever mellow and clear?

Spin the wheel! Spin the wheel!
Our next two guests, who need no introduction -
- Hey, you up there, less noise for God's sake!
- Turn down that racket!
- How can a man get any rest in this chaos...?
- Crazy motherfuckers!
- Is there anyone in charge around here...?
- Can I feel the warmth of the womb of the morning...?
- Give us a hand here for God's sake!
- Take hold of my hand, you Goddamn worthless Gypo...!
- Lift him up!
Up!
Up!

- We stood on the ledge, breathing heavily after our exertions, clutching the portly sweating figure of the Egyptian as we dragged him out of the dark. We all moved back from the overhang, Ibn Battuta, the Traveller, leading the way with the torch. Once we reached a calm section, midway through the Pancreas, we called a halt and reviewed the situation.

There were four of us, in this particular conclave, after Jesse had wandered off: Ibn Battuta, Lincoln Korombane, Nep (Merenptah-Pharaoh), and myself, Arnold Flint. Winner of the Truman Capote Hardnose Fiction Award three years running. A first, if anyone wants to know. Thank you for asking. Nep was trembling, as is his wont after a night running from his demons, and we threw an old army blanket round him while Battuta brewed up some coffee in his battered old *finjan*. We sat there in silence, letting the old gypo get his breath back.

This confinement within the body is becoming a real chore. Locked up with a bunch of unpredictable lunatics, it's not long before one's own mind begins to falter, to run dry and begin imagining even more things that aren't there than weren't there before. If you get my drift. These are the remnants of a mind that was once sharp as a knife, and always honed... No use crying over spilt pus, is there?

I would have preferred to have driven my companions back home with me, unhinged as they are, out to Westchester County, in my old Caddy Convertible... Easing through the foggy jams of Midtown and the perils of Route 87 thru the crumbling projects of the South Bronx, past the ragged tramps and threatening adolescents rushing to squeegee your windscreen. Anything for a buck in this city. And Yonkers, what can you say about Yonkers? But pretty soon you're into Greenburgh and Mount Pleasant, skirting the Reservoir and Pocatinco Lake, the softly rippling waters, the birds and the bees, the angler's paradise, smallmouth and largemouth bass and so forth... Turning off the main road down the tree lined archways, the sunlight dappled red, russet, roseate leaves, the rows of detached houses, with their porches and porticos, lawns and lawnmowers, woodchucks and squirrels in the eaves, kiddies' tricycles on grassy verges, German shepherds straining at the leash. I loved the turn in to the grounds, the soft buckle of the car as the tyres skid over the join between asphalt and gravel, the satisfying crackle of tiny pebbles thrown to either side, ricocheting off the chassis. The tall beeches lining the route up the hill, and then the old colonial house, with the old wood porch and the rocking chair and benches, the leaves nestling up to the steps. The wisping chimney smoke of a real fire in a real fire place... It's astonishing what you can afford when you're in the New York Times Bestseller list eighteen weeks running.

But we are locked in this regurgitating pit, and have to make do with a little bistro in an atrium I discovered just behind the spleen. The food is undistinguished, but palatable, and there is a small fountain whose tinkling waters drown the beat of Beatrice's hellish dungeon drums. We took a small table for four. I had no wish to entice that dill pickle, Jesse, from the contemplation of his Messiah, the Great Teacher, who, like the plumber, is always just about to fetch around the corner with his bag of wrenches and plumbs. Ann Hedonia the female Oblomov and Jaime of the Colon were as much a dead loss. Battuta always tries to get me to rouse the Alchemist, Mordecai, but I won't discuss my private business with the phantom "Regulator", whom Battuta has never convinced me was ever anything but a figment of his oriental imagination. The Eternal Jew. Some people never give up.

"Well, if you got it folks, flaunt it!" I put on a brave face as the waiters, two young faceless acolytes, boy and girl, dressed in crisp white with black butterfly bow ties, brought us the menu. I chose the escargot with whipped cream. I waited till Lincoln ordered his usual T-bone steak with french fries, and Battuta the kofta kebabs. Nep, shaken if not curdled by his nightly runaround, said he would make do with a little light green salad. We all called for Chinese green tea. I didn't want to open the discussion until the butterfly youth were gone. It was not clear where, in the first place, they had crept from, nor what role they were playing in the greater scheme of things. One has to hug one's cards to one's chest.

"We gotta get outa here," I whispered to my colleagues as soon as the waiters were out of sight, and hopefully earshot. "You must be aware there's been a lot of snooping going on lately. Prying eyes. Probing questions. So called Therapy. A little bird tells me our Names have been given out, and written down in official documents of the New York Social Security System."

"Is that so?" Merenptah perked up, "was it an ibis or a lesser crested gull?"

These ancient duffers are so literal. "The Mongols excelled at using carrier pigeons," Battuta added, "they could deliver a letter from Karakorum to Tiflis in three days. It was the secret of their success."

"Pigeons," said Lincoln.

"Specially trained," said Battuta, "they were shown maps, and away they went."

"Are you guys gonna give me a break?" Hell is other people. Wasn't that from Sartre's *Huis Clos*? All these incompatible clashing egos. It was Beatrice who had put me in the know. "There's a lady psychiatrist who's got her hooks into Mo," she said, hanging her whips out to dry in the red heat of her charcoal braziers in her anteroom. "There are several interrogators. A Jew. An Arab. A crazy Armenian. A Professor of History and some bitch who runs an art gallery in the East Village."

"You don't say." I am always circumspect with Beatrice. She has ambitions of her own, to be the Regulator in place of the mythical Jew. She claims to know the exits from the body, but then, that's a familiar scam in here. The spick, Jaime, always offers to show you the way out for ten dollars, and then strands you in the lesser caecum. I might as well join Nep in his mumbled mummy spells. It's a den of iniquity, a viper's nest in here, though I have a soft spot for Link and Battuta. Battuta's travelling tales are as shaggy as Sinbad's, but in the important things he's straight and narrow. Lincoln has been dumped upon by life too much to lie to a buddy. I put a lot of store in a good drinking partner, spade, spick or kike. Merenptah is too scared to lie because it all counts against him in his imagined journey through the Underworld. It's a trip through his underpants if you ask me. But different strokes for different folks.

We're all brothers and sisters under the skin, ain't we? Except Jaime, who is closer to the orangutan than to man, and rips off anybody who comes near him, and Jesse, who I wouldn't wonder is in league with the snoops. His symbiosis with that tub of lard, Ann Hedonia, is positively repulsive. I once went into her room for ten minutes and was sick for ten days.

No, it's the Tax Men who are after me. Those gravediggers from the Infernal Revenue. One is never allowed to be a success in this country. The moment one begins to properly ride the system those injuns are out there, moving in for the kill.

We hold these truths to be self-evident: Life, liberty, and the pursuit of happiness. Let's face it, it's all a crock of shit. Your life's in the hands of your neighborhood mugger, your liberty's in hock to the CIA and all the other manipulators of our unmanifest destiny, and the pursuit of happiness, you can shove that up your ass. I thought I had found it with my first wife. Then with Numero Duo. Tell me about it.

My only really happy day was the day a big fat check arrived from Random House for the first magnum opus. That was a rebirth day, no shit. "The Crimson Trash." How I out-Mailered Mailer. It all came out of true stories of the German army at Stalingrad in World War Two, which, I can now reveal, I read in the Readers' Digest. This is how it happened: In the depth of the Russian winter, soldiers who wanted to survive had to crap in their uniforms, because if they unbuttoned their trousers to shit their rectum froze up and their accumulating excreta blew up their bowels. Kaput kamarad. I wanted to call the book "The Frozen Assholes", but my editor, Random head honcho Eldon Griffith the IIIrd, talked me out of it. I suppose he was afraid his staff would think it was about him.

It's amazing, but Americans still like nothing better than to read about both Germans and Russians dying horribly in gruesome detail, as told by my young OSS officer, Dale Burroughs, attached to the Russian partisan forces. His coupling in the snow with the beautiful Ukrainian commissar, Katarina, was noch besser for business. But a young couple who tried out Katarina's method for melting ice with naked passion, in Montana, were found by their shocked parents the next morning, frozen in each other's embrace. Mum and Dad sued both me and my publisher, a case which made both Time and Newsweek and my fortune. I won the case and offered the losers an ex gratia settlement, out of compassion for their pain, but they turned me down. I learned then that you can't be responsible for the entire world...

At least the young folks died happy. Rayette Glass and Ulric Dietenhoffer. Poor bastards. Sometimes I see them, threshing about in my dreams, trying to melt the ice floes...

But I digress from the pre-eminent theme: My success. My second book, "Jamaica Pass", was the epic of George Washington's campaigns in New York, serialised in the New York Times Sunday Magazine. Five weeks running. First and only instance. The tale of the bloody battles with the British in what is now Brooklyn and Manhattan. The Battle of Long Island, August 1776. The sun rose on that day with "a red and angry glare," and the Americans were bombarded, bayonetted and chased into the redoubt of Brooklyn Heights, where they held out for several days, eating biscuits "hard enough to break a rat's teeth."

A tale of privation, betrayal, agony. Blood and guts wrapped in the flag. That book sold two million copies and was made into a mini-series starring Paul Newman, Anthony Hopkins and what's her name, the chameleon woman – Meryl Streep? It was at that point, when the cash started flowing, that I began to pay attention to the urgent need for an appropriate portfolio... A little Savings & Loans, a chunk of aerospace, a few futures, a few pasts, a reasonable piece of the present... Something to put by for a rainy day. Damn the bastards! In which article of the Constitution does it say that an American citizen and taxpayer can't enjoy the fruits of his labours?

"A man can't allow himself to be pinned down nowadays," I told my companions, through the bites of escargot, "there are too many enemies waiting to do you down. Divorce lawyers, infernal revenuers, Jehovah's Witnesses, insurance salesmen, parasites, blackguards out to take you for every penny you've got."

"How do you expect us to bust out of this joint?" says Lincoln, easing off his T-bone, "I've been in Pretoria jail. That's the ultimate. But this place is a real labyrinth."

One is always surrounded by defeatists. I leaned forward:

"Where there's a will there's a way."

I could see from their blank faces staring at me that I was not getting through. Battuta at least should see my point. A man who has traversed the civilised world and carried on far into the dark realms of barbarism should understand the main chance. Merenptah is hung up not just on getting to the "other side" but with the right way to get there, all those spells and mumbo jumbo. But Lincoln is still so anxious to hide from his troubles outside...

"Every journey of a thousand miles," I reminded them, "is just one short step. It only requires the decision to get up off your ass and hit the road."

"What do *you* know," says Lincoln, launching his usual spiel: "I walked fifteen hundred miles from Joburg to Dar es-Salaam. By the time I got to Dar my feet were like two rotting marrows. My shoes had worn into two thin strips of leather which I had to take off and chew on the last leg of the journey to stave off the hunger pangs..."

I know, we're going to get the whole shebang. The flight from Boer oppression after the Sharpeville massacre, the despair of exile in "Independent" Africa, the poisoned sanctuary of Ghana's Kwame Nkrumah. Osagyefu - the Redeemer, and his corrupt acolytes. Merenptah's eyes glaze over and Battuta, connoisseur of the bizarre, smiles politely, baring his teeth. I just settle back and let my ears droop. I'm going to hear the whole story all over again, how he failed to gain support for the "revolution" in Africa, and how he failed in Paris and London, and how he ended up being "trained" as a guerrilla in the Soviet Union, and how fate made him, in the fullness of time, a double agent for the CIA.

"None of us had ever travelled north of the Equator," he droned, "but there we were, freezing our butts off in northern Kazakhstan, being trained for defence against atomic, bacteriological and chemical weapons. We had naively volunteered for ABC training, thinking it was some basic course. They dressed us in plastic suits and gas masks and threw us out onto the icy steppes, sending down Tupolev air-planes to spray us with indelible dyes. My friend, Nga Moholo, lost three toes and his left thumb to frostbite. In the evenings, despite our numb exhaustion, we had to take lectures on Marxist-Leninism from a hatchet faced lady in a stiff uniform which seemed to have closed around her like a glacier on a mammoth..."

But I was already wandering elsewhere, in my thoughts, mulling over my third, prospective novel, my grand epic, "The Sabbath", a saga of the Salem Witch Trials, with my own ingenious twist. No Milleresque allegory of McCarthyism for me. My devil, like Mark Twain's, or Updike's, perish the thought, was real, but no stranger in town. I had gone back in my researches to the source, to Cotton Mather, the Boston clergyman who wrote the original tract which inflamed and encouraged the hunts. He called his book "The Wonders of the Invisible World". To Mather, you see, the world was seething with legions of the unseen Enemy, a legion being, he reminds us, twelve thousand and five hundred demons, in this case. "Multitudes in the valley of destruction," like the frogs and plagues of Egypt, ever increasing. They were everywhere, in the fields, tempting men to sloth, in the shops, tempting merchants to dishonesty, in the bedroom, tempting women to lust, and in the churches, tempting all to heresy. Both Jews and Catholics were, according to Mather, agents of the Hellish pestilence. He was a man deeply tormented by these perils which he claimed only he could see clearly. The Devil, truly at his side, imbuing the cleric with his vital mission to save the New Jerusalem, made manifest in New England...

This was my personal twist: The old gnostic heresy - the world as Satan's creation, not God's. Who is the one tempting us to turn towards our inner voices, and who is He who wrote society's rules? Round and round the old conundrums we go, scratching at all the old sores. How refreshing to meet someone like Link, who became a perfect Benedict Arnold. It must be so satisfying to know you have sinned the ultimate political sin. Cotton Mather's Satan also knew that a terrible liberating force lay somewhere in that kingdom of absolute fear, of irretrievable transgressions...

Measured against that, my own were so petty. Spiking the drinks at the PEN annual jamboree. Cheating on my wives and children. Hating my neighbour as myself. Savings and Loans. Traditional vices. In my first visit to Beatrice's Dungeon of Torment, at the entrance to the duodenum, I gave myself over to her free offer of chastisement for beginners, but could not fully enjoy the pain. I had myself strapped to a cod-medieval crossbeam, with manacles round my wrists and ankles, a leather mask and wooden clothes-pegs snapped on to my nipples. Another strap was tightened round the base of my testicles and attached to a chain which rubber-clad Beatrice tugged fiercely when she thought I was not paying sufficient attention to the matter at hand. The entire House of Pain was throbbing to the rhythms of something called Death's-Head Thrash, which in itself was painful enough. I had put myself down for G.T., only realising too late it did not mean Gin and

Tonic but Genital Torture. The buxom madame laid about my naked flesh with a selection of whips, paddles and straps, and then proceeded to apply a tube of sandpaper to my exposed cock. But all I could think of at the time was the folly of having my Diners Club card debited for this...

Sins against the flesh and heresies of the spirit. They must have all been down there, one time or another, my fellow inmates of this fleshy stockade, Battuta, the mythical Mordecai, Merenptah, even Jesse, and Link, atoning, sure as eggs is eggs... A man's a man for a' that...

But I woke with a start from my own reverie to find Lincoln still droning on: "Now Comrade Nga," he continued, "never refused a challenge. He was determined to fuck this Comrade Commissar free of her arctic carapace. He stalked her down the chilly corridors with their pale walls covered with exhortations by Lenin and Stakhanov, and portraits of great Marshalls of the Red Army like Timoshenko and Budenny and Voroshilov, armed with a bottle of vodka he had stolen from the Russian officers' mess. He caught up with her in the barracks gymnasium where she had shed her outer armour to wrestle with dumb bells in a scarlet track suit emblazoned with a great golden hammer and sickle. He pinned her round the neck with a World Federation armlock, but she threw him over her head and smashed him with a drop kick. He grabbed her again and pinned her to the mattress but she managed to knee him in the groin. They circled each other, panting like animals, as he dangled the unbroken bottle of vodka in front of her quivering nose. She closed in to finish him off with karate kicks, but he dodged them and fended her off with a head butt, which sent her reeling, blood pouring down her face. They both burst through the doors of the gymnasium into the cold, hard yard, where the flag of the Soviet Union was a rigid sheet of red ice against the black sky. He grabbed her, she grabbed him and they clinched, she biting his chin and his ears as he greedily licked the blood off her face. The dawn patrol found them like that the next morning, encased in an iceblock of congealed blood, vodka and semen. His penis had frozen inside her, and it broke off, like a stalactite, when they moved them. They were defrosted and she was sent back to Moscow. Our entire group was disbanded and put on the next Aeroflot flight to Berlin."

The vagina dentata of Faith. Rayette Glass and Ulric Dietenhoffer. Poor little kids. Lincoln thought I was sighing for him and his castrated friend, and gave me a wan smile, taking my shrug as a cue to continue, as if I gave a fuck. Let him steal my stories if he wants. Leaning back in his bistro chair and sighing like the Azanian Job he makes himself out to be -

"Years later, at my initial debriefing at Langley, the Company agents wanted me to describe every detail of that period. Every spot on the wall, every zit on the pale Slavic cheeks of those Soviet instructors. What do they know about our nuclear capability? What do they know about our missile trajectories, our response strategies and target options? They haven't a clue, I wanted to tell my CIA handlers. They are so incompetent they will fall apart on their own, your invading troops will need no more than massed brigades of men with brushes and pans to clear up the drunken bodies, and pumps to suck up the great pools of vodka. But you couldn't tell the Company that in 1968, no, not with the alarms over the Middle East and tanks in Prague and students carrying the faces of Ho and Mao in the streets of Paris and London and Berlin. Do you understand me, Arnold? They had killed Che Guevara in Bolivia but were terrified of his ghost stalking the jungles and veldts from Benguela to Bengal. So I gave them what they wanted to hear: A great tale of collusion stretching over the globe, a web of conspiracies leading from the Kremlin to trade union tea parties in Liverpool, to teacher training courses in Paris lycees, to dopehead communes in Wyoming. I painted lurid pictures of camps in Tanzania where long haired Germans received secret training to poison wells in the Western Capitals come the approaching Red Day of Wrath. They were crazy to know whether I was a double, triple or quadruple agent, and whether I could be turned back by the other side. But I was simply careening blindfold down the path. Trying to survive. Trying to figure out what I could turn to the advantage of the Liberation Movement back home. After all, everybody made deals. Our capitalistic Boer zealots, we already knew by then, worked hand in glove with their communist enemies to corner the world market in diamonds and gold...

"Let me tell you this story: In Omsk I met an Afrikaaner named Ventner who was liaising between BOSS and the KGB's Southern African Economic Unit. He threw his boozy paw over my shoulder in a local shebeen in which a red forty-Watt lightbulb disclosed a row of catatonic muzhiks slumped over their own vomit, and greeted me like a long lost brother. `Mein kamarad!' He chattered at me in Afrikaans about his own mad vision of things. We were all wrong, he said, we revolutionaries. The Brotherhood of Man would not be realised by idealists, utopian dreamers and rebels, but only by a cabal of the world's secret services. They were the only true custodians of the true facts of history, all the way from Babel and the Flood. This was the terrible Truth: God had given the gift of political knowledge and understanding not to the prophets or the proletariat or the aristocracy or bleeding heart liberal academic pederasts, but to the police. For all the rabbins and priests that are worth their salt know that the Bible, the Five Books of Moses and the Gospels of Jesus Christ are inscribed in code, which only the initiated can decipher. And throughout history, the primal codes have served as bases for all subsequent knowledge: The secret tables of Isis, the ancient mysteries and symbols, the hieroglyphs, the formulas of alchemy, the hermetic books of Francis Bacon, Paracelsus, Robert Fludd, the Rosicrucians. In our day this crucial data was preserved, Ventner insisted, by the Masons, who kept, within the innocuous mainstream organisation, hidden chapters which, through an elaborate and concealed network, controlled what was left of any coherent genuine authority in world affairs.

"`At first we thought it was the Jews,' Ventner whispered to me, his Boer spittle licking at my ear, `then we discovered the Elders of Zion were merely a sideshow, a shadow play of puppets. Real knowledge transcended all our petty fears, our ethnographic prejudices. It is beyond the questions of colour, race, gender, creed. Real knowledge was and is located in a sphere of total terror, a place in which all our so called received wisdom evaporates in the pure fire of the nuclear spiritual energy that ties us to the Origins of Life. Not the heretic Darwin, of course, who was assigned to turn science away from Truth and into Error, on the very brink of the era which could have liberated Mankind.'

"I could not understand what he was talking about, as his speech became more and more slurred, until eventually he slid mercifully off my neck into the spew and muck on the floor, where he threshed about like a stricken eel for some minutes before going into rigor. Later I was asked to reconstruct this incident for my CIA handlers at Langley, and they took down every word carefully, with a deadpan look and pursed lips. They showed me a book of mugshots of BOSS agents from which I was expected to pick out Ventner, but they all looked alike to me, with their plug mugs, their chiselled shaven heads and farmboy chins."

Lincoln sighed once more. "I was so naive then. I believed I could tap into sources of power to play realpolitik against itself. I knew I was taking the highest risk of being denounced as a traitor by my own people. This was a burden I had to bear alone, and I expected no help if I failed..."

Indeed, the old Talmudic adage. If I am not for me, who is for me? And if only I am for me, who is for me? And if not now, when? Battuta squeezed his hand in sympathy, though Merenptah was already long gone, emitting short popping sounds from his mouth and twitching, back, I presumed, in his demon infested netherworld. But there was now a distinct chill in the air, and a growing rumbling noise. The chairs and tables shaking. The wind, picking up all about us, vibrating the atrium, slapping us with the fountain's fetid stream, rocking the table, throwing the cold food off our plates... I could feel the sleeper shifting around me, rustling in his New York Times pages... The body tossing and turning in that limbo that just precedes awakening... I could hear the crockery smashing in the kitchen, the cries of the waiters as they slid in torrents of spilled soup, the howl of gusts in the oesophagus...

"Bodyquake!"

Merenptah tipped out of his chair, Battuta catching hold of his hand and Link's. Everyone pulling and pushing to safety, falling over each other's torsos and feet.

"To the belly button!"

The stern but lithe figure of Jesse the Essene climbing up over the liver with a lantern, waving to show us the way... Even the sedentary Ann Hedonia seems to have been cast out of her bed, threshing and slipping in her mess of pottage, banging her feet and arms against the door...

Blind, dizzy and deafened, we were sliding towards another temporary oblivion, as the body turned, stretched, retched, yawned, kicked out against the piles of wooden crates, scrabbling for purchase on the hard concrete ground, farting, spitting, rolling its tongue round the dry chapped lips, prising apart the hardened mucus of filth encrusted lashes, opening its bleary punch drunk eyes to the blare, the smoke, the rush of traffic, the tumbling cardboard boxes borne by the wind...

IN THE NAME OF GOD, THE MERCIFUL, THE COMPASSIONATE:

I, MUHAMMAD ABU ABDALLAH, KNOWN AS IBN BATTUTA, bear witness to the truth of these astonishing events that God, in His Infinite Wisdom, has ordained that I should observe. For seeing the world through the eyes of the Sleeper, both asleep and awake, is a prodigious paradox which none of the scientists of old, nor even the poets, could express. Perhaps the Sufis, who spoke of the world of the imagination as seen by the adept through his magic mirror, predicted such a singular perception. The Philosopher Ibn Rushd argues that in our essential being we are all One, and individuality is only an accidental element. Ibn Sinna, on the other hand, argues for the immortality of each rational soul, rejecting the incarnationist ideas of the *hululi* Sufis. Even when disembodied, Ibn Sinna proclaimed, the soul retains consciousness of its own separate history. Our experience, says Ibn Sinna, provides us with an identity that is not dependent on the body.

But Ibn Sinna lived when experience was a more direct thing than it is now, if now is the time of the Sleeper. I note that I am both embodied, as I am within the Sleeper's body, and disembodied, when I am seeing his world through his eyes. My limbs are his limbs, my senses his senses, my taste his taste, my smell his smells, the toxic odours of his own surroundings...

At the moment he wakes, I am assailed by these odours, and by a multitude of ear splitting sounds. A mass of human cries, and the terrible shrieking and pounding of mechanical engines. For a moment, I am back in Cairo, Mother of Cities, the teeming quarters of the Bab el-Khalq, the Ghuriyya with its din of artisans' workshops, and the traffic jams which always afflicted al-Azhar. Great modern minarets rise up high as the Bab Zuweila and higher, except that no call of the *muaddhin* echoes from them. The crowds push, shove and yell in much the same manner. The same proliferation of stalls, markets and diverse eateries, though the kind of foodstuffs available are often foreign to a Believer's palate, if not actually unclean and forbidden: "Ham and pickle" sandwiches in "Oshri's Deli." "Hot dogs", a risible thought even to the famished. But the Sleeper's mouth slavers. Wobbling on the corner of the "Specialist Car Radios", the glut of strange, incomrehensible signs across the road: UNCLE! UNCLE! UNCLE! EVERYTHING IN ELECTRONICS FOR LESS! CANAL RUBBER - IF ITS FOAM WE HAVE IT!

Verily one is in need of "Crystal Ball Readings - Past, Present, Future - Lucky Days and Numbers, Three Dimensional Sculpture Readings, Crystal Energy - Only $20!" I can recognise the abundance of Chinese writing, but we are clearly not in the China of my own travels. There is none of the manifest sense of order that pertains in a Chinese city: The regulated roads, the fine houses set in their own individual gardens, the conspicuous discipline of the inhabitants. Here everything is in disordered flux. The merchants' shops are piled one on top of the other: Luu's Food Market Sun Say Kai Restaurant An An Trading Company Maga Jewelry Engagement & Wedding Rings Gem Avenue Hing Wong May Choeng Tai Fook, New Wah Yin Hong Enterprises Top Stars Skin Care & Beauty Center Lei Sung Corp We Buy Gold Diamonds Pay High Price.

These are not as high as the buildings we passed since our initial emergence from the Ocean. The twin towers of the "World Trade Center" alone were almost as high as the peak of Sarandib. I was told, in my travels, of a mountain range, in the north of India, bordering upon China, so tall that the Angels are able to step onto it in without descending more than a short step from Heaven. But it is guarded, according to reliable reports, by a tribe of fierce warriors who keep their heads in armoured cages separate from their bodies, so they can fight without risking decapitation. I cannot verify the existence of these paragons from my own experience, but I did witness, south of Lake Tchad, in Africa, a tribe of infidels whose heads were in their groins, and who conducted sexual intercourse primarily with their tongues. Manifold are the ways of Allah.

As regards tall buildings, I have seen in Hadramaut vast edifices carved from high mountains, which stood twenty-five storeys high behind ramparts which could not be breached by any catapult. In that land the men were ruled by the women, who were astoundingly well versed not only in the arts of war but in the divine words of the Holy Quran, which they could recite from the first verse to the last. The Queen of that land, who was named Tiwalisasa, wished to procure me as a breeding slave. I barely escaped with my life from her amorous clutches, but that is a tale which still awaits the telling...

Other tall buildings, of course, include the Pyramids of the mystic Egyptian Kings of old, Khufu and Khefren, which still stand in the barren plain of Geeza. The Great Pyramid of King Khufu stands 675 cubits high and contains subterranean chambers which descend to a depth of a further 570 cubits. Its bulk above ground is composed of 2 million tons of stone, which contain, within the stones and hidden by massive plugs, over 800 cubits of uncovered tunnels and passageways leading to secret rooms which conceal vital secrets of the unknown universe. The subterranean chambers have, in the course of time, all been looted and blocked up by ancient tomb robbers, who have, notwithstanding 3,000 years of their efforts, been unable to find the hidden shafts within the colossal monument itself.

These things, and many others which I have mulled over in the centuries that have passed since my death, were related to me by the illustrious Cartographer and Alchemist, Mordecai Ben Suleiman of Cairo. For both before and after my exhaustive journeys I sojourned with this man of great learning, whose library was one of the largest I have ever seen and whose laboratory was equipped with divers marvels at the cutting edge of science. It was situated close to the great mosque and mausoleum of Saydna Zeinab, sister of the Shi'ite Martyr, Hussein. When I arrived to visit this master for the first time it was the feast day of Zeinab, her *mulid*, and thousands of people were out in the streets banging drums, playing upon musical instruments of all kinds, watching the dervish dances performed in gaudily decorated tents and indulging in all manner of boisterousness, within the bounds of the Faith.

My friend the Jew walked through these crowds with ease and familiarity, since he was a venerated person in his quarter. With his long grey and black beard and turquoise skullcap he was like a figure from an old book of legends. I had been recommended to him by my friend, the Shaykh Abd-el Khalil Qarsh, of Tripoli, who said the Jew owned one of the original Magical Mirrors, with which he could look into the landscapes and streets and even the houses of distant countries.

I did not see this Magical Mirror in the apartments of the Jewish wizard, but he did show me into one of his work places, with its abundance of glass vessels and pipes, endless rows of jars with strange contents, shelves of maps, manuscripts and scrolls, instruments of measurement and great charts hung on the walls of all the countries of the world, the celestial zodiacs, the human body, ineffable alphabets and ancient runes. A slave girl brought in a tray of marvellous sweetmeats and a cannikin of an extremely dark wine which he decanted into two long ampullae, having poured their somewhat effervescent previous contents down one of his porcelain sinks.

"You have not tasted slivovitz before?" he queried. I confessed this politely, aware of a streak of mischief which made him flaunt his faith's inadherence to our own prohibition of intoxicating fluids – even the new-fangled coffee-shops of Cairo were frowned upon by the *ulema* at that time.

"It is a fermentation," he related, "from the land of the Bogomils." They were, he explained to me, Christian heretics who had developed the most disturbing beliefs. They claimed this world was of Satan, not of God, and that all Creation was tainted by demonic sin. Even the heroes of the Holy Scriptures were, according to them, inspired by Shaitan. Abraham, Isaac, Jacob, Moses, peace and the blessings of God be upon them, all were evil to them. The Lord God Himself, if such a thought could be uttered, was an assassin, for He had slain Pharaoh and destroyed the cities of Sodom and Gommorah. Only the so-called Son of God, Jeshua of Nazareth, was in their view free from sin.

This was an evil doctrine which proclaimed the corruptness of all matter, said Mordecai, but nevertheless they made a nifty wine. I watched him down one ampullae-full after another, his eyes growing larger and larger all the while. They wished to free the soul from the body, he declared, and ideally might all wish to starve to death, leaving no progeny, but old habits died hard and they appeared to condone feeding and sexual intercourse, as long as this did not involve conception. Their preferred mode of copulation was, therefore, the unnatural entry, for which, among other things, they were being persecuted by the Byzantine Church.

It was not clear to me at the time why the Alchemist was telling me this strange tale, except in the vague sense that I understood he was preparing me for the manifold, and often disgusting, wonders of the world beyond our mundane view. Outside, the Sufi devotees sang out the multiple names of God, celebrating the divine gifts of music and speech. But the Light that shines, said Mordecai, is a light in the darkness, and beyond the edge of brightness ancient forces, which still were without form and void, played in the recesses of God's mind...

I was not at all certain where the Alchemist's argument was leading, but was growing increasingly dizzy from his piercing gaze, despite the fact that I had not touched the booze. The slave girl had melted away, and we remained alone in that dim lit hall of strange vessels and pungent liquids bubbling in murky flasks. He took me by the hand and led me into even dimmer recesses in that grand chamber, in which, lit by strange buzzing lamps, there hung large charts and maps of heaven and earth, dating from the earliest masters of the Art: The rectangle of Anaximenes, maps of Sargon of Akkad, the projections of Eratosthenes and Claudius Ptolemy, the fabulous illustrated maps of Solinus, which portrayed the four eyed people of Upper Ethiopia, the dog-faced tribe of Limuria, the basilisk of Syrtis, the race with only one giant foot, which they used as a parasol to keep the sun off their heads. He had an exquisite Chinese map which showed the location of the kingdoms of Gog and Magog, and there were star charts illustrating the fabulous beasts who dwelled in the celestial spheres.

"All maps and diagrammes," said the Alchemist, "are exemplars of the original template, which remains hidden. All maps aspire to the design from which God, the Primal Architect, fashioned the world, all inanimate and all living things deriving from the same mathematical principles. The essence of the map is not only to draw the world as it seems to be, but to uncover the hidden principles. See here."

He led me on, to a dark brown lectern upon which he unscrolled a detailed plan of the Great Pyramid of Khufu, whose majestic and mysterious outline I had seen upon my entrance to the City. The plan included a vastly complex array of cross-sections, perspective views and equations of the various proportions of the artifact, relating to minutely detailed astrological calculations drawn in the margins of the scroll.

"You might be aware," he said, "of how the Caliph al-Mamoun, son of Haroun al-Rashid, decided, in the 198th year of the hejira, to excavate into the Great Pyramid, in order to find a secret passageway into the hidden burial chamber of the Pharaoh. He expected to find there not only thirty great rooms filled with the pagan King's gold, but also the magical stones and ancient runes which revealed the place of the other worlds beyond Time, to which our Father Suleiman was later to banish the jinns and demons who were at the Pharaoh's beck and call. Other carvings would, according to the secret Greek texts which Haroun al-Rashid had purchased during his reign from merchants in Smyrna, unravel the occult way which led from the center of the Pyramid into the afterlife, the Pharaoh's passage to his Elysian Fields. But al-Mamoun, having broken in through the old tomb-robbers' entrance, could only find, at the end of his excavation, a hollowed out and completely empty chamber, with the open stone sarcophagus which is still in that chamber to this day, despite the fact that no other passageway could be found leading out of the structure.

"The Caliph's masons also found the two other passages that led to what we know as the `Queen's' chamber and the underground chamber, both as empty. In a niche beside the `Queen's' chamber the Caliph's masons found one chest of jewels, which was sufficient to pay the costs of the Caliph's labours but not one single dirham more! Chastened by God, al-Mamoun abandoned the Pyramid. The secrets of Khufu remained hidden."

The Jew turned and suddenly seized my shoulders with two hands that had the force of giant pincers. "What is a journey?" he demanded, "how big is the universe? Why do we wish to know? Is it not a simple matter of our own incompleteness, the pettiness of our conscious mind? You wish to travel to the ends of the earth and see with your own eyes what lies far away. But what if the world shrunk, and was brought to you on the head of a pin, or the surface of a glass? What would you seek then?"

"Only God can tell our ultimate fate," I said, warily, "we are but poorly made clay."

"Platitudes," he said, releasing me, suddenly weary, slumping back into a bench by the lectern. "Go in peace," he said, "return to me at the end of your journey and tell me what you have learned."

The slave girl appeared, to lead me out, silently. I returned to my quarters, and two days later, left the city, proceeding up the Nile, into the center of Africa, and then on to Asia and China. God granted me, in his infinite mercy, many astonishing adventures, blessings, and miraculous escapes from misfortune, until I could return to my homeland, to Fez, to dictate my memories to my faithful scribe, Ibn Juzzay. Then, having unburdened myself of this duty, I was able, in the following year, to respond to the Jew's original invitation and visit him in his abode in Cairo.

Over twenty-five years had passed since our first meeting and the Mother of Cities had changed almost beyond all recognition. Disaster had visited her with his blight and she had been beset by dynastic disputes which saw eight different Sultans in as many years, with rivals deploying their Mamluk soldiery to fight their battles inside the city walls. To add to her misery, old Mother Cairo had been visited by that terrible plague called the "Black Death", which had spread from the infidels of Europe across the Mediterranean Sea. Disease and famine had decimated the city, and the streets around the Alchemist's abode echoed no longer to the cries and songs of the dervish *zar* but to the piteous wailings of the many starving beggars who stretched out their emaciated hands for alms.

The Alchemist's house stood among the ruins like a dark oasis, behind closed doors and guards. Shuttered windows kept out the pitiless light of the sun. But Mordecai himself did not seem a single day older. His skin was unblemished and his beard was completely black with not a single strand of white hair.

"Have you discovered the Elixir of Life?" I asked him boldly, since I had learned to be blunt in my travels. But he only laughed and said: "It was only yesterday that you left me."

I told him bluntly this was not the case. I did not need a mirror, magical or otherwise, to tell me how much I or the city or the entire suffering world had aged.

"What have you learned?" he asked me.

I had prepared a long catalogue of my enhanced erudition, of the marvellous sights I had seen, the good and bad men I had met, the women I had loved, the slaves I had owned. But I fell silent, struck dumb by the fresher sights and sounds of misery that I had just encountered. He gave me a long, scornful look and, taking me by the hand, led me to his lectern.

"Do you remember this map?" he once again unscrolled the ancient chart of Khufu's Pyramid. "Many have wondered at the method of the construction of these monumental tombs. Some said prisoners must have been used in enforced labour, like Our Ancestors who built Pithom and Rameses. But in fact the Great Pyramid and its successors were built as a labour of love and religion. For the entire lifetime of King Khufu his people paid him the tithe of their back breaking labour, contributing sons, fathers, brothers to the work gangs which hewed out the great stone blocks from the quarries of the Upper Nile, then transported them downriver on giant barges, dragging them from the riverside quays to the site, manouevering each stone up onto the ramps and pulleys, repeating the same struggle over two million times. And then they raised the stones, step by step, plane by plane, higher and higher, laying each in place precisely to the specifications of the engineers and masons. There was not a year in those people's lives in which this toil was not enacted, towering over their daily strains and travails, casting its shadow over their small joys and passing comforts, their pleasure in domestic or family occasions, the birth of a child, a marriage, a pious anniversary, a feast day, the dedication of a house, a field, a fishing boat, a farm. Always, every day and in every hour, as they toiled, ate, slept or fornicated, or entertained and educated their children, the giant tomb rose higher and higher.

"And then the tyrant died, and all his people ceased work for ninety-five days and mourned him, wailing and gnashing their teeth, ceasing all work, abandoning their homes, fields and cattle, neglecting their children, leaving their own houses half built, tearing their clothes, smearing mud on their heads and limbs, abstaining from all material benefits, refusing ablutions, and coming together in their hundreds of thousands to pay homage to he who was the fountainhead of all their deprivations and miseries. And then they carried him into the tomb, and immediately began the work of raising the next tomb, for his designated heir."

He pulled me by the arm, back to his table. "Do you understand this?" he said, "do you hear the cries outside my window? Can there be any Message which can relieve this burden? Can you consider any Messenger of comfort? Can you believe in the cackle of glad tidings? Can you be lulled by the sooth-sayer's balm? Do you still believe in the incorruptness of matter?"

The Jew appeared to me to be skirting close to blasphemy, but I did not wish to enter into a religious polemic. Now that I looked into his eyes I could see that, although he had not physically aged, it was as if a great chasm had opened in time, to agitate his mind. I took my leave of him as soon as politeness allowed, and walked outside, in the desolated alleyways. Children who were merely ragged wraiths came up to tug at my robe. A blind man who appeared a mere skeleton sat motionless in a doorway. I could not imagine this as the Cairo I knew, the City of infinite life and compassion, the centrifuge of mutual aid. I gave out all the money I had and left the City, on the first available boat down the Nile.

"Any spare change for a cupocofee man?"

"Help out a brother who has lost his way..."

"My baby's starving, we ain't had nuthin' to eat for five days..."

"Help a man who's down on his luck..."

They're everywheres, you have to swat 'em away like flies... And so the Man rises, out of his deep, disturbed sleep...

"YOU CAN'T SLEEP HERE, SIR, THIS IS CITY PROPERTY!"

Just a light tap of the nightstick. In the old days they might beat your brains out. Who says life doesn't improve, day by day?

Groggily we stand on the brink of the thoroughfare, the crowded pavements and phalanxes of yellow cabs, motorised vans, trucks and containers, the glut of pictograms and signs: NO PED CROSSING. LOCAL TRAFFIC THIS WAY. TRUCKS, BUSES, VANS... CITIBANK. CHASE MANHATTAN. LI XING JEWELLERY. MANHATTAN SAVINGS BANK. THE WIDER, SMOOTHER TASTE OF CAMELS.

Clearly some aspects of cuisine do not change, though I remember them as being fairly tough. I thought, when I took leave of Cairo for the last time, as an old and tired man, that I had seen the last of the Alchemist, but when I awoke, inside the Sleeper, it was his unchanged, mocking countenance I perceived standing over me. I had eked out my last days in Fez, enjoying the company of my wives, my children and their children, putting the storms and furies of the world behind me. I had made my peace with God and felt the soft hands of my retainers closing my dried out eyelids, and I prepared, at the last moment, to meet the Destroyer of Lives and the Grand Maker of Dreams. But when I awoke, rudely, in this shifting, noxious cavern, it was the familiar face of Mordecai, the Jew, that I saw above me. He, of course, appeared no older than before.

"A man never listens to good advice," he told me, "until he has exhausted all the possibilities of the bad."

There were various figures, all around me, threshing about knee deep in swill, their bodies and faces covered with a thin film of slime. They were crying out and, I am sure, cursing, in strange tongues I could not at first make out, but in time, using my well tried linguistic skills, I was able to learn. My first terrible thought that I was to pay for my sins despite my piety and charitable works soon faded, to be replaced by a hope that I had perhaps recovered, miraculously, from my terminal illness, and been transported to the closed section of the *maristan* in Marrakesh, that excellent hospice which cares for those whose mind has been disturbed by physical illness, as well as the insane... Was Mordecai the surgeon? But I was soon disabused of this thought, as I learned the names of my new companions, Arnuld, the self-esteeming scribe, Jessai, the harbinger of his "Teacher", Lincoolen the exiled rebel from the southernmost tip of African, Umar-Neptah, who claims the mantle of Pharaoh, and the young street singer, Jai-Meh, who fluttered his eyelashes at me, but then vanished back to his den. Not to mention the two women, wrapped as they are in their separate harems - slothful Ann and the procuress Beatriz. Verily, it is the house of the mad, the *majnun*, but where does it lie, within or without my universe?

"You bet your life, brother... You better believe it..."
"Can you stop a minute here, Mo-says?"

The body is completely awake, now, marching, with its usual willful, staggering step, across Baxter Street, Mulberry, Mott, Elizabeth, past the hanging lanterns, oriental vegetables, fresh fish, crabs, mussels, oysters, shrimps, lobster, Chinese newspapers, t-shirts, umbrellas, electronic organisers, Mickey Mouse and Swatch watches, Kung fu videos...

The corner of Canal and the Bowery. The Greek columns and mock Arc of Triumph leading onto the Manhattan Bridge. On the south-western corner, a street stall festooned with gaudily colored heretical Nazarenes, Buddhas, Ganeshas, Vishnus, the Rabbi of Lubavitch, the Holy Virgin... "Blessed Art Thou Among Women". The glowing scarlet of the Sacred Heart. Bleeding droplets, each pierced by its own arrow. 1 Dollar the drop. All this under a dilapidated political flyer drooping from the corner lamp-post: VOTE VELASQUEZ FOR CONGRESS! LA CANDIDATA DEL PUEBLO!

- *How on earth can a virgin be a mother, Mo-says?*
- *It's an effable mystery, Battuta.*
- *Even mysteries should not confound logic...*
- *Can I move on now?*
- *As you please, brother Mohammed.*
- *Thank you brother. Have a nice day.*

Veering north once more, up the Bowery. SAYONARA - 14K LUCKY CHARMS. We Buy Gold, Silver, Platinum, Diamonds. Wai Hong's Fu-Jow Pai-Kung-Fu. Wah Men Enterprises. AAA Noodles. Pressing forward in the gathering squall. The rain whipping against the face, in horizontal dashes. Forlorn figures, leaning into the swell, faces pushing, arms flung behind for balance, farting for a little smidgeon of counter-propulsion...

- *Where are you, Mordecai? God fuck your Jew arse!*

Silence within. All the voices dropped away, for the moment. Only the muffled beat of mariachi music wafts with the colonic wind -

" - *Aiy aiy aiy aiy,*
mi corazon, my lonely heart,
lost in the shadows of your dreams - "

Gathering pace, with the lashing of the rain, that whining voice, complaining, demanding, lamenting, above the shreds of the drowned...

Jaime.

MARICONS. ALL THOSE BASTARDS SONS OF WHORES. They can crawl up my ass and lay eggs. Life is enough of a bitch anyway, without these assholes rapping all the time. They wanna keep me quiet, but it's my turn now, hurricane or no hurricane.

I don't really like the daylight. The cops are everywhere. People shove you off the sidewalk. Your enemies can see you coming a mile away. Everywhere you go the shops are full of stuff that you can't get at, food that you can't afford to eat. Everywhere people are stuffing their face: Steak florentine with grecian style spinach and scallions, veal stew parmigiana, baked manicotti with meat balls and sausages, Sicilian pizza, triple enchiladas, provolone omelettes, hot pecan pie, baklava with honey and cinammon, fancy Indian and Vietnamese food. I ain't got nothing against the Vietnamese but hey, I thought we won that war, right, so what them sons of bitches doing over here? You know what I'm saying? Once all those people come in off the boat have taken their slice of the leftovers, there ain't much of the pie left to go round.

But later, in the night, the streets belong to us. The yuppies are all bundled up in their big new coats as they step out of their restaurants, looking from side to side, rushing along like they've been stranded behind enemy lines, throwing out a hand: "Taxi! Taxi!" That wild frightened look in their eyes. You know what's they're thinking. Wild animals out there, in the jungle, muggers, junkies, psycho dingbat crackheads armed with guns and knives and razor blades to cut through their fancy aftershave.

You better believe it. Me, I don't carry a weapon, except sometimes, nunchaku stick. A homeboy client of Beatrice showed me once how to use it. All the moves, where to strike to cripple or kill. The five places in the body you can waste a man with one blow. Terminate with extreme prejudice. All right! I ain't never used it yet in anger. But nothing is for ever in this world.

The time I was procuring for Beatrice was a high point. I got to dress real fine. I had an Armani suit and George Letelier cufflinks and Gucchi shoes and Sardi socks. I had me a pair of Raybans that could stop the light from a nuclear explosion. You know what I'm saying? That's called hyper- bole. Arnold Flint taught me that word. It means when you're exaggerating for effect.

Arnold Flint is a real motherfucking son of a whore. He is a Jew bastard from some ghetto shithole but he has made himself a regular wasp. He got himself a shit colored sun tan and silver corners to his hair. A regular *maricon*. But smart. He has managed to fuck life right up the ass and still come up smelling of roses. But I can smell a rat. It takes one to know one. I always like to learn new things. I'm smart and I have learned to wait in my life. I am not going to spend my time in the Tombs, yakking about some shit detox project with a faggot from Columbia University who is majoring in wiping shit from his ass.

That's why I prefer to live *in* the ass. Living in the shit, nobody can track me down. You take your tracker dogs and your bloodhounds and your doberman pinchers and you can shove em up your crack. Because I am in your crack. You know what I'm saying? I am hiding where I can't be found. Only in the small hours of the night I can crawl out into my own world, like a special forces commando crawling over the wire, behind enemy lines. It can be tough sometimes. The body has piles. Sometimes I have to wade through blood. Then I crawl down the buttock, holding on to the hairs. I hit the ground running and then I'm off, man. Then I am in my element. Up the Avenue of the Americas, across Canal, towards SoHo and Greenwich Village. All us freaks come out at night, man. The fags, the dopers, the trannies with their Uptown pervert clients. What some people won't do to get fucked up the ass by a guy-gal with silicone tits. They don't care about the diseases, man, it's all part of dicing with death. Sometimes I lie in wait till they stagger past with their sphincters bleeding and take what's left in their wallets. Sometimes I let them suck my cock for the appropriate fee. But I hate stubble and moustaches. Its difficult to imagine that you're being sucked off by Beatrice in her best bondage gear when your dick's being scraped by some bastard fat boy's bristles.

I met a man once who wanted me to tie him upside down to a girder on the Williamsburg Bridge while I poked him and whupped his thighs with a steel wire. He wanted to do it over the edge but I won't die even for fifty dollars. It was a weird bang, with the cars rushing by and the drivers looking straight forward, trying to pretend they ain't seen nuthin.

When you're a creature of the night, you can be damn near invisible. The only people who see you are the ones who have gone through the looking glass. People have all sorts of different ideas about how to have themselves a good time. There was a man who came in my ass shouting that I was Jesus and he was Judas Iscariot. There was another who only wanted to look at my bare foot while he ate pellets of his own dung that he had brought from his house in a little plastic bag.

They say there are twelve million people in the City, if you count all the five boroughs, Brooklyn, Queens, Manhattan, Bronx and Staten Island. Each one of them evacuates his bowels at least four or five times a day. That is a lot of shit. If they all put it in a plastic bag it would fill the ocean, which would spill over and drown us all. I got caught in a course once in a shit detox program, in which they tried to teach us History. They told us it all started with a Dutchman, Pete Minute, who bought the island of Manhattan from the Indians for twenty-four dollars. They called it New Amsterdam. Then the English came and called it New York. New this and New that. But all I see around me is old and decaying, broken down, beat up and worn out. Yards filled with stinking rubbish and bits of rusty corrugated iron, dilapidated fences, broken brick walls running with damp and sewers, graffiti and dried blood. Down towards the river, under the bridge, small charcoal fires light up the tired faces of the bums, as they sit scratching their scabs and warts, pulling roaches from their crotch and roasting em over the flames. They are only one step from cadavers. You can always tell em from the way they walk, the way they sway from side to side, as if they're trying to get picked up by the wind, at least to give them some direction. Or when they are walking very very slowly, like they're trying to grind down the sidewalk, looking in every shop window as if they are millionaires in disguise who are thinkin of buying the joint.

They all look the same, the men, the women, the kids. Stunted like those desert trees you see on the Discovery Channel, with lizards licking at dry bark. They even have names, which seep out mumbling between the cracks: Zoos, and Herpes, and Afrotight, Ape-Olo, Helen, Oriole, Dietnices and Herms, Borax and Pussydun, Tartare and Medium, Castrate and Poleaxe, Belltelephone and Ourchillies. Then there is the group that hunts together along the banks of the East River: Eamon and Ozzy-Rees, Icies and Nut, Chorus and Kishter, Seth and Tar-Baby, Crazy Ray, Mad Hatter. It's difficult to make out what they're saying. Most of them have lost their teeth, and some of them have even lost their lips and their tongues. Toothless gums are said to be good for a blow job, but you don't want your meat anywhere near there.

I had a man once who wanted to chew on my foreskin. He said he used to be a Jewish ritual slaughterer who had been barred from circumcisions. He offered me three hundred dollars to chew the thing off completely, I think they call it the prepuce. I told him to get lost, and ran. He ran after me, bawling and crying. I had to hide in the late night subway. The labyrinth under 42nd Street and Times Square. Where the troglodytes live and frolic, men with frog's heads and women with crocodile's feet. There is a whole group, on the third level down in the tunnels of the A and C trains, under the Port Authority Bus Station, that have scales like fish and faces with long tapering snouts that have adapted to suck the garbage that has fallen between the tracks.

I have seen the most amazing sights in the tunnels. People live there who have never seen the light of day. Making babies that can see in pitch black, and have fur all over, and catch rats with their paws. The tunnels stretch as far down as you could imagine, and then more, deep into the bowels of the earth. Legends tell of a whole network of hidden shafts that go on forever, subterranean cities where all sorts of people who have run away and escaped from poverty and oppression all over the world have settled, and travel, miles underground, even under the seas and the oceans. I even heard that these tunnels intersuck with the shafts built by governments to hide their secret projects, chemical and biological warfare an all that, so that the homeless people are always there, hiding in the ventilation ducks, watched on all the top secret screens.

I don't know about that, but once, when I was hiding from another client, who pulled out a knife as he grabbed at my dick, I saw a sight in the Canal Street subway that really affected me to the heart, you know what I'm sayin? A slim, straight backed black woman, dressed in a deep blue kaftan, leading a line of ragged, starving men, women and children out of a hole in the ground at the end of an abandoned platform. I knew at that moment that I was having a vision, the kind of thing Father Bruce used to talk about in the Midtown Mission of the Immaculate Virgin, except the vision he had most in mind was his fat dick rammed up a twelve year old boy's tight ass. He said it was the poorest and the most deprived people who would see what the satisfied and the ef-feet, whatever they was, couldn't reach: The Divine Snatch. The woman led the vagrants to a ladder which led from the platform up a rusty pipe. She disappeared, with her followers, in a shaft of golden light that came down the duck.

I thought about this woman often, when I was alone, in the body, listening to the gastric juices. All the sluice of liquid garbage that comes down the intestine. Her beautiful profile as she turned: In just a moment she was going to see me and beckon me to follow her up the tube. But I just stood there, paralysed. I missed my chance to get away from it all...

I told no one of this woman, this Black Goddess, except Beatrice. You can't keep anything from Beatrice. She has her spies everywhere, in the spleen, in the pancreas, in the occipital lobe, the eyes, the nose, the tongue. I know, because I have been her advance guard, recruiting clients for her in the crumbling edges of Times Square. Hell's Kitchen. Den of thieves, pimps, boozers, dopers and cokeheads. Around the porno theatres and peepshows and magazine and video shops there are always people looking for the ultimate. I lead them down the sleaze racks, along the tenderloin, up the colon to Beatrice's Dungeon of Torment and Pain.

When I walk into her parlour I know I am in another world. The low red lighting and the steam rising from the heavy grates in the floor. The chandeliers and lamps covered with scarlet gels. All the furniture is bay-rock and racacoon. Loudspeakers around the walls relay the cries and whispers of the clients down below, their hisses and shrieks, their pleas for mercy, the crack of paddles and whips. The music is thrash and heavy metal, rising and fading under the cries. I volunteered to play some nostalgias and maybe do some rap to jazz up the joint, but Beatrice said no. She is a sight, coming out from behind her counter, covered with silver chains and handcuffs, in knee high leather boots, with nothing else on except two small gold stars on her titties and a black steel panel fastened by a leather strap over her twat.

The Undivine Snatch. Not even God was going to get in there, to immaculately conceive. She stands, with her magnificent blonde wig and flashing black eyes, swishing her cat o'nine tails backwards and forwards like a hungry snake, facing the client:

"What's it gonna be, baby?"

The client screws up his eyes to look at the blackboard of current charges:

GENITAL TORTURE - $300.
CORPORAL PUNISHMENT - $125 - $220.
ANAL DILDOS - $125
FIST FUCKING - $185
ENGLISH (WHIPPING WITH RIDING CROP, TAWSE, QUIRT) - $200
DOMINANCE TRAINING - $180 - $325
RIMMING - $160
GOLDEN SHOWERS - $180
HIGH HEELS ON SCROTUM - $220
BULLWHIPPING, CAT - $250 - $300
GOLDEN ENEMA - $200
INFIBULATION (piercing, cock & balls only) - $280
SHIT EATING - $300
VERBAL ABUSE (with any of above) - $50 extra.

"Aren't these prices a little steep?" asks the mark, timidly.

"GET DOWN ON YOUR KNEES WHEN YOU TALK TO ME!" The poor jerk starts to lick and suck on her boots. Then she drags him down to the basement, as he yelps on: "Thank you mistress! Thank you! Thank you!"

I'm not allowed down there. I can only imagine what The Mistress and her Acolytes do to the wretched stiff before he staggers back into the world, missing half his teeth, with cigarette burns all over his cheeks and earlobes, and often brutally shaved all over, clutching his bleeding bare skull. Sometimes they have lost the power of speech and utter only meaningless fuff-fuff-fuff noises as I lead them off back to the colon and shove them down the shute, shit-spattered, back into the

Outside. Sometimes I have to give them a subway token, outa the goodness of my heart, they have been so properly fleeced.

So I spend long hours in the lobby, under the red lights, sipping a beer from the icebox, listening to the sounds from below an watching out for the Morals Patrol, the private dicks who are always trying to break into the body from their hunting grounds in Times Square. The "plain clothes" detectives, in their shabby anoraks or bulky hip-hop pants and scuffed sneakers, rings in their eyelids and drool dripping down their stubbled chins. Pretending to look for a score. They stand on the stoop, in front of the big steel door of the Dungeon, pressing the bell. Ring ring! Ring ring! I can see them through the hole in the door. I know em all by their names now: Inspector Haemoglobin an Sergeant Thanatos an Officers Scoopy Lamine an Tommy Lobo. Or the graveyard shift: Officer Thora Zinn, Lars Gactil, Syde Effekt an Hal Peridol Jr. The "Swedes." I hate their guts. But I just lay there, watchin them, till they get fed up an leave, shufflin off towards the duodenum.

And they are only the tip of the iceberg. The bloodstream is full of cops, narcs, feds and snitches. There ain't anywhere safe anymore. I used to spend happy hours in the colon, strumming *nostalgias* on my guitar and recording my own rap into my cassette recorder. But nowadays, almost every day, when I'm asleep, somebody comes along and erases my songs.

Maricons. Sometimes, when I look in the mirror in my little makeshift shack, with my few meagre belongings that I have managed to steal in the night, a lady's scarf, a Casio organiser, some useless plastic, a half-eaten sandwich, some moth-eaten dollar bills, I am startled to find that I can't recognise myself. Sometimes I see different people in the glass: a strange Arab man with a beard and turban, a tired looking nigger with heavy eyes, a fat slut who looks like a lump of dough with acne, a suspicious looking wop, even Arnold Flint and sometimes, Beatrice, staring at me with devil's eyes.

And then, when I dared to look again, I saw this stern, dark face, an off- white man with a huge shaggy beard and a strange pointed hat spangled with stars and banners. His eyes were like two black coals that had been burning quietly for as long as anyone could remember. I looked round and there he was in my room, fingerpunching the personal organiser.

"Every interior decorator from Staten Island to Scarsdale," he mused, keying through the database. "This could be the burglar's bible. Do you want to rise in the world, boy, or do you want to be a punk forever?"

"Hey man," I said, "I'm game. Anything for the right price."

"Follow me," he said. He seemed, like me, to know his way in and out of this joint. Pocketing the Casio in his shimmering robe, he led me out down the colon, ducking our heads to squeeze through the sigmoid flexure, into the rectum, past the prostate and into the anal canal. This was a man who really knew his way round the asshole. The prostate was so enlarged that we had to wriggle through on our stomachs. The bearded man had brought a gas mask so he was surging ahead, but I was coughing and spluttering as usual, till we reached the anal orifice.

We stepped out onto the corner of the Bowery and Delancey Street, just under Schacht Lighting and opposite Alexander Butcher Black Supplies. The wind was howling like a banshee and cardboard boxes, upended trash cans and rubbish tumbling and flying past. We could hardly see for the rain which had turned the day into a flying bath. A couple of bums were huddling together in a doorway, trying to hold on to their blankets, snarling and swearing, as these bums do. "Goddamn motherfucker..." The Man dragged me across the street under a sign which said "Seneca Distribution Inc. Pool Tables. Billiard and Bowling products. Trophies. Placques. Awards." He stepped up to a rusty iron door and unlocked a padlock with a large brass key. We pushed our way through a garbage strewn corridor to a gloomy cracked flight of stairs. The snap crackle and pop of street signs banging against the walls came from outside. The bearded Man bounded up the steps with the spring of a young athlete. I was gasping by the time I reached the fifth floor. "Drugs and cigarettes," he said, "they sap the health. And incessant ass-fucking, that really slows you down." He hurried up, to the seventh floor, waiting before a dirty grey door that he unlocked with another key when I finally made it to the top. I stepped through the door, into a long thin corridor with rotting floorboards and grey peeling walls, bloated with rot and fungus. At some points there were actual mushrooms growing from the walls, huge sinister twisting stalks with stinking, gaping caps, blotched and speckled with red dots and green slime. I had to tread carefully along the floorboards as gaps in the wood fell sharply down into dusty black holes.

At the end of the corridor I was glad to step through a narrow open doorway into a cavernous loft. The sort of thing rich artists in the city love to rent to show they are close to reality in all its musky depth and emptiness. But this loft was dominated by two long tables piled with strange instruments and tools. Glass bottles, tubes and pipes, twisting in a cat's cradle and full of bubbling liquids flowing from jar to jar. The shelves covering the walls of the loft were filled sealed jars, labelled: Mercury, Sulphur, Alum, Arsenic, Vitriol, Nitric Acid. Other jars were filled with strange plants and animals floating in a thick fluid, lizards, tiny bats, toads, cows' udders, aborted babies, tongues, eyes and ears. Jars of butterflies, beetles and moths, grubs, roots, and what looked like magic mushrooms.

"Got any dope?" I asked him, "I don't do anythin stronger than coke, you don't have to worry about that."

He ignored my question but motioned me to follow him up the space between the two tables. I passed by the antique instruments, iron scales, wooden beams, rulers and rods, compasses and metronomes, filing cabinets and shelves of old books, manuscripts, rolled up blueprints and maps.

"The zodiac," he pointed them out to me, "symbolic schemes of the universe, sephirot, heiroglyphs, labyrinths. Tables of Isis, the Periodic Table, the Tetragrammaton, the Mundane Monochord, sections of the Great Pyramid, Yggradsil, the Tree of Noah, the Rosy Cross, the Ineffable Alphabets, Navaho and Aztec runes. The journeys of Herodotus, the lost kingdoms of Prester John, Saint Brendan, Antichthon and Atlantis, plans of Paradise, Purgatory and Perdition. Seacharts of Oronce Fine, Mercator's projections, plates from Blaeu's Grand Atlas, celestial charts from Ptolemy to Cellarius, astrolabes by Muhammad Mahdi al-Yazi and plans of all the voyages of Ibn Battuta."

"Got a spare subway map, man?" I asked him, but he just froze me with a glare. He swept to the end of the two tables and began rummaging in a broken down cabinet attached to the wall by two bent pegs. "Where did I put the coffee?" he mumbled. "Ah!" Pulling down an old cardboard box and throwing out old monkey wrenches, scissors and screwdrivers. Finally getting out a jar. "Foulger's Crystals, O.K.?" I nodded, what the fuck did I care, he had left me far behind. He dragged out a kettle and some chipped mugs. "Solids to fluids. Pig-iron to silver. Everybody wants something from nothing. Desire out of apathy. Pleasure from pain. Dollars from dross. Gold out of lead is simple economics. It's usually the other way around. But of course it's really a matter of the quintessences. Fire, earth, air, water. And the *quinta essentia* makes five. It's not just a matter of sticking in something this end and getting something else out the other. Do you want half and half? I only have powdered creamer."

He mixed the brew and poured it into two filthy cups from which he had flung out some yellow liquid. "The essential work of transformation, compadre. It's more complicated than you think. Any amateur chemist can produce a dead body from a live one. But the other way around... The Egyptians spent millenia refining the process of preserving the dead. But it took the Christians to claim a true resurrection in real time and within history. The Christian alchemists were always trying to recreate that golden moment. See Jung about the Lapis-Christ parallel, particularly the chapter in *Psychology and Alchemy* in which he discusses the *Wasserstein der Weysen*, which defined the Philosophical Stone as a `veritable Harmonia, Contrafactur and Prototype of the true spiritual and heavenly Stone Jesu Christ.' Jakob Bohme dealt with this a great deal. Or see Maier's argument on the Trinity, Father, Son and Holy Ghost. God the Son is the Philosopher's Stone produced by the two former entities. The whole point of that alchemy was to produce a *corpus subtile*, a body which was also spirit. In this context the Christian alchemists also tried to rope in our Jewish concept *elohim*, or God the plural, as a prefiguring of the Trinity. It's all what you can do with words. The Chinese, on the other hand, had a different ambition: Immortality through transformation of the body. Look up your Jung, it's all there. Or did the spirit of God sit upon the undivided waters and hatch the earth, like an egg? The feminine principle of the prima materia. The Alchemical Marriage."

I had no idea what he was talking about, but I kept quiet. Looking around me, I was thinking that, in this junkhouse, there must be something worth a few bucks. You can't believe what people will buy in this City. If they're willing to pay for my ass, anything goes.

"Whatever you say, man." I sang out to him, as I wandered off down the room as the kettle heated up on a tiny one ring hob, taking a more serious audit.

"What we are all arguing about," continued the Alchemist, "the different path to unity. E pluribus unum. The I at the top of the pyramid. All the old Masonic dreams. We are seeking keys to a room which we are already inhabiting. Does that make sense to you in any way?"

"Sure, man. I'm with you all the way." I stopped short in front of a life sized drawing of the outstretched figure of a man, his arms and legs spread out, and framed inside a six pointed star. The man was covered all over, head to toe, with a whole load of crazy writing and inscriptions:

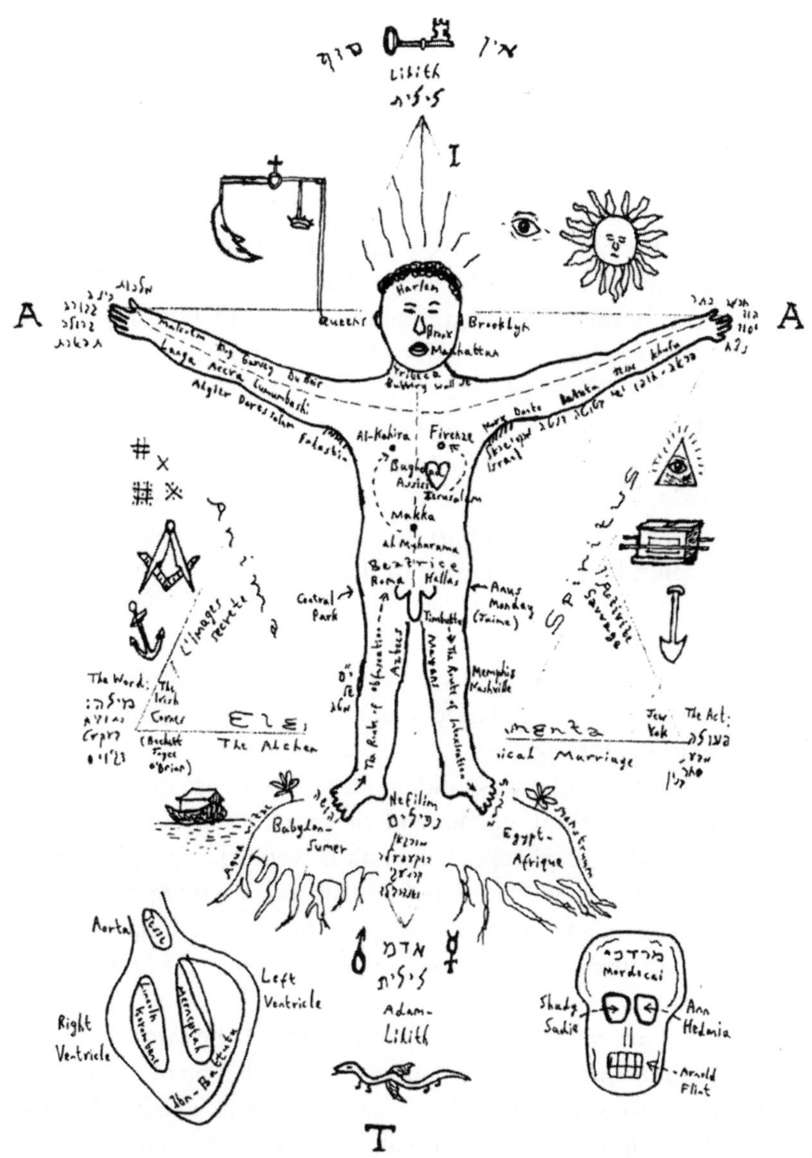

It was like something from a Santeria ritual, where the obeah man or woman sticks pins in a doll and kills a chicken. I wondered why Harlem was on the forehead and Manhattan on the mouth, but I was more worried by my name that I noticed, in what do they call it, () - underneath anus monday.

"Recognise the image?" the Man came up behind me, carrying the two mugs of Foulger's Crystals, steaming in his hand like magic potions. "The Microcosm. Consider how far have we advanced. People talk today about the `human genome' project, the complete mapping of the human chromosomes. We who knew the Microcosm and the Macrocosm have long known that everything corresponds. The soul of the world, the logos, and Adam Kadmon, the creature wrought in primal clay. He was the first work of Art that could explain itself, up to a point. The sages tell us the divine sparks rise from the feet of Adam to his head, in a constant but infinitesimal process of mending the world that was broken in the primeval cataclysm. The *tsimtsum*, or shrinking, of the Godhead. We are trying to put Humpty Dumpty together again. Modern science will tell you that there never was a complete whole, a primal harmony, a perfect start. First there was an infinitesimal dot and then the greatest of explosions. And they call me a crank. Partical physics, quarks, muons, bits of cosmic fluff that move backwards in time, is it the observer or the observed? The old saw. It's all in the primacy of mathematics. Godel's incompleteness theorem... Georg Cantor believed that concepts and theorems are not invented by the mathematician but exist independently of human thought. In the mind of God? Cantor regarded himself simply as a reporter assigned to the outer limits of thought. A transcendent world, in which the Creator weaves marvellous shapes out of numbers. Is this not the case? Einstein, Bohr, Rutherford, Szilard made marks on paper and forty years later American generals made their own big bang in New Mexico. Should there be things Man is not meant to know? Or is that just another old saw..."

"Hey man, you got the edge on me there..."

He suddenly reached out and pulled me round towards him by my hair. He put the cup of Foulger's Crystals down and pulled open the belt of his robe. The robe fell off him, displaying a lean, hard body, browner than mine, matted with strong black hair. His breath smelled of sulphur and brimstone as he tugged my mouth to meet his. His free arm swept a row of glass bottles and pipes off the table, smashing onto the floor. A thick white cloud of smoke rose up to surround us, as he threw me down and tore my pants.

"Knowledge is power," he said. His dork was stiff and large as a policeman's nightstick. "Hey man, take it easy," I breathed, but he climbed on top of me like a goat and shoved his dick up my ass fast and quick. The smoke was clouding my senses. It seemed to have a weird perfume.

"Hey man, no rubber's extra."

"Shut up and fly," he said.

I flew, propelled by his giant wand into the upper stratosphere. All around me there were clashing cymbals and huge pyramids of sound, welling up and smashing like breakers on a rock. Trumpets were blaring like the Last Judgement, out of the center of the earth. I felt myself torn apart, like the broomsticks I once saw in a Walt Disney film. Tiny parts of myself were shooting off in all directions, shrieking and laughing...

The Divine Snatch. I was rising above the world, speeding past the moon, Venus, Jupiter and Mars. I saw the Black Goddess, sitting on the rings of Saturn, naked and magnificent, with her string of stinking subway acolytes writhing beside her in glass jars. Every now and then the jars would get unstoppered and the doomed souls would fly off, screaming, to be burned up in the clouds of red, orange and purple fires scudding over the dark planet's surface.

"What's your name, sister?" I shouted out to her as I shot by, but she only waved lazily.

"Lilith," said the Alchemist, "she was Adam's first wife. But she wouldn't obey the Man and flew off in a frenzy, to fuck with all the demons of hell."

He pulled out. I don't even know if he shot his load in there. I was someplace else, then I came to on the table. The smoke was gone, the loft was cold and gloomy. The loose signs rattled in the wind outside, on the Bowery. The wail of police cars fought with the storm.

"You're a good boy, Jaime. We'll do great things together."

"Hey man, you bring the jelly next time." My ass felt like a split watermelon. Something was oozing out there, pus or blood. He wiped me gently with a handkerchief.

"You're safe with me," he said. "Fire purifies. The putrefactio and nigredo precede calcification. The falling dew ignites the true stone."

"You're crazy, man." I looked at his dingle, which had shrivelled to the size of a french bean. After they get their rocks off they are always shrunken, fading away like echoes of a dream. I pulled my pants back on and he helped me off the table. I had to take care, the floor was strewn with glass.

"We will go far, you and me," he said, "we have to contend with powerful forces plotting against us. The body is under threat from all quarters. Enemies within and without. Unhappy God created diversity and look where we are now. A cacophony. Is harmony lost for ever? I will teach you all the tricks. I will teach you to recognise the Enemy, the traitors and the invaders. Come."

He pulled me back to the front of the loft, to a small window just by the door to the corridor that I'd not noticed before. He pushed it open with a creak and I looked carefully out. The rain was whipping past, horizontally. The road was practically deserted, except for the bums, who were trying to fight their way uptown, perhaps towards the richer pickings of Cooper Square, though there would not be much to pick up today. Lamp posts were skewing over, lightbulbs shattered by the wind. A yellow cab was crawling down the road, buffeted by the heavy gusts.

"You see that cab?" That sulphur breath was at my cheek. His black beard brushed against my skin. "Why is that driver out there, in this weather? What is he looking for? Why is he prowling in this neighborhood? He'll be lucky if he doesn't smash his vehicle to pieces, or be flung up and thrown over the Bridge, into the River. But I know what he's after, I can tell you. He's looking for Mo Smith."

"Who the fuck is Mo Smith?" I asked.

The Alchemist looked at me, with infinite pity in his soft glowing eyes.

?

ThE GRID

CLINTON OR BUSH?

Chicken or pork? Rice or salad? Toffee apple banana or ice cream?

"There are fish moving past your twelfth floor window, Frances."

"They have a right to do what they want, Benjamin."

Trying to figure out why Benjamin has adopted my apartment, at this point, as his port in the storm. Israelis fetishize irrationality. It becomes the excuse, the cause, the symptom and the cure all rolled into one. But I have taken all the proper precautions. The camera tape on the window panes, all bolts bolted, the icebox filled with enough for three days, the fullest complement of Pepperidge Farm Cookies, Entenman's donuts, Bakery Light bread, Low Fat Granola with Raisins, Rice-a-Roni mixes and Healthy Choice Low Fat Stuffed Pasta Shells as recommended by the American Heart Association.

"I'll be with you in a minute, Benny."

"You're not short of reading material, Frances," he has already settled in his old favourite armchair, as if things have never changed. "All these Village Voices, New York Times Book Reviews. I see you still keep all these local freebies. The Manhattan Spirit, the Upper West Side Resident, even the Jewish Sentinel, God help us."

"Forearmed is forewarned."

"Thought you might be at the gallery this morning. Making sure it's all still there."

"I'm not that obsessive."

"You could do a show, Empty Space, Blown By The Wind. There could be queues round the block."

"Don't give me ideas. I have enough already. Is Caroline at work?"

"Doctor's appointment. Women's stuff. I should be at the Film Co Op but I'm sure there's nobody there."

"Well, you can stick around till it blows over, Benny. Just don't move things round too much." One can't argue against the forces of nature. But he is riffling through the piles.

"The world goes round but here everything stays the same. Listen to this: `Latest results in the Democratic primaries: Nydia Velazquez leads Stephen Solarz in the 12th District 33% to 27%.' Hope yet for the dispossessed. But listen to this: `Congressman Ted Weiss is leading his rival Arthur Block in the 8th District by 88% to 12%, despite the fact that he has just died.'"

"I'll make a coffee," I offer, "do you still take regular?"

"I'm still holding out against the ersatz. I see you got the Weekly World News. Maybe this is what Ted Weiss's been taking: Secret New Drug Which Brings Back the Dead: ABRAHAM LINCOLN'S CORPSE REVIVED FOR 95 SECONDS. Civil War President Asks Amazed Doctors: `Gentlemen, Where Am I?'"

"As well he might. I don't know if I have any sugar."

"Look in that upper shelf on the left. It was there four years ago, you never throw anything out. Did you know, Frances, that the Pyramids of Egypt are actually upside down? They were originally balanced on their tips to provide launching pads for alien UFOs. When the aliens left for good they flipped them over. `Scientist Abdel Gallad is currently soliciting funds to turn at least two of the three Great Pyramids onto their points again. "If we could see what is on the bottom of these pyramids it would be absolutely conclusive proof of my theories. I am sure there would be evidence of UFO landings and takeoffs."'"

"Send him your collection of old Israeli shekels. They must be worth at least five cents now."

"Two point three U.S. pennies for the whole lot. But one day they'll be museum pieces."

Like the rest of us. I come through bearing two mugs of coffee, with no ideas as usual where to put them. My whole life the failure of pre-planning. Benjamin turning to the Village Voice Bulletin Board:

"Eliminate Stress, Strengthen Immune System. Free Bulimia Treatment - take part in a Federally funded research study. Jewish Mysticism, South Street Seaport, Pier 17, behind `La Compagnie

Internationale' under the open skies... Or how about the Transvestite Image Salon?"

The flotsam in this apartment has increased exponentially since our last success at the Gallery, post-kinetic art by Selina Hasek. Selina is a Czechoslovak immigrant who lives in a geodesic dome on Long Island. She makes chairs with no seats to sit on, shelves slanted so that everything slides off them, sealed jugs and a giant Warholesque Coca-Cola can with the imprint of a human figure trying to escape from the inside. In return for the exhibition she gave me a number of her pieces, all completely useless, which now clutter all my space.

"`Is your cat your significant other?" Benjamin riffles on, "`Call today for that very special someone...' Or how about this as a tale for our times: `Pretty woman, with slight accent, asked me directions to Village Voice on Saturday 7/24. I was sitting in front of antique store on Lafayette near Bleecker. Our eyes met and you looked so interesting...'"

He has to be humoured in this mood. "This one sounds more like you," I peek over his shoulder, handing him his mug. "`Krav maga: The Israeli way of self-defense. It could save your life.'"

"Every stupidity eventually migrates. Now this currency question. Did you ever read that short story by Robert Louis Stevenson? The Bottle Imp. A sailor buys a tiny demon in a bottle which can grant him three wishes. But after he's got his wishes he has to sell the bottle for less than the sum he paid. The price of the bottle falls and falls, till there's no coin small enough to buy it, and the buyer who dies owning the bottle goes straight to hell. But in our day and age there would never be a last buyer, with currencies getting worthless by the hour, so that the bottle would be flying from Buenos Aires to Moscow, from Kiev to Cameroon, without ever hitting rock bottom..."

"An imp in a bottle is an aborted foetus, Benjamin. It's a different kind of primal anxiety. Selina Hasek did a facsimile once."

"It's all facsimiles. Isn't there anything real anymore? How's your lawsuit going?"

"No real answers yet."

All the leftovers of lost causes. It's now a year since I first became involved in this class action launched by radical Jews and Palestinians on the West Coast against the Zionist lobby group, the Anti-Slander League. It had been a nine day scandal: The good friends of Zion had been caught spying nationwide not only on alleged enemies of the Jewish State but also on a whole range of civil liberty committees, trade unions and other groups. The San Francisco Police raided the Anti-Slander League's California offices after a tip off had led them to a briefcase in a luggage locker at San Francisco Airport, which turned out to be stuffed with Anti-Slander League lists and illegally obtained police files. The briefcase belonged to a private detective named Frank Ox, who was, it appeared, on extended vacation in the Philippines. The SFPD requested his extradition, but no sign of the man so far. The impounded bag contained 12,000 names of Arab, Jewish and Israeli dissidents, trade unionists, civil libertarians, and campaigners for everything under the sun from single mothers to Free the Trees, as well as fake passports and driving licences under six different names, blank birth certificates, Army discharge papers, official stationery from several government agencies including the FBI, the CIA and the National Security Agency, files on Central American death squads, a black hood, two whips and photographs of blindfolded and chained men.

In an interview he gave the San Francisco Examiner from Zamboanga in the island of Mindanao, Frank Ox admitted spying for the Anti-Slander League for forty years, collecting information on anti-semites, anti-zionists, Communists, gay activists and "environmental terrorists", with the co-operation of high ranking police officers. Having been alerted by friends in the Israeli-Palestinian Peace Committee out West, I filed, at their suggestion, a request to the Department of Justice under the Privacy Act, requiring the San Francisco Police Department to release all and any papers detailing my name and activities, political or cultural, from the files in Frank Ox's stash. But nothing turned up.

"No thrilling tid-bits? Snapshots of you kissing Yassir Arafat?"

"I leave that to Salim. I need to show cause that I might have been personally affected by dint of personal danger or fear of retaliation by any extra-legal organisation. I don't think being spat on by the Jewish Defense League at the gala launch of our Palestine Under Occupation show is really enough to qualify."

"What about your reputation?"

"Oyf kapoyres. Where is Salim today?"

"He went out in the cab to look for Mo Smith. Caroline asked him to. He doesn't believe in hurricanes."

"Only the human kind."

"Turn on the T.V., Frances. Let's see what's happening out there."

A flash of heavy waves and bent trees and a man in a soaked orange anorak standing at a sharp angle, cradling his mike, warbling -

" - gale force gusts and waves of up to ten feet battering the eastern seaboard you can see the boardwalk behind me is taking quite a pounding but this is not the hurricane that we have been talking about we are only picking up the tailwinds the full force of Hilda has in fact just clipped the city and moved to the center of Long Island where I understand we have a report from Jake Matsuiakama are you there Jake? - Yes Mike I can barely hear you I don't know if you're picking up the noise out here it is quite awesome like someone or something is trying to uproot the houses of this quiet seafront comunity from their roots - "

"This has been going on for three days, it's absolutely pointless, Benny. The anticipation overtakes the event. Like the red king in Alice through the Looking Glass, who screams before he pricks his finger."

"Forget that crap. How about this in the Voice Bulletin Board: `Do You Want to Know: Where He or She is? What He or She is doing? Who are They with? Call 212-566-FIND. Discrete Investigations, East Side Office.'"

"You should have seen the forms I had to fill in." Request of information under the Privacy Act, in accordance with 28 CFR Section 16.41, personal data sufficient to identify the individuals submitting requests by mail under the Privacy Act of 1974, 5 U.S.C. section 552a, failure to furnish this information will result in no action being taken on the request of the System Manager. "I thought of writing to the Director of the F.B.I.: `Federal Bureau of Investigations Washington D.C. Judge William S. Sessions Dear Sir, After the death of J. Edgar Hoover and the dismantling of the House Unamerican Activities Commiteee a citizen of the United States might have cause to presume that paranoia, suspicion, mistrust and destabilising of ordinary citizens going about their legal business in accordance with their constitutional rights was a thing of the past but -'"

"I told you to hack into the program, Frances. I have one of my kids down at the Film Co Op who can do that sort of thing blindfold. Hack into the Pentagon mainframe deflect satellites from their course send the space probe scuttling from Neptune to Uranus and back pull out troops from Somalia and redeploy them to Uruguay from his dump in

Avenue D. It's easy as pie. Or you can buy all this cheap equipment to spy on them spying on you, all sorts of tiny gadgets you can hook on their pants or point at them from your window. Anything goes now."

"I just wanted to know. All the gossip and tittle-tattle about myself. Everybody wants to be a victim these days. Nobody wants to fail on their own. It's the fashion." I am not immune.

Turning down the sound on the TV. The wind wailing outside the windows like a demented ghost. Might as well join Benjamin on the couch with the small ads. Flicking past Explode with Pleasure, Sensual Body Rub Creative Hands, Custom Tattoo, Body Piercing by Martha, Unwanted Hair Removed, Make Serious Money, Erotic Rub For Men. You can get anything in this town.

He picks up 'The Learning Annex,' that freebie cornucopia of evening courses for everything under the sun: Be the Person You Want To Be, Making It In the Film Industry, Skin Care for Black Women, Mastering Your Phobias, Progressive Dinner Parties, Hip-Hop, White Collar Boxing, Sexual Harassment On the Job (for this you need instruction?), Fetishes and Fantasies. "How about this? How to Start, Own, Manage or Invest In Your Own Topless Bar. You Will Learn:

" - How to get a liquor licence and do you even need one.

" - How to get business permits for the adult entertainment industry.

" - What to look for in a dancer and how much to pay dancers.

" - How dancers can make the most money from customers in the least amount of time.

" - Do dancers ever date customers and is it appropriate?"

Oh yes, fly me to my Club Med Free Vacation Hot Air Balloon Intro Lesson How You Can Make Money Reading Unbelievable But True Garry McGarrett has made a living as a story analyst since 1980 working for clients such as CBS/Fox Video, 20th Century Fox and HBO. He's read over 25,000 scripts and also reads product labels for a reputable baby food firm.

Blow wind blow. So many options. But it's always the same with Benjamin. A wild search for some excuse for what's already been and done. Caroline is his ideal lover, for how long only God knows. Most of us have to put on some kind of mask to get us by the day. With Benjamin you get the raw symptoms. I could only take it in small doses. I'm an American, I need my portion of delusions.

"I'm going to make something to eat, Benny. I'm starving."

"From those slops? I'm amazed you survive."

"The stuffed pasta shells are not at all bad."

"No thanks. That wind is driving me crazy."

"I can put on some music. Some jazz? Miles Davis?"

"Too cool. We need something to fight back. Wagner."

"You took away all your tapes, remember."

"Gotterdamerung. Tristan und Isolde. The Nibelungen. My ring and magic helmet."

"Wasn't that from Bugs Bunny?" To the radio, twiddling the tuner dial. A burst of piano, Beethoven. Fading out, followed by a low, rasping voice:

" - That's what I really call music. It warms the heart and uplifts the soul. Not that I have anything against rock music. We all like to let down our hair now and again. Its good to just be boys again. But sometimes its good as well to start thinking where we came from, what we really care about. What we are in the depths of our soul - "

"What on earth is that, Frances? Who is that lunatic?"

"Its Crush Limbo. Don't you read his column in USA Today? He's syndicated all over the country. He thinks Bush is a soggy liberal."

"I know who he is. Why are we listening to him?"

"It sometimes helps to know the other side. This is what most of America listens to. Its verbal Wagner."

"Verbal drek. Turn it off."

" - today, and every second day for a few weeks, we're going to introduce to you a new voice, a man I really like to listen to, who can really tell it like it is. I'm going to give him a guest spot on my show, because I believe that we need somebody who can not only talk about the nuts and bolts of what's wrong with this country and what the shock troops of political correctness and the liberals and the proto-socialists and the feminazis are doing to eat away at our moral fabric but who can also understand and analyse these maladies at the root. We need a philosopher of the disease, and, ladies and gentlemen, I have found him for you. Without further ado, I'm going to hand over the microphone to our new guest star, Flint Arnold."

"Thank you very much Crush. Folks, I won't mince words. The people who control the secret agenda of the United States of America don't mince words in their secret communications, but these will never see the light of day. The bleeding heart liberal socialists who have bought their way into Congress with your tax dollars have made sure they put up one hell of a smokescreen. And it's a beaut. They've set up their so called Freedom of Information Act so that you can snoop on the daily efforts of the F.B.I. to track down criminals and crack merchants but they make sure their own efforts are securely hidden from the public gaze. The crucial example was the so called scandal of Irangate. You read a lot of New York Times Op Ed pieces about Oliver North and Admiral Poindexter and President Ronald Reagan and how they were supposed to have taken your money and handed it over to the Hizbollah terrorists in order to get our boys out of jail, and then `illegally' diverted that money to the Nicaraguan Contras, but they would never publish any Op Ed pieces which would reveal the real truth. How many of you have heard about the Groundnut Barons of Iran and their hold on the hard shell fruit industry in this country?"

"What the fuck is this?"

"God knows, Benjamin. There's a new one every day."

"...how many of you have gone down to your favourite groundnut vendor only to find the sign NO PISTACHIOS UNTIL NEW CROP COMES IN, or NO CASHEWS until further notice, or BRAZILS AND PECANS UNAVAILABLE AT THIS TIME? Now we have to go back to the links between the Democratic Party and the peanut growing industry in the American South, and we all know the price the American South has had to pay for the profligacy and bankrupt policies of northern politicians, particularly those who owe their seats to the tax dollars milked from you, the American voter, in socialist inspired and discredited schemes, policies that go way back to the time of the Civil War, and long before that, when the specter of anti-trust laws was first sighted haunting the dinner tables of ordinary men and women ekeing out a living on the wide open frontier, long before the Salem so-called witch-trials..."

"Shut it off, for God's sake, Frances! Turn it to the weather, Liberace, anything..."

"O.K., O.K., Benny, don't panic..." Give the poor man the jingle jangle of soporific pop.

"You could cause a man serious brain damage..."

"We have to live where we live, Benjamin."

"We can dream a little, we don't have to remind ourselves all the time. What about this, Frances: `Ask Ellen, a column on sex and relationships: Dear Ellen, I love my boyfriend, but sometimes while making love to him I let my sexual fantasies start running through my head. I imagine he's a prince and I'm one of his harem girls, or he's a rich and powerful man and I'm his mistress and we're making love on his yacht. Does this mean there's something wrong with our relationship? Dear Susie, there's nothing wrong with fantisizing during sex. Why not go another step and consider sharing your fantasies with your lover? He might well have his own fantasies that he would love to share. Play together and share your fantasies, and your love will only grow.'"

"Nothing wrong with that, Benjamin."

"What do you mean nothing? I don't want wisdom dispensed to me in free hand out magazines, matchbox covers and little bits of paper pasted on lamp-posts. I want to discover wisdom in the words of a great philosopher, someone who's thought about these matters on top of a mountain in the Himalayas with a twig of the Bodhi Tree up his ass, not some superannuated yuppie Ellen on East 23rd Street. She's probably a hairy bald bastard anyway called Stanislaus Kowalski, a super in some basement wrestling with roaches and burst pipes and overflowing washing machines. Where's the real romance nowadays?"

"What's eating you today, Benny?"

"Nothing. Just the usual Fear."

"Well, I'm going to fix some of those pasta shells anyway. I'll make enough for two."

"Not for me thank you." Back to the kitchen, banging a pot, filling water from the tap, lighting the hob. "Shit, I'm out of parmesan. Listen, Benny, can you do me a favour? Turn the radio back to that show."

"What show?"

"You know, Crush Limbo."

"What?"

"Something just struck me. I'd like to listen..."

"You're not yourself. It'll pass soon..."

"O.K. I'll do it myself."

" - Somalia, Haiti, Bosnia, Korea, all the links in the chain. The world at their feet, and us, the poor suckers, licking their boots and giving thanks for the taste of dirt and mud."

"Thank you very much Flint. Now I think that was food for thought. We all need a kick up the pants now and again to make us think about what really matters, the way things are and the way things ought to be in this besieged Republic. Ladies and gentlemen, that was my very special guest, Flint Arnold. And he'll be back, with me, next Monday, that's in three days, not two days as I said at the beginning, Monday morning, ten thirty a.m., on the Crush Limbo Hour, 703 kilohertz 965 megahertz f.m. here on ACHR American Christian Hearts Radio Monday ten thirty a.m. keep the faith!" the piano roll of Beethoven's Number One.

"You hear that, Benny? Flint Arnold! I knew I'd heard that name. That's one of Mo Smith's alter egos, isn't it - Arnold Flint? The so-called wasp best-seller? The irrascible voice, talking about nuts. Remember, in your apartment?"

"So? He got it off the radio. It figures. It's all a con trick after all."

"No, but this was the first time that man was on the radio, didn't we just hear?"

"So what, first time on this show, he must have been broadcasting all over, maybe for years, we don't listen to all these crazies, lunatics, mad evangelists, Ku Klux Klan..."

"You don't, but I do, Benjamin. I never heard that name."

"Maybe it was another city. There must be ten thousand of them..."

"No it doesn't make sense."

"What are you trying to say, Frances? Mo Smith's alter ego has broken loose and is broadcasting on local radio? That would be one for the hall of fame."

"No, but..."

"Or is Crush Limbo sitting there with a homeless black African-American tramp spewing out mad white right wing trash? Maybe Crush Limbo is black."

"He's certainly not. You've seen him on T.V."

"Could all be make up. Whiteface. Another big con on the American public. Maybe white is black after all."

"That was definitely weird. It gave me a funny tingle in the ear."

"That means somebody's walking on your grave."

The inner and outer selves, self and object... Differentiating one from the other. Or are we all inside Mo Smith? Is the wind dying down? Or does it only seem so? It's doing strange things to my brain. I put the pasta shells on and then remember. "Is the wandering phone in there, Benny?" He fishes it out from whatever pile and I slide into the living room to take it. Poke around for the old Roladex on the table. Dial the number.

"Hallo, is that Rostashvili's Gas Station? I can't hear you. Oh yeah, the wind, are you O.K. out there? What? I can't hear, can you speak a little louder please. It's Frances Stein here. Stein. S-T-E-I-, Frances, from the Acme Art Gallery, Selina Hasek's friend. I was just wondering, is it too windy for you to get a message out there? To the dome. No, not the HOME, the DOME - yeah, the geodesic dome, I think it's your wife who usually takes the messages Mr Rostashvili, oh, you're not Mr Rostashvili, what's that? You're Mr Shalikashvili, right. It's nice to know you. I just wanted to know if she's all right out there. You know, the Community, the people who are living inside the dome? Mrs Rostashvili usually takes an envelope and puts it in the mailbox just outside the tunnel. The one that leads into the dome. They collect it from there and they leave their own messages. No, I'm not from the State Police. About what? Your dog Shevarnadze? I don't know anything about a dog. I'm sure it must be, sir. But the dome is O.K.? You don't know about the dome? But it's just across the road from the gas station. That big round criss-cross thing. Uh-huh. Look, it's O.K., don't worry about it, I'll call back when Mrs Rostashvili... yeah, O.K.... have a nice day..."

Total futility. "Sometimes I wonder, Benny, whether it's all worth it. Maybe Len Loons had the right idea. Just fakes and rip-offs. Cater for the insipid rich."

"I don't know, Frances. It's a bad patch."

"Caroline?"

"Ah. I don't know. I feel I'm grinding her down. She gets so tired. But with everybody else she's so full of life and - life. You know."

"Well, she does work eighteen hours a day. All those head cases. The poorest of the poor. It's like shovelling the sea with a spoon."

"It's not just work."

"Well, Benny. You're a bedouin and she is a *fellah*. She likes to plant seeds and watch them grow. You like to graze and move on. The cowboys and the farmers. Did you ever see Oklahoma?"

"Was that with Howard Keel?"

"You're thinking of Seven Brides for Seven Brothers. This is the one with Rod Steiger. `Poor Judd is dayd'?" Sudden recall of the pasta. It's all shrivelled up, little black lumps definitely not al dente. But something might be salvaged from the wreck. "People follow the same pattern. The same with us, the way we used to be, Benny. You have to give her space."

"This is New York, Frances. There isn't any space. Maybe I should just chuck it all in. The Film Co Op, the kids with all their fresh dreams. Maybe I should get on a Greyhound, go out west, around the world, shave my head, chant my mantras, go to India, climb the Himalayas, find Shangri La, hang glide from Everest, bay at the moon. Have I stopped dreaming, Frances?"

"Getting homesick, Benny?"

"For the Land of un-Promise? the curdled milk and sour honey? the muddy alleyways with ammunition belts and pouches? suffer the little children? forget it. Let them sort it out at the top."

"It's the wind, Benjamin. It sets up wierd vibrations. Especially the rain against the airconditioning. I get it at night, it's like Chinese torture. Are you still hyper-acute?"

"Yes, I hear everything. A dog peeing against a lamp-post, pins dropping at a thousand miles, a homeless man coughing on the riverside. At least the louder sounds drown out the worst ones. The low level hum. Generators, power cables, the subway. Caroline says its nothing to do with the ear. It's how the brain processes sound. Not to speak of the teeth."

Bruxism. Nocturnal gnashing. There are, apparently, aversion therapies available. Hypnosis, pills, gestalt. All the millions with sleep disorders, insomnia, disorientation, pseudo-hallucinations, hypnagogic fugues. Seeing what isn't there and refusing to see what is.

Was the wind dying down? Perhaps it only seemed so. Just gathering its strength, trying to tempt the unwary out of doors, into its path, so that it can strike out, with all its sight-impaired fury...

SALIM.

The Bowery looks deserted tonight. Cardboard boxes flying everywhere, thrown by the wind across the street. No point in checking out the World Trade Centre, where we first found Mo Smith, that's as windswept as the Gobi desert.

I draw up the cab, at the corner of Prince Street. I thought I saw a figure on the broken stoop of the dilapidated building on the corner. 190 Bowery. But it's just a hooker, too addled by junk or desperation to figure out that this was not a night to turn tricks. She is trying to light a cigarette in the wind. But I can't rescue all the lost souls. Even Caroline sometimes walks by, on a night when the weight is just too heavy.

Give me your poor, your huddled masses... I remember my first night in America. The Immigration room at JFK. John Fitzgerald Kennedy. Ask not what your country can do for you, ask only what you can do for your country. Those three poor people who were in the room with me: The Nigerian woman who had lost her passport, the Kashmiri man they suspected of being a terrorist, and the Palestinian who had been evicted from Kuwait because his name was Saddam Hussein. We sat there not speaking to each other for most of two hours. The Nigerian woman weeping and searching her bag for the hundredth time, laying out all her meagre possessions on the floor. The room looked like a garage sale in Lagos. She must have had fifty coloured handkerchiefs, wrapped round little gifts, tiny figurines and children's toys. The Kashmiri sat silent as a rock, with a fixed gaze, as if he was trying to direct a secret force field down his moustache to melt the walls of his cell. The Palestinian from Kuwait had told me his story in the first five minutes but then shut up, shaking his head and spreading his hands in resignation. He was a simple man, a motor mechanic, who was trying to join his brother in Detroit. Every now and then he let out a soft prayer for God's forgiveness of his parents, who had failed to foresee the dreadful coincidences of the future.

Finally my name was called and I was interrogated in a tiny cramped office by two men, a little crew cut white guy and a big hefty African-American with a sheepish look and sad eyes. They asked me why I had come to America. I said I had a letter of acceptance from Flatbush College, signed by the college authorities, as well as Professor Allan Darwish. They asked me what I had done before in my life. I told them I had worked with the PLO office in Tunis, but I had crashed with my leader in the Libyan desert and had survived by drinking his urine.

They had obviously heard so many stories this one didn't even make them blink. The little white guy asked me if I drank urine on a regular basis or whether it was a special occasion. I said it was only the one time. The African-American asked me what my leader's urine tasted like. I said it was brackish, not very different from the tap water at Ein el-Hilwe refugee camp. They questioned me about my time in Lebanon. Did I know any terrorists? I said I had nothing to do with all that, and that I was now a committed pacifist, and abhorred all violence, even in a just cause. They asked me, if I were to become a U.S. citizen, would I fight for my adopted country. I said I could not tell a lie, I would not fight for any country in the future. Then the white guy asked me: "If you crashed in the desert with President George Bush, would you drink his urine?" I said I couldn't answer that question. Each event depended on its circumstance, in the pain and moment of its occurrence. But I was sure I would have no prejudice, for all men were created equal by God.

They stamped my passport. The black officer even shook my hand and said: "Welcome to the United States." Outside the detention room, Allan Darwish was waiting for me. I went past him at first, since he looked, sitting alone on a red plastic chair, like a clerk at any Middle Eastern Ministry of Traffic Control. Except for that mischievous smile:

"Salim Halimi?"

We left the Immigration building. I never learned the fate of the other detainees. There are so many of us, waiting in locked rooms, with our few belongings laid out in small piles...

Up, from Prince Street, towards East Houston. The entire side of a building advertising Chef Restaurant Supplies. Pot Belly Stoves. Pizza ovens, sinks, steam tables. Dough Retarders, whatever they are. This was really what they call a wild goose chase. The man was not likely to be outside in the storm. These homeless people are resourceful. They have all sorts of holes to crawl into. He might have gone deep into the subways tonight, or broken through a grille in some doorway. I had some wild thought of taking him round the corner to Benjamin's apartment at East 4th, since he told me he would be staying with Frances. At least to rest up for an hour and see if he would agree to go to the Shelter...

Recalling the day we tracked him down, on the World Trade Center concourse: We hadn't been cruising the area long, when we spotted him, that first time, among the Japanese tourists craning for snapshots. Caroline recognised him immediately, rummaging in a trash bin opposite the Millenium Hotel. It's hard to avoid the symbolic. Signs without meaning, they're all around us. But there was no sign, at that moment, of the voices, just a mumbling complaint about the shoes, that he had just bought, which he said were pinching his toes. He took them off, and Caroline measured them against his feet, telling him they were perfectly all right, but there was a big hole in his sock, and an ugly corn on his sole. The stench of the foot flowed out over the concourse, causing the great Twin Towers to shimmer and shake in the sun. "It just don't fit me," said the homeless man, "you hear me?"

"I hear you," said Caroline, "but if we just take you to a drugstore, we can get you something for the foot. We have our own cab here. These are my friends, Salim and Benjamin." But he just grunted and waved his sock at us. We couldn't come all that close.

He didn't want to go in the cab, so we walked him across the road to Burger King, where we bought him a Double Whopper with extra ketchup and cole slaw while Benjamin went off to find some foot lotion. I had myself a Double Whopper as well, while Caroline just sipped a coffee.

"I hear you have some stories to tell," I said to him. "You must have seen plenty in this City. It's never a dull moment."

His teeth chewed jaggedly on the charbroiled hamburger, his tongue flicking in escaping strands of lettuce, lapping a stain of tomato ketchup spreading like blood down his chin. His eyes met mine just for a moment but I could not read anything there, in those blood shot veins. Another set of bleeding hearts. What religion were we selling? The low thump of muzak over the empty plastic tables...

If you crashed in the desert with President George Bush, would you drink his urine? At odd times, this question jumps into my mind. I tried it a couple of times on guests at Frances' opening nights. But they just moved away edgily, these art enthusiasts, avoiding my gaze and my touch. It was a question that often came naturally watching the kind of stuff that Frances put on at her SoHo Gallery - the Acme. "Con-ceptual" Art. Accent on the con. Everyday objects, taken away from their everyday setting. Mo Smith could have been a perfect exhibit in one of those shows. They could have mounted him stuffed in a glass case with his lips still wrapped round the Double Whopper. Adam - God's first work, a rejected prototype.

The ghosts of the times... Sometimes, as I flow up and down the grid, from the Battery to Baker Field C.U., at 220th, from the FDR Drive to the Henry Hudson Parkway, and all the built-up boxes in between, I imagine the indigenous victims, the Manhattan Indians, the Americans' own "Palestinians"... Professor Darwish once gave an evening class on the subject: This island before the white man. The Algonquin, who hunted and fished up and down the island, across the unspoiled glades that are now the Bronx, Brooklyn and Westchester County. The forests and hills filled with wild game, foxes, bobcats and deer roaming the woods. Until a ship called the Dauphine arrived, in April, 1524, captained by Giovanni da Verrazano, an Italian adventurer working for the King of France, only 28 years after Columbus first set eyes on the "New World..."

Darwish taught a course on Columbus, too, whom he called "the biggest bastard who ever set foot in this part of the world, until the coming of even bigger bastards." He gave us a book to read called "The Harp and the Shadow", by a Cuban writer, Alejo Carpentier. It was above the heads of most of the class but I read it, as a Palestinian, avidly. Columbus came to the "New World" to look for gold, which he never found, so he made money out of the inhabitants, by setting up slavery. I remember Carpentier's description of the captive Indians Columbus shipped back to Seville and Barcelona, crying with fear and begging to be sent home. I could imagine their terror at being plucked from their familiar world into a hell of alien plenty and cruelty. Starving in the sight of feasts they couldn't eat composed of foods their stomachs vomited out. Columbus entrancing the King and Queen of Spain with his tall tales about the golden kingdom of Cipango, making his desperate sales pitch, begging for more money to go back and pillage the land of myth and magic...

Instead of Columbus's chains we had our own *fidays* sailing into exile to Tunis on their Mediterranean cruise of despair. I thought also of the exiled Jews and Moslems of Spain, embarking for unknown shores... At the end of the day, everybody turns up here, in Mahattan, driving a yellow cab, with those name tags which so unsettle the white Yuppie passengers: Ghassan, Mohammad, Mohtashedi, Patel, Mendoza, Ahmadou, Ndebele, Cheung, Tran Van Ang, Rutskovitch, Vilathswami, Halimi, Hovsepian. Unless they're taken away, in handcuffs, to the next flight out...

After Columbus and Carpentier I became very interested in maps. The idea of the exploration of the unknown. The search for the means to draw things together. When the planet was the universe, and all the rest was God's domain. Pushing back the frontiers of knowledge. And was that good or bad? From Eratosthenes of Cyrene, through Ptolemy's meridians and parallels to Al-Idrisi's celestial sphere, the fabulous maps of Solinus, Mercator's projections and the great Atlas of Willem Blaeu. All the strange and wonderful speculations of men who could not, like our generation, send up spaceships to take snapshots of the real thing. They had to crawl upon the earth, or toss about on its apparently endless oceans, looking for a safe haven and calculating their way by the stars...

When our own great voyagers, Sulaiman the Merchant, Al-Maqdisi, Ibn-Jubair and of course Ibn-Battuta travelled, their mission was to celebrate the utmost limits of the Faith, though they had respect for infidels like the Hindus and the Chinese. The marvels of the world were indivisible to them. But when Mercator and Columbus and the dutchman Blaeu drew the world it was divided into the known and the unknown, the familiar and the exotic, the Christian and the Savage, the eaters of their God's body and blood against the eaters of men...

Exotic lands, peopled by cannibals and four eyed men and women, men with dog's heads, ruled by hyenas and apes. What brought out Ibn-Battuta from the mouth of Mo Smith, in that first meeting, at

Benjamin's apartment? Is it all coincidence, or perhaps something else?

The kingdom of the irrational. Frances and Allan Darwish tried to lead me on by Reason. Frances, in particular, took on my artistic education. She wanted an intellectual in bed with all the proper angles, and my rough edges had to be smoothed down. She took me around the City's great museums, the Metropolitan, MOMA, the Frick, the Guggenheim, the Whitney. Of them all, I loved the Met the most, with its million and a half square feet of nested galleries, a grand labyrinth of the whole world. Later I would just go there by myself, and lose myself for hours in the crowds, wandering through the Graeco-Roman and Near-eastern sections, into the hall of the Pacific Islands and pre-Columbian artifacts, the fabulous wooden totem poles of New Guinea with their great carved phalluses, the ritual masks of the Andes, then climbing up to the European paintings, room after room of the Old Masters, three thousand works, the visual sign-posts of a civilisation that saw itself as the world's true soul. From Masaccio to Manet. I would sit in the room of the Rembrandts, watching those pudgy faces watching me. The light of the eyes. I understood the difference between the reproduced and the real thing. The direct touch across the ages. When there is only one of a thing, not endless, useless copies. And then I would wander on down, through the American Wing and Musical Instruments, back to the Medieval Art and into the Egyptian Galleries, where I could spend whole days.

When I used to pass through Cairo, fetching and carrying for our Chairman, I always wanted to go to the Egyptian Museum, which my mentor, Abu Hamid, had told me was one of the building blocks of the human brain. The treasures of Tut-Ankh-Amun, the great sarcophagi, stelas and hundred thousand household things which showed us where we all came from. But I never had the time. All I managed was one hour at the Pyramids, while the Chairman was closeted with the President of the Republic, and I rushed round the colossal monuments, gaping and wondering, while all the camel drivers, horse wranglers, postcard touts and would-be guides dogged my steps, cursing my parents and all my ancestors going back to the stone age for ignoring them. At the Met, at least, I have the time and space to catch a glimpse of what I might have seen. The massive stone heads and bodies of the Pharaohs, the hieroglyphic Books of the Dead, the funerary inscriptions and ornate coffins, the scattered loot from the temples of the ancient world.

I don't know if any of Mo Smith's Pharaoh, Merenptah's, belongings are there, but I read that he was among the actual mummies that had been on display in Cairo, in the Museum I never had the time to check out. And then there's his tomb, in the Valley of the Kings, just across the Nile from Luxor...

So small are we in the scheme of things. I know it's a cliche, but it impressed itself on me as I walked among those dry bones and shreds of vanished empires. I sat at the tables provided below the exhibits in the museum, reading the illuminated translation of the long papyrus scrolling the length of the wall above. The incantations of the Book of the Dead: *"I come forth to heaven and sit myself down by the God of Light. Hail, I have become helpless! Hail, I have become helpless! but I go forward. I have become helpless in the regions of those who plunder in the underworld..."*

Yes, I know how they felt. THE CHAPTER OF A MAN TRANSFORMING HIMSELF INTO WHATEVER HE PLEASETH. Did Mo Smith sit here like me and read this? Certainly Professor Darwish believes that Mo's personas are the result of years of reading, in places such as this and the New York Public Library, where anyone can come and go. The product of a prodigious memory, not of some magical possession by other souls. How much would we not give to be able to climb into other skins, other times?

THE CHAPTER OF A MAN TRANSFORMING HIMSELF INTO WHATEVER HE PLEASETH. How very American. What was once available only to Pharaoh is now the birthright of us all. Even the Blind Sheikh Jedid of Queens got into the act, complementing his spiritual enterprise with the spreading web of his more earthly business: The garages, parking lots, hardware stores and video shops bought to fund his mosques and educational charities throughout the East Coast. It was not for a small cog like me, without a Green Card, to figure out how "A Fistful of Dollars", "Nightmare On Elm Street Five" and "Motel Nurses" could fit in with the divine plan. I just took home the merchandise in the evenings, to my crowded little den of Palestinian exiles, my friends Rafik, Ghassan and Khalid, putting on our borrowed video the full portfolio of the west's fat dreams. From John Wayne to Arnold Schwartzenegger, from Alfred Hitchcock to Charles Band, from Paramount to Troma Pictures. Later, after Frances, and Allan Darwish, and Benjamin, the film buff, got hold of me, I began dipping into the

World Classics section. But at the beginning it was all just blood and guts, vicarious reliving of the old days in Beirut, when not even the most heavily armed Chuck Norris movie could match the mayhem in the streets. More guns among the audience than on the screen. Even there, the cinemas kept going through the worst shelling, until the roof caved in... That's entertainment.

I missed the guidance of Abu Hamid. The stern love of the old comrade. It's all crying over spilt blood. The ancient Egyptian prayed that his body would be resurrected in the underworld, that he should cross the waters whole. He needed his name, his spiritual body, his spiritual shadow, his vital force, his heart, his heart's soul, and the *ka*, the incorporeal double. So many disparate bits. I would sometimes feel, in my video days, the various pieces of me peel off, detach and melt into the muggy air of our crowded exile den, escaping through the jammed windows into the fetid city, like Mo Smith's own splintered selves...

I remember one movie classic I took off the shelves, an old British film: The Man Who Could Work Miracles. The Gods, betting on the maturity of Man, decide to give an ordinary guy the power to make miracles. First he tries simple tricks, like making a girl's pimples disappear. Then, as he starts to understand his potential, he becomes more and more ambitious. He decides to remake the world in his own image. But things get so hectic that, in the middle of his creation, he stops and calls for time to stand still, for the earth to stop rotating around the sun. Immediately everything flies off the surface of the earth, trees, houses, palaces, humans and all. His last wish is for everything to return to normal, before he got the Gift...

Normality. A wife, two childs, a dog, a cat, a pet tortoise and a little house in Westchester County. What might children of mine grow up to? My father's dream, the little bucket of earth from the homeland, in which dead flowers grew... Sitting in a ploughed field, with a flute, thinking about eternity. No miracles required. Or are they?

But as the rain pours down around me now I am stuck on the corner of Bowery and Prince. I'm not going to find anybody in these streets tonight. I turn the engine back on and make a U-turn, back towards Canal. Visibility practically non-existent, the car bucking in the wind like a wild horse. If things get any worse I'll be washed away, over the Williamsburg Bridge and into the river, reversing Verrazano's route, back to Spain... I turn right into Canal. The waters are rising and my windshield is being battered by a hail of loose fruit, grains of rice and frozen fish swept from stalls or delivery vans. A tiny old Chinese woman is plastered against the glass for a split second, her mouth puckered in a silent pout, before she too is swept away. I am beginning to feel like Dorothy of Kansas, another movie discovered courtesy of the Blind Sheikh, before she is swept up by the tornado, houses, bicycles, carts, chimneys and all, into the sky. Perhaps they might welcome a Medallion cab in Oz, to cruise down that yellow brick road...

I know what they felt like now, all those people who were not taken on board Noah's Ark. The unrighteous. The stiff necked and the unbelievers. Those who would not heed God's word, who did not believe a blind Sheikh could see past his own cataracts. I battle on across what I guess must be Mulberry, Baxter, Center Street, Lafayette. The fish have stopped raining down, now it's just water, overwhelming my poor wind-shield wipers. Cardboard boxes, loose planks off road workings, banging against the sides of the car. Car and shop alarms, set off everywhere, wailing like trapped djinns. They are designed at frequencies that disrupt the brain cells, not much of a problem for the thief but agony for any law abiding mortal...

It was King Solomon who, it was said, had chained all the djinns and demons in jars sunk in the bottom of the sea, where they shrieked and gnashed their grisly teeth. They would be let free, on the Day of Judgement, to make obeisance before their Master and be cast out, forever, or redeemed. Chinatown seems as good a location as any. But I make it up past Broadway to Sixth. Turning up the Avenue of the Americas, the wind now buffeting the cab at my back. Shooting me up, like a bolt in the pants, past Grand, Broome, Spring and Prince, across Houston and up to West 4th, where it suddenly changes direction and turns me towards Washington Square. The square itself is a gushing, rippling whirlpool, in whose hub a man stands holding up frisbees, which are whipped up one by one in the wind to disappear in the grey pudding of the sky. Just another bum, a tall, emaciated pony-tailed white man with a hook nose, definitely not Mo Smith.

Finally a customer stops me, flinging himself at the bonnet of the car as I try to steer my way back round West 8th, just outside B. Dalton's. Banging his fist against my window. I roll it down just a little, to shout: "Don't you see? I'm off duty?" But he shouts back: "I'm a lawyer! I'll sue you and your fucking company!" So I let him open the door and climb in.

"What you have to do to get a cab in this City!" he snarls, shaking the rain all over me. I loose the brake and begin coasting up the Avenue of the Americas. I know when to stop arguing. The man sinks back in the back seat, mumbling. Pretty soon, I'm sure, he'll tell me where he wants to go.

And if not, man, the meter is running.

ONWARDS! ONWARDS! Ploughing on up the Bowery, coughing, retching and spitting into the tempest, dragging one foot after the other, wiping the snot off his nose with his sleeve, his coat and fatigues already soaked through to the skin, the sinews, bones, marrow. Pressing on, past corrugated shuttered frontages, coated with graffiti and pasted with peeling flyposters for long past events, Desmond Dekker & The Aces, S.O.B.s, Jimmy Z Funky Flute, Motorhead, Sonic Youth, The Boredoms, Public Puppetry, Sabado the Festival of Love. Music under the bridge. Across East Houston, past Intergalactic Art, across Bleecker and the Sunoco gas station (Attendant Does Not Carry Cash), across Bond and the Bouverie Theatre, across Great Jones Street, pausing on the corner of East 4th at the trash bin stubbornly clinging to its post, with its stern "WARNING: LITTER ONLY, NO HOUSEHOLD OR BUSINESS TRASH $100 FINE," but the wind has blown out all the contents, leaving only a soggy indeterminate mass clinging like a putrid jelly to the wire mesh, in the lee of the grand arched building with the flapping pennants of the Village Voice. NYU, New York University, another font of all knowledge abandoned in the storm, leaning into Cooper Square. Here ends the Bowery, splitting into Fourth and Third Avenues, diverging to the Village and Uptown. Crucial decisions. Whether to endure the slings and arrows of the East Village, up past Saint Marks to the opulent climate of Park Avenue and Murray Hill, or to take arms against the eastern clip of Greenwich Village, towards Union Square and from there onward, onward towards the nub, towards the invisible spire of the Empire State Building, hidden in the dull grey cloud. Where great apes climbed to destiny. Make up your fucking mind Goddamit! He stood at the foot of the big conceptual cube, slowly turning on its concealed axis by the force of the wind. Gathering speed, it spun faster and faster. He waited for it to show its hand and cease. It kept on spinning. The buses had deserted the bus stop on the other side of the square. The NO STANDING sign was bent over, the ONE WAY pointing towards the ground. A small van bearing the legend THE BEENIE WEENIE AND BURGER MOBILE had keeled over against the entrance to the Traffic Violations Bureau. Mo hovering waiting, tamping down the restless hordes tearing at his lining, scratching his viscera, hammering on his adam's apple.

"Give us a break, Mo, Goddamit!"

PUSH! PUSH! PUSH!

GO GO GO!

"THE BODY IS HISTORY AND HISTORY IS THE BODY," said the Alchemist, blowing out smoke rings, which curled up among the stacked pool tables, racks of billiard cues, boxes of coloured balls and bowling pins, wreathing the paradigmatic placques covering the walls of the loft. FOR STALWART SERVICE IN THE AMERICAN CIVIL WAR. LUTHER T. MANDRAKE, FOUNDER UROLOGY INSTITUTE, UNIVERSITY OF WISCONSIN. JONATHAN B. WONDERFUL, PHILANTHROPIST AND HUMANITARIAN. THIS INTEGRATED OFFENCE-DEFENCE CAPABILITY DONATED BY HOMER LATHROP, FORMER PFC US MARINE CORPS SEMPER FIDELIS. TO MY MOTHER, ESME H. FRUPP. "Just consider it all from the beginning: The birth of Adam. Was he indeed created by God from mud or was there a shameful secret right there at the start? Did Satan have a hand in the original Act or did he just foul the ingredients? How well do you know your cosmology?"

Jaime was poised over the single functioning pool table, the cue thrust through his left armpit, its tip hesitating over the eight ball. The ash from his cigar drooping over the felt top. "Fuck me, man."

"I already have." The Alchemist leaned back in his rattan rocking chair, beaming at his protege, "primeval monsters roamed the void before the Creation, are you aware of that? Rahab, the Great Dragon, Leviathan and Behemoth. At the End of Days, they will be slaughtered, to provide a feast for the Wise. Why only the Wise? Always exclusion, even beyond the bounds of Time. The rest of us will have to scavenge round the dustbins, picking out a drumstick here, a little piece of gristle, a wishbone, some shrivelled offal or tripe. Why should not we, too, have a seat at the grand table, with the maitre dee fussing round our neck with a napkin and slipping the wine list into our hands?

"On the third day of Creation Lucifer rebelled and was cast down to earth. But it was not until the sixth day that Adam was formed, what do you think of that, eh, icho? One has to deal all the time with Johnny Come Latelys. But Adam was made in the Image, as you know. The only original, in fact, was Lilith, did you know that? She sprung up at the very same time. But she refused the missionary position, and flew off, determined to be his equal. She was the one you saw in the stars. The true authority of beauty. God built her up from tissue and bone, muscle and blood, the true slithy elements of life. But Adam was disgusted. He turned away, and God removed her, nobody knows where to. It's only then that he put the bum to sleep and made an obedient helpmeet out of the bastard's rib. So she could rib him for evermore. Ha ha ha. Rib him, get it? Boy, do you ever do more than grunt?"

Jaime grunted, potting the green and moving on to the reds. The Alchemist rose, knocking his way through the piles of trophies, silver cups, memorial tumblers and goblets waiting in vain for the inscriptor to mark them with names and fields of glory, kicking the vessels aside with crash and tinkle, reaching the shuttered window and pulling the blind, wiping the grimy pane with the sleeve of his gabardine coat. The dull glimmer of the stormy day was giving way to a more limpid glow, the wind noticeably dying down from a shriek to a growl.

"The most ancient traditions known to us say that man's first sexual encounters were with animals. A man spent more time with his sheep than his wife. I can't vouch for the feminist viewpoint. The great hero of the Epic of Gilgamesh, Enkidu, was androgynous. There is a great suspicion in Biblical exegesis of hairy legged women. The fear of backsliding to paganism. The old temple rites, where anything goes. From Adam to Foucault: The soul is the prison of the body. But we who are the prisoners of the body should not therefore be prisoners of the soul. We should be free of both. Don't you agree?"

"Yeah, sure, man, no problem." Jaime, giving up the pool table, moved among the silver cups, picking them up and casting them aside. "It's all junk here, man, all junk. I know a man who'd give us fifty bucks for the lot. But I tell you, if we could transport the tables..."

"Forget money," said the Alchemist curtly, "it's an old anal fixation. Money is an effect, not a cause. A symptom not a source. What we are looking for is the Pleasure Principle. Now there's a goal worth pursuing.

We haven't even scratched the surface in our quest up and down the body. From Harlem to Babylon-Sumer, from Khufu to Malcolm X, from Cairo to Rome. Do you think we are the only ones to live in the web? It's a constant struggle, not of opposites, but of sames. I won't say equals, I'm not playing that game. Are you with me?"

"I am with you man, but I don't understand a word you're sayin."

"Good. Just follow me blindly." Turning and striding purposefully back down the length of the warehouse, past the billiard equipment and through the laboratory, the maproom and past the vas mirabilis, into the top floor corridor, ushering the young man out and shutting and locking the door with twelve heavy bolts, pocketing the great ring of keys. Rushing down the five flights of stairs. "Come on, sonny boy, chop chop." Out into the street, the pale afternoon light, the storm abating to gale force, the tops of the buildings beginning to show through the swirl of dispersing clouds.

"This way." The Alchemist led Jaime round the corner of Bowery towards the Spring Street-Lafayette subway. In his black gabardine and homburg and loping gait he seemed no different from the familiar vision of the orthodox Jews whose turf this used to be, before the Italians, the Chinese. Jaime hurried in his wake, the wind still whipping his face, reluctantly rushed by the lush galeterias, their windowfulls of great shanks of ham and giant cheeses, Provolone Tipico Caesaria Bresciana Aurricchio Parmegiana Reggiano. The collossal hanging salamis, Milano Napoli Toscana. Hurrying, hurrying as his black clad mentor clattered down the steps of the Number 6 Uptown.

The platform was almost deserted, with only three lone passengers hunched over the gap. The wind from above echoed in the tunnel with the whistle of a disgruntled ghost. "The Fall of Man," continued the Alchemist, as Jaime scavenged along the platform, picking up three cigarette butts, two nickels and a handful of discarded pennies, along with a sodden rubber condom which was no longer fit for its job, "the Tree of Knowledge and the roots of sin. Was Paradise merely a hallucination produced by the fly agaric? Heim and Wesson's *Les Champignon Hallucinogenes du Mexique,* read and discuss. The God Tlaloc was in another aspect the magic serpent himself. In short, Adam and Eve were framed. But will you see CBS and CNN mount a proper investigation of this fraud? Not bloody likely. According to tradition, the Messiah still lives in Eden, sipping nectar and eating grapes until the generation is ready. That would be one hell of an exclusive, wouldn't it? But nobody has real guts any more."

The Number 6 Lexington Avenue Local City Hall to Pelham Bay Park clattered up, its doors springing open. The train moderately crowded, even on this tempestuous day, so that Jaime and the Alchemist had to stand by the Metropolitan Transportation Authority's new poster castigating panhandlers and tramps, a large thought balloon emanating from nowhere revealing the day to day traveller's innermost fears:

Uh, oh. Come on, **not** me, **NOT ME.**
Oh Pleeeeeze don't come stand in FRONT of me ASKING for money.
GREAT, Now the whole *CAR'S* staring.
What do I do, WHAT DO I DO????
I know, I'll pretend I'm reading my book.
Look. I feel bad. I **really** do.
But HEY, its MY MONEY.
And HOW do I know what you'll spend it on anyway?
I DON'T. SORRY. No money from me.

"The Judeao-Christian tradition, as you know, laid the rap on the Archangel Samael, or Satan, for doping Adam, out of jealousy for his beauty and grandeur. Samael refused to worship Adam, but tricked Adam into worshipping him as the snake. The snake, as you know, sheds its skin on a regular basis, a proper model for us all. There is a confusion in the midrash between Samael and the original Prince of Darkness, Hallel Ben Shahar, alias Light, Son of Dawn, alias Lucifer, who claimed equal property rights in the Creation. God banished him and his minions to the Pit of Darkness, where they languish in silence, waiting for their liberation. They are known as The Watchers. What they have not seen ain't worth seeing. They are the origin, I have no doubt at all, of the later Greek oracles, who prophesy out of the depths." The train juddered to a stop at Bleecker Street, to allow on some more brave souls who had chanced the storm, batting no eyelid to the disembodied cry "Numbersixuptownextstopastorplacewatch-theclosindoors!" jerking on back into the tunnel.

"Demons and devils, dragons, witches and djinns. Inccubi and succubi. Not the kind of succubi you're thinking of, young man. But the orgiastic powers inside. The walpurgisnacht of the belly button, the black Sabbath of the ureter. You have barely touched the surface, with your petty crimes and transgressions. Just wait until you meet your retrovirus. The faceless force that destroys all in its path. The true malignancy of regression. After the murder by Cain of Abel, the demons pestered him in his sleep, causing him to dream forbidden dreams and give birth to the twisted seeds of night emissions. They also assaulted Eve, raping her repeatedly, producing countless litters of little devils. Some say these were the unfinished spirits made by God on the sixth day, just before he ceased work for the Sabbath at sunset. So there is a certain responsibility there, that can't be easily shirked. But betrayal indifference and lassitude are universal maladies. God is not exempt. Omnia non mutantur, common belief notwithstanding. But we have to change next stop, my honey."

14th Street, Union Square. The glut of corridors. Up steps, down steps, switching levels, criss-crossing platforms. This way for the B, N, Q, R. Broadway Express, Broadway Local. The cars are clean and efficient these days, not like the graffiti covered trucks of yore. 23rd, 28th, 34th Street change for PATH trains watchtheclosindoors. "One more stop, boy. The Sons of God, son, the Angels, were sent down to teach the right and the good to mankind. But they were seduced by the pretty women in fishnet stockings and lipstick and kohl with their steamy thighs and heaving breasts and milky nipples and honey tones and gave birth to a race of bastards, the Fallen Giants, the nefilim. God destroyed them in the Flood, leaving only Noah and his quarrelling family, with all their fancy menagerie. The sinful and the righteous. What a dichotomy." The doors sprang open at 42nd Street Times Square, giving vent to an ingathering and outpouring of humanity, the Alchemist stepping out and nodding his head for Jaime to follow, into the flow, threading the red painted columns, past the blind saxophonist cooling the fetid air with his riffs, up the steps and into the main concourse, the newspaper and magazine stands, the donuts and danish stall, the souvenir and pischifke vendors, skirting the crowd gathered round the black teenager drumming the universe into tremendous syncopation with his collection of plastic trashbins, catching Jaime's eye in a sly wink, waving his drumstick, pushing through the turnstile, up the steep steps to the corner of 42nd and Seventh Avenue, by the leather styles shop under the shut down Victory Theatre. The iconic electric news of Number One Times Square rotating behind them. BUSH AND CLINTON GAP CLOSING - HURRICANE HILDA SMACKS CITY - LONG ISLAND DISASTER AREA. By the subway entrance, the Brothers of Islam braved the dying wind to set out their regular stall, incense sticks, silver bangles and lucky charms, alongside The Koran, The Truth, The Prophet Muhammad, Leviathan 2000 and The True Faith of Jesus and Moses. The white clad vendors of the Word sitting patiently behind their display on little folding stools.

"Noah built the Ark," said the Alchemist, "and God Flooded the land, and killed off whoever he killed off, and spared whom he spared, and the descendants of Noah built a city, in the Plain of Shinear, and said: Let us make a tower that will reach to Heaven, and let us make us a name, lest we be scattered over the face of the earth. One descends to banal and obvious metaphors. The sons of Noah, Shem, Ham and Japheth. Ham saw his father's nakedness and was cursed. That is the origin of anti-black prejudice. In fact just seeing his father's pee pee would never warrant such a penalty. The midrash tells us the real crime was castration. We have the same thing in the emasculation of Uranus by Cronos. In Hittite myth, according to Graves, the rebel son Kumarbi bit off his father the great God Anu's genitals. It's a classic case of bowdlerisation. The true Original Sin - not munching apples but nuts. Are you still with me?"

Jaime hurried to keep up with his mentor, who was striding in seven league boots past the gutted lobbies of the long closed theatres, the New Amsterdam, the Selwyn, the Harem, the Harris, the Roxy and the Joy, whose marquees had been recast by local projects with a melange of strange messages, replacing the long gone titles:

IT IS EMBARRASSING TO BE CAUGHT AND KILLED FOR STUPID REASONS.

LAUGH HARD AT THE ABSOLUTELY EVIL.

YOU ARE TRAPPED ON THE EARTH SO YOU WILL EXPLODE.

A LOT OF PROFESSIONALS ARE CRACKPOTS.

SLIPPING INTO MADNESS IS GOOD FOR THE SAKE OF COMPARISON.

DEVIANTS ARE SACRIFICED TO INCREASE GROUP SOLIDARITY.

SAVOR KINDNESS BECAUSE CRUELTY IS ALWAYS POSSIBLE LATER.

WHAT URGE WILL SAVE US NOW THAT SEX WON'T?

What indeed? Running the gauntlet of the porn shops, videos, peep shows. Turning in at a particularly narrow passage under a cacophony of signs pledging XXX Discount Multi-System Audio Video Lotto Color Copies Beer Cold Drinks Adult Movies Foreign Oriental German Transexual Amateur Anal All-Male All-Female Hero Souvlaki Non Prescription Drugs past two large vendors seated on high stools on a raised dais by the store, surveying their kingdom from a height of nine feet, glaring at the intimidated customers browsing along four long racks of videocassettes and magazines depicting all the lustful visions the devilled flesh is heir to, Punk Tarts, Sex Fuckheads, Wet Cunt Number 6 thru 12, Prime Pussy, BangCock She Males, Hog Tied Hookers, Hot Filth, Scrotum and Taboo, Of Human Bondage, Death Swish, Blow Job Special, Assholey Sinner, The Cunterfitters, Warts and Piss, Chicks With Dicks, Jailbait Jism, Nausea Monthly, Little Dorkitt, Slagtime, The Big Slit, Group Porking With Lady, Finnegans Wack, Suckaberry Finn, Satanic Nurses, Cunt Twenty-Two, Lord of the Flies, Rimming and Punishment, Tristram Shaggie, Hard Times, Paradise Lust, Remembrance of Things Pissed -

"And God said, let us confuse their language, that they may not understand each other's speech. And so He did, and the builders of the tower could not speak to one another, or convey meaningful instructions, so that if one asked: give me a mortar, he would be handed a brick, and if another asked for a hammer, he would be handed a pile of schmutters. And so the builders of the tower fought among themselves, and their work ceased, and the tower fell into ruin and destruction. Luckily they never tried to take a cab in this City." The Alchemist led Jaime, reluctantly whizzing by the gaudy images of concupiscence and shamelessness, through into the bowels of the shop, past a swing door and a long corridor sloping down, between rows of peep-booths whose customers' eyeballs were glued to thin slats beyond which nameless simulations writhed to a wild synthetic beat. Jaime nodding in approval, slapping the wriggling haunches as he passed: "Cool, man. Way to go."

"Grow up, little street urchin," said the Alchemist, stopping short before a dilapidated door, scarred and scuffed and marked with graffiti but appearing to have no handle. At its top it had a small frosted glass window, with the legend "EMPTY ROOM." The Alchemist knocked on the door, three times, slowly, then another four knocks in quick succession. There was a long pause while the heavy metal thrashed behind them. Then the Alchemist pushed the door open with his foot.

"Come in, the door's open."

The man within sat in a caricature of the sanctum of the seedy eye. The walls pitched at crazy angles and the light of a single fly specked light bulb illuminated an old teakwood desk covered with dusty files and yellowing papers, half eaten sandwiches, cigarette butts, marijuana roaches, a tin army mug of rancid coffee, a cracked magnifying glass, a jewellers' eyeglass, a metronome, a chisel, balls of string, rubber bands, jars of pills, a blackjack, an abacus, a pot of glue, a framed portrait of J. Edgar Hoover and an assortment of miniature wind up toys. The man behind the desk, sunk in a flabby mauve armchair whose blotched upholstering was bursting out from numerous cracks, was a gaunt, almost emaciated figure, shaped by the chair into a question mark, his large head drooping over his meagre body, the fedora hat dragging it down, shadowing a sea of stubble. A black patch was fastened by a black band over his left eye.

"Cool, man," marvelled Jaime. The Alchemist pushed the door shut behind him. The man waved a pale hand towards two rickety wooden chairs before the desk. The Alchemist sat, motioning Jaime to follow, and extracting from the pocket of his coat a battered tin of Schwartzgebbar Tobacco, slowly rolling a peck in Rizla paper.

"Good to see you, Frank, how's business?"

The question mark sighed, soft as a snake's fart, his right eye balling from one to the other of his visitors. The Alchemist inclined his head to Jaime.

"This is my friend, Jaime, my Archie Goodwin, as it were. Jaime, this gentleman here is Frank Ox."

The private eye sighed again, like the last gasp of a horse at the glue factory, stretching his spidery thin hands to wind up the little toys. A tiny hamburger advanced, pudgy arms waving. A mouse backflipped, holding a morsel of cheese. A set of plastic teeth began chattering and two feet wobbled forward, each capped by a ten cent piece.

"The March of Dimes," grated the detective, "how d'you like that?"

"It's a honey," agreed the Alchemist. The two feet, stopped short by the coffee mug, kicked out in dumb frustration. The hamburger toppled over, waving its legs feebly and the mouse, miscalculating, flipped off the table. The gaunt man bent to pick it off the floor, which was covered in a thick film of dust and fluff.

"It's when they start talking you begin to worry," said the Alchemist, with his eye on the still rattling teeth. "Remember the Glockenspiels of Frankfurt? Shadowing Mephistopheles for Faust. *Ich mocht' mich gleich dem Teufel ubergeben - Wenn ich nur selbst kein Teufel war!* Eh? That was one hell of a report, mensch. You really burnt your fingers on that one. And remember the time you got the goods on Caligari? Some wheeze, hiding in his cabinet. The Dusseldorf child murderer - a classic. And how about the Mysterious Stranger? Yes, those were the days. The Salem case. You lived that one for how many years? Four, five? Skulking in the underbrush, hiding up chimneys, curled up in basements, taking notes, setting it all down, the damning plots, the devil's dolls, the transformations into pigs and monkeys, all thoroughly documented in huge dossiers, twenty thousand pages of parchment for the Commonwealth of Massachusetts."

"A man has to make a living," rasped the dick, unbending slowly to grab at his coffee mug, but his grasp fell short, the dimed clockwork feet still kicking vainly at the tin.

"Indeed. What was it the good Doctor Faustus used to say? -

"*Wie nur dem Kopf nicht alle Hoffnung schwindet,*
Der immerfort an schalem Zeuge klebt...
How strange that he who cleaves to shallow things
Can keep his hopes alive on empty terms,
And dig with greed for precious plunderings,
And find his happiness unearthing worms!"

The gaunt man grunted, his large head bobbing suddenly, his stubbled face going even bluer as he succumbed to a coughing fit, beating his tiny feet on the table leg.

"Our friend Frank," the Alchemist explained to Jaime, as he finished rolling his spliff and giving the seam a good lick, "is actually supposed to be in the Philippines, hiding out from the S.A. and L.A.P.D., who are after him for various violations of the Privacy Act, the Anti-Voyeurism Act, the Foreign Invasion Act and another bushel of laws. Surveillance is not what it used to be."

"Regulation," rasped the dick, "they want the end but shrink from the means. Under the table, everybody's at it. They want the message on the messenger's corpse."

"And how is Mephisto nowadays? Drunk in some local bar, probably. Too much competition from humanity. You didn't burn the witches, did you? It was the magistrates, the clergymen, the good burghers doing their civic duty. Responding to the wishes of the electorate. It makes you puke. But if everything that made you puke made you puke you would be bent over a bucket all your life. The little people haven't lived up to it. The golden promise. The dawn of a new day, beckoning to newer shores. *Zu neuen Ufern lockt en neuer tag. Ein Feuerwagen schwebt auf leichten Schwingen, an mich heran! Ich fuhle mich bereit, auf neuer Bahn den Aether zu durch- dringen:* Piercing the ether, new born, I aspire to rise to spheres of pure activity... Scribble scribble scribble, eh, Mister Goethe? Now and again, there have been insights. Little sparks of fire amid a sea of embers. And Ole Man River, he still goes rolling along."

"What do you want of me now?" the thin man ground between his teeth, "I'm busy. I got a full caseload. I'm up to here. I'm swamped. I'm swept under. I've got enough work to last me till the trumpet sounds." He motioned at his faded files, which glinted for a moment as if brushed by an invisible Tinkerbell. Ping, ping. The teeth stopped chattering, the plastic hamburger was still and the marching dimes twitched fitfully.

"Desire!" mused the Alchemist, "here in this temple of lust where every lewd longing is catered for. What should we wish for? Knowledge like Faust? Power like Joseph Stalin? Limitless sexual gratification like the Marquise von O? To be loved by you and nobody else but you, like Marilyn Monroe? I think we'll settle for modest survival. After all, we have plumbed the depths, and all that has happened is we have lost our plumb. We are adrift in the great sea of verbiage. Have you read six characters in search of an author? Pirandello. Very fashionable in the twenties and fifties. Today nobody expects characters to have an author any more. The text is bouncing free, gnashing its false teeth and wailing. Metaphors cannon loose in the meadows. Hyperbole climbs up Jacob's Ladder. The individual voice is so still. What do I want? I want you to be the invisible man, without bandages. I want you do what you've always done: Creep around corners, lurk in dark alleys, burrow away beneath the fabric of society, hide in designated refuse collection areas, infiltrate unsuspecting organs, penetrate secret cabals, worm your way into intimate confidences, sneak into exclusive circles, prowl in backyards, slither in basements, crawl along rooftops and drainpipes, slide between the sheets of distracted lovers, wriggle under beds, slip into a thousand and one disguises, evade the clutches of the law cosmic and temporal, monitor, bug, pry, snoop, eavesdrop and wiretap, decode and decipher messages, elucidate the obscure and construe the recondite, interpret the inexplicable and the arcane, illuminate dark nasty corners and leave no slimy stone unturned. In short, Ox, I wish to engage your services."

"Seventy-five bucks a day plus expenses," said Ox. "All laundry and medical bills included. Four weeks retainer."

"Fifty tops," said the Alchemist, "laundry excluding underwear. One week's retainer."

"Sixty-five," said Ox, "briefs included, but boxers optional. Three weeks retainer."

"Fifty-five is my absolute limit," said the Alchemist, "boxers, but no briefs. Detergents extra. Two weeks retainer."

"Sixty-two-fifty, briefs every other week. Eighteen days retainer."

"Fifty-six fifty. Sixteen days."

"Sixty-one. Seventeen days."

"Fifty-eight."

"Sixty."

"Fifty-eight seventy-five."

"Fifty-nine fifty and not a penny less."

"Fifty-eight ninety-five."

"Fifty-nine twenty-five."

"Done."

They leaned across the table to shake hands and the Alchemist unpeeled one thousand and seven dollars from a thick wad and counted out another twenty-five cents. Leaning back in their respective seats with a mutual glow of satisfaction, while Jaime stared at the ceiling, upon which two robust red roaches were chasing each other in ever decreasing circles.

*

*

*

*

*

Several hours later, Frank Ox sat alone in his room in the National Hotel overlooking Times Square. Looking out wistfully at the lights blazing, glistening on the rainsoaked streets, the fiery furnace of marquee signs and advertisements transmuting one into the other in the consumers' great bacchanal. DRINK SHADRACH. EAT MESHACH. SUCK ABEDNEGO. BELSHAZZAR'S FEAST XXX SHOW FOLLIES 25 CENTS LIVE NUDES MOVIE HITS FANTASY BOOTHS TABLE DANCING 1 ADMISSION PRICE OPEN 24 HOURS. The rotating news strobing disaster politics sports and weather around the clock. Japanese products upon the frontage of buildings replaced the man who used to blow Winston rings. The smoke that used to curl in through the skewed shutters of the hotel. On off on off. And does anything endure? Across 43rd to 46th, plumb in the crossline of the X of Broadway and Seventh he could see the squat shape of the statue of George M. Cohan at the apex of Duffy Square. 1878-1942. Yankee Doodle Boy. Give My Regards to Broadway. You're A Grand Old Flag. Over There. It's no use crying over spilt blood. Behind Cohan, just below the awnings of the Discount Ticket Center, Father Duffy himself stood framed boldly against the stone cross erected by the Catholic War Veterans of the U.S.A. A Life of Service For God and Country. Around this oasis of patriotic memory swirled the hapless crowds and their predators, the hookers, pimps, butt artists and transexuals spreading their venereal scourge onwards, from this nodal point into the furthest sites of the body. Ox sat down on his creaking single bed and examined the charts unfurled from the scroll the Alchemist had handed him in his office. The anatomical study in which the mouth was Manhattan, the Bronx stuck in the nostrils, Queens and Brooklyn at each ear. Harlem, emblazoned across the forehead, emanating rays towards the sign of Lilith and the Macrocosmic Key.

"Boloney!" the private eye snarled to himself, discarding the map onto the floor. He turned to study the mimeographed profiles the Alchemist had included, with names and addresses provided wherever possible, but no photographic evidence. Ox sighed. It is not surprising, with such amateur resources, you need the professional touch. Putting the file aside for closer study, he rose to cross over to the kitchenette, where his weekly wash was bubbling in a blackened pot over the single ring hob. If one could save on laundry bills alone the savings could amount to at least four dollars per week. He lifted his underpants with a wooden spatula but dropped them back in the stew. The pot rattled like a furious djinn on the ring. His dead eye was aching and he removed the eyepatch, examining the crater of the socket in the mirror over the cracked handbasin. Accustomed as he was, he recoiled from the face that stared back at him pitilessly through the film of grime. It looked like a snake which had shed its skin so many times all that remained was a lump of gristle with warts. A worm crawled out of the pit of the eyesocket and slowly wriggled down his cheek. He lifted it carefully off and laid it on the sink, turning to his toolkit to extract a pair of surgical tweezers and his jeweller's eyeglass, which he screwed into the functioning eye. He examined the beast with a professional detachment, then flushed it down the sink.

"Yes Mordecai, Frank Ox has fallen on hard times." He spoke to the wall but the wall did not answer. It shimmered and heaved, but remained, somehow, in place. I am seeing sober what William Burroughs saw through the distorting lens of smack and cocaine, he considered. Addiction and abuse are no longer necessary. All lunches are naked now. I can close my good eye and see Hell's Kitchen the way it was, before the Lincoln Tunnel and the Port Authority Bus Station bulldozed the bars and tenements. The Thieves' Lair, every vice catered for and practised, the poor preying on each other like demented wolves, in Babel, before the fall. The tongues were always confused. But was there nevertheless a camaraderie then, that we have since lost? Memory can't be trusted. If you wish to serve your client, you have to get your mitts on the goods: Documentation, tapes, fingerprints, footprints, fotographs, forensic data, genetic codes, dental records, birthmarks, stigmata, tattoos. Metaphysics are no guide to effective action. Though your young Hispanic hoodlum, Mordecai, might be of some use...

He tipped the boiled briefs into the sink. Strode across the room. Chose from the wardrobe the most ragged raincoat. Put on a pair of cracked army surplus boots and tied them round his feet with frayed string. Folded up the eyepatch and donned a pair of opaque wraparound sunglasses. Replaced his teeth with an old set from the South Bronx morgue and carefully packed the necessary tools in a nested set of plastic Red Apple bags. By the time he reached the street the wind had died down almost completely. The rain washing down the gutters and spraying off the wheels of the cars. The Moslems on the street corner overshadowed by the stall of the Black Hebrew Nation, tall and stern in their garment of pitch black sweaters festooned with gold chains and stars of David, their speaker blaring forth his challenge against the general roar of the square:

"Moses the Liberator was a mighty King in Africa. He was a black man. Joshua, his viceroy, was a black man. Samuel the Prophet was an African. Isaiah, Jeremiah, Hosea. These were the true People of Israel. The mightiest People in Africa. The white man is a descendant of insects. He was a primitive barbarian when we were Kings."

Tell it like it is, brother. The growl of assent followed Frank Ox as he dived down into the Times Square station, hopping over the prone pile of human rags on the steps and inserting one of his tokens into the turnstile, commending the foresight which led him to stockpile them three years before at a dollar-fifteen a pop.

Passing like a ghost in the crowd. The mass moving to and fro, oblivious of what lay beneath their feet. Should I open my mouth and blurt it all out? The underground nations, the shifting earth, the drifting foundations, the clashing tectonic plates, the impermanence of matter, the tangible meltdown, the collapse of proper order. Can't they hear? Can't they feel the vibrations? No, they think it's only the Number 2 train rumbling up from Flatbush to White Plains. Independent Rapid Transit. They have eyes but see not, ears but hear not, senses but sense not. Why did we ever hatch from the egg? The usual crowd of malcontents, maladroits, malignant and maladjusted malingerers packed the Uptown 123 platform, leaning over the rails, staring down the dead eye of the tunnel, paying scant attention to the blind saxophonist and the large black man lambasting himself in tongues, beating his breast and dashing his head against the encrusted steel columns. The train comes, preceded by its glowing Cyclops eye, rattling in to the platform, opening its hissing doors to engorge and disgorge, closing over the invisible man as he is borne north by the Number 3 7th Avenue Express, New Lots to 148th Lenox Terminal. Squeezed below the usual exhortations:

STOP THE AGONY OF HEMORRHOIDS, HERNIAS, WARTS.

**THE SUN TRAVELS 93 MILLION MILES TO GET TO THE SEA -
ALL YOU HAVE TO DO IS TAKE THE TRAIN -
JONES BEACH, CONEY ISLAND, FIRE ISLAND -
PEOPLE BEING CURED OF AIDS - 000,000,000,000.**

The cup bearers, rattling their scant nickels and dimes, passing down the carriages with their tales of infinite woe... I once could walk, and now can barely crawl, I never had a chance to rise, but only to fall, All I need is one good break, Where is the caress that once was nigh, I waited for the voice to speak, but it stayed silent. I called for light and only darkness showed. In my distress I cried out but there were too many cries, How can I be heard in the multitude, Out of the depths I call thee, Lord, gimme twenty cents and I swear to God I won't bother you again ever again...

If you ignore them, eventually they go away. But they will return, in greater numbers-

"Seventysecondstreetchangetolocalnextstopninetysixthwatchtheclosin-doors!"

He disembarked at 96th, rising overground in the post-hurricane mist, carrying his little pile of curiosities, his little sack of violations, his magic bag of intrusions and trespasses that might, or might not, be forgiven...

BZZZZ!

"Allan Darwish here. Who is it?"

"It's me, Caroline."

"Come on up!"

The slow rise in the lift, with its plaintive notice: ON MONDAY MORNING SOMEBODY STOLE MY DETERGENT FROM THE LAUNDRY ROOM. WHAT'S NEXT? ARE THEY GOING TO STEAL THE LAUNDRY? To which some smartass had added in a scrawl: YES! LA MANO NERO!

His door was ajar as the lift arrived. She pushed it open.

"Allan?"

"I'm just finishing something. Come right in." She entered into the small tenth floor apartment, the whole complex of nested rooms about the size of her kitchen, the central bed-living-room with its folded sofa and TV, the recessed bedroom with its folding doors on the left side and the study on the right, the messy table with its stacked files and loose papers, the wiry white haired man hunched over his obsolete portable computer, fingers flying over the keys.

"Saving! Saving! Obey, stupid machine...!" Rising to embrace her with a hug as she still hovered, wondering which pile of newspapers to remove from the sofa or chairs, to where, as he rushed over to the little recessed kitchen to scrabble about for frozen bagels in the ice box and fiddle with the cafetiere: "Coffee, squash or something stronger? It's so unusual, coaxing you out of your cave."

"You've done a lot since I was here last, Allan."

"Oh, yah, moving things around. The sofa was there, wasn't it? I didn't have this partition. I got those paintings up last month. They're by my research assistant, Mahmoud, aren't they something? He really captures the colour of Cairo. The dust, and all those rushing dots. I think he really should exhibit, Frances is willing, but he says he's not ready yet. There are still some patient people in the world. Did you say coffee?"

"Dekaff. No sugar. It's all verbotten anyway."

Looking at her out of the corner of his eye as he bustled. Nodding at the piles, "just put them on the floor. I have to clear it all out anyway. All the news that's shit to print. I need to get a scanner, and a really huge hard disk. You can't believe how much it eats up," seeing she was seated comfortably, "what did the doctor say?"

She was still looking at the two paintings, "yes, I can see the shape of the city, right enough. Isn't that the Citadel? Or was it the Hassan Mosque? It was a long time ago. I should go again. I should go lots of places. Catching up. You know that line from Alice in Wonderland, you have to run as fast as you can just to stay in the same place?"

"You need to slow down, I been telling you for years. Take Benjamin on a holiday. Or just go yourself, have a spree. You're free, black and over thirty- one..." he stopped there, unwilling to go further, bringing the coffee over, seating himself on the straight-backed chair facing her, putting his mug down on the adjacent stool, knitting his hands together, cocking his head. "Tell me."

"What's there to tell. It's no mystery. It's in the blood, didn't we always know that? You can't fight your own cells." He said nothing, but cocked his head further, pursing his lips, widening his eyes. We know each other long enough, Caroline. We've been through it, we've seen the cold dark nights, the bleak sunsets, and a few dawns.

"What does medical science know? It's all primitive stuff, placebos, mantras, we might as well be back with Galen. Acute lymphoblastic leukemia. You know the acronym? ALL. It's most common in children. Maybe I failed to grow up. But at least I got this far. You know it's very uncommon among black people. Touch of the whitebrush somewhere? Great oaks from little acorns grow. A single malignantly transformed progenitor cell begins to proliferate in the haemopoietic system. The blood stream to you yokels. The blast cells have abundant cytoplasm. Merrily increasing by the day."

"Oh shit Caroline."

"Oh shit indeed my friend."

"It's what you suspected."

"It's what I knew. I had all the symptoms. Malaise and anemia, mouth ulcers, unexplained bleeding, pain in the bones, headaches, nausea. It was quite something to hide it all from Benny, acute paranoid that he is. He just thinks its overwork."

"You haven't told him?"

"I suppose he'll have to know sometime."

"But these aren't the middle ages, Caroline. People survive, people are cured..."

"The history varies. The remission rate is seventy percent with chemotherapy but long term survival is not so hot. Fifteen to twenty percent survive more than five years. I need to go in to the hospital for a couple of million more tests. Only then they write the date on the death certificate."

"Bullshit, Caroline. We're in New York City, the hi-tech center of the world."

"Yeah, babies are born with congenital syphillis, t.b. is rife all over the city and people are bedding down in newspapers. Tell it to the Marines. O.K., I'm insured to the eyeballs. There's a special programme at Mount Sinai I can get on. But I still have to do my work, Allan, Goddamit. I'm not going to spend my life on tubes."

"But it's your fucking life, Caroline."

"My fucking life, what is my fucking life? I had to escape from the house, Allan, to come over here to be able to talk to you in peace and quiet, do you realise how many messages are going to be on my machine when I get back? I have twelve patients who have my home number, each with a list of syndromes long as your arm. Somatization and personality disorders, bipolar disorders, you name it. I have a woman who has already drained three therapists and likes to call up at three in the morning, she loves to be shouted at so much. I have the reputation of being the lion-tamer in the department, all the hardest cases."

"But that's what you love to do, you fruitcake..."

"And this new case, this Mo Smith. I shouldn't have let him slip. I've been rewriting my report on him, looking at all the precedents. Male Multiple Personality Syndromes are very rare, Allan, and those that have been diagnosed have been invariably violent. I should have booked him in to a program. But it was so unusual I was hesitant. It sounded like malingering, but now I'm not so sure. It's all such a fad nowadays. MPD's become like M.E., everybody's got it. I need to do the proper tests. Bring in a clinical team, proper assessments. Real MPD's are self-destructive. They have a raft of comorbidities. Munchausen's syndrome, Briquet's, Borderline Personality, PTSD. I was probably wrong to keep him out of the system."

"You can't save the world, Caroline. And even if you want to, you can't do it if you're dead."

"It worked for Jesus Christ, didn't it?"

"Wrong sex, wrong faith, wrong era."

"You're forgetting my Baptist mother." She got up, looking out the window at the night, the line of lights below of Riverside Drive, stretching to the black swathe of the Hudson, and the fairy lights of New Jersey beyond. "Some view, Allan."

"You should have been here in the storm. The wind really whistles, like the devil's steam train. You can hear it blow five hundred miles."

"The Chatanooga Choo Choo. I know I should be scared to death, Allan. But you know what I feel? I feel really pissed. I feel really really furious. I mean I have fucking things to do, for God's sake."

"You have to fight it, Caroline. I know you. This is one thing you can't ignore. You can't just go on as if it'll just go away. You have friends. You just tell us what we can do to help. Don't they have bone marrow transplants, things like that?"

"It's not always appropriate. They have to do their tests. Renal function, serum uric acid, calcium, electrolytes. Testing the blood to destruction. Then the drugs. Corticosteroids, Prednisone, Methotrexate, Mercaptopurine, the combine POMP. Possibly cranial irradiation. It's like exploding a nuclear bomb in your blood. Shit, I really hate to be ill."

"You're a typical doctor, Caroline. At least you don't drink to oblivion, like the Angel."

"The dead past, Allan Darwish. Even deader than the future."

"Does Karim know?"

She walked away from the window. His was not an apartment she could pace about in, so she just reached the study and sat in his writing chair, surrounded by paper flotsam.

"Karim. He'll see it as the judgement of Allah on my profligate life. How should I know what's in his head? How... What am I supposed to do? Hand out mimeographed bulletins? Put an ad in the Times? Or in the Bulletin Board of the Voice, beside the acupuncture and the Shaman from SoHo: Doctor Caroline Dexter announces her impending death. Don't send wreaths on account of hayfever. I don't know, Allan. I've counselled so many people I don't know what to say to myself. I just don't want pity. I don't want to be dependent, you know what I'm saying?"

"Nobody can pity you, Caroline. You've made your own life."

"I don't mind the whole flock seeing me as the crazy mother bitch, suckling her young, I can take it. Just so long as it's not the other way round..."

"Even in the heavyweight champeenship of the world the contenders have to rest between bouts. Life hammers you you build defences..."

"This one will have to be a honey..."

"I didn't..."

"Look, if my time is up it's up. Maybe it's the truth: God's throwing his weight around in my direction, because I didn't pay my respects. I should have listened to my mother. Gentle Jesus, meek and mild. The lamb that came with a sword. I never could abide that mixup. If it's so it's so. I'll go down fighting, not trussed into an intravenous web."

"I know it sounds like crap, Caroline, but let's face it together, like we've done before. It just got that tougher."

"It's not crap, Allan. You know I appreciate it. It's just so fucking unnecessary! Who needs this?"

"Nobody. Listen, before we get really heavy..." He rose to the kitchen cabinet and took down determinedly a bottle of Black Label and two glasses. "I think this is the prescription, before they cut you off... Or are on anything yet?" She shook her head and made no objection to his handing her the half full glass.

"I should call Aram. Sometimes you need the Armenian view. The long look across the centuries."

"Sure Allan, why the hell not?"

"Do you want to eat? Should I call in from the Gourmet Szechuan?"

"Whatever." He found the menu stuck on a board by the kitchenette, beside the monthly brochure of the Museum of Modern Art, an offer of discount reading spectacles and an invitation to a conference on North African Poetry and the Fundamentalist Siege at Columbia. Dialling on the kitchen extension: "Hallo, yes. I want to order out, for delivery, I have one of your coupons. Yes, I want... shall I choose...?

Yah, we'll have the crystal shrimp dumplings, one order of steamed pork shiu mai.... one lamb with Szechuan ma la sauce... one empire three delicates... yes, and I want one white rice and one brown rice... no..." She shook her head, "make that two brown rice. And can you make the lamb not too spicy. That's right. It's Darwish, 443 West 97th... it's the last house before Riverside Drive... apartment 1003. Yes. How long? Fifteen minutes." Hanging up the phone. "Is that all right for you? Or is it too much?"

"It's O.K.. It's fine. Maybe I should get everybody together and have a party. Make it an official announcement. God, this is insane."

"Isn't it. What can I say, Caroline? We'll fight. We've always fought. What else can we do? God knows, I know I've been so lucky so far. I've brushed by so much pain and suffering and somehow I've been spared. And no guilt, Caroline. If only I can still do some things..."

"D'you think we should have asked for spring rolls?"

"D'you want me to phone them back? There's still time."

"No, don't bother. Call Aram, its time I got really smashed. The last hurrah. Or is it the lost weekend? Wasn't that a movie, with that guy, what the hell's his name, Benny would know, him and Salim, with their endless video gossip... Delirium tremens, beetles coming out of the walls..."

"You remember that time we got smashed in Cairo? That was in Subhi Atrash's house. The architect. He took us to that hotel building his client wanted him to add three floors to. But there was a family of squatters living on the roof, up above the city, with their uncles, aunts, grandma, chickens and the goat, remember the goat? On the roof of the Nile Continental. And they couldn't be got out for love or money? The client was furious. Subhi was so delighted. He called it the `revenge of the sans culottes.' The poor would prevail by sheer numbers. Anwar Sadat couldn't stop them. It was after Camp David, remember?"

"Jimmy Carter, who could forget. Well, almost everybody forgets everything. But I thought he was a good man. They ate him up, the Zionist lobby never forgave him for that. And then Iran."

"The `students following the line of the Imam.' I was going to ask you, among the books I left, I think somewhere on the second floor, in the stairway, those booklets I found in London, the `Documents From the U.S. Espionage Den.' You know all those compilations of the CIA stuff they found when they took over the embassy. The CIA clerks tried to shred them but the Iranian students stuck them together, strip after strip. That was some labour of devotion, eh? Anyway, I was going to come to look for them. I'm working on my Irangate piece... But it's not important..."

"Everything is important, Allan, every Goddamn thing. Every trivial word, jot and tittle. Every sigh and burp and fart. The streets of Cairo, all that dust and crowding, those alleys just about wide enough to take a donkey, with two full streams of traffic and masses of people in between - that taxi, that tried to force its way through a gridlock of five lanes of cars, the cities of the dead, and that guard who tried to seduce you in the Islamic Museum..."

"What d'you mean tried? You know me Caroline. I came back the next day and we did it in a closed section. Just beside Muhammad Ali's crown jewels. I never pass up a hunk like that."

"You're incorrigible, Allan. I hope to God you take care nowadays. Sometimes I can't believe you're still alive."

"I told you, I'm Mr Lucky. But luck..." he refilled her glass, and his own, then turned and picked up the study phone. "Aram, its Allan. Caroline's here. There's a crisis. We're drinking whiskey. Can you come?" Replacing the phone. "He'll be right over."

"With his occult skills. That's what I need. Wasn't there an Armenian hero who had his head cut off but kept fighting in the battle of Marzipan, or whatever?"

"The battle of Manzikert, could be. Armenians are always doing that. But what can you do against the storms, honey?"

"Just rage against the dying of the light. Dylan Thomas. And death shall have no dominion. There was a fighter for you. Didn't he drink himself to death?"

"Did you ever meet my friend Rashid Hussein? The Palestinian poet. He got drunk in his apartment and it burned down with him inside. The crazies of small nations. They always burn the brightest. The Palestinowelsh. I can remember that poem: 'Though wise men at their end know dark is right, Because their words had forked no lightning they Do not go gentle into that good night.' He wrote that about his father. They were not close, to say the least. What can we do? We all fail to live up to the hopes. But its when you know you've let the young folk down that you despair..."

"I never knew you to despair, Allan."

"Dissimulation. It's in my heritage. The old Shi'a tradition. *Taki'a.* When the Faith is threatened you are allowed, no, commanded to pretend to conform. 'Whoever disbelieves in God after believing, except those who are compelled while their hearts are firm in faith...' that's the Koranic formula. Allowing the weak to survive. Like the Jews who converted to Christianity but kept their faith in secret, in Spain and Portugal, the marranos. What's important is what you feel inside. Isn't that so very Unamerican? McCarthy zeroed in on that."

"You think American Communists were Shi'as?"

"Absolutely, my dear. They had all the hallmarks. Self flagellation, martyrology, a fanatic belief in the Ayatollah Joe Stalin. It's all a perfect fit. You know it, you're a psychiatrist, honey. Fabulation, isn't that what you call it? Believing in the Elysian Fields. They still call me up, asking me to meetings to discuss how the CIA recruited Gorbachev. How the Soviet masses were robbed of their birthright and how can we reverse the trend."

"How to build a better past, it's always the same story. But it makes sense if you don't have a future."

"It never makes sense, Caroline. If we lie to ourselves, how can we make any claim for what we tell others? It's the first sin of scholarship."

"It's still a sin in psychiatry too. You have to get at the traumas, the worse the better. We're all still in hock to Freud, except now its all concrete, not fantasies. The return of the repressed. If you can't remember how your parents raped you when you were two years old, even under deep hypnosis, then boy, that must have been a lulu."

"But you've always fought against that."

"I fought for common sense. But that's not in the textbooks. It's all tests. MMPI, DDIS, DSM-Three-R, the SHSS. Stanford Hypnotic Susceptibility Scale. The search for diagnostic validation. We make up syndromes and then try to fit reality to our theories. When I delivered a paper about this at the ASP in eighty-eight they nearly struck me off the register. You should have seen the conversion syndromes: People coughing, rustling papers, creaking chairs. If they could have pointed the bone at me and wished me dead they would have done it right there and then. Careers are built on categorization. It's Adopt-a-syndrome out there. That's why MPD's become so popular. You get to be on Oprah, Letterman, Larry King Live. You know the drill, Allan."

"Sure. It's sexy. People want to escape. In an individualist society if you don't have the right kind of identity you make another one up. If you're a failure you need to blame somebody else. You're cut off, nobody will help you. That's why self-help is such an industry. Nobody can be a loser."

"Right. Which is why Mo Smith fascinates me so much. His syndrome is so unique. MPD's alternates usually serve to take on all the blame. A rapist-killer blames his alternate. A self-mutilating woman is coerced. Alternates are often as pathetic as the mother-person. But this man's alternates are so robust. The Arab traveller, the best-seller, the mysterious Alchemist, the sadist domina, the all-powerful Pharaoh. It doesn't fit the profile. But if he's acting out, where did he get it all? If your theory's right, and he read it all in the library, how does he retain it? That's savant territory. I've read up on that. It doesn't fit. The categories are defied."

"Thank God for that. That's the buzzer, I'll get it." Getting up, a little unsteadily now, to the intercom. "Hello. Yes, I ordered a delivery. Come right up. It's the tenth floor." Turning back to her. "Dinner."

"About time. I'm fucking starved. What do I tell them all, Allan? They all expect me to be different. They all think I'm so fucking strong. Look at me, I can't even lift this glass."

"That's because it's not full enough."

"To Karim."

"Karim."

"Our son."

"Yes, Caroline."

"Goddamit Allan! All our fine words. What have we done for the boy? What have we done for him?"

"We kept an open door. Was I wrong? I probably was. Remember, you wanted it this way. We were both so fucking young. You did what you could. He's chosen his own way. He's not in jail, he's not mugging people, he's not on drugs. That's a miracle in this city."

"He should have had a father."

"It's a little late now."

Knock knock knock.

"Hello. Who is it? What?" Opening the door to confusion. A pudgy Chinese boy with a carrier bag in collision with a tall, falconlike Armenian with the biggest beak on the Upper West Side: "Hey, Allan! We got here together. There's a weird ragged white man lying across your main doorway with his ear pressed against the brickwork. Hi Caroline. Ooh, Black Label." Heading directly for the bottle. "This looks like a Palestinian wake." Eyes darting about, trying to catch the situation hanging in the air, while Allan counts out twenty-five dollars and thirty-five cents, handing another three dollars to the delivery boy, "thank you, thank you, enjoy." "Don't mind me, Allan, I've already eaten." "There's enough for three, no problem." "Hey, you put those paintings up."

"Aren't they something."

"He has talent, Mahmoud. He's wasted on you. He's wasted in this fucking country. He'd do well in Germany you know. They have a thing about Middle Eastern art. It's all part of their guilt complex. Arabs, Jews, the whole thing. You'd be amazed. But here we're just lemons, do you know. Strangers in paradise. How are you doing, Caroline?"

"Well..."

"Sit down, Aram. Keep the bottle. You'll need it. Caroline has been to the quack. She's had the first test results in. They confirm what we thought."

"Oh shit."

"She has to go in to the hospital for more tests, then the treatment starts. It's going to be tough."

"Oh shit."

"You're both saying the same thing. I'm sitting here with two college professors with a dozen degrees between you and all you can say is oh shit."

"Oh fuck. I'm sorry Caroline."

"So am I Aram."

"We're past all that. We're getting drunk, and we're pigging out on Szechuan Gourmet. So here's the plates, forks, chopsticks anyone? Some water, for a chaser. Now this is how it stands to date. Lamb Ma La sauce, Empire Three Delicates, this must be it, Crystal Shrimp Dumplings, this is the Pork Shiu-mai, no, these are the shrimp dumplings, so this must be the Pork Shiu-mai. Let's eat before it gets cold."

"I want to hear everything, Caroline. The symptoms, the causes, the etiology, the precise diagnosis, the form of treatment, the prognosis. It's best to face these things absolutely square. You make them a concrete enemy. You get to know its every facet. You learn its strong points and its weak points. Then we can discuss strategy."

"This is not a political problem, Aram. Its cancer."

"Good, you said the word. Savor it. Cancer - a cardinal element: Water. The moon. The crab. The retrogade movement of the sun after the summer solstice. The sideways movement symbolises crookedness and evasion. In the ancient Sumerian myth the crab is an aspect of Nina, Mistress of the Sea. In buddhism it is the period between incarnations, death, between births. In astrology, the gate from the Milky Way into manifestation, the waning power of the sun. But it is also a lunar aspect of love and inspiration, purity and tears. The pearl, constancy and domestic happiness. Nothing is ever all bad."

"Don't come all new age on me Aram."

"New age fuck. These are the oldest timbres. Echoes of primeval fears. The immolated kings. In the month of Cancer the king went up to the top of his ziggurat and in the full view of all the people began cutting off his lips, nose and ears. He cut off bits of his flesh and threw them out to the multitude, till he could cut no more except for the last slash through his throat. You have to understand these echoes, Caroline. The fear of pain, not of death. Death is the easy part. It's the pain."

"I can be afraid of both if I want to."

"You have to get used to your fear. I'm not talking any nonsense about making it welcome. Hate the bastard. It's a male thing. Pain is female."

"Thank you very much."

"Is this all the whiskey you have, Allan?"

"It was nearly full when we started. Let me take a look. No, that's all the whiskey. But there is, my friends, the Tunisian fig wine! Bouka l'Oasis. And the Lebanese Arak."

"Then we are all set."

The sweet drumroll of juiced up remembrance, rolled back time, the way we never were, the music of the temporal lobes. The night the Cubans came to town, the day Richard Nixon said I am not a crook, the great Social Deviancy ball of 1971, the benefit for the Outlaws of Amerika, you were fifteen Caroline and raring to go remember that's where we met Aram, oh Caroline every fucking heart was broken, you should have seen her in the March on Washington Aram, twelve years old with your father Sam, Caroline, Goddamn I miss him so, what he didn't know about African- American history not worth even thinking about, all that mass of people, Yes, I remember he took me see Martin Luther King I was ten then I was really awestruck, it was just after the Speech, it was like meeting God, and to know my father was his buddy, it really made it very close, God does not make great speeches Caroline, read his book God was the Crush Limbo of his time, Oh shit Aram fill my fucking glass man, when was it we first met Allan shit my memory is all shot to hell it wasn't Washington it was, no wait, it was at home wasn't it, that's right, on 138th Street, Andy Young was there and Jesse and all those people from the SCLC, I was rather hot on Andy Young at that time, then my father introduced me to his best friend Freedom Rider from the old days, I don't know what I expected I'd never met an Egyptian American before, you weren't quite black enough, I remember, I treated you with due suspicion I was a strict Malcolm fan, oh God that man, look at all the idolisation that's been going on Spike Lee and all that, He was a smart kookie Caroline he was constantly evolving he would have eclipsed them all, moving away from Elijah Muhammad and all that crew, Well here they are all back again Allan stronger than ever and, the conversation skirting close to forbidden faultlines, she stopped, waving an empty glass at Allan, who replenished warily, while Aram drank down the last Black Label, sticking his finger in the bottle then laboriously wiggling it out, the black experience, African-American, when will people decide what to call themselves for God's sake, it's a crisis of identity, always has been Aram, well look at the Armenians, Oh God Aram I knew we would get there soon enough, No but, you understand, an unbroken history running for five thousand years, from the first kingdom of Urartu that was king Aram I will have you know, absolutely, from the beginning we had our troubles with the Assyrians, the Persians and the Medes we saw them all off they would come into the mountains, burn a few cities, leave their own corpses and slink off, Tiglath-Pileser, King Midas the Phrygian, Ashurbanipal, Sargon of Akkad, we saw them all off, it was only the Scythians who finally got us, the barbarian Russian hordes, we had a treaty with them but they stabbed us in the back, Armenians are always being stabbed in the back Aram, It's because our back is so broad Allan we carry the whole fucking world around on it, wherever we are, scattered to the four corners of the earth but still we know who we are we've kept our history, our legends and our language that's what an identity is, Well we won't go into that now Aram, Why not it's what these arguments are all about now who's blacker than who who's more African than the Africans the sun people and the ice people all this total bullshit, I agree with you there Aram but it's the madness of nationalism not of not having enough nationalism if you see what I mean, no, it's all the craziness of America, this decline and fall, the loss of empire before you even had a grasp of it, That's bullshit Aram the empire is still holding fast it's just the appearance of chaos they're still going strong, No but look at this thing in Somalia look at Grenada nickel and dime invasions what's the point, No but look at Iraq that wasn't small change five hundred thousand troops when it's important they pull out the stops the rest is just for show the empire isn't done yet, Somalia that's just a trap Bush set for Clinton it's just an election ploy, You're wrong there Caroline I've been reading the literature, the databases, oil company reports there are deposits out there in the desert and it's the horn of Africa after all, The ho-o-orn of Africa, Oh yes man, No but, I was going to say something about nationalism but what was it I forgot, more Arak? No I remembered all this Back to Africa shit, Marcus Garvey, he called it Black Zionism but now they've dropped that phrase they've written it out of the history books it's all rewriting the past to suit the present, Nothing new in that Caroline everybody's at it, No but Allan my point is it's much worse when it's the victims who do it, the only people we're fooling is ourselves puffing us up with all this crap about being descendants of Pharaoh when if you read nineteenth-century black writers they all identified with the Hebrew slaves, Nobody wants to be identified with slaves these days people want to be victims *and* proud of their heritage it doesn't go together, Why not, Armenians have managed to be both, well, you're noted schizoids Aram sorry to insult your whole nation, It's nothing new Allan we are the original stiff-necked people nothing gets through apropos Pharaoh we should ask the horse's mouth your new patient Mo Smith - Pharaoh Merenptah, son of Rameses, he should have the answers, we were just talking about him, Multiple Personality Syndrome, Well you remember that old sixties' joke - you're never alone with schizophrenia, That's a clinical misunderstanding Allan, schizophrenia has nothing to do with it, totally different syndrome, About George Bush, how did we get to George Bush, Somalia, Allan, he knows he's going to lose to Clinton so he leaves him this little time bomb did you ever see anything more ludicrous than those troops landing in blackface on the beach with all the world's cameras live on CNN and all those people starving for food not for Abrams tanks and M-16's they've got plenty of those, It's the global pillage Aram, What, I think you've been mixing your drinks there have some oh shit it's finished, You finished it half an hour ago Aram, What the fuck's the time? I'm supposed to phone my colleague at Amherst there's some intrigue going on in the department can you imagine I'm being done for political correctness, Well you can certainly plead not guilty there, No it's this woman this writer Cymbeline Ozark, the super-Zionist, she's been after my hide for years now she says I've been banning Jewish authors from my curriculum, its outrageous who is there except Jewish authors it's all Israelis on my list Simha Flapan Benny Morris Tom Segev, all the revisionist historians she wants me to give them Menachem Begin's The Revolt I don't mind but you can't find it anywhere who will print that trash? Do you know any feminist fascists I can assign? Plenty, Aram. Oh, don't you two get started you sound like Crush Limbo already. No, but... They want to impeach me, faculty hearings, nail my hide up on the door they don't know what dealing with an Armenian means... You will prevail Aram, You bet your sweet ass but I'd better go oh shit Caroline we haven't talked about... you'll let me know won't you, blow by blow, fight the good fight, don't let the bastards get you down, what's that they used to say, fuck 'em and feed 'em beans, you phone me tomorrow you hear me, I'm off now, No Aram that's the door to the bathroom, oh is it, my God, so it is it's the Tunisian fig-wine I don't know what they put in it, it's only thirty-something proof but there's a mule kick in it somewhere, right, I know my way, it's just round the corner, oh Allan I was meaning to tell you but the Chinese delivery wiped it from my mind they're stealing the laundry in your basement I saw a notice in your lift, That's all right, we know about it Aram, well bye Caroline for God's sake keep the flag flying the sun still comes up in the morning look at the storm we had but now it's over nothing left of it but upturned crates and some smashed trees on Long Island who wants to live on Long Island anyway yuppie new age layabouts what a man needs is some genuine mountain air the Blue Mountains remember Allan the lake the lodge the writers' colony what was that woman's name who runs it Grace Keighley her father was in the CIA wasn't he, owned all that land and then she inherited it and gave it over for subversives and enemies of the state like us, ah well, Allan, we should all go up there Caroline breathe some good air God's own country remember when we saw the bear? Not to speak of the flies. The lime tick, yes, now I remember we couldn't dare take our socks off up there, wandering around like boy scouts in short pants, you will keep me posted won't you, Caroline? O.K., I'm off now, yes, it was you, wasn't it, Allan, who wrote LA MANO NERA on that notice in the lift? I recognised your handwriting, take care they don't evict you, these co-op people they can be damn fierce don't I know it I'll tell you some other time all those soft-hearted ecologists but when they get started it's like the KKK in action, O.K. bye now - oh and, don't forget to ask Pharaoh, personally - Merenptah - his father exiled the Israelites - let my people go, and off they went, out into the wilderness, with all their children and their kine, what the hell is kine Allan? out into the uncertain future, with nothing but the faith in who they are, of course they were Armenians, I'm going to write about that some day. Bye Aram, that's the emergency door. You don't want to walk all the way down, ten floors. That's the lift. I'll phone you in the morning. Without fail, Allan. I promise you Aram. Bye Caroline. Bye Aram, see you. Bye.

ONWARDS! ONWARDS! No thanks for all the memories. The wind has stopped completely, its ghost hanging in the air like any one of the City's latent threats. Don't fuck with me, baby, or I'll be back. You can bet your life. The way the traffic oooozes past, like a long gob of metal chewing gum. UP! UP! UP! From Cooper Square and the Traffic Violations Bureau, up 4th Avenue, over Wannamaker Place, East 10th, East 11th, the Grace Episcopal Church and the Corner Billiards cafe, over 12th, 13th to the corner of 14th Street, the main thoroughfare of Discount Centers, from rags to Rolexes, from abacii to zithers, looking across towards Union Square. Remembering her cool suggestions at the Welfare: Try the Shelter at 14th Street, Mr Smith. Just so we know where to find you. I know it can be a tough place but... the winter's coming, the deep deep cold, the blizzards' savage bite...

But why should I be found if I'm not lost? North South West East. I'll detour West. Crossing Broadway and University Place, past the Grand Discount Center, the Jackpot, Kids' Tower, Gina Fashions, Woolworths, across Fifth, by Island Sportswear and Sotshun Corporation Cameras, Jeans and Sneakers, the City of New York Social Security Dept Waverly Income Maintenance Center, American Dollar Store, Jay's Bargains, Price Busters Electronics Beep Me Beepers, across Sixth to Il Cappo Spanish Food (Hoy Comida Latino), the Asson Bazaar and Titanic Fashions.

On one side of the street the Armory. On the south side, the iron gates of the Salvation Army Centennial Memorial Temple: NEW YORK'S LONGEST RUNNING EVANGELICAL CRUSADE. Etched on the wall, the founder's resolute pledge –

"While Women weep, as they do now, I'll fight.
While men go to prison, in and out,
in and out, as they do now, I'll fight.
While there is a drunkard left,
While there is a poor lost girl upon the streets,
While there remains one dark soul
Without the light of God, I'll fight - -
I'll fight to the very end."

- General William Booth.

- A man after my own heart!

- Shut up Jesse, when did you ever fight for anything sitting there scratching your nuts in the dead sea sun, scrolling away the only reason you didn't booze yourselves to death out there you couldn't get any, waiting for your nailed up saviour to turn the water into wine, and not even any water anywhere, just that brackish salty sludge... Oh ye of little faith! Don't mock the poor man, he's only trying to do his best in a wicked body. Who was that, Ann? Beatrice? Anyone seen Merenptah around? Still thinkin he can get out of here, out of the darkness into the light? Good ole General Booth. The Watchtower. No, that's the Jehovah's Witnesses you're thinking about there, shut up Arnold, good solid friends of yours Jesse, did you know they believed that Abraham Isaac and Jacob would come back to earth back in the 1920's, and they actually bought a house for them in San Diego - Beth Sarim, house of the Princes. No really? It's amazing what you learn if you hang about in here. Stick around with me, babe, you'll learn plenty.

- Shush shush shush. Don't all talk at once for God's sake. Settling wearily down on the wet steps leading up to the Salvation Army Memorial Temple gate, where already a group of wayfarers tarry, some sitting cross armed and gloomy, others stretched out on soggy newspapers that had soaked up the rain. Behind the gate, those who had sheltered in the temple doorway from the storm secured with battered thermos flasks, rusting kerosene cookers and their sodden parcels of food. With a sigh, Mo took the weight off his feet. Waiting for nightfall. This is as good a place as any. The soup kitchen opens at eight-thirty.

Chicken broth and noodles, yum yum yum. You should be so lucky.

Who's that, Lincoln? When I was in the training camp in Tanzania it was sadza, day in day out. We lay awake at night, wracked by hunger pangs, half-dreaming of surrender to the Boers and great breifleisches of boervurst and beefsteak. Not that it was like that in their jails, I can tell you. They mixed in cockroaches with your mealie-meal. Those big African motherfuckers, ever seen one Arnold? Eight fucking inches long, and fat as your arm. Must have been nourishing enough Link. Way to go, man, way to go.

Too many fucking memories. Here come de judge, the wandering Pharaoh, glooming up from the catacombs. " - *hail, the night watchers of the crocodile, whose faces are hidden and who dwell in the divine temple of the north...* Give us a break. Never wake a sleepwalker, Goddamit, just humour him it's only a passing phase... Come on brother, take a moment's rest, Thank you Battuta, at least there's a mentsch here somewhere... nobody helps anybody, there's no solidarity...

But now the rain has stopped and the night lights have bounced on. No diminution in the blare and screech of the traffic, the headlights dappling Booth's Covenant - I'll Fight to the Bitter End... ZZZZzzzzzzzzzzz.....

The body sleeps, as night falls Uptown as well as Down, far away from the hub, and a tense silence falls on Riverside Drive, punctuated only by the rush of the Henry Hudson Parkway and the car alarm sirens wailing emptily. The occasional chugga-chugga-chug of hip-hop booming out from a brother in transit. And all the usual thuds, hisses, and sighs. So many trumpets blaring the last trump, but no corpses dare to stir. At the corner of 97th street, a gaunt figure in rags shifts none-the-less. Hugging the walls, Frank Ox peeks from within his derelict disguise, observing the one-dimensional world with his live eye while his dead eye peers back into the soul.

Is anyone looking? Between the motion and the act. Slipping in to the sanctum of number 443, in the instant between the entrance of a keyholding resident and the quick exit of another, slurking through the narrow lobby into the laundry room, freezing a while in place alongside a basket of rumpled linen and shirts. So successful his subterfuge that a tenant from floor Five picks him up and deposits him in the dryer along with her own grubby apparel. Like the fine and professional eye that he is Frank Ox cavils not, revolving in somber silence. The fires of the furnace heating the drum and turning his skin beetroot red.

- Ah, but it was a mere nothing, Mordecai, compared to the Mephistopheles Case... Cavorting down there in my asbestos demon suit, waving a pitchfork and shaking my tail. Hanging out in the eighth Bowge of the Nether Hell, between the Counsellors of Fraud and the Sowers of Discord... Blend in, that's the whole Torah on one leg... The fly on the wall, the worm in the wood, the snake in the grass... I lectured once at the FBI Hiding School. Those were the days, I was respected then. Those young Christian Scientist pip-squeaks hung on my every word as I held forth on illusions and camouflage... Oh, yes...

Stepping out, at the end of the drying cycle, before the launderer returns for her clothes, Ox summons the service lift and rises, rises, rises to the tenth floor with the brooms, the mops, the empty pails and bags of flotsam left there by the somnambulant super... Slooping up to the door and attaching his pseudopoda to listen for the soft tones of the old friends baring their souls to each other within. Muffled mumbles about Jimmy Carter and the streets of Cairo and Muhammad Ali's crown jewels. Ooooh those private confessions... Darting into the emergency stairway as the lift disgorges a Chinese food delivery and a dishevelled Armenian... Reattaching himself to the wall as the drunken seance flows on, and then, when she left, accompanied by the professor to the lift, upon somewhat unsteady legs, Ox attaches himself to the rim of her coat, and slimmering into her duffle pocket, as the good night embrace is cut short by the elevator's arrival, and she descends, with Frank Ox in situ, down, down, down to the surface of New York, back to the street and the wailing car alarms crying out at their real or imagined violation to an indifferent night, which wraps around Caroline, hooting and flaring, as she picks her way over the running gutters, across West End Avenue and down Broadway, ignoring the happy crowd behind the plate glass of the Szechuan Gourmet and continuing to Amsterdam, down towards the corner of 93rd. Unlocking her door and pushing aside the affections of the giant hound, who barks in an inexplicable panic and paws at her coat pocket, but Frank Ox has already darted away, slithering up the wall and attaching himself by suckers to the ceiling, utilising the shape changing faculties developed in the FBI's Defence Against Extra-Sensory Perception program (DAESP) to excrete an opaque odour, so that the dog darts about, frustrated, and she slaps it away and climbs the stairs, exhausted, to collapse into the bath, almost forgetting to close the tap before the water over-runs, sinking, sinking, as Frank Ox sloops through into her bedroom-study, ignoring the hand woven tapestries of West African scenes and motifs, the Moroccan mirror and decorated brass plates, cote d'ivoire masks and Yoruba ivory, the Zairienne figurines, the hermaphroditic gods with giant phalluses and immense dugs hanging to their knees, making instead straight for her work table, the lamp still lit, casting a pool of dusty illumination upon the scattered pages of her unfinished - **Interim Report: "Mohammad Ndabaninghi (Mo) Smith" - Multiple, Misappropriated, or Mistaken Identity? by Caroline Dexter, M.D.. 2nd Draft.**

Does Multiple Personality Syndrome exist? Or is it an invention of therapists who have over-invested in an exotic disorder? The pendulum has swung to and fro many times since cases of "co-consciousness" began to appear in the late nineteenth century. In 1887 the French case of Felida X surfaced, in which the patient, diagnosed as "hysterical", threw up a number of alternative personalities during fits of "involuntary spasms and vomitting." More cases were reported by Dessoir, Binet, Myers and others. These cases were discussed in the context of the emerging ideas of a dichotomy between the "conscious" and "unconscious" spheres of the mind, leading directly from Janet to Breuer and Freud. But the "discovery" of multiple personalities was closely tied in with hypnosis, which was dismissed, in 1909, by Freud, as a "method of doubtful ethical value." The most prominent case in the literature of this period was that of Christine Beauchamp, reported by Morton Prince, who described her condition:

"Miss Christine R. Beauchamp... is a person in whom several personalities have become developed; that is to say, she may change her personality from time to time, often from hour to hour... Two of these personalities have no knowledge of each other or of the third, excepting such information as may be obtained by inference or second hand... The personalities come and go in kaleidoscopic succession, many changes often being made in the course of twenty-four hours..." (Prince, pp 1-2)

Prince's methodology, and the suspicion of transference and over-investment, have been criticised by McCurdy (1941), Coons (1980) and Sutcliffe & Jones (1962). Narrowing diagnostic criteria backgrounded MPD for many years, and there has been criticism of the prevalence of the syndrome in the United States (57% of global recorded cases - Taylor & Martin, 1944). Skepticism about MPD has

lasted well into the 1970's, when the pendulum swung sharply to encompass a veritable "epidemic" of new cases. Coons (1986) estimated that 6,000 cases had been diagnosed in the preceding ten years. The number of alternates reported has also escalated. Early cases report between two and four personalities, but recent reports have cited cases of 300 or 400 personalities, and the matter may be clearly getting out of hand. The excess zeal on the part of therapists may well play a part in this increase. The validation of the disorder has occupied a great part of the literature on this subject. (Pro: Herzog 1984, Coons, 1980, Kluft 1985, Ross & colleagues 1989, Bliss 1984, Solomon 1983, etc; Con: Fahy 1988, Spiegel 1988, Putnam 1986, Thigpen & Cleckley 1984, Simpson 1988 etc). Simpson wrote:

"The extent of the patient's pathology is directly proportional to the amount and intensity of the therapy... It appears to be the norm that further `personalities', often more rewarding and entertaining for the audience, emerge in therapy..."

The issue of MPD has been particularly problematic in the relatively few cases of male MPD recorded, which have been highlighted in legal defences of high-profile serial offenders, such as the Hillside Strangler, Bianchi (Schwartz, 1981), who failed to have his MPD recognized as a valid defence for multiple murder. On the other hand, the case of Billy Milligan (Keyes, 1981), who claimed to have 24 alternates, who caused him to commit a variety of crimes ranging from theft and vandalism to robbery, drug dealing, kidnapping, rape and murder was recognised as a valid MPD, leading to hospitalization. The case of Milligan, with its graphic evidence of severe abuse in childhood and sociopathic family environment, appears a textbook instance of the syndrome.

In the case of "Mo" Smith, on the other hand, we face a challenge to the prevailing perspectives. It would seem highly unprofessional to even contemplate an analytic report without carrying out a single one of the standard test procedures. IQ tests, MMPI (the Minnesota Multiphasic Personality Inventory), the Lachar-Wrobel Critical Item List, GAS (Global Assessment Scale, DES (Dissociative Experiences Scale), SCID-D (Structured Clinical Interview for Dissociative Disorders) and DDIS (Dissociative Disorders Interview Schedule) - none has been applied to this subject. Tests of comorbidity, tests to quantify borderline personality disorders, Briquet's syndrome, or PTSD, have not been done. The methodology, such as it is, has been to begin to compile an anecdotal history, from the horse's mouth, as it were, of the alternates as separate entities, withdrawing any special techniques, such as hypnosis or any form of suggestion, from the entire process. (The drums of the American Analysts' Association, rolling Caroline Dexter out on her ass...)

I have no doubt that, in a clinical environment, the subject, "Mo" Smith, will be encouraged to fabulate on a scale commensurate with the most extreme, or "colorful", cases in the existing literature. I cannot rule out the possibility, proposed by one of my colleagues, that the subject is displaying massive recall capabilities of reading up his "subjects" in public libraries (and so would be perfectly capable of reading up on the literature of MPD, as other recorded cases have indicated [Casey 1991, Harris, in Spencer 1989, Biaggi, in Bliss & Bliss 1985]). This would stipulate, from the scope of the histories of the eight (so far) alternates, a memory almost on the scale of those individuals described as having "Savant's syndrome." It would indicate an almost eidetic capacity to absorb written material, and re-organise it in memory to provide consistent and separate identities as a wilful fabulation. Clearly, without testing for intelligence quotient it is not possible to form a valid view on this issue, but it appears to be a circular argument: if "Mo" Smith is smart enough to remember and fabulate on such a scale, he can certainly fool the standard IQ.

In "Savant's syndrome" (Treffert 1989) it is thought that the special, almost miraculous skill of the savant, such as the ability to play any piece of music that is heard, or calculate dizzying calendar counts, or draw or sculpt astonishing likenesses from memory, is an integral part of a handicap which impairs the ability to live a normal life, from minor retardation to severe disability, such as the blind musical prodigy Lemke. The existence of Savant skills in an otherwise functioning person is rare, apart from those gifted individuals who become great scholars and artists, such as Mozart. But it is difficult to admit what we call "genius" residing together with the socially dislocated reality of such a person as "Mo" Smith.

How many geniuses are wandering out there? We have case histories by the thousands of persons who could blossom out if given "a break." Among the tens of thousands unable to cope with the pressures of bad housing and unemployment, untreated disease, drug abuse and family breakdown, there are incredible losses of our human resources... (omit? elaborate?) We are aware that a range of dissociative disorders are

caused by childhood deprivation, abuse and trauma. It remains to be seen whether "Mo" Smith can be cajoled into revealing family background, given that I am unable to trace his existence in the available records. (still drawing a blank on the SS, Police records, Army records, Missing Persons... not the first time, Caroline, but at least the others told their stories... still waiting for "Ann Hedonia" to reveal more about the "commune" in Vermont...) **There might be early physical trauma which might be ascertained from medical tests, to explain the "savant" skills...** (A little absurd, is it not, to search for childhood trauma when the trauma of the City is all pervading... "Treating" the mind when the body is decaying...)

MPDs have been known for their destructive behaviour either towards themselves or others, compulsive crime, self-mutilation and Munchausen Syndrome, as well as Munchausen-Syndrome-By-Proxy. There appears to be no sign of any of this type of behaviour in our relatively few meetings so far with "Mo" Smith. We would appear to know what he is up to: Wandering the streets of this City, this grand metropolis, this hub of finance, this refuge for the poor, the huddled masses, yearning to be free... But Felix kept on walking, walking the grid, heading on into the dire dawn of winter... the killing time of the unsheltered...

We know that Mo Smith is just walking, walking, inoffensively, with his new boots and paper cup. But what, we might ask, are his alternates doing, in the rippling shades of his soul?

Click click click. Click click click. The shutter of Frank Ox's miniature camera snaps away, leeching page after page onto a tiny strip of silver halides, which twinkle and shift to the rapid variations of light and dark. Knowledge is power. Information is currency. The customer is always right. Forewarned is forearmed. When, in the course of human events, it becomes necessary for a body to dissolve the bands which connect it to itself, and to assume among the powers of the earth, the separate and equal station to which the outlaws of Nature and Nature's God entitle them... We hold these truths to be the self's evidence...

SHANTI,
SHANTI,
SHANTI...

Here endeth the First Cycle of the Wanderings of Mohammad Ndabaninghi Smith. In the Second Cycle, Mo Smith will proceed in winter to traverse Manhattan, while his Alternates make their bid for freedom, strengthened in their will to achieve self-determination in a world of mutually irresponsible entities...

Book 2:

Ice.

The Music of Our Time.

WHEN I DIED, ALL EGYPT GATHERED TO MOURN. I could not see them, or hear them, as I lay, debrained and eviscerated in my bier, with the liquid natron drying out my veins, waiting to be stuffed and wrapped. But I could, indefinably, sense them, shuffling and rustling towards the funerary temple in their tens and hundreds of thousands. The shnooks and shmucks, the ordinary men and women, carrying their papooses of children, their offerings of chickens, goats and ibises, their pitiful little bags of grain, perfumes and oil. I am lucky my organs of smell have been removed already, so that I am immune to the intense odour of the populace which has not bathed or washed for seventy-two days in mourning at their beloved Father's demise. They are also supposed to refrain from drinking wine or beer and any sexual congress in this period, but *oyf kapoyres,* I do not need my sensory organs to detect the hanging droplets of booze and sperm that waft across the Nile. The cosmic reek that permeates the universe.

Who better than a Pharaoh knows his people. The poor peasants, fisher folk, builders and scribes who labour to the harmony of earth, river and sky, and to the glory of their King. On second thoughts, omit the builders, the tomb wallahs, masons, carvers and calligraphers whose sole job it is to see that their master's tomb is completed and ready for the day and hour of his death. A worse band of chisellers, shirkers, goof-offs and scroungers cannot have been imagined by the Gods. The overseers are the worst, pocketing their ten percent, if not twenty, of the entire works budget to stash away for their own tombs, keeping the best painters and artisans back to decorate their own sarcophagii and that of their tarted up wives. Labour disputes, stoppages, outright strikes, diluted building materials, even sabotage at the most delicate level of the inscriptions dogs a man at every turn. You have to watch them like a hawk, going over every phrase and heiroglyph with an enlarging glass, making sure you are not diverted before the Fifth Division of the Tuat towards the abyss of souls or the pit of the serpent Apep.

Building your tomb consumes the best years of your life. Rameses at least had the time, but I was 64 years old when I ascended the throne... I lived and died in the shadow of my father. He was the sun. I was the afterglow. After me it would be downhill all the way. The usurper Amenmesse, my son Sethi II, Siptah, Sethnakht and all the mini-Rameses, III thru XII, without even the imagination to think up their own individual names.

I was the last, and after me, the desert. Everything was an uphill battle against Time. But at least the tomb was done before my death. Chamber after chamber, it descended into the rock of the Valley of the Dead, the great sealing slabs poised over the corridors and false cavities, ready for the final phase of my journey. There at least I could be alone, away from the chattering blag of the priests, the incessant whining of the court mourners, the crocodile tears of my family and all the extended clan which only waits to tear my great inheritance to pitiful shreds.

But there is a way to go, yet, before that final stage. The endless wrapping of my mummified body, each fold of the linen accompanied by another stanza of the priestly rap:

> *"The doors of the sky are opened,*
> *The doors of the firmament are thrown open for Horus,*
> *That he may ascend to bathe in the field of rushes..."*

Everything has to be just so. Everything has to be repeated the requisite number of times, not one repetition omitted, on fear of remission, regression and obstruction at any one of the manifold Halls of the Dead. The wrapping proceeding, limb by limb, up to the left fist, which is closed and covered with the oil, ankh-imy plant, bitumen and natron concoction, the gold seal placed on the index finger, the hand then gilded and tied with the thirty-six packets of seneb-netjery and the branch of the aru-tree placed firmly in it, and then the outer bandages, leading up to the head. And then, when it was finally over, the priests placed my corpse in the great coffin and the people could at last gather, at the necropolis, to witness the river crossing.

It was a sight to see. I remember it from Rameses. The great funerary boats, crossing the Nile. The women, in the first, turned towards the sarcophagus drawn in the second boat, keening and wailing, while the eldest surviving son (myself) stands in the prow, calling out to the helmsman: *"Steer west, to the Land of the Justified... When eternity comes, we shall meet again, for you go to the land where all are equal..."* Death, harmony and the pursuit of eternity. In the second boat, drawn by mighty oars, the bier, with its ornately coloured inscriptions, covered with flowers and soaked in perfume. Two more boats filled with the deceased's relations and courtiers follow in the majestic procession. So large the boats that a man could cross by foot over the Nile simply stepping from each stem to stern.

On the eastern bank, the people line the riverside, waving palm fronds and bullrushes. Imagine four hundred thousand people weeping, the waves of woe rippling along the crowd, engulfing rich and poor, man and wife, children and idiots, the educated with the illiterate swept along in the vast tide of grief. Only the Great Pyramids themselves, at Gizeh, stand indifferent, but who can figure them out anyway. The boats draw up to the western shore, mooring at the foot of the great ramp upon which the coffin is unshipped. Four oxen draw the funerary sledge up the ramp, towards the Valley, the mourners following with their cargo of flowers, baskets and boxes of their final offerings. Slowly the procession winds up the hill, the musicians playing the songs of departure.

It is the most beautiful sight in the Empire, enacted upon the one man for whom it is designed, but who cannot witness its glory. Still, its essence carried through to me, in my bier, as the ox-team drew me up the mountain. I felt as if I were going home, for this tomb had consumed so much of my time and effort, so much of my hopes and my dreams. For I was already so weary, when I became Pharaoh, so bowed down by the chores of survival, the shoring up of Dad's empire, the Syrian campaigns, the Hittites, the Hebrews, the Libyans, endowments at Karnak, taxation, public works. The great race against Time and the working class. At the end of the day, the legends are true, it's only the giant turtles and the snails who win that race. Man is too speedy. He trips over himself and falls, stricken and dried. The little water that is left sucked out by the priests. At the door to the tomb they perform the last ritual. The Opening of the Mouth. The priest sticks his monkey wrench into the opened coffin and prises the dry gullet ajar, for without this the soul, the double, the *ka*, cannot return to resurrect the body.

Why should I care. I felt no pain any more. I just wanted to get on, finally, with the crucial stage of my journey. The exhaustive rituals completed, the mourners withdrawn, the priests silent, the coffin drawn down down the corridors of the tomb into the burial chamber. The sarcophagus closed, and, with it, all contact with the outside world severed. The workmen, the last to withdraw, pulling after them the great stone plugs sealing the tomb from thieves and bandits. (In the old days, they used to have the workmen killed by loyal soldiers at the exit, so that no one could retrace their track, but these days so many people are in the know, scribes, architects, masons, overseers, the game is not worth the candle. The size of the slabs is what really matters. Nothing is sacred any more.)

At last I am alone! The chattering mob departed, the mourning stilled, the night of Death transcendent. Above my stone, the painted stars and undulating inscriptions and images of my coming journey. My figure, hand in hand with Isis, guiding me towards the portals of the Underworld. The Gods, Hathor, Khnum, Ptah, Anubis, Horus, Thoth. At the end of this night, I will be reunited with Osiris, or know the reason why. Not for nothing have I spent four years checking every jot and tittle, every dot and scratch –

> *"The doors of the sky are opened,*
> *The doors of the firmament are thrown open...*
> *That I may ascend to bathe in the field of rushes..."*

I am freed of my tomb. The sarcophagus lies behind me. The *ka*, the *ba*, the *khu*, the *sekhem*, the "shadow", and the Name, all the scattered elements of the spirit, are coalescing, into my immaterial entity. I wave goodbye to my body, which I shall re-enter once I arrive safely on the Other Side. I can't say I miss it much at this point. The inscriptions all about me show the way - *"Awake, Osiris, awake! Throw off the earth which is upon you...! Gather my ancestors to my side..."*

All ye who have gone before, guide me... The way is long, the darkness rising. Open the sky. Open the earth. I am alone. No priests, no guides, no servants... Help me, Dad! Are you there? Silence. You have to stand on your own two feet. Not very easy, without a body. You just drift. Go with the flow -

For millions of years, the Gods have sat, waiting for men to make this journey. They have seen it all before, every hope, every thought, every fear, every feeble invention. What can be new under the sun, or in the night? The moon appears near, but it remains a mystery. The Gods are said to dwell in the stars of Orion. When the Great Master, Imhotep, built Khufu's Pyramid, my brother Khaemwasset told me, he constructed the secret shafts from the death chamber so that the light of the stars would strike the Pharaoh's open mouth, drawing his *ka* up into the sky. Just to make sure, Khufu had buried seven solar boats, and a troop of reluctant boatmen, in case he had to go the hard way. They had style, in the old days. But now it's every man for himself. Oh ye Gods, who dwell in this, and that, and the other, show me the fucking way. Oh brother. If only I had gone with the Hebrews, and their pillar of fire. Their desert God. Just One, instead of this multitude. It makes sense. What do they call it, Occam's Razor. Nothing should be multiplied beyond necessity. Freedom is the recognition of necessity. Marx. Or was it Lenin? I can't remember any more. THE CHAPTER OF MAKING A MAN REPOSSESS HIS MEMORY IN THE UNDERWORLD: *If any God should advance unto me, may I be able to pronounce his name forthwith...* Osiris, Horus, Set, Thoth, Jehovah, Jesus, Allah, Tammuz, Ishtar, Vishnu, Kali... Hormuzd and Ahriman, Ahura Mazda, Kronos, Aphrodite, Mumu, Enlil... Buddha, get up off your ass from that bodhi tree and show me the way... Or at least give us a drink, Finn MacCool... So fucking many of you and nobody can spare a thirsty man fifty cents for a cup o'coffee...

But there is no God at all, only Commerce. Gilgamesh, in his great quest through the underworld, comes across a five and dime. Key chains, watches, canvas shoes, compasses, Chinese kites, hold-all bags, wallets, razor blades, plastic windup toys, kettles, teacosies, pocket calculators, filofaxes, organisers, breadknives. He turns out his pockets but there is nothing there except a magic charm for warding off serpents. He offers it to the shop-owner, who shakes his head sadly. In a parallel aisle, Hercules is shopping for a sturdy dog collar and chain. He is wearing the myrtle wreath bestowed on him in Eleusis in preparation for his descent to Tartarus to bring back the hellish hound, Cerberus. This would be the last of the Labours imposed by the Pythoness at Delphi after he had gone mad and slaughtered his own children by mistake. Or was it Eurystheus who imposed the Labours? It's so hard to think clearly in all this noise. Children buzzing round and round on rollerskates, Chinese matrons conversing at the top of their voices, the booming voice of Crush Limbo on National Christian Radio, the roar of the 14th Street traffic.

Hercules was promised immortality if he performed all his twelve Labours. I was promised nothing but a kick up the ass, Pharaoh thought, passing a calloused hand over his stubble. The corridor twists, down the aisles of worthless gew-gaws. Glass jewellery, doorknobs, door numbers, name tags. Cynthia, Samantha, Johnny, Sadie, Arnie, Betty, Jo, Marty, Beth, Dino. If these are the Gates of Death, where are the Gods? Instead a small Hispanic man with a moustache, at the exit, stops me and passes a metal detector over my arms, legs and balls. I step out into the street.

The icy cold hits me like a bolt from the depths of the earth. It wraps round me like a winding sheet, gripping my throat, forcing my breath back down my gullet. It freezes the spittle on the frost of my lips and the droplets of snot hanging off my nostrils, creating tiny stalagmites. It hardens the warts, pustules and scratches of my face to brittle wedges, which crumble and break off. It dries up the lachrymal fluid of my eyes, icing up the tear ducts and canals, freezing the mucous membrane, obscuring my sight. All around me, passers by are likewise tottering, gasping for air, trying to pluck a breath out of the frozen sky. The ground is a sheet of slippery ice, thrown across pavement and road alike, so that the passing cars, trucks and buses slide and slither dangerously over invisible lanes, honking and hooting, their sputtering engines wheezing and rasping to suck at the last heat escaping from the bowels of the earth to be stripped by the sub-zero wind.

"Turn back, turn back, O Nut,
In this your name of 'City'...
The Eye of Horus is on the wing of his brother Seth,
The ropes are tied, the ferry-boat is ready..."

No use. The words freeze on the tongue, breath falls in chunks of ice to the ground, the gusts of whipping snow thrash the skin and cheeks like chips of molten iron. Nobody's listening. You just have to walk on, into the blizzard, past the row of shuttered restaurants, hazy in the whipping white flakes: Yofee-Chai, Meson Vasco Spanish Seafood, the Quatorze... Plat du Jour: Tomato Eggplant Soup, Bacon Gruyere Omelette, Salad Nicoise, Fillet of Ocean Perch. NOTRE PATISSERIE EST GARANTIE PUR BEURRE FERME - LE MAISON N'ACCEPTE PLUS DE CHEQUES OU CARTE. Damn. And I was goin' to try out my Amex Gold. The corner of 14th Street and 8th Avenue is a windswept prairie of howling Arctic gusts. To the South, Ali H. Abli Grocery and the Girls From Ipanema Bar. To the North, the Republic National Bank and La Taza de Oro Cafe Espresso. To the West, Manufacturer's Hanover and the New York Savings Bank. To the east, all our previous excursions. We must decide.

Even a journey of a thousand mires starts with a single stop. What if your feet are frozen? The soles stuck to the ground, the toes devoid of feeling, the ice floes rushing up the legs towards the groin, rushing to meet those rushing in towards the abdomen from every corner of the earth - the fingertips, the elbows, ass-cheeks, shoulders, neck.

Chill out. Goddamit, who turned off the steam? Super! Super! Fuckit, even the veins are frozen. Everything is icing up. Ann, are you there? I can't get this door open, it's frozen solid! Fuck, you guys, this is the last straw. A normal person can't bear it in here for one more minute. It reminds me of... Just shut up, Bat. Lincoln, whadayasay? Do we make a run for it? I'm not moving an inch in this climate. If only there was a stick of wood in here, at least get an old fashioned fire going. Timber! The snowy forest of Vermont... A long time ago. Now is here, here is now. Do something about it! Gimme those blankets. At least the pus has congealed. Goddamit, this is not bearable. I'm calling for a counsel of war. There have to be certain minimum standards. I say we take a vote now. Whaddaya mean not everybody's here? No show no go, that's constitutional. How many others? You're shitting me Jesse. Where have they been all this while?

The body whirls. North South West East. The hands flung out, wildly flailing. Drivers, desperately trying to control their vehicles, wind down their windows, mouthing rage that dies in mute icicle howls.

Getoff the road! Getoff the road! The junction spins all about him. The banks, the grocery stores, the coffee shops. THIS WAY. THAT WAY. LOCAL TRAFFIC.

His foot twirls, toecap flying. His body follows, against the traffic, oblivious to the lights, leaning into the swithering snowstorm.

**@@!!! Fuck! Shit! Asshole!

The body turns towards the North.

Washington D.C., January 20, 1993:

- MY FELLOW AMERICANS. Today we celebrate the mystery of American renewal. This ceremony is held in the depth of winter. But by the words we speak and the faces we show the world, we force the spring. A spring born in the world's oldest democracy, that brings forth the vision and courage to reinvent America.

When our founders boldly declared America's independence to the world, and our purposes to the Almighty, they knew that America, to endure, would have to change. Not change for change's sake, but change to preserve America's ideals - life, liberty, the pursuit of happiness. Though we march to the music of our time, our mission is timeless. Each generation of Americans must define what it means to be an American.

On behalf of our nation, I salute President Bush for his half century of service to America, and I thank millions of men and women whose stead- fastness and sacrifice triumphed over depression, fascism and communism.

Today, a generation raised in the shadows of the cold war assumes new responsibilities in a world warmed by the sunshine of freedom but threatened still by ancient hatreds and new plagues. Raised in unrivalled prosperity, we inherit an economy that is still the world's strongest, but is weakened by business failures, stagnant wages, increasing inequality and deep divisions.

Profound and powerful forces are shaking and remaking our world, and the urgent question of our time is whether we can make change our friend and not our enemy. The new world has already enriched the lives of millions of Americans who are able to compete and win in it. But when most people are working harder for less, when the cost of health care devastates families and threatens to bankrupt our enterprises, great and small, when fear of crime robs law-abiding citizens of their freedom, and when millions of poor children cannot even imagine the lives we are calling them to lead - we have not made change our friend...

Thomas Jefferson believed that, to preserve the very foundations of our nation, we would need dramatic change from time to time. Well, my fellow Americans, this is our time. Let us embrace it. Our democracy must not only be the envy of the world but the engine of our own renewal. There is nothing wrong with America that cannot be cured by what is right with America. So today we pledge an end to the era of deadlock and drift, and a new season of American renewal has begun...

"SHREDDED BEEF WITH GARLIC SAUCE, lamb with Szechuan Ma La sauce, prawn and scallop combination, aromatic Chinese eggplant, Empire three delicacies sauteed... my God, that should be enough."

"And start with the dumplings."

"Pork or prawn?"

"One order of each."

"That should stuff us completely. Wait, here's Aram. He'll want to add his own ideas."

The warm cackle of the Szechuan Gourmet Restaurant, the white shirted waiters and waitresses weaving between the tightly packed tables with giant trays of steaming chef's delights, from Special Hors d'oeuvres to Ho Fun, the loitering take away crowd at the bar, the waiting line for tables crushed in between the rushing waiters and the cold frosted door, the figure pressing through to the waving threesome seated at the table waiting for the fourth -

"Greetings guys. What a ghastly night. There are stalagtites dripping from the moon."

"Glad you could make it. We were just going to order."

"Hi Aram."

"Hi Frances. Benjamin. Where's Salim?"

"He couldn't make it tonight. He's out on a job."

"In this weather? Either a brave or a poor man."

"What are you having, Aram?"

The fourth guest settles, peeling his coat, great muzhik hat and two scarves, wrapping them round his chair.

"I'll have anything that's going, but no broccoli. In Szechuan in the Cultural Revolution we had nothing but broccoli for six months. The Red Guard commander in Dengsheng had cornered the market. We had to beat off several assaults, some with tanks, by the Yellow Faction of Chengdu."

"Then how about General Tseng's Historic Chicken. Waterchestnuts, celery, strawmushrooms and red pepper, but no broccoli."

"Suits me fine. God, it's steaming in here. What is it with America, Allan? Only extremes."

"Only extremes Aram."

- To renew America, we must meet challenges abroad as well as at home. There is no longer clear division between what is foreign and what is domestic - the world economy, the world environment, the world AIDS crisis, the world's arms race - they affect us all. As an old order passes, the world is more free but less stable. Clearly America must continue to lead the world we did so much to make.

While America rebuilds at home, we will not shrink from the challenges, nor fail to see the opportunities,

> of this new world. Together with our friends and allies, we will work to shape change, lest it engulf us. When our vital interests are challenged, or the will and conscience of the international community is defied, we will act - with peaceful diplomacy whenever possible, with force when necessary. The brave Americans serving in the Persian Gulf, in Somalia and wherever else they stand, are testament to our resolve.
>
> But our greatest strength is the power of our ideas. Across the world, we see them embraced, and we rejoice. Our hopes, our hearts, our hands, are with those on every continent who are building democracy and freedom...

"And how is Caroline?"

"She's still in the hospital. Another week, then she continues the treatment at home. It rips you up, chemotherapy. But she's fighting."

"It's in her blood."

"You're damn right, Aram. Leukemia, what a horror. It wants to eat every single cell."

"Who needs new plagues when we have all the old ones. But she's an honorary Armenian, Allan. You give her my love."

"I always do."

"This weather makes me feel so primitive. The ice age. These kinds of temperatures are inhuman. Minus fifteen Fahrenheit. That's minus twenty- six centigrade, isn't it? That's a different kind of breathing. I went into a store for cigarettes and I thought I'd gone blind. My spectacles had iced up."

"Well, I'm glad you're all here, those who could make it. Miss? We're ready to order now."

The smiling face and poised arm bearing a refill of iced water cutting through, receiving the Professor's order with the easy certainty of perfect recall. "That all?" "That's all for the moment, thank you."

"How is the cutting edge of art these days, Frances?"

"Getting blunter every day. You've heard about Len Loons' giant Hershey Bars? They're a hundred and fifty feet high, and made of pig iron. He's setting them up in Binghamton. They are Granola Nut, Pistachio and Plain."

"Not my flavours. What did you think, Allan, about Clinton's speech?"

"At least the man can parse a sentence. He's articulate, he can read and chew gum at the same time."

"I was not impressed. It's Kennedy ersatz. But you're right, he can jog without total collapse. That's a big plus in America. Motion and youth. The sun came out for him, the lucky bastard."

"Democrats always start well, before they're bogged down. It's all the health bill. If he can get that passed, he gets a second term. If he doesn't..."

"America, Allan. So many resources. So much power, so much waste."

"Don't expect anything different in foreign policy. On the Middle East he could turn out worse than Bush."

"Things will work themselves out, Allan. You're too pessimistic."

"Realistic, Benjamin. It's too dangerous to believe what you want to believe."

> - Today, we do more than celebrate America - we rededicate ourselves to the very idea of America: an idea born of revolution and renewed through two centuries of challenge, an idea tempered by the knowledge that, but for fate, we - the fortunate and the unfortunate - might have been each other; an idea ennobled by the faith that our nation can summon from its myriad diversities the deepest measure of unity; an idea infused with the conviction that America's long, heroic journey must go on forever...

"I don't want to believe anything. I just believe things can't go on the way they are. Look at what's happened in the world. Russia. Eastern Europe. South Africa's changing. Even Armenia is a country now, Aram."

"A rump, fighting for its survival, like Bosnia. It's an elemental balance. Progress is always countered by regress. The ups and downs. Cancers and cures. You defeat one disease another crops up. Or the old one, in a more virulent form. Light and dark. Hormuzd and Ahriman. Learn your Persian Mazdaian myths, Benjamin. Don't listen to these Marxoid rationalists."

"Nothing more Marxoid than Hegelian dialectic, Aram."

"Hegel was a brute. All those German pessimists. Even Nietzsche was a Lutheran pastor, or his father was. You don't get rid of cultural miasmas that easily. At the other extreme, the Chinese went for manic optimism. What you will is reality. If the crops fail while you're forcing everyone to make old pots into fighter planes you just deny it, and proclaim record yields. Production up ten thousand percent! I saw the results. Mass starvation. It cured me of optimism forever."

"You're mixing up hope and despair, Aram. There are different routes to the same emotions. One way leaves you open to new ideas, the other closes down all the escape ways."

"You are talking about stupid hope, Allan. Silly speeches about trumpets blowing. Answering the call. Like that poor crazy man, what was his name, Mo Smith. He heard plenty of calls. They were all calling him, inside his head. What became of him, do you know?"

"Caroline arranged for him to go into the 14th Street Shelter for the winter. The Armory. Benjamin saw him there, right?"

"I was there with Salim, just before Christmas. You should go down to that place, Allan, sometime. It's just one huge empty space of a warehouse, filled with rows and rows of single beds, just stretching out as far as you can see. The homeless men walk around and around the place like zombies. There's no point putting your stuff in the lockers, everything gets stolen, so they all carry their bundles or bags or rucksacks with them and tie them to their belts at night. They put their boots underneath the legs of the beds, to keep them from being stolen. Imagine a whole hall full of beds with boots on, waiting to walk, but no place to go."

"I had an exhibition of boots once at the gallery. We called it `Walking.' It was by Gregg Roonee. He collected them all over the world from tramps and vagrants and wanderers and painted them in bright colors. But the homeless got wind of it and came off the street and took em. The artist loved it. He wanted us to keep the show open till the last shoe was gone, then put up a notice saying `Sold Out.' All over the city you could see the boots, all year, people tramping in bright yellows and blues."

"You'd be amazed what people pay money to see in this town."

"Ahhh... Here comes the food."

The steaming dishes. Historic chicken, aromatic eggplant et al.

"Ohhh... the prawns and scallops are divine...!"

"We should just stay in this restaurant till the summer. Eat very slowly. Pace ourselves. Order smaller and smaller portions, then build up to larger ones again. We can have long periods of steamed rice. Wait till asparagus is in season. Stay put, just like your friend, what's her name Frances, in her geodesic dome. In Long Island, wasn't it?"

"Yuh. Selina Hasek. They sealed the dome completely just before Christmas. They took a vote and decided on a `test to destruction' for one year. She stopped sending me exhibits or answering the phone calls. There are fifteen people, I think, now sealed up in there, like the astronauts from 2001. Lets hope their computer isn't called Hal. They'll all come out on New Year 1994."

"I hope they like each other."

"They hate each other's guts. But they believe in the cause."

"Insanity?"

"Saving the planet. Recycling what little that's left."

"Utopias are getting smaller all the time."

> - And so, my fellow Americans, as we stand at the edge of the 21st century, let us begin with energy and hope, with faith and discipline, and let us work until our work is done. The scripture says: 'And let us not be weary in well-doing, for in due season, we shall reap, if we faint not.'
>
> From this joyful mountaintop of celebration, we hear a call to service in the valley. We have heard the trumpets. We have changed the guard. And now - each in our own way, and with God's help - we must answer the call...

The sound of chopsticks, clicking merrily away in the shade of the invisible scythe...

STAYING ALIVE! THAT'S OUR AGENDA. HE HAD OPENED HIS EYES, IN THE MORNING, and there she was, making her way towards him in the 14th Street Shelter, threading through the maze of beds under the great bank of lights high in the ceiling of the great warehouse. The cacophony of morning sounds, spitting, retching, clearing of a thousand and one male throats. The clatter as the awakening sleepers lifted their beds up to retrieve the boots they'd deposited for safety under the metal feet. The rustle as two thousand and two hands felt for the vital stash of money, tobacco, keepsakes that might have been pilfered in the night. Sighs of relief or cries of bitterness. "Goddamit! Motherfuckers!"

She was dressed in a neat black jacket and trouser suit, with a red coat hung over her arm. "Mr Mo Smith? Do you remember me? Doctor Caroline Dexter."

"Sure." He bent to put his shoes on his feet.

"My friends Salim and Benjamin were asking after you. They haven't seen you for some time. I thought we could have some breakfast."

"Sure." He gathered together his little bag of belongings, the battered blue shoulder bag with the sheaves of news clippings, the rolled up rags, the old broken windup clock, the empty plastic food container, the paper cup, the roach-clip, the little sewing packet of needle and thread, the spare shoelaces, the clear plastic raincap, the threadbare mittens, the blunt penknife, the keyring without keys. He followed her through the maze, marvelling at the poise and firmness with which she navigated in the mass, up to the guards by the metal detector.

"Checkin out man?"

"We're just going out for some breakfast. You keep this man's bed for him please. He's still residing here."

"It's all the same to me, lady."

"Well, it shouldn't be. But have a good day."

This was before the snow. And it was only raining. A steady downpour out of the steelgrey sky. She unfurled a black umbrella over the two of them. "I know a place just round the corner," she said. They crossed Seventh Avenue to the Mykonos Restaurant. Through the double doors, she shook off the rain like a dog. "Brrr! Man, it's foul out there. Look, there's a free booth, let's grab it." The battered leather seats, the burnished brown table, the bright framed photographs of the sunkissed Greek island on the wall, the row of patrons' behinds settled on the high stools at the long curving counter, the stove, the griddle, the smell of frying eggs, ham, bacon, onions, fresh coffee and donuts, buzz of voices high, low, loud.

"So what'll you have today?" His heavy hands turned the menu. "Don't stint yourself," she said, "I'll have the number two over easy hold the potatoes, brown toast, english muffin. Orange juice, dekaff." He gazed at the menu. "You want me to choose for you?" He nodded. "Give this man a large cheeseburger platter with a Greek salad and a gallon of coffee. Regular? Orange juice? That clears that out the way." She gave him a long hard look. "I don't want to choose your life for you. Just saving time. I have a hospital appointment at ten uptown."

"Anythin wrong?" he said. Sixth, seventh, eighth senses alerted.

"We came here to talk about you. You want to know my troubles? That would be only fair, I suppose. But a waste of our time. Are you O.K., at the Shelter? Any unusual hassle? Health holding up?"

He shrugged. The waiter brought the coffee, giving them something to do with their hands.

"Who am I talking to?" she said, "am I talking to you, Mo Smith? I think I'm talking to you. I don't think the others are with us now. I know they're always there. But you know what I mean. You're in control. I can sense that. How does it feel?"

"O.K. I guess." His voice like an amplified whisper.

"You remember, the first couple of times that we talked, at Benjamin's, our third meeting, in all, remember? We talked about MPD, the Multiple Personality syndrome. You said you knew all about it, but you wouldn't say if you were treated before. The thing is, you have to ask for help. I can get you into a program, which will take you off the streets for the winter, and you'll be away from the shelter as well. It's located upstate, in Mount Pleasant. It's a small place, they only take twenty patients. Warm rooms, comfortable beds and good food. But you have to ask for it. I know the Armory's no long term solution."

I remember l looked at her, in the dull light of the coffee shop. The coiled intensity of her glance. I could feel the tension of her small body. But there was something there wasting away.

"You're ill and you ain't letting on," I told her. The others stirred but I slapped them down.

"Yes, you're right," she said. "I've been diagnosed with acute lymphoblastic leukemia. Do you know what that means?"

"It's cancer of the blood."

"Right. Usually children get it. I'm still getting the tests. It's a treatable condition, these days, but it's a war, in the body. I have to take a cocktail of drugs. Chemotherapy. It fucks up your system. It's like trying to nuke the bad cells and only leave the good ones intact."

"You goin to die soon?"

"Not if I can help it. We all gotta die sooner or later. I'm sorry, I know that's not original. But we want to fight to live, don't we? Everybody wants to live forever. How about you, Mister Smith?"

He shook his head.

"Or should I ask - don't *they* want to live forever? The traveller Ibn Battuta, Arnold the writer, Jesse the Essene, Beatrice and Ann, the boy Jaime, the Alchemist Mordecai, the Pharaoh, I can never remember his name?"

"He's been dead a long time. He's just stubborn, is all."

"You see, even the dead want to live. That's what MPD is all about, Mister Smith. You remember we talked about symptoms and causes. We believe the syndrome is the result of a childhood trauma, severe abuse. Things that happened to you as a child, which were so bad you had to bring out separate personalities, imaginary people, to seal it off, to protect your basic self. As time goes on, they become more important. But do you really need them? That's the question."

She was leaning towards him but the waiter appeared suddenly, splitting them asunder with large plates of fried eggs, cheeseburger with giant french fries, salad, toast and muffins on a side plate and a host of tiny tabs of butter, grape jelly. "More coffee?"

"Sure. Mine's the dekaff." She leaned back, as he grabbed hold of the food. "Do you really need them? I know real friends are hard to come by, when you're down and out. I know what your friends inside are thinking. You get into the program, the psychiatrist will kill them. He'll leave you without protection against the memories, whatever they are. He'll leave you all alone in the world, a blank slate. That's not how it should be at all. All those people are a part of you, of what you are, Mister Smith, they are not separate entities. I've talked about you with my friends, remember that group - Benjamin, Salim, Frances, Professor Darwish, Aram. They all think you're a genius. The way you've picked up information, the detail, the history. You could be a scholar. You could work on research. I guess that's what you've been doing. You're a smart man, Mo Smith."

He was devouring the cheeseburger with the fixed determination of someone who might not get a second chance. But I was listening to her. The sound of her voice, the sibilance of her consonants, the music of her vowels. The resonance of her compassion. He paused for a moment.

"Childhood." he said.

"Yes, Mo?"

"I never had no childhood." And he resumed eating, finishing off the burger and fries and ploughing his fork through the Greek salad.

"Everybody had a childhood. You just don't remember. We can work on that."

"No." You still don't understand. We were meant for each other. When I made you, among all the others. The first two. Adam and Lilith. Before Eve came along. Ann Hedonia. The first mistake, opening up the flood. And then the deluge, which engulfed its Creator. "I was the First."

"You're God, and you made us all? That's crap, and I ain't buying it. You're too smart for that. God don't wander about with a torn coat and tattered bag and boots that he got from the Welfare. That's Jesus Christ. I don't want to offend you. But you should get your story right. That part of it is just malingering, Mister Smith. I can't help you if you don't play straight with me."

It's the old challenge, Lilith. You wouldn't play the game, you wouldn't accept reality. You wouldn't acknowledge power and meaning. You just blasphemed and went off, leaving me with the spare rib. But I will love you to eternity.

"I'll think about it." The eyelid droop, the paranoid glance of Arnold Flint. Either fuck her or furl your dick, maestro. We'll book a session with Beatrice. Propitiate our sins, strapped to the rack and paddled with a prickly tawse or cat-o-nine-tails. $350 normally, discount for the unwaged. Mea ultima culpa. Pain is love, agony is desire. Nipple clamps, high colonic enemas, rubber fetishism and vibrators up the ass. Best prices in town. Group rates available.

FUCK OFF, ARNOLD. We're laying the base here. The grand cosmic reunion. But she didn't come back. She missed her next appointment. The supervisor brought me a note, in my bed, number 1543: It's from your shrink, man. She says she can't make it, she's had to go into hospital. She wants you to call her after the holiday, at this number. She's sent you fifty dollars. Sign here, so they know I handed it over. Use this pen. What the fuck...? Who the hell is "Ibin Battuta"?

Thanksgiving. They said the Mormons were going to bring us all some turkeys. Hold the relish. There's enough cold turkey in here, God help us. The cries and shrieks in the night. The vomit. The weeping. We've had a meeting, Mo, and it's unanimous, we can't hold out in here a minute longer. A man can't hear himself think in this hell. Time to move on.

Staying alive. No thanks for all the memories. The rain washed out the autumn and turned to ice. Cold Christ mass. Yuppie New Year. New Presidential dawns. Keep moving and at least you won't freeze. See, the lumbering corpus of Mo Smith, staggering up Eighth Avenue, from the turn of 14th Street, past the Republic National Bank, the Cafe Espresso and the Taza de Oro, dragging one foot after the other, head lowered against the blizzard, leaning forward into the stinging white flakes.

Yukon do it. Heaving across 15th Street, past the Zodiac deli, Smile NY - Your Dental Center, the Chelsea Army and Navy Store, over 16th, past Blockbuster Videos, pressing on, over 17th and 18th, the Video Blitz, Chelsea Gym and Gascogne Food, Spring Joy Chinese Cuban Cuisine, Burns, Tears, Moth Holes Repaired. Stopping to glower at the frosted news headlines: "FURORE OVER CANNIBAL KILLER RELEASE." "CAPITAN PIRATA MATA 2 MUJERES." Caramba.

If a man crams in to the barred doorway, he can gain some small respite from the wind. A triple layer of New York Times Weekend Real Estate plus the Arts and Entertainments Section next to the skin can provide insulation. Those old blue Navy coats close round the mouth. What's really required is one of those Arctic zootsuits, with full Defence for chemical warfare. Little tubes and plastic warmed sacs to piss in which can be stockpiled till the all-clear. Did you know the Defence Department spent a billion dollars on research to find out how many of these sacs could be accomodated before they had to be vented outside? Calculating on a three week stretch of chemical battlefield inundation the future U.S. trooper will move about the combat zone with up to one hundred and thirty five sacs of his piss dangling underneath his sealed suit. If they all burst at once the poor grunt will drown in his own pee or choke to death on the fumes.

Are you listening, Mo? The man is out for the count. Trying to cocoon himself in himself. Anybody there?

Just this silent muttering...

Time for us all then, the Prisoners of the Body, to make our plans before he wakes...

*

- I know, my friends, this isn't the best place to meet, this clapped out, nicotine stained lung. Not a pulmonary lobule that's free of caked grot and grime. The cold blasts coming down the trachea. The fingers freeze even through double mittens. A man can't feel his own dick in here. But where else do you suggest? The spleen's flooded. The intestines are full of muck. The colon's full of shit. Even the bloody asshole's frozen. Remember the German troops at Stalingrad? Their assholes froze tight, nobody could empty their bowels and they just swelled up and bust like rotten marrows. This is a Grade A emergency and I don't think any of you can deny that.

I think we should open this meeting with a roll call. I can see only four of us standing here, but it's so foggy there might be some others lurking behind the oesophagus or the diaphragm. Everyone present say I.

Lincoln, Merenptah, Battuta. Is that it? And I, Arnold Flint. What about the rest of yez? Jesse? Ann? Beatrice? Jaime? Where are you, you Puerto Rican runt? I've always known that boy was up to no good.

Baring his ass to that fucking Jew Mordecai and anyone else with a couple of bucks. It's no wonder disease is so rampant. Do we need some medieval alchemist telling us when to speak and when to shut up? Are we men or are we mice?

You know what Groucho Marx said about that one? Put a piece of cheese on the floor and you'll find out. But I don't expect you people to know about that. What am I doing down here with this bunch of dead beats? Anyone care to contribute, to make some serious decisions? Jesse, are you there? You lily-livered stargazer. Fucking dried up dead sea scroll. You're the one who's been shitting me about there being more people down here than we know. Apart from the waiters, flunkeys and invading shamuses, or Beatrice's clients. Are you there, Queen Bitch? Or that other sack of female lard, Ann Hedonia, I can hear you snoring in the duodenal. Wake up! Stand by to repel boarders. Party poopers, breathing our air, filching our food. Where are these bastards? I say we have a right to know. Or are we just puppets jerking off on a vein?

I for one am not going to stand this much longer. I can at least remember self respect. Ten weeks in the New York Times Top Ten Hardbacks. Five weeks in the Paperback Top Twenty. When I signed at Scribners the queue stretched out round the block. I got work to do, the public awaits my next masterpiece. I have commitments. Talk to me, friends. We gotta get outa here. There's no point skulking in the flesh. A clean break, and damn the consequences. We should move now, while the body's defences are low. We can all feel it, can't we? The breathing laboured. The blood stream sluggish as mud. The whole metabolism grinding down. Listen to that heartbeat. Any slower it's going backwards. Face it, this body is practically a corpse. And then what do we do? Barricade the membranes against the seething maggot tide? Do we live on when the body dies? Just think about it, fellahs, huh?

The Great Escape. I'll tell you a little secret now. I have been preparing the ground. That Hebrew cunt Mordecai and his spick faggot are not the only ones who can make contact with the outside. I have had audio hook-up for about four months now. Broadcasting twice weekly on the Crush Limbo Show. National Radio. Guest spot, Monday and Thursday mornings. Ever listened in? A bit right wing for your tastes? But hey, the man really cares. He wants to make the country great again. The United States of America. You know what I mean?

They called me a maverick too. Crush Limbo takes a moral stand. The evils of abortion. The disarmament lobby. Feminutsos. Liberal bleeding hearts. Hey, don't we know there's pressure everywhere? You've been to Moscow, Lincoln. You saw the cold winter light. O.K., so the Commie Empire has crumbled, but they're still skulking around. Deep in our gut. Isn't that what you mean Jesse? You know, all that stuff about chastity and poverty. No bang for your bucks and no bucks either. Now that's not just unAmerican, but unhuman. Everybody has the right to self-defence, and to enjoy the fruit of his labours, without the Groundnut Barons of Iran muscling in on our life, with their lackey socialist-feminist President. Am I right?

I know what you're thinking. Radio. That's small potatoes. In this day of the information superhighway. Cable, fiber-optics, internet sex. One drop of sperm can go a long way. We all want to bang the cosmic egg. I had Crush on the line just the other day. "Arnie," he said, you know he likes to get familiar, "Arnie, have you ever been to Chicago? Have you ever been in the city in the dead of winter, when the wind comes boogeying over the frozen Lake, and even the snow-ploughs are bogged down? Ever sat here, in your shirt sleeves, in the studio, wondering what the world would be like if it were really run by your environmentalist wackos, with everything back to the horse and buggy, no nukes, no electricity, no power? Ever think about the bodies piling high on the ice floes, the frozen lumps of social welfare clients? Don't you think we should do something about it?"

The short and the long of it is, I have been offered my own TV show. Crush is to get two hours a week, I get a solid ten minute slot. Ten fucking minutes, eh? I can bring on any guests that I want. Even you can have a go, Link, with the 'liberation struggle.' The man ain't as prejudiced as you think. An equal crack of the whip. Battuta, you can tell your globetrotting stories. Don't know what you want to talk about, Nep. Those Egyptian spells get a bit wearing after a while. But hey, the royal pedigree. People are bored with the Queen of England, the King of Saudi Arabia, the Sheikh of Kuwait. The King of Egypt: That's one hell of a deal. We all have to get out of this shithole. The sooner the better. Hey, folks? Whadaya say?

It's pointless. Nobody listens down here. Every bastard's talking to themselves. A man can't think clearly in this cold. Despite I've wrapped myself in every spare blanket I could find. My feet are ice blocks. What

I need are those Russian army puttees. I remember researching that for the first novel. "The Crimson Trash." The Russian army knew better than to depend on boots in the snow. They wrapped the feet with what amounts to swaddling cloths, wind upon wind, really trapping the heat. Boots congeal and become like cement plugs, rooting you to the ground. You can't run, you can't fight, you can't hide. You just plod on. Ya gotta keep going. The uniformed muzhiks, pushing the guns. The frosted up 155 milimeter cannons, sinking in the snow to the barrels, which are stopped with rags to be removed when Fritz gets into sight. The city may be starving, but it must be defended at all costs. The city of ice, which has no mercy.

Stalingrads yet to come. Keep us awake, friends. Lincoln, come on. Tell us your tales of the struggle. Your days of guerrilla training in Kazakhstan. Why did you exchange the African sun for the snow? When did you decide to become an agent for the CIA? Was it a sudden decision or did it creep up you unawares? What was your first contact? When did you decide to betray your friends for the greater good? Or was it just for cash?

Who wants to know?

The public, Lincoln, the voracious masses. The eye and ear of gossip, slithering all over the globe. The National Enquirer. The Sun. The Weekly World News. The Alien Bulletin. The Body Politic. News On the Hour Every Hour. Whatever it is, wherever it is, we'll be there. Tonight, on the Crush Limbo Show. Our first guest, Lincoln Korombane, previously a member of the Pan Africanist Party (PAP) of South Africa, and now a swimmer in the polluted bodily fluids. Having fought the cruel apartheid regime of his country he accepted the role of a double agent for the Central Intelligence Agency when invited for training in the Soviet Union.

Now you know it's not how it was, Arnold.

Well, tell it to our sixty million viewers. Sixty million God-fearing Americans who drink the blood of freedom with our mother's milk. Unsanitary as it may seem. What was it took you to the Evil Empire, Lincoln? Was it the Devil? Did the Devil himself come to you while you slept, in your little shanty-town shack, breathing in the fetid air of oppression, with the cockroaches crawling over your eyes? You can tell us about the Devil, Lincoln. We all know his sneaking, sniggering ways. He is, as you know, the subject of my work in progress, 'The

Sabbath, A Tale of New England.' The Devil, and the Reverend Cotton Mather, Witch-hunter Extraordinary. Of course, I can hardly make any progress in this hellhole, this Dantean chaos, this ninth circle in which the traitors writhe in their great lake of ice -

The hues of shame, livid, and with their teeth
Chattering like storks, the dismal shades stood here...

Good old Dante Allegory. He had four types of traitors in his icy hell: The traitors to their lords, the traitors to their guests, the traitors to their country and to their kin. The sins of the wolf, he called these. What brought you to this pass, Lincoln? You who were named after the great freer of slaves, Honest Abe. In other words, are you or have you ever been? You get my drift? And in this bottomless pit in which you were mired, shivering in the eternal shade, came to your aid the Saviours of the C.I.A., with their shimmering lances of chalcedony and gold, bearing the Great Seal of the United States upon their gleaming, depilated breasts, with the glorious code of the Marine Corps on their brow: Semper fidelis! They came to save you from yourself, wasn't that the way it was now?

Fuck you Arnold.

That's all they can ever say. Fuck you this, fuck you that. The English language, the finest means yet produced by Mankind for the articulation of ideas, concepts, impressions, analysis, erudition. The light in the darkness of ignorance. And this is what it all comes down to.

Double fuck.

Give it a rest Arnold. Stick those puttees up your congealed ass.

Did I ever tell you how I rescued the abducted wife of the Grand Sultan of Constantinople, Muhammad Uzbeg Khan?

Oh not now, Battuta, for God's sake...

ABBRRAAAAHHHH! GOD DAMN THE MOTHERFUCKIN LOT OF YOUZ!

The body, unfreezing from its torpor, flailed out, kicking an empty squashed can of Diet Coke out of the trashstrewn doorway at 20th Street and Eighth Avenue into the street, just as the snow plough rumbled by, its treads squealing, its gears clashing, its funnels spewing out muddy ice. Mo shook his head, banging it against the bars of the shop, the sign for Keys Cut While You Watch...

GET THE FUCK OUTA MY BRAIN! Don't none of you motherfuckers ever give a guy a break? Running TV shows out of my lungs. You gotta licence to do that? You gotta certificate from the Department of Paradigmatic Synergies, U.S.Reg.Pat., to fucking mess with my neurons up there?

GET OUT MY WAY MAN!... The street was empty, as he crossed 25th to Kyung's Fruit and Deli, next to the parking lot and the graffiti-scrawled wall of Danieli's Ristorante, on which the owner had affixed the plaintive sign:

"IT COST ME $25,000 TO CEMENT THIS WALL. PLEASE DO NOT WRITE ON IT - I WOULD NOT DO THAT ON YOUR WALL."

Across the road, on the diagonally opposite corner, the snow capped sign of McDonalds. The big M. They've given up telling us how many billions sold. A stream of cars slithered up to the lights, squealing brakes and puffing exhausts. Walk Don't Walk. His leaden feet sliding on the ice. Crossing over to the Big Mac. That blast of stale hot air in the door. Clatter of trays, the odour of french fries. The shuffling queue. Extra Value Meals, Salads, Chicken. $1.99 Special.

Any requests down there?

- Make mine Boervurst.

- Humus and kibbeh mishwieh, fried ladies' fingers...

- My kingdom for a melohieh...

- I'll have the tartare de loup et saumon aux condiments, feuilette de Saint-Jacque, souffle chaud et cacao...

- Just a little cracked wheat for me.

Hey Jesse. Ann with you?

- She's asleep.

Always asleep. Ann Hedonia. Bloated and slack on her bed in her sealed room behind the tear ducts, filled with empty or discarded cans, decaying fruit, shrivelled TV dinners, watching the game shows on her fizzling strobing old TV set with its broken aerials, dreaming of long gone days of glory. When she was slim and willowy in her coloured kaftans, back there when...

Love and loss. Losing and love.

"Can I help you?"

"Oh yeah. Special platter man." Extracting from the inner sanctum, the little bag hooked round the neck, the last of Caroline's wad, two folded dollars, waiting for the glaring counter-boy's penny change. It didn't last long, all that stash. Saw me through the Christmas drought and the New Year, don't tell me about the free trimmings. You're even more invisible when people are havin a good time. Settlin at a corner table overlooking Eighth Avenue through an ellipse of frosted glass. Like a vignette of the city in doldrums. Mid-winter in Neuw Amsterdam. The tinkle of sleighbells and the trudge of miserable burghers bringing a scrawny snow-shoe rabbit home to their old Dutch and wee Nederlanders. Trading in furs. In those days the smugglers sold muskets to the Indians for twenty beaverskins a piece. The Iroquois Injuns came down from Westchester and chased the Algonquins into Manhattan. Then the Dutch invade Westchester County. Blood and cash, same as always. He bit into the thin meat patty. Yes, the memories were swirling. Back to the Day of Creation. As I lay, wracked by burger-pains, in the miserable night of Trinity Churchyard, giving birth to the world. All the billions welling out of my tear ducts, slashing like glass slivers through my belly button, drifting down out of the primeval slime of the nostrils, shat and farted out in whole nations and tribes. Only the old Irish janitor, O'Connell, tending my agonies, wiping my brow. "Are you right, Mr Smith? Shall I call a doctor?"

Absolutely not. Tossing and turning, Ann. All those overgrown tombstones: *Here lies X, who departed this life... the Patriot of Incorruptible Integrity...* Keep off the grass...

And when I'm laid low in the filent grave,
Where the monarch is equal with the flave...

When we were together, eh, Ann? Up in the hills, in our own log cabin... till The Man came...

- I have to hand it to you, Mo. Not everybody can use a McDonalds as a madeleine...

Fuck off Arnold.

- If only I could. Set me free. Let my people go!

- Our Wasp scribbler is getting more and more difficult isn't he? Time to get rid of him, Moses...

So there you are, Mordecai...

- Don't listen to *him*, Mo, fucking bastard scheming kike!

- Beware, Moses, the strong cannot give way to the weak...

- Where's your little catamite, Mordecai? That little feigaleh, Jaime?

- Fucking maricon...

- Don't worry, Moses, he's under my absolute protection...

- Under is right...

- Untermensch... ferkakte buffoon...

A body divided against itself cannot stand... The Black Goddess. Lilith. She needs to meet all of you. To bring us all together. We are the only cure for her disease.

- There's no disease, Moses. Just the life force. Just the blood coursing through our veins...

Cancer of the blood...

- That's her problem, Moses. You have to look after yourself. Defense. Security. Dissimulation. *Taki'a.* Never show your true face to strangers. One slip and they'll be walking over you. Scavenging in your guts, slurping up your cranial fluid. Mounting search and destroy missions in your cells. I have already taken precautions. A good man to watch over us from outside. Somebody reliable and discreet. Frank Ox, Private Investigator. Believe me, he has eyes and ears everywhere. The FBI, CIA, NSA, Interpol, he has his finger on every pulse. You can't move an inch today without security. They've had their spies inside you for years. Jaime has seen them. Crawling about in the colon. Coasting up and down the anal canal. We're keeping tabs. Nil desperandum. I'm on the job, Moses. Trust me -

- Trust an alchemist!? A man who crushes frogs' legs and mixes bats' blood with diluted formaldehye! A man who paints iron bars with gold leaf and tries to pass em off as kosher? Don't give him an inch, Mo -

O.K., that's enough boys, knock it off...

He rose, leaving the crumbs of the hamburger, taking the styrofoam cup of the drink, just in case. Tightening the coat around his neck, stepping out of the restaurant into the icy blast of the street. Crossing over 27th, along the Fashion Institute of Technology and the David Dubinsky Student Center. On over 28th. Club Cinco Happy Hours 4 Till 7. Over 29th. Holding out the cup. Spare some change, man. Workin on my plans for world conquest. Start up investment required. Settle for a dime. Any brothers to spare? The street is empty, bar the swishing cars. Windscreen wipers battling frost. The screeking slipping tyres. A bus sliding by with its cheery sign:

THIS BUS IS HEADED FOR EASY STREET -
CASH XPRESS WIN $2,000 INSTANTLY!

Settle for twenty. A man wants a proper pitch, he has to move onwards. Across 30th, past the Molly Wee Pub, Charlie Mom Express Deli, Hiyee Realty, Condos, Apts, LEASE, BUY, RENT. Sure, man, lemme just consult my broker. Across 31st to the south-western wedge of Madison Square Garden. Penn Station. On the other side of the Avenue, the General Post Office. The imposing facade, steps, columns, the pediment boldly proclaiming in carved stone:

NEITHER SNOW NOR RAIN NOR HEAT NOR GLOOM OF NIGHT STAYS THESE COURIERS FROM THE SWIFT COMPLETION OF THEIR APPOINTED ROUNDS.

And all I have with me are jerkoffs. Nothing but moans, cries and complaints. Go! Go if you really want to! You are bringing me nothing but grief...

Along the wall towards Seventh Avenue. Down the steps into the Penn station concourse. The hustle of the Long Island Railroad travellers. Level B. The floor slippery with the snow and slush the people bring down with them off the street. In and out, in and out. Going or coming from Hicksville, Ronkonkoma Beach, Babylon, Cold Spring Harbor, Amityville, Little Neck, Great Neck, Manhasset, Patchogue, Sayville, Valley Stream, Freeport, Locust Valley, Millstone Round the Neck, Far Lockaway, Deadpan Gulch, Lostwood, Flat Mountains.

He put his last dime in the slot of the telephone. Dialling her home number.

Ring ring ring!

"Hallo?"

"I wanna speak to Doctor Dexter. Caroline Dexter."

"She ain't in. She's at the hospital. Who wants her?"

"Who are you?"

"I'm Karim. I'm her son."

Impossible. There can be no son. For if there's a son, there has to be a father. Unless...

"Hallo? You still there? What do you want me to tell her?"

He put the telephone down. Shuffling into the hub of the concourse. Holding out the cup.

- Ladies'n'gennelmen. Spare a few coins for a man who has no home to go to. I used to be Rockefeller but now I'm down on my luck. My skin turned black along the way down. Just twenty-five cents from you, kind sir, and the light can shine again on my face! Yes, ma'm, I am a poor orphan, I don't remember my mother and father, they left me on the doorstep of life. I just need a little help to get on the first rung of the ladder and then I'll be home free. I don't mind the upper rungs, I gotta good head for heights. I'll just fly away and be no trouble. Thank you ma'm. The good Lawd bless you. Don't forget to wrap up warm now! I do agree ma'm, He watches over us all. The Lamb of God! Sweeeet Jeeesus, meek an mild! Thank you ma'm.

Happy motherfuckin Valentine's Day!

Ibn Battuta's Tale: How I Rescued the Abducted Wife of the Sultan of Constantinople, Muhammad Uzbeg Khan, in the Icy Land of the Bulghars.

A tale to pinch and chill the heart: As I set out across the land of the Bulghars towards the Kingdom of Darkness, with only four trusted companions, travelling upon sleds drawn by dogs, the only means of crossing those icy wastes that lie across the River Oxus. The only guide to those empty lands was the lead dog, who knew his way with his uncanny hidden sense. Such a dog is never beaten nor coerced. Rather it is spoken to in low and respectful tones, fed with the best cuts of meat, even when the traveller goes hungry. Some might say, were it not on the verge of blasphemy, that the spirit of long dead wise men such as our teacher The Master Mawluni, al-Rumi, lives in the dog, guiding its actions. Late in those dismal cold nights, wrapped in my furs, I even tried to speak with the animal, as it lay, curled peacefully in its heavy silver coat, but it only gazed at me with deep and sorrowful eyes, and said nothing.

Forty days and forty nights we travelled into the vast interior, even though the dogs were pulling our two sleds at an amazing speed. The Sultan's wife, who was his youngest *khatun*, and the apple of his eye, was being held by a fierce tribe of golden eyed cannibals, who had captured her in an ambush when she was on her way to visit her father, the Sultan of Turkestan. They were known as the Chi-Chins, and at that time had not yet been converted to the True Faith, but worshipped wolves and bears.

One night, when we had travelled so far we thought we must be approaching the rim of the earth, we were surrounded, as we slumped, exhausted, by our camp fire, by the Chi-Chins. They were short, stocky, hunched men in bearskins, pale as the ice, who spoke in guttural growls, snorts and whistles. They kept a healthy distance from our lead dog, who ignored them, but took the rest of us captive. I tried to explain the reason for my presence in the fifteen alien tongues I had learned in my previous travels, but they spoke no known language. Nevertheless, they must have guessed our mission, for they brought us directly to their chief, and his captive, the Grand Sultan's kidnapped *khatun*.

She reposed, at the chief's side, on a pile of silver wolf furs, dressed in a magnificent sable coat. When our eyes met, I knew I had been smitten for ever. Her eyes were black gems that glittered in my soul, and her pouting mouth was like the cavern of desire. I spoke to her in our native Arabic, and she translated my words into the chief's uncouth tongue. I told him I had come from across the ice and the moon to bargain for the return of the Sultan's *khatun*, offering gold and precious gems and a set of state of the art arquebuses powered by a new method of internal implosion. He responded, dismissively, inquiring what recompense could there be for a creature who was beyond any material value or price? I answered that the friendship of the Sultan, who ruled a hundred nations and a hundred million men and women, was also without price. He said that he refused my offer, but would send me and my companions back unharmed, so we could tell the Sultan his former wife was in good hands.

I knew I had but a brief moment that night in which to make my move. Three out of four of my men were unwilling to set their lives upon such risk. They took one of the sleds and left that night. The fourth, my faithful Greek slave, Uterus, chose to stay at my side. We each took one of the powerful arquebuses and crawled in the dark past the guards. Rushing into the chief's tent I shot him dead with my first dart while Uterus dispatched his two guards. I swept the Sultan's *khatun* up in my arms and made for the remaining sled. My lead dog, sensing the urgent need, rushed up, pulling the sled, to my side. I called to my companion but he had been surrounded by the savage horde. He killed another two with his weapon before they fell upon him with their sharp lances. I saw them pierce my Uterus through and through.

I placed the *khatun* gently on the sled and the faithful dog pulled us away from the camp at breakneck speed. She clung to my neck with her arms, her soft face laying on my heaving breast. As we sped across the ice, I spoke in her ear, mouthing insane words of love. I told her that she was the sun and the moon and all the stars. I told her that I was honour bound to return her to her illustrious husband but even heaven itself could not force me to deny my undying love.

I cannot recall her saying anything but her head pressed more firmly at my breast. I felt as if I were floating on air, and the dog was carrying us through empty space, leaping among the stars. I could clearly see the constellations: Andromeda, Cetus, Cassiopea, Virgo, Sagitarius, Orion. The constellations seemed to be calling me, but I awoke from my reverie with a start to realise it was the cries of the Chi-Chin as they pursued us across the ice.

As they came closer, despite the speed of my dog, I saw that they were riding sleds drawn by wolves, great monstrous brutes with glowing eyes and fangs that glinted in the moonlight. The leading Chi-Chins were holding poles on which were impaled the heads of my unfortunate companions, who had been caught fleeing along the way. I called out to the dog to redouble his efforts. I called out verses from the Holy Quran: *All that you give for the cause of God shall be repaid you, you shall not be wronged.*

But it is also said, in the same chapter, The Spoils: *You seek the chance gain of this world, but God desires for you the world to come.* Despite the speed of my dog, the pursuers closed in on either side of my sled. The one on the right threw his lance. I turned my body, to place myself between the spear and my beloved. The lance missed, but another, thrown from the left, struck her unprotected ribs.

She cried out, and stiffened against me. I called out to the dog, dropped my reins, and fired my arquebus at the pursuers. In my fury I demolished six of the savages, blinding three of the tugging wolves, who fell, in their howling pain, upon each other and upon their drivers, rending their limbs and throwing hacked flesh into the snow. The pursuers fell behind me, flailing and crashing in a melee of fangs and blood. I clutched my beloved, the lance protruding from her rib cage like a giant hook thrown from the skies.

When I judged the pursuers were far behind and routed I called on the dog to stop. He stood there mutely, looking at us with a sagging tail. I laid the *khatun* gently on the ground. We were both soaked in her blood, which gushed out, staining the ice and congealing to a frozen red crust. I could not dare pull out the lance, lest her blood poured out completely from her wound. But I could see there was no repair or cure.

She lifted her head to me and tried to speak, but could not. I held her in my arms and wept. Blood welled up in her mouth, and her body shivered, in the death rattle. The dog came up, and squatted before me, with his deep, compassionate eyes. There we remained, frozen in place, throughout the entire night. In the morning, the sun came up, a pale creature, bathing our dismal scene wanly. My tears and her blood had frozen into long icicles, brilliant red and dazzling white.

- What was her name?

Her name?

- Her name, Battuta, Goddamn, it, the Princess of your dreams...

Her name? Her name? What's in a name? Her name? Now hang on just a moment... it's on the tip of my tongue....

BENJAMIN.

WHEN IT GETS REALLY COLD, my central heating ducts talk to me. Benjamin, Benjamin, they call out, then subside in another fit of hissing and thudding, gasping and gurgling in their woe. Sometimes it feels as if the whole twelve tribes of Israel are prisoners in the ancient cylinders and tubes. Sometimes it sounds like my old dead grandmother, Nehama, wheezing on her aerosol inhaler. I used to hear her gasping in the night, at three a.m., when I was a small child, her bedroom was next to mine. I used to imagine that she was being attacked by the demons which afflicted the very elderly, the incarnate secrets of their past.

Perhaps, when my mother developed Alzheimer's, back in the Holy Land, it was a defence against those demons which had shown her the vision of utopia but only delivered the mundane realities of a "normal" state, with all its political warts and carbuncles. These fancies, it turns out, are no match for the realities of medical fact and decay. A documentary on the Discovery Channel told me that the disease is caused by a single brain cell mutating into a "prion", which then replicates itself ad infinitum, destroying all the healthy tissue. No one knows why the primary brain cell does this but they are catching up on how. Soon they will be able to scan our genes and tell us if our cells are prone to do this, but they will not yet be able to do anything about it. This is scientific progress all over. We will soon all be like Socrates: We will know only that we don't know.

The snow is still drifting outside my window, down onto East 4th Street. Locking me into an apartment which is heating up like a steam bath. Nothing but extremes. Angst and ambition. Desolation and desire. Solitude and satu-ration. Love and leukemia.

In lieu of a Discovery program, I looked the disease up in the medical dictionary. *Acute lymphoblastic leukemia - ALL. The aetiology of the majority of leukemias in humans remains unknown.* Thank you very much. Genetic factors: the sins of our fathers and mothers, again. *Low frequency of ALL in black children.* Not much help to be an exception. Environmental factors: Radiation, Chemicals, Drugs, viruses (HTLV type 1). Symptoms: Easily noticeable to anyone except sclerotic, blind, deaf, dumb lovers. Fatigue, anemia, malaise, headache, nausea, vomiting, mouth ulcers, blurred vision. And I thought it was just the City. The workload. The pressure. God damn it. Or is dim perception in the blood?

Why didn't she tell me?

I sat with Allan Darwish in the Keywest coffee shop over breakfast, bagels with cream cheese, Broadway and 99th. Crammed in among the regulars. The elderly and the generally decrepit. Difficult not to eavesdrop on the adjacent tables. One old guy who had stopped off on the way to the graveyard trying to chat up the old biddy opposite. "I always like to come here. Their bagels are soft, they don't break your teeth. The other places, the bread is hard. Do you come here a lot?" But she was not biting.

"Why didn't she tell me?"

"You know Caroline. She didn't want you to panic. She wanted to be sure. She wanted to plan."

"But you knew about it."

"That's different, Benjamin. We got off the boat together."

"The teeth I had before, they fit better," said the old man. "But my orthodondist said they were no good. He charged me three thousand bucks for these and now I can't eat meat. They say you shouldn't eat meat anyway. But I like a good steak. He's a ganef, that dentist."

"I don't know," said the old lady. "I've had my teeth for twelve years."

"I like it here, though," said the old man. "When it's not crowded, I like to sit and play cards. Do you want to come to my place? We can play some gin rummy."

"I don't know."

Some people just won't accept that knock on the door from Father Time. The old bastard with the scythe. Good luck to you granpaw. "What do you think, Allan? How does it look?"

Where there is rapid destruction of leukaemic cells, liberation of phosphates and other intracellular components results in hyperphosphatemia, hypercalcaemia, hyperkalaemia and hyperuricaemia - the so-called tumor lysis system. It may be rapidly fatal. It is avoided by hyperhydration before administering chemotherapy and careful biochemical monitoring at frequent intervals.

They can do wonders with words nowadays. And with the drugs. *The remisson rate in adults with ALL is of the order of 70%. Long term survival is, however, much less satisfactory than in children, with only 15-20% surviving more than 5 years.*

The old saw: What would you do if you knew how long you had to go? That Japanese film, by Kurosawa - Ikiru - To Live. The stiff, spiritually dead bureaucrat finds out he has stomach cancer, and has six months to live. He decides to ram through the plan of a children's playground for some slum dwellers who have been ignored by the City. After his death his colleagues gather to weave together the web of his last days. In the last shot of the film he is swinging on a child's swing, in his playground, alone in the snow, crooning a sentimental song. "Live your life with all your might..." or something...

It's easy to find solutions in art that you can't find in life. Or even in central heating. Thok - wheeeee - ploop... This is ridiculous. I'm sweating in my underpants in the middle of a snowstorm. It's so easy to lose the thread. Tangled in the cat's cradle of our uncollective memories...

"Was it all simpler in the sixties, Allan, or was it just another myth?"

"It was simpler and it was just another myth. But people believed they could make a difference. That was the difference. And we did, up to a point. What we couldn't figure were the consequences."

But Allan Darwish is a a freak. He really wants to know what's going on, objectively, and is not primarily concerned with his emotions. In a country obssessed with feelings, not thought. People here say I think when they mean I feel. Land of the irrational rationale. They can put a man on the moon but still argue that the earth was made in six days.

Wasn't it Voltaire who said Faith consisted in believing not what appears to be true, but what appears to our understanding to be false?

What do you believe, Benjamin? My stupidity consists in my continuing to ask myself this question after the age of fifteen.

"Ben-Ha-Meen... Ben-Ha-Meen..."

"Yes?"

I am going mad, talking to my central heating. It has nothing to say to me, being simply the marriage of turn of the century plumbing with state of the art Puerto Rican maintenance. I asked Esteban, the super, if he couldn't stabilise the system at a pleasant twenty centigrade. But he said the building's oldest tenant, Mrs Yugo of apartment 2c, threatened to report him to the owner if the temperature drops below 90 Fahrenheit.

Time to go down to the Film Co-op, round the corner, on East 6th, to see if any of my students have turned up. The only snag is, to go out you have to put on clothes, in this schvitz-bath. If I put on my pants, shirt and sweater, and wait until I'm out the door to the corridor before I put on the coat, I can just about manage the transition, but then when I'm down the lobby it's into the high steam again, as Mrs Yugo sometimes sits and reads last year's paper on the sagging old sofa there. So it's either off with the coat again and on out the main door, or a quick mad dash across the flaming Sahara.

Going for the latter option, I'm out, the beads of sweat freezing to salty ice on the steps outside, floundering through the unswept snow. The snow is so high it's practically covered the entrance to the basement, location of the Hermetic Bookstore, whose proprietor, a Mr Linowicki of Krakow, is usually so deeply buried behind his piles of fifth hand volumes of everything from Astrology to Zoomancy that he would hardly notice the Flood. I've bought some curiosities off him, a Latin Book of Beasts full of griffins, salamanders and the bizarre sucking fish Echeneis, which holds a ship fast in the strongest storms although it is only six inches long. Also a book of "Hebrew Alchemy", The Great Pyramid Decoded, and a more recent book, The Art of Memory, by Frances Yates, a fascinating trip through the lost arts of pre- print memory, Giordano Bruno, Raymond Lull and other Renaissance esoterics. There's more to history than meets the eye and ear.

In the book I bought about the Great Pyramid the author proves that the angle of the slope of the Great Pyramid, when taken as a "rhumb line", whatever that is, describes the direct route of the Children of Israel as they passed over the Red Sea, and continues straight to Bethlehem, that distance, in Pyramid furlongs (1 Pyramid furlong equals

8000 Pyramid inches), corresponding to a time scale which points to the very date where Jesus the Nazarene was born.

Faith again. Lying in ambush, as on the day, when the leukemia tale erupted, and Allan phoned me to say Caroline had just returned from her hospital tests, that I rushed up to 93rd and Amsterdam to find, behind the Hound of the Baskervilles straining round the open door to wrap its huge paws round my midriff, the unfamiliar figure of an earnest young man in a clean cut black suit with one of those razor edged haircuts which made it look as if you could land an aircraft on his head. Behind him, Caroline hovered.

"Hi Benjamin. This is Karim."

So this was the prodigal son, who had seen the light in the eyes of the Reverend Louis Farrakhan and decamped into the Nation of Islam at the age of thirteen. Now he was sitting beside his mother on the old red battered sofa on the ground floor living room, you could see the kinship, although he was twice Caroline's size, and had that healthy look that comes from clean living and certainty. But they both had that stubborn pouting expression. The quickness of the eyes, and the calm hands, stroking the dog that sprawled between them. Behind this tableau, the dismal rain of October ran down the grimy tall windows.

"Hi," he had said, "how y'doin man?"

I put out my hand and he shook it, after a slight hesitation. I sat in the only available seat near them, which happened to be the old wood rocking chair. It's impossible to sit in it without feeling like Grandma Moses on a roll. We sat, bobbing our heads at each other as if they were on creaky springs. Or maybe Karim was shaking his head. His pout was at the edge of distaste. Small wonder if she had told him she had been sharing her bed and board with an Israeli, representative, if I understood the Reverend Farrakhan correctly, of the pretend Jews, usurpers of the true claim of the authentic Black Hebrews. Ice People pretending to be Sun People, the ultimate seducers and race rapists. But whatever his thoughts, he was keeping them well hidden behind that surly countenance.

"Karim's come down for a couple of days from Chicago," Caroline said.

"I've heard a lot about you," I said inanely. "I hope you're doing O.K. out there." His presence set up a shield, emblazoned with experiences, trials, traditions, images and blood I couldn't cross. It reminded me of the day I was shipped up to 138th Street in Harlem to meet the folks, but then it only lasted for a blink, as they sized me up, then poured five fingers of grappa into a glass they shoved at me, and then continued pouring, to hell with the consequences.

Color is skin deep, but religion... After some inane chit chat about her tests and reassurances of good prognoses she walked me out onto the pavement in the rain, giving me a peck on the cheek and a whisper - "he'll only be here a couple of days, Benjamin. You know I haven't seen him for two years. You know how it is."

If I knew how it is... We had this tacit agreement. She never discussed Karim with me, or either of her two ex-husbands. I didn't even know which one had fathered the prodigy, if either. When you find some human contact in this city, you just say Thank you God and hold the questions. "I'm just glad," she said to me once, in the night, when her thoughts wandered off the agreed rails, "he's not out there pushing drugs or worse. I don't believe what they believe but they keep the kids from self-destructing. In this country you can't put that down."

No, he's only learning to separate, to forge an iron clad identity to keep out all intruders, flaws, blemishes. Purity and wholeness, as opposed to Mo Smith, who glories in his fragmentation. Maybe if those two could meet, the sparks would fly, though probably the one already contains the other, or vice versa... What do I know?

The Art of Memory, Frances Yates wrote in her book, was an attempt to pull together the strands of human knowledge in such a way as to obtain the cosmic power, the rational magic, to be able to tap into the underlying harmony of the world that could be known. The root of learning, alchemy, music, mathematics, language. The Renaissance ideal. Not much point of that here in America, where nobody remembers anything...

Slipping and sliding through the snow, I reach the glass doors of the Co- Op, galloping down to the basement studios, which are hardly warmer than the street outside. The coffee machine isn't working but my angular colleague Vera Lompoc is encamped in the office, her question-mark shape wrapped in a mangy fur coat, and surrounded by posters for a slew of programs old and new: New Video & Film From Finland. Lewis Klahr: Tales of the Forgotten Future. American Exploitation Festival: Herschell Gordon Lewis, Ted Mikels, Abel Ferrara. Jean-Marie Straub revisited. The Chantal Ackerman Retrospective. Yep, we go all the way.

At least here, at the Film Co-Op, I can sink into my own esoteric world, dust off the vintage reels of Stan Brakhage and project those old classic "underground" movies for myself: Reflections on Black, Zone Moment, Anticipation of the Night and Dog Star Man. Those endlessly repeated sequences, superimpositions of sun spots, moth wings stuck onto the film and somewhere in there the dog, the star and the man, the repeated birth of the child, the man climbing up the hill, the sun, the moths, the star, the man and so on. I find Dog Star Man very soothing, though I invited Allan round for one of our screenings and he vowed never to set foot in the studios again. But Brakhage is still at it, and we have booked him in for two evenings next month, to show his latest works: Christ Mass Sex Dance, City Streaming, and Delicacies of Molten Horror Synapse. Looking forward.

"Morning, Vera. What happened to the heat?"

"Super's day off, Benjamin."

"Anybody in today?"

Our Co-Op works to an informal system. Members register for a year and pay a fee which entitles them to full access to our equipment and facilities or a part fee for just the evening programs. Then there are the special evening workshops on editing, video equipment, cameras. I handle the full members, the kids who come to use the equipment to make their own movies. The Keen Machine. At the moment the roster is twenty-four souls, all shades of the City's human rainbow.

None are in this morning. No trace of youth but a show reel, left for me with a short note by the Tango Twins Javez and Roz, the raw footage of their documentary about the Hispanic murals on the walls of alphabet city - Avenues A thru D. These amazing frescos, collages of Latin American history, street life, prison, drugs and dreams, all painted by ordinary street kids, sometimes as part of rehab projects, but apparently protected by the local gangs, who keep them from being defaced or destroyed. It's strange the mix of care and callousness.

I suggested to Frances that she could adopt these murals as an external exhibit to be sponsored by her Acme Gallery, but she found that not many people were keen to traipse down to Avenue C and 8th, one of the universe's most dismal junctions, to be ogled by the crack pushers hanging about with their gold rings and silver rimmed Ray-Bans.

But there is talent out there, festering, burning. Flickering before me on the old Kem editing table, a five storey high rainbow riot of hues swirls about a huge hand grasping a multitude of people streaming out from a landscape of lush fields and green leaves into the jazzy, multi-lit towers of a Caligari-like Manhattan, vignettes of street festivals, entertainers, musicians, clowns, jugglers, and strange creatures lurking in the undergrowth: fabulous men and women with the heads and limbs of animals, lions, panthers, iguanas and eagles, sharp claws emerging from tailored suits and dashiqis, tails curling from human behinds. Here is a lizard playing the cornet, there a beast of myth, is it a salamander? - selling holy icons from a tray. The camera pans, nice and steady, thank you Roz, across the road to the opposite side, which has been razed to the ground, like a landscape after a nuclear attack, an empty field of garbage on which the ragged homeless graze, gathering indefinable bits of flotsam and dropping them into plastic bags. One man is slumped over a folding chair, with a gutted car engine dumped in a supermarket cart beside him, while others roam with pointed sticks, picking up trash. Cut to the artists, four Hispanic kids, three boys and one girl. Their stories, without sound on this reel. But I have heard the tapes. The boys have all done time for offences of existence below the poverty line - two on marijuana busts, one for robbery of a liquor store with a toy pistol. The girl, Jacinta, was on probation after squirting aerosol paint into a cop's face. She has a black mane the size of the Empire State Building and the graceful, cautious movements of a stork. You could see where all the strange animal figures came from. Javez and Roz took me to see her, in the chaotic apartment she shared with six other kids on Avenue B, chock-full of dozens of her amazing miniatures of the jumble of street and fantasy life: Lizards and lechers, schoolboy werewolves and voodoo housewives, devil cops and beggar-saints. Salim accompanied me, that time, and fell in love with her. But she turned out to be a lesbian, and was only interested in him as another representative of an oppressed nation.

"I'm so tired of it," he complained to me afterwards, in the Dojo Coffee Shop on Saint Marks Place, among the usual freaks and punters, riffling through the souvenir stalls, the neo-punk ex-hippie trashbins of overpriced memorabilia of times that never were. Redwood dreidles, my God, I haven't seen those for years. "It's like being the point of a pyramid which is upside down and the whole weight of history crushing down on you. Who needs it? What I need is a good fuck."

"It's no use Salim. It's biological."

"Does love count for nothing?"

"Nada."

It was a bright but cold fall day, I remember, just after the election, Day One of Clinton. I tried to console him with politics. "At least they got that bastard Bush out, Salim."

"Bush was better for the Palestinians. Clinton belongs to your lobby, Binyamin. Whatever it is we'll lose out."

"Things have to improve, Salim. They just have to."

"You've been in this fairyland for too long, Benny."

"Where else can we go?"

"San Francisco?"

Climbing up Jacob's Ladder. If only wrestling with angels were the problem. But I'm not looking for the big bright light any more. All I really want is to survive the winter.

"Why don't you tell her your story? The day you crashed with your Chairman in the desert. The barren dunes. The terrible price of survival. You've stacked up enough bone fide hours of suffering. It might count for something, if not the old one two."

He shrugged: "You never can say what works in this City. I once had a woman passenger who peed over her boyfriend in the cab. Of course, I threw them both out. It's sometimes when they shit that you don't notice till later, when the next customer gets in... This is a sick town, Binyamin. If I could go home I would. But your people are living in my house. So what can I do? Don't you ever want to go home?"

Again and again, the same old tune. Any more pounds of flesh off me I'll be a skeleton. "You can have my house, Salim. Only you'll have to live with my parents." And listen to all their soured dreams. The fouled promissory notes of a tainted utopia. No, the whole point is, to live without illusions. To get by day by day without expectations. Just living for the frozen tick of the clock...

Back to the murals, on the dim Kenco screen, a golden griffin, lurking among garbage cans. The camera moves in, to a glow of red eyes, a demonic and startled look.

BOOM. The building suddenly vibrates. A muffled thud, which seems to have come from under the earth, follows, with a second's delay. The editing table takes a little leap. As does my heart. I've heard that sound before. But I stick by my post, until, over the ratchet clatter of the editing table's cams and springs comes the wail of ambulance, police and fire truck sirens, one howl at first, and then a cacophony of lamentation. Vera Lompoc whipping open the door of my cubbyhole -

"Hey Benjamin - did you hear the explosion?"

I, who can hear a toothpick snap at eight hundred yards... My ears already ringing with the sirens louder now through the opened door, rushing down 4th Avenue. And another roar, the growl of speeding helicopters.

"Is there a radio around?"

We have tons of equipment in our basement, but not to connect us to the real world. We used to have an old TV set, with mickey mouse aerials, but it was thrown in the junk long ago. In this place we're tuned to our own private transmissions. Closed circuit dreams. But Vera turns up an old Walkman, and we press our heads together, sharing the tiny earplugs, twiddling the dial through all the usual cacophony: Talk shows, scream shows, offers of cut-rate furniture, discount boloney, second-hand clocks, ambulance-chasing lawyers, Howard Stern's Big Boob Bonanzas, Crush Limbo rants, the beat of pop, pap, rap, techno, house, country, classical clips, and the whole Babel of Greek, Italian, Spanish, Japanese, Albanian, Hebrew, Polish, Russian, Uzbek, Apache, Hopi stations. I might as well be listening to my central heating ducts, which are at least more soothing. But the news show finally does break through, the event unfolding in its frenetic dolour - "ten thousand people still trapped in the buildings... There appears to be no accurate count of casualties at this time... I can still see people high up there, on the seventieth or eightieth floor... smoke still coming out of those broken windows... people streaming out of the buildings... it seems that all of the electrical systems of both towers have been knocked out..."

An old acquaintance, in a new setting. I nodded at Vera, and she nodded back at me.

"They've blown up the World Trade Center."

Two days later, they arrested Salim.

REPORT NUMBER ONE -
by Frank Ox, Private Investigator. *(Primus inter non pares.)*

WE HOLD THESE TRUTHS TO BE SELF EVIDENT. The forces of entropy and destruction are closing in upon us... Everywhere, and at every moment of the day or night, plots are being hatched. Invisible ears are quivering at every gate, wall and doorway. Every blind spot conceals invisible windows through which hidden eyes can see into our soul. Under the carpet, strange tiny devices with digital nostrils scurry...

But I have now completed the first phase of my research, Mordecai. Addressing your request to be appraised of those individuals who constitute a threat to the integrity of The Body. To wit, in the first instance, the Primal Adversary - **Doctor Caroline Dexter.** Extensive surveillance and acquirement of personal files and reports reflect the highest possible level of proposed intervention in the affairs and destiny of The Entity, alias Mo Smith. (Alias, and so on and so forth.) The immediate danger of interference is, at present, mitigated by the medical condition of the subject *(see attached notes, p.4 thru 8, lab reports, urinanalyses, haematomologies, CSFs, CT scans, X-rays, hospital management transcripts)*. Excess caution advised due to the Entity's cognitive affective bonding matrix with this subject as object of the most recondite desires. I.e., in Jungian terms, his exteriorised anima, in neo- Freudian terms, his feminised totem, in Runyonesque terms, his dame, his chickadee, his doll. In 'hood argot (or rap), his queen-bitch.

Subject Number Two: Benjamin Gaberman, of 44 East 4th Street, NY 10011. Born Tel Aviv, Israel, 1962. Two years and six months old exactly at the date of the Kennedy assassination. (Note!!) Army service in the period of the Lebanon War (1982). Excused army reserve service after incident in Occupied West Bank town, 1988 (threatening fellow n.c.o. with armed retaliation after alleged assault by same on stone-throwing child). Established subversive instincts but no overt political affiliations. (Check possible connections to deep-cover occult and cosmo-zygotic associations.) Dental records (physician Dr Jesus Maria Indelicato, 66 East 8th, Apt. C.) checked against those of all known Foreign Agents in FBI Files (U.S. Code Sections 739-743, Executive Orders 11907-11908), results negative match. Present occupation: Tutor/Manager at "East Side Film-making Co-Op", workshop studio, running check on members, guests and affiliates still in progress. *(See Adjunct, section 34/b-5/d.)* Until current medical crisis of Subject Number One (above), in intermittent sexual relationship with same. Previously in sexual relationship and cohabitation with Subject Number Three (below). No extant venereal records. No recorded convictions. 15 Parking Violations *(New York City Transport Ordinances 24/j thru q)*. Vehicle owned by Subject Number Three, sold February 1991 to a Mr Wladislaw Woczeczowski (alias "Vlad"), unemployed painter, of Happauge, Long Island. Vehicle totalled in non-lethal motorway collision September 1991, records end. $2000 insurance paid. Investigations of possible insurance fraud optional but not prioritised.

Subject Number Three: Frances Stein, of 139 West 79th Street, NY 10024. In recent times involved, sequentially, in sexual liaision and co-habitation with Subjects Number Two and Number Four. Currently Director/Manager of Acme Gallery at 42 Prince Street (at Mott). Born Bellevue Hospital, 1959, to Sophie and Gerald Stein, schoolteachers. Member of Habonim Jewish Youth Group, 1973-1974. Membership of subversive organisations, from 1975: Palestine Solidarity Youth Committee Houston East (Note acronym - PSYCHE!!!), New Jewish Agenda for Peace (NJAP), 1976-77, Friends of Peace Now, 1978-, Delancey Street Community Association, 1981-85, Ad-Hoc Committee for Peace in Lebanon, 1982-3, Jews for a Democratic Palestine, Jews for Peace, Artists for Peace, Radical Issues for Radical Art Forum (RIFRAF!!!), et cetera.

It should be noted that Ms Stein is an accomplice to the malicious "class action" suit filed against me in Marin County, California, which forced me into my supposed exile in the Philippine Islands, alleging breaches of the Privacy Act, the Daid Act, and the Natural Justice Act, concerning my work for the proto-Zionist Anti-Slander League, which, as you are aware, was carried out on assignment by the Government of the United States in order to keep an Eye on both sides and report, from the inside, on the long standing activities of the Illuminati, the Nine Unknown Men, the Manichaeans, the Cabal of the First International, the Bilderbergers, the New Hashasheen, the Neo-Sufi Order of Ka and of course, the Elders of Zion themselves. No offence, Mordecai, but a Private Eye has to call a spade a spade.

It is in this context that one has to look at the Acme Art Gallery's consistent mounting of exhibitions which are either incomprehensible or pornographic, or both. In the past year it has become a showcase for the dubious constructions of Selina Hasek, under the facile rubric of "non-kinetic" art. Miss Hasek is a "refugee" from Czecho-Slovakia, known, until the shadowy events of 1989, as the lynchpin and hub of the world communist cabal. The ignominious defeat of the communist cabal which has been trumpeted by the Bilderberger-controlled press *(the New York Times, the Washington Post, the Los Angeles Times, etc, the London Times, Le Monde, the Suddeutsche Zeitung and others)* being, as we well know, a ruse, the ultimate manouever before sweeping back, as the Free World's back is turned, to a victory greater than any it might have previously imagined. Miss Hasek's domicile in a so-called "geodesic dome" in Long Island, together with 12 other (note - 12!!) deep-cover long term Czecho-Slovak and other foreign agents cannot pass un-noticed by the watchful and vigilant Eye. As a matter of urgency, I intend to move, in the next phase of my investigation, against this hidden center of the intrigue against the lucidity of our vital bodily fluids.

(Supplemental notes: See under Conceptual Art, Connectivity, Convergencies, Deconstructionism, the Gaze, Len Loons, MoMa and the Masons, Object Art, Post-Post-Modernism, Simulacra, Warhol's Brillo Pad, etc)

In this context, I should add the following: It is, apparently, little known that John Wilkes Booth, Abraham Lincoln's assassin, did not die in a fire in Garrett's Barn, as the prevalent historical myth has it, but escaped the blaze, and lived in various hiding places in the United States until his death in Illinois in 1904. The soldier who claimed to have fired the shot that killed Booth, Boston "The Crab" Corbett, was an adherent of a religious sect which practised self-castration, and is known to have been placed in an asylum in Michigan from which he eventually made his escape. Corbett's connection to the sinister Skopotsi sect of Bulgaria which practised self-castration as a path to salvation, in continuation of the infamous Bogomil Heresy (see the Albigensian Rebellion, etc, notes 35 thru 37), has still not been established. But this is clearly only a matter of resources. One would need to penetrate the "geodesic dome" at Patchogue, and subject the occupants' genitalia to the closest possible examination.

Do you read me, Mordecai??? Do you feel the pain, the agony?? Till when, O Lord, must we countenance the counsel of malefactors, and all the afflictions of our youth? Why art thou so far from helping me, and from the words of my roaring? I who have done it all, in my time, from Autopsies to Ziggurats, from Bugging to Witch-hunts. I who wore a dry-cleaned black suit and a white fedora with no trace of birdshit on its brim, I who shot it out with Baby Face Nelson, Fancy Pants "Bugsy" Moran and Lou the Big Fish of Kansas City. I who sipped peppermint tea with J. Edgar ("Big Eddy") Hoover, commiserating with all his woes and his wobbles. I who hid under Marilyn Monroe's bed, listening to the low buzz of her ovum. I who had a bug in Lee Harvey Oswald's pocket and in the brain of Jack Ruby. I who know the secrets of the assassinations of Lincoln, the Archduke Ferdinand, Walther Rathenau, John F. Kennedy, Anwar Sadat and General Zia ul-Haq. I who know the meaning of the caduceus symbol of the so-called medical fraternity. I who poisoned Lenin, and know in which old age home the rescued Hitler is lying, a dried out husk of 103 years, fed on strained yoghurt and royal jelly, still awaiting the Call to Return. Yea, though I have walked in the valley of the shadow of breath, I have always had my concealed microphones and fish-hook lenses in the deadly nightshade. You know my bona fides, Mordecai. The Faust Agenda, the Beelzebub Dossier, the Salem Portfolio, the Dante Allegations, the Jehovah File. How I hid in the Burning Bush to mislead Moses. How I spirited Jeshua of Nazareth off the Cross, and put Judah "The Man" of Keraioth, heavily drugged with opium, in his tomb. How I concealed myself under a rock in the Arabian desert and dictated the Holy Book to Mohammed. All the Black Arts and Psy-Ops. I always aim to give good value for money. An honest day's work for an honest day's pay. What can't be cured must be endured.

Till when, O Lord, till when? I who cry in the daytime, but thou hearest not, and in the night neither am I silent... As I sit here, writing in the frozen doldrums of my dingy room in the National Hotel, watching my underpants boil and bubble in the blackened pot upon the single oven hob. For I am a worm, and a reproach of all men, and despised of the people. Even my pot sneers at my kettle, shouting out: Kill the white nigger! I, who have known the secrets of the seed corn, have become the most abandoned of all. I...

THE ALCHEMIST MORDECAI PUT DOWN THE DETECTIVE'S REPORT FOR A MOMENT, facing the youth Jaime across the pool table. "Frank Ox is cracking up. He has completely flipped. Can't the man pursue a simple assignment? I give him names and addresses to check on and he gives me this crock of tamales. What has John Wilkes Booth got to do with the price of eggs?"

Jaime paused for a moment, cue poised over the eight ball. "Hey man, you paid the man, you expect some service. He can't get somethin for nothin." He slammed the tip of the cue against the ball, which bounced, over the edge of the table, disappearing into the dust on the floor. The dust, rising, diffusing the dull glow cast by the single lightbulb hanging over the flotsam of the loft like an executed prisoner.

"Come over here, boy. I want you to suck my cock." The Alchemist unzipped his fly. The heat in the loft was unbearable, despite the sub-zero temperatures outside. Every shutter had been sealed shut, banishing the day. Mordecai turned his pants down and unfurled his member, whose tip hummed with anticipation. Jaime sighed, reluctantly shelved the cue, knelt down and grabbed the Alchemist's thighs, applying his tongue to the target area.

"If there is one thing that I can't abide," breathed the Alchemist, "it's when things go out of control. The whole fucking point of Alchemy is that you get all the ingredients right. The salt, the morning dew, the oil, the powdered ashes, the pubic hair of a red haired left handed man, preferably a eunuch, but not compulsorily. I used to use little dabs of my own, my personal signature: Powdered emu eggshells, anal mouse hairs, the dried sperm from a lifelong member of a Trotskyite organisation, with just a little dash of unicorn horn, a mere soupcon, so as not to blow the whole schmeer out of the water. Everybody thinks we were just after the elixir of life, the philosopher's gallstones, or just greedy for gold, but there were so many other dividends. The creation of homunculi, who would do your every bidding, was very popular in the 16th century. Palingenesis, restoring a plant from its ashes, that would lead the way to resurrecting the dead. The *spiritus mundi*, the force that moves the world, the divine spark innate in matter. None of that's a simple business. Work work work, not shirk shirk shirk, comprendo? You may just think you're just sucking another lousy dork, compadre, but what you are doing is raising the life forces of the universe. The cosmic sperm, gurgling in the root, the most ancient truths, the oldest subterfuges and deceptions, the cosmic follies, the demiurges of the old Adam, the entrancements of Eve. The whole secret is to suck that apple, not bite. Aaah, yes... Lower down, boy, get that tongue round the balls. Whatever you can dish out, I can take it. Life should be an eruption boy, the endless gushing of the volcano. But Adam gave birth to Man and then stuck around in the Garden, eating grapes and communing with trees. Playing chuck-a-luck with Lilith's successor, Eve. Cutting the grass, polishing the microwave, doing nectar and wild berries. If you were a self- respecting serpent what would you do? Eh, icho? Get a little action going, man, sow a few seeds, some wild oats. Are we men or are we mice? Put a few fire-crackers under the Old Man's bed and blow the sucker sky high. Out of the Garden of tiresome dreams and into the big wide, awesome, dangerous, sexy world. Ohhhhh, SHIT!"

Mordecai ejaculated, directly into Jaime's mouth. The boy pulled back, to avoid taking the blast, but the Alchemist's powerful right hand held his tousled head, trapping his lips round the stalk. The boy bit down, sharply. The Alchemist's head snapped back with a piercing howl. His hand pulled back, his right foot kicking the boy away with overwhelming force, knocking over the pool table in a great cloud of dust and blood, as the boy fell back, the tip of the Alchemist's organ shorn off in his teeth, his mouth foaming red and white. The stricken man staggering about, shooting a parabola of blood and semen into the murky air. Bellowing like a stunned bull, the Alchemist lurched about the loft, overturning chairs and tables, crates of billiard cues, boxes of coloured balls and bowling balls, which cascaded on the floor, rolling about like wild demons, colliding and dispersing. Blood flecked the walls, racks, empty showcases, trophies, plaques: FOR LIFETIME SERVICE TO THE ALLIED REFRIDGERATION COMPANY - DONALD F. KRUPP. A MAN OF VISION - OGDEN B. SNATCH, PRESIDENT HOHOKUS ELK LODGE.

"AAAAAAAAAHHHHHHHHHHHHHH!!!"

Jaime spat out the bloody mangled tip. "You break the rule, man - " The Alchemist turned, lashing out, crashing his elbows into the walls, tearing the nailed shutters off the broken jagged windows, tearing his fingers on the glass as the great icy blast of the city ripped through -

"FUCK! SHIT! FUCK!"

On the floor of the toilet of the Pennsylvania Station, Mo Smith thrashed about with his feet, kicking and squealing in the drying pools of piss spit and vomit, the other customers edging carefully around the sprawling body of the homeless man, in his soaked layers of shirts, threadbare sweaters and coats, as his hands desperately fumbled at his undone fly, clutched over his tormented groin.

"GODDAMN! SHIT! BASTARDS!"

Passengers coming in to relieve themselves turned back and fled at the sight, as the tortured man propelled himself round and round on the floor by the kick of his feet. A few, who were too tight to wait, stepped over the circling human starfish and popped their load in the encrusted sluice.

"GAAAAAHHHH..." Stopping his gyrations with his mouth pressed to the floor, his tongue attaining purchase on the grimy scuffed tiles, Mo pressed his elbows, then his palms, to the floor, raising himself painfully, first on one knee, then the other, scrambling to his feet, doubled up, pressed against the peeling wall. Dragging himself, hand over hand, to the door, then out into the glut and hustle of the railway station's lobby, the moving masses blurring to and fro. His hands clutching again at his groin, the burning pain shooting through and through. A wide empty space forming about him, the crowd magically parting to allow him on, towards the nearest escalator. The blast of freezing air swirling down like an invading force -

"They should be taking care of these poor people in the shelters... they shouldn't be allowed to just walk around..."

Cutting his way through the voices, bursting out at the top of the escalator, up the last flight of steps, into the roaring traffic of Eighth Avenue, spewing steam and ice. Clawing at the air opposite the General Post Office, with its stone carved sign incongruously honouring CARDINAL DE RICHELIEU, PUBLIC POSTAL SERVICE, PIERRE D'ALMERAS MDCXXI GENERAL DES POSTES - Crying out in the supreme agony, he whipped his penis out from under his multiple folds, thrusting it forwards into the path of the whistling, greedy, shrieking wind. Hurling himself down to the pavement, the thick coating of fresh snow, pressing his injured organ into the cauterizing flakes -

"Aaaaahhhhhh..." The red blood flowing, hardening, congealing in thick whorls in the white ice. A sanguine whirlpool liquorice. His fist jabbing down in the cold -

"YOU MOTHERFUCKING BASTARDS! IF YOU WANT TO GO, GO!"

The Alchemist lay, face down, naked in the snow. Hands stretched out, clutching snowballs, his face flicking back and forth in the icy crystals, his mouth and tongue cooling to the balm. The shamefaced boy standing a little tentative above him, holding, in his brown hand, the little reddened sliver.

"Hey man, I kept the cut. You can get it sewed back on, if we can find a quack..."

Another roar of rage welling up, from the end of the anus, through the torso, tearing through the lungs towards the mouth. The implosion tearing through his teeth, as, one mile downtown, another savage explosion shook the pavements and buildings, emitting a great spew of fumes and splinters, knocking out all electrical power for forty blocks on every side, north west east and south, of the Trade Center's Twin Towers...

Dog Star Men - the Great Escape.

Jacinta and her assistant Miguel walked the zig-zag blocks from their apartment on 10th Street across Tompkins Square to 8th and Avenue C. The snow was thick on the ground and the few derelicts sprawled on the benches wrapped up head to foot like bundles of rags. There was a cop car on the corner of B, but the two occupants remained inside, unmoved by the familiar sight of the lanky girl and the amazing hulk carrying her folding ladder and her pots of paint in the grey morning light. Even the thought of a quick cocaine bust could not draw the policemen from their heated metal womb today. Far from the bombed Trade Towers, there was no property to protect in this barren waste, long abandoned to the wretched of the earth.

There was one wall still to be attended to. One stubborn moss grown surface, whose crumbling bricks had long evaded the restoring power of Jacinta's brushes and paints. She had spent days repairing the cracks and filling in the gaps with plaster and putty, but it was like pouring freshwater into the ocean. The house itself was a shell, and in its jungle interior the dealers and pushers plied their trade. Today the snow had crushed the foliage into a melded soggy white mass, into which no-one in their right mind would attempt to climb unless they hankered for an icy tomb.

The buildings on either side had already succumbed to the project, and, even in the dull light, shone with the brassy eloquence of Jacinta's frescoes of the heros of the ages: Moctezuma, Tupac Amaru, Manuel Belgrano, Jose de San Martin, Simon Bolivar, Toussaint L'Ouverture,

Emiliano Zapata, Pancho Villa, Agustino Sandino, Che Guevara, Mao Tsetung, Amilcar Cabral, Eduardo Mondlane and Samora Machel, gazing defiantly upon the bleak streetscape. There had been no room left to celebrate Nelson Mandela, and she had drawn up a blueprint in which the hero of the South African liberation struggle would be the centerpiece of a new cycle of faces, focusing on women, notwithstanding the illustrious leader's impending divorce from his wife Winnie, which some of the comrades considered a potential threat to the entire concept.

Moctezuma and Tupac Amaru were killed by the Spanish, Manuel Belgrano and San Martin and Bolivar triumphed, Toussaint defeated the mighty French empire, Zapata and Villa and Sandino live on, Guevera bequeathed us the glory of his martyrdom, Mao raised the East's standard, Cabral, Mondlane and Machel were all martyred, too, in the name of Africa's renewal. Here on Avenue C they have little to look forward to but small bands of jaded gangstas selling brief vulgar dreams in white packets or tiny folded slivers of silver paper. Perhaps it would be best to keep Mandela out of this.

But as Jacinta and Miguel approached the wall, her assistant's heavy boots thursting the snow aside like shovels, she spied a figure lying at its foot. At first she feared it was a dead body, a familiar dry husk fallen from the urban tree, but as she crunched closer along the snow she could see the body was trembling, the feet kicking slightly like a sleeping dog, a large German shepherd or even a Great Dane. As she looked more closely she saw that it was however a human, male figure, clad in torn corduroy pants and a frayed jacket, covered with a layer of what appeared to be a kind of congealed slime, almost a half frozen placenta, now dripping off him to dissolve in the snow. It had a pungent smell which was evaporating in the freezing air, but that reminded her of nothing on earth. For a moment she had a fantasy of a "man who fell to earth," a being from a half-remembered science-fiction movie, dropped from the stars. A face peered through the melting cocoon at her. A thin, wiry black man, who might have once been handsome but whose skin was drawn taught on his bones, an ashen colour, as pale as a black face could be, as if starved of light, unlike the burnished rough features of the homeless men and women flayed by the open air, the wind, the sun, the rain, the frost, the sleet.

"You O.K. man?" Miguel, the hulk, kneeled, laying down the ladder, pots and rucksacks, putting out a massive paw to clutch the prone man's ragged shoulder. Wiping the layer of slime off on the snow. The man's lips moved in tiny puckering, popping sounds.

"It's weird, this stuff is warm, but he's ice cold," Miguel held a slimy hand up to her. She hesitantly touched the man's face, peering into his eyes, which seemed blurred and unfocussed.

"What we gonna do with him?" asked Miguel.

"I don't know." She looked up at the bulk of the wall, above them. The empty, plastered space. Moss twining in and out of new cracks, like climbing ivy. She looked back at the man.

"Can you talk? Do you have a name?" she asked him. Then in Spanish. But he shook his head. His lips formed words.

"Lincoln," he said. "Lincoln Korombane."

Miguel felt down and round his body. "He ain't been hit, or shot, that I can see. Just this slime all over. Nothin in his pockets, no papers, keys, knife, nothin. Not a nickel."

"We doin no work today." She got up, tossing her mane at the wall, which growled at her, flouting its flat mangy face. Miguel sighed. Hefting the man, onto his broad right shoulder. Jacinta lifted the ladder and placed it under his left arm. She gathered the pots of paint and rucksack. "Lincoln. I didn't think of that. Why not a white man, if he was a good one? Just paint him black, and make him one of us." She turned to the man, gasping on the hulk's back. "Don't worry man. We'll take care of you. Nobody dies under one of my walls."

Not too disconsolate at not having to spend the day freezing his butt off in the deep midwinter, Miguel loped ahead, with his burden, as Jacinta trailed behind, chewing her lip and thinking of outlandish images. The two cops in their car barely gave them a glance.

The authorities are always slow to respond to miraculous births.

*

HE'S OUT! AND THIS TIME IT'S REAL!!

Oh Shit!

Arnold Flint stood gasping for breath on the corner of 41st Street and 8th Avenue. Clasping his thin pajamas around him as the icy wind swept through his bones.

Jesus Mary and Joseph! And Abraham, Isaac and Jacob and all the rest! He looked down at his bare feet, which were sinking, sizzling and giving off steam into the thick layer of snow. He looked at his hands, which were gnarled and blue knuckled, the fingernails a dreadful purple hue.

"This is not the right way!"

But the words turn to ice cubes in the air, falling uselessly to the ground. He looked round stiffly. Behind him a garish red light flicked on and off the legend "XXX NECTAR - MALE & STRAIT - BI - TRANSEXUAL - EUROPEAN VIDEOS." On the floor above a sign said "WIRE MONEY IN MINUTES - ENVIE DINERO RAPIDO." A tramp bundled in the doorway wearing six Navy blue greatcoats eyed him strangely, shaking his head. "Man, you a long way from the Waldorff Astoria." He looked down, glancing at the hotel legend on the pocket of his red striped top.

"Fuck! Piss! Shit!" He swung round again, realising the grey maw of the Port Authority Bus Station on the other side of the road. "Move, feet!" They responded, shakily, to his command, carrying him into the path of a two way stream of traffic, which had just been released by the lights. Waves of slush and hooting horns battered him on his way. He swatted them off. "Bastards! Nazis! Fucking Polacks!" He blundered to the other side, collapsing against the hood of a yellow cab which was just swallowing a bag-laden customer. The driver swung to face him, eyes ablaze, but he staggered on, into the Bus Station concourse.

A steady stream of travellers passed by him, trailing melting white crystals into the building swept away immediately by the eternal mop of the weary blue-coated attendant. Too much transience. And those with nowhere to go, huddled along the shopfronts and corridors, shuffling around the restroom entrances. The patrolling policemen, swinging handcuffs and mace cans, lacking the heart to evict them into the icy outside. The relative warmth loosened his locked limbs and ungnarled his frozen fingers. He could see the breath in front of his eyes. Slinking away from the policemen's quizzical gaze he lurched towards a bank of Bell telephones. Managing to lift the receiver to his ear at the third attempt. Finding zero with a numb forefinger.

"Operator! I want to make a reverse charges call. People That Count Corporation, 65 East 65th Street. It's a radio station. I don't have the number. I want to talk to Mr Crush Limbo. Limbo - El-Eye-Em-Bee-

Oh. My name is Arnold Flint. Ef-El-Eye-En-Tee. Flint. Yes, I want to speak to him personally. Make sure you get him on the line. What? Well, do what you can. It's an emergency. Yes, I'm waiting, but the circumstances... O.K., right, well, do it." The pause, of electronic rustling. The unsettled void. "Yes. What? Whadyoumean, they won't take the call? Are you sure... did you speak to Mr Crush Limbo...? What, no I didn't ask for his secretary, we have a personal... what's that? I know he's the President of the Corporation. I'm the President of Arnold Flint Communication Enterprises. I want to speak to him, not... They won't take the call. You get them to... you ask... No, listen... I have this spot on his show... Two hours, Mondays and Thursdays... We have ten million listeners on the East Coast alone, not counting our subsidiaries and syndicated... Hey, no, I am listening, you're not... Fuck you bitch! Oh God!"

The empty buzz of non-contact. Pressing his head against the wall. At least it was warm, reverbrating with the thrum of the buses rolling to and fro above, in and out of their bays. To Manhasset, Hicksville, Brookhaven, Teaneck, Hackensack, Passaic and all points out-of-state, Greyhound- Trailways to the four corners of the earth. Steadying his shaking forefinger, stabbing at zero once again. Relieved to find a different, male, voice.

"Happy Valentine's Day to you too, sir. I want to make a reverse charges call. To a Mrs Elaine Shainberg-Flint, 365 Larch Avenue, Pleasantville, telephone number 203-XXX-XXXX. My name is Arnold Flint. Now listen, it's my ex-wife. The thing is, she can be a little ornery at times, particularly if she's been at the minibar, dyou get my drift. Mano a mano. You don't take no for an answer. Sometimes it takes a little push. You know, seventeen years can't be just tossed down the drain. There's always something left. You have to dig for it. Get down to that soft layer, where the old days swell and glow. True love is a star forever shining in the heavens and all that sort of crap. You know how it is. Thank you, you're a real trouper, what's your name, Gustave? That's a hell of a name. Has a real ring to it. O.K., do it, I'll hold on."

The minutes tick away. The loudspeakers call out the roll call of altered platforms and departures. The telephone line clicks and hums.

"Hallo? Hallo? What's your name, Sydney, Fred, Abdul... Come on Elaine, you know I didn't mean to poison the dog... stupid lop-eared mutt... Hallo? Yes? What? No, that's not possible. What do you mean she's never heard of me? If she's never heard of me how have I heard of her? Gave you the right number, didn't I? You sure you spoke to the right person? Shainberg-Flint, O.K., Shainberg, 365 Larch... got that right didn't I? Bet I did, worked my ass off on that porch, climbing up that roof, pulling those damn squirrels out with my bare hands, still got the scars on my fingers, bastards bite down to the bone, fucking damn vermin, fixed those goddamn roof slates... Now listen, Sydney, whatever your name is, this is just one of her tricks. Seventeen years. I know every crease in that body. Love handles you can really get your mitts on. That wart on her left buttock. The one she thought was turning nasty after Puerto Rico, when was it, 1985? Rushed back to Doctor Talehban, fucking Iranian quack. Laughed in her face. No way melanoma, neither malignant nor benign. Said it was going to fall off in three days. On the money. Had that thing since she was thirteen. Hid her ass in the shower. Ask her about that. Why not? Fucking Valentine's Day. No, listen... well, see... No, I understand your procedures... Don't want to get you fired by the company, asking women about their warts... Hey, there's no need to take that tone with me! I'm an American taxpayer, damn fucking I.R.S., skin a louse for its pelt... shirt off my back. Listen man, I'm freezing to death out here... No, I don't want you to phone the Washington Street Shelter, whadyou take me for?"

Slamming the receiver down on its hook. Now here's a fine kettle of fish. But can a man of this calibre just give up and die? How long was I in that diseased fuck's kishkas? Probably smell of pus and urine. Bad vibes, travelling down the lines. Those miserable German soldiers. Froze their ass off at Stalingrad. Iced up bowels. Spontaneous combustion. Have to work this out. Get rid of these fucking pajamas. Get a wash. Warm clothes. Money. Get up there to Westchester County. Show that bitch who's boss. Crush Limbo. East 65th Street. Must be a way. This may be a setback, but it wouldn't have stopped the Wermacht. Certainly not the Red Army. Marshalls Tikhonov and Timoshevsky. Put another Tartar on the fire. Sacrifice the weak to keep the strong going.

On into the restroom. Warm water, splashed on the face, neck, arms. Put the right foot in the basin. Bliss. Now the left.

It's not as easy as it seems. To knock down some fellow human. Steal their clothes, shoes, money, and get away, body and soul unscathed. Easy to put down on the page. But most of these passing dead beats, shuffling about with three coats, could well do with two, far too large, black, ornery, hands like shovels, probably knives hidden in those tatty folds. The cops armed to the teeth. Travellers passing too quickly, none of them daring the toilets. And one cop already mumbling into his intercom. Taking notice. Gotta move on.

Make believe you're going somewhere, even in this ridiculous attire. Head, down, towards warmer quarters. On the escalator down to the lower level, past the Greyhound Ticket office with its languid, morose line. The chocolate fudge shop's delights hidden behind bolted shutters. Through the swing doors into the long underpass leading to the Times Square subway. The long, dolorous tunnel through the vibrating earth. Deep below the ice we might reach the sulphurous depths, the steaming lava flows. Somewhere along the way, behind a broken bolt, an abandoned old barber's stall, a shoeshine niche, there might be a pathetic bundle of rags, a peripatetic, lost soul, someone in direr straits than oneself, worn out by spirits or drugs, who can be knocked out, robbed, despoiled of the small stash of coins in his pockets or boots. The survival of the least unfit, in this purgatory, in these tunnels of the halls of the dead. Where are you, Merenptah, dead Pharaoh, schmoozer in the underworld, when I need you? On second thoughts, what's the point, you lost your way in any case too. I'll probably end up back in the intestines. At least it's warmer here.

Maw of the subway. 42nd Street. Just managing to slip through the turnstile. The galloping hordes. Shops, stalls, the begging saxophone players. A man belting out some fearsome blues lyrics, a capella, glaring at the crowd. His bag filling up with coins and dollars. What the fuck can I perform? Old school poems: Byron. Frost. The Gettysburg address. Or a reading from the new opus - selected rants of Cotton Mather: *"The very Devils are broke in upon us, to seduce the Souls, torment the Bodies, sully the Credits, and consume the Estates of our Neighbours... as if the Invisible World were becoming Incarnate, on purpose for the vexing of us!!"*

So what else is new? Never learned an instrument, Goddamit. Sing for my supper. How did that Cotton Mather piece continue? - *"The Devil, exhibiting himself as a small Black man, has decoy'd a fearful knot of proud, froward, ignorant, envious and malicious creatures..."* Always knew this was his stamping ground... It all makes sense. But oh, the smell of those Hebrew National frankfurters!

Sometimes a man is just inspired. His feet planted just within odour range. His arms, rising to the occasion. From unknown depths, the voice bubbled, an unexpected basso profundo with an unexpected Robesonesque timbre, plucking from forgotten wellsprings the weeping, compelling cadence of the Cantor calling forth the service of the Funeral of the Dead:

"*El maleh rahamim, shochen ba'meromim...*"

O Lord full of compassion, who dwells in the sky... slow to anger and abounding in loving kindness... grant pardon for transgressions, bring salvation near, and perfect rest under the wings of the divine... open the gates of righteousness and light, the gates of pity and pardon...

Something in the voice cut through the rush and bustle of the subterranean chamber. The babble ceased, and the wailing sound of the sax from the lower level died away. The crowd gathered round the middle-aged, silver haired man in the Waldorf-Astoria night dress, hushed and perplexed, as the dirge rose over the unceasing rumble of the trains.

"*Be'seter kanfechah tastirehu...*" Under the cover of thy wings give him shelter, and let his soul be bound up in the bond of eternal life...

He fell silent, sagging in his thin pajamas after the exertion of his startled larynx. His chin falling down upon his racked chest. The hair falling over his eyes. And then the crowd stirred, throwing a shower of coins, placing a mound of notes at his feet, then melting away, to continue their interrupted journeys.

*

At first there was only the darkness. Then he perceived a dim glow from afar, sillhouetting a host of strange figures, like columns of headless torsos, stretching in every direction. He was lying on a cold, hard floor, which nevertheless appeared to creak lightly under his hands.

He lifted himself to his knees, and raised his head. His eyes adjusting to the dimness. The racks of torsos seemed to be fixed on hard metal stands. He stretched his hand to touch them. Fingers brushing fabrics. He could recognise now the shapes of the clothes he had seen people wearing in the streets, through the eyes of the Sleeper.

Softly, Ibn Battuta rose, padding carefully about the enclosure. Moving stealthily between the racks. The store appeared to extend into endless alcoves which led in turn to a maze of others. Some sections contained clothing for men, others for women, others a large variety of handbags and luggage, others strange undergarments remarkably smooth and delicate to the touch. One thing was certain, this was not the world of the interior of the body to which he had become, by force of necessity, rather than choice, reconciled.

"I have returned into the world," he murmured to himself. But still not the world of his own time and place, but that, he surmised, of the Sleeper, of the shop windows he had peered in upon his long passage up the thoroughfares. Like a cat, he could now see in the semi-dark, making out the names spelled in Latin letters on each set of the alcoves: Donna Karan, Elen Tracey, Giorgio Armani, Liz Clayborne, Calvin Klein. It was clear to him these were the names of the stall owners who would return, come daylight, to attend their wares. The store itself was an endless bazaar, with metal staircases leading up and down to further floors, with a variety of goods, modern apparel, comestibles, a "Health Food Restaurant" and a dazzling display of jewellery encased in caskets of glass, which would have enticed the *khatun* of the Sultan Muhamed Uzbeg Khan at a distance of six hundred paces.

Unable to know how long he had before daylight, Ibn Battuta nevertheless proceeded, as the experienced traveller does in a new country of whose customs he has but little knowledge, to accoutre himself according to the mannequins he noticed placed at various spots within the store. Collecting an appropriate number of items from different racks he found, by opening doors marked "PRIVATE" - noting his comprehension of the language used as a lingua franca in the Body - a cubicle with clean washing facilities, in which he ran a hot bath and then proceeded to dress himself: Commencing with the softest silk undergarments in a deep velvet black, followed by a white linen blouse and an oversuit taken from Mr. Armani's stall. Matching pants and boots chosen after a short but uncomfortable search completed his attire, but he could not decide between the hats which he had taken from an upper floor. Eventually he decided upon a large fur cap of the kind he recalled from the Transoxanian wilderness, and, having shampooed and combed his beard with the implements found in the washroom, exited towards the stairways. It was at this point that fortune truly smiled upon him, as his boot came upon and kicked aside a small wallet which was lying by a rack upon the floor. He picked it up. It was bulging with recognisable banknotes, of denominations rising from the modest "One", with the Masonic eye over the pyramid, to the delightful "100"s, with "The White House" and "In God We Trust" upon the back. A folder of hard, embossed cards and a number of paper documents were also included, and a number of small portraits, depicting a smiling bald man with spectacles and a family of two women and three small children who all looked similar, albeit with hair.

"All praise to God, the Almighty, the All-seeing, the Provider," he murmured, raising the wallet to his lips. All that remained now was to exit the enclosed bazaar before the vendors Liz Clayborne, *ustaz* Armani and Klein arrived to open their stalls. (I knew an Al-Omani once in Tripoli, he recollected, a seafarer of Sindbadian proclivities - but that's another story.) Descending the staircases, arriving at a large entrance hall dominated by eight clocks, each showing a completely different hour. This, he thought, was oddly appropriate. But he could hear the rumble of traffic coming from the street beyond a series of glass partitioned gates. He tried to push them open but they would not budge. Taking hold of one of the stands, he stepped back, then heaved it with all his strength at a glass window. It shattered, setting off the hellish cadence of an excrutiatingly shrill siren. Using the stand to sweep aside the glass fragments, he thrust himself swiftly through the doorway and ran down the sidewalk, passed the rushing, oblivious vehicles, down past the lighted shop windows and the immense emblazoned sign, "BLOOMINGDALE'S", across the wide sidestreet, ignoring the irate honking of drivers, putting as much distance as he could between himself and the unbearable sound.

*

THE BLIZZARD, WHIPPING ONCE AGAIN ACROSS THE WINDOW. The drying laundry, slung across the room. Undershirt, longjohns, socks, jockstrap. And Mordecai the Alchemist's bloody under-pants, scrubbed but not cleansed in the cooking pot.

"Lie down, you need your rest."

Frank Ox's good eye gazed solicitously upon the man thrashing in the bedsheets. His right hand poised with the needle.

"I can double the dose, if needs be."

"You taking elocution lessons, Frank? I don't fucking needs be the needle. That stuff has no effect on me. In 1349, in Florence, I had a hundred and fifty leeches feeding on me, sucking out the plague. I don't need any shit in my veins. I need my fucking penis back."

"Most of it is still there, Mordecai," said the private eye, "he only got the very tip. I've seen worse mutilations."

"Sure. I've seen men with both arms and legs blown off get up and win the Congressional Medal of Honour. I've seen headless men sing the Marseillaise. I want that fucking spick bastard! You hear me, Frank? His ass is mine."

"I thought that was the point at issue."

"Very funny, Frank. On second thoughts, give me that needle. I don't care where it goes in. I took a lance in my ass, in the Siege of Vienna. I was fighting on the Ottoman side. That Polack jerk, Jan Sobieski, stuck me in the right buttock in a sneak attack. I was the Grand Turk's chief physician. I operated on myself. No snow or smack at that time. A Muslim army, no booze either. I just remembered all the humiliations of our faith. So fuck you."

"It's all right, Mordecai. I'll find the young man. Nobody escapes me in this city. No matter how deep they burrow or how high they climb."

"This is no ordinary grudge, you get me? This is fucking elemental. You can't bite off a man's cock and get away with it."

"It's just a small part, Mo - "

"Nothing is small. Everything is gigantic. Everything is the whole world. The smallest speck of shit is cosmic. Every fucking quark tells a story. There is no beginning, middle and end. The slightest is the most. Now!"

The Detective lunged with the hypodermic syringe at the Alchemist's raised left buttock. He pushed in the piston to the full and withdrew, as the stricken man sank back, emitting low whispers and snorting growls. Surveying the slimy preparation he had stirred up in a grimy wineglass, he considered refilling the needle for his own use but then set it aside upon the cluttered worktable, among the quiet wind-up toys. Surveying the boxes and piles of clothes, disguises and manuals of everything from nuclear engineering to raffiawork, he looked out the window again, trying to peer through the storm. The infinitude of white crystals, blasting out of pitchblack sky. The struggling lights of Times Square, the news sign rippling round the Number One tower. BOMBERS TARGET U.N., TUNNELS - PREZ PLEDGE TO ARMY GAYS.

Indeed, as we approach the millennium, the contradictions can only increase. Ox pressed his nose up against the pane, his breath fogging the glass. He wiped it. But the image was still obscure.

Where are you, lost boy? I know you're out there, somewhere.

It's always the same. People think they can hide, from their enemies, friends, lovers, creditors. In a city of twelve million souls, surely you can disappear, vanish as surely as if you had never been. But he who knows you may not have been in the first place has no problems smelling you out.

Frank Ox licked the filthy pane, and crooked his stained forefinger.

Just come to me, my little lad...

*

The snow comes out of the sky in a flurry of white needles. Picture postcard white on the trees of Riverside Park. The squirrels are in complete hibernation. Stalactites hanging from branches. The abandoned railway sidings frozen in ice. The Hudson river itself not quite solid, but sluggishly pushing filthy grey floes.

And yet there is life in this desolation. At the rotunda of the Soldiers and Sailors' Monument, a strange crowd has gathered. Snow has capped their duffle coats and hoods. Their feet stamping to keep warm. In regular flourishes, they raise and shake their fists at the sky, calling out in unison the refrain: "Fuck you! Fuck you! Fuck you!" Their bestial cries echoing across the park, across Riverside Drive, through the double glazed windows and blinds of the condominiums on the other side, through the knocking and hissing of the steam in the heating ducts, through earplugs, triple blankets, and pillow covers.

"Fuck you! Fuck you! Fuck you!"

The sleepers toss and turn, assuming, perhaps, that the cries are inside their heads. Others, more alert, rise stiffly, staggering to the icebox to get something for their parched throats, wondering about a pre-dawn snack.

"Fuck you! Fuck you! Fuck you!"

Jaime, pulling the collar of his thin jacket tight around his trembling chin, his fingers and toes feeling like lead bullets grafted onto his arms and legs, climbed up the steps of the monument to mingle with the crowd, to warm up at the heat, craning forward to try and make out the cause of their agitation. He had thought it might be something like an illegal dog fight, perhaps with beasts who'd had their larynxes removed, so as not to alert the cops. But there was nothing there to see. The crowd huddled around the base of the rotunda, it appeared, for the mere companionship of their immaculate passion. There seemed to be no object of their desire, save its own expression. Pretty soon, Jaime was shouting, too, waving his fists and stamping his feet back to life. But something in their eyes made him lower his fists and draw back towards the edge of the crowd. Although it seemed the expected mixture of the city's types, races, ages, shapes, all were men, whose faces gleamed, despite the pitch of night, their eyes lit with an emberous glow from within. He backed away, down the steps, to the snow- drifts of the covered paths leading to the road. Across the sludge swept Drive and up 97th Street he might find, he thought, past West End Avenue, along Broadway, some foolhardy souls braving the elements on leaving the all-night drinking and schmoozing clubs. Perhaps there might be among them one righteous soul in Sodom who, even after the rave, might nurture a gleam of compassion for a boy desperate enough to brave the arctic night in quest of a few quarters and dimes. Maybe even someone crazy enough to pay for services rendered, though in minus 15 centigrade...

And then - The Miracle of Riverside Drive: No star in the sky to guide the enlightened, but, nevertheless, there he was, a small, hunched figure, wrapped in an army surplus overcoat, with a thick scarf and a bobbled wool cap, emerging from one of the apartment block buildings and ambling across the road to the Park. Braced against the snow, with quick chopping movements of his heavily gloved hands to propel him forward, the man leaned against the storm, which crusted his spectacles, causing him to pause and try and wipe them clear with his glove. He stopped short at the blur of the young man's trembling frame.

"You O.K.?" The man put his spectacles back on, examining the still wavy, unclear shape before him. "You don't look equipped for this kinda night. Are you with those people?" Nodding his head towards the still chanting crew.

Jaime began to speak his mantra but his teeth chattered: "Ya ga-ga-ga any-ny ch-ch-ch-ch-ch...?"

The overcoated man examined him, took his spectacles off again and wiped them with a large handkerchief extracted from one of his coat pockets.

"Shit, man, you're freezing. Someone take your clothes? Well fuck it. Come with me."

He turned and walked back across the Drive through the slush, turning only once to beckon the youth on. Jaime followed. They climbed up the steps to the apartment block and the man unlocked the main door to the lobby with his key. As they entered the heat of the lobby the man's spectacles frosted up completely, blinding him with an instant layer of ice. He took them off and peered at the young man intently.

"When did you last eat?"

Jaime flapped his arms around to get back his circulation. He looked like a wounded bird desperately trying to fly.

"I, ah, well, man..."

"What's your name?"

"Ah, Jaime."

"I'm Allan. Well, Jaime, I'm going to take you up to my apartment, then I'm going to fix you something to eat. You can stay a few hours, then we'll see." The man pressed the lift button. It began cranking down slowly, from the 17th floor. "I'm going to trust you, Jaime. That cuts both ways. You know what I'm saying? Nobody owes anybody anything except trust. I don't have to tell you how much of that you can expect in this city."

The lift arrived. They rose in it, silent, until the tenth floor. Allan unlocked the door to his apartment. Jaime stepped in to the clutter of a room lined with bookcases, piles of books and files and loose papers held with rubber bands on tables, piles of newspapers, a recessed study with all the writing machinery, desktop computer, printer, copying machine, stationery and yet more books. A leather sofa which Allan cleared of more books, newspapers and files. The only free wall, by the TV, dominated by a large painting of dusty ochre and brown lines and scrawls. Reminding Jaime of something, but he could not think what.

"I like that, it's weird," he said, as Allan took off his coat and moved towards his kitchenette, carrying more papers off the work surfaces. "That your own work, man?"

"Oh no. A friend of mine, from Morocco. A student. He's very gifted. What does it make you think of?"

"I don'know, man. Looks like..." His hands made shapes in the air, then dropped.

"It's Cairo. In Egypt, Jaime. You ever travelled out of the States? Were you born here?"

"I, I don'know where I was born, man. It was a long time ago."

"Right. You know what Chico Marx said? `I don't remember, I was only a little baby.' The movies - the Marx Brothers, know any of that stuff?"

"Not really man."

"You don't have to stand there. Sit down. I'll have to see about those clothes. I got some stuff somewhere. It's just got a bit cluttered lately." He opened the icebox. "I got some Chinese food that I kept from yesterday. We can heat it up. It's real good food. The Szechuan Gourmet. Empire Ginger Chicken. Aromatic Chinese Eggplant. How does that sound?"

"Sounds great man."

"I had some dumplings but they've all gone. My friend Aram gobbles those up. We've been a bit distracted lately. A friend of ours has been arrested. We've all been buzzing about arranging lawyers, all that sort of stuff. You probably know the drill. How long you been living on the streets?"

"Me? I don't really know, man..." His head slumped back on the seat. His eyes closing then opening to take in all the unfamiliar surroundings.

"Listen, if you want to take a shower the bathroom's there. The water's hot. It's up to you. Get out of those freezing clothes. I've got a dressing gown somewhere..." He left the kitchenette and rummaged in a cupboard, struggling to hold up falling cardboard boxes. Jaime sprang up to help him get them back into place on upper shelves. His hand brushed against Allan's shoulder and squeezed it slightly.

"Here it is," said Allan, "I have a friend who uses it sometimes, but it's in good shape. There's also a Tunisian djellabah, but it's a little thin for this climate. I've got some ordinary clothes you can wear. You're about the same height as I am, but you look in better shape. I'll heat up the food. Shall I wait till you have the shower?"

"O.K., man."

The sound of the shower almost drowned out the shouts still rising from the Park. The storm, too, was gathering pace, lashing against the walls and window. From this height the howling wind was like a ghost, whipping up the chant of the Park and adding it to its repertoire of moans, shrieks and lamentations. Hours of the wolf. Allan Darwish punched on the television. CNN Business News from Asia. The Heng Seng Index is up twenty three and a quarter points. Tokyo is still buoyant at close of trading. South Korean stocks are tipped to rise. Taiwan was still depressed overnight.

Aren't we all. Jaime walked out of the bathroom, with the mauve dressing gown open to reveal his wet tousled pubic hair and half gorged cock. His right hand was absently caressing his balls.

"Inside Latin America is next," announced the firm blonde female announcer, whose eyes were glazed over in that early morning autocue look. Allan sighed and reached for the remote control.

Outside, the warmup session continued:

"Fuck you!
Fuck you!
Fuck you!
Fuck you!"

SALIM:

THEY CAME BUSTING IN MY DOOR, at five o'clock in the morning, with guns drawn and mouths blazing.

"DON'T MOVE!"

"HANDS BEHIND YOUR BACK!"

"GET DOWN ON THE FLOOR!"

"SHUT UP!"

"TALK NOW - WHERE'S THE OTHERS?"

Hordes, rampaging through the apartment, physically removing the door, blocking every window, pulling back the bedclothes, opening every drawer, jerking the mirror off the wall, along with the bedou saddlebag, the ornamental oud, the Moroccan painting by Allan Darwish's research assistant, the woodcut of Central Park with snowsleds.

"WHERE THE GUNS? WHERE THE EXPLOSIVES?"

"No guns here, no explosives. I'm a taxi driver."

"Just don't get smart." A square crewcut face with a drooping moustache and a bull neck clamped into a bullet-proof vest bulging with pouches thrust itself into mine. There were the traces of a cheeseburger on his whiskers. His eyeballs practically brushed my eyelids. It was like looking into the depths of the sea. Another clipped voice spoke up behind him.

"You are Salim Halimi, of 54 Stanton Road, Brighton Beach?"

"It's my name, yes. I haven't done anything."

As soon as that left my lips, I knew it was a lie. I knew they had me, in the grasp of that metaphysics. I have done so much in my life, and yet, nothing that can be marked down by posterity for any great reward, or great punishment. Not, at any rate, by Man. With God, I have to take my chances.

But he was not the listening type. Or the Merciful. Droning on in my ear: "What I'm saying is for your own safety, and for the safety of innocent residents. You have a duty to tell me where any weapons or flammable materials are stored on the premises, and dangerous chemicals, poisons, plastic explosives, Semtex, CF5s or any other potentially lethal items. We don't want innocent people to get hurt."

While this jabbering was going on I could hear the rest of the mob trashing my apartment, crashes, thuds, loud ripping and tearing sounds, the hammering of what must have been large mallets, knocking out the cupboards from the walls. Everything I ever owned since I arrived here with nothing but my delusions seemed to be flying across the bedroom, shirts, pants, underwear, jackets, suits, socks, video-cassettes, tapes, cds, books, papers, boxes, keys. I could see out of the corner of my eye one hulk with overalls with "NEW YORK STATE POLICE ENGINEER" in white all over his sleeves and chest down on his knees unscrewing the back of my TV.

"I don't know what the fuck you looking for, man," I told the eyeball, "there's nothing of those kinds of things here. You got the wrong address, the wrong man, man."

"Is that so?" The voice materialised into a smallish, dapper man with his body armour incongruously fitted over a dark suit, his tie immaculately fixed, his hair glistening with a thick black cream. The eyeball pulled back a fraction to allow him to thrust a loose photograph in front of my face. "How about this?"

"What about it?" I asked, "there's nothing criminal there. We're all talking about peace these days." It was a portrait of me in more committed days, smiling, with the Chairman's straggly-bearded grin under his head- dress beside me and his arm draped around my shoulder. "Secretary Baker met with him fifteen times." I didn't know the number but it sounded O.K.. "There's nothing secret about that. It's all in my Immigration records."

"Oh yah?" he said, "and this?" He flourished, like a magician producing a rabbit, a pamphlet I had probably stuck long ago in a drawer, with a photograph of the old Sheikh Jedid and an Arabic text of one of his favourite sermons: The Backsliding Evil of the American

Jahiliya. I got it for Allan Darwish's collection but forgot to pass it on, God knows when.

"It's bullshit," I said. "I'm not with those people."

"You attended his mosque," the man said, "you ran his video shop. He got you a job. What other jobs has he asked you to do?"

If I hadn't guessed at the start what this was all about I could guess now. I started sweating. Despite myself, despite the enormity of the thought, the error, the outrage of their suspicions, I saw the scenes on TV, the smoke rising from the Twin Towers, the naked people running in the snow with shredded clothes, the covered torsos of the dead... The anchormen's frenzied speculations, about Serbian, Haitian, Arab, Muslim terrorists -

"Listen," I said, I babbled, "I haven't done anything. I'm just a taxi driver, trying to make a living. I've been a student. You can check with my college..."

"You have the right to remain silent," the little dapper man said, "if you give up the right to remain silent anything you say can be used against you in a court of law..." I had heard it so many times, seen it on TV. Kojak, Starsky and Hutch, Hill Street Blues. I was being Mirandized. But I was not there. I was no longer in Brooklyn, no longer in New York. I was back in Beirut, back in Sidon and Ein el-Hilweh, rushing to the shelter of heaps of rubble when the warplanes came crashing over. Crouching with my hands over my head waiting for the blast of the bombs. Thinking of all the comrades in prisons, the captured martyrs of the struggle. You think you've escaped the harsh realities, the dread and drag of need and woe. You think you've managed to switch off, to start to heal the jagged wounds. You think you've managed to become someone else, another life hacked out of the ruins of the old. You think you've escaped the common fate.

"You have the right to retain a lawyer of your choice. If you do not have a lawyer, one will be appointed for you by the court..."

They tied my hands behind me. They no longer use handcuffs. They have a kind of plastic wire. Their beefy hands grabbed hold of me in six different places, as if, like Houdini, I might slip through the net of half a hundred agents with their automatic weapons, their pump action shotguns, their cans of tear gas, batons and armoured cars. As they took me out, past the undoored doorway, and the ruins of the tiny lobby, strewn with my coats and shoes, into the dim dawn of the street,

I could see, behind the barricade of cop cars with their red revolving lights, the hastily erected "Police Barrier" fences, my neighbours, bleary eyed and swaying in the snow, wearing whatever strange concoctions they put on to rush out and bear witness, sweaters put on the wrong way, woollen hats askew, coats inside out, thin bare legs in bedroom slippers, their breath pushing out in wisps of steam in the freezing air, their bulging, wet eyes. I could see it all, as if looking through both ends of a telescope at the same time, both near and strikingly far, all in a strange, strained silence, as if my ears had gone completely dead. But I could smell the cold, like the sweetness of a sea-shore winter, that lay behind me, on the Brighton Beach. All my Russian, Georgian and Armenian neighbours, who had come out to watch a Palestinian being taken away, accused of blowing up the symbols of his refuge, in the land of the free and home of the brave. I could imagine the interviews they would be giving in only a few minutes time, about how they had never guessed, and he was such a quiet young man, and so inoffensive, so ready to fix your stalled car.

Benjamin, Benjamin, where are you, my Israeli friend? Allan, Caroline, my American friends? I know people in this country officer, not quite in the highest places, closer to the bottom than to the top, but... is this not the land of opportunity?

A blanket was thrown over me, as they led me down the steps of the porch, someone must have realised I was naked except for my shorts in the cold. I hadn't noticed it at all, as, like a sack, I was propelled through the back door of a van, into a darkness filled with pressing bodies in their armoured uniforms. They pressed me to the floor of the van, my head down, my tied hands behind me. Great boots pressing down on my back. Then suddenly I heard the wail of the sirens, the clanging of doors, the muffled shouts, the megaphone orders to the crowd to disperse, the hawking and coughing of the men around me, the rubbery smell of the body armour, the engine's reek, my own fear. The van jerked and moved off, the sirens following, the mocking dirge for the life I thought I knew, serenading me back into the past...

*

*

*

"SALIM? YOU'RE KIDDING ME!"

"I wish I was, Benjamin. They arrested him this morning, early. I just came back from the Tombs but they won't let me see him. Nobody's giving out information. I called this lawyer friend of mine who works all the hard cases. It seems they arrested twelve people in all after the Trade Center bombing. Most of them are going to be charged as accomplices. It sounds like they're going to package the whole thing as conspiracy. That way they don't have to prove participation in the act itself. Only in knowing about it in advance. It's all tied to this blind Sheikh Jedid in Queens. Though he hasn't even been picked up as yet."

"But Salim! He's not even a Moslem! He just worked in the man's video store!"

"Tell that to the FBI. We're getting my friend appointed as his attorney. I don't know if it's the best move but we can't afford anyone else at this stage. My friend is like a red rag to the bulls. Gerald Gittlin. The Great G. G. Gittlin. He defended us at the Chesapeake Trial. You know, when we were accused of plotting to kidnap Henry Kissinger, back in sixty-nine? He also defended the Weathermen. God help us all."

"But this is ridiculous, Allan. What do you think's going on?"

"I don't know. Aram thinks the whole thing is a set up. But we've been down that road too often. The Plot. Conspiracies. Agent provocateurs. The F.B.I. and the Mossad blowing up the Trade Center just to prove we still have deadly enemies. But I know these people are capable of doing it. The Islamic Jihad. Show them a bomb and they slaver. Revenge against the mighty of the earth. The great Satan. The problem is how far the police want to go. If they've planted evidence then we are in real trouble. If they're just fishing we may have a chance. Of course Salim was never a member. But they can dredge up that whole PLO stuff. You know Americans, they can't see any differences. It's all black and white."

"What do you want me to do? Have you talked to Frances? And Caroline?"

"I'm calling them next. Let's meet at Caroline's if she's up to it. I don't have room here as you know. Seven o'clock. Can you make it?"

"I'll be there."

After the snow, the rain. The post-blizzard thaw turned the pavements and streets into a churned black mush, topped up by the downpour. The rain undecided when it hits the ground whether to turn to ice or not. Nightfall will bring another freeze to create the famous ice shoe shuffle, when navigating across the roads becomes a roulette game of slips and plunges. The dark brooding sky matching my mood perfectly. Having slipped out of the house without an umbrella, I let the flood whip over me, plastering my hair to my skull, drenching my face and clothes. The cold clammy clasp of The Fear, that miasma of all the malignness of the City, working its way into the bloodstream, moving up from the old Reichian vegetative center up the spine and into the brain, eyes and nose, drying the mouth, wiring the entire body. My first host in the City, Mad Nathanel, warned me about it, but then, he had been mad before he hit this City. Then it hit me, a few weeks later, on just such a day as this, a black sky spewing ice cold rain, the tall buildings wreathed in a spray of steam, the streets full of drowning strangers, the shops and cafes and restaurants almost empty, the opaque vehicles crawling by with windscreen wipers desperately trying to slash a wedge through the wet muck.

First Caroline and now Salim. The undefined plague which seems to be devouring my friends, one by one. The thought of Salim, of all people, caught in the steel trap of the "law", with its absurd omnipotence, stupidity and barbed cages, was too much to bear. And yet here I was, bearing it, once again the beneficiary of the chance roll of life's dice which placed me above and him below. Our own Jewish sins and misfortunes transferred upon the Palestinian. The old survivor's guilt. That ugly, inevitable tinge of relief - that life grabbed his balls, not mine. And Caroline?

Israelite morbidity. But Allan Darwish is having none of this. A whirlwind of activity, he works the phone at Caroline's sanctuary like an old-time stoker feeding the coals of an antique warship. Phoning lawyers, old university colleagues, sympathetic journalists, deep throats in the diplomatic corps, the State Department, even disaffected FBI agents who now run radical think tanks in darkest Georgia, tracking the web that once they wove. Tracing the interconnected infamies of government from domestic scams to foreign intrigues, pork barrels to the Bay of Pigs, from the Watergate Cubans to the JFK mystery, from E. Howard Hunt to Haiti, from Panama City to Tel Aviv, from Atlanta to Afghanistan. "You have to take what these people tell you with a pound of salt," Darwish warned me, "some of them have completely flipped and see UFOs landing on the White House lawn at night, but some have kept their heads screwed on." From all these, he was hoping to make out the pattern of events which might lie behind the unexplained bombing, and the chain of arrests which was still, according to the TV news, going on... As we sat, in the dim gloom of Caroline's basement kitchen, watching the pundits of the tube peeling off their theories and hanging them out to dry, talking with absolute certainty about things they knew absolutely nothing about, Islamic Fundamentalism, the Middle East, the Palestinian cause, the hidden hand of Iran, Sudan, Libya, all the current Evil Empires of the day, now that the Communist threat has expired. Me sitting on the rickety, half collapsed chair that everyone always assumes I will take, along the long scuffed table, with Allan and Aram between me and Caroline, and Frances watching from the sofa, wedged between piles of medical and other magazines that clearly made her feel at home. The Hound of the Baskervilles, Fluppy Puppy, sprawled under the table at our feet.

Since the Revelation, I had not slept in her bed. This was Caroline's decision. She could not take on, she said, the Benjamite angst as well as her own at the same time. Before, we had agreed that our anxieties had cancelled each other's out, leaving a kind of mutual space. But this was something she had to fight alone, in the cold dark of the night, in the pale dawn by the cracked mirror in the bathroom, confronting the little demons in her bloodstream. Already she had the whole extended clan of her family pouring in from Harlem, Denver and Saint Louis, not to speak of the visitations of Karim, wearing his own opaque guilt. There was also talk of her mother moving in for the duration of the primary struggle against the disease, which could last from six months to two years. But then we knew that the disease was now a condition of life, like the fingers on her hand, the shades of her face. No return to status quo ante.

And the blizzard locks in once again. So reluctant to leave us be, even though the calendar says enough already. The ides of March. Caesars beware. Everybody in this city should beware, any time. Only the bloody dog is blissful, snoring away underneath Caroline's kitchen table, dreaming of God knows what. The steam turned up to over eighty Fahrenheit. Hoping to get Caroline's blood count up. The new cocoon. Caroline exhausted, in bed early, her mother departed back uptown to Harlem, Karim, Allah be praised, departed back to Saint Louis, and only the thirteenth son alive and awake in the cavernous house, alone with the dog, amid the flotsam of a Gourmet Szechuan takeout and the latest issue of the American Journal of Ortho-psychiatry which still merrily arrives month by month.

"Reaching Vulnerable Populations"; "Trauma and the News Media: Critical Considerations"; "Child Sexual Abuse Histories Among African-American College Students"; "Children of Survivors of the Nazi Holocaust: A Literary Overview"; "Attention Deficit Hyperactivity Disorder" - that sounds the ticket - "Out of Mind, Out of Sight: The Homeless Mentally Ill."

Leafing through: "Each night more than 160,000 persons suffering from mental illness face the dangers of living on the streets and in shelters nationwide." Half of them at least seem to be lining Broadway between 72nd and 96th Street, the gauntlet of supplicants holding out their styrofoam cups, wagging their woes in your face, flapping in the city's gaunt mourning. "Society has a basic responsibility to provide living conditions that ensure human dignity and offer refuge..." M.D., Ph.D.. Whadaya know, whadaya say.

All my insomnia returned. Already gutted Newsweek. "TERROR HITS HOME: THE HUNT FOR THE BOMBERS. How the Experts Keep Tabs on Terrorists." You'd think if they kept tabs they'd been able to prevent the act. But this is not the way an expert thinks at all. I need only look at "Doctor Death", page 48: "Dr Kevorkian, the `suicide doctor', plans to carry on, despite a murder investigation and a law aimed to stop him." Dr Death has been rushing about the state of Michigan helping terminally ill patients to end it all, by inhaling carbon monoxide, his favourite method of painless exit. Question: "Do you feel that you're accomplishing a larger goal, other than helping individuals?" Answer: "No. I have never cared about anything but the welfare of the patient in front of me. I don't care about the law. I don't care about injunctions. I don't care about legislators." How absolutely American. And not even invoking Jesus Christ. There at least is a breath of oxygen. What else has Newsweek got to reprise? The Crash of 1993: A reader's guide to the lowest interest rates in 20 years. Drugs: Is the Price Right? Not in this stretch of town. The ordinary price of any reasonable weed has doubled but you can get enough crack for five dollars to stick your head through the stratosphere.

I can't read any more about the "Massive Manhattan Manhunt." Bullshit alliteration always floors me. This morning's visit to The Tombs was enough. I always marvelled at that name for the downtown prison but never quite visualised it. I saw in my mind's eye an old Victorian dungeon, all high damp walls and rusty bars. Wretched hordes in Auschwitz uniforms and chained feet shuffling in lines like the condemned in a medieval Last Judgment. Hatchet faced guards, looking like "Jaws" on quaaludes, standing by with shotguns and wraparound shades. But The Tombs, I am informed by Darwish, was built in the '20's on the site of an even earlier, pyramid-shaped jail, sunk deep into the ground so as to cause the minimum eyesore to the crowds of ordinary folk going about their business between the financial center and Chinatown. Now it complements the "ziggurat", the gruesome Criminal Courts Building on Worth and Baxter, all jagged edges and opaque windows, looming over an innocuous city playground where children frolic on swings and old Chinese men play chess on trestle tables. Columbus Park, can you believe it.

The new Tombs itself, the "Men's Detention Center Complex", is just behind the Ziggurat, connected to it by a series of closed walkways which enable the accused to be shunted back and forth from their cells to the courts without any contact with the outside world. The prison is a tall mass of brown concrete, with vertical buttresses on every side, no windows up to the upper floors which are covered with an impenetrable steel mesh. The official address is 125 White Street. The back of the Tombs abuts on to a very ordinary Chinatown alley, with Chinese Health Clinics, restaurants and a sushi bar, and a tall apartment building whose side facing the prison is completely smooth and windowless. Just round the corner is Canal Street itself, the loud hustle bustle of the marketplace, fishmongers, Chinese grocery stores, joss-sticks, black-bean sauce, sticky rice and pak-choi. Liberty and penitentiary entwined.

But we got nowhere trying to see Salim. In the lobby, all glass booths and polished benches with morose black sisters, mothers, sons, brothers, daughters, fathers waiting for their number to be called through into the visitors' section, we cooled our heels for an hour under a huge logo of an immense cog and fulcrum with the legend "Correction Department

City of New York" in yellow on a blue background. Eventually the lawyer, G.G. Gittlin, came in to meet us through the main door. He had just been in the Courts, performing his usual ritual of trying to chip away at a cast iron wall. We adjourned to the sushi bar, which was filling up with lawyers taking an early lunch break before the next gruelling bout. A large flamboyant man in a crumpled grey suit and the obligatory shock of snow white hair, with a face that had seen it all and liked none of it.

"Up to their old tricks," he told Allan, having ordered a sashimi deluxe, "I've filed eighteen separate writs. But they just invoke the Conspiracy laws. Gives them a thousand ways of not letting go. We've been here so many times. On the other hand it could be a good sign they haven't arraigned him yet. It means they're not so sure. They're pretty confident on some of the others, but I think this one could be a foul ball."

"How is he taking it?"

"He was pretty shook up, the first time. It's easier to deal with if you're guilty. It's the innocent who foul themselves up, usually. If you're unprepared, it's pretty devastating. With the politicals, in the old days, at least you felt part of something, even if your client was an asshole. Remember Chesapeake, Allan? That little twerp from Princeton who wanted to be found guilty in order to expose Capitalism? Just like the Baader-Meinhof. They thought if the people would see how oppressive the state was they'd turn against it. But instead the people just clamoured for more and more effective oppression. And the Weathermen? That firebrand, Katharine what was her name, Beddows, Biddel? My memory's definitely not what it used to be... I remember I lost ten thousand bucks bail on her account. She absconded, and went and lived in the Subway system for seven years, living on rats and God knows. I defended her when she came out, but she still wanted to make a speech to the jury. Thank God by that time nobody gave a flying fuck. She got four to six, came out in three. Married a computer engineer in Fresno but left him to go and live in Oregon somewhere. With the Bhagwan. I defended him as well, for a while. At least he paid his bills. They were only allowed to have sex with rubber gloves, his followers. I hear it's loosened up since his death. I won't take any more Messiahs on anyway. Some folks called me the other day, about this man Koresh, in Texas. I took a raincheck. I don't need the money. I'd rather work for those who really need the help." He swooped on his sashimi platter with his chopsticks. Faster even than Caroline.

"This whole business. I have no doubt they're all involved. The CIA, the National Security Agency, they used these Islamic militants in Afghanistan. Three of the detained were in that war, trained by us to fight the Russians. I have reliable information that the Blind Sheikh, Jedid, was a major conduit for CIA aid to the Afghan guerrillas. Our government poured eight billion dollars into their coffers, through Pakistan, to get the Russians out. So what are these people doing here, in Queens, and since they are here, why should they be blowing up things in the place that gives them refuge? It doesn't make sense. These are very muddy waters, ladies and gentlemen of the jury. Very muddy. Would you buy a used terrorist conspiracy from the same people who gave you the Bay of Pigs and Watergate? But we're a long ways from that yet. We'll have to truss 'em up with the law. Hoist them on their own petard. Improper warrants. Entrapment. That FBI agent they had in the mosque for the last two years. They had those people under surveillance. So how did they fuck up? Or did they let it happen? I'm trying to subpoena tapes, documents. But they will fight it tooth and nail. When the state fucks up, that's when the coverups start. Don't we know it, hey? JFK, Bobbie, Martin Luther King."

"It's not going to be easy," said Allan, bearing down on a portion of raw eel. "Public opinion's against you."

"When was public opinion for us, hey? In Alabama? In Chicago? When we tried to get the Panthers a fair trial, when they sent Otis down for killing that cop? And he was in another town at the time? The boy is still there, in Soledad."

"The Blind Sheikh is not Huey Newton. Let's not get things confused. My priority here is personal. I know Salim is not mixed up with this group, whether they did or didn't do this deed. I know the people who introduced him to the Sheikh in the first place. It was just a courtesy call. Even an American court can see the absurdity of accusing a Christian of being a Muslim fanatic."

"I understand, Allan. But you're not seeing the picture. Religion doesn't count a damn here. It's race. It's all sheer bloody minded racism. An Arab is an Arab. He's on the wrong side of white. How long have we been fighting this system? I don't have to teach my grandmother how to suck eggs."

"Of course not, Jerry. But you know as well as I do there's never dark without the light. There's still a liberal constituency in this country that can still be mobilized. Even in this day and age they elected a Democrat President, shitty as he is. We should never give up."

"Who's giving up? Excuse me, I'd like some more tea." Clatter and crash across the counter. "I never gave up when Nixon and Kissinger were sending this country to hell. I cut my teeth on McCarthy, remember? That creep Roy Cohn came into my office. I was a strapping young lad at the time. He gave me the eye and said he didn't believe I was a communist and he would like us to be real friends. He wanted to stupp my ass, no offense, Allan, but this was not my game. I told him to fuck off. Bold as brass I was in them days."

"You told J. Edgar Hoover to fuck off, or so the legend goes."

"It was the Hoffa case. Bobby Kennedy and Hoover had ganged up on Jimmy. He was a crook, but he did well by his men, for a while, at any rate, before he got really greedy. Then Bobby and Hoover fell out. What can I tell you, Allan? In the snake pit. Can you wonder I liked all those rebels, those men and women who wanted to change everything, even by violence? We support it elsewhere: Vietnam, South Africa, Palestine. Why not here, where all the chickens roost? I know, we have our democracy. Our checks and balances. I know it's no solution. But sometimes even old men dream. I liked Huey. And Bobby Seale. And Stokely. You need some passion in this world. I know, you adored the pacifists. Dan Berrigan, and Jerry Rubin, Abbie, Ginsburg. The howlers and the pranksters. But I was a Bolshevik in those days. I didn't believe the ruling clique would be laughed out of power. Still, I don't see any point in blowing up the World Trade Center. Killing and maiming innocent people. They trap us by our own scruples, don't they? And then they have us in the palm of their hand. What do you think, Mister Benjamin?"

"Me?" I was running around in short pants while all that was happening, helping my Pa stick black adhesive tape across the windows of our Tel Aviv apartment to protect against Egyptian bombing raids. The armies of President Gamal Abd-el Nasser were going to march up along the route of Moses in Sinai to nip our own poor resurrection in the bud, unless we zapped him first. This was the way we saw it, caught in the old blood feuds. And now the Arab bombing raids have finally reached me in Manhattan, in a new mutant form...

No way I can help you, Salim, except to listen to these tales of old struggles and hope this old dinosaur can claw his way through the bars of steel and law towards you. G.G. Gittlin. They made a TV film about one of his cases. I can't remember the title, but he was played by Gene Hackman. I suppose they could have Omar Sharif to play Darwish, in the present. Who would I choose to play me, now that Paul Newman is past it? Wired and awake in Caroline's kitchen, these kind of musings come natural. Banal thoughts keep tripping up the mind. The heat is so high inside the house I am dripping sweat while the ice age clings on outside. Does this make sense, Caroline? Politics and disease. Any help here from Orthopsychiatry? How I would I cope if I were in your shoes, Salim? Do they allow you shoes in The Tombs? Or do they take out the shoelaces so you don't hang yourself, as in all the best jails?

This can't go on. I will go upstairs. I will undress methodically and get in under the quilt with Caroline, despite the prohibition. I will take care my gnashing teeth and wired up tension don't wake her up. I will lie beside her and listen to her breath as she fights her deadly microscopic battle. I will try to transfer whatever rude health subsists in my body to her own. By metamorphosis. The alchemical marriage. Hypnotise her blood back into life. Mending the world, knitting together the broken vessels of Creation...

ONWARDS! ONWARDS!

Picking himself up, scrabbling off the snow to stand, swaying at the corner of 34th Street, opposite the New Yorker Hotel, in the lee of the Home Savings American and a giant advertising mural with a jazzy quartet representing CAMEL - THE HARD PACK. Garment suppliers trundling their barrows through the drifts. The pain beginning to subside in his groin. Some kind of non-specific-agony. NSA. National Society of Assholes. 25 cents Peep Show Private Booths. Flailing his arms. Gotta keep moving. Across the street. Jackie's Department Store, Favourite Donut. The Sunset Coffee Shop. Billiards. Gifts. A framed portrait of Malcolm X. Give us strength, the red haired prophet. If I am not for me, who is for me? Up, the swathe of 8th Avenue. Loans. Fabrics. Foods. Deli. Pizza. American Valve Center. XXX Nectar Male & Straight, Bi/Transexual European. The Port Authority Bus Terminal. Gotta keep moving. The eternal corner of 8th and 42nd Street. Up against the car park fence, the Evangelists have replaced the Black Hebrews. GLORY TO GOD, JESUS IS LORD. All the bright lights of yesteryear. Give my regards to Broadway. I'm just a Yankee Doodle boy. The fire in the penis. The throbbing tip. Jesus died for your sins. He didn't care if you were a junkie, a crackhead, a thief, a murderer, a faggot, a honkie, a nigger, a greaseback, a spick. He didn't care if you were ugly or beautiful, or rich or poor, or man or woman. The one certain thing is that Jesus loves you. His love is unconditional. You just have to open the door and let him in, that's right sir, just open the door and let him in. You don't have a door? Just spread your arms there, just spread your arms and welcome Him. Because if you turn your back, as sure as night, the deep abyss will welcome YOU! E-ternal Dam-nation! Who is the man so dark or lost that he will risk that?

Where are you boys? Anybody in down there? Even in the storm, all human life is on this corner: the Mexican Caffe, King's Fried Chicken, Adofi's Deli and Grocery, Times Square Photo, Entrance to Subway Arcade Stores. More Adult Videos than you can shake a stick at. Live Erotic Male Shows. The hand of Time and the New York Municipality's New Cleanup Policy hanging over it all. The dead kingdom of the peeps. Stir yourselves! Up and at em! Merenptah! Lincoln! Arnold! Bat!

An ominous silence below decks. The whiplash in the groin. Beatrice and the House of Pain still in residence. The low moaning snore of Ann Hedonia. The slosh of bucket and pail. Who's that? Jesse? At least someone's minding the store.

Don't Walk Away From Jee-sus!!!

Crossing the road, past Show World Center, the Fan Emporium, Big Top Lounge, Electrics, Delis, Mogali Candy Store, Lingerie, Handbags, Luggage, Manufacturer's Hanover, Adonis Male Theatre for Adults Only, and on, across 44th. Mama Leone's. Smith's Bar and Restaurant. Beefsteak Charlie. Milford Plaza. The placque "Dedicated to the future of the City of New York, July 31, 1980." Over 45th, slush and traffic. World's largest Collection of T-shirts. Eros. Venus. 4 Adult Hits. Capri - New Show Every Tuesday & Friday, Clean, Safe, Best in New York. No one biting for the moment.

Still nothin to say down below? Whassamatter with you guys? Gone shopping? Try Scruffy Duffy's, or how about Happy Deli, all Boar's Head Brand Sandwiches, Cajun Joe, City Knickerbocker Lighting Fixtures, Ray's Famous Pizza, Stores for Rent - call Mr Rosenthal 212-207-3000. The Little Rascal's Restaurant - "The Original Oldies" - Singing Waiters, Deli-Chops- Salads, that should bring you out of your cells.

Not a chance. Hey Jesse, seen any of those other louts? Those belly-aching farts - forget about Jaime and the Alchemist, well rid of them, motherfucking beasts. Where is my Ibn Battuta? My friend Lincoln of the Mournful Countenance? My wandering Pharaoh? That son of bitch wasp faker promising to get me on T.V.? The cable hookup. National Radio. With or without sponsors. Fuck em all. Past the Ramada Inn 24 Hour Indoor Parking, World Wide Plaza, 50th Street. Elite Value Center

Health and Pet Foods - cybergenic, Green Magma, dried juice from young burley leaves, Soy Lectithin, Brewer's Yeast. Muscle Mac Pasta Cyber Trim 6 week mega fat-loss system. Try walkin these streets for ten years. Dr Edward H. Miles optometrist. Hyde Park Tarot, E.S.P. - I will tell you the past as it was; I will tell you the present as it is; I will tell you the future as it will be...

Do I feel lighter for this absence? The maricons have fled the coop. The bastards have cut loose, slipped the knot, blown the ghetto, rocked their cocks. Freebased on air. Chilled out. Departed this bale of sin. Lincoln. Arnold. Nep and Bat. Definitely gone.

- Good riddance, Moses.

That just leaves you, Jesse and the dames. Motherfucker. Leavin me with those two ballbreakers. Beatrice an Ann. This is bad news man. Those two will eat me up alive. I need the others. Checks and balances. The yin and the yang. The good the bad and the ugly. Something for everyone. The whole enchilada. I gotta think this out.

Up, dragging one boot after another, leaving deep footprints in the snow. Across 54th, 55th Street. Past Paramount Loans Pawnbrokers, Pioneer Piano Sales, Roy Roger's Roast Beef, more Macdonalds, the Symphony Cafe, Mariella Pizza, West Side Luggage, the Pottery Barn. The Fisk Building. 250 West 57th Street. In sight of Columbus Circle. The Great Discoverer, perched up there on his pedestal, head and robes capped in white under the dull grey sky.

All the way from Palos, Spain, to this. Enough to weep frozen tears. Icicles forming on the eyelids. Cataracts of ice. The frozen fountains. The wheel, with spokes east, west, south, north. Decisions once again. The diagonal spoke of Broadway heading off nor'-nor'-west. No point in holding up a licked finger, which would simply freeze and break off. Turn against the wind, buffeting the blow. Lurching over the crossings. The sign: KEEP RIGHT. PEDESTRIANS PROHIBITED. ONE WAY.

Mo turned the other way and pressed on, into the 60's, up Broadway.

Do the Dead See Scrolls?

JESSE.

I like it better in here, now that the louts have gone. Pity the poor Pharaoh though, he at least was the silent type. Kept himself to himself. He must have finally found the right turning in the labyrinth of his Halls of the Dead. I don't regret Battuta. Civilised as he was for a heretic, he turned out as much a blabbermouth as the others. Now, at least, there is some time for meditation, some peace of mind between the chores.

Now it is just I and the women. The Righteous Man, in the middle. Between Beatrice and Ann Hedonia, the Mistress of Pain and the Somnolent Martyr. I use this last term not in its stricter theological sense. For Ann Hedonia has not given up her place in the world for a painful death in the defence of faith, but there is certainly a cause, for which she suffers, if I could only find out what it is.

Beatrice is the Enemy. Like a spider in the center of its web she sits, with her whips and chains and instruments of voluntary torture, brooding over her lost clients and planning to ensnare new ones. One should not underestimate the female lust unbridled. I have been thinking a great deal about this.

In the desert, on the banks of the Dead Sea, one was free, in most part, of temptations. They came to us in dreams, as they did later to the Egyptian hermit Antonius ("Saint" Anthony), who was pursued by a host of demons, mostly of a sexual nature, vying to deflect him from the True path. The Teacher himself was said to have suffered these attentions. I myself never had those dreams in the desert. In my worst dreams I was tempted by food. Great carts of delectable dishes were wheeled down the rugged slopes of the Jebel Harmun, sumptuously wafting the odours of roasted meats - lamb, water buffalo and quail, bison and beef, even forbidden pig-meat - towards my famished senses. Waiters in immaculate white robes and turbans with brilliant red sashes stood by, with freshly laundered cloths odoriferous with soap and perfumes, their green scarves whipping in the dry wind. Then they removed the coverings, and my poor senses were overwhelmed, at which point I would awake to find myself lying with a parched throat, in the lee of the Qumran cliffs, under the clean velvet canopy of the stars.

And so I have never been impressed by the false and fetid delights which lured my fellow consignees to fall under Beatrice's spell, enticing them to be strapped down upon her wooden racks and crossbars and to be beaten about their most delicate parts with an assortment of paddles, bamboo canes, leather straps, ping pong bats, cat o'nine tails and whips that would flay the skin off an ox. Their cries, whether of pain, pleasure, a combination of both, or a kind of strange animal cry that appeared to come from some prehuman spirit, a reptilian caw, as of an eviscerated iguana, were not conducive to a contemplative climate.

Never is humankind a greater mystery to me than at these moments, when I am climbing up around the pancreas, with my pail of water and a sack of fresh bagels, to tend to the Sleeping Unbeauty, and hearing those desperate sounds coursing up from below. But what does Beatrice herself gain, apart from the vigour of her physical exercise, and the promise of financial emolument, which is in any case no use to us within this ragged twomb? The empowerment of her unchained femininity against the chained males? Whose desire was being served here? This was not something I could discuss, or elucidate from my boorish companions, slaves as they were to their basest passions, their slack jawed palour bearing witness to the degeneration of the intractable libertine. The multiple sins of Onan. Not to speak of the heavy weights Beatrice liked to attach to their testicles which made them sag and brush upon the floor. And now that they have gone, I have lost my chance to understand. Or have I?

It was Jaime, the teenage catamite, who alerted me to the possibility that there are, lurking in the recesses of the body, new intruders, waiting to appear. He claimed they coursed about the bloodstream, the "plain clothes" detectives of the New York Moral Patrols, and he gave them fanciful names: Inspector Haemoglobin, Sergeant Thanatos, Officers Thora Zinn, Lars Gactil, Hal Peridol, Scoopy Lamine. Of course, he was a grade A liar. But sometimes, even I could be brought to doubt, wondering about the fleeting flash that could be seen out of the corner of the eye. Who knows through what levels one might have to wander in search of that elusive, Final…

I pushed open the door of Ann's room, against the muddy slush which had, as always, accumulated inside at its foot. The dingy chamber, with its peeling, blown out plaster walls and leaky ceiling. The great sagging four poster bed with the figure lying under that moth-eaten quilt which had once been as multi-coloured as Joseph's dreamcoat but was now a faded grey mess. The face, bloated and decaying, with her mouse coloured hair in wisps all over the pile of propped up cushions, encrusted with mouldy food stains, and leaking moulting grey feathers. It lifted towards me, the right eye closed, but the left staring, like the eye of a rotting potato.

"Hey, Jess. I lost the remote."

"It probably fell on the floor." Which could hardly bear scrutiny. The eternal glut of empty food cans, crumpled silver foil of gutted TV dinners and takeouts, the mass of airmail letters, pages spilled out, some torn across, others shredded or crumpled into little balls, the paper trail leading across the slush to the dilapidated TV with its broken bunny ears, the screen transmitting a sea of fuzz and static, through which odd bloops and belches erupted. She waved a pudgy hand wearily towards it.

"The off switch ain't bin workin for a while now. But I could change channels. I think it's under the bed."

This is the chore I least enjoy. Perhaps, if I were a genuine Saint, it might be the one I most prized: Getting down on my elbows and knees, sticking my head carefully under the bed without actually drowning in the sludge. The space beneath the bed was a mound of clotted muck, in which a number of small red cockroaches scurried, backstroking away towards the wall. And all this in vain.

"I can't see it."

"Ah." She grunted, let her head fall back on the grimy pillows. I opened the small icebox in the corner and put in the bag of bagels, brushing away the frozen corpses of intruders intrepid enough to climb in there through the cracks.

"I'll try and clean up."

I went to work, with my bucket and mop. The thankless task. She muttering away, repeating lines I had already heard time and time again - "I was not always like this, you know... You better believe it... once upon a time... I was the belle of the ball... slim and fit as a fiddle... I swam across lakes and dived... sat on mountaintops and let the wind thrill through my silken hair... I smoked home grown keef and read Herman Hesse and Doris Lessing and Richard Brautigan... I had unblemished skin and infinite vision... living in teepees, like the Indians... we were the rainbow people, up with the dawn and merging with sunsets..."

Her voice, surprisingly mellifluous and resonant, as if coming from another source entirely rather than those cracked lips. A totally incongruous song, in these lower depths. "Are you there Jesse?" "I'm still here, Ann." "You know the poet's words?" "Which poet, Ann?" "Whitman, Jesse, Walt Whitman:

"`I have established nothing for good
I have but established those things,
till things farther onward shall be prepared to be established
And I am myself the preparer of things further onward...'"

This seemed to express my own thoughts regarding The Teacher, whom we awaited in the caves of Qumran. For the others in the Community, all was immutable, and our obligations to the Holy Spirit had been set down in the depths of time. We were all judged singly and collectively as to whether we had adhered or deviated one whit from the Spirit and the Letters of the Law. The Teacher was he who was whole in spirit, and represented the True Path to the world.

But it seemed to me, when I contemplated these matters in the night, with the white shroud-light of the stars and the moon casting its ghostly glow on the mountains, that all of the Almighty's Book was concerned with His striving to make the universe whole. That is, out of the scattered sparks of the original creation, which had been broken, at its moment of conception, by the impurities of the world of matter, God desires to restore what should have been made in that grand instant of invention. Why he chose Man, the most imperfect of his inventions, as the vehicle for this work of restitution, I am too ignorant to imagine. Therefore it is Man, not God, who is the Mystery, and God who is the seeker of the truth.

A neverending work, as I wrung out my cloth into the bucket, trying to at least reduce the level of the flood. Collecting the shreds and shards of paper and tucking them in my pants pocket. She had discarded them, but perhaps later I would have the chance to dry them out and find the clues to her affliction...

Jesse left, closing the door softly behind him, as the sound of her renewed snores echoed from the vast bedridden mound. But, as soon as he had gone, the mound shifted, as if by some sudden, recalled urge, groping about beneath the bedclothes to locate the lost remote control, pulling it out to point it at the buzzing screen. The television suddenly came into life, revealing a cheerful young Chinese featured woman, clutching a microphone, her words rising and falling amid static:

"In a moment, we will be going live to the Floor of the House, where the debate to ratify the Thirteenth Amendment to the Constitution is about to commence. In other headlines, the Federal Fleet is still besieging Charleston, and General Sherman's March through the ravaged southern States is almost complete. In the House, polls suggest that the Amendment abolishing slavery will pass by the required two thirds majority..."

The massive frame quivered, and the bloated face of Ann Hedonia lifted in a spasm from the pillows. Her elephantine legs twitched, then thrashed up and down, knocking the tattered quilt off the bed. Her great abdomen heaved, splitting the frayed off-white gown with "Property of the State of New York Mount Sinai Hospital" still inscribed upon it. Under the torn fabric, the mottled skin began to split. Beginning at the belly button, and ripping up to separate the two flaps of sagging breasts, tearing at the neck, the chin fracturing, the mouth opening wider and wider to engulf the nostrils, nose, eyes, emitting a great spume of black, yellow, green and red bile. As the wattled, worn flesh fell away, two strong, sun-browned long fingered hands pushed from the depths to pull the parted folds away, followed by powerful but slim muscle-toned arms, elbowing off putrid gut and viscera, and the taut, firm breasted figure rising, pulling free, the head, with glistening raven hair, clean symmetrical features, the determined mouth and coal black eyes, spitting away the muck and mucus.

"MOVE OVER, DAMN FUCKING BITCH..."

Climbing off the bed, slapping off the slime, shaking her head and hair into the small washbasin by the whirring icebox, giving only a cursory glance at the live transmission of the burning of Atlanta, the cries of the soldiers, the flinging of the torches, the screams of the victims running anguished from burning buildings, the dreadful howls of combusting horses.

"What a way to make a living..." Gathering her hair in a knot, Beatrice stepped forward to the door, opened it a little, cocking an ear for any intrusion.

"I know you're there, you bastards."

Nothing but the slow drip of time. The empty cavity of the stomach infested with stalagtites and stalagmites. The icy blast of the outside forcing her to wrap her arms around her as she hurried down towards the safety of the House of Pain, its dull beat of preset heavy metal loops reverberating in the duodenum.

From gastric follicles, glands and fibres, tiny heads peep, crablike hands shuffling binoculars, broomsticks, muffled bells, quivering antennae. Dry quills scratch on slates and notebooks. Keyboards click. Low voices waft information across the ripples of the mind...

SALIM:

The door is steel, the walls are steel, the ceiling, the floor is steel, the bedframe steel, bolted to the floor with steel bolts, the mattress might as well be steel, the toilet is steel, and there is even a steel shower cubicle, with steel water dripping out of a steel nozzle. Everything is self contained. I arrived here after being marched through tier after tier of steel doors, whisked open and shut by invisible switches, shutting me off further and further in steel Chinese boxes. You read about it but you can't imagine. You imagine it but you can't understand it. You experience it and you don't believe it. But the cold truth closes about you. Cold in metaphor, because there is no winter in here. There is no season, no day or night, no hours.

I came in here with nothing, and even that nothing was pawed over and examined intensely. My torn sleeping shorts, fingered and patted and dismembered, the seams ripped open to find the secrets I might have embedded inside. A steel cattle prod was passed through my hair, my groin, my ass. A pale faced man with a surgical glove searched my cavities to see what else I might have concealed. Another man shoved a pencil light into my nostrils and ears. They handed me a blanket which was totally devoid of any smell, marked "MEN'S DETENTION CENTER NEW YORK DEPARTMENT OF CORRECTIONS."

I stared at my grey steel cell for hours, or years, suspended in my own thoughts, which made no sense whatever. Jagged fragments. Streets in New York. A bunk in the old barracks in Ein el-Hilwe. A coffee shop on the Beirut Lido, with a bunch of corpses drifting by, glued together by some terrible solidarity, bobbing on the deep blue waves.

Or was it blue? I can't conjur colors. Everything floats in monochrome. Abu Hamid, and the baking heat of the Libyan desert, the dryness in the throat. I had to piss. I knew the moment I began using the utilities of the cell I would be finished. I knew that would signal my acceptance of this place, this fate. I held on for as long as I could and then surrendered. The body always does this to you. I remembered the old man of Lebanon, Kamal Jumblatt, the Druze leader, who went to India to study Yoga methods of material denial. He wrote a book called I Speak For Lebanon in which he mentioned his Yogic quest. Soon afterwards the Syrians blew him up in his car. I remembered his son, Walid, and his big bulging eyes. The Druze believed in the oneness of all faiths. In reincarnation. But if you are dead in life, how do you make that transition, into the next, fresh, unspoiled body?

I thought of Mo Smith, with his eight or more personalities, hidden away like swallowed sacks of cocaine. If only I could bury myself deep in his lungs, his heart, even his bladder, at this point. Anything to be somewhere else. After an age, they called me out to ask me questions that could not possibly be answered. These were questions that were addressed to another person, who did not exist, except in their imagination. A figure of orientalist fantasy, a slavering towelhead beast with hairy sweaty arms and a sack of bombs slung over his shoulder, who burst up from some medieval slime pit to pollute the honourable streets of peace loving folk, a stain of blood on the pure white paper of democratic constitutions. A frothing fanatic, waving a holy book, mouthing guttural syllables of hate. They were courteous and polite at first, genuinely pained and eager to understand what had made me so. What was it, embedded deep in my genes, my eyes, my culture, my religion, that made me thirst for so much blood?

It was completely vain for me to tell them that I had no religious feelings to speak of, that I was the very apostle of non-violence, and that there was no hereditary taint that I was aware of, programming me towards demonic crimes. They looked into my eyes and saw a mirror reflecting their own fears and desires. I was Benedict Arnold, the traitor who had almost nipped the American Revolution in the bud. I was John Wilkes Boothe, the assassin of Lincoln. I was Sacco and Vanzetti, the swarthy dago anarchists. I was the Jew Rosenberg, who sold the bomb to the Russians. I was Lee Harvey Oswald. I was Saddam Hussein and Yassir Arafat and Abu Nidal and Abul Abbas and Abu Everybody rolled into one. I was their doom and their nightmare. They sat in their nuclear bunkers with their warships and Stealth bombers and tactical MIRVs pulled up over their ears and trembled at the thought of my hand closing on their throats in the dark. They had sent Rambo after me to the depths of the desert and the jungle and the seven seas and he had failed. Now there was only them, and the New York Department of Corrections, to stand between my omnipotence and the lives of their loved ones, their little babes struggling in the cradle of freedom and market forces everywhere.

I was, in my complete helplessness, expanding into a bloated, fearsome giant. I was a Golem, come to revenge past slights and massacres against my people, the Wretched of the Earth. I was Geronimo and Sitting Bull, avenging the slaughter of the Red Indians of the great west plains. I was the buffalo, come back to life and snorting, pawing the ground. I was the wrath of the enraged, emboldened lamb, and the Sword of the Prophet, wielded high over the heads of the cowed infidels.

Except that I was none of these things. The dream, the nightmare crumbled, as it formed, cascading around me in tiny shreds and flakes, melting in the heated hum of the interrogation box.

"Tell us about Sheikh Jedid."

What is there to say? An old blind lunatic who talks about the kingdom of God and runs some video shops and garages. Lost, gaping young men go to his lectures and hang on to his angry, wispy words. Then they go home and masturbate over the videos they have hired from his stores. I remember one Italian film I took out once, The Erotic Adventures of Frankenstein. It was an old black and white feature, very weird. I was never one of his disciples, I told them. I paid him a courtesy visit, and he helped me out. I am not a Muslim, do you understand? My mother kept little dolls of the Holy Virgin, with little tiny plastic donkeys, and straw. This whole blood feud on modern materialism, the West, the Great Satan, it's not my style. I love modern materialism, consumer goods, Steven Spielberg, Star Wars, Bloomingdales. I am a confirmed pacifist, and have been ever since...

"Ah, yes," they said, "tell us about that cup of piss."

It always comes back to the same thing. What we might do or not do to survive. If these guys had whipped out their cocks and made an offer I would have stretched my lips any time, just to get out of this trap, to turn the clock back one day (or is it one year?). Humiliation is not the issue. Humiliation was our mother's milk. Humiliation was the heritage we tried to annul by blood and fire. We were not the first, nor will we be the last to try this. But try explaining this to these clones. That I went down that path and grew sick and weary. And I could no more head that way again than grow wings.

"If you are a pacifist and a Christian why did you visit the Sheikh?"

Go talk to these people about obligations, the tangled skein of kin and clan. About sharing a history that ties our separate veins together into a cat's cradle even if we share nothing else. About being the wretched of the earth and knowing it. About the loop of hate and love. About the memory of hunger. Here in this grand guzzling city. About being the nation with the paper cup in the midst of plenty. About sharing from the root. Anything I say would just tie me in deeper in their minds to the blind old rabble rouser.

"I never discussed politics there. I came here to study. I got my green card. Now I drive a cab."

They had reams of computer print-outs and schedules of every fare I ever took. I couldn't believe it. They unrolled a huge chart of my movements across the city in the past six months. All arrows and trajectories of movement across the Manhattan grid. With different coloured tags covering destinations all over the map, from Brooklyn to the Bronx.

"Do you remember these journeys?"

I remember nothing but journeys. From the first one I took as a gleam in my father and mother's eye when they ran from their coastal plain village ahead of the Jewish Haganah's tanks, all the way across the mountain ranges to Jordan, crossing the river like Moses and Jesus walking backwards, and then from the refugee camp in the desert up north, to Damascus, then Beirut. My journeys from camp to camp, then the long retreat in the Greek holiday ferry with our leaders, from Beirut to Tunis, that long, dismal summer cruise. Flying about at the Chairman's side from tarmac to tarmac, from handshake to slippery handshake, from kiss to kiss, stubble to stubble, spit to spit. How he epitomises our people, our Chairman who has no chair to rest, no home, no hearth, no closed door, no bed to call his own. Like the Flying Dutchman, or the Wandering Jew, he is cursed from pillar to post, from land to land. And then, my flight from his side...

Do you remember these trips?

Out of the land of milk and honey, out from the dry brown furrows and the dark green olive groves... across the desert and the wasteland and the shifting dunes to the Big City, bent against the wind, the rain, the snow.

We hold these truths to be self-evident...

How can you remember every wire of the grid? 4th Street to 208th. Debrosses to Dyckman. Lincoln to Queens. Long Island and New Jersey Special rates. You don't go anywhere man, you just go. The schedule is routine, not retention. It's all a blur.

"You know these men?" Four Arab mug shots. Wild eyes and beards. As are we all. Guilt ever etched in our eyes. We stare at the camera that steals our souls and seals them in the police files. No, we all look alike, don't we? We are all interchangeable. The great madness of the Orient.

"You don't know these people?" They rattle off names that sound vaguely familiar. Young stalwarts, hanging around the Blind Man for directions. The Holy Word of God in Babylon. Perhaps indeed they were me, in other times, in other twisted possibilities.

"I don't know them." They show me another one. This one I do know. Stupid Majid. He was one of the assistants at the first video store, at Prospect Park. He was devout. He couldn't stand the wrappers with the undressed ladies and the form hugging tights, I could see him, mouthing some Koranic verse against all the temptations as he handled the merchandise, very carefully, with the tips of his fingers, over the counter. "That will be twenty five dollars ninety nine plus tax madam." One day he just failed to turn up. And that was over two years ago.

"I haven't seen him since then."

The Erotic Adventures of Frankenstein. Nirvana Nurses. Jailbait III. The Female Bunch. Feast of Flesh. Hot Rods to Hell. Lovingly gaped at at three in the morning, just to pass the time. Feasting on America's garbage. The Gourmet Szechuan was yet to come... I switched off from the insane interrogation and began imagining the menu there: Shrimp, pork and wonton noodle soup, barbecue beef szechuan style, crispy sesame shrimps, empire ginger chicken, empire three delicacies sauted, seafood riot, sliced rainbow, aromatic chinese eggplant, scallops among black pearls...

They took me back to my cell. I lay back on the steel mattress and listened to the water drops leak from the shower. I remembered my mentor, Abu Hamid, talking about prison, about the mental disciplines necessary to stay sane and to endure. The creation of an inner world, which can't be violated. None of this seemed to stop the uncontrollable shaking which overtook my body on the bunk. At the most vegetative, biological level, my body was rebelling against me. Every cell shrieked out in despair, bubbling, seething, bursting. My feet were kicking against the steel frame of the bed, my hands vibrating, my eyes blurring and rolling. The bile was rising to my throat, swamping my mouth, flecking down my chin. My bowels were exploding. I dragged myself off the bed, lurching to the steel toilet bowl, stuck my head in it and let the panic rip. I lay there gasping, listening for Abu Hamid's voice. Slowly slowly it began breaking through to me, from the greatest possible distance: Salim! Salim!

Out of the burning bush. But my tongue is not free from its impediment... Salim! Salim! Free your mind! Make your mind work for you. Let it roam, slide, slither, ooze through the walls and bars and gates, slip past the electronic sensors, the multiple fail safe alarms and tripwire sirens, the eagle-eyed guards bolted into their razor edged uniforms, into the sky, dancing with the blizzard, fighting the flakes, blowing up the snowswept steps of the Metropolitan Museum of Art, bowling down its labyrinthian galleries. Try and map it out Salim. Pay a dollar, or as little as 25 cents, for the day badge, red, yellow, blue or green, pin it on your pocket and march past the blueclad guard, up the wide internal staircase to the European paintings: The Florentine, Sienese, Venetian paintings, the Dutch, the Flemish and the French. The eyes of the Rembrandt portraits, greeting you as you walk through their home. Van Dick - what a name for an artist. The miniature reality of Vermeer. Light from exquisite windows. The Portrait of a Young Woman. That grabbed me when Frances first walked me through it. The luminous, delicate face, the big eyes. They swim at me, across the air. On towards the great landscapes of Venice, the Turner, Canaletto, Guardi. The gondolas and sailing boats, packed on the canal in an aquatic rush hour. I can walk into the picture, stepping from boat to boat, across the water, towards the Piazza San Marco. Continuing, up the steps, under the glorious turrets and towers, into the Cathedral itself. Sanctuary! Sanctuary! I have never been in one of these great European Catholic monuments, our churches at home are small and cosy, not to speak of the Holy Sepulchre itself with its dingy multiple grottos. But I can see, as I step into the Venetian Cathedral, the great transept, the immense stone columns and vaulted arches, all decorated with mosaics and jewels and colored lamps, illuminating the vast interior, leading me forward, towards the altar, towards the figure shimmering in the shifting light. But I walk straight through him, passing right through his navel, into the glittering room beyond, upon which, on a slab, Abu Hamid is laid out, in his guerrilla uniform. His face is pale and blood spattered, his uniform riddled with the bullet holes left by the Mossad raiders who swooped down at dawn upon his home in Tunis seven years ago. He opens his eye and winks at me.

"Salim. Salim."

His left arm is clutching the dried severed head of a cat. The Enemy gives us no mercy, we give no mercy to the Enemy.

"At least I died fighting," he tells me, "how about you, Salim?" I place my right hand under his head and lift him, slowly, upon the slab. His stiff corpse seems to weigh a ton. I prop him up with a brass candlestick. Blood continues to trickle from his wounds.

"They are accusing me of blowing up the World Trade Center," I told him. "Six people were killed and many injured. They claim it was ordered by that man, Sheikh Jedid. But I'm not capable of harming a fly."

"If you don't harm flies they take over and wipe you out," he said calmly. "But you mean Thou Shalt Not Kill. If only we could all have been so noble. I was shot while I was still asleep, you know. I barely heard a commotion but before I could move they were in the doorway, spitting fire. My hand reached out for my pistol, which is always on my bedside table, but I didn't make it. At least my wife, Soraya, was away at the time. She is a true heroine of the Revolution. But now it's all backdoor deals and diplomacy. The end of our time is nigh, Young Salim, we old dinosaurs. We who fought for a cause that could be grasped. The Young Ones who come after us are fighting for God, not Country, for the Book, not for Man. Everything is regressing, towards a much more primitive war: The battles of Gog and Magog, at the beginning and at the end of Time. Everything comes full circle. After my death, our ideals will be sold to the highest bidder. You are caught in the coils of our failure, Salim."

I clutched his cold body to my breast and wept, my tears flowing over his congealed blood. Then I left him on his slab and walked, unsteadily, out of the church through a small, creaking side door. The

Grand Canal was behind me, on the other side of the Cathedral, and what faced me now was a narrow, muddy stream, straddled by an ancient, crumbling stone arch. I walked across this bridge into a dingy alleyway between grey, decaying houses. I felt a certain comfort at being lost in the hidden depths of the picture. Far behind me, I could hear the muffled cries of the museum guards calling me back out of the painting. But I soldiered on, round the bend of the alley, squeezing between the damp windowless walls and coming out into a small piazza, surrounded on all sides by those leaning old buildings struggling to avoid sinking into the waters. There were a number of shuttered coffee shops and taverns around the piazza, with some iron tables and upended chairs scattered about the cracked paving stones. All the alleys between the buildings were narrow except for one, a wide opening which led to another canal, beyond the piazza, crowned with sails. I walked up onto this wharf, cluttered with sailors and tradesmen in silk baggy pants and turbans. Wooden gangplanks led up to the sailing ships. A mixture of languages caressed my ears. Italian, French, Greek, North African and Middle Eastern Arabic.

I followed the sound of my people, and walked up to board my fate...

*

From the New York Times, 3/6/—, etc:

MORE ARRESTS IN TRADE CENTER BLAST.
NEW YORK, N.Y. - The FBI announced three more arrests on Friday in connection with the World Trade Center bombing. Two of the men, who were arrested in Queens, were members of the mosque headed by the blind preacher, Sheikh Jedid. Both men had Jordanian passports. The third man was detained after police were called by the managers of the Pilgrims' Arms Hotel to investigate a guest who had attempted to authenticate his identity with another man's credit card. The guest, who paid for his room in cash, claimed he had found the card lying on the floor at Bloomingdale's department store. He appeared to

speak only halting English, and investigators say they are having difficulties identifying his Arabic speech, which they described as "archaic." The suspect, who has been named as Mohammed Abu Abdallah Ibn Fatuta, has not asked for legal representation. His court appointed lawyer, Seymour Simkin, said he had no idea why his client was being linked to the Trade Center bombings, as the only legitimate cause for investigation might be his inability to produce proof of identity, other than the documents "found" at the department store. These have now been restored to their rightful owner, Mr Bohumil Krinkl, of Pacific Heights, Brooklyn, N.Y. It is understood, however, that Immigration Officers have not yet interviewed Mr Fatuta, who is being questioned by the team in charge of investigating the World Trade Center blast. Mr Simkin has entered a writ of habeas corpus, which will be heard in the District Court tomorrow morning.

In further developments yesterday, Sheikh Abu-Bakr Jedid refused to be interviewed at his home in Jackson Heights, but a representative denied all allegations of his involvement in any act of terrorism, and denounced what he called "a criminal conspiracy by Zionist agents and western Intelligence agencies to tarnish the name of Islam."

TEXAS CULT COULD HOLD OUT FOR MONTHS.

WACO, Texas - Accounts from former cult members, federal officals and a neighbour indicate that there are enough supplies inside the fortified compound of a self-proclaimed Messiah to enable him and the more than 100 people with him to survive for weeks and possibly months. Even as hundreds of law enforcement officials with tanks and weaponry kept the property surrounded, the federal agent in charge, Mr Jeffrey J—, said there were no plans to storm the compound and that he wanted a peaceful resolution to the standoff. That is what 33-year old cult leader David Koresh says he wants, too, but he insists that the only one who can tell him just when to come out is God.

When federal agents attempted to arrest Mr Koresh Sunday on a weapons charge, four of them were killed by shots fired from inside the compound. A federal source said as many as 10 of Mr Koresh's followers may also have died in the exchange. Hours after the gun battle, Mr Koresh, head of the Branch Davidian sect, a breakaway from the Seventh Day Adventists, told CNN News that he had been "shot through the guts" and was lying on a sheet soaked with his own blood. But he has been talking away since then, quoting the Bible for hours in telephone conversations with professional FBI negotiators. "He seems to have recovered miraculously," Mr J— told a press briefing.

Local people familiar with the sect have been talking about its eccentric founder, Vernon Howell, who later changed his name to David Koresh. "He had a kind of arrogant air about him," related Calvin Ross of the Lone Star Music and Sound Company, who said Mr Koresh often came to his shop looking for guitars and invariably drove a hard bargain. "He was a frustrated rock musician who wanted to be a rock star, gave up on that dream and then wanted to be Jesus Christ."

ROUGH PATCH MARS CONGOLESE DIPLOMACY. N.Y. - Roland Ojukwu-Ndole, cultural attache in the consulate of the Congolese Republic, has been having his fill of the seedy side of life in New York City. The Republic has fallen back so far in its payments to its embassies around the world that it has not paid its diplomats for several months, in some cases years. Six months ago Ojukwu-Ndole had to leave his luxury apartment in Turtle Bay and he has since been living rough in the City, sleeping in Subway stations and mixing with the City's homeless. All this while he continued to fulfill his official functions, keeping his dress suit in a luggage locker in Grand Central Station. His desperate plight was discovered by 22nd Precinct officers after he was robbed of his suit one night on returning to his regular patch on a disused platform of the IRT line. Ojukwe- Ndole became abusive when police at first refused to accept his unusual story and he spent 48 hours in the cells before a friendly cop humoured him by calling the Congolese Consulate.

According to fellow diplomats, Mr Ojukwe-Ndole attended almost all his assigned official receptions, which may have been his main source of food in this period.

"He always was very polite and respectable," said a colleague, Emmanuel Dlamini, "the amazing thing is that he carried on working, and none of us suspected the truth."

In an unrelated incident, reporters seem to be unable to find another legendary inhabitant of the New York subway system, a man described as having the "white-haired mane" of an Old Testament patriarch, who has been regaling passers by with renditions of Jewish liturgical songs in the voice of a top quality Cantor. The man, who first appeared dressed only in thin silk pyjamas inscribed with the logo of the Waldorff-Astoria Hotel (!!!) later acquired a heavy army coat due to the enthusiasm of a Jewish Navy Officer, who was reduced to tears by the rendition of the great prayer of the Day of Atonement - *Kol Nidre.* Further sightings of "The Subway Cantor," as he was instantly dubbed, were at stations as far afield as Grand Central and Flatbush Avenue. Witnesses say he was always showered with banknotes, some even pressing hundred dollar bills into his hand. No doubt he has now retired, to enjoy his rhapsodic earnings in better locations than the downtown N platform.

FRANCES.

On Sunday night I dreamed that the Mad Hatter in the statue of Alice in Wonderland in Central Park spoke up and told me that Art was redundant. He said he was representing an insurance company called Mutual Assured Destruction, which had decided that works of Art had no value and were therefore uninsurable on the global market. (It's true, I have been trying to rejig the insurance rates for the Gallery.)

The Mad Hatter went on to tell me that Art was a regressive game played by elites to kid themselves there's more to life than neverending struggle and brutality. "Art is literally crap," he said, in that highfalutin' English tone I always expected him to have. "Babies playing with their kaka, nothing else."

This was a bit rich coming from a piece of sculpture made by an artist inspired by fictional creations. I looked round at Alice herself, but she remained in stone, although the March Hare, beside her, wore a frightening, widening grin. I looked back at the Hatter, who was now holding in his hands a distinctive, fur-covered cup of tea. I recognised it as the famous Meret Openheim "Luncheon in fur," circa 1936, which should have been in the Museum of Modern Art on 53rd Street, the one that Robert Hughes called "the most intense and abrupt image of Lesbian sex in the history of art."

"What did he mean by `abrupt'?" I asked the Hatter, but he had metamorphosed into Salim, holding, instead of the tea, a golden *finjan*, from which the strong aroma of what I knew was Chairman Arafat's urine emanated. He was trying to move towards me, but his left foot was caught in the coils of a giant stone snake, which was sliding up his leg in the manner of the Roman Laocoon. The head of the snake was rearing towards Alice, whose head, I now saw, bore the face of Caroline. As both my friends were being devoured, the March Hare, who now had Benjamin's face, leered at me, calling out:

"Are you taking all of this down?"

So much for Sunday. Monday morning I decided to brave the snowdrifts and go downtown to the Gallery. The Mad Hatter still echoing in my head. You should trust your dreams because, like your mother, they are telling you things you don't really want to know. In fact my mother, who had been let down by my father, by the Communist Party of America, and by her Savings and Loan Company, the Federal Alliance and Loans, had come to the conclusion that you can't trust anybody in this world. Her dream was to open a musical instruments shop, but now she lives off what's left of Grandma's dividends from the stock portfolio she built up sneakily while Grandpa was selling hot dogs at Yankee Stadium for twenty five years. My family are not an object lesson in mutual confidence and understanding. My first response was to rush off to Israel to pick oranges on the Communal Farm. That lasted all of three months. It should have cured me forever of Israelis, but then Benjamin came along. And went. So don't take this away from me too.

Though where is the balance? When one of your best friends is struck by leukaemia and the other is in jail falsely accused of mass murder? The rest pales into insignificance. So what if Len Loons can make millions reconstructing porcelain kitsch?

New York in the snow still is the Magic Kingdom. An eerie silence in the domain of noise. The stranded cars, the snow ploughs geysering white, the gallumphing, Doctor Zhivago-like people, the popping of ice snapping off up on the fortieth floors. People are constantly being hit by splinters falling off tall buildings in the thaw. I read that one poor shmuck was killed by a jagged piece dropped off the top of the Empire State Building. Committed perhaps by the ghost of King Kong.

Where is Lewis Carroll now that we need him? Our modern rabbit holes - the steaming subways, the platforms covered in slush and coughs, everyone's leaping Beijing Flu. It used to be called the Peking Flu, but the Chinese-American community insisted on the new transliteration. Everyone is sensitive to the merest pin-prick on their paperthin identity, but nobody cares if a good man rots in the Tombs. As long as he's an Arab, the new pariahs. He should have changed his name to Slim Helms. Like Bernie Schwartz becoming Tony Curtis. But now it's too late.

Downtown. I usually get off at Astor Place and walk down Lafayette, past the Astor Place and Joseph Papp theatres on either side of the road, Tower Books and Videos and Screaming Mimi's and the Time Cafe, with its inverted clock. Time running backwards, if only. All the places that tempt me to delay, espeically on this ice cold morning. A strong non-dekaff slowly sipped among the non-mobile non-radical not-quite-so-chic, with the occasional spiky hair do or nose ring. Riffling through the piles of leaflets and free magazines - Subterranean Sounds & Culture: The Devil Dogs, Deadguy, Madball, Pillbox, The Bleeding Hemeroids, White Trash Barbecue. "Music with no socially redeeming values, don't forget your ketchup!" Shootyz Groove - "Jammin in Vicious Environments." What goes round must come round: "Godflesh have made it their life's mission to wreak havoc on the traditional structures and boundaries of extreme music."

Party on dudes. I like the leaflet for Witchcraft, though, advertising the Old Religion Supply Store: The Goddess is Alive! (Open 7 Days.) Ritual knives only $13. Blended incense $4 an ounce. Astrological charts, altar clothes, cauldrons, ritual swords, scourges, crystal balls, witches' bottles. Motto: "Where There's a Witch There's a Way!" I can spend whole days in these flea shops. There's one just down the block from the Acme Gallery, Marty's Cool Stuff. You can take two hours just looking in the window, even with the snow falling. The Woody Woodpecker Golden Book (oh my God...), the wigged plastic skull with cigar, the Vietnamese coffee can, the china pussycats, old Kellog's Cornflake packets with their tiny plastic gifts of Tiger Moths. Rag dolls and old tin soldiers refighting the battle of Waterloo all over the display, among the medieval map books and rabbit- nibbled vintage copy of Uncle Remus' Tales. "Dead men they lifts up their legs an' hollers Whahoo!" Not where I live they don't.

The Acme Gallery is closed. As I'd supposed, my assistant, Ada Em, hadn't tried to toil uptown from Brooklyn. Monday is a funny day. It's not the money. Our owner, the shoeshop Tsar of Brookhaven Long Island, doesn't mind as long as something happens during the week. Another connoisseur of the redundant. I unlock the door and am alone in the display.

The Mad Hatter was not allegorising. The present exhibition is literally trash. Toxic Waste by Una Sturridge. She is an English artist who has been exhibited all over Europe, as far east as Bulgaria, and in Australia and Japan. Each exhibit is drawn from local materials. But trash, of course, is universal. Garbage enclosed in glass cases, with chemical and nuclear signs. Most of it is, I suppose, innocuous despite the heading. Choice pieces from the Staten Island landfill, where all the city's rubbish ends up. Pieces so mangled they might be Claes Oldenburg's cheeseburgers thirty years on, except that this is the real thing. So at least we've moved on.

But it all seems pretty unsatisfying, after the Mad Hatter upset the delicate balance of my disordered brain. Moving alone among the exhibits. "Little chunks of unwanted reality which take on a different meaning when shut in their glass shells." Or so the Village Voice was kind enough to say. The public can be more down to earth: "I can see this any place outside for nothin'!" "Hey, that looks like Henry's balls!" Well, it is called Melancholy Scrota. Just by the crushed paper packs entitled "23 billion sold." Len Loons would do it all in cement three hundred feet high. But Una Sturridge is "aux nature." I had to get a replacement for Selina Hasek, whose supply dried up after she sealed herself with her colleagues in their geodesic dome. Perhaps, when the winter's over, and the first buds of spring, the fresh sea breezes and the pavement cafes open, she might venture out, like a cautious squirrel... But a proper business woman can't count on such outbreaks of rationality, not in this neck of the woods.

Going into the empty office, I make myself a cup of peppermint tea. Like Proust's madeleine, it puts me in mind of lazy mornings with Salim, sipping his favourite tea with *na'na*, fresh mint leaves, the Arab style. It's strange when people you know well disappear. Of course, the physical absence. But the subtle change in your mind. Suddenly they become idealised, like Len Loons memories done in porcelain, painted in brighter colours. Behind the paint, a touch of resentment: Why did he get into this mess? He always was naive about the Blind Sheikh - "that old man who drools in his beard." If these people do you favours they'll expect something in return. Yeah, Frances, free porn videos, under the counter. Or maybe, Salim, to snare you in the trap of their own dire dreams.

Guilt by association. The tea with *na'na* was your Proustian madeleine. It took you back to those imaginary fields of bliss in which you never lay, listening to the corn grow that you never heard and watching the Palestine birds that you never saw flit through the blue sky. The most you could conjur authentically might be images of the beach at Beirut, with the happy- go-lucky nouveau-riche bathing while the Mirage bombers shrieked overhead to bomb the shit out of the poor.

Pick up the phone and dial Allan Darwish. A Puerto Rican voice answers. "Allan ain't at home right now. He'll be back at two o'clock." We're back to a recurring phase. The old urge Darwish gets every now and then to redeem a lost youth from the streets. When I first met him it was a Haitian youth, Jean-Pierre. Then it was that Chinese boy, Ang. The last was two years ago, Juan. This one, apparently is Jaime. There's no point in warning Darwish. One day he'll pick the wrong kookie and'll be too old to outrun the maniac chasing him round the bed with a knife. But I shall have to wait until two to find out whether the famous G. G. Gittlin is having any luck getting Salim transferred to a civilian hospital, so we can find out the truth about the recurring trances that have baffled the prison doctors.

Working the phones nevertheless to try and rustle up new recruits for the Defence Committee. At the end of the day it's all the same people who have always come forward for Palestinians' rights in America. The nice elderly socialists of the New Jewish Agenda, some old Communists, a sprinkling of new Trotskyists, non-denominational Good Souls, the radical Reform Rabbi Benson Bloom who wanted to flood the occupied West Bank with like minded American Jews, as if they weren't flooded enough with our brethren already, and the usual tally of sympathetic priests, church workers and Christian earth-mothers who considered all lost people an extension of their own massive families, a host of unruly kids who had to be fed. Caroline, undergoing another bout of chemical assault on her blood cells and hospital tests, is out of the running, disqualified from her usual Queen Bee role of rallying the city's dispossessed in solidarity. Our other nexus of support - my co-litigants of the class-action war against the Anti-Slander League in California - busy raising as much Cain as can be raised on the West Coast while still enjoying the mid-winter sun. That mellow outrage.

The snowfalls have stopped and the Weather Channel has said thaw is in the air. We might actually be emerging from another worst winter in living memory, with temperatures below minus 100 in Michigan and the wind chill factor below human tolerance. No sign of thaw yet here in the Gallery. I can never figure out how to restart the heat. I need Ada Em, but she doesn't answer her phone in Brooklyn. Gone out tobogganing, maybe. My mouth is going blue working the lines. Darwish wanted to call a full Defence Committee meeting for Friday night. Four days away. But he forgot that our Jewish religious friends are into the Sabbath then. So I'm trying to bring it forward to Thursday. Every day that passes Salim could fall deeper into his prison malaise. I call the lawyer but he's in court. I call the Rabbi but he's out taking food to children cut off by the snow in darkest Flatbush. I chat for a while with Marina Hathaway, who is carrying on a protracted negotiation with one of her teenagers at the same time. When they were smaller, she used to threaten her kids with giving them non-racist, non- sexist toys, but now the times are tougher. Now they are fully equipped with state-of-the-art, Modem-connected personal computers, on which they are busy writing their own software that will transform the world.

Party on. I'm looking straight at one of Una Sturridge's "installations", a stack of crushed Budweiser cans made into the walls of a nuclear shelter. Perhaps if I crawled inside the world would just keep out. Instead, just to annoy myself further, I called Benjamin.

"Any news?"

"I can't take this any more," he said, "I want the heat, the sun, the dancing."

"Go to Florida. Any news on Salim?"

"I can't enlighten you, booba. But something odd has turned up. Have you seen the Times?"

"I've stopped taking it. I'm on homeopathic stuff now."

"It's in Newsday as well. You know they're still arresting people. They picked up some guy at the Pilgrim Arms Hotel. I stayed there a couple of nights once, on the ground floor, with my ear right up against the central heating boiler. It was like sleeping inside an aircraft engine. Anyway, this man they picked up, he claimed his name was Ibn Battuta. Remember, Frances, Mo Smith's alter egos? Remember your theory that they were seeping out into the world? That radio programme? Well here's another one."

"You don't say. I'm not really in the mood for this now, Benjamin. I'm freezing my butt off at the Gallery. Ada Em hasn't turned up. Allan wanted me to call people and change Friday night to Thursday."

"It's O.K. for me. But wouldn't that be a story? All these alternative personalities, getting into the real world. I mean what would you do if you were a fourteenth century traveller suddenly stuck in New York City?"

"Give it up, Benjamin. What else is new? Some of the people we have to deal with would think the fourteenth century is real progress."

"I don't care about the century, only the season."

"Have you seen Caroline?"

"Her condition is stable. That's official. The cells are not getting better, or worse. A chemical standoff. Science and disease just frozen in limbo. She said she'd try and come to this meeting. I know Allan doesn't want her to get involved. But you know Caroline. I hate it, Frances. I hate it when there's nothing I can do."

"I know."

"Mortality. It sucks. You know these people in California who say they're going to live forever. They're going to halt the ageing process by positive thinking, and by refusing to think about death. Don't they also live in a dome, somewhere in the Mojave Desert? Naturally they are all gentiles."

"I have to go now, Benny. There's someone at the door. I'll call you later."

It was Ada Em, fumbling as usual with the three keys, although the two lower locks were open.

"Ada?"

"Is that you, Frances?"

"I thought you weren't coming."

"I wasn't. But my appointment was cancelled. I was at the Heights so I thought I'd just go on. I'm behind on the books."

"Forget the books, Ada. Let's do an early lunch."

Ada is textbook New Age. Alternative Health, Holistic Triangles, Light and Color Therapy, Crystals, Chakra balancing, Iridology, Chelation Therapy, Circles of Life, Breathing Power, Rebirthing, DEP (Deep emotional release), Tao, Tantra, Past Lives, Insights of the Ancient Kahunas, Heartsong, Feng Shui, The Great Gong Experience, Reflexology and Self Hypnosis, the works. She goes off on weekend courses, conventions and endless workshops. Thank God she hasn't discovered religion. But it's only a matter of time.

Gallumphing down Lafayette towards Bleecker, past Marty's Cool Shop without batting an eye. Up Bleecker towards Washington Square Village. The Noho Coffee House. Where the aspiring East Village writers go to soak up an espresso confidence. Sitting at the tiny tables, dragging on their Gauloise-sans-filter (last choking gasp before the anti-smoking bans) poised with an untidy manuscript and an impressive array of pencils and pens - nothing so modern as a typewriter, God forbid a laptop, to disturb the Henry James or Virginia Woolf-like gloom. Gazing out at the snow, waiting for the ghost of Chekhov to tap them on the shoulder. Go, muzhik, go. But the odour of pasta and pesto from the kitchen ruptures the Siberian dreams.

"Going anywhere this summer, Frances?"

Ada hates to talk about bad news. Another soul in strict denial. Taking her comforts from the battering of the city by floating out there in the void. A refugee, too, from a bad marriage, with an abusive lout whose stock in trade was pulling out clumps of her hair.

"I thought I'd stay in the city this year. See if I can survive without my brain melting."

"It's a dangerous experiment, Frances. The very air you breathe is toxic. The heat captures all the pollutants, the spiritual and the physical. The scavenging radicals."

"I lived with those when I was young. It's nothing new." Last summer I allowed Ada to take me to a jamboree upstate for "Gaia." The slogan was "Drum, rattle and heal the Earth!" We each had to bring some noisy implement and shake 'em all at the same time. Three hundred men and women sitting in a field and being three year olds. Then we had to drive our own prams back.

"You can't let all the bad things in life drag you down." Her credo. And who am I to argue, crawling along the ice, hand after hand. Ada has really had a bad deal. Her first husband became a Jewish Repentant, grew a beard, sidelocks and black gabardine coat and homburg hat and went to train with the fanatics of the Jewish Defence League to kill Arabs in case the Israeli army went soft. He divorced her by spitting three times and throwing a shoe at a hat stand in lieu of her presence at a Rabbinical Court in Crown Heights.

"You're a cynic, Frances, but there are marvellous things in the city, if only you know where to look. Even if people are faking, they're inventing new worlds. It's like their lives are Installations. You know my fortune teller, Madame Cropfin? She's found a new assistant. A male seer. Egyptian Pharaoh. She told me he was the real McCoy. Maybe she's really gone off her head this time. But she's helped a lot of people. For ten dollars for thirty minutes it's a better deal than you'd get from a shrink at a hundred dollars an hour. I was going to see them today, at Brooklyn Heights. But she was closed. The note on the door said 'Have taken Merenptah to the dentist.' Apparently he is the son of Rameses the Second, you know, the Pharaoh of Exodus."

"Oh, I have met him."

"Really, Frances?"

"No kidding. He was a homeless man, who was a client of Caroline, for a while. Then she got ill and lost sight of him. His real name is Mo Smith. He seems to be leaving bits of himself all over the place. I'm not surprised his teeth are ferkakt."

"Was he an Egyptian?"

"African American. Very much the local variety. It was only one of his voices. Multiple personality, poor bastard."

"Then it can't be the same guy. Madame said this man was like the old figures. Very tall, lean, majestic features. Very light skinned. Talks no English at all, only ancient Egyptian. Madame had studied it with the Learning Annexe."

"Where did she find him?"

"It was very spooky. She saw him coming out of a tunnel, at the end of the D platform, at Atlantic Avenue. Naked as the day he was born. She said he has authentic hieroglyphic tattoos on his right shoulder, left forearm and buttock. She took him home and he's been living there since."

"It's fantastic how soulmates meet in this city."

"I'll give you a full report when I see him."

It's too cold to consider all the ramifications. Even inside the Coffee Shop, with the heat turned full on, and the steaming fettucini. What do I see, in my own steamed up crystal ball? The Rosetta Stone of my life, with three different languages. Demotic, hieroglyphic and petrified. All my friends appear to be either going nuts, desperate or lost in their own stone Wonderlands. And where will you summer this year, Salim?

Perhaps I need the fortune teller, after all...

*
*
*

THINGS FALL APART. THE CENTER CANNOT HOLD. And what rough beast, etcetera, slouches towards Bellevue to be born?

Whadayasay, Frank? Frank? Motherfucking dickhead. Never there when you need him.

The blurry eyes, trying to refocus on the contours of the room. But there are no distinct lines, everything is wavy and grey. Trying to track sensation in the limbs. Feet encased in cement. Hands tied in lead filled boxing gloves. Brain of quicksand. The weight of the world. Only the pain, at the tip of the penis, still burning bright, but now an almost welcome reminder that the body is still vital.

"Frank!"

No answer. Manoeuvering to lift the cement blocks off the bed. A superhuman effort. The Alchemist became aware of a loud hissing sound, and a clamour like the rapping of a thousand fists on glass. The rain. The pouring rain, rattling against the windows of the National Hotel. The agent of the Thaw.

"Frank!"

How long have I been here? The weight of the limbs lightens just a little, then a little more. A vice lifted off body and brain. The hand pulls aside the grimy bedclothes, heavy with dried pus and blood. The cement foot grinds against the floor. The second follows. Pins and needles. Up, and drag a couple of steps to the washbasin. The detective's underpants and socks have gone, leaving a black smudge. Above, the encrusted mirror.

The glass mirror is merely the material aspect of the metaphysical place in which the Image of the psychic Interval, or *barzakh*, in the Persian tongue, is located. The sufis, and before them the Mazdaean adepts, knew that the forms produced by the absolute psychic activity of the soul reside in a place between the two worlds, the material and the divine, and the adept, whose eyes are open, can see in this mirror the Forms that are invisible to ordinary mortals. These Forms are the *prima materia*, the mold from which the material forms on earth were made. The Artworks of God.

But nothing gazes out at me now from the Other Side, observed the Alchemist, but my substantive, puffy punim. A far worse image than any prison mugshot, weary, wicked and careworn. Coalsacks under the eyes, crow's talons, blackened teeth, swollen gums, cracked lips, the beard thick with dried vomit, the cheeks striped with sooty tears. An absolute wreck.

The Adept knows that the Forms continue to subsist in their own manner even if the mirror is faulty, or broken. Or if no mirror exists at all. This will be true as long as the duration of the *barzakh*, or Interval, continues. The sufis held that this duration was eternal. But I, who was there long before them, can tell you that this is not the case. The Interval, in which the Forms which enable earthly material and the life of the flesh, is finite. This is made quite clear in Genesis. For if it had a Beginning, then it will have an End. In this regard the mystics of all the theistic faiths, Hebrew, Mussulman or Christian, have gone up the wrong path.

If you know the Truth, it merely binds you in tighter and tighter chains. To be free is to join the Chaos, the glorious Chaos, before it all began.

The Alchemist turned on the washbasin tap, a twist of the fingers which seemed to wake up all the demons in the pipes to rattle and vibrate the walls. A thick mucus trickled out, which transmuted, after a drumroll which almost shook the peeling plaster loose, into a thin flow of yellow water, which then yielded and became clear. He washed his face in this trickle, wiping away the grime and blood with an old rag hanging on a rusty hook by the mirror.

In fact, he thought, the entire history of humanity is a rebellion against the imposed forms. From Adam thru McDonalds Man refuses to accept the pre-arranged, the tyranny of God or instinct, and strives for his own options. At the same time, Man always loathed and feared his own self-determination, longing for his past structures. The old com-mandments, do this and don't do that, fearful and blown with the wind.

The Alchemist was shaken from his reverie by an almighty crash on the wall. He staggered over towards the window, but was thrown off his feet by a second impact, clearly coming from outside. Hand over foot, he pressed to the window, raising his head to look out.

At first he could see nothing but the rain, slamming against the window pane. He could hardly make out the contours of the building across the other way, with its shuttered and sealed windows, and, at the other corner, the neon lighting of the orbiting news sign on Number One Times Square. It seemed to be saying something like - DOOM-POUR SET FOR THREE DAYS -

But he was hurled back from the window by another giant slamming blow against the side of the building. He lifted himself once more, and this time could see, at the right hand side, the great iron sphere of the wrecking ball hurtling forward again. The massive three storey tall crane swinging it on a gargantuan chain. The sphere struck the side of the building and sent a deluge of bricks flying in a cloud of dust instantly swallowed by the rain.

"Frank! You slimebag bastard!" Leaving me here to die absurdly in the ruins of the National Hotel. The window shattered this time at the impact, and the Alchemist wrapped the rag around his fist and dashed the glass shards from the window-frame, leaning out and calling:

"Goddamn you sons of bitches! People still paying rent in here!"

There was no reason to believe there was anyone else in the building, but something had to be done to hold back the forces of savagery and destruction. His voice, however, which had in the past shaken cities and emperors alike, came out as a rasping, feeble wheeze, utterly lost in the screak and slash of storm and machine. The iron ball, once again, battered the Hotel, smashing through the adjoining room. It became stuck, somewhere in the wreckage of bricks and plaster, and the crane's engine roared and wailed, seeking to dislodge its bulk. The connecting wall between the rooms shattered, filling the space with a cloud of dust which choked his mouth and clogged his nostrils. The rain rushed, hissing, into the cavity, squelching the dust, but soaking his entire body. He could see, through the smoking hole, the wavering, shimmering shapes of the edifices of Times Square, the strobing signs, the neon billboards. YOU GOT THE LOVE? COCA COLA. SUNTORY WHISKY. HOWARD JOHNSON'S. WHAT AMERICA IS SAVING BY USING MCI INSTEAD OF AT&T.

The looming pit. Staggering back from the abyss, he fumbled at the door of the room, which came off in his hand. He threw himself out into the corridor just as the entire room, the rickety table, chair, the grimy washbasin, the filthy bed in which he had spent the last God knows how many days, weeks, or months, and all Frank Ox's rusty kitchen utensils, dropped down with a great crack into the street below.

"Mongol barbarians!" He shook his fist at the destroyers but retreated, ignoring the arrows for the Emergency Exit, which had become displaced and were pointing directly up at the ceiling. The ceiling itself was not going to survive much longer, riven by rents and gashes, coming apart at the beams. The floor was buckling under his feet. He found the stairway door and pushed it open. Thank God the stairs were at the back of the building. He stumbled down, as the walls of the National Hotel crumbled to dust all around him.

"I'll get you, Frank Ox, for this!" He should have known at the outset that the shamus could not be trusted. Past pride in a job well done was one thing, the slips and slides of present day greed and amorality had driven out the last vestiges of virtue. Someone must have paid him more, Mordecai thought, to betray me, to leave me in that room to rot and die. And if that's so, then there are forces out there, extant, sinister, which have not been taken account of in our previous assessments...

Slithering down the stairs, the Alchemist noted, with some satisfaction, that his groin was no longer throbbing, at any rate manifesting no more pain than the rest of his racked, battered body, and that he had given no thought for Jaime, or the other lost Companions of the Body, since his last awakening. But he had little time to develop these reflections, reaching the ground floor just as the wrecking ball, breaking through above him, smashed the upper stairway to smithereens. Plaster, brickwork and iron beams cascaded down three floors. He rushed through the deserted lobby and pushed open the cracked glass main door.

The rain cascaded out of the heavens, drenching him right to the bone. The giant crane was edging forward up against the building, it's chain tracks climbing up new piles of rubble. A low line of ramshackle plyboard fencing separated it from the road outside. The fencing was haphazardly joined, and the Alchemist crawled through a gap between two boards.

There he stood, on the corner of 42nd Street and Seventh Avenue, realising, for the first time since he rose off his bed, that he was completely naked, devoid of even the merest slip of cover. Only a thin gauze on his cock, which was unravelling and peeling off in the flow of the rain which cascaded down his head and chest, breaking into two streams at his thighs and gushing on the road.

He raised his face to the flood, gulping water. Washing the dust out of his mouth. The strobing light of the Times Square sign played on his eyelids. He opened them to read the latest - WACO SIEGE: "JESUS" STILL DEFIANT.

As well he might be. For the Eternal, the twists and turns of fate are only pin pricks, droplets of fire on the road to glory. If Frank Ox was unable to help in Re-integrating the Body with its Scattered Souls, I, Mordecai, will have to do the job alone.

Behind him, the wrecking ball continued to demolish the National Hotel, its walls collapsing in upon themselves, the old fin de siecle pipes and fittings crushed into a fine powder. All along 42nd Street, the great theaters of the golden age were shuttered and sealed, their marquees either blank or filled with the obtuse drivellings of the champions of the "42nd Street Haiku" - WITH A FLOURISH THE WAITRESS LEAVES BEHIND REARRANGED SMEARS. HIGH ABOVE THE LITE DAWN FLARES FROM A WINDOW WASHER'S PAIL. INTO THE LAUNDROMAT SHE PEERS AT MIDNIGHT'S TATTERED GLOOM. The sign over the old New Amsterdam Theater, once the glittering home of the Ziegfeld Follies and then a Kung Fu fleapit, declared: ON THE 12TH FLOOR A LIFE'S WORK HOLDS OPEN THE BOOK REVIEWER'S DOOR.

He strode out, across the road, regardless of the traffic which jarred to a halt, hooting and howling. The gutters were still filled with the last remnants of the slush of the melting winter snow. The vendors of The Truth, Koran, the Life of Muhammad and the Proofs of the Visitations From Outer Space were still out on the corner of 43rd, their wares and their bodies encased in cellophane wrappers. Other stalwarts of the streets hurried past, hiding their startled glances under their umbrellas. The Alchemist hesitated a moment at the doorway to a Dunkin Donuts, but then stalked on, across 44th and 45th. The traffic having halted, he followed the WALK sign across the confluence of Seventh Avenue and Broadway to the mid-road triangle of Duffy Square. The statue of George M. Cohan at its apex, the Discount Ticket Center, at its base, closed for the day. At the right, behind a clump of bushes,

Lieutenant Colonel Father Francis P. Duffy, stout before his Croix de Guerre - Distinguished Service Cross, Conspicuous Service - For God, For Home, For Country, To Those That Served That Others Might Live. Erected by the Father Duffy D.S.C. Post 54 Catholic War Veternas of U.S.A., A.D. 1954. But someone had already affixed a sign, to a lamp-post, behind the gang-busting priest, which read: YOU CAN BE ALL YOU PLAN - DON'T BELIEVE THE PIPE.

A steel lid, by Father Duffy's feet, yielded to the Alchemist's grasp. He pulled it up and away, lowering his head to peer into the black hole. He could see nothing, but the rumble of the subway trains echoed eternal from below. He sat and dangled his legs in the cavity, his feet finding the top rungs of a ladder. Testing it gingerly, he lowered himself, slowly, into the hole, checking the rungs one by one. As his shoulders reached the rim, he pulled the heavy lid over to cover the opening. The rain pouring in making the rungs increasingly slippery. Father Duffy leaned over above him and fixed him with a jagged bronze gaze. Mordecai glared back.

"Fuck you, the Pope, Jesus, Mary and the rest of 'em."

Father Duffy unfurled and shook his fist. The Alchemist stuck out his tongue, and closed the lid, which settled with a muffled clang. He turned his head, waiting to adjust to the dark. Then his feet sought out the rungs.

In order to rise, one must first descend. To find the sparks at the feet of Adam Kadmon, one must dig deep in the embers. To prise out the prima materia, imprisoned in crap, you have to muck in there and get dirty. Real alchemy is not for sissies. The job demands dedication, resolution, endurance and a stubborn tenacity, to find and force together all the escaped fragments of the Whole: the Hebrew, the Mussulman, the Christian, the Male and the Female, the androgynes, the loose cannons, Arnold, Lincoln, Ibn Battuta, Jaime, Merenptah, not to speak of the flitting shadows of the unnamed. The manifold Forms, yearning to be redeemed in the One. The mirror images longing to be real. If I, Mordecai, Hermes Trismegistus Thoth, Pythagoras, Hiram, Judah Lev Ben Bezalel, Faust Magus, Ramakrishna, am chosen, then so be it, this is my burden. To go down, step by step, rung by rung, into the echoing unknown, the country of the lost and the damned, delving deep into the recesses of memory, beneath the space of Time Squared...

Book 3:

Fire.

Upon the Flat Earth.

THE SUN IS MELTING! THE SUN IS MELTING!

Nobody pays attention. But I am not alone! The breath and sweat of the masses - the choking fumes of a million cars, cabs, trucks, buses, Veterans Refuse Collectors emptying their dumpsters, their belching, coughing vehicles covered with painted slogans: MAKE LOVE NOT WAR, AMERIKAN OUTLAWS, RECLAIM THE EARTH, FREE NATION. Stripped to the waist, their battle scars rippling perspiration, massive gloves plunged into mounds of rubbish tossed into growling metal teeth.

I hear and see it all! I, who was here before any of you. I, with whom it all began. The whole long, interminable trek. Long before any of you were even thought of, I crawled up from the sea onto the dry land. It was not dry land at first. It was swampy and wet, and everywhere you moved you made loud sucking noises, as your limbs broke free of the mud. The Delta, stretching from the Mediterranean down through the tributaries of the Great River to the empty desert beyond. But when I landed there, there was no Rosetta Stone of three languages for me to figure out the rules. When you're the First, you have to make things up as you go along.

I crawled onto the land and blinked at the sun. No sun cream to protect me, no Ray-Bans, no Ambre Solaire, no parasols or awnings. Just my bare flesh under that pitiless heat. And no trees to shelter under neither. Nothing but low scraggy shrubs, a poor apology for vegetation. And no voice speaking from a burning bush. When bushes burned, they burned, leaving nothing but ashes. Only the flip flap of pterodactyl wings offered any sign of progress.

But I was not one to be disheartened easily. Tearing strips off the shrubs, I fashioned a pair of wide mud-shoes and proceeded to walk forth upon the swamp. My progress was perforce slow as my feet still kept sinking back into the sludge and I had to exert myself to pull them free. And so I dragged myself on, as around me signs of life began to bud and quicken, new shoots pushed through the soil, insects jumped, small furry creatures swithered through the underbrush, small birdlike beasts fluttered, men emerged from their caves, beginning to construct mud huts, then, emboldened, moving on to more ambitious structures, family shacks, outhouses, barns, log cabins, hovels of corrugated iron, houses of straw, clay and bricks, tenements, chalets, bungalows, fortresses, domes, palaces, chateaus, ziggurats, temples, pyramids, Alcazars, churches, synagogues, mosques, nickelodeons, grand hotels, bingo halls, bowling alleys and vast stadiums in which tens of thousands could gather to cheer at worthless things in unison.

Soon, all around me, the sounds of hammering, sawing, drilling, smelting, blasting and forging echoed ceaselessly, until I could see in the dull haze of the sun ahead of me the city rising, with its turrets, battlements and spires punching up to scrape the sky. I hailed a passing cart and accepted the kind offer of a farmer to take me in through the suburbs. Already vast shanty towns had risen all about the perimeter of the city, composed of all those for whom the land could no longer provide sustenance. Beggars, mendicants, traders whose credit had been revoked by bankers, the mentally ill who had escaped from their tribes and families, the young who spurned the stifling security of their home life, fallen women whose virtue was becoming cheaper by the minute, misplaced matriarchs and pulverised papas, scabby scholars dreaming of great universities, and would-be cafe dwellers awaiting the invention of the taverns, whose boisterous sounds and pungent smells assailed me as I entered the main gates and passed into the city's inner quarters.

Iftah el bab! The great doors of the metropolis creaked open, blasting me in the face with the cries, shrieks, colors, the blazing air of the mid-summer rolling the exhaust fumes of a million vehicles into nose, mouth, eyes. My vision blurred, and all the towers and minarets of a thousand mosques and seminaries danced around me, like shimmying giants, so that at one point I even thought I saw a colossal ape, climbing up the tallest. It stood at the top, shaking its fist at the hordes of flying vehicles, which buzzed about the tips of the spires, grinding through the skies and rumbling in to land at the two airports that flanked the expanding, swelling skyline, under the burning hammer rays.

The sun is melting! The glass hitting 105 degrees Fahrenheit, and humidity pushing 89 per cent. The hammer and the anvil... Ibn Khaldun (Abd-el Rahman Abu Zayd Ibn Muhammad) stated that man first seeks the bare necessities. Only then does he proceed to the comforts and luxuries. The toughness of desert life precedes the softness of sedentary life. It is only in the cities that lineages become confused, races mixed, descent forgotten, bloodlines fudged, family ties disintegrate, mere anarchy is loosed upon the world. Ibn Khaldun wrote that savage nations are better able to achieve superiority than others.

His proper pupil, Christopher Columbus, demonstrated this theme perfectly, with his genocide of the native Americans. Now, having replaced the naive with the enterprising, the slow with the quick, he looks down upon his sweating acolytes and can admire his handiwork, facing the traffic jam of Eighth Avenue, the greasy haze of a thousand and one yellow cabs glistening in the stagnant air. His back to the Gulf and Western Building, and Central Park off his left shoulder. The fountains below him switched off to prevent the wayward youth of the city frolicking naked in the cooling cascade. Nevertheless the populace is stripped, with loinclothed rainbow youths and Amazon women jogging along the Park trails, their ears plugged into the beat of synthetic love and rage, bicycle fanatics with shiny plastic helmets and thick ripening thighs, the roller skaters weaving in and out of the Hecksher Playground, the Wollman Rink and the Pond. Groups sprawled on the stone rim of the monument at the Park's entrance to THE FREE MEN WHO DIED IN THE WAR WITH SPAIN THAT OTHERS MIGHT LIVE. The stone greek figures stretching in the sun, garlanded with birdshit, facing the homeless encampment on the other side of the plaza, in the shadow of the Coliseum. A knot of overladen supermarket trolleys, tattered blankets, mounds of reclaimed soda pop cans surrounding the swaying, lurching denizens of the mini-shanty town.

"Hey, Mo. Long time."

"You know what they say."

"Every day's a holiday, right?"

"Heard about Zoosman? Got caught last night by some mean kids up at the Lasker Rink. Beat him to death with baseball bats. Man had no face in the morning."

"Didn't he have an old lady?"

"They took her to Potter's Field. Long time ago."

"But we are still here."

"Got any refreshments? Special of the day?" A big plastic bottle of Coca Cola.

"Hey Mo. That bitch was lookin for you. Shrink woman. What was her name. Doctor Dexter. Aksed about you."

"Is that so?"

"She was talkin about some program upstate. Said to tell you they's still a place for you, if you want."

"What program man. Shit."

"I would take it man."

"Breakfast in bed an round the clock nurses. Ain't all bad."

"Didn't Crazy Ray go there? Ain't seen that fucker for a while."

"Nobody comes back from upstate. They just stay there forever, moonin around in white pajamas. No drugs man, just the birds and the bees."

"No drugs? Shit."

"You get your head straight. An you get paid by the State. Per diem."

"Wha's that?"

"It means you get a dime every day. Tellin you man, you much better off in the streets."

"Motherfucker."

Once upon a time, there was a man, Oedipus, who did fuck his mother. The story goes it was by mistake. Up in the Bronx, they will fuck anybody without even thinking. So shamed was Oedipus, he poked his own eyes out. Drastic stuff. As the Jews say, Oedipus schmedipus, who cares, as long as the boy loves his mama! But I can still hear the cries of pain, as the light goes out suddenly, and there is nothing but the pit...

Vanity, vanity, saith the preacher. The eye is not satisfied with seeing, nor the ear filled with hearing. We are too ready to take our senses for granted, until the voices come along. All my life, they have been crying in my eardrums. Rapping and wailing and bemoaning their fate, like a pack of wild djinns. I have seen all the works done under the sun, and behold, all is vanity and vexation of the spirit. King Solomon subdued the djinns, packed em all in jars and chained em at the bottom of the sea, keeping the keys. I told that story in my previous book, the "Arabian

Nights," otherwise known as *Alf laila wa lailah*, in the tale called "The City of Brass:" A traveller, Talib Ibn-Sahl, set out to the westernmost reaches of the desert, to find the lost jars of the djinns in the Kingdom of the Amalekites. The traveller dies, trying to awake the sleeping Princess of the City, but his companions, fleeing in terror, find the jars among a group of poor fishermen, who have been using them to cook fish.

The fishermen gave the questors the jars, as a gesture of friendship, to take back to the Caliph in Damascus. But when the jars were unsealed, in the Caliph's presence, the djinns flew out of them, begged forgiveness for their rebellion against their master and flew off through the ceiling. They have been at large ever since. The djinns had risen in rebellion when King Solomon had demanded the hand of the daughter of their King in marriage. But despite their awesome power, they were defeated, and they can be defeated again.

I did not fuck my mother. I was born, fully formed, out of my own endeavours. Of course, this is not easy to accept. It was a matter of much puzzlement, to Doctor Caroline, when she questioned me during our first meeting at the New York Department of Welfare, that day I went to get cash for my boots.

"Tell me about your parents, Mister Smith. Your father and your mother. Where did they come from?"

I shook my head. She was not ready to understand me, and I was not sure who she was, then.

"There must be somebody in there who wants to tell me," she said, with that flash of the eyes, "somebody who wants to tell me where all this started."

I will tell you the tale, Lilith, when you acknowledge who I am. You who would not bow down to Adam. The self-made has to have some pride.

But how can I judge myself? If I look down on my creation, and see that, lo, it is no good? As the signs proclaimed, upon the City of Brass:

"Enter and learn the tale of the rulers,
Who rested a while in the shadow of my towers,
And then passed, driven like straws
Before the wind of death."

Nothing endures. But everything is recycled. If not as gold, or brass, at least as shit. Spare a few dimes, you fucking sons of bitches! Let there be light, goddamit!! Let there be boundaries, barriers and breadlines! Alms, for the love of Allah! Spare cash, weighting down your pocket! Liquefy your assets! Melt your hearts!

But they all trudge by, drooping in the sun. There is no rest. A man must carry on. Shouldering the rucksack and the day's pile of plastic bags, the cullings of the Park's wastepaper baskets, leaving the encampment of the Coliseum vagrants behind, and crossing over West 60th. A model with a hairy chest and a Burt Reynolds leer peers from the window display of the Pharmacy & Cosmetics shop at the corner, over the legend -

BE A SENSUAL MARATHON MAN! MASCULINE NUTRITION! THERA EXTRA STRENGTH MEN'S VITAMINS! HAVE MORE CONFIDENCE IN YOUR STAMINA AND ABILITY!

Absolutely, man. Ever onward. Past the boarded up wreck of Martin's Tender Beef Steaks, Coffee & Muffins at $1.25 a mere mockery to the parched. Across 61st, the American Bible Society - A Translation Everyone Can Understand. In the window of Melissa's Gourmet Deli, an array of jars of different pickles shimmers in the light. The Lincoln Plaza Cinemas, across Broadway at 62nd, offer three premiere shows: *Swoon ("a great movie" - Rolling Stone), La Discrete ("Wonderful, exuberant" - Molly Haskell)* and *A Brief History of Time ("Compelling" - the Village Voice).* What came first, the chicken or the egg? The slow croaking of a paralysed voice.

The Bank of New York - "WE'RE A NYCE BANK - Liquid savings annual yield 3.148. 6 month credit 2.988. 12 month credit 2.890. 18 month credit 2.800." The Harkness Atrium, shady space under glass and potential marks sipping ice coffee. Spare a quarter, man, any loose change, put a smile on a poor man's face, thank you very much have a nice day.

The Lincoln Center. Honest Abe. Mecca of the Arts, crowds circling the Avery Fisher and Alice Tully Hall. The Empire Hotel, O'Neill's Empire Grill, Fiorello's. Houlihan. Liberty Travel. Cosmetics Plus and Chemical Bank. The Visitors' Center at the Church of Jesus Christ of the Latter Day Saints. Public Welcome - Free Guided Tours. YOU ARE THE SUM TOTAL OF YOUR ANCESTORS. WHO ARE THEY? Who indeed? FREE! A GREAT FILM - YOU ARE NOT ALONE! BEFORE

COLUMBUS! LOST EMPIRES OF THE AMERICAS - 15 MINUTES. Salvation and truth on the fast track.

So where were You when I *was* alone out there? Spilling my guts in the Trinity Churchyard, straining to give birth to the world? Alone in the night, with no one but the old janitor, O'Connell, to ease my pain and soothe my brow. No father, no mother, only the guardian angel, gouty and ugly, with his bad breath and warts.

RECLAIM THE EARTH! Onward, onward. Look out for the djinns. They may have escaped, but I feel, in my burning bones, that they can't have gone very far...

THE BREATH AND SWEAT OF THE MASSES. The choking fumes of a million cars, cabs, trucks, buses. I hear and see all! From the sidelines, the trashbins, the dried up gutters, slithering, glopping along the baking pavements, I, Frank Ox, Private Eye, Ear, Nose and Deep Throat specialist, meddler, moocher, magi, malodorous and mangy man of straw, follow in the wake of misfortune like a scavenger trailing an old tramp steamer. A classical castaway, bereft of home, office, hotel room, welfare support, investment income, even employer, after the vanishing of the treacherous Mordecai into the Times Square tunnels. I wallow along, lamenting the latent loss of 42nd Street, the proscribed pornographers, prostrated peep shows, doomed dementias of a thousand and one fleapits, fuckshows and flicker-parlors, closed down by order of the Times Square Renewal Project. Hell's kitchens to be mopped clean and disneyfied. The New City, rising over the ashes of the old, a rededicated hub of commerce, gleaming new towers to replace the old. Even if the World Trade Center had been blown up, we would have rebuilt it, twice as high as before! America, from sea to shining sea!

O beautiful! O beautiful! But Frank Ox is adrift and floating, the shamus shivering in the sun. The light! The light! I want my shadows back, my frosty nooks, my turned up overcoat. But a man of destiny must soldier on, in sticky shorts and shabby undershirt and tennis shoes, to slide on in and out of trashcans, slither around lamp posts, bus stops, scaffolding and traffic signs.

Everything shimmers in the heat which wraps around me like an iron overcoat. The air is blurred. The eyeballs glaze and bubble. But none of this should keep me from my mission. Keep on truckin'! Drooping at the corner of Columbus and 74th, the Eurotrash shop:

Picasso, Dali, Magritte, Klimt, Monet, Warhol, Miro, Chagall, O'Keeffe, Man Ray, Weber, Lichtenstein, Avedon, Adams, Hopper, Doisneau, Hockney, Haring, Canetti, Cezanne, Klee, Cartier-Bresson, Matisse, Brassai, Renoir, Degas, Kandinsky, Estes, Sewada, Christo, Sieff. On the other side of the street Pioneer Supermarkets are offering Italian Prune Plums at 69 cents, Macaroni Cheese at 99c, Sour Cream 89c, Peas 79c, Yoghourt 2 for $1, Chuck Steaks for $1.49, Veal Chops and Rib Steaks $2.99 and Laundry Detergent at 99 cents.

There must be a meaning somewhere among all this data, but a man needs shade and cool to think. Slithering up past Kenar Clothes and Frank's Barber Shop and the Chase Manhattan Bank and Variazoni Gallery and Nancy's Wines, the Shamus slides gratefully into Skimpy Heaven, Soups, Salads, Sandwiches, and orders a tall freshly squeezed juice. Orange, tomato or rhubarb. Wiping his sweat off the table with a rolled napkin. A young beanpole of a girl dressed in a scrap of tush-hugging denim on a stool digging her way out of a Greek Salad. The waitress, dressed in diamond shaped reds and yellows, brings him his ice cold tomato juice. The frozen haemoglobin. This place was even hotter than the Philippines, Frank Ox reflected, hotter than Hades on the Faust job. Now there was a risk, tweaking Mephistopheles' tail. The Big Guy didn't like it. "Looking for loopholes, Mister Ox? You want to know my secrets? Down here it's what you see is what you get. A deal's a deal. I had you with your first unkind thought. You wanna see how many saints I have in this neighborhood? You wanna meet the Big Boy, Mister Nails himself?"

Curiosity is my business. I cannot reveal, at this point, the facts, or otherwise, about the final ignominy of the Christ. The Devil is such a proven liar. But I refunded Faust's retainer, as I could do nothing for him. I was an idealist in those days. No fix, no fee. Not any more. The blood-red liquid cooled me down sufficiently to take my bearings.

The entire nub of this case, thought Frank Ox, is the Inherent Paradox. If Mo Smith's predators and carers are emanations of his own will and testaments, why should he feel threatened by them, and if his remaining demons had escaped, should he not rejoice? One personality is enough trouble for the rest of us. Or does the problem arise from the Alchemist's nature: the naked urge for power, the sheer reluctance to accept that he too is a puff of smoke? The bottom line, that this too is a political issue. The race for shrinking metaphorical resources. Karl Marx's tendency towards Monopoly. The One that swallows the All.

It might be the time, Frank Ox thought, to consult the Secret Powers Which Control the World. The Keepers of the Ultimate Knowledge. The problem being, of course, Primary Contact. This wasn't as easy as it once had been. Drawing a pentragram on the floor of the Lower Level toilet at Grand Central Station and scattering pinches of sulphur and some snatches of gibberish might have been good up to the nineteen-twenties, but now the Keepers have become much more elusive. They might have even left town. Unthinkable as it may be. The Global Village. One would have to dig deep for The Clues.

Ox finished his drink, counted two soaked dollar bills out upon the table and left the cafe, crossing over 75th Street and the main road to face the Animation Gallery, pausing only for a moment to take in the cel drawing of Tweetie Pie confronting Sylvester and Yosemite Sam: YES, WOBBIN, THESE ARE THE SHEWIFFS WHO WOBBED FWOM US POOR WITTO SWOBS AND GAVE IT TO THE WICH - THEMSEWVES! Jeepers. Sweat pouring again, he turned left at 76th Street to pass by the residential blocks with desperate notices affixed to their outside railings: STOP! NO MORE MENUS! NO MENUS PLEASE! DEFINITELY NO MENUS! Past the Riverside Memorial Chapel, corner of Amsterdam. A black itinerant held out his hand in supplication. Frank shook his head and staggered on, across the street, the Exxon Park and garage, the Beacon Theatre Parking - NEW OR OLD, WE TREAT YOU LIKE GOLD! the Avis office and across Broadway to the Koo-Joo-Roo California Kitchen - original skinless flame broiled chicken, but bypassing that and Belleclaire's Cleaners and Cohen's Optical and Tano's Bags and Shoes, the Westside Gourmet Meats, pressing open the door of the Original Big Nicks 100% Charcoal Grilled Burgers and entering the cluttered steamy space within.

The airconditioning was on full blast, thank God, though it failed to dispel the pungent blast from the hot grill just inside the thick glass door. The row of burger barflies perched on leather stools flicking their eyes to flash him a glance. The blue jowled waiter waving the menu. "Back here sir!" leading the Shamus to the furthest corner, conveniently placed below the rows of framed photographs of all the celebrities who had patronised Big Nick's from time immemorial. From Fiorello La Guardia and Jack Dempsey to John Lindsay and John Travolta, pugilists, politicos and stars. The panels at eye level plastered with the joint's printed enticements: ANY ONION RINGS? ANY CHILLI? TRY OUR BLUEBERRY YOGHURT. ACIDOPHILUS CULTURE. SPUMONI SUNDAE WITH WILD CHERRY SYRUP IMPORTED FROM GREECE. The brown mahoganny table in front of him bore the establishment's testimonial under a plastic wrap: BIG NICK'S GUARANTEE: "In my joints we cook in front of your eyes. You can watch us. I pay attention to details and I am committed to quality."

I called for the Burger menu and studied it intently. Time marches on, and it is always possible that procedures have been changed, but, in Nick's Burger Joint, this would necessitate a shifting of the earth's axis so profound as to leave global signals, which, needless to say, the Ox snout would have picked up.

In the normal course of events, one might have expected to find the clues within the core, beefburger menu, to wit -

AMERICAN CHEESEBURGER: Covered with melted American cheese.
AVOCADOBURGER: Snappy, South-of-the-Border Burger, Caramba!!
BACON BURGER: Strips of crispy bacon for an extra mouthful.
BARBECUE BURGER: Zesty, with Barbecue Sauce.
BLUEBURGER: Sauce with blue-cheese chunks & olive for gourmets.
BOSTON BURGER: Served with Boston baked beans on the side.
BURGER FLORENTINE: Topped with tasty Grecian Style Spinach, Olive, Feta Cheese & Scallions. A BJ Original.
CHILIBURGER: Served with a spicy side dish of chili con carne.
CHILLI CHEESEBRUGER: Cheeseburger with home-like chilli con carne on the side.
FETA BURGER: Tomato and Feta Cheese with Olive. A BJ Original.
FRENCH ONION BURGER: Savory onion sauce with Parmesan cheese and olive.
GARLICBURGER: Covered with thick garlic sauce, spices, olive.
GRECIAN BURGER: Stuffed with Herbs, spices & onions. A BJ original.
HAWAIIAN BURGER: With an Aloha lei of Grilled Pineapple.

MADRID BURGER: With Olive, Feta Cheese & Pimento.
MEDITERRANEAN BURGER: Grecian Burger with Anchovies, Feta Cheese and Tomato, Second to none.
MOZZARELLA BURGER: A bellisima burger with the Italian touch.
MUSHROOM BURGER: Topped with Hearty Mushroom-Onion gravy.
PHILA BURGER: Topped with Cream Cheese on English, Olive.
PIZZA BURGER: With thick Mozzarella, smothered in pizza sauce on a toasted English muffin.
PORT CHEDDAR CHEESEBURGER: Topped with good Cheddar laced with delicious Port flavor.
SWISSBURGER: Covered with melted Swiss Cheese.
TEXASBURGER: Topped with an Egg for "egg-stra" energy.
WESTERN BURGER: Capped with a tasty slice of Grilled Danish ham.
**BEEFBURGER: THE SIMPLE CLASSIC, COOKED TO YOUR TASTE.*

A host of possibilities here, as one could ponder the erratic use of capitals, the mysterious emphasis of "BJ Originals", the clues inherent in the English muffin, the "Aloha lei" or sudden lyrical emphases on Mozzarella, Mediterranean and "Hearty" Mushroom-onion gravy. But there was too much here to go on. The codes are usually more compactly devised. I called for the "Special Menu", and had to object firmly to the menu of the adjacent Pizza Joint which the Hispanic garcon tried vainly to press into my hands. "Tell the manager I said the SPECIAL." Nonplussed, he called the Man himself, who breezed out from behind the counter, nasal hair and moustache abristle gamely. I gave him the nod, the wink and the twitch, and he nodded back, swept back behind the counter and produced the required article, dog eared and grease-stained. This time the job was far easier, as the stains formed the pattern of the Rosicrucian Mysterium Magnum, with the lowest blotch falling over the heading of the boxed menu at the bottom of the mid-panel of the menu - GREEK GYRO W/TSATSIKI IN PITTA BREAD. The text as follows:

> Yoghurt dressing adorns slices of roasted gyro loaf with authentic seasonings. In the pocket, with shredded lettuce, tomato, onion & touch of feta. Topped by tsatsiki.

Now at last we were cooking with gas. This was child's play. It appeared a simple inverted pattern, in which the first two letters of each word, from the start, are matched with the first two letters of each word, from the end, converging to the middle, i.e. YO DR AD SL OF RO GY LO WI AU SE IN TH PO WI SH LE TO ON TO OF FE TO BY TS will make -

YOTS DRBY ADTO SLFE OFOF ROTO GYON LOTO WILE AUSH SEWI INTH PO.

This leaves us with some letters reformed into words and others gibberish, to wit -

TOYS TOAD FOOF GOYN WILE WISE BYRD SELF ROOT TOOL SHAU THIN (or HINT) OP.

A closer scrutiny reveals another key. The "Special" menu contained, in fact, a print error, one of the "of"s put down as "ol". This made the nonsense FOOF into FOOL. The proper words then constituted: TOYS TOAD FOOL SELF ROOT TOOL WILE WISE HINT. This could be an old fashioned Kabbalistic "atbash" cypher, in which the Hebrew letters of the alphabet are inverted, so that "Aleph" becomes "Tav", "Bet" becomes "Shin" and so forth, which, allocated numbers, reveals the true message. But, after half an hour, I was stymied on that route. The waiter returned, insisting on my order, so I fobbed him off with a sardine platter. This alone should have given me pause for thought. But I would get there. Next, if I took the four remaining gibberish words - counting the corrected "ol" to "of", I emerged with the following square –

GOYN
SHAU
BYRD
FOOF

Applying "atbash" here, this gave me:

TLBM
HSZF
YBIW
ULLU

Which, diagonally from the bottom, gave me "LIST", and then the following words in sequence - THIS LIST WILL FILL BULL FIBS WISH BILL FISH.

The moment I wrote this last word my sardine platter arrived, garnished with crisp lettuce, tomato, olives, potato salad, cole slaw, radish and house garnish. Clearly I was on the right track. Sure enough, as I moved up to the "Fishermen's Net" segment of the menu, there were three clear grease stains in classic triangle on the section, which was short:

FRIED JUMBO SHRIMP: Plump and crisp, served on a bed of lettuce with tangy Cocktail sauce, Lemon Wedges and Creamy Cole Slaw, Tomato and Olive.
FRIED BREADED FLOUNDER: Light and Flaky with Tartar sauce, lemon wedges, Tomato, Olive and Creamy Cole Slaw.
FRIED CLAMS: Sweet and Crispy, with Cocktail Sauce, Lemon Wedges, Tomato, Olive and Creamy Cole Slaw.
FISHERMAN'S PLATTER: Deep Fried Flounder, Shrimp and Fried Clams with Tartar Sauce, Cocktail Sauce, Lemon Wedges, Tomato, Olive and Creamy Cole Slaw.
(All the above served with Thick French Fries, Crisp Tossed Salad, Beet Salad or Chick Pea Salad, Choice of Bread.)

The omens were clear (and note the Creamy Cole Slaw motif). It only remained to tot up the prices on these 4 items, which totalled $41.80 cents together. In letters these formed DAH - with the zero forming perhaps infinity, or the Hebrew "Aleph". In English this gave me "HAD", which was redundant, but in Hebrew the word spelled out "AHAD" or "One", implying I had hit the jackpot. (Note, too, that "Da" if one omits the silent "h", in Hebrew, is the word "Know." This does not involved transmuted "atbash", which itself would transmute "Dah" into "Khad", once again the word "One." Q.E.D.)

41.80 was, in that case, the answer. Clearly, if precedent was anything to go on, a location in the city. 80th street was clear, but 41 was useless as a cross-street. However, adding 4+1 we have 5, therefore arriving at 5th Avenue and 80th, without doubt, the location of the Metropolitan Museum of Art.

Once again, Frank Ox comes up trumps. An inversion of the figure, 08:14, also provided me with an appropriate time. I polished off the sardines, toasting the eponymous owner with an ice cold pitcher of tap-water. Accept no substitutes. All that remained now was to pass the period between this lengthening afternoon and the following morning, when I could proceed to the rendezvous. I thought perhaps of perusing the Pizza menu after all in case it concealed the week's winning lottery numbers, but that is an old mug's game.

It's back to the old Central Park bivouac, northside of the Reservoir. There are quiet nooks, though one is disturbed, frequently, by the bestial grunting of the city's pederasts assaying anal sex. The entire idea of penetration, male or female, is dismaying. Bodily fluids have long been a problem, well into the Age of Enlightenment. It has always seemed to me that Mankind is far too sticky.

The night is almost as hot as the day. Sweaty bodies squelch and pummel each other behind bushes, like a brood of giant frogs. One can hear the city honk, squawk and squitter from all four borders of the park, a vast restless bestiary, gryphons growling, salamanders sighing, phoenixes scrabbling out of ashes. All the little people whimpering, giggling and gasping, rattling tin cups against the bars of their cages. Predators prowling, and the victims waiting, crouched in corners, their hot fearful breath expelled into the fetid air. No wonder the Keepers remain hidden. Who can bear the revolting mass.

Trying, in my soggy mind, to muster the roll call of the usual suspects: The ailing Queen Bee, Caroline, and her buzzing hive - Darwish, Benjamin, the occult Armenian, my tormentor, Frances; the imprisoned Arab, Salim, and his new companion, the *djinn* Battuta. The *djinn* Jaime, now installed in the professor's apartment. The *djinn* Flint, at large. And the greatest threat of all, the awakened Pharaoh, Nep, ensconsed in the fortune telling business in Brooklyn, sitting pretty now that his mentor, Madam Cropfin, mysteriously disappeared in the night.

Ghosts and demons. They are everywhere, behind every wall. They walk the streets, brazenly, under the brightest streetlights, ride the subways and buses, regale the new immigrant drivers of taxicabs with their pathetic tirades. They sit in bars and singles clubs, sharing their pain with whoever might be slumped within range. Sometimes they are packed so tight in the spaces between apartment block walls that the cracked plaster can be seen shifting, in the small hours.

But I am so fatigued that even with this swirling in my brain, I drop off, and awake when the sun has already cleared the trees. Startled, I look at the time - 07:45. Less than half an hour to the rendezvous. I rise to my feet, kick over the legs of the slumbering pederasts and crawl under the reservoir wire to dunk my face in the brackish waters of the lake. Padding over the dewy grass, shooing the squirrels away, across the Transverse Road and round the back of the Metropolitan Museum to the exit of the Park to 79th. By 08:10 I am ensconsed on the corner of 80th and Fifth Avenue, looking towards the Museum. Having checked this location the evening before I was pretty sure the next Clue, whatever it may be, would occur in the street, not in the Met itself, whose main entrance would be construed as being between 81st and 83rd. I curled up by the wire wastebin on the south-east corner of the crossing and settled down.

At this hour the Museum itself was not open and so pedestrian traffic was sparse. Buses and other vehicles rumbled past, gasping by the traffic lights at Fifth and 79th. No one but I seemed to be pausing at this next corner.

But one should have faith in the universe. If not in its inhabitants, at least its mathematics. At 08:13 precisely a vagrant, of Hispanic visage, dressed in a tattered short sleeved shirt and torn pants, walked up with rather a jauntier air than might be expected by his circumstances and began affixing small strips of paper to the lamp-post at the north-western corner. He completed his work just as my watch clicked past 08:14. I remained slumped by the trash. He walked on without looking back, pacing past the great front steps of the Museum and on up the pavement of the Avenue. I waited for a full ten minutes, watching the lamp-post and the small strips sagging limply in the still air. Then, at 08:24 precisely, I walked across the street, in a traffic gap, up to the post.

The strips were printed slips, of the familiar kind which dot every pole and post in the city. I tore one off. It read:

GOVERNMENT JOBS NOW OPEN
Paying $9 to $25 per hour. No experience or test required. Free applications available for over 2000 job titles. For a complete list of jobs available and instructions on how to receive application forms, call 24 hours, 7 days at - - - - - -
Your satisfaction guaranteed.

I have not divulged the number, to prevent unwarranted intrusions. But the way forward was now clear. I tore all the strips off the lamp-post and, in a slow shambling gait in keeping with my subterfuge, moved up and down the road (consecutively) to check the other posts along the way. The lamp-post at Fifth Avenue and 80th Street had been the only one to which the Message was affixed. I had correctly read Big Nick's Menu.

Frank Ox proceeded, to stage two.

VERY LIKE A TOMB, is this, old Bertha Cropfin's living room. The blinds permanently drawn, and nailed in to the wall, so that even at the height of the summer only the thinnest shafts of light ooze through, poking a couple of inches at most into the room, tiny slits of swirling particles of dust. In order to banish even this infraction, thick purple drapes are available to close upon the besieged window. The furniture within the room is uniformly dark, two old black leather settees and the hardbacked soothsayer's chair, up against the deep mahogany table. The single lamp on the desk is so veiled and dim that only the outline of the sitter can be discerned. The client, sitting across the desk in a shabby sunken lounger, is usually in total darkness. Only his, or her, thoughts can be seen.

Merenptah, after Madame Cropfin died, did nothing to alter this setting. He sat, alone and silent, for many hours of each day, surrounded by the paraphernalia of her craft. The tarot packs, the playing cards, the cups, the saucers, crystals, jeroboams and jars, the cheiromantic charts, the salt cellars, chalcomantic bowls, the mystic keys, the laurel leaves and dampened cloths, the simmering incense, the rows of coloured eggs, divining rods and dried out mummies of local fauna, the neighbour's deceased cat, the stray dog, the rat and tray of old roaches. The complicated bell pulley Madame had used to warn her of the sudden visits of the Park Slope sanitation inspectors was still operational, but it had not tolled since her death, as the bureaucrats had apparently assumed her business had ceased to function.

In fact few clients jangled the front door bell since Merenptah had entered his mistress' bedchamber, his royal organ ready and rampant for her insatiable if septuagenarian appetite, to find Madame stretched out, stiff as a board, upon her unruffled sheets, her hands crossed upon her thin and scrawny breasts, a rose stuck between her teeth, one eye closed tight shut and the other wide open, staring at the zodiacal ceiling. The goat, the water carrier, the fish and the ram were directly over her sightless eyes. The scorpion's tail pointed towards her feet. According to tradition, it was feet first the *ka* whipped its way to the celestial homing grounds. This did not bode well for Madame's soul, in the swampy nests of the night house of Mars, the planet of frozen waters and nocturnal mumblings. But perhaps she would pass on, towards happier climes. Who could tell? Certainly not one who had become marooned, half way between this world and the next.

Merenptah was unable to remove the rose, which appeared to have grown out from within Madame's larynx, and he instructed the morticians to inter her with it, placing an old copper English penny on her open eye. He excused himself from inspecting the embalming process, the very mention of which filled him with nauseous feelings, so that he had to exit the chapel and leave the body to the Cardozo Brothers and their reeking unguents.

For a time Merenptah had occupied himself in Madame's library, poring over her esoteric collection, her alchemical volumes, Secret Books of the Egyptian Gnostics, Mazdaean Magic, the shelf of Pyramidology, Masonic Secrets, Hermetic philosophies, the Teachings of All Ages, Albigensian texts, Secret Maps of the New York Subways, Christian and Judaic Kabbalah, Sufism and Buddhist commentaries. But inevitably he would go to bed with a Zane Grey paperback, a tattered pile of which he discovered under a loose floorboard underneath her sagging bed. His first volume was *Riders of the Purple Sage,* a tale of violence in a rugged frontier setting which reminded him a little of the Nubian campaigns. He lay awake, allowing the ramshackle fan above the bed to agitate the muggy air, trying to recapture in memory the zest and vigour of his youth compared with his present after-life. The only vigorous activity he undertook nowadays was his weekly trip Uptown to indulge in sexual passion with Miss Ada Em, a loyal client who had foregone her annual Catskills summer escape to remain in the stifling heat of the city to rendezvous with her unusual paramour. Thus he would drag himself up, of a morning, throw on a t-shirt and jeans and lumber out, triple locking the door of the Seventh Avenue apartment, traversing the corner of Lincoln and up past the Brooklyn Academy of the Esoteric Arts towards the subway. Floundering in the infernal platform heat, then gratefully gasping in the air-conditioned balm of the D train with its rainbow passengers, as if the entire planet had dumped one of each of its types and exemplars, flopping with fatigue, onto the plastic seats. The train clattering by Atlantic Avenue and De Kalb, slowly lumbering up from ghost-lit iron pits, screeching and caterwauling, onto the Manhattan Bridge. The massive steel latticework, crossing and crisscrossing against the panorama of the East River, the Brooklyn Bridge and the sungleamed towers of Fulton, Pearl and Wall Street, and then the slow cluttered plunge into the old unreconstructed maze of nineteenth century blocks across the South Street Viaduct, the brick walls peeling ancient painted panegyrics to long lost Chinese restaurants or accountancy firms either long foundered or hopped across the grid to pan-global power. The gaunt decay of Rutgers' Houses or the Knickerbocker Village, with its quaintly Washington Irving title - and was it here where it all began - the Cosmic Creation, and the Famous Navigator Noah coming to earth, the Heroes of Communipaw, and the dream of the founding of the great city of Neuw Amsterdam out of the primeval mud? Fleeting visions vanishing in an inkling, if they were ever inkled, as the D train plunges back into the pit and on towards its first Manhattan stop, Grand.

Merenptah alights at Broadway-Lafayette, walking east down Houston a few blocks to Wooster, and Ada Em's apartment. Her block one of the oldest in this neighborhood, a seven-storey climb of blackened fire escapes and pediments that were once ornate but are now black as soot. No elevator, just a long, stifling slog up flight after flight of blackened stone steps, with dried up corpses of Raided roaches buried in the scum at the bottom of each stairway, the walls looking as if generations of vermin had carved their individual names in their blisters. Tiny hieroglyphs in beetle or mouse language. But Ada had transformed her portion of Inferno into a haven of

At this point there is a break in the narrative, perhaps in the tradition of Laurence Stern, or possibly the Dead Sea Scrolls, as all that remains of the 1993 text for the next section is a number of fragments, dealing with singular pharaonic sexual positions taught by Merenptah to Ada

Em, along with irregular lessons in hieroglyphic writing, which she insisted upon but he imparted reluctantly, not being accustomed to the arts of communication by example rather than by decree. This segment is then again abruptly curtailed, to be followed by disconnected fragments concerning the Alchemist, Mordecai, wandering in the subway tunnels beneath the city. There follows part of a rambling monologue emanating from a disembodied mind, possibly in an eighteenth level shaftway midway between Canal Street and the Center of the Earth, followed by a segment in which Ibn Battuta and Salim, while being transferred from Riker's Island prison to a secure Anti-Terrorism enclosure in Ossining, are involved in an autobus accident and escape, relatively unscathed, by crawling through the smashed windows of the overturned vehicle before teams of SWAT officers and night-black helicopters begin trawling the Upstate woods along the Hudson from Greenburgh to Yorktown. This is followed by the transcripts of a number of newspaper clippings reporting a spate of unexplained arson attacks upon Manhattan bookshops, concentrated on Dalton's and Barnes and Nobles superstores, all occurring upon the hottest nights of the year but leaving plain evidence of foul play, petrol soaked rags and inflammatory devices left in nearby alleyways, testimony of either a deliberate goading or a particularly moronic intelligence. Mixed among these fragments are pages copied from Washington Irving's seminal "History of New York" by the fictitious "Diedrich Knickerbocker", first published in 1809, when the events of the Great American Revolution and the eviction of the Colonial Power were still fresh in the minds of the public, including the following segment:

BOOK I. CONTAINING DIVERS INGENIOUS THEORIES AND PHILOSOPHIC SPECUATIONS, CONCERNING THE CREATION AND POPULATION OF THE WORLD, AS CONNECTED WITH THE HISTORY OF NEW YORK - Chapter I. Description of the World: According to the best authorities, the world in which we dwell is a huge, opaque, reflecting, inanimate mass, floating in the vast ethereal ocean of infinite space. It has the form of an orange, being an oblate spheroid, curiously flattened at opposite parts, for the insertion of two imaginary poles, which are supposed to penetrate and unite at the centre; thus forming an axis on which the mighty orange turns with a regular diurnal revolution.

The transitions of light and darkness, whence proceed the alternations of day and night, are produced by this diurnal revolution successively presenting the different parts of the earth to the rays of the sun...

The Brahmins assert that the heavens rest upon the earth, and the sun and moon swim therein like fishes in the water, moving from east to west by day, and gliding along the edge of the horizon to their original stations during night; while, according to the Pauranicas of India, it is a vast plain, encircled by seven oceans of milk, nectar, and other delicious liquids...

Besides these, and many other equally sage opinions, we have the profound conjectures of Aboul-Hassan-Aly, son of Aly Khan, son of Aly, son of Abderrahman, son of Abdallah, son of Masoud-el- Hadheli, who is commonly called MASSOUDI... who informs us that the earth is a huge bird, Mecca and Medina constituting the head, Persia and India the right wing, the land of Gog the left wing, and Africa the tail. He informs us, moreover, that an earth has existed before the present (which he considers as a mere chicken of 7000 years), that it has undergone divers deluges, and that, according to the opinion of some well-informed Brahmins of his acquaintance, it will be renovated every seventy-thousandth hazarouam; each hazarouam consisting of 12,000 years...

*

But the heat... the unbearable heat...

"JUST LET ME TAKE THIS IN," SAID BENJAMIN, "you're telling me that your friend Ada Em, Miss Fruitcake of 1993, is having an affair with the Pharaoh Merenptah, the same Merenptah that our own vanished wanderer, Moses etcetera Smith, claimed as one of his alternative personas, looking for his way out of the old Egyptian Halls of the Dead? Doesn't she have another excuse for fucking some alte kaker that she picked up on the streets?"

"He's not any kaker, he's her fortune teller," said Frances, "and I don't know what to believe," holding the fridgidaire door open, as she rummaged for a Diet something-or-other, lingering as long as possible in the ice cool blast. Benjamin lying upon the sofa by the open front window like a starfish, shirt open and stomach hairs itching for a trace of wind. "Whoever he is he knows his onions. Aram verified the script as authentic."

"What did it say? What's the old Egyptian for Kiss my ass baby?"

"You're not that far off. They were erotic passages."

"Inshallah. My first summer in the city, it was all a massive open air turkish bath. The world's only urban nudist colony. But all the energy is lost now."

"It's all in the mind, Benjamin. Ada Em is scarcely any younger than you are and she has the Kama Sutra beat to hell."

"Have you met this ancient paragon yet?"

"He wasn't there when I turned up." She had found the Diet Coke and reluctantly closed the icebox door.

"Are you O.K., Frances? You've been here before, I remember. What about that other character, the author, what was his name, the one who was broadcasting on NPR?"

"It was the Crush Limbo Show. Arnold Flint."

"Oh yah. And of course the Arab guy - Battuta. Arrested at the Pilgrim's Arms. It was in the Times, so it must be true."

"I don't know, Benjamin. It's just too hot to think."

"It's him for sure who's burning down the bookstores. The writer's revenge. Transformed from an imaginary person into a real one, he goes out into the book stores. Not a sign of his writings. Not a single volume, hardback or paperback. He looks up, what do you call it, the Books in Print - not a single listing of his name. He's been wiped out from history. He never happened. If he exists, it's only in a different time-space dimension. His entire life's work is invisible. He's nobody."

"Enoch Soames."

"Excuse me?"

"Enoch Soames. He was a character in a short story by an old English writer, Max Beerbohm. He was so neglected as an author he made a pact with the devil to transport him a hundred years into the future to the reading room of the British Museum where he could check up on his posthumous fame. But he discovered that the only reference to him was as a fictional character in a short story by an old English writer, Max Beerbohm."

"If he burned down the British Museum then he is our man."

"No. I think it just ends there."

"That's UnAmerican. There can be no action without a reaction. Or without a reactionary."

"Very alliterative."

"How long before your air-conditioner gets fixed?"

"They promised it for Friday afternoon."

"Two more days. That's too much. I can get the same thing in my apartment. The eternal shvitz-bath."

"You can stay or go Benjamin. Whatever you want."

"Decisions. I could leave but I can't get up. Is there any ice in that icebox?"

"I just filled the thingie."

"I can't wait. Give me anything cold. Frozen schnitsel, iced yoghourt, snowballs, the heart of Golda Meir, cryogenic capsules, lemon popsicles, stalactites, great speeches of Labour Zionist leaders, anything from Canada, Grace Kelly, memories of childhood, portraits of old Jerusalem, Ronald Reagan's testicles, *tisha b`av*, tundra, polar bear's tits, any kind of fish, except octopus..."

THE HYDRA HEADS AND TWISTING TENTACLES... Having called the number on the torn slip of paper upon the post south of the Metropolitan Museum of Art, Frank Ox found himself standing in line in a dismal bunker in the basement of the Manhattan District Office of the Internal Revenue on Church Street and Murray, waiting his turn in a line of glum, wheezing unfortunates, to be interviewed for unspecified government service. No one spoke or comunicated except by cough or spittle. After an hour the entire line was called in to a bare brick walled room lit by one harsh neon bar. The interview consisted of a rudimentary examination of the teeth and genital areas, followed by a thermometer thrust up the rectum. Those who protested were invited to leave. The Examiners, a row of bullet headed white blonde men in what appeared to be blood-spattered white coats, spoke only in monosyllables: "Here. Mouth. Pants. Bend. No. Yes. Go. Take." The most gimlet eyed of the men gave Frank a printed slip which referred him to "The Harbor-master", at a Hudson River pier at the end of 57th Street. This proved to be the point where the Hudson Parkway leads off from the pitted swathe of 12th Avenue. Frank crossed the street, under the shadow of two massive chimneys overseeing the bleak scape of storage warehouses, towards a vast parking lot of city garbage trucks. Giant cranes were unloading containers of refuse onto the cargo ferries which were to convey them down the river to Staten Island, curling around the promontory of southern Manhattan, past Ellis Island and the Statue of Liberty, down the Kill Van Kull and Arthur Kill to the vast dumping grounds of New York's Sanitation upon the banks of Fresh Kills creek.

Riding with the refuse, Frank and eleven other of the chosen, encased in sheer-white overalls and gas masks, slowly approached, softly chugging on the hot mid-morning, the massive mound of debris and household rubbish fed by its fleet of squat ferryboats like a termite queen by her incessant brood. They alighted, led by black-garbed riflemen into a harshly lit cabin, where an even more gimlet-eyed bullet-headed man, whose skull was cracked and pitted as the city's asphalt, laid down the law of their employment. He projected, upon a screen, a series of old fashioned epidiascopic sketches of what appeared to be two egg shaped steel capsules, which, in closer section, were revealed to have a series of tiny, strange carvings upon their narrower ends.

"This, gentlemen, is what you are looking for," the Cracked Skull told the garbage men. "We can call these the Cosmic Eggs. What they are, or how they came to be here, is not your business or concern. All you need to know is they are somewhere in the Unsorted Mound, which will be the object of your searches. In case the thought crosses your mind, the Eggs are not traceable by any known scientific method. Our mighty technology, at the threshold of the twenty-first century, is no use whatsoever to us in locating these two motherfuckers. Each is between three and four inches in length, seven inches in diameter at the median. You need not be afraid of damaging them by your searches, they are, to all extents, indestructible. As you might guess, unless you are absolute morons, we have handled these kinds of babies before. Once located you will remain in place, and contact me on your mobile communicators. Do not attempt to bring them in. Don't even think of misinforming me. You will be searched rigorously at every shift end. If you try swallowing the Eggs or hiding them up your ass, they will be extracted by the most brutal methods. You will be paid one hundred and fifty U.S. dollars for every day's search. The person who locates an Egg will receive twelve hundred dollars bonus. You will be asked to sign the Oath of Silence and the consequences of any transgression will be dire. Wherever ye may run or try to hide, howsoever ye may disguise yourself or conceal your identity, ye will be found and chastised severely. You who are the lowest of the low, ye may think ye know pain, despair, anguish and suffering, but you ain't seen nothin' yet. Go to, and may the best men prosper."

Encased in his white overalls and breathing apparatus, Frank Ox ventured forth upon the Mound. The mid-day sun was scorching, and the sweat poured in rivulets down the inner tubing of the suit, to be vended out above his shins. The Mound faced him in its glorious putridity, a dense packed mass of all the city's waste, stretching ahead as far as the goggle eyes could see, shifting through stinging tears. The proverbial needle in a haystack seemed to be child's play, a mere finger flick in comparison.

Frank wondered, how long had this quest been proceeding? How long had men, dressed as he, or before, in unprotected clothing, been struggling like ants over this vast pile of rubbish in search of these mysterious objects? Clearly they were not alone. The Mound, in fact, was home to an elusive population of parasites who seemed to be living off its meagre and dreadful pickings: strange, stumpy, or hunched, ragged beings who scampered off before they could be approached, climbing over the piles of dreck and debris and burrowing into its depths. In the days that followed, Frank caught glimpses of the outlandish struggle that these creatures fought for their pathetic habitation, as they were chased over, around and through the Mound by the Cracked Skull's SWAT teams, armed with stun-guns and tranqilising darts. On two occasions Frank witnessed a catch, as first two, and then three of the Mound dwellers were struck in the open, and dragged clear by their pursuers. The two figures laid at his feet, he could see before he was prodded away by the riflemen, were a man and a woman, of totally indeterminate age, both bearded, and gnarled like distorted figures of Red Indians in fading old photographs. They seemed of no known race, but were undoubtedly human, or humanoid. The Searchers were not encouraged to socialize, even in their common lunch breaks, but once Frank did manage to snatch a conversation with an old withered lifelong vagrant, who introduced himself as Clarence, and told him he had been working the Mounds, on and off, for fifteen years, without finding a single Egg. There had been, nevertheless, a Finding, six years ago, by a new recruit who had only been working the Mound for a week, and had been whisked off, with his Find, never to be seen again.

"Some of them are Searchers," Clarence told Frank, about the Mound dwellers, "who couldn't stomach life off the Mound, and came back, on the sly, through the perimeter. Now it's electrified and booby trapped, but still there are some ways through. Life is very different here. Soon enough you'll get used to the smell. But if you work here too long your lungs get used to the gases, and then you can't breathe non-toxic air, no more. I went away, to Pennsylvania, but I couldn't breathe the country air, so I came back. It ain't the twelve-hundred bucks, of course. You can make that in an hour selling dope. But they say if you touch the Egg, it has a special energy. Like that film Cocoon, you know. About the old folk that touched these shells from outer space, and they made them immortal, so they went off to this far off planet, where they'd live forever."

"Have you talked to anybody who'd actually touched an Egg?"

"Told you, there was just this one guy, and he was taken off-Mound. But they say our boss, the Skull, he touched several. He is one hundred and sixty years old. He was an army executioner, in the Civil War. They say he hanged a hundred Yankee deserters."

"They say? Who?"

"You know, word gets around."

"And the Eggs? What do They say about the Eggs?"

"You take your pick. There's so many stories. The usual outer space stuff. Grey aliens. Secrets of lost civilizations. Ancient Egypt. Guy came once, said the markings on the eggs were Sumerian. He was a Professor from the City Museum. Kind of a spy, it turned out. They found him floating face down in the Upper Bay, with his hands, feet and penis cut off."

"That sounds like unnecessary savagery."

"You better believe it. This job marks you for life, one way or other."

But the Captain of the Guard, who had been taking a leak, interrupted them, and Frank redonned his breathing mask.

Life on the Mound attained its own routine. The Searchers slept in confined, cell-like bunks, clean but austere, with cable television and pornographic and Chuck Norris videos to keep them occupied during the night hours. Newspapers and books were not provided, apart from those few dog-eared volumes the employees themselves had brought in. Frank was grateful to Clarence, who had for some reason brought in the Personal Narrative of a Pilgrimage to Al-Madinah and Meccah by Sir Richard Burton, in two facsimile volumes, including the first proper map and measurements of the Holy Ka'abah or *Bayt Ullah*. One of the other men was a solemn Muslim, and practised the five daily prayers, even when upon the suppurating Mound. But Clarence, as far as he could gather, was simply a street polymath who had never turned his wagon to any particular path, simply voyaging as fate took him. He had been in parts of the Bronx never frequented by strangers, and had a half-bitten left ear-lobe left over.

In the morning, after reading of Burton's journey from Cairo to Suez, with his two dromedaries, his Indian boy, and his Bedouin *chibuk* pipe, lit with cotton dipped in a solution of gunpowder - those people really knew how to travel, at the mercy of nature, *the sky terrible in its stainless beauty, and the splendours of a pitiless blinding glare, the poison wind of the samun caresses you like a lion with flaming breath... What can be more exciting? What more sublime? Man's heart bounds in his breast at the thought of measuring his puny force with Nature's might* - - Frank ventured out again to the hunting grounds. The men were equipped with a probe, rather like a long cattle prod, and a machete to cut through the detritus, which was often all but impenetrable. Once he came upon a hollowed out enclosure, lit by dim battery-driven torchlight, and realised he had chanced upon a Mound dweller's site. There was no-one at home, just a bare filthy mattress stretched out on a floor of stomped junk, a suprisingly strong surface made out of compounded peels, junk food packs and old newspapers dating, from the few scraps of still readable print, from 1956. HUNGARIAN REBELS CRUSHED. THE DEATH OF LIBERTY IN BUDAPEST.

Frank hesitated over his communication beeper, but after a few moments stayed his hand, and followed the hollowed out tunnel which led from the small chamber through the matted growth. The strangeness of this environment had begun to seem normal, and, as Clarence warned, he found he could breathe without the mask. It is ever amazing, he considered, how adaptable the human form is to conditions which at first appeared completely unbearable, and incapable of sustaining life. He wondered whether this might not be the hidden purpose of his employers, whether they be the United States' Government or the Skull's own private scheme, to train a new mutant form of expendable humans, perhaps to colonize the Solar System's planets. Various speculations already aired, as Clarence had noted, in movies, novels, so-called science-fact fantasies and other jaded forums, came to mind. But he was still no nearer, Frank realized, fathoming the mystery which he had inherited from the Alchemist, Mordecai, of the Host Body, and his own place in its Plan.

Frank Ox began to have serious misgivings about his acceptance of this literally shit-kicking post on an eight week contract, as specified by the Skull. This would entail spending the entire summer, through the stifling days of what was left of July, and August, on the Mound. His previous retreat from the world, hiding out on the island of Mindanao, in the Philippines, had been a far less onerous exile, involving, as it had, discount services from the adjacent cathouse. Lying on his bunk, ploughing through Sir Richard Burton's trajector, he tried to turn his mind to other times and climes:

> *Our Pilgrim Ship, the Silk al-Zahab, or the "Golden Wire," was a Sambuk, of about 400 ardebs (fifty tons), with narrow, wedge-like bows, a clean water-line, a sharp keel, and undecked, except upon the poop, which was high enough to act as a sail in a gale of wind... She had no means of reefing, no compass, no log, no sounding lines, no spare ropes, nor even the suspicion of a chart... Such, probably, were the craft which carried old Sesostris across the Red Sea to Deir; such were the cruisers which once every three years left Ezion-Geber for Tarshish; such the transports of which 130 were required to convey Aelius Gallus, with his 10,000 men...*

No, one could not stay cooped up any longer. Frank lay awake all night, making plans. This should, after all, not pose too much of a problem for he who had slipped in and out of besieged Richmond in the guise of a Flemish courtesan. It was all a matter of uniforms. The white clad Searchers, the black carapaced guards. Every day, dozens of ferryboats cruised the Kill, offloading New York's garbage, and returning empty for more. The major problem was the sixth sense of the Skull, who roamed the area, clad head to foot in black leather, his grimacing face open to the elements, as the most toxic air was sweet to his muck-clotted lungs. He seemed to sense nuances, changes and eddies in the stench which clogged everyone else's nostrils. He could smell fear, rage and ambition at a distance, and his eyes would suddenly settle upon you before the thought you were about to think took form. Eyes which, Clarence had said, had feasted upon the terror of the young men whose necks he had adorned with rough hemp nooses in a time of blood and fire.

In mute dissimulation, Frank Ox set forth in the morning upon his appointed round, swinging his machete through the tangled scum in the quadrant allotted by the overseers. Progress was always slow, as every hard object, metal fragment, bottle, lump or casing had to be pulled away and handled, carefully, avoiding sharp tetanus-bearing edges. Lockjaw, Clarence said, was an occupational hazard on the Mound, and fatal casualties were bagged in haste, carried off, and, it was said, silently dropped off the ferryboats on their return journeys, sometimes, or even perhaps often, not as innocently empty as they might seem.

Cautiously, taking care that the guards were not taking notice, Frank edged up and around his part of the Mound, so that he could climb high enough to view the landing sites and the mouth of the Kill. From this point he could see the New Jersey town of Carteret, the railway line of the New Jersey railroad, residential houses and the cars and trucks rumbling up and down the main road of Roosevelt Avenue. The grey works of the Con Ed Company were to the north, beyond the inaptly named Victory Boulevard. Out of sight, the bird sanctuary of Prall's Island, whose greedy inhabitants skirled and cawed above the Mound, swooping in swift raids and then rising as far up as possible to gulp clean air before the next dive. The whole scene had a kind of putrid beauty which made him twitch, performing an odd little dance upon the refuse, as if his legs were invigorated by the fumes wafting invisibly upwards. As he danced his eye caught something at the furthest corner of his vision. He turned his head. There was a glint of strange in the debris. He lumbered over. It could not be. After all the digging and the delving. Nothing could be that simple, that obvious.

But it was. Bending down, he cleared the muck away from the object. It was not embedded very deep. It was as though it had just arrived, or else, as it was slag covered, it might have been pushed by an overwhelming force, or even pushed itself, by some unknown power, out of the bowels of the earth. He cleaned the dirt away with his glove. There was no mistaking it. It looked exactly as shown on the Skull's charts and sketches, as described in his lecture. A hard ovoid thing, three and a half inches long, about seven inches in diameter. At its cone, a series of strange carvings, definitely not Egyptian, but of an ancient kind. Little pictographs of unfamiliar things. He looked closer. The thing seemed to shine with a glimmering inner lustre. He took off his gloves and ran his fingers over it. It was completely smooth to the touch.

He looked around him. There was no one near. No one had seen him. The nearest guard was about two hundred yards down the curve of the Mound, and only the back of his thick neck could be seen. His fellow Searchers were out of sight.

Frank Ox cradled the Egg, turning it over and over. He removed his mask and rubbed it against his cheek. It was oddly warm, and pulsing. Or was that his blood pounding in his own vessels and arteries?

Frank Ox took the Egg and placed it carefully in the left pocket of his overalls. The he straightened up, and resumed his labours, brushing the topside sediment aside with his prod, trudging on across the Mound.

Caroline:

WHEN YOUR BODY BECOMES YOUR ENEMY, all your priorities shift. Everything else fades into the background, hangs in the air, just out of reach. Like a besieged town, you become obsessed with defence, shoring up every crumbling battlement, plugging every empty hole. So many different ways to be healthy. Always the same way to be ill. It's not so much the capital sentence itself. It's all those slow years on death row.

Still, the expectation of others: The heroic Carolingian mode. That girl, she never gives up. Such a shining example of courage. Fit to appear before the cheering millions, on Oprah: Women Who Fight On to the Last Breath. But in the creaky silence of one's own bathroom, with the haggard reality in the mirror... Until so many weeks and months have passed that you just look and say: That's me, that's what I am.

Your friends, your work, your memories, everything that has wrapped round your life. At least if I was a researcher, or a writer, I could concentrate on completing a project, a book, something that could say Finis. But field work has no real closure. The comforting myth, Freudian or un- Freudian, of a cure, what Sigmund himself called transforming the agony of a neurosis into "ordinary unhappiness." An entire metropolis of the cured. Cue those analysts who have latched onto MPD, Multiple Personality Disorder, because it seemed to offer the prospect of that golden moment - when all the alter personalities are convinced of their own irrationality and persuaded towards the goal of "integration." E pluribus unum - out of the many, the one. Or just an easy way to please your shrink?

Doing something about Mo Smith: Allan Darwish's proposal. "In any case, Caroline, you can only work part time. You've already passed on most of your case load. Maybe we can help you find the man. He'll still be out there. These people survive in the streets forever. Jaime can help. He knows the jungle. He can locate Mo Smith for you."

More Darwish summer madness. Every now and again he takes it on himself to save a street boy from the grind. Juan the Salvadorean. Chiang, from the Village. "You won't get them to trust anybody if you don't give a little trust yourself." And then the rueful shrug of the shoulders at the sight of a cleaned out apartment: The PC, the laptop, the TV, video, portable radios and CD player, all gone, leaving neat dustless rectangles where they had once reposed. "It's only material things," he would say, "I've got back-ups. At least he hasn't touched the files." I know how to avoid the dangerous ones. That was another mantra. Misremembering the Moroccan youth, Naseem, who had chased him round the bed, in the old house in Brooklyn, with a kitchen knife, accusing him of stealing his thoughts from his head while he slept. That one at least was found a well- kept institution in Maine, where he could contemplate the birds, the bees, and the Big Feet, who passed regularly just before the first glimmers of dawn.

"I can't just fuck 'em and say goodbye, Caroline. I have to make the effort. Reduce the odds against their staying out of jail."

The immediate problem in this case: How to keep those tales from Karim, the born-again Islamic progeny. "The boy has enough reasons to stay away from me, Allan. Let's not put another nail in this coffin."

For suddenly he has returned to me, my home grown Saint. In Saint Louis, he had approached his spiritual mentor, the Secessionist Reverend and Mentor of the Oppressed Black Masses, and inquired what to do now that his wayward mother, the secularist and miscegenating pagan, had been stricken with a life-threatening illness. "Why are you asking me this question?" the Reverend had told him, "the Prophet, who is in your own heart, has given you the answer." And so the Young Muslim packed his bags and presented himself at my old dark house, eager to do his filial duty. Becoming, as the summer sizzled on, a perpetual, glowering presence in the living room, sitting bolt upright in the hardest chair, as all my usual exiles and vagabonds milled about sympathetically, till I had to tell them to stay away. Even the dog, sensing both his mistress's exhaustion and the prodigal son's disapproval, gave us both space and slunk round the walls, or curled up in the disguise of a ragged black rug behind the sofas or in the cooler corners of the room.

Even as an invalid I could not keep away from the weekly Salim Update. This was held at first at Allan's apartment, but then moved to the traditional venue of the Szechuan Gourmet since the news of Salim's escape, en route to Ossining, from the overturned prison bus. While teams of FBI agents combed both banks of the Hudson all the way up to Albany and undercover NYPD units squirmed and squittered through the Bronx, the Defense Committee reverted to the regular banquets and data-starved speculation.

"Paranoia has now been replaced by reality," offers Benjamin, "now we know we're all being watched." No great act of deduction or fancy required here, as the drooping, sweaty figures slumped in parked cars outside our homes were making no effort to hide.

"He must have found a way to survive," says Darwish, "not a sign, for a month now. What most worries me is if he's had to go to ground with the people who are really to blame for this mess."

The minions of the Blind Sheikh Jedid, the "Afghanis", the mercenaries recruited by the United States government to fight the Russians in Afghanistan and now eager to bite off the hand that had fed them. "Eight billion dollars poured down their throat by the C.I.A.. Even the mullah with the longest beard in the hemisphere can keep going with that boodle. If Salim is with them now, he's lost. The smartest lawyer in the universe won't get him out of that fix."

"But Salim knows that," Benjamin, "he hates those people. He'd find a way to come to us."

"You don't know what it's like in jail," Darwish, "It can change you, to the roots. He's no longer the man we knew, Benjamin."

"This other guy..." Frances begins to speak but then stops, interrupted by the old guilty pleasures. Scallop and Prawn and Scallop Combination, Empire Three Delicacies, Chicken Five Flavours...

"`Ibn Battuta!'" Darwish waves his hand, "we can only take one lunacy at a time. The lawyer did what he could but drew a blank. Either nobody knows or nobody's talking. In this hysteria any Arab immigrant without proper papers can be swept up. We just have to keep our nerve. Just let the watchers watch. We've been here before..."

On those Vietnam mornings, the night armies and jailyard singsongs... But there's no glory any more, no clear sense of direction, not even the glow of delusion. Sisyphus, rolling the stone, pitted and barnacled with old memories, once again up the hillside.

The steamed dumplings. Brown and white rice. Toffee apple banana. And a more bitter background. The F.B.I., flush from the Waco Siege, determined to make no errors this time. In ending their standoff with the armed acolytes of the new Son of God, the forces of the law had rushed in with tanks, setting off explosions which gutted the Texas compound and killed 84 people. This time, they swore, they were determined to catch the two "Islamic terrorist" escapees alive...

Hold the Aromatic Chinese Eggplant - it was Salim's all-time favorite. Let's take the Takeout menu, just in case he turns up. One for each, for good luck. Benjamin walks me home. More a demand than an offer. Things that need to be got off the chest. Except that it's impossible to lift any burdens in this stifling, humid night, the temperature reluctantly dropping a floppy degree or two from the day.

I don't want you to come in, Benny. Karim sits up late, like a prison guard. He puts my food in a tin plate through the bars. The Prophet said that even if you carried your mother on your back for seven years, you could not repay her for the time when you were her burden. Can you see it? Him walking me about the city, my legs wrapped around his neck, the Old Woman of the Seven Seas.

"The Old Crone of Manhattan. Well, you're not there yet. What do you want of me, Caroline? You won't allow me to do anything."

I don't want anything of you, Benny, that's the whole point. Pausing on the corner of 93rd. I'm inundated with nurses. People standing in line to carry my bed pan. I don't want it. I know my limits. "What can we have together, Benny? Sex with the dying? I've lost it Benny, I don't have the energy. I don't want the self sacrifice. I don't want your self-restraint. I'm sorry if it's brutal but I have to take short cuts. I don't have the time Benjamin. I don't have the time to enjoy moments. I still have work to do. I resent every minute of rest. I'm not going to convalesce. You understand what I'm saying? We had good times and now it's over. Just accept it and spare the cliches. I'll work till I can't work anymore and then I'll go on working. It's the only thing that gives me the buzz. And don't look at me like that, Benny. This is just me being me. You understand me, Benny? I have to take enough shit from my son. When he was thirteen he came home from his Muslim meeting and called me a whore and walked out for five years. So what's changed? Maybe he thinks I'm just paying the price. A redemption through suffering. Stamped with the Seal of Allah. I can't mix you with him, Benjamin. It's fire and water. You think I can tell him it's still me who's carrying him, and not the other way around? I can't carry anyone else. Not now I've got to carry my blood stream.

"Maybe I understand Mo Smith much better now. The weight of carrying a load of strangers around, inside you. All your blood cells, each one complaining. Fighting off the chemical bombs, like those scenes in that film, with Raquel Welch? Remember we saw that once?"

"Fantastic Voyage. It's a Richard Fleischer. From Isaac Asimov."

"Right. The ship miniaturised in the blood vessels. The antibodies, chasing Donald Pleasance. Wasn't that it? They killed him off."

"But Raquel Welch did survive."

"She has stronger bones than I have. That solid ribcage."

"All right, Caroline. I get the story. So forget about the bedpans. If you don't want the boy there, why don't you just send him away? Forget I said that. It's just Benjamin, the uncouth Israeli."

"No, Benny, you're absolutely right. I just can't afford to be rational from this point on. Things happen. I have to bend with the wind. You'll just have to go with the flow."

AS ACROSS THE ROAD,

two bored watchers in a maroon pontiac munch their Dunkin Donuts, sipping coffee from large styrofoam cups, their moustaches dipped in sweet brown liquid. From chinks in frayed curtains, a young Muslim and an old dog watch the watchers.

But not everything can be watched at once. Twelve blocks downtown, along Broadway, inside the locked and secured Barnes and Noble bookstore, an intruder is cunningly hiding. Wearing plastic sucker boots obtained by mail order from the Magic Warehouse in Kansas City, Arnold Flint has attached himself to the ceiling of the staff toilet and, thus concealed, has been waiting for two hours for the store to close and be vacated. By the time he felt safe to move his every bone, muscle and pore was aching as if he had been pummelled with clubs by Kurdish tribesmen. This was no way for a mature son of New England, a Massachusetts Brahmin by nature, if not blood, to spend his declining years. But sometimes, nevertheless, there is no choice. The die is cast.

The runes have been displayed.

Releasing the sucker boots, and twisting in fall, managing to land on his side, merely sending an agonising pain through his ribs and arm, rather than cracking his skull. He takes up a rigid position by the wall just inside the door, in case the crash has alerted a human watchdog in the store, but only the electronics are live. Turning the latch of the door he presses through into the dimly lit cavern of the bookstore proper. The shelves! The shelves! Rows upon rows of the oblong paper objects, stretching ahead in a wooden maze, all the combined wisdom and stupidity of the modern world contained in brightly coloured packages. All neatly organised in categories and arranged by alphabetical order. Was this always how knowledge had been organised? Sometimes one yearned for a more savage age. Or even just different. Somehow all our ills have come out of this tyranny of classification. If I follow the signs to the Philosophy section, I could no doubt work some of this out. Or to the Computer books, and try to understand the new dispensation, when all that is required has been pre-digested, and just a few flicks of the keyboard will bring forth the meaning of any random thought or moment's fancy. The problem being that all one can find, at the immediate instant, is the Transport, Sport and New Age section, filled with utterly useless and competing fish-hooks for the jaded imagination.

Faced with an endless choice, one is completely paralysed. Particularly when one's own self has been wiped from the equation. Where the world of Arnold Flint should be, the neatly stacked, reprinted volumes of the award winning "Frozen Asshole", the perennially bestselling "Jamaica Pass" running it a close second, not to speak of my reprinted early volume of short stories - "The Intense Bowel," nothing but a vacuum, as "Fleming" whups up against "Florey" on the Fiction shelf. Nada!! Wiped, removed, banished, excluded, erased, eliminated, purged, voided, vanquished, dumped, deposed, disposed of, deleted, demolished, discarded, defenestrated, obliterated, drowned, abrogated, cancelled, annulled, quashed, rescinded, disowned, denied, dissolved, divested, degraded and discontinued, as if I had never been...

The Invisible Man! As the old tale was told, once the bandages are removed the power of revenge, unseen and unsuspected, shines with a bright, inner lustre. The atomic trigger, fission-fusion inside the nuclear banana. And now, after the sparks - the fire! The great lava flow of the burning, the demons purging the world - the red hot heart of destruction! Who said revenge was a dish best eaten cold? Not, for sure, a red-blooded American!

Burn, baby, burn! There is nothing like the great fiery whoosh when volume touches off volume, the myriad tiny red glows and the great rush of scattered ashes! Up it goes! The Cookery department, Furniture and Furnishings, Glassware, Antiques, Art and Architecture, Music, Popular, Classical, and Jazz, Broadway Shows, Pop Biographies, every single Renaissance Artist, from Aarne to Zygo, all the scribblers, playwrights, poets, versifiers, librettists, diarists, self-dramatisers and endless hacks, penpushers and keyboard-kickers. Shakespeare, Schumann, Schweitzer and all Shmendricks, the famed and the infamed, the great and the ghastly, all the gibbering ghosts, publishers' pets, printed pischers. As the petrol soaked rags are distributed about the shelves, the matches poised to be struck. Pangs of regret? Remembrances of things past, of solitary delights of times gone by, of other realms of being? Keats, Shelley, Byron and the Romantics, Rabbie Burns, Walt Whitman? *I think whatever I shall meet on the road I shall like... I think whoever I see must be happy...* Oh me oh my. What, even Mark Twain? Tom Sawyer and Huck Finn. Even they must burn? Even they. One weak spot and they'll all crawl through. The darkness with the light, the ugly with the beautiful, the bad with the good, the chaff with the wheat, the styrofoam with the polished silver. No, kill 'em all, turn a deaf ear to the shriek of Anna with Ahab, of Bloom with Brutus, of Josef K with Karamazov. Yossarian shot down in flames. Even Svejk, looking dolefully out of the pyre. All the imaginary immortals. All those yammering Greeks, who lasted so long. Sancho tries to beat the blaze off Quixote. Not a chance! Quasimodo bellows and Esmeralda shrieks, but in vain. Leopold Bloom looks up from his Guiness reproachfully, and Beckett's Unnameables mutter darkly in their burning jars. But only I am untouched, the Invisible! Arnold Flint, the man who never was. I survive it all, dancing amid the billows. The fireball consuming Nietzsche with Nixon, Aeschylus with Archer, Goethe with Grisham. The All Consuming which does not discriminate. The Unforgiving, the Unmerciful. And, as the New York Fire Department's engines blare, blast and wail their way through the midnight streets, the Invisible Man, redonning his bandages, slinks away, towards Riverside Drive...

IBN BATTUTA AND SALIM LOOKED DOWN from the mountainside over the black expanse of the lake. The moon was classically crescent in a clear, star-studded sky. The ghostly light picked out the tips of the forest pines peaking on the other side, on Blue Mountain. The campfire was low, close to embers, as the remains of the rabbit Ibn Battuta had trapped were slowly being reduced. Salim wondered, as he watched the older man gutting the last of a hind leg, how much longer this savage existence could last. Could this be, in fact, the end of the journey, living wild in the belly of the beast, reduced to the status of a caveman in the richest country on the globe?

For several weeks now the fugitives had been making their way across the wastes of New York State, but this was the first time they had bagged wild game. Salim could make a shrewd guess that the SWAT teams whose helicopters they could often hear and sometimes glimpse roaming overhead were tracking their progress by the disappearance of the household pets which they had been capturing and devouring, from Scarborough to Cherry Valley, from Ephrata up into the Adirondacks. On towards Canada, eating cats and dogs. Ibn Battuta had started this, grabbing and strangling an errant moggie in Franklin Delano Roosevelt State Park, telling Salim how he had survived on this diet once when cast out in the Maldive Islands, after an edict he had produced aginst usury, ostensibly on behalf of the local Sultan, had led to his expulsion from that Far Eastern kingdom, in 1347 A.D.

Nothing seemed strange to Salim any more, not after his transformation from yellow cab driver to the FBI's Most Wanted felon. He had no mirror to look into now, but had once examined his rippling features in the waters of the Cherry Valley Creek and failed to recognise the gaunt, bearded and shaggy haired creature that stared back at him with crazy eyes. I have become that which they have always seen me as, he thought, the mad bomber, the terrorist Arab fanatic, who should not be approached under any circumstances. Contact your nearest police or FBI officer, subject is probably armed and certainly dangerous. Public Enemy Number One.

I am the genie in the water, he thought at that moment, but I can grant no magic wishes. Not to myself, not to anyone. I might as well be back in the bottle.

On the other hand, he thought now, in the moonlight, there have been some magic tricks after all. Despite the trail of lost pets, the massive manhunt, the growling helicopters, the police roadblocks on almost every road, they had, against all odds reached over half way to the border which might be their salvation.

Salim, in fact, knew nothing of Canada, except that it was another world. But for Battuta, all these worlds were strange, ever since he had awoken in the Sleeper. But, despite the vast towers, the loud horseless vehicles, the streets more crowded than the bazaars of Urganj, he had discovered, more rapidly than he had wished, that the fears, follies, misfortunes, and iniquities of human nature remained as they had always been, untouched by time. And prisons remained prisons, in any age.

Earlier in their getaway, they had hidden by day, crouched behind bushes, or by secluded creeks, or in caves concealed in the undergrowth, venturing out at night, although the whirr of what Battuta dubbed the "mechanical vultures", and their scanning searchlights, were constant. Without Battuta, Salim would have been lost, for the old wayfarer was well able to navigate by the stars, whereas the Medallion Cab driver was completely helpless outside the grid of the City. During their second day, in their enforced layby, he had related to Battuta the tale of his own wanders, the story of his exiled and oppressed people, and of his first remarkable transformation from warrior clerk to pacifist student. Ibn Battuta displayed no doubt or mistrust at this narrative, but merely commented on the curative values of the imbibing of a potentate's urine as a known medical fact in the Far East, referring to the properties of the bottled piss of certain Buddhist priests or ulema, known in remote Indo-Chinese regions as "lamma", which was sold to travellers by their followers, and tasted much like brackish water with some added sweetness, like a strong whiff of almond baklava.

"I had an ample supply with me," he told Salim, "during my sojourn in the Mongol realms of Kipchak, Persia and Chagatay. Many of these regions still showed signs of the devastation caused by the invasions of Genghis Khan which had taken place one hundred years before. In Transoxania, the great city of Bokhara had been sacked and burned three times by the Tatar hordes. All Muslims of any authority or learning had been executed or exiled. The Illkhan demanded that I should change my religion to his own, which was Nestorian Christian, or be impaled upon a pointed stick. But I demonstrated to him my superior knowledge both of my own religion and his, whereas he himself had no schooling whatever in the principles of the pagan Nestor. Thereupon he appointed me his tutor, and became a secret Muslim, though when his conversion was discovered, he was impaled upon the orders of the Grand Khan, Tamurlane, and I had to escape, by the skin of my teeth, once again.

"The Muslims have to bear the sorrows of Mankind upon them," Battuta added, "because we alone know the truth. We can afford to be forbearing and magnanimous because we know all of Mankind will come to our way in good time. That is why we are not murderous fanatics as the infidels of this land seem to think. But these are the familiar fantasies of policemen. If we could meet the civilised rulers of this country we could speak to them as equals, I am sure."

"I'd rather get to Canada first if you don't mind," Salim said. "Then we can make some telephone calls." He hesitated, trapped in a cave with a man from another age and mode of thought, before deciding that a man could not entrust his life to another, and be dishonest. "I have to tell you, I am not a Muslim. I am a Christian Arab, from Ikrit. Not that I am a believer, myself. But both my parents were devout Christians."

"It makes no difference," said Battuta, clapping his strong, calloused hand upon the youth's shoulder, "it only proves my point. All men are brothers under the skin."

The conversations between Ibn Battuta and Salim, after this, teetered over many topics. Battuta was particularly keen for Salim to reveal to him the inner workings of the society in which they were now fated to survive. What kind of faith underpinned it? What was its economic system? Who were its enemies? What was the nature of its cuisine?

How did it handle the relationship between town and country? What were its political aims? The machines themselves did not pose a major challenge. "In my day the celebrated engineer, Umar Ibn al-Khas, of Khurasan, was experimenting with flying machines which could carry cauldrons of greek fire to pour upon an enemy from above. He had studied the movements of birds for thirty years and displayed to the Sultan a device made of light wood and toughened parchment which, when pushed off a cliff, hovered for several minutes in the air. Of course, it could not carry heavy weights. But this was only a matter of time. Systems of pulleys which are self-sustaining were said to be used in China, though I did not see one in action. And of course, explosive devices are common throughout the civilised world."

But Salim could not explain the essence of the United States to Ibn Battuta, despite trying to dredge up garbled segments from Allan Darwish's lectures. "It's a country to which people came from many other countries who wanted to live a freer life. In theory everyone is supposed to be equal before the law. This has obviously not worked in our case."

Battuta dismissed the idea of democracy. "What is the point of allowing those who own no property to have equal rights with property holders? Since the former vastly outnumber the latter, their desire to overturn the economic system can only lead to revolutionary conflict and a complete paralysis or even overthrow of the state."

Salim tried to explain to Battuta that, by means of manipulation of the powerful organs of "communication," the press, television and the culture in general, the rich were able to convince the poor that property and wealth in the hands of the few were a natural requisite of the general good. "In which case," said Ibn Battuta triumphantly, "why pursue the charade of `democracy' at all if the result is the same as its opposite?"

"It makes people feel better," Salim said lamely.

He fared even worse in explicating the principle of freedom of religion, and the agnostic nature of the law. "If the state is so indifferent to the faiths of its subjects, why are we hiding in a cave?" Battuta asked. Salim soon realised the main obstacle to the understanding of his well travelled friend was not the particular but a general principle: the idea of the duality of secular thought. The enfolding of the true within the false, the charitable within the callous, the civilised within the savage, and the ability to reconcile irreconcilables within a self-sustaining frame. In Battuta's day, the state did not pretend to virtues it did not possess - this was the domain of religion. But Salim did not wish to challenge Battuta on this point. Eventually, therefore, their philosophical discourse was slowed down, and they returned to their immediate concerns.

Slowly, foot by foot, mile by mile, they made their way north-west, having stolen a boat at three in the morning from a jetty at Georges Island and crossing the river to Stony Point. A change of clothing to army fatigues conveniently found in the boat stood them in good stead for the following week, in which they were able to skirt the perimeter of the West Point Military Academy and proceed over Schunnemunk Mountain, through Blooming Grove and Hamptonburgh, Walkill and Mamakating, meandering up towards the Catskills. But the biggest stroke of luck occurred three days later, when, stymied at the banks of a lake which seemed to stretch endlessly east and west, they tripped over the Dead Man.

The Dead Man was sprawled in tall grass overlooking the lake, his hands outstretched as if embracing the darkness. He was like a pudgy starfish, dressed in a grey t-shirt with a large rucksack weighing him down to the earth. Battuta removed the rucksack and turned the man over, prising his eyelids open in the pale moonlight. He looked asleep, but was stiff and cold to the touch. There were no obvious signs of violent assault, by man nor beast. He seemed to have succumbed, while trekking alone in the wilderness, to a heart attack or similar seizure.

The Dead Man's rucksack was a cornucopia, manna from the sky for the fugitives. It contained spare clothing, boots, a compass, detailed maps of New York State and hiking guides, a pair of binoculars, a cheap automatic camera, a wallet stuffed full of cash, identification documents and credit cards, as well as two unused tickets for the National Baseball Hall of Fame in Cooperstown in Otsego County. The Dead Man's name, according to his papers, was Bartholomew Simpson, and he was a native of Springfield, Ohio. He did not seem to have either wife or children, as the only snapshots found in the rucksack were portraits of baseball stars and of an elderly couple who were both as pear shaped as he.

The cash amounted to six hundred and forty six dollars. Salim raised the wad to his lips and kissed it fervently. He was about to explain to

Battuta the irony of their being succoured by Bart Simpson, iconic American working class hero, but on second thoughts realised he would have to enter the tangled dual domain of explicating to his companion both the unreality and the reality of animated cartoons. Mickey, Donald and all the barnyard animals. Time enough for that later. Taking the marvellous bag, they left the Dead Man still worshipping the lake that had become his own personal River Styx, now unburdened by his last earthly possessions, and continued west along the shore of what the map revealed to be the Pepacton Reservoir. In the night, Salim imagined Bartholomew waving them goodbye, as he rose and looked out across the waters for the boatman gliding in to the shore.

In the next few days Salim introduced Battuta to credit cards and tried to explain American baseball. "It sounds similar," said Battuta, "to a game played by the Khwarizmian Turks with the severed heads of their enemies. The Afghan Pashtuns have a similar game, on horseback. I think it is called Pooloo. The winning team gets to batter the 'balls' to a pulp at the end of each session."

"That is not the principle of baseball," Salim said, "although some of its fans might wish otherwise."

"I would like to see this `Hall of Fame,'" said Battuta, "is it a kind of Court, to which one applies for justice? We cannot live like animals all the time."

Nevertheless Salim persuaded Battuta to keep off the beaten populated tracks. The miracle of the Dead Man had given him confidence, for at least a fleeting moment. He had become accustomed to the great outdoors, to the deadly heat of the day, the loneliness of the night, and all the myriad pricks and bites of insect life which filled each copse and hill like a miniature Manhattan. The flies were the worst. He remembered listening to Darwish's tales, of this region, or further north, the Adirondacks, where, at a lake called Blue Mountain, he often spent a few weeks in mid-summer at an "Artists' Colony" in an old wood mansion which had been inherited from a Republican Senator by his daughter, a 'sixties Vietnam rebel. "The flies! The flies!" Darwish intoned, like Kurtz invoking the Heart of Darkness. "It's the tiny tiny ones you have to beware of. They come in swarms and fill every hole. Not to speak of the lime tick, but that's no problem if you wear proper socks. It's the red ring on the shin you have to watch out for. Once that's appeared, all is lost."

But Salim had met the flies and they held no terrors for him any more. It was as if he had taken on the leather skin of Battuta, who seemed impervious to bites, scratches and sores. Men of an earlier age, unpampered by the hygienic shields of the sanitised modern age. Perhaps it was the jail that turned my skin into armour, Salim mused, the steel carapace of the Tombs, where no kiss of softness could penetrate. At any rate, I am now a genuine wild boy, and Man, not Nature, is now my singular foe.

In his new moment of exultation, Salim even began to enjoy the landscape. The rolling hills and forests, the winding rivers and creeks, all ashimmer in the midsummer sun. He remembered Darwish's exclamations about Blue Mountain: "It's God's own country, Salim! You have to get your nose out of this cesspit sometimes! This human anthill - look upon the wide open spaces."

This Other America - the pastoral dream of tramps and poets, woodland, wildlife and sky. Whitman, Thoreau, Frost, and I, I took the path least travelled by - and will it make any difference?

Northwards, northwards... *Having turned towards Broadway at 76th, turning at the corner of Body Shop, AVIS RENT-A-CAR and the Koo-Koo- Roo Original Skinless Flame Broiled Chicken, the body squelches, in the matted heat, past Belleclaire Cleaners, Cohen's Optical and the Westside Supermarket, pausing for a moment by the entrance to the Original Big Nick's, mouth slavering at the prodigal Burger menu, but sensing some unwelcome presence within, and up, past Allon's Fashions and the Hotel Belleclaire, across the road the LOVE store, Discount Health and Beauty Aids, Greenberg's Desserts, Mendeal's Meat Market and Deli, the Pita factory, Shawarma and vegetarian Falafel, Westside Laundromat, La Caridad Restaurant, comidas china y criolla, over 78th to Apthorp Pharmacy and Federal Express, packages to any part of the globe, night and day, via the hub of Memphis, the ornate gates of the Apthorp Building, 2211 Broadway, next door to Chemical Bank, and the wide swathe of 79th, waiting for the traffic, the East-West bus, dragging slowly over to join the raggedy men slumped on the steps of the First Baptist Church - "POWER IN THE GATHERING" - the heat slamming down upon the stone...*

The Pursuers seem to have been thrown off the trail. Perhaps they couldn't believe the objects of the FBI's mass manhunt could have progressed so far from their starting point. Perhaps they had lost the trail of lost pets (Battuta caught a sheep, up Cherry Valley, which sustained them for ten days before they had to resume their regular domestic prey). Perhaps they had guessed the fugitives' objective and were massing on the border, north and west. The two pronged choice. Head for the tourist logjam of Niagara Falls, or risk the longer, possibly easier crossing somewhere along the line with Quebec, like Palestine, the domain of secessionist troublemakers and malcontents.

Dreams of escape... Battuta: "When I was waylaid by bandits, south of Delhi, during my mission to the Grand Moghul, Hindu rebels under the holy deaf-mute Ramakraskanan scattered my escort and I was separated from my men and unhorsed. In fact, it was on a sweltering August day, such as this one, almost six hundred and fifty, no, almost six hundred and sixty years ago. But I can recall it as if it were yesterday. I had to take refuge in a deep ditch and watched as my assailants rode past, waving their swords and shouting, and holding aloft the head of one of my escorts, whom they had ridden down and beheaded. I tried to make my way on foot to a village which was known to be loyal to the Moghul's amir, Al-Hawari. But another band of dacoits captured me and stole my sword, robe and pantaloons, leaving me only in my underclothes. I was taken into the rebel camp where discussions were held as to the disposal of my head. But they apparently thought I might be worth holding for ransom so I remained, with my head, under guard. One of the guards, who turned out to be a Muslim, offered to help me escape. I exchanged my rags with him, and, wearing only a blue loincloth, the guise of a lowly labourer, I was able to walk out of the camp and into the fields.

"For twelve days and nights I wandered, ten thousand miles from home. Lost among a people who did not only worship three Gods, like you Christians, but thousands of them, whose ancient battles they recalled in their endless poems and sagas. But mainly they were worshipping, like men of all religions when the madness overcomes them, the common God of War, Plunder and Destruction. Your 'democracy' could only have been, for them, the right to kill without discrimination.

"Unlike these mountains, this was a place of barren deprivation, with only grass and bamboo shoots to soothe my hunger. Eventually, emboldened by starvation and thirst to venture out by day, I came across a well at the outskirts of a sleepy village. I lowered my boot into the well to try and trap some water, but my boot was caught below and I raised up a frayed and empty rope. Just as I was trying to cut the other boot in half to fit both feet a dark, large man appeared, carrying a pannier of water, and a small basket of rice, and offered me his food and drink. He told me he was a Muslim and had heard of the fugitive from afar. This man not only saved me by this kindness but even carried me, exhausted as I was, upon his back, across the bamboo fields, through enemy lines and into a loyalist village. Thus I was reunited with the survivors of my former escort, with whom I continued, apace, upon my journey...

"So you see," Battuta waved at the grand sweep of the Blue Ridge, which challenged the sky, ahead of them, "things could be far worse and still, God, in his Mysteries, sustains us."

But Faith still could not move the mountains which rose, ridge after ridge, before them. By the time they had crossed the road, and climbed over the fence of the Blue Mountain Lake's Artists' Colony into the grounds, Salim felt he had reached a state beyond exhaustion, of a complete and total depletion of his physical faculties. His feet had begun to swell some days before, and he became convinced that, despite Bart Simpson's thick hiking socks, the lime ticks had got his measure. Battuta removed his socks by the light of their campfire and examined his shins and ankles closely, but there was no tell tale ring. Just a mass of tiny ordinary bug bites, that had been his burden for weeks.

"How long have we been on the road? I've lost count. I'm sorry, Bat, I don't think I can make it."

They opened up the maps, and Salim passed his finger over the terrain still to come - seventy miles, as the crow flies, of more mountains, lakes, ridges, valleys and even swamplands, before the flatlands of north Franklin County leading to the Quebecoise border. And we have to hop every step, over ground...

Just leave me, friend, and save yourself... But this cliche, too, is worthless; Battuta cannot go on alone. It was even more futile than being lost in India, and the likelihood of a kind Muslim samaritan, bearing rice, and willing to carry you on his back to a friendly village, is zero, even in God's Own Country. Salim realised that he had been gravitating to this point with one purpose, with this kind of failure in mind. In this day and age - and which day and age am I living in, Salim wondered - one can fly from New York to Canada in about fifty minutes - if one can reach the airport in less than two hours - and drive there in sixteen hours, or less - but "Shank's pony", the old bipedal route, the ancient footpaths, could stretch into an eternity. One of Bartholomew Simpson's dogeared guide books had warned him, in fact, of the unchanged perils of the Adirondacks:

"Although the mountains are deceptively gentle in appearance, the terrain is, in fact, hazardous. Add to this the sheer size of the wilderness, and the result is the nearly annual tragedy, often involving an experienced, lone hiker who wanders from the established trails. In the summer of 1982 35 year old Gerald Fresbauer was lost while on such a hike along the Northville-Lake Placid trail. He left on June 6 and died in early August after trying to survive on insects, snails and plants. The final entry in his journal, found after his death, records the words: 'What happened? Ran out of food, no water, got sick, flies everywhere... where is everybody?...'"

The skeletal trail of pioneers... In the midst of life we face our mortality, in the midst of plenty we starve, in the midst of beauty we despair... But perhaps, after all, there is human compassion, the dark rescuer, with his basket of rice... Down there, on the banks of the Lake, where the jagged shape of that old fashioned new world moghul's mansion can be discerned against the forest pines. The Colony of Artists. The moghul's rebel daughter. Darwish's old acquaintances, the cream of Liberal America, the learned, the sensitive, the empathetic, the creative, the flagbearers of intellect, reason, understanding, wisdom and openness of character... Asleep now, after an exhausting evening debating the immensities of life, the quality of prose, the fineness of musicians, painters, sculptors, the ferocity of cutting edge playwrights, the centrality and meaning of Art...

Friends of my friend. Will you carry me on your backs? Just for one short step?

Down by the lakeside, slumbering in the House of Peripatetic Art, were the following: Jemima Finklebloom, vendor of poetry to the anthologies “Archaeos”, “Parmesan Review”, “Arthritic Review” and “Tikkun”; Armando Click, whose real name was Aaron Lipshutz but who wrote short fiction set in the *favelas* of Brazil and Argentina, usually involving visitations from outer space to the very poorest of the poor; Jonathan Lunk, backwoods poet and methodone addict; Paula Passion-Fruit (nee Prescott), erotic miniaturist, and her lesbian lover, Inca Kahlo-O’Keeffe, Irish-Hispanic hairdresser and modernist dancer, who shrieked at every clitoral touch; Eldad and Oded, Israeli gay gentlemen, craftsmen of silver menorahs and other sacred objets-d’art, who moonlighted as exotic performance artists in Greenwich Village bars; Cash Nuggets, winner of the James Baldwin Memorial Prize for African-American Pain; Jo-Bobette Neiman-Lafayette, ex-Louisiana Sun-shine Queen whose first novel, “Bayou Fever”, had been described by the New York Times’ critic, Thomas Meurtherstern-Biel, as “so erotic I could not get sideways through my doors”; Elsa Unbounded-Joy, self-described “Rapturist”, who was fucking Cash Nuggets into insensibility on a nightly basis; Frederick Mainscotting, Professor of Linguistics at the University of Bethlehem, Mass., who was studying the click-language of the Kumba-Kalimba people of southwestern Zaire as the possible Original speech of the entire human race, and was spending his nights awake, sweating, and masturbating over Jo-Bobette; Jim Beeme, Professor of Northamerican Literature at Syracuse, masturbating over Cash Nuggets; Aviva Garibaldi, painter, poetess, sculptress, interior decorator and high-flying Wall Street broker, seeking inspiration in the fly-swept wild, present with her ten year old kleptomaniac boy, Ari, who crept along the dark, creaking corridors of the mansion every night while she slept and stole small items such as keychains, watches, pocket torches, insect repellent, drugs, underclothing, tampax, KY jelly tubes, other knick knacks from the rooms, as well as corkscrews, small knives, salt cellars, cheese-graters, forks, spoons and ashtrays from the communal kitchen. Suspicion fell on the scullery-maid, Anita, who, infuriated by the reproachful glances of politically correct-impeded silent accusers, took to leaving her room, twice weekly, taking her canoe out and rowing fiercely into the depths of Blue Mountain Lake, cursing all the guests and her employers in passionate Guatemalan slang. Then she returned, storming into the room of her current lover, Victor Cardozo Hecht, guitarist, raconteur and scribbler of unpublished diatribes against anyone and everyone, rich or poor, oppressor or oppressed, and screwing his brains out until their next door neighbours hammered on the wall with their fists.

Further along the shore, in little isolated log cabins nestling among the trees, thirteen other colony tenants stirred and shifted in their beds; nine who had been spending the entire summer, from mid-May, as virtual recluses in the woods while banging out their respective epics upon old fashioned typewriters or even more slowly, carving out their words by hand with sets of ballpoint pens, or even pencil, so that entire weeks' work could be erased by the rubber ends - with no electric supply in the cabins, modern laptop computers or other electronic means were banned. These nine long-termers: Elisha Frug, novelist; Aloha Smith, poetess; Zephaniah Marley, rap writer; Jehovah Clam, political philosopher; Jumbo McTavish, anarchist; Veronica X., still at work on the largest novel ever written, which had already reached thirteen thousand pages, of which she had published some fragments in the literary journals ibid; Boris Borisovitch, pointillist painter; Imre Kovacs, avante-garde playwright and Sigfrieda Kohlbacher, troubadora. The four temporaries, spillovers from the main mansion, were Kalinka May, composer and folkloriste; Brian Boon, Australian environmentalist; Professor Emma Gluck, political scientist of the University of Baltimore; and Clive Sinclair, visiting Anglo-Jewish novelist, from Saint-Albans. The only person awake in the cabins was Veronica X., who worked in longhand, twenty-two hours a day, ate yoghurt and fresh fruit, a total of eighteen minutes per day, meditated for forty-two minutes and slept the remaining, exactly one hour, from four until five a.m..

"Can you hear what I hear?" Salim whispered to Battuta, "someone shouting, it sounds like curses in Spanish, from the other side of the lake?"

"Pain is inevitable," said his companion, quietly, "even in Baghdad, the most prosperous city in the *umma*, if you passed at this time in the night you would hear both men and women crying out in anguish, in the midst of their deepest sleep."

"YEEEE-AAAARRGGGHHHHHH!!!"

It was not the ejaculation itself that made Merenptah cry out, but the sheer exertion caused by the position adopted in accordance with Ada Em's bedside book, Sex In Atlantis, that had made him exclaim as his wizened, three thousand year old seed shot forth into her receptive cavity. Despite her enviable collection of rubber prophylatics, in all colours and shapes and wattled surfaces, she had decided that three millennia of abstention made him reasonably infection free. He rolled back, extricating his left calf from the back of her neck, while removing his right ankle from the cleft of her buttocks, sighing with much needed relief. I'm too old for this, he thought. I should never have boasted about the secret Pharaonic postures. After all, they were only a small repertoire of manouevers retaining the compulsorily dominant setting. A Pharaoh could not have anyone, not even his Queen, astride him, as if he were the steed. My father Rameses, of course, was said to have ignored these strictures, but Rameses could afford to do whatever he liked.

"That was fantastic," said Ada, "Oh God, Nep. You're the only man who could ever do it that way. These New York hunks are so useless."

He lay back and gasped, clutching the pillow.

"Do you want a glass of water?" she asked.

It seemed almost hotter at night than during the day. In the daytime, at least, you expected it. But at night you might think the sun, having gone around the earth, could not retain the power of its rays while invisible. On the banks of the Nile, the desert night was almost invariably cool, if not cold, in Thebes. Giza was another matter, but legend had it that in the days of Khufu even that plain had enjoyed a moderate climate. But in this place, everything was extremes. Wind, ice, or fire. What could be next?

"Do you think I could become pregnant with your child?" she asked. "And what on earth could he or she be like?"

"I don't know," he said. "I had eighty-five children, but I only ever met forty-six of them. They were all in perfect health." Of course, he neglected to tell her about the fifth son of Nefertut, who had been born with a club foot, and had been disposed of, by the palace disposers, who then had to dispose of the distraught mother, who was strangled with a curtain cord and secretly buried in a gorge beyond the Valley of the Kings. Some matters ordinary people misunderstand.

"Oh Nep, you're something else," she said, turning over to him, with her mischievous, wondering smile. "You say things that nobody else ever says. Let's do it again."

He shook his head. "I am too old. Much, much too old."

"You're the youngest man I've ever had," she said to him, "tomorrow, remember, you got to start teaching me the real secrets of the Book of the Dead."

"You would need a priest for that."

"I've had one. Believe me, they're nothing special. At least what you keep for a long time you remember."

"I do?" Lying prone, sweating on the bedclothes. But everything is becoming so blurred. Even the solid objects in Ada Em's apartment were fluttering like exhausted moths. Her peerless collection of magic crystals, amulets, lucky charms from all five continents, including Melanesian cowrie shells and a genuine aboriginal necklace of platypus claws and tiny pebbles hewn off the underside of Ayers Rock, Uluru, the epicenter of the world. The Bolivian shaman's poncho hanging on the wall by the window leered at him with a toothless haggard grin. The three rows of multi-coloured memorial candles of all nations danced a rainbow dance on his cones. It was not possible to tell, with his present eyesight, which were his floaters and which real objects. The priests of Thoth said that Pharaoh's destiny was written on the whorls and specks that swirled in scarlet and tourquoise whirlpools when the eyelids were tightly closed. But Nep could never read anything there except chaos. He remembered the private advice of his father, Rameses, upon his deathbed: "Nothing a priest says should ever be believed.

Whatever they counsel you, do the exact opposite. Kill them if they get out of hand."

But all that now was left were Ada Em's knick knacks, and the tools of old Bertha Cropfin's fake trade. Nep could not bear the thought of returning to that, preying on the gullible misery of mostly poor black and Hispanic women who wished to believe there was some lightening of their burden just a tad beyond the veil. The cards, the crystal ball, the tea leaves and coffee grounds, palms and phrenologies. Loved ones, pining in the ether, poised to emit Madame's own patent ectoplasm, a secret formula concocted from banal ingredients found on the local Pathmark shelves. "We are the court of last resort, honey," she told him as she trained him to the task. "After us it's only lawyers. Or the little bottle of poison. The little bottle being cheaper, if you know what I mean."

So many of the common people swarming upon the surface of the earth. My father knew what to do with them, putting them to honest, useful labour, building the cities of his glory. Who was the Rameses who built this City? He had been excited, reading through Madame's reference book, at the idea of The Republic, something touted in embryo, he remembered, by the heretic, the so-called Sun God, Akhenaten. "That pot-bellied transvestite," as Dad called him, and all his works ploughed over, after his overthrow, his name removed from all the holy tablets, his cartouche erased from every wall that could be found, even the public toilets. The whispered themes of my poor brother Khem. Pharaohs are nothing but parasites on the living body social, he mused. But was it for this kind of thinking that I have been expelled from the Halls of the Dead?

Whatever the case, he began to enjoy the City, prompted strongly by the charms of Ada Em. Just a block up from her Wooster Street apartment he discovered the Espresso Bar, a cavernous meeting place of the strange characters who formed the vivid tapestry of the streets. They seemed to walk with an odd loping gait, and reminded him of nothing so much as the young acolytes of the sacred temples of Karnak. Their rituals were as mysterious and meaningless. Many of them were artisans of avocations which appeared to have no actual value. They were "artists", "writers" or musicians of varying kinds, whose work appeared internally motivated and was exhibited solely to each other. They were serving no higher cause except themselves. Nep would wander in, with or without Ada, order a double espresso or a "latte", sit at one of the tiny round tables and watch the inconsequential dance of the troubadors, the waving hands, the excited faces, the feet drumming the tiled floor. The young men and women would embrace promiscuously, with a happy familiarity. They seemed unworried by their immediate needs. Nothing that happened here would matter.

"I like it here," said Nep, "but Ada, I would like to pay my dues to this society, now that I am no longer a person of consequence. I would like to become a citizen of this Republic."

"That presents some serious problems, Nep."

Ada confided in Frances, a few days later, on a sweltering morning when Nep was too lethargic to travel Uptown from Park Slope. They left the Gallery in the care of Frances' new assistant, Martha B., and turned the corner to The Clock. Frances leafing through the free magazines advertising the local clubs and dives. Frances nursing a Decaff Latte. Ada making do with a freshly squeezed orange.

"You're getting in too deep, Ada," Frances warned her. "This isn't something you want to deal with. What documents does the man have? Where is he really from? Who is he? Unless you get some serious answers, you just have to stop right there."

"I know you don't believe, Frances, but I do. There's no lying here. The incredible is simply true. I've got the money. What I need are papers. Green card, social security, passport. We'll say he's an Armenian. I'm sure Aram can help."

"Aram is crazy but not that crazy. Forget about Allan too. They did all those wild things twenty-five years ago, but times have changed. If this man of yours really is Pharaoh, he should have some pretty good contacts himself. Isn't Egypt a major U.S. stooge?"

"Don't laugh at me Frances."

"I will if it's funny. And this is funny, Ada, you can see that. Let the man sort himself out. I'm your friend, Ada. I'm supposed to tell you when you're going over the rails."

"You don't understand. He doesn't realise that we have to do something illegal. It's just the way he is."

"What about Hay-sus? He got Selina Hasek her papers when she was a refugee from Czechoslovakia. He's probably still in business. I can give you a number to call. But then you're on your own, Ada. I'm not going to get involved."

“That’s fine. I just wanted your advice.”

“Then take my advice. Keep away from Armenians. The next thing you know, they’ve got twenty-five relatives living in your bedroom, kitchen, toilet, in the cupboards and under the bed. I’ve been there, Ada.”

“I know.”

“Have you learned how to say Fuck Off in ancient Egyptian yet?”

“🙘🙚🙜🙞🙵 🙵👍🙵🙴[!”

“Well, you learn something new every day.”

Frances sat for a while after Ada left, idly riffling through SoHo’s delights, trying not to reflect too hard, on another scorching day, on the jumbled cross-currents of her mind. The psyche still battered daily by the continual reports of the manhunt for Public Enemy Number One. Blurred memories of the FBI interrogation, the first week of The Escape, when she was summoned at the gallery by a polite plain clothes couple, who seemed to be eyeing each other adoringly in the car ride to the 19th Precinct, and whom she had dubbed secretly Kathy and Heathcliff, so electric was the atmosphere of denial of physical contact that surrounded them. But they only ushered her into a brightly lit interview room and left to moon on elsewhere. This was Frances’ first experience of police interiors, which she had previously imagined on the model of the kind of television series whose titles ended in “Blue,” characterised by an intensely waving camera. But the interview room was rock steady, metallic grey and hung with framed photographs of famous New York persons. She recognised past Mayors Fiorello Laguardia, William O’Dwyer, John Lindsay, Ed Koch and the present incumbent, David Dinkins. Her interviewer was a smart black woman whose hair was pulled so tightly back it seemed to have stretched her face too into a metallic sheen. She took notes on a small standard pad.

“This is an informal session, thank you very much for attending, Miss Stein. I am going to ask you a series of questions regarding your acquaintance, Mr Salim Halimi, who, as I assume you know, is now a fugitive from justice. Please feel free to extrapolate and add any material you consider relevant. All your legal rights are reserved.”

“So I told her what I had to say about Salim,” Frances told Allan Darwish, later that day, in his apartment. “I thought there was no point playing dumb. Anything that can be damaging they’ve already piled up. I followed Gittlin’s guidelines. I only talked about what I knew directly. I told her I wouldn't be drawn into discussing Salim in Beirut, or Tunis, or any other hearsay. I did mention some things in general. The Palestinian case, his pacifism. Of course she was all sympathetic."

"Of course."

"It's obvious they think he's going to contact one of us. Probably you. Maybe me. Even Benjamin, the safest bet maybe, as an Israeli."

"Did they drop any hints about the other guy?"

Aye, there's the rub. She looked out of Allan's window overlooking Riverside Park. The glistening Hudson, and the heat haze beyond. Allan blinked at her from his chair with owlish eyes. There was no trace of Jaime in the apartment, apart from an extra toothbrush in the bathroom. She was aware Allan had been trying to find him a job as an assistant doorman in one of the nearby blocks.

"Sometimes," said Allan, "life is full of coincidences. You walk around in a city of ten million people and meet a friend on the street whom you haven't seen since you met in another country. You think of a person and that person calls you on the phone ten seconds later. We meet a homeless man who speaks in eight different voices and then you see these people in real life. You think my friend Jaime is one of them. You hear that man, Flint, on the radio. Your friend Ada is having an affair with the Pharaoh. You think the phantom Ibn Battuta is the man with Salim. It's a great novel, Frances, you should write it. Mabe this is the theme you've been looking for so long."

"Maybe it is."

"Life is a cabaret, my friend. Or a horror story, take your pick. You know things are happening in the Middle East. The grapevine is humming and all the tom toms are drumming. The Israelis are making a deal with the P.L.O.. Secret talks are going on, in Sweden or Norway. The White House troubleshooter, Dennis Ross, is out there."

"We've heard it all before."

"War and peace. The difference between them, discuss. But there are things in the air, even in August. Remember August three years ago - when Iraq invaded Kuwait. It's when you least expect things, they happen."

"How does this affect us and Salim?"

"It might have, if Salim hadn't escaped. The case against him is really flimsy. Gittlin says they were on the brink of dropping charges.

They've been trying to link the other man, 'Battuta', into the story. The computers have been zinging like mad trying to fit his face to some known activist. But you know the drill. All Arabs with a beard look the same to them. He's probably some Egyptian refugee with a mental history. Gittlin wanted to speak to him but the prison authorities shut him out. Those people could elevate Prince Mishkin into the Most Wanted. We just have to plug away at the campaign, and wait for the recapture. They will get them, Frances. We just have to hope they don't shoot first and make up the story afterwards."

The unspoken dialogue: And if we hear from Salim?

The usual drill.

How you, too, can make paranoia your friend.

What she really wanted to know, my FBI interviewer, whose name, it appeared, was Agent Balla, was about drinking the piss. They all do. "Now this story about drinking Yassir Arafat's urine in the desert after an air crash. Is that true?"

"Well, it's not the sort of story somebody would make up, don't you think?"

"That's what I'm asking, Miss Stein. Was he involved in left wing circles?"

Everyone involved in the left wing is in circles, honey. "He was part of the Fatah, the mainstream Palestinian movement. They're nationalists, sort of like the Democratic Party." Only without the democracy. Speak no evil.

"You know if he calls you you have to call us. This is my card. Failing to inform us is a felony. You become an accomplice to the act. Friendship is not a mitigating factor."

That could do nicely for a motto. The truth was, I would have stayed longer in the Precinct, because, unlike on TV, it was fully air-conditioned. That raw blast of New York's mid-day summer wrapping round as she came down the steps. Even Allan's apartment, though cool, was not cool enough. The coolest non-air-conditioned place was Caroline's. But there the air was stifling in another way. Caroline, unable to function properly in the August furnace, lying on the reclining armchair, with bottles of fizzy water and yoghurt, and Karim, ready to fetch and carry. Solid as a carved hunk of mahogany, his presence a bulwark and a reproach against all that Caroline's friends personified: diversity, confusion, laxity. He tolerated them for his mother's sake and for their function as possible sources of information about Salim, whom he had only met once, but whom he regarded as an honorary Muslim, victim of an Islamophobic society, as were all the World Trade Center bombing suspects. The air was thickest, naturally, when Allan Darwish was present. For Frances alone, among the friends, knew the facts of Karim's paternity, and his devout denial of Darwish as his father. Even Benjamin, despite his two years as Caroline's lover, was not in this loop.

And so, despite it all, we have secrets from each other, Frances thought, as she sat in The Clock, among the latte quaffers, failing to make sense of it all. Trying to draw up enough energy to face the walk down Broadway to Spring Street and the Acme Gallery, to deal with life's real necessities - calling the Gallery's accountant, Cliff Seers, of Seers, Jackson & Bloomenthal, to query, again, whether there might be some angle, in a good light, or by astigmatic glancing, in which the Acme's books might look as if the Gallery would remain open into 1994, or close permanently, October-November at the latest, say on Halloween. Trick or treat. The only way the Gallery could be saved, Frances reflected, would be if Selina Hasek, its previous star turn, could be coaxed out of the Geodesic Dome on Long Island, with whatever new masterpieces she had achieved in the last year, isolated from the rest of humanity. But since March, the Dome had been cut off, since, as enquiries elicited, the dome-dwellers had neglected, or deliberately refused to pay their telephone bill. And so they remain within, as the days weeks and months pass, forgotten and forgetting, with their shiny Buckminster Fullerist construction gleaming under the sun and the moon.

Friendship Is Not a Mitigating Factor.

Legends of "The Skull" -
An All-American Hero.

How he had become, by chance, as always is the case in battle, an executioner for the Union in the Civil War: The official hangman, Zebediah "Noose" Stringer, had been killed in the Battle of Yellow Canyon, having had his head blown off by a stray cannon shell which had for some reason, known only to itself, decided to spare the poor, pant-shitten seventeen year olds of the Fifty-Third Michigan Infantry and scurl off for the Ordnance Support tent in the rear, shielded from the main action by a formidable wedge of a hundred casks of Tennessee Sour Mash whiskey, which had been miraculously rescued unscathed from the ambush of a rebel supply train one week earlier, of which eighty casks were commandeered by the officers and twenty handed down graciously to the n.c.o.s, sergeants and auxiliaries, among whom Sergeant-Major Noose sojourned, so that when the stray shell whistled by, setting the tent on fire by its trail, it took the head of the hangman off, with the bottle of whiskey he had just raised to his chapped and gruesome lips, leaving the rest of him, torso up, his right arm raised, hand severed at the joint, before it toppled over in the dust. It so happened that the battalion, on that day, had custody of three young scallawags who had slipped away from the ranks the night before the coming Battle of Yellow Canyon, which had been touted for several weeks as the make or break tussle of this crucial phase of the War, the Big Push that would unseat Stonewall Jackson and push his forces back across the Tangahasee Creek, but had been captured by the night guard and sentenced that very morning, at seven a.m. sharp, to death for desertion in a trial lasting a full three and one half minutes. Sentence postponed till dawn the next day as the adjacent Rebel forces began their bombardment promptly at 06:54.

The three condemned youths, shivering in their mud-caked underclothes, guarded in a three by six foot foxhole by two massive Massachusetts militiamen whose power of empathy and imagination had been completely erased by months of hand to hand fighting and who had been rendered totally deaf by cannon-fire, crouched and prayed for the destruction of their entire battalion, but were instead rewarded with the pyrrhic success of the hangman's decapitation, as, following the victory and rout of the Confederate Forces, the hanging was reset for the same afternoon, at one o'clock sharp, and volunteers were called to take the executioner's place. A young man, a war orphan, whose parents, poor farmers in the Nangahasset Valley, had been shot down by Rebels with their entire extended family, except the boy who hid inside a haystack, breathing through a two foot long reed, and whose name was not recorded, though everyone referred to him as Chick, stepped forward, and dispatched the three youths with such expertise and enthusiasm that he was offered the hangman's post, and handsome salary, in officio, which he fulfilled to the complete satisfaction of his superior officers, and of the Union of the United States of America, from that day on. On April 12, 1865, he won a personal citation from President Abraham Lincoln, signed two days before the Great Liberator was shot by his assassin, John Wilkes Booth, in Washington D.C..

The Skull, which became his name well before his nineteenth birthday, due to the shape of his head which was accentuated by his clean shaven scalp, preserved perforce because of the fondness of lice for his hair whenever he was rash enough to allow it to grow, continued to perfect his manifest destiny in the Indian Wars which followed the peace, as the spearheads of the U.S. Army, and its famed Seventh Cavalry, pushed west, to protect the new railroads, the iron beams and foundations of a newly envigorized nation, pounding coast to coast, from New York to California and back again, Atchison, Topeka and Santa Fe, and all the mythical beasts. He became part of an elite, secret and deniable force of the Union Army, designated to spread terror among the indigenous tribes of the as yet amorphous Territories, in the manner of gouging out an Eye for an Eye, and entire mouthfuls for a Tooth: In "retaliation" for native atrocities, scalpings and massacres, they would range far and wide into Indian lands, falling upon encampments and teepees pitched in the rear of marauding braves, killing and mutilating old men, women and children, cutting their scalps, ears and intimate pendulants, disemboweling the pregnant and nailing unborn foetuses to trees, and divers other ferocious deeds, committed among the Arapahoe, the Apache, Comanche, the Sioux, the Nez Perce and other enemy groups.

In the late 1880's, as the Indian Wars ceased, and the remnants were hustled into their bleak reservations, The Skull returned for a while to his profession as Dispatcher in the U.S. penitentiary system, but the bleakness of prison walls and drudgery sapped him, and he returned to active service in the Cuban-American War. From then on, he continued aiding his country to the best of his abilities in the shadowland of Special Services, serving in Panama, Nicaragua, Mexico, Haiti, the Dominican Republic, the Philippines, in Europe in the First World War, slicing off blonde German ears instead of swarthy Latino or Asian appendages, returning both to the Latino and Asian spheres between the wars, then with the O.S.S. in Europe, and then back again to Central America, Guatemala, Mexico and Nicaragua again, and off to South-east Asia, Laos, Cambodia and Vietnam in the Sixties, then back to his old beats again, and southwards, to Brazil, Argentina and Chile, and finally being judged so jaded by these hundred and ten years of brutality that he was re-assigned, States-side, to the ever more clandestine niches of the National Security Agencies, Alien Watch, Occult Support Systems (O.S.S. II), and on to the Staten Island detail, nicknamed the "Hen House", grubbing for the "Cosmic Eggs" in New York City's Sanitation Depository and Reclamation Hub.

*

With a sigh, the Director of the Central Intelligence Agency, Orville Dullest, put down The Skull File and rubbed his knuckles vigorously into his eyes. This is exactly the kind of thing, he reflected, that brings the Agency into disrepute, creates jangled nerves throughout the system, engenders layers of coverups, prompts the most severe Presidential skepticism and threatens budgets, ops, careers. The most stringent evaluation had to be called for. Every angle had to be carefully looked at, from computer error to operative bungling, clerical mistakes deriving from previous epochs, possible sabotage, of foreign or domestic origin, or of some kind of criminal nature (could The Skull have been boosting his potential pension payments??), mischief engendered by mental breakdown or incapacity somewhere along the line...

The Director cleared his throat, looking out from his great mahogany working desk, across the booklined room, exquisitely bound volumes of the Classics, from Aeschylus to Zoroaster, and out the elegant French windows to the open space lawns leading to the electrified fence and the soft hues of the Maryland woodlands beyond. Here I sit, virtually in Paradise, contemplating the Abyss. The weight of his responsibilities dragged down the bulbous and stringy dome of his head. His broad, glistening forehead, almost sunk to the polished level of the desk, the In-tray of U.X. files towering up at his right as his eyes sank down. But I am to destiny born. Third in an illustrious line, from the time the Agency was only a modest Office, not the giant hydra it had now become - Dull, Dulles, Dullest, this was not a lineage that could be traduced. Noblesse oblige. From August Dull down, we had never shirked from presenting the evidence of our Information Gathering brief to the Chief Executive, as our Prime Directives obliged. This was mandatory, whether the Chief Executive and Commander of the Armed Forces and Keeper of the Faith liked what he often reluctantly heard, or not.

So it was with the current incumbent. Conspiracies, foreign espionage plots, terrorist alliances, U.X. satellite data, even the ongoing Cosmic Watch, in all its sixty-three centers, did not phase the President, but the innocuously named Smith File was well over the fence. "Why are you bringing me this?" the President asked, spreading those strong palms, wagging his forefinger, "my calendar shows me July 10, it's a long ways from April Fool's day."

"I am obliged," said the Director dryly, "whenever data analysis and manual over-ride produce the same set of variables, I have to present. It's your decision."

"Right. So you're telling me that your best minds and machines are seriously considering the option that we are all, this office, this town, our country, imaginary constructs, fictitious people dreamed up by a mentally disturbed homeless person dragging New York City, which, I presume he had dragged up too out of his own gut. This Mo Smith.

That our entire existence is a solipsistic fantasy. And how does Mo Smith exist? In the eyes of God? No, but you're telling me he is God."

"That is not concluded. But too many random factors converge. You will note the exhaustive enquiries involving the denoted names Frank Ox, Mohammed Ibn Battuta, Arnold Flint, Lincoln Korombane, Jaime and Pharaoh Merenpath. The cross-referenced listed and verified U.S. citizens and aliens as filed. Note that Mr Salim Halimi and Mr Ibn Battuta are both suspects in the World Trade Center bombing, currently at large and subject of a major manhunt. This is of course our primary trigger. I am in this case, Mr President, merely the Messenger. All variables such as error, fraud, criminal tampering and all the usual components having been factored in. You will note the probability of validation is thirty-five percent, well above my obligatory threshold, which is, as statutory, fifteen."

"Well, I admire your candour and indeed your guts in bringing this to my attention, Orville, but I am I think pretty sure I wasn't elected by the American people to be a figment of the imagination, whether it is of a poor homeless African-American or of the President of Texaco for that matter. You gotta review your procedures, Orville. We are agreed this one is over the fence?"

A forest of nodding heads around the table. Sympathetic glances in the Director's direction. Barely hiding the quivers of malicious glee. Orville has done it this time. A gross miscalculation. But guarded suspicion: What is he up to now? The tumour in his skull, which had been kept at bay for over two years by chemical bombardment, must be thursting its way to the fore. Can he be counterfeiting his medical records, the bi-monthly all-clear required by his boss? Even the greatest tree must shake before the buzzing chainsaw whine.

The Director's forehead hit his desk, with an odd rapping sound, prompting him to start and draw up his neck. This was the same response elicited from the report on the Feminization of Nature, and that one was supported not only by the most rigorous agency forecasts backed by tons of independent scientific research from bona fide, untainted, world wide and impeccable sources. "Just keep this one away from my wife!" Very funny. Within a hundred years, all male sperm could be completely enfeebled and all normal procreation come to a halt. Of course, you can't interest elected persons, however smart or even dedicated, in the long term, whether you are the head of the

C.I.A. or a long-haired bleeding-heart environmentalist lobbyist dribbling outside the door.

What does He want of us after all? The Director pulled at his lip, which, he sometimes imagined, was becoming excessively rubbery, so that he could almost pull the lower lip out a full four inches, like those Amazonian warriors who put a plate inside, why he could not for the life of him remember. Is this too, a symptom of that kernel, that hard nut, that lethal cocoabean waxing and waning inside his head? But this is what we have been asked to do, Ingather Information, Intelligence, Analysis, in lieu of all the rest of the stuff we have been ordered to refrain from, assassinating foreign leaders, depilating their beards, poisoning their morning coffee with toxins, rubbing out recalcitrant trade unionists, student militants, activists annoying those we wish to honour with our gifts. Destabilising countries which are already so unstable they only need a little, cheap push to topple over into the pit. Making sure the Russians never rise to challenge us again. But of course this is all nonsense. They want us to do it all, but not to tell, and take it on the chin if we are found out. Self-righteously and zealously "revealing" all the renounced atrocities of the past: The projects on hypnosis, "brainwashing," telekinetic and psychic projection, clairvoyance, "practical spiritualism," ghostbusting, necro-plasmosis, the Tuskegee research, the LSD experiments, but they still insisted on flying that charlatan, Ulrich Geistner, over Baghdad in the X20, hoping he could pinpoint the bunker where Saddam Hussein was hiding, so he could be taken out. It's all a matter of what you can get away with.

Still, I cannot ignore what is imperative. The UneXplained too close to home. This is more essential than the Cosmic Watch. Admittedly, the Skull had an Egg astray, this was worrying, whether it was in the hands of an imaginary character or not. But the concatenation of forces that linked these Subjects with no possible material source of identity simply cannot be ignored. From the "impossible" facts of the Skull's longevity, to the sudden "manifestation" of Ibn Battuta at the Pilgrim's Arms Hotel, Merenptah in Park Slope, Lincoln Korombane, picked up in downtown Manhattan, whose tales of C.I.A. involvement had checked through, to immense surprise, within the system, on to the admittedly shaky "Jaime" file, which might be nothing more than the case of another lost subcontinental waif, another moth flitting against the light, though the contact with the old radical Darwish, mentor of the suspect Halimi, added another coal to the fire, and through to the interrogation of the "Unaburner", the bookshop arsonist caught in the act... The endless ravings of Arnold Flint about his vanished bestselling status, his mythic divorced wife and perfidious agent, his bizarre diatribes against "the ground-nut barons of Iran," none of this could be completely discarded. Not when the mainframe, again and again, came up with only one consistent conclusion - the factual basis of the claims of Mo Smith.

The only other conclusion was as unthinkable: Scrap the entire system, shut down the mainframe, put all the corroborating officers under intensive psychiatric and indeed political surveillance (all sixty-three of them for the identical syndrome!), return to manual filing for as long as it takes to reprogramme and walk blind through the shadow of the valley of death until it is considered safe to switch back on? And considered by whom? The same fucking fourteen year old Siamese-twin fruitcakes we relied on to set it up in the first place - now the nineteen year old Fretillini Brothers?

The nut, the nut inside my head... The Director rose from his desk, walked across the deep plush carpet, turning into the corridor towards the bathroom. It seemed to stretch out, far in front of him, the panelled walls hung with the portraits of his predecessors as well as all the most important strategic thinkers of the ages: Clausewitz, Napoleon, Nhong-Ti-Giap, Genghis Khan, the Mamluk Sultan Baybars. His first fore-runner, August Dull, scowled at him with busy beetled brows. Allen Dulles seemed to smile, acidly, revealing a set of yellow, rotting teeth. His threadbare sweater, patched pants and battered, filthy plimsolls were quaint legends in a safer age. Help me, you bastards, for God's fucking sake! But they just shook with scornful laughter, rattling their frames.

I'm only doing my job! He finally reached the bathroom, staggering against the ornate jamb. The suite beckoned within, the great heart-shped bath, the gold taps and piping, the gleaming multi-level shower head, the white sink with its pristine towels, bathsoaps, shampoos, oils, the red cross on the medicine cabinet.

He opened the box, scrabbling for his pills. The pain killers, the fifty-carat guarantees, as touted by Doctor Heinz Baskerville, of Georgetown. Nothing can resist these. All the pain will stop, as if flattened by an express train. That's what I'm afraid of. But no choice.

He filled a glass of water and downed two. Contemplating the rest, the seventy odd left in the jar. Perhaps this is the solution. The Old Fashioned Way. A hundred years ago I would take my service pistol and just end it all with a ball in the brain. But I already have a ball in the brain. And I have no pistol, service or otherwise. All I have are half a hundred sharpshooting, eagle eyed, fighting fit bodyguards hidden about all over the underbrush. Just beyond the quiet lawns. The trees used to come up almost to the porch, but they had them cut down to the perimeter for obvious security reasons. Obvious to them, but why should I care. When Margaret and the kids were here I had people to really worry about. But now the birds have flown, and mama vulture is away on a tall branch somewhere in Italy scouring the land for some new poor near-corpse... Still, we had some good times, had we not?

Just say goodbye, and swallow the lot. The "coward's way out." But maybe hallo to some new adventure, if I am really just a figment of Mo Smith's imagination. Isn't there a creation myth of some kind, is it of the Polynesian islanders, that all are images in the dream of the primal giant, who must not be wakened, under any circumtances, for his waking marks the end of the world? He pinched himsef. It hurt. He lit a match from the secret smoking box and held it over his palm, then cried out and shook it out, cursing. He scrabbled in the drawers, there must be a sharp knife somewhere. Why bother? There was pain enough as it was. At least fifteen minutes before the pills would start working. Spreading that soothing, glowing balm.

Something caught his attention from the corner of his eye. He turned his head. Yes, there was something, crawling along the perfectly polished creamy marble floor. A twisting, whitish form, almost invisible against the similar color, but definitely there. He moved up closer. It was a slimy, foot long worm. He shook his head. Is this it now, what they've all warned about, the daytime hallucinations, the tumour's moment of triumphant takeover? The fortress breached, the enemies about to all come tumbling through?

Despite his revulsion, he bent down to touch it with the tip of his right forefinger. It was mucously moist, and recoiled to his touch. It seemed to increase its speed, side-winding like a desert snake across the marble, towards the wall adjacent to the bath. The wall was tiled, in matching cream colour. A pure white towel hung by a ring fixed at face height. He grabbed the towel, knotting it to flick at the intruder. Is this some new device? Some deep penetration surveillance, or even assault weapon, developed in some deep-dish biological bunker, by the Russians, the Libyans, the Iranians, even the Israelis. Or even our own side, finally come to deliver my comeuppance, a rival agency, the N.S.A., pricked by my intrusion into their domain with my investigation of The Skull?

In the world I have conjured up, out of my strictly rational and scientific principles, anything could happen, anything could be. Perhaps I should dash back into the study, call up the database of Maryland Fauna, Invertebrate Section - there must be something, in the children's old book-form encyclopedias, still further up, on the untouched third floor? It's simple of course. I'll whup it, kill it and pin it up, hand it to the S.S. for analysis. Better to be safe than sorry. But before he could strike, the worm seemed to crawl into the wall, directly into the sealed, cavity-free skirting tiles, vanishing out of sight.

He blundered forward, putting his hands towards the wall. They pushed as if through a viscous surface. There was no wall. He pushed on through. The bathroom disappeared behind him. All the normal, hard, safe accoutrements of his everyday life. All around him was red, mucous, palpitating, the surface under his feet slick with sticky, thick moisture. He slipped and fell. The smell was appalling, like a hundred thousand borehole latrines. The worm was ahead of him, swimming through the mixture with a bouyant, almost vivacious alacrity. It seemed to turn its head, or at least its front end, and smile. Then it wriggled out of sight.

"Get me out of here!" The Director's cry was swallowed in a tomblike echo, wrapping back all round him. No one answered. He floundered forward, looking for a way out. A reddish, undulating valve-like tunnel seemed to open up before him. He dived in, despite the fetid stench. His feet, unslippered, slipping and sliding in a muck he was too fearful to examine.

"Is this it?" he said aloud, "are you my tumour? Are you the thing that's eating my brain?"

"Just come this way!" He turned, abruptly. A dim light wavered from the tunnel's depths, behind him. "Take small, careful steps. You'll be all right!"

The voice was firm, if foreign sounding. He turned, and blunderd towards the light.

"It takes some getting used to, you could have chosen a better entry point!" the voice said, more airily than could be warranted by the circumstances. "The inner caecum. That's a pretty messy place. But if you come this way it's easier, behind the spleen."

A hole, and a dark, though friendly face lit by a kerosene lamp, held up to flashing eyes, straggling long hair, an unkempt beard.

"I am Jesse," said the face. "It's good to see another man round here. Since everyone else left. Except the women. Come on, you're quite safe here. Just stretch out, and take hold of my hand..."

* * *

STATEMENTS, DEPARTMENT OF JUSTICE:
Lincoln Matatu Korombane, Holding Facility 346/8, NYC.

It is factually true to state that I have been resident in the City of New York, functioning as an assistant muralist to the "Puerto Rican Decoration Front," for approximately six months, though I cannot vouch for the precise date when this phase of my life began, without proper identification papers, social security number, visa or "green card." These events took place under circumstances completely beyond my control, as is my presence on U.S. soil, which, despite the above, might seem totally justifiable in the light of previous matters.

It is also factually true to state that I have been an agent of the African Bureau of the United States Central Intelligence Agency since 1966. When Kwame Nkrumah was overthrown in Ghana I was approached by a young American called Greene, who convinced me that without a major U.S. input no possibility of change existed, and that continued Afrikaaner rule was only a U.S. interest so long as the African opposition movements were Soviet backed - the so-called Moscow-Khartoum Axis. In 1968 I was able to perform a major service for my employer, Greene, in joining an African National Congress task force being trained in the Soviet Republic of Kazakhstan.

I took the extreme risk of being discovered and denounced by my own comrades as a traitor, although every act that I did and every fibre of my being was committed to the liberation of my people from the yoke of Boer domination. My experiences in the Soviet Union convinced me that the Communist regime was not interested in the liberation of Africa but only in establishing their own bases of support to challenge and subvert the free world. I considered that I had proved my commitment to the liberation struggle by the scars I still bear all over my body from beatings by the brutal Afrikaaner police, my deteriorated eyesight due to my years in detention in the dark cells of prisons in Bloemfontein and Pretoria and the callouses on my feet from the thousand miles of my enforced walk, after Sharpeville, across desert and veldt, all the way to Dar Es-Salaam.

The following two decades were not velvet years either. Tramping the cold European corridors of exile, chillblains and creaking bones in dank Berlin dosshouses, even in the sunny climes of Los Angeles, where Greene found me a sinecure in 1970, I was reduced to the status of walking old women's dogs for a living, suffering the bites of the little canine brutes on my ankles as I tried to drag them up Beverly Drive. (I was travelling on a legal visitor's visa at that time.) In this period, too, I was executing work for the U.S. Government, as Greene had requested me to report on the activities of certain so-called revolutionary groups which were suspected Soviet or Chinese fronts. I recall being introduced to no less a personage than Mr Henry Kissinger, Secretary of State, by Mr Greene, in a restaurant in Washington, I think it was the Belvedere. Mr Kissinger listened for fifteen minutes to my analysis of the Southern African situation, and impressed me by his incisive questioning and penetrating mind, though he embarrassed Mr Greene somewhat, I recall, by dismissing the threat of certain "Trotskyite" organisations as "Shnipishocker shlimazels," "shnorrers" and "shnooks." This meeting took place, as I recall, in November 1970. Soon afterwards I was flown to Europe to infiltrate the Pan Africanist Congress, but I could not find it, and I had to take various menial positions in London, Paris, Brussels and Amsterdam. It was at this period that I became a doorman at a Dutch brothel, with subsequent offers of employment of a less salubrious nature. As these took place before 1980, I can safely say that I have not suffered from any incurable long term ailments which might invalidate my claim for a United States visa.

During the late 1980's, when the United States became more actively involved in supporting the South African liberation struggle, due to the change in the political climate which followed President Reagan's meetings with Soviet Chairman Gorbachev, I had hopes that I might be able to draw on my past services for the United States' Government to obtain an immigrant's visa. I wrote several times to Mr Greene, at all the "safe" addresses I had been given, but received no reply. I feared that Mr Greene might have retired or even passed away, and sent copies of my letters directly to Mr Kissinger and to the Intelligence Liaison Office in the Department of Justice. Still no reply. News was continually coming in of winds of change in South Africa, of encouraging speeches by the new Afrikaaner leader, Mr F.W. De Klerk, and the possible release of the A.N.C.'s leader, Nelson Mandela. But rumours regarding my own American contacts had led me to be regarded as a pariah by my own exiled comrades, and it seemed that change might come, but I would have no benefit, and remain forever a wanderer between three worlds, the world of my birthright, the frosty rejections of European exile, and the receding dream of a tangible return for my secret past. I yearned to come in from the cold.

In 1989, when the Berlin Wall came down and the communist regimes of Eastern Europe were overthrown, I was overjoyed, because I could see my ultimate dream of return to my homeland was nearer. Then, in February the following year, Nelson Mandela walked free from his imprisonment. I was watching on a small black-and-white television with chopped aerials in a freezing basement in Battersea, London. I remember it well, because one waited for an hour, and then almost two hours, while the cameras rolled, and the great man was not yet revealed. Finally a small dot was seen in the distance, and the man himself, clutching his wife, Winnie Mandela's hand, emerged slowly from the crowd and came on towards the waiting lenses. I leaned forward, in order to adjust the broken aerials, as the picture was becoming extremely fuzzy, I recall my frustration as I tried to pull the little rods this way and that, thumping the box. But Mandela's image was indistinct, blurry, breaking up. I reached round the set to the small ring which connected the aerials to the box, and at that point, I remember, a shock running through my fingers up my right arm and into my body, a blinding white flash, and then oblivion.

I came to, as I have described repeatedly to my various current interviewers, within the strange location which I still cannot define as anything other than "The Body." I have described my companions. The location, site, arena, scene, however it may be named, was fetid and enclosed, quivering and palpitating, a nightmare of dark, living flesh. I cannot tell how long, in real time, I spent in this location. The events I have described, and the conversations with my "companions" in this distinctive predicament, are as accurate and factual as I can recall. Having reread the transcripts, I can neither add or deny any substantive parts, as recorded.

As suddenly as I had found myself transmigrated from Battersea, London, to the "interior" of "Mo" Smith, I found myself, once again, evicted, onto the streets of downtown Manhattan, New York City, about six months ago. For a time, which I was informed was three weeks, I lay, exhausted, in the apartment belonging to the named Jacinta Guevara, and her assistant, Miguel Ortiz. Then I began my labours as their assistant muralist, mixing paints, fetching and carrying ladders, cans and other equipment. We have, I understand in furtherance of a legitimate grant from the City's Municipal Education Project, executed murals on buildings within Alphabet City, that is, Avenues A thru D, and on sites around the Jacob Riis, Lillian Wald and Bernard Baruch Houses, down to La Guardia, Rutgers, Albert E. Smith Houses and Knickerbocker Village. In the last six weeks of this period I had graduated to adding various smaller points and embellishments to the murals themselves. I have drawn and painted images of Nelson Mandela, Robert Sobukwe, Samora Machel, Julius Nyerere, Robert Mugabe, Kenneth Kaunda, Eduardo Mondlane, Jomo Kenyatta, Kwame Nkrumah, Haile Sellassie, Albert Lutuli, Nana Mahomo, Vusumzi Make, and other struggling stalwarts. I even painted a few white faces to be venerated, such as Trevor Huddleston, Ruth First and Joe Slovo. They appeared a little out of place among the lush Latino jungle foliage that Jacinta specialises, but they evoke the spirits of our times. These last few months have been the happiest of my life, when I have felt free of burdens, free of confinement, and, I can admit, enamoured, though my adoration has not been reciprocated, of the magnificent Jacinta, the portraitist of freedom. I accept my new confinement here, stifling as it may be, with equanimity, for I have seen the open sky, beyond the great towers of capital and mammon, and even, on some clear nights, obtained glimpses of the stars. I await the disposition of my interlocutors quietly, faithfully, with absolute harmony of head and heart, and with a strong belief in the Free World's ability to transcend its detrimental origins in the dark past of slave ships riding the high Atlantic breakers, the selling blocks of the human markets of Massachusetts and indeed New York City, the cotton fields of Confederate America, and the crack tenements of a thousand and one downtowns and projects, the corridors of welfare, misery and desperation.

Forwards Ever, Backwards Never!

Your comrade in arms, Lincoln Matatu Korombane.

Prisoner No. 9864387, Pretoria Gaol, 1961.

Arnold Adler Flint. Interrogation Room 3, 25th Precinct, Manhattan.

In this infernal heat, I understand completely, the purpose is both metaphoric and oppressive. The idea is to recreate the heightened temperatures of the fires, 451 Fahrenheit, the point at which paper catches fire. But I refuse to be intimidated. I am proud of my sweat. Honest moisture, it is not worthy of this filthy, spit-strewn floor on which it trickles, down the tips of my toes. Flowing from my scalp down my forehead and ears, around my lip and down my chin and neck to gather in the curling hairs of my chest. Weighing down my hirsute groin.

But I will not submit. All these reports of my so-called capture by the rapier-brained detectives of the N.Y.P.D., blue and bloated, are complete canards, outright falsehoods. Total fabrications, fibs, deception, perfidy, hypocrisy and mensanges. Let the truth be known and properly announced: That I surrendered of my own free will, disgusted at the utter incompetence and incapacity of the New York Police to find me, determined that my acts of justice should be seen and known to have been done as they have been done, and not only rumoured, and whispered about in corners, misunderstood and misattributed.

I am the "Unaburner." If this is a "confession," then so be it. I would define it as an "affirmation." Just as some affirm Christ, and others Mohammed, and others the Lord God Jehovah, and many other deities too numerous or obscure to be included here, and still others affirm their faith in reason, or in the biological imperatives of man, or in the eternal truths of mathematics, or in the ever-changing flux of chaos, or in Elvis Presley, or in the trivial and passing tremors of their momentary desires. In this same sense I affirm my self. The irrevocable expression of my identity, the "I", from which all else flows. If this central, first object of perception is denied, impugned, constrained, confuted, then a vehement and, indeed, savage response is inevitable.

I, myself and me. The Pharaonic Egyptians had the conception of the various different spiritual and physical identities of a man - the *ba,* the khat, the *khu*, the *ka* - or double, not to be confused with the *khaibit*, or shadow, the *skhem* and the *skhu*. To which we in our idiot times have added the *klutz*, the *schvantz* and the *shmuck*, to name but a few ingredients. I am a world within myself, and then, the others - multiple worlds, each within their own I's, without end - for, even mathematically, one must compute those still unborn, those potential, and those discarded behind, in the passage of time, the dead, their zombies, ghosts and husks.

We each require our place in the scheme. And if we are denied, shall we not take revenge?

I know the old Italian adage: Revenge is a dish best eaten cold. But I have never had a liking for salads. I prefer my vengeance red hot, well over 450 Fahrenheit. I want to see my enemies not only burn, but shrivel, and even their ashes perish.

I am not a fiction! I am a free man! *Instar omnium!* As Propertius stated aptly: *In magnis et voluisse sat est!* In great things even to have wished is enough! Does this sound like a figment to you? And yet that insect, that invertebrate carpetbagger, the self-styled Radio Ranter, Crush Limbo, comes into this precinct, bold as brass, and to my face, swears on his Bible that he has never known me before! I, who increased his audience share on KBXX from 48 to 76 percent! Off peak! Now he claims I am an impostor, those tapes came to him sui generis from Punka City, Ill.! Producing affidavits from all his staff that I had never set foot in the studio! How could I, encased and imprisoned inside the corpus of that shambling mendicant, welfare scrounger and bum, Mo Smith, or whatever the hell he calls himself, at any day of the month. This is not a racial point, but since I am being honest, and telling the truth, exactly as I see it, it's all very well for black and white to live together, I am an old fashioned unreconstructed liberal on that count, but not inside one another! I would be the first to acknowledge that any poor bastard black Afro-African American whatever the hell he wants to call himself is stuck inside of me he damn well has something to complain about! We may fuck, but we are not interchangeable, if you see what I mean.

(There follow two more pages of intellectual rambling, picking up points allegedly made by Plato, Aristotle, Propertius, Protagoras, Diogenes, Epicurus, Marcus Aurelius, Saint Thomas Aquinas, and Saint Francis of Assisi, on whom Flint pours the most excessive scorn. A sudden leap from Francis Bacon to Nietzsche is too bewildering to explore. Finally, the statement comes full circle, finding, in the semi-populist interpolations of Douglas Hofstadter concerning Godel's Theorem and the proposition that no system can be examined from outside its own boundaries, an echo of Plato's iconic "shadows in the cave", and returning to the themes of betrayal and deception -)

The Groundnut Barons of Iran, among other forces directing and manipulating U.S. foreign policy, the ancient power of the peanut and the real causes of the Civil War, the pistachio and the Salem Witch Trials, the dispossession of the native Indian population and despoliation of the Nez perce, the Sioux, the Apache, the

Sawaneequaw and the Hiawatha, the pecan and Pocahontas, down to the teutonic hegemony in recent times of that horror, the ubiquitous meat patty, the so-called Hamburger, the destruction of the Amazon rain forest and the spreading of insidious, lethal and incurable cattle diseases, which threaten to reduce the brain cells of millions of carnivorous citizens to complete mush, the comeback of the English (and talk about revenge eaten cold!), all the encroachments of dumb semi-socialized industrial conformity, the way we all look alike, talk alike and think the same moronic television induced thoughts, the tyranny of the machine, technomania, instant communication of one utter stupidity with another, the total degradation of the Word, the cheapening and debasement of meaning, the remaindering of fine art and the invisibility of actual quality, the magical disappearing act performed by books, authors, agents, publishers and readers. All these cannot be forgotten or condoned. The revenge is not the revenge of me, the *ba*, Arnold Flint, but of the *ka*, the spiritual side, the "real" Arnold, the memory and that part that memory plays in reality. For if what I, Arnold, recall in the most vivid senses, can be ordained to vanish, and stated to have never been, then I, the *sekhem*, the material body of Arnold, risen Phoenix-like from the ashes of my own immolation, condemned and burnt at the stake as a heretic, must rise to do the deeds that must be done.

And fuck you, Crush Limbo. Republican party reptile and reprobate. I repudiate all your works, and stratagems. And don't get behind me, don't think I don't know your kind. The way the sun is, at night, creeping behind the backside of the earth, dreaming, skulking, thinking of the scorching torments that can be applied next day. While the ship of the dead glides by, in the dark, hoping that a cooler dawn will reveal a balmier, hospitable shore.

Yes, I torched the lot of them. Daltons, Doubleday, Barnes and Noble. All of them. Ex debito justitiae. Exitus acta probat - the outcome justifies the deed. So perish all tyrants.

Arnold Flint, Political Prisoner.

P.S.: More steam, o super, more steam!!

Meanwhile, in the pitch dark mosquito night of Blue Mountain, this is what had so far occurred: Comin slowly down the mountain towards the lake and the Art Colony, Battuta and Salim were suddenly confronted by the scullery maid Anita, who had just moored her canoe after paddling back and forth across the lake in the night, mouthing curses in Spanish about the Anglo-Yankee denizens whose furtively suspicious glances exposed their suspicions of her being the sneak thief who stole their watches and pocketbooks and underwear in the night, whereas the real culprit, unknown to any of them, was the kleptomaniac boy, Ari. Walking across the lawn to the house, Anita felt, rather than heard or saw, movement in the trees, and, rushing back to the canoe, extracted its paddle and stepped forward, calling out: "Who goes there?"

Battuta, who was more versed in this kind of situation, called back in the Spanish dialect he had learned in Andalusia: "We are neither thieves nor murderers, but only travellers who have lost our way!"

Not understanding this dialect, which had not been spoken on the planet for at least five hundred years, Anita stood her ground, brandishing the paddle and yelling: "Come out and show yourselves sons of bitches! I'll crack open your fucking skulls!"

The fugitives came forth from the trees, sheepishly, resembling, after their long hard journey nothing so much as the Wild Men of Borneo, or extras from the primal version of King Kong.

"It's O.K. ma'am," said Salim, softly, "we just need a place to shelter for the night. Then we'll be moving on."

"You're the escaped terrorists," she said, lowering her weapon. "Shit, why didn't you say so at the beginning. Just shut up and come inside."

She took them round the back of the house to her quarters, the old servant's cabin by the kitchen, now supplied with the modern conveniences of electricity, hot and cold running water, and round the clock cable T.V.. As they rubbed each other down in the shower she threw a couple of steaks which made their heads spin like tops into a pan upon her cooker. "Soup's up, boys!" They rushed forward, wet and naked, as she threw them a couple of towels.

Meanwhile, the proprietress and manager of the Blue Mountain Art Colony, the Boston Brahmin heiress Grace Keighley, who had been lying in a state of semi-awareness as the cries of "icho de putana!" and "maricons!" rippled across the lake, had been startled into full waking mode by Anita's yells at the jetty and, throwing on her kimono, stumbled out onto her porch. The powerful odour of frying meat drew her to Anita's bunker. Hugging the log cabin walls, she crept along the stoop, to the window, bobbing her head to sneak a peek. The two wild men were tearing into their steaks with gusto, holding the food in their claw-like fingers, utterly ignoring knife or fork.

"All right, girl, this time you're out!" Ms Keighley muttered under her breath. She turned to go, but the same revelation that had struck the scullery maid stopped her dead, and she turned back for another look.

"I assure you ma'am," Salim was saying, "that we are both completely innocent of all charges. If we can just get across the border to Canada, we will fight this in the court of public opinion. But you shouldn't get into trouble. If we could only find just a simple change of clothing we can be on our way as soon as possible."

"Don't talk crap," said Anita, "There's an unused cabin up the lakeside. Nobody comes there and you got a boat you can hop into if somebody does turn up. I'm a falsely accused person myself." She opened the fridge and cast about for two cold beers. Buds, matured over beechwood.

"Now hold it, missy!" Grace Keighley, having nipped round the hut, pushed the front door open and stepped in. "If anyone's going to hide the F.B.I.'s Most Wanted on my property, it's going to be me." Anita frowned, and Battuta leaned back and fell off his chair. Grace Keighley was an imposing figure of a woman, six foot tall and with her leonine mane over her kimono could appear quite daunting. She held out her hand as Salim helped Battuta up to his feet. "I'm Grace Keighley.

I own this place. My father had it built with his ill-gotten gains from thirty years of screwing the third world on behalf of the Central Intelligence Agency."

"I'm pleased to meet you. I am Salim Halimi. This is Mr Battuta."

"An honour." She clasped their hands, almost dislocating Salim's knuckle bones. "Anita, go get the cabin ready. You'll have to change the sheets. The floor in that place is filthy. The raccoons have shat all over the place. It needs a new lock on the door. I'll see to that. We don't want to involve anyone else in this. Comprendo?"

"O.K., Grace." The familiar between gritted teeth.

"Let's do it then." She hustled the two fugitives out of the maid's cabin, turning off the light first, pausing on the stoop to look right and left. Her warm hand was firm on Salim's forearm. "I know all about you, Salim. I'm on your Action Committee. I'm a good friend of Allan Darwish. You have to tell me the whole story. I want to know exactly what goes on in the jail, in the Tombs and Riker's Island. We're preparing a report for Amnesty."

Night, the heiress, the maid, the mosquitoes and the moon. It stood over the lake, bathing the treetops and the ripples of the lake with its ghostly glow. Cicadas were absolutely rampant. The Spanish curses had abated to a subsonic low. Hippety hop, hippety hop, the two fugitives and their two rescuers flitted over the grassy lakeside. A dog barked, from somewhere over the other side, but stopped short as Ms Keighley raised her head sharply. And can that have been a distant wolf howl?

Grace Keighley left them helping Anita sort out and clean the cabin, a snug, if ramshackle room with bunk beds, an old fashioned stove with two cooker rings, and an attached outdoor latrine. Most of the space in the room was taken up by a magnificent old teakwood desk, with little drawers and paper holders, ready and waiting for a new Walt Whitman to celebrate its rustic glory.

"James Mohoney wrote his Pulitzer Prize winning play, The Woodpecker, at this very desk," Grace informed them, before she left. She returned, in less than half an hour, with a duffle bag from which she extracted two complete sets of proper hiking clothes, with multiple pockets filled with spare bootlaces, mending kits, first aid, Swiss Army knives and compasses.

"I'll bring you more stuff either tomorrow afternoon or after midnight," she said, "there's enough canned food here to get you through at least three days and nights. Just stay indoors. If anybody sees you moving about don't worry, you'll just be another two working playwrights. There's one of James' old typewriters in the wardrobe. It's not the one he used for The Woodpecker, but I think he wrote Bring On the Dawn on it."

She paused at the door before leaving again, "I'll have to get word to Allan by personal message," she said, "we can't trust the phone or fax. It'll take me a day or two. Just stay cool. Come on, Anita."

The maid followed her out, throwing them a private glance. Salim threw himself down on the bottom bunk as Battuta swung himself up above.

"You see, Bat, the entire world is not hostile."

"Allahu akbar," said the Traveller.

Salim fell asleep almost immediately. But he was awoken, rudely, by two strong hands shaking his shoulders. A torch shone in his face, then turned to light the scowling face of the scullery maid Anita.

"Come on," she said, "we gotta get moving. We'll wake your friend in a minute."

"I am awake," came the voice of Battuta.

"Well hold on a few minutes while we sort this out."

She pushed the naked Salim back on his bunk and pulled off her pants and t-shirt. "How long since you've fucked?" she asked. But her lips closed down upon his before he could answer.

"Allah is merciful," Battuta commented. Loud grunting noises came from below. The bunk beds creaked, rattled, quaked.

"Oh Holy Mary Mother of God!" croaked Salim.

"You fuck! You fuck! You fuck!" cried Anita. He shot his load, feeling as if it could have the force to reach to the stars. Didn't the Pharaohs aspire to fuck the universe? Or at least the constellation of Orion. He lay back, exhausted.

"O.K.," she said, wiping with her hand, "let's go."

"What's the hurry?" breathed Salim. The sudden intensity had left him flattened.

"You're not gonna trust that bitch, are you? Little Missie C.I.A.? Her Pops was the grandest white motherfucking son of a whore in the entire fucking world. She's exactly the same. She'll sell us out before the day breaks. Get all the stuff. We're goin now."

He had no grounds to question her assessment. "Let's do what she says, Bat," he wheezed.

"Ah, the fickleness of women," breathed Battuta. Anita was already gathering up the clothes, the cans of food, the hiking gear, the spare boots.

"Get a move on, Speedy Gonzales," she prodded Salim with her right sneaker. Shaking his head, pulling on the new pair of pants, he rose up. She lead them out of the cabin, moving furtively along the lake, to the small jetty. A three seater canoe was moored, the moonlit ripples lapping softly at its prow. The fugitives climbed in, Salim facing Anita, Battuta behind her, facing forward. She unhitched the rope and cast off, wielding her paddle with expert ease.

"You there in the back can help," she said. Battuta picked up the second paddle, and dipped it smoothly into the water. "This reminds me of..." he mused, but thought better of it, sensing the hostility of her shoulder blades.

"Row, row, you motherfucking bastards."

The canoe shot forward, towards the silvery moon.

From the New York Times, August 28, 1993:

DISAPPEARANCE OF C.I.A. CHIEF FAILS TO WORRY WHITE HOUSE. By Wilf Kibitzer.

The disappearance Thursday of C.I.A. Operations Director Orville Dullest continues to baffle F.B.I. investigators, but the White House says it's business as usual. Director Dullest, who was due to retire at the end of this year, was known to have suffered from recurrent depressions linked to a recently diagnosed brain tumour. His wife, the English-born Theresa Wilkes-Dullest, daughter of the nonagenarian beverage baron Lord Skelmersdale, raised the alarm early Thursday afternoon when, entering the study where she assumed her husband was working, she found him absent, and a search by the Secret Service guards who patrol the Maryland mansion failed to locate the missing masterspy.

Reports of clues found on the scene, such as signs of a violent disturbance in the adjacent bathroom, dislodged cabinets and even a damaged wall, were dismissed by Secret Service spokesman Alvin Keen as "idle speculation." Presidential spokesman Peter Pipsquikopoulos, questioned by the press corps at the White House Friday briefing, said that Mr Dullest was known to be under severe strain caused by his illness and pressure of work prior to his Christmas retirement, and may well have taken an unscheduled trip to one of the family homes in Maryland or Pennsylvania, and become lost on the way due to his recorded memory lapses. He could not confirm whether the Director would have been carrying the C.I.A. "black box," equivalent to the Presidential briefcase, but repeated the assurance that even if he had, this did not contain any nuclear or other strategic codes. All relevant police forces, said Mr Pipsquikopoulos, had been alerted to be on the lookout for a sixty-five year old, confused old man, dressed either in a casual jacket or possibly a bathroom gown, who might be wandering about the public byways.

Questioned about the wisdom of entrusting the nation's most crucial secrets to "a brain damaged old coot," Mr Pipsquikopoulos replied that such comments were unworthy slurs on all of America's senior citizens and reminded the press corps that President Ronald Reagan had been elected at the age of seventy-one and re-elected at the age of seventy-five. He assured the assembly that Deputy-Director Kevin Spivak was firmly in control of C.I.A. operations and procedures and blamed Congress for delays in confirming the President's first choice for Mr Dullest's New Year replacement, former Senator Jabez Woghammer, adding that ribald comments about the family names of both previous and projected incumbents was detrimental to the proper functioning of legitimate appointments made in the public's best interests. The Presidential Spokesman then left the podium, ignoring a barrage of questions about the competency of the secret service, the state of the Director's bathroom, and reports allegedly about to be published in the National Enquirer that Mr Dullest had been picked up by a spaceship from the galaxy of Alpha Centauri, which had called to take him home to die in peace among his own kind.

*

CAN THERE BE ANY BOUNDS TO HUMAN FOLLY? Frank Ox thought, as he folded the newspaper carefully and burnt it to ashes in the kitchenette sink. Anything that increased the heat in the room was deadly, but long-applied procedures die hard. At least it was not the Sunday edition. Conditions in the Deacon Hotel apartmentlet were just a tad short of infernal. Although the streets outside were still sweltering in 96 degrees Fahrenheit, the supers in the Hotel had actually turned on the steam, responding to the demands of the little old ladies who were the building's longest term clients. The chief super, Eliakim Zaks, was habituated to the squawks of anguish from the uninitiated, drawling out in soothing tones, "it's the old girls, they keep saying it's cold. You know those old bones, whatever the heat, they're freezing up."

Frank Ox had indeed ignored the glances they shot at him, as they sat in the lobby's sunken armchairs like wizened mummies, giving him the evil eye. He felt sure one or two of them recognised him, and seemed to have a vague recollection of one, a shrivelled bag of bones with the right eye of a hammer-head shark, whom he thought he had last seen mounting the scaffold of burning faggots at Salem, in 1649. But clearly she had cheated the hangman, more than once. Now she and her sisters were enjoying their revenge.

"Godfrey Daniel!" haggardly exhaling, the detective returned to the rickety table on which the Cosmic Egg retrieved from Staten Island stood, looking like nothing so much as an innocent and useless souvenir bought for a dollar from some old curiosity shop. Even its glow, which had been so apparent at first, had faded with the squelching heat. Again, for the thousandth time, he passed his fingers over the hieroglyphic markings that adorned its perfect shape. He had copied them out, spent long hours at the Public Library and even consulted an old informant, Elisha Worms, at the Metropolitan Museum of Art, who confirmed to him that to all available knowledge this was not a language hitherto known to science.

Perhaps, he thought, it is one of these alien tongues that U.F.O. fanatics always talk about, the language of Our Visitors From Outer Space. Perhaps the language that recalled Orville Dullest to his "home" amidst the constellations. "O.D. phone home." But Frank Ox had enough knowledge and experience of Inner Space to know that its external equivalent was, at most, a moot speculation, and, to most intents and purposes, a permanent Unknown. Detectives, he mused, do not deal with the Permanently Unknown. Our whole stock in trade is in providing answers. We are humanity's last defense, against infinite gullibility, duplicity, stupidity, mendacity and the entire gamut of deceptions. But to be truth-tellers, we have to traverse the whole journey, and be the Enemy, to tease out and confound his wily tricks and schemes.

Looking at the Egg, he considered once more whether to emulate Faust, again, if he could recall the whole tatterdemalian ritual, the drivelling invocations, the patterns of chalk, the salt and pepper pentagrams. Recalling his last meeting with Mephistopheles: "The world is now a cultured place, my friend, where the devil has evolved accordingly - " *"Auch die Kultur, die alles Welt beleckt, Hat auf den*

Teufel sich estreckt. Das nordische Phantom ist nun nicht mer zu schauen, Wo siehst du Horner, Schweif und Klauen?" - "That nordic phantom can no more be shown - where seest thou his horns and tails and claws?" Exactly.

Oh but it's getting hotter and hotter. Ox clutches the Egg, which is nevertheless cool, if not exactly cold, to the touch. Is this what we used to call The Philosophers' Stone, the holy grail of so many centuries of Alchemy? And if so, should I not go in search of my own employer, Mordecai, and risk sharing my secret for his knowledge and experience of all those aeons of the quest?

But Mordecai had disappeared, before even the first shafts of spring, into the city's deepest subways, which, of all the city's hiding places, were the least attractive in this climate. And I have to confess, I still fear The Alchemist, with his crafty ways and buried hates. Worst of all, he might actually know the Answer, and snatch the fruits of my long arduous endeavours right beneath my blurry eyes.

Methodically, Ox began to prepare the ritual. The chalk, which he always carried in his pockets in case of challenges in snooker halls, drawing on the chipped Deacon tiles the Double Triangle or six pointed star of Solomon, the Tetragram and five pointed Pentagram, the circles enclosed and enclosing from outside. The Kabbalistic words: Yefim, Akim, Eglon. The divine name, inverted, thereby making of Ioah - HooHee. The ineffable word, in Hebrew - Jabamiah - the Word Which Produces All Things. The seventy-second spirit - Mumiah - around the circle, the word for "mummy" or "flaw." He then ransacked the kitchenette cabinet for its few ingredients, the salt, black pepper, paprika, vinegar, and undefined "mixed spices." One would have to be much more precise, and be in possession of the alchemical vas as well as divers other instruments if one wished to even think of producing the Philosopher's Stone, but, on the working assumption that the Philosopher's Stone was present, he placed the Cosmic Egg in the very center of the entire schema and began to scatter the salt and the black pepper methodically along the straight lines.

"Aloo! Ignat! Mahout! Shadwallah!" He danced about, wielding a bent kitchen fork in lieu of the required trident. Stamping his right foot, then his left, within the appropriate circles. The room became hotter and hotter, but he could not tell if this was a physical fact or his body temperature raised by his exertions.

Down below, in the lobby, the old ladies began twitching and stirring in harmony. Their heads wobbled upon stringy necks, their thin shoulder blades quivered, their sticklike joints unfurled with strange clicking sounds and they rose from their chairs, stumbling on chicken legs towards the old fashioned revolving front door. The eldest incumbent, Mrs Clarence Terwilliger the IIIrd, widow of the thrice bankrupt tin baron of Terwilliger-town, Kentucky, who was said to be 98 years of age, spun like a top, two entire revolutions, fetching up under the nose of the startled desk clerk, Ippolyte Alvarez, and screeching at him: "The master is coming! The master is coming!"

"Are you O.K., Mrs Twig?" he asked anxiously. He had long given up trying to pronounce her name.

"Der meister! Der katsengeister!" She spun again, towards the door, in which three of her colleagues were already helplessly entwined. The momentum of her arrival freed the stuck door, which whirled forcefully, catapulting the old ladies out onto the pavement amid the hot swirl of Broadway, corner of 82nd Street, just outside the Bridal Boutique.

"Akhnashtun! Meshobab! Tetragramatton!" Frank Ox stamped his foot heavily upon the center of his ineffable circle, upon the chalked words MELKIAS, EMMANET and MAGISTER. He flung a handful of paprika in the air, which settled about the room like piquant red dust. His nostrils twitching, he doubled up in a sneezing fit.

"Achoo! Achoo!"

The air in the room quivered, or was it just his eyes inflamed and watering? Down below, passers by halted in their languid progress down the sun-splashed street as the six old ladies, spinning like ballerinas, thrust their way into the bridal emporium and emerged with their scrawny hands full of wedding gowns. Shrieking and mauling, they proceeded, in full public view, to tear off their widows' shreds and don the bridal gowns, clutching crushed bouquets and laurels.

"Der meister! Der meister kommt!" A uniformed policeman, who happened to be passing by, lunged hesitatingly forward but was seized by the invigorated harpies, who stripped off his shirt, pants and weaponry, and sprayed his own mace in his eyes. "Aaargh!" he cried, staggering down the pavement. The inflamed women allowed him to escape, turning the tear gas on the gathering crowd, which scattered, with howls of pain and alarm.

Frank Ox had reached his peroration.

"Shodak! Shodak! Shodak! Ianoda Htoabas!" he cried, inverting the Hebrew invocation of holiness. A great whoosh of flame rose from the crisscrossing, circled lines he had drawn on the floor, scouring the shapes and writings into the ceiling in instant, sooty black. Luckily the flames had rushed straight up, bypassing the bed, chairs and divers flammable objets d'hotel and turning instantly to acrid smoke. Frank gasped, choked, rushed to the open window. Thrusting his head out, he saw with blurred eyes the growing commotion below, as police sirens heralded the closing in of New York's finest upon New York's eldest, in a flurry of white gauze and lace.

"What the fuck?"

Shrilly, the room telephone burst into ring. Aark Aark! Aark Aark! He blundered over.

"Hello?" The desk clerk's voice came over the line:

"There's a gentlemen here to see you, Mr Bull." Not the best of aliases, but mine own. "Yeah? Now? Who is he? What's his name?"

A pause for garbled off line dither. "He says he is Alpha and Omega, the beginning and the end. Shall I tell him to come up?"

"Oh shit." Frank looked around, in the smoke, at the smudged floor, the written ceiling, the soot stained furniture, and the Egg, reclining totally unscathed, unmarked and unstained in the center of the room. "What does he look like?"

"Excuse me?" Ippolyte was clearly straining to take in several developments at once, his visitor, the excitation in the lobby, the commotion outside with the convergence of thirteen wailing police cars. "Is a tall dark stranger. I don't know him. Shall I send him away?"

"No. Yes. No. Just wait a minute. Tell him I'll be right down. No..." Hearing the siren squalls. "What the hell. Tell him to come up. Room 1134."

Frank rushed about, waving the smoke towards the window, scuffing the remaining chalk marks with his feet. The floor was red hot to the touch and he cursed and roared as needle pains shot through his heels and toes. "Fuck! Fuck! Fuck!" He picked up the Egg, looking at all the hiding places he had been using in the past few days - the tall thin wardrobe, the rickety kitchen cupboards, the bedside drawer, the crack in the wall over the lavatory, the sluice itself, the usual place. He slammed it into the bedside drawer, beside the Gideon Bible, which, he noticed, had been reduced to a single cinder. "Well, whadayaknow."

His hands were soot black. He rushed to the bathroom mirror. His face was too. He looked like Al Jolson on methadone. He turned on the tap, splashing the cold water on his hands, neck and face, which only spread the dirt. But he could clear his eyes.

"Well fuck you, whoever you are. I'm ready. And I want some answers. No fucking weasel heut deutsch this time!"

He re-entered the room, the scene of his labours. It looked like the aftermath of a mine disaster. He closed the window, preferring to trap in the smoke than to tempt the crowds outside to add the fire brigade to their chaos.

"Never say Frank Ox isn't ready for anything!" He remembered the Philippines, Patagonia, Salem. What haven't we done, where haven't we been. And yet a man's a man for a' that. He heard the footsteps outside. Heavy. Clump clump clump. A pause, and then the bone-knuckle raps on the door.

Knock knock knock.

"Come in."

*
*
*

"The door's locked. Don't you trust me, boy?"

Jaime stood back, casting his eyes around the kitchen cubicle, stepping up to extract the sharpest of the kitchen knives in the wooden block by the oven hob. Holding it behind his back, he advanced to the door, turning the top and bottom bolts. Then he stepped back again, sharply.

The Alchemist glided into Allan Darwish's apartment, nodding shrewdly at the boy, half-dressed in his new doorman's uniform, the tunic open over his smooth brown chest, pants unbelted. Mordecai smiled, casting his eyes about the bookshelves which dominated the compact space, bedroom and kitchenette to the left, open sofabed filling up the living room space straight ahead, study with paper-strewn desk and PC to the right. The books, everywhere.

"The man of erudition often has his weak spots. Sometimes he's nothing but weak spots. You've fallen on good times, my Chaimie."

Jaime edged along the sofabed, still clutching the knife behind his back.

"Are you afraid of me, Chicko?" the Alchemist drew closer to examine the shelves. "Just put that thing away and relax."

"I'm sorry about that time, man," Jaime tried to sound as sincere as possible, "it was just an accident. I didn't mean you no harm."

The Alchemist waved a dismissive hand, "how could you mean any harm, biting the tip of a man's cock off? It grows back, like everything else. Now look at this guy. He thinks if he can read all this stuff, just take it all in, into the bloodstream, he'll understand what's going on. You know what I mean, Chicki-Chuck? Look at this: The Middle East Reader: History, religion and politics. Chapter One: The Dawn of Islam. Mohammad's Message. Empire and Culture. The Abbassids and their System of Government. The Crusades and their Impact. The Ottomans and their Tax Collectors. Now there were some smart bastards for you. Spreading their tentacles everywhere. Maximum results with minimum force. There's a lesson for the world today. But today nobody wants to be a real student. Do you know what I mean? They all think they can find the keys to the kingdom easy, flick a switch and hit the keyboard. Just ask the question and the answer pops out. When I started out, you had to search out the manuscripts. Really search, you know what I mean? Journey to the ends of the earth, through fire and ice, wind, mountain and desert, and then sit down and copy it out by hand. With a feather quill. Copy or memorise. To be a real scholar in those days you had to know by heart at least one thousand manuscripts. And that was just for starters. Suleiman al-Alfassi had seventy-thousand manuscripts committed to memory. Can you understand that? Tomorrow afternoon they'll have as much of that in a chip as small as a flea's egg, but will they know anything? Really know?"

"I doanow man."

"Of course you don't sonny, your very charm is that you are ignorance personified. But here you are, among all this data."

"This is all the Professor's shit. He don't like me touching it."

"Not a Pygmalion, is our Darwish? But I see he's got you enrolled."

Jaime buttoned up the Doorman's jacket with his right hand, still holding the knife with his left. "Got me a job. Ain't much but I get some legitimate money. Buy me time to work things out."

"The only thing that's being worked out is your tired brown ass, boy. Here, you should be reading this." Tossing the boy a paperback, which fell on the sofa, earning a brief sidewise glance. "Travels of Ibn Battuta, A Medieval Traveller. Know your brothers under the skin. We should have been sticking together, shouldn't we. But no, everybody wants to be somebody, these days. Nobody wants to be a part of the whole. Seen any of the boys, Flint, Lincoln, Merenptah?"

"I got nothin to do with all that now, man. I got a proper roof over my head."

"Oh yeah? And your good friend, the Professor, does he know all about you? Does he know where you came from? Does he know how you lived in the asshole? Does he know you were engendered in the colon, as an act of diseased will?"

"He's O.K., man. We have an understanding."

"Sure. You bend over and he shoves it in." Mordecai threw him another book. The Journal of Foreign Affairs. Is a Breakthrough on Palestine Possible? The New China, Fact or Myth. East Timor, Still Invisible. Clinton, the First Virtual President?

"Born not of man or woman, Chaimie. Just a beast from the depths. If I hadn't pulled you out of the mire you would still be turning tricks in never-never-land, and running messages for Lady Pain in and out of the Body. I showed you the everlasting secrets of the universe. How to enter and exit the world of Nefesh and Ruach. But how do you repay your benefactor?"

"Told you I'm sorry man. Moment of panic. I couldn't help myself."

"That is the whole point my boy. What are we without help, without comfort, without a hand to render us assistance?"

He pulled out another book, a hefty hardcover tome, "Majnun: The Madman in Medieval Islamic Society," by Michael W. Dols. "Boy, I could tell this man a thing or two about that. Possession by djinns. Are you listening, Chaimiekins? `According to an *hadith* of the Prophet, these demons are found in every person as blood circulates in his veins.' Absolutely, sonny boy, you can't keep a good djinn down. `According to one legend, the jinn were believed to be the first inhabitants of the earth. God sent down an army of angels against them and forced them under the earth.' Positively, Mr Gallagher, absolutely Mr Shean. And I have been there and I have seen their faces. It takes a long time, to get used to seeing in the pitch dark. The first few days, you just stagger along like a blind man, tearing your legs on the rusted, sharp girders and raking the crumbling tunnel bricks with your claws. The scurrying sound of the rats and larger, more ominous vermin. The pitter patter of feet, and sniggers in the dark. Then the voices, almost, but not quite like animals, calling out to each other in the depths. `Yo- hoooo... Yo-hoooo....' Some of them sound like the rams-horn calls of our brethren to the New Year prayer. Sometimes it's just wind in the hundreds of smaller shafts. And the echo of the trains, rushing through their bore holes. Did you know that deeper, deeper still, the seventeenth level below Broadway-Lafayette, you still hear the trains rushing by? Just the other side of the tunnel wall. So who are these deep-earth travellers, whose boisterous cries you even hear, sometimes. Or are they the desperate shrieks of the condemned? Does hell provide its own transport system? Are there A lines, B lines, or maybe X and Z lines to the real end of the track? Or do they just loop, endlessly, filled with fellow New Yorkers, crammed to the gunnels, with no air-conditioning, like the bad old days, in a stifling summer inferno in the Tombs, just going round and round, in eternity, without stopping at any station? Don't bother to step clearothaclosindoors - they never open! And all the while, the ads for Jonathan Zizmor, Board Certified dermatologist, mock you with their promise of that silk-smooth skin. Now that's what I call true damnation! But, eventually, your ears screen it all out, and your eyes begin to make out all the jagged shapes and contours of the underworld. The red eyes and the clammy touch of your fellow sufferers in the cave. The `mole people.' Down there, of course, there's no divisions, no race, no color, no beauty or ugliness, no rich, all are dirt poor. Or maybe you could have called us dirt-rich. Though there are of course male and female. You can work it out by touch and feel. There is always male and female, you can't escape that. And there are the kids, born and reared in the darkness. The baby djinns, lithe and quick and horrible. Of course, their feet are always hoofs, as it says here in this book. I would read it if I were you, it's all true."

The Alchemist paused, sighed, closed the book and returned it to its place on the shelf, between the sufi "Kashf Al-Mahjub" of Al Hujwiri and Frances Yates' "The Art of Memory." He turned back to Jaime.

"If a man is blind, at least he can feel the sunlight. He can hear the birds sing and the bards strumming on their mandolins. If a man is deaf, he can see beautiful sights. If a man is stricken in all his senses, terrible as that is, his mind may still create wondrous worlds for himself.

But if you are in possession of all your senses, but they have no use, you can go truly mad. I was imprisoned, a long time ago, by the ruler of a city, in another continent. If I say it was Venice, you'll think I'm talking about California, you poor stupid ignorant little boy. If you know even that. But the doge, the prince of the city, was a little annoyed at some advice I'd given him that had not panned out. He put me in this tiny cell, which had no windows, for three and a half years. There was no light. Outside, I could hear the rustle of life, even through the walls, the passing of the jailers, the hint of life without the palace walls, all the tourists who walk those corridors today licking ice cream and whirring their Japanese camcorders. But at least then I could be kept alive by thoughts of revenge. I could conceive the future. Not, I have to say, the stupid pound of flesh demanded by that idiot compatriot of mine, that grocer, but a real revenge, hatched in the depths, nurtured carefully over so many years. It kept me alive. Just as in my incarceration in the subway tunnels, through these filthy, lice-ridden months, I just looked forward to this day."

"I'm not sure I get your drift," said Jaime, edging away again along the sofabed, trying to make his way towards the bedroom and following the walls, all the long way round towards the main door. Still clutching the knife. "I'm just an ordinary guy, tryin to keep out of trouble."

"The Doorman, eh?" The Alchemist followed, closing the distance between them very slowly, "yes, mam, no man, how are you doin today sir? Apartment 12-A? I'll see if the gentleman is in sir? Mr Hammarshoeld, there's a drooling, kak-stained bum who wants to see you? Throw him out? Certainly sir. Do you want your golden arsehole licked clean sir? Tickle your cunt today madam? Oh, those buttons look good enough to eat."

"It's just a job man. Least it ain't shovellin shit. Cleanin out the toilets man, you hear what I'm sayin?"

"I hear so much dreck and drivel it's not worth switching on the brain to take it in," the Alchemist was closing the distance between them, at the bedroom door. Jaime ducked inside the Professor's inner sanctum, the unmade bed, the newspapers and magazines everywhere, and more books, piled around the floor. "I'm tellin you, my friend'll be back any minute."

"Oh no he won't," said the Alchemist, "he was called away to the Adirondacks, where he thinks his bosom buddy the Palestinian piss-drinker is hiding out, together with our brother Battuta. But lo, the birds have flown again, though he won't know that till he gets up to Blue Mountain. But you will be blue enough down here."

"You're bluffin man, you can't know all that."

"We brothers resonate, like so many voodoo drums," purred Mordecai, "it's only you who's too fuck dumb to hear it all. Or maybe you heard, and heard me too, but waited for me, because you knew the time of reckoning was due. For each man kills the thing he loves. Oscar Wilde, the Ballad of Reading Jail."

"I'm warnin you man, just don't come any closer." Jaime held the knife out, blade ready. "I don't wanna hurt you man, I told you."

"Silly boy. You can't hurt the Controller. Or rather, yes, you can hurt your brother and keeper most egregiously, but only in the soul, for, of course, the Body is not here. We are merely illusion made flesh. Did I not show you all the diagrams and formulae? The putrefactio and the nigredo? The coming together of the prime elements? The Body is still toiling up the road, Chaimie, still dragging his feet, step after step, holding out his paper cup. Spare a quarter for a man who's down on his luck? You look like a goodhearted soul to me man. Thank you kindly madam. Have a nice day. Fuck."

The youth was up against the window now, backing up over an immense pile of New York Times, Washington Posts, Village Voices, Financial Times and Le Mondes. He tripped but caught his balance, catching the bedroom blind, which whipped up, curling with a tight snap around its upper rod. The hazy hot vista of Riverside Drive, the Hudson Parkway, the lazy waters of the river, and the urban clumps of New Jersey beyond.

"Stay where you are man. I swear to God, I'll stick you man. I don't wanna do it, but you keep away from me."

"The child is shy. Of his progenitor! But I always knew that it would come to this. It always does. From the beginning. And Cain slew Abel. But Abel should have got the drop on him and slain Cain. You have to get up early in the morning if you're going to be able to get to bed at night. Even the closest to you can't be trusted. The microcosm and the macrcosm are both full of bile. Enemies everywhere. But I gave you my best shot. Like the others. But now you've all turned bad it's up to me to put things right. Restore some order. Get rid of the dead wood. Know what I mean man? We can't have people burning down bookstores, alerting the F.B.I., blurting it all out to the C.I.A. and causing all sorts of ructions. Biting off men's cocks. You understand me boy? I was there before you and I'll be there after you. Just put the knife down and we can make an end of this episode in love, instead of hate."

"Fuck you, man! I'll cut your cock and balls off completely this time. Don't fuck with me!"

"These verbal contradictions. What a horror."

The Alchemist lunged forward. Jaime thrust the knife in an intense stabbing move. But the Alchemist had stepped aside, easily, treading down the mound of newsprint, grabbing the youth's arm and twisting. The bones in the arm snapped. The boy gave out a terrible cry. The knife dropped.

"Love me and the world is mine..." crooned the Alchemist. He pushed Jaime down, onto the bed, dropping on him, knee thrust in his back. His powerful forearm closed round the boy's neck, pulling up.

"They used to execute criminals like this once, in Java," he said softly, almost without exertion. "There was a blacksmith's strike, a sudden shortage of swords. Or was it because the Sultan was a kind old soul, who was sick of the sight and even thought of blood? He had seen so many wars, and battlefields, and legions of corpses, hacked and mangled and dismembered. I hear they use the `humane' injection in quite a number of the federal states now. Sorry I don't have my needles with me." He paused, as the youth's back was pulled into an unbearable and totally unnatural arc. "Sorry I can't allow any last words. How about the thought: Father, forgive me, for I knew not what I did?"

The youth let out a terrible wheeze, a last, choking protest of the throat. Then his neck snapped, like a wooden stick breaking. His bulging eyes looked forward, at the off-white wall.

The Alchemist laid the twisted corpse down, gently, wiping the froth flecked mouth with the sheet.

"No more terrible dreams for you boy. Lucky bastard." He moved off the bed, around the newspile, looking back once from the bedroom door. Shaking his head in sorrow.

"What a fucking waste."

Looking around the flat, the books, the files, the desktop.

"Just ask the questions and you'll get the answers, eh?" Shaking his head, opening and stepping out the front door. Closing it behind him and punching for the elevator. It stopped and a flustered middle-aged man in t-shirt and shorts, with tufts of sweaty black hair all over his calves, arms and neck, fumbling with a small holdall, waited impatiently for him to step in.

"Ground floor?"

The Alchemist nodded. The elevator descended, slowly, to the street.

From the New York Times, August 30, 1993:

SATANIC RITES SUSPECTED IN HOTEL CORPSE MYSTERY.

Police have so far not been able to identify the remains of a man found dismembered in the Deacon Hotel in Upper Westside Manhattan on Wednesday, in what promises to become one of New York City's most gruesome crimes this year. The man was found by hotel cleaners in the morning, but police forensic experts have established that the time of death was between six o'clock the previous evening and midnight. Identification and laboratory testing are made difficult by the fact that the murdered man's head has not been found. The occupant of the room, who checked in three days before as a Mr "Bull," was not known to the hotel staff, and police are sifting through thousands of missing persons' files to attempt to find a tentative match.

The body was found in circumstances which Detective Harold Opatoshu, of the 25th Precinct's homicide squad, described yesterday as "bizarre." The floor of the room had been marked with various occult circles and triangles, which were matched by similar symbols literally burned into the hotel ceiling. Most items of furniture in the room were either burnt or singed, but no hotel fire had been reported. It has been speculated that an unexplained disturbance at six-thirty p.m. the previous day, which involved a number of the elderly female long term tenants, may have deflected attention from events in the eleventh floor room, though police refused to speculate on any possible connection between these disparate events.

At ten thirty a.m, hotel cleaner Mrs Grace Parker unlocked the door of room 1134 at the Deacon Hotel in order to conduct a routine change of bathlinen. What she saw caused her to scream loudly and alert the other members of the hotel staff. She told our reporter: "It wasn't just what I saw. It was the smell. It was like all the sewers in the City had bust. It was awful." Mrs Parker added: "It was the smell of evil. The Devil himself must have been in that room."

Other hotel staff who entered to view the horror also commented on the acrid odour, but strangely, no one in the rooms adjacent to room 1134 had heard or smelled anything unusual that night, although both adjoining guests did not return until the small hours of the morning. The acrid smell had evaporated, staff said, by the time the police arrived, through opened windows. Police only reported the strong odour of burnt fabric, paint and plaster. As to the Devil, he is reputed to be a long term resident of the City, and long past the time when he might easily be recognised in the streets...

An "Occult Specialist" invited by police to examine the markings in the room told the Times: "This definitely was a Satanic ritual. The victim appears to have been seized by a ferocious and superhuman power which literally tore him limb from limb. The disappearance of the head might indicate some connection with Caribbean `santeria' rituals, though you would expect to see some trace of sacrificed animals, such as chickens, weasels or small cats. None of these were on the scene. The person who did this, if he is a person, is an extremely dangerous individual who may well strike again."

The most mysterious element, according to police forensic specialist Fred Neuberger, is the complete absence of any materials which might have been used to start the fire in the room, and the fact that it did not spread to any other rooms or corridors of the hotel. The door to the room was almost untouched by the fire, and was reportedly locked from within. It is, all in all, as terrifying a mystery as New York City has seen since "Son of Sam."

Sun of Man.

Dear Diary:

Sometimes I feel that I am resurfacing from the deepest trench under the sea. Encased in one of those metal spheres, a bathyscaphe – is that what it's called? – I rise, very, very slowly out of the ooze, where I have seen nothing, and where I am absolutely aware of the pressure, hundreds of pounds to the square inch, that could crush me from outside.

Strange fish live down there, as National Geographic Magazine never fails to remind us. Lying in tattered piles in so many waiting rooms, the wonders of the world stare at you from their beautifully colored plates: Great scaly things with hammer-like snouts, serpents twining round gold luminous algae, octopii that could have sunk the Nautilus, diving off abyssal cliffs. Down down down.

But as I surface, clear water all about me, bubbles, the sudden gasp of air, the searing heat, chased off by the whirring fan Karim has placed at the foot of my bed. Blowing a breeze into my face. My son, sitting beside the bed, looking up solicitously from the Koran.

"Don't you read anything else?" I tried asking him once, not just to needle, but I had to believe he was for real. "The house is full of books. Thirty years of the Dexter-Darwish collection. Millions of words on the Middle East. We must have about a hundred books on early Islam."

"This is The Book that counts." Oh boy. A dozen years ago who would have expected it. The little rapscallion running around the house, pulling the new puppy's ears. Now they both tower over me. The Dog with his melancholy giant panting, the Boy with Allah's word. Maybe when I'm asleep, or drugged, or down there in the bathyscaphe, he sneaks off and picks up a paperback from the pile my mother keeps for when she's around. Robert Ludlum, Tom Clancy, Sydney Sheldon, all the real garbage. Or, a mother prays, let it be Toni Morrison, or Alice Walker, or James Baldwin. No chance.

"I seek of you no recompense, my people... for only God can reward me..." Sura 11:29, the tale of Noah, who was told to build an ark, for all of Mankind had sinned and was condemned. But Noah's own son would not believe him, and stayed behind, as the ark departed. Still, Noah told God: *"You are the most just of judges."* But God told Noah: *"He was no kinsman of yours, he acted unjustly."* So I suppose it is ever more touching of my son to sit beside his sinful mother, waiting for her to emerge from the depths.

When the cancer is in the blood, it saps everything. No part of the body is spared. Everything can be overwhelmed at once. And the thin medical lifeline, pulling you up, up, up.

If only the Muslims had taught him how to cook. But that is the woman's task, obviously. In good time there will be an obedient Sister, who will man the oven and prepare her loins. For the moment it's takeaway shwarma from the Lebanese down on Broadway. My faithful and cheerful Jameel. Circling round Karim warily as he comes in, like a dog who's once been bitten, nevertheless wagging his tail. Another one of Allan's conquests? What I don't want to know I don't ask.

Jameel is always asking about Salim, but I can give him no answers. The whole thing has escalated beyond the absurd, with SWAT teams combing the hills and valleys of six states for the escaped fugitives. Frances has tried to spare me her strange speculations about Battuta and the Barnes & Noble arsonist, Arnold Flint, but Benjamin, who is as yakkety as any market stall mama, gave me the whole story. Reigniting my curiosity about Mo Smith. Where has he got to now?

Down in my depths, I can believe anything possible. Time slows to a crawl, or stops altogether. I feel in touch with some strange tactile field which seems to connect all things. I assumed these are the drugs talking. Sometimes only medical science anchors me to reality. But I remember all the strange, convoluted, mad stories my patients told me over the years, and my feeble attempts to coax them back to "reality." Benjamin once told me a quote from the Spanish film-maker Luis Bunuel, talking about religion: I don't need the hypothesis of God if I accept the reality of the imagination. I suppose this has been my bread and butter. But my delusions, I know, are chemical, like Timothy Leary's. All my molecules being rearranged.

Two days later:

(Or at least I think it's two days.)

Talk about rearrangement of molecules. Cataclysm. Benjamin calls at the door, unannounced, unusual in itself, as he's usually careful to alert Karim of the Hebrew invasion thereof. I'm sitting in the front hall, doing my medical journals. Determined to get back into the swing.

The gist: Allan left two days ago, having had some news of Salim in person from Grace Keighley, of Blue Mountain. She wouldn't use the phone, for obvious reasons. This morning, at ten, the Haitian cleaning lady, Fanny, came to do his weekly cleanup. She found Allan's friend, Jaime, dead in the bedroom. Apparently his neck had been broken. All hell breaks loose. Police, F.B.I., you name it. Search parties out for Allan now. Calls to Blue Mountain. Benjamin tells me he's on his way back. He looks at me as if he thinks this news will kill me on the spot. But I live here. I've always been afraid that one of Allan's little friends will bring an unwanted cargo with him. That flash of relief that it wasn't Allan lying broken necked on his bed. Worked the phones - amazing how a crisis energises - raising an old friend in the N.Y.P.D. with contacts in the right places. Turns out there is a witness, a neighbour, who almost certainly saw the murderer getting in the lift from the 9th floor, at about the right time. A heavy-set, bearded man dressed oddly, in a raincoat, on a day of 95 degrees sunshine. Not very inconspicuous. In any case, only an immensely strong individual could have killed a vigorous young man in that way. My contact said they obviously knew each other, as the door had not been forced, and most of the apartment was untouched.

But there are bound to be endless questions, and I can't predict Allan's reactions. The Arab-American combination. The surface cool, the inner rage. I can't write about this any more, tonight. Sent Benjamin away. Karim silent. But what's bottled up inside. Stop now.

Friday:

I know it's Friday because Karim is off to the mosque, to hear whatever hellfire sermon the local chapter has in store about America and its evils. Boy, don't we know about these. My mother came but went out of her way to avoid discussing The Event. Having to swallow the whole story with me and Allan, and Karim, it's been her cross forever, but she's never been able to take the sexual issue. Deep deep denial. A frightful morning.

Allan doesn't call till the evening. Seven o'clock. Just released from questioning. They don't care about Jaime, he said, all they want to know about is Salim. But that's no secret any more. He and the other man turned up at Blue Mountain and then left, with one of the staff, a girl who worked in the kitchen. Canoed off down the Marion River, towards the other lakes. It's only a matter of time. I told him to come and see me immediately. He gave me the usual: You don't want to know.

The roster of things I don't want to know seems to grow by the minute. I dredge out a promise from him that he'll show up in the morning. He's obsessed about burying Jaime. No trace of next of kin, the boy never wanted to talk about that, he's not going to just drop him in the pauper's ground. Old Potter's Field.

The whole thing nags me. Overwhelming madness. Going back to my interrupted notes and treatise on Mo Smith. The multiple personas. Ibn Battuta. Merenptah. Arnold Flint. Jaime. Again, coincidences.

It must be the chemicals. But at least it gives me a proper goal. Locate the man again. The needle in the haystack. After all, the city isn't all that big, when you've always lived in it. If he's still in Mahattan. And by the rate he was ploughing the streets, up from the Bowery, he should be practically next door by now.

Working the phones again. Homeless shelters. Welfare offices. Human resources. The grapevine. The street cabals. The homeless, even in their despair, are a community. Nobody is completely invisible. Only the dead can vanish, into their own sombre limbo. Which I shall find out about in due course. I have put out the word. Doctor Caroline Dexter seeks Mohammad Ndabaninghi Smith. Or whatever your name is this week. I know you're out there. And I know how to snare him. I told everyone: Tell him Lilith wants to speak to him.

He'll come to me, I know he will.

*

*

*

IT CAN'T GO ON. IT GOES ON...

...the August heat, a scalding blanket. Above, below, it's all the same. Inside the 86th Street subway, the citizens' sweat drips on the platforms. Bring on those air-conditioned carriages! A black man with a plastic bag begins singing the old Beatle tune again: Yesterday, all my troubles seemed so far away. A pretty good voice but no prospects. On the street, the pamphleteers are out. Blimpie Buck - $1.00 off any sandwich, salad or blimpie lite. Buy one, get one free! Grand opening, coffee and donut, just 99 cents with this flyer. Roy Rogers, $2.49 2 pc fried chicken with purchase of soda at regular price. Ask our manager about discounts on large orders, corporate accounts. Pathmark shop smart, Ajax dish detergent, 99c, Lucky mint toothpaste, 99c, Lavoris Mouthwash, 99c, Wizard air fresheners, Nail polish remover, Lady's choice antiperspirant, all under one dollar! Afrin nasal spray $3.89, Aleve pain reliever/fever reducer $3.99, baby fresh ultra guard $3.49, Kellog's cracklin oat bran $2.39, Progresso soups, 89c, Rice-a-roni 69c, Zing liquid detergent $1.99. Sister Debra, spiritual reader and advisor tarot cards palm reading Sister Debra can help you in all problems of life such as love marriage business health answers all questions solves all problems if you are seeking a surefire woman to do for you the things that are needed or wish to gain financial aid or peace love and prosperity in the home you need to see this woman of God today don't go through life miserable and in sorrow when you can be happy and content guaranteed results in 24 hours one visit is all you need to remove all evil influences... Witchcraft the old religion supply store - "if there's a witch, there's a way!" - the God and Goddess are alive open 7 days 10 am 11 pm, brass mortar and pestle $13.00, ritual knives $13.00, fresh herbs, candles, pullouts all kinds of roots blended incense astrological charts and readings $40.00, we buy used books and oddities silver jewelry ritual swords crystal balls t-shirts, Baphomet, pentagrams tarot cards scourges witch bottles...

There's so much to do in the City That Never Sleeps, art, bookshops (those that have not yet been burned down), windowshopping, museums, pre-natal pizza, female boxing, gambling, S & M parlours, squash courts, boat trips round the island, raquet clubs, cosmetic surgery, movies, video rental, cds and cassettes, old vinyl, personal training, body scrub and waxing, encasement in latex, star watching at ellen's, lesbian and gay classes, horse-riding in the park, flea-marketing, roller-blading, skating, jogging, check-cashing, beauty salons, eating chinese, italian, sicilian, tuscan, french, armenian, afghani, indo-pakistani, burmese, malaysian, thai, singapori, tibeti, kosher, vegetari, vegani, soul-food, west-african, american, russian, german, polish, goulash, sour-mash, fucking: new sex secrets from China that really work, the most complete package for small penis and erection problems ever offered, Fok Mo Off super pump-it, In Go Tok Chinese sex energy pills perfect for either man or woman gives you boundless sexual energy any time of the day or night, Wac Ma Coc Chinese stay hard pills, Sip Cow Yat Chinese sex hypnosis pills puts your partner under your domination, eager to perform any act you wish, artifical vagina and rectum money back guarantee if for any reason you are not completely satisfied in any manner shape or form all you have to do is return this refund coupon to us with the unused portion of your merchandise for a full refund fill in this rush order form now...

MONEY BACK GUARANTEE!
Please rush me by return of mail the following certified items:
Eternal Life Forevermore Abiding.
Freedom From Fear, Pain, Oppression, Tyranny, Backache, Muscular Spasms, Heartburn, Impetigo, Arthritis, Skinrash, Piles, Athlete's Foot, Moral and Actual Blindness, Unemployment, Cracked Nails, Coprophilia and all Carnal Desires.
100 Tablets Herbal Laxative.
The Wisdom of Solomon (as Interpreted by His Highness the Guru Maharish Shred Rajnee).
Instant Success in Every Possible Endeavour, Financial, Domestic, Personal, Emotional.
Unlimited Sexual Potency.
100 Do-It-Yourself Tattoos.
Do-It-Yourself Cosmetic Surgery Kit.
Joy Everlasting. Heavenly Comfort. Complete Serenity. Total Happiness. Wrinkle Prevention Amniotic Orgone Gel. Holistic Health Mental and Physical. Lightning Reflexes. Perfect Prognosticative Proficiency. The Ability To See Round Corners and Be Prepared for Anything. The Absolute Right to Sit by the Right Hand of God and Perceive the Pitiful Follies and Foibles of

Mankind, Male and Female, Young or Old.
Please include free shipping and handling. Enclosed is my cheque/money order/promissory note/i.o.u. for 25 cents U.S.. I am aware that should I not be totally satisfied I may within 30 days of purchase return the goods and receive full restitution of my investment forthwith.

Above 86th Street, the baking swathes of Upper Westside beckon to the sweaty unwashed: Paper cup land triumphant! Up by the Hollywood Cafe, the Broadway Deli and Grocery, Belle's Gourmet Deli - Hot and Crusty Fresh Bread Coming Out of the Oven Now! Manna! Manna! But not for us. Over 88th to the Marine Midland Bank and Red Apple and Leroy's Pharmacy and Ray's Pizza, sweat dripping off hairy bodies onto the Ziti Parmigiana, dribbling through the Hawaiian Slices, Tangy Tomato & Cheese, Baked Macaroni... aaaahhhhhhh!!!! and over 89th to ogle at Dock's Oyster Bar, only for the elite, the cog-no-scenti, next door to Murray's Sturgeon Shop, the Food Emporium, Your Caviar Today...

Oho say can you see, in the dawn's early light... But with the sun right up there in the sweltering sky... the Argo restaurant Chops Steaks Seafood, Barzini's Special Foods... Twin Donut, the Keyfood store - Mrs Adler's Gefilte Fish $1.79, 9 Lives Cat Food 4 for $1 now that's more like it. The emporium of choice. We find these truths to be self evident. Pintchik Paints and Le Sportif. Happy Burger Best Home made Shawarma $3.49, Baklava, Kataif. By the doorway of Lachter's Housewares a brother lies inside a mailbag, his arms wrapped round his knees which are curled up to his nose. Blissfully snoring away. It's amazing what people will find to do with their leisure hours.

Coming up to the Uptown nexus of 93rd to 96th Street, the 96th Street Station, all change for the 2 and 3. Lenox Terminal and 148th Street, or all the way thru the Bronx, 241st Street, in unimaginable climes... A well-wisher presses a pamphelt into his hand: Save Lives! Keep This Handy! AIDS Threatens Us All, Find Out or Die! AIDS is transmitted: A) Sexually: by male/female intercourse (use condoms); by anal intercourse or sodomy (use condoms); by oral sex or 69 if skin is broken; B) Non-sexually: by sharing hypodermic needles (use disposable ones); by blood transfusion (solution: medical control); by pregnancy if the mother is a carrier (use contraceptives). AIDS IS NOT

TRANSMITTED by: shaking hands, sharing toilets, or family life. PROTECT YOURSELF AND OTHERS: avoid contact with secretions (blood, mucus, semen).

YOUR SEX LIFE: A) Nudity: The normal human body is beautiful, and contemplating your own body and that of others should be ordinary too. Under the right circumstances (swimming etc) collective nudity should be normal. Erotic arousal by nudity in certain situations is also normal and healthy, as is the sexual instinct that causes it. It has bad results only when accompanied by feelings of guilt or when lacking respect for others.

B) Love and Falling in Love: The strength of passion, like drunkenness or drugs, blinds the lover, who tends to see more what he wants than what the other person is and wants. So falling in love can consist more in self- esteem than esteem for the other's well-being. It is crazy to use this blind feeling to choose your mate, have children and so on, because you're only setting yourself up for a highly destructive letdown within a few months or years. But falling into a carefully measured dose of love can be highly beneficial <u>after</u> making your well-thought-out choice. "Before marrying, keep your eyes open; afterwards, keep them shut" (Benjamin Franklin).

No kites are flying in the sky.

*

GIVE ME A BREAK! The problem of being a ghost in the City in midsummer, thought Frank Ox, is that one's ectoplasm can't stop melting. Unedifyingly merging with the molten chewing gum speckling the pavements like a million and one dalmatian spots. As the melting gum adheres to shuffling shoes my ectoplasm is picked up with it, to be scraped off on curbs and manhole covers. The one advantage of all this is that one can no longer feel pain. Not, at any rate, the physical kind. The mental anguish continues unabated. Now, more than ever, when I can flit about, whether at will, or buffeted by exhaled air and exhaust fumes, up and down, east and west, north and south, to the topmost skyscraper penthouses and into the bowels of the earth, skittering along the rusty rails of the abandoned subway sidings, dipping down down

down where even rats fear to tread. The subterranean oceans. Dante's realm. Not that I have not died before. This has happened to me twice, both violently, the first when I was burnt alive after the inhabitants of Chleppa, in Bohemia, alleged they had caught me trafficking with the devil in the Taverna Ludovicem, and the second when crazed latent homosexual German Freikorp officers beat me to death with their rifle butts during the Berlin uprising of 1919.

Death, and resurrection, tend to leave serious scars upon the psyche which are not easily healed. One moment you feel you're on the brink of the everlasting balm and restfulness, the next you're back in the melee, dodging spit, sweat and dog do. But for the moment, in between this and that, sludge and spirit, I can look at things from a multitude of angles, from every face of the host. Now for a brief while I can see everything, and be in several places at once. Is it a bird? Is it a plane? No, it's Superplasman Frank Ox, streaking across the hazy towers. Gazing down like King Kong before the aircraft came upon the screaming city. Peeking into top floor windows, at the squelch of naked, urgent bodies. The surreptitious secrets of solitude, self flagellation, sloth, wife and husband battering, the acting out of impossible dreams. Shunning the hi-decibel sounds of youthful exuberance, diving through impenetrable sealed doors and bank boardrooms, listening in on the plots and cabals of the wealthy and watching the dance of numbers on the edge of a byte. The virtual cosmos, where everything is interconnected, and invisible bugs fell cities and plains far away. A cough, and seven hundred thousand Hyderabadi farmers choke, stagger to their knees in the dust. A fart, and ten million Russians take to the streets, yelling about their increased bread prices. When the heart falters, the entire body stumbles, eyes watering, hands flailing to keep the balance.

After the Alchemist, Mordecai Mephistopheles, killed me, I watched him, from my departing spirit's perch, on the ceiling, gruesomely dismembering my body with his serrated kitchen knife and piling the pieces about the charbroiled room. Then, gathering up the cosmic egg into the folds of his loose black coat, he departed, taking the emergency exit, down the ten flights of stairs into the street, pressing past the milling cops and windmilling old ladies stumbling in their newly stolen bridal gear. Rushing into the downtown 86th Street station, breathing heavily, his bearded chin dug into chest as his arms hold the egg like a mutant pregnancy upon his heaving stomach. Straphanging in the crowded Number 9 all the way down to Time Square, where I lost him, temporarily, in the crowds rushing to and fro in the stifling maze of corridors. Down in the dark, where the rats are gnawed by those who have never seen the light of day. But I can soar, soar over the entire city like a commuter rising from La Guardia, almost touching the spires and winging northwest over the rivers, lakes and mountains, up over Monticello and Liberty, over the Catskills and the Susquehana, Chenango and Madison Counties, over Oneida Lake and the Black River, opening out onto Lake Ontario, where, an infinite dot upon the calm azure waters, scuds the tiny boat carrying Salim, Ibn Battuta and the scullery-maid Anita, impelling them with vigorous strokes of her oar towards the invisible border, the cloudless blue sky merging with the lake, so that, like latterday Baron Munchausens, they may as well be floating up upon the atmosphere, towards the moon. Only the night-time will tell. Meanwhile, back in the City, the other part of my ectoplasm veers further down Broadway, past Union Square, over Canal Street towards the offices of the New York Department of Immigration and Naturalisation where, amidst a line stretching two and a half times around the forbidding cracked grey building, the ex-Pharaoh Merenptah, alias Neptune Phocopoulos (Ada preferred a Greek to an Arabian cognomen) stands patiently, shifting his feet, his arm draped over Ada's shoulders as she looks adoringly into his beaked, long suffering face, among the human driftwood and flotsam fetched up upon the Promised Land's shores, the rainbow hopeful, silently moving their lips in rehearsal of the pledge of allegiance, clutching their sheaves of documentation, real or false, proofs of identity, good will and unblemished souls.

She: "I think the line's moving, honey."

He: "I have all the time in the world."

Oblivious as they are to the husky, hoarse voice calling out from the clammy depths:

"Merenptah! Arnold Flint! Battuta! Link! Jaime! Where are you??"

Echoes stifled by the abdominal ring and the ribcage, the folds of flesh not yet fully melted -

"There's nobody here but us now, and the two women. Ann and Beatrice. Unless there are more following, where you come from."

"The sooner I get out of here the better. I am a person of some consequence, I must tell you. My disappearance won't go unnoticed for long."

"I'm glad to hear that. Even I get lonely, with this sort of company. Did you bring any Hershey bars with you?"

"I did not."

"That's a pity. Ann adores them. It might wake her up. She's been dormant all through the summer, you know. If only the snoring weren't so loud. Which leaves us with Beatrice. I should warn you about her. Unless she is your cup of tea."

"I know all about you people. Jesse the Essene. The pimp Jaime. The Pharaoh, the old Traveller, Flint, the Alchemist. I've been studying you for some time. My name is Orville Dullest. Director General of the C.I.A. The Central Intelligence Agency."

"I have never heard of it, I'm afraid. The only central intelligence is in the Godhead. The only true Agent is the Teacher. The Master of the Mysteries. Are you He?"

"Some people have called me that. But I'm no teacher. I've barely even begun to learn."

"Come along then Orville Dullest. Just follow me."

Slippering and sliding along the viscera. The intercostal arteries. Where are we going? After a lifetime of service, fighting for my country, lying, cheating, manipulating, making sure we don't come second, let alone last, the world carries on, regardless, while I slip into oblivion. The tumour in my head. The cosmic egg, hatching in my brain, to produce, what? One last, dramatic hallucination, slithering and sliding down the sliproads of the mind. Hey Mister Tambourine Man, just stop that damn drumming for one minute!

Kaboom! Kaboom! Are we approaching the heart, like those miniaturised voyagers in that Hollywood movie, what was it, she of the bounteous bosom - Raquel Welch... Down in the Inferno, is this what preys on the mind?

Midway this way of life we're bound upon,
I woke to find myself in a dark wood,
Where the right road was wholly lost or gone...

ABANDON HOPE, ALL YE WHO ENTER HERE!

Dante had his Beatrice, so am I to have mine? We have nothing to fear but fear itself. But we have so many things to be afraid of. Old age, poverty, disgrace, sickness, sudden death or worse, mutilation, loss of loved ones, the Big C. The Buddhists may claim it's all illusion, but look at them in a dogfight. We are such a poor species. The bigger picture. And all our follies back at home. Kennedy, Nixon, Carter, Reagan, Bush, Clinton. Imagine Truman deciding about the atom bomb. Like giving your five year old child your bank books. Woe is us.

When the chips are down, you have to accept the place you're put in. The good place, or the bad. There is not only me, but all the mystery that surrounds me. Except for Mo Smith, who surrounds himself. And the ectoplasmic detective, who is everywhere. As long as one is not alone.

That is the deepest, darkest place of all,
And farthest from high Heaven's all-moving gyre;
I know the way; take heart - no ill shall fall.

There is always a way out, if only you can learn to find it. Wherever you are, somebody knows the answer. The point is to figure who it is.

"If the others have escaped, why have you remained here?" I asked the ragged figure in front of me. His thin shoulders shrugged.

"I have to stay until Ann wakes up. You wouldn't understand."

"Loyalty. I understand that."

"Necessity. What has to be. You understand nothing."

In the kingdom of the blind, the one-eyed man is king. But what about the blind, among the one-eyed? Racking my brains to reconstruct the file. The need to make the right connection. Then Comprehend, Cajole, Control. The four "C"s of counter-intelligence. And then the question of ultimate goals...

Squeezing on, through a contracting, expanding passageway, a blast of fetid air from a sideshaft. The glimpse of a supine, mountainous shape amid a tangle of torn quilts and soaked blankets. A fleshy face, with a bulbous nose and blubbery lips, a cascade of matted black hair. The buzzsaw exhalation and inhalation. Jesse tugs me by the hand.

"Come on now, we don't want to keep Beatrice waiting."

Why not? What on earth can be urgent here? Except to exit - *On every side, the vast and reeking mire, Surrounds this city of the woe-begot, Where now's no entering, save with wrath and ire...* A pounding sound, increasing and approaching. Not, as I'd thought, the heart, but a familiar synthetic sound, the deep repetitive beat of what my grandchildren call I think "techno" or "rave", I could never tell them apart. The tawdry flashing lights, shimmering about something which reminded me of nothing so much as Hansel and Gretel's gingerbread house. Except that it was not gingerbread, but seemed to be a kind of fold in the abdominal lining, into which my non-Virgilian guide led me, thrusting aside a bamboo curtain, under a garish red light. The beat pounding into my skull.

"Shut it off, for God's sake!"

The sound cut out, leaving the dull hum as of a generator, a low incessant buzz. "Come in and sit down." The voice behind a low receptionist's counter beckoned me forth. The woman sitting behind it on a wicker chair was certainly dressed for the part. A red rubber corset-like thing rose between her thighs to wrap about her somewhat protruding torso and cantilever her bared breasts, which might otherwise have succumbed to gravity, even in this peritoneal sac. The woman encased in this constrictive membrane might have been aged between thirty-something and fifty, her forearms massive and muscular almost in the Popeye mold, much the kind of build that certain army generals manifest when they have gone to seed. It was difficult to ascertain the tincture of her skin in the red light, but her face with its veritable beak of a nose and flashing black eyes gave her a definitely Mediterranean look. Her hair was a mane of velvet black curls, but that may have been a wig. She was holding across her lap a heavy, multi-thonged whip. Above the reception desk a row of hotel pigeonholes was barren, with a heavy key hanging from every empty box. Very much the Madame of an old-fashioned Turkish brothel.

"Well, it's about time," she said to Jesse, who had stood aside to let me pass into the narrow lobby. "Business has been slack this summer. What sort of pain is your pleasure, Mister?"

"I'm too old for pain to be pleasure, ma'm," I told her. "All I would really like is for the headaches to stop."

"Don't I know you from somewhere?" she said. She did look alarmingly like a lady whose services I had engaged, as a honeytrap, in Istanbul, when I was just starting out in the trade. But this was fifty two years ago, and even miracles do not age that slow.

"I doubt it," I said. "But I wouldn't mind lying down for a while. If you can do me the courtesy. I've had a really difficult day."

"Sure, baby," she said, "just come in to my parlour. Jesse, buzz off. The gentleman and I have business."

"I'll call in later," he said, ducking out through the bamboo curtain. The Madame opened a flap beside the desk. "In here." I passed through into an even dimmer room, this one lit by strobing purple. It was a cell-like chamber, with walls lined with instruments of infliction, whips, chains, canes, paddles, hoods, barbs, crossbars and cuffs. I reeled, in a sudden nausea brought on by the strobing and the fetid air. She caught me as I fell, hefting me up upon her powerful forearms, and carrying me, despite her diminutive stature - she couldn't have been more than five feet five - into an adjoining room. This was a smaller cell, with brick-like walls and one low, padded couch, on which she laid me down. She opened a concealed cabinet in the wall and poured out a glassful from a decanter of red wine.

"That was like the vestibule to hell," I croaked, after I'd downed the drink. It was good Burgundy.

"A good title," she said. "I should rename the place. Get some new flyers printed. 'Cept now I don't have Jaime any more. Can't reach the clients."

She switched on a soft, yellow-lit side-lamp. Drew up a rocking chair and sat, swaying. "Thinking of changing my meter. Getting out of all this sorry business. Like to have a farm somewhere. Get myself some chickens, dogs, mink maybe, maybe rabbits, even cattle. And a husband with some animal sense. You ever had a farm?"

"I own a ranch, in Vermont," I wheezed, accepting a fill-up. "Breeding horses. Got some good Saudi Arabs. Racetrack business. But too little time to enjoy it." I gulped the wine down. "I run the Central Intelligence Agency. Protecting the Free World. Or so we thought. Don't know what it means, nowadays. After the Soviets bellied up. Just janitor work now. Castro, Saddam, drug wars. Not the America we loved."

"Everyone should do the thing they love," she said, pouring herself a tall portion. Hesitating. "Yes, everybody."

"Is this what you wanted to do? What were you before?"

"Before? I don't remember. We don't have proper memories, in here. Ann, you know, she keeps it all."

"Ann Hedonia? The sleeping woman?"

"The Sleeping Ugly. She keeps it all. There used to be letters, documents, forms. But they got washed away. Then everybody left. Even Mordecai. That Jew fuck. The controller. Are you a Jew fuck?"

"I'm an Episcopalian. Virginia born and bred."

"We could do with some blue blood in here. It's always been scum. Jews and niggers."

"That's New York City for you."

"I could really go for a man like you. Top material. Somebody not eaten with guilt. Everybody who comes here wants to be punished. You want to be punished, Mister?"

"Not if I can help it."

She leaned over me. "We can make good music together. Ever hear two whips singing the same tune? We could clean up. Get that bastard Jesse to get out there and rustle up johns. We could make a go of it. There's plenty people out there dying to be fucked up the arse by a real Master. I'll cut you in on the deal. Fifty fifty."

She was breathing in my face. Garlic and onions, and a trace of rancid kebab. Her hand gliding over my thigh, squeezing my groin. A vain attempt at raising the dead.

"You could be the new Controller. Fifty-five forty-five. Yin and yang. What do you say?"

Today the oesophagus. Tomorrow the world. Get out of a tight spot. Figure the way out of here later. One has not been trained by the best for nothing. And despite it all, the old snake stiffens.

"You got a deal." She climbed on top of me, pushed my pants way down and slid on my prick. The heavy whip lashing down, slashing my thighs, my face and my chest. How can the world endure, half slave and half free?

"I love you, Beatrice! I love you, Lilith!"

The pain in the head increasing, exponentially.

"Lilith! Lilith!"

The barking dog leaps up at the window, waving its massive head. The Prodigal Son walks forward to haul the dog back by its leash.

"Some bum out there, ma. Brother with loads of shopping bags."

"I know who it is, Karim. Let me hold the dog. Let him in."

"You serious, ma? Just let me deal with this."

"Let him in, Karim."

"I love you, Lilith! I love you! Open the door!"

"Take the dog to the kitchen and lock him in, Karim. I'll handle this. He's one of my patients."

"I don't like it, ma. You want me to call the cops?"

"Lilith! Open the door!"

THE DOG, IN THE KITCHEN, keeps on barking for a while, then stops, for some reason, mollified.

The Son, still suspicious, perched on the hi-backed wooden chair, ready to intervene.

Caroline, gaunt, in the red plush armchair.

Mo Smith, slumped, a pile of street rags, on the old black leather sofa.

"You look sick, Lilith."

"I'm dying, Mo. I was dying when we last met, remember, in the shelter? Before you left. I'm just dying faster. Some times it slows down. You got my message? I spread it round, everywheres I could."

"I heard."

"I like that 'I.' Who am I talking to, Mo? Is it Mo? The real Mo? Or who else?"

"I can stop you dying, Lilith. What you have to do is come inside me. You know what I'm saying. Get within me. Then you can live forever."

"You better watch your tongue, man." The Son stirs.

"Do me a favour, Karim. Can you get in the kitchen, without waking the beast, and get us a coffee. Heat up a couple of those bagels while you're at it. I might even eat one. The plain one."

"I shouldn't leave you alone with him, ma."

"Just get in there."

Alone, gazing at each other.

"A couple of old crocks," she shifted in her chair, every movement an effort, sighing. "Crocks before our time. How long you been on the street, Moses? I think I'm talking to the real one here. I know I am. Moses Smith, or was there another name?"

"Thomas."

"Thomas. First or second name?"

"Thomas. Moses Jeremiah Thomas."

"That's good. We're getting somewhere. Tell me about yourself. Where were you born?"

"I don't remember. Beatrice. Beatrice Alabama. Monroe County."

"Mother's name?"

"Ann."

"Father's name?"

The head shaking.

"Brothers? Sisters?"

"I don't remember. Jesse. Jaimie. Annie. Link."

"What happened to them? Where are they now."

"Gone."

"When, Moses? Do you remember when? Dates? What was your Dad? Was he a soldier? Was it the War? World War Two?"

Head shaking.

"When did your family move north? Your mother, when did she move?"

"Don't answer her, Mo, you're not obliged."

"Who was that? Who was that speaking? Name yourself."

"Orville. You don't have to answer any questions. You keep your secrets."

"I can help you, Mo. I know you want to be helped. Or you wouldn't have come here. Do you want me to help you right now?"

"Don't talk to her."

"Get the fuck outa here, Orville. What happened, Mo? Swallowed a lawyer? Keep him right down there. We're talking now. Caroline Dexter, your doctor."

"Lilith."

"There ain't no Lilith. It's all a game played by your mind. These secrets you want to keep. These are chains, Moses, holding you down. keeping you from being yourself. All these other people. You just told me. Your brothers and sisters. What happened to them? It's all there, Moses. I can help you to remember. But only if you trust me. I can put you under hypnosis. First I can give you a safe drug, to relax you. Then you drift off, and we talk. We get together a little conference, of all the siblings. All the voices. We work it out between us. We can do it here. It's borderline ethics but they can strike me off. Expelled from the A.P.A.. Big deal. I'm soon going to be expelled from the A.L.P.A. The American Living Persons Association. Whadayasay?"

"No drugs. No Pnosis."

"O.K. We can just talk. Let's start with Lilith. Why am I Lilith, Mo?"

"Lilith. The first wife. Before Eve."

"You know your mythology, Moses. Before Eve, Lilith was created equal to Adam. But she refused to obey him, and flew away. She copulated with demons, if I recall correctly. Which is more than I've ever done. Bar the occasional goblin. You were married, weren't you, Moses? What was your wife's name? Was she Lilith?"

"Bea."

"B.? Bee? Beatrice, Alabama? O.K. All these people that you had inside. Pharaoh Merenptah. Battuta. The white writer, Flint. You read a lot, don't you, Mo? Where do you read? The Public Library?"

Head shaking. "You gotta ask Ann."

"Ann? Your mother? The other Ann. Ann Hedonia. The sleeping one. You want to wake her?"

"Speak to Jesse."

"I don't want to speak to Jesse, Mo. I want to speak to you. You are a real person. You're the one who loves, feels, lives in the world. You're the one who's afraid. What we have to deal with, the fear."

Head shaking.

"Everybody's afraid, Moses. I wake up at night shivering. Even in this fucking heat. I'm shaking and shivering like it's freezing cold out there. All the lights are on but I'm screaming, scared out of my wits of the dark. Scared of the pain. Scared of the poison eating up my blood. The things I can't see, gobbling up my life. Being dead. Not being. What if all the worst religions are right? What if my sins have bought me everlasting pain and suffering to come? What if it drives me mad? Madness, Mo. Not `mental illness.' That place from which you can't escape. Where there is absolutely no choice. The most terrible things. Fear, Mo. Nobody is fearless. Is Orville fearless?"

"Fuck Orville."

"And who else is there right now?"

"They're only trying to help. Jesse. He brings me Hershey bars."

"Who is me now? Is that Ann?"

"All my children. The whole world, in my hand. Lilith as well. Before Adam. But then they both died."

"They died? Your children died, Moses? How did they die? I want to know, Moses."

"I am the Resurrection and the Life. But those who said, this man is a mortal like yourselves, nourished by the same food and drink, there is no other life but this, he is an impostor. Do not believe him."

The dog, barking again in the kitchen as Karim maouevers through the door, carrying a tray with coffees. Pushing the animal back with his foot.

"And he said, help me Lord, they will not believe it. But I replied: They will rue it before long. The Cry will overtake them in all justice, and they will be swept away like withered leaves."

Karim, pausing in his tracks, with the coffee, picking up the slack:

"Gone are those wicked men... and then - then we sent Moses and his brother Aaron, to Pharaoh, with our signs and our power, to Pharaoh and his nobles - but they received them with contempt... And we gave Moses the Book, so he be rightly guided..."

The puzzled look, from mother to son.

"Holy Koran," said Karim, "he's quoting from the Book. You are a Muslim, man. Is that true?"

"Your religion is but one religion. And I am your only Lord. Therefore fear me."

"Yet men have divided themselves into factions, each rejoicing in their own doctrines. Leave them in their error till the appointed time."

Karim pressed the hot coffee mug into Mo's hand, the great calloused paw closing round it. But Mo's eyes dropped, and his head shook again.

"What the fuck is wrong with that dog?" Karim hesitated, putting down the other two coffees on the rug, moving towards the kitchen door, the scrabbling sounds and howls emitted behind it.

"Maybe he's allergic to religion." Caroline sagged in her chair. The effort proving too much.

"I'll have to tie him to the table," said Karim, "maybe he wants his fucking dog food. Move back, dog!" Pressing back into the kitchen. Mo rose, crossing the six foot gap over to Caroline's armchair, leaning over her like a crumpled giant.

"I can protect you, Lilith."

"Nothing can protect me, Mo," she whispered. "I got all the state of the art twenty-first century medicines lined up. To keep me going. Where? Do *you* know where I'm going, Mo? Does Orville know? Jesse, or Ann?"

"Those who are reborn in me shall never die."

"You're not Christ, Moses. You're not God. You're not the Prophet. You're just a man in pain. Is that not enough?"

"I can make you live forever."

"Don't Mo. I don't have the energy. Why doesn't that fucking dog stop?"

Karim, in the kitchen, wrestling with the huge black hound, scrabbling to bind the leather lead round the leg of the heavy dining table.

His lips were now close to her ear. The heavy fetid breath of every imaginable detritus, of all the hot ashes -

"They were burnt." The voice, harsh, laboured, wheezing, female. Caroline's answering whisper: "Is that Ann?"

"All of them, dancing in the flames. Little screaming figures. Dancing."

His lips brushed her ear, her hair, then her forehead.

"I'll show myself out."

The breath withdrew, shifting its weight away from her face, the shuffle of plastic bags retreating, as the dog's protests wound down to a peevish whine. The door lock turning, squeaking, and the slam, as Karim, perplexed, reappeared.

"What happened?"

She turned her head. From the ceiling, a dark, sticky blob dropped on her arm. She shuddered, throwing it off. A glue-like fluid, on the carpet. Caroline looked up. A shadow, on the high beams, flitting out of her peripheral vision.

"Gotta do something about this house before the winter," she sighed. Karim gathered up the unused coffees, returning them to the kitchen, where the dog looked at him reproachfully, with a lolling, dripping tongue. He took a cloth from the sink and walked back to the carpet. But the fallen stain had gone. His mother, slumped back in her chair, was snoring.

He wiped the carpet anyway, and, as an afterthought, wiped down the couch on which the tramp had sat. Then, holding the cloth by its tip, he carried it back into the kitchen and, as the dog watched approvingly, placed it in the garbage can.

Book 4:

Earth.

Apotheosis of the Geodesic Dome.

In this area of natural beauty, just on the outskirts of the Connetquot River State Park, the pliant night sky, normally domain of the magicicadas, reverbrates with the blaring discord of two dozen power drills hacking into reinforced concrete. The softly falling snow, drifting in the light breeze, is illuminated as an infinity of crystals by the great crane-borne lights blazing at the workmen below, the cameras and microphones of the national and international press poised for the instant of the breakthrough.

These are tense moments down here, at Holbrook, Long Island, a couple of miles southwest of Ronkonkama. An unlikely spot, perhaps, for billionaire environmentalist Bookbinder R. Cruller to have erected his experimental Life Dome, an artificial and controlled habitat in which, he argued, human beings could live fruitfully without the need for contact with the polluted atmosphere and toxic by-products of what he called our "Age of Waste and Disorder." In late November, 1991, two years and one month ago, his twenty-four disciples shut themselves inside this Dome, vowing to live their lives, grow their own food, and recycle their own purified atmosphere, without any contact apart from voice communication with the outside world, until Thanksgiving Day, 1993, now twenty-six days past.

Among the twenty-four who volunteered to turn their back on the world were academics, teachers, artists, short-order chefs, a bicycle repairman, a prima-ballerina, two doctors, three engineers, two biologists, two botanists, a professor of philosophy, a dentist and an electrician. All were sworn vegetarians, and the few animals they took with them, a handful of dogs, cats, parakeets, and a pot-bellied Vietnamese hog named Archibald, were taken for companionship alone.

The final addition to this valiant band of pioneers was the astronaut, Nehemiah Snead. Commander Snead, the third man to walk on the moon, declared himself delighted to test the conditions which might enable man to embark on the great voyages of discovery of the twenty-first century, to the outer planets, Saturn, Jupiter, Neptune, and beyond. His smiling, white crowned face and waving hand were the last sights we saw at the Dome's single hatchway before it was bolted and sealed.

For eighteen months all seemed well within the dome, and monthly telephone calls - only outgoing calls were possible - reassured loved ones in the outside world, until, on the 6th of April, the leader of the Long Island Pioneers, as they came to be called, Dwight Deeblethwaite, a New Jersey sanitation engineer, telephoned the news division of the local radio station, KSCR, to announce that henceforth the line would be disconnected, and no further communication would be made with the outside until the Pioneers left the Dome. Asked when this would be Deeblethwaite answered: "When the world is worthy," and then terminated his call.

For three months, local inhabitants and curiosity seekers walked by the strange, silent construction, this giant golf ball with only its top curve protruding from the surrounding grassland, and its bulk buried underground. Since the Pioneers entered, many protected species of birds from the Connetquot State Park, the Horned Grebe, the Red-necked Grebe, the Common and the Red-throated Loon, the Gannets, Ospreys, Plovers, Sandpipers, American Coots, and various Boobies and Storm-petrels, took to perching on the white plastic struc-ture, some even building nests and rearing their young in its pitted shallow cavities. The smooth surface of the dome made it a perfect sanctuary from predators, foxes, weasels and bobcats, who could not climb up to catch their prey.

But then, late in July, the mother of one of the Pioneers, Mrs Letitia Windstrom, whose daughter, Pat, had been a teacher at the Metuchen Infants' Training College in New Jersey, petitioned the Suffolk County Court in Long Island for an order giving her access to her daughter. She claimed that in her last telephone call, in March 1992, Pat had told her of her worries about the mental health of some of the dome volunteers, including their leader, Dwight Deeblethwaite. Mrs Windstrom argued that Suffolk County had a responsibility to investigate allegations of either crimes or misdemeanours which might be occurring within its jurisdiction, and that the suspension of communication from inside the dome constituted an obstruction of justice. As silence continued throughout the summer, other parents and children of the Long Island Pioneers joined her call for the dome to be breached by force, if no other means of communication could be established with its occupants. They invoked the memories of Jones-town, Guyana, and the mass suicides of the followers of cult leader Jim Jones. A number of relatives of other Pioneers opposed them, invoking the more recent and painful memory of Waco, Texas, in which a massive FBI invasion resulted in the tragic death of over 80 followers of the self-named Son of God, David Koresh.

Three days ago, three judges of the New York Supreme Court upheld the decision of Judge Miller Huxtable of the Suffolk County Court of Sessions, that given no evidence that the Long Island Pioneers were armed and liable to provoke any violent reaction to a forceful breach, and given the unusual disposition of the land and property of the dome itself, which was bequeathed by billionaire Cruller to "Planet Earth/ Gaia and All Her Species," which was deemed to include the Sheriff and other law enforcement officials of Suffolk County, the Sheriff was empowered to engage the Hindenburg Destruction Company of West Babylon to breach the dome and gain access to the intrepid Pioneers.

I am interrupted now by a message from our Woman on the Spot, Jess Iodine. The engineers have drilled a hole in the reinforced surface of the dome. Over to you Jess. Thank you Jebb. The engineers have managed to break through the three layers of ruggedized plastic which surrounds the dome on all sides. In the initial stages, fears were expressed about the nature of the atmosphere inside the dome. Some said there might be at least some areas in the dome in which an artifical weightless condition had been developed as part of the deep space aspect of the experimental endeavour. But other observers argued that the kind of power required to create that environment with earth's gravity would prohibit the low energy objective of the entire experiment. No source of such power was in any case identified either in the planning or construction of the dome. The Judge at Suffolk County ruled that it was safe to assume that the air inside and outside the dome was compatible with normal human life needs. I am at the opening now and we cannot sense any difference in the quality of the air, except for a slight rush of warmth, which is to be expected given the artifical climate inside and the very cold, bitterly cold in fact conditions we are experiencing out here in the open.

There is in fact a warm glow, as we enter, Sheriff Koons of Suffolk County leading. I am here with Mrs Letitia Windstrom, whose persistent devotion to her daughter's well-being has brought about this extraordinary event Mrs Lindstrom what are your thoughts now that the dome has finally been breached?

Well, Jess, I believe this is a victory for common sense and for the ordinary citizen against the forces of money and influence which sometimes try to hide behind the cloak of good causes. We have nothing against the ideas of Mr Bookbinder Cruller or the nobility of purpose which led our loved ones to place themselves within the power of his acolytes. We just feel we have the right of access to our daughters, sons, brothers, sisters, mothers and fathers so that we can get their direct testimony as to whether they are functioning with their free will.

Wow! Sorry for interrupting you, Mrs Windstrom, but isn't this really something? I mean, we seem to be passing through some kind of jungle, these plants are really thick in here I can see the Sheriff is trying to hack his way through. I'm a bit of an amateur botanist but I sure can't identify any of these species, we might as well be in the Amazonian jungle! This thing here, can it be? I think it's a real Venus flytrap, if I put my finger here - ow! That thing really bites! Just look at these vines! You can almost expect Tarzan to come whooping down one of these. Are you O.K. with the camera, Hank? I'll just hold these aside. Are you receiving me out there?

We're receiving you loud and clear, Jess. I'm glad to hear that Jebb, we've barely been in here a minute and already I feel as if I'm in another world. But you know what suddenly strikes me? There are no animals in here. Just this low kind of hum, the dome's internal generators I guess, but no sound of any creatures - no insects, either, have you ever heard of a jungle without insects? - There's something not right here, Jess, just as I always thought. This is not the way God intended life to be. No, it doesn't seem so Mrs Windstrom. But we can all remember all the discussions about Bookbinder Cruller's dome when it was being built - all the talk about a proper ecological balance and the need to conserve the planet's manifold species. Several hundred species were being destroyed in the earth's remaining rainforests every day. Or was it thousands? But there don't seem to be any around here today. Maybe the flora will inherit the earth. Is there anything ahead there, Sheriff?

I think I'm reaching the end of this chamber, Miss. There is a door. I am about to turn the handle here. It's a bit like an aircraft door. I hope I'm doing the right thing. - You're authorized to gain access, Sheriff, you can't stop now. There may be dead bodies behind that hatch! - There's nothing to indicate that, ma'm. Nothing untoward here at all, it seems to be some kind of airlock. - It's like a kind of spaceship in here. What was that film, with Bruce Dern? Do you remember Jebb? - No I'm afraid I don't Jess, what do you see? The lens seems to be encumbered by those leaves. - Well I think we've passed through the vegetation now Jebb. We're in some kind of empty chamber, there's nothing here but bare grey walls and, oh, there are some strange carvings on the ceiling, can you get a light on those Hank, they are a bit like old Egyptian carvings, but not quite hieroglyphs, oh this is weird, we have these figures, in spacesuits, with uh animal heads - birds, lions, a monkey, what's that? looks like a hippopotamus head on a woman, that one is a woman, you can see the shape of her breasts, then there's a small dog faced child oh boy this is really something. Now there's another door here, are you sure you should open that Sheriff? O.K.. I don't have a good feeling about this. - Oh my poor baby! - Just hold on, Mrs Windstrom, nothing has happened yet. Just let me do my job Mrs Windstrom. - The Sheriff is now opening the door. We're in another chamber, this one looks like some kind of storeroom, can you get by all these boxes, Hank? Just look at all this stuff! This isn't what we thought this place was all about, is it? All these sound- systems, amplifiers, T.V. sets, personal computers, just look at these Bugs Bunny telephones, what on earth was going on in here? We've got shelves and shelves of all kinds of radio equipment here, walkmans, CD players, this looks like transmission equipment, boy, they sure could have talked to us if they wanted to, or did they set all this aside? I thought the whole idea was isolation, so why would they have needed all this in the first place, can you make head or tail of this Hank? Yeah, neither can I. These boxes and boxes of stuff, hundreds, maybe thousands of video cassettes. Look at this: Every single Little Rascals title, Johnny Carson show, All in the Family, Soap, I

Love Lucy, boy, they certainly weren't letting go of that world outside! Or maybe there was some kind of internal argument about this, some kind of power struggle which ended we have no idea how, but it's time I think we found out. There must be another door round here, over there Sheriff. Now this one seems to be locked. The Sheriff is calling the demolition experts, you can see them going to work on this door. I'm beginning to get a bad feeling about this. This isn't what we expected to find, this group of Pioneers setting their back on our fast consumer society and looking for a balanced ecology well I suppose if you lock people up, I remember when my mother locked me up in the closet for two hours - but that's another story, I think they have the door open now, Sheriff Koons is going through. Mind your head, Hank, this hatch is pretty low, God knows what lies behind this doorway, that's all right, you go first Mrs Windstrom, is anything wrong? Can you let us through Mrs Windstrom, please get out of the way, we're trying to record this for our viewers millions of people around the world are waiting to see what has been going in here for the past two years, O.K., just move aside Mrs Windstrom let me get in so Hank can get through the door, that's fine Mrs Windstrom, right, I'm through now this looks more like it, I can see a great circular chamber very dim light though can you get the light in here Hank -

Holy moly! WHAT THE FUCK IS THAT SMELL?????

*

- Two months earlier, sitting on the jumble strewn couch at Frances' apartment, watching a very different event unfolding on the T.V.: Hundreds of American, Israeli, Arab, Hollywood and other Global Village dignitaries gathered on the White House lawn, as, out of a doorway in the President's house three men emerge, walking down the pathway: the President of the United States, flanked by the Prime Minister of Israel, Yitzhak Rabin, and the Chairman of the Palestine Liberation Organisation, Yassir Arafat.

What can I say? "My God, they've all drunk the Chairman's piss now." But Frances can see that my eyes are welling over. A kind of sob breaks from the assembled guests at this incongruous sight, this unreal vision of two sworn enemies brought together by a shared fatigue. The weariness of wars without end. Can there be hope after all?

"You can't deny it, Benjamin, it's happening."

"T.V. trickery. It's all opticals. Quantel graphics. Digital fakery. Just like the landing on the moon."

In slow motion, the principals step up to the podium. One small step for ageing men. How many strides for those yet to come? The President, the hushed commentary reveals, has chosen a special tie to go with the big day, a blue strip with little yellow trumpets, symbolising the bugles which brought down the stubborn walls of Jericho. But Jericho is now just a small, seedy ruin surrounding a tiny oasis, and the empty mudhuts of refugee camps long since drained of their hopeless charges. Symbolically, it will be the first town in the Biblical Land of Israel to be handed back to its present Palestinian inhabitants, together with the sumplands of Gaza.

Peace in our time. "We the soldiers who have returned from the battle stained with blood, say to you today in a loud and clear voice: Enough of blood and tears!" Was it not Winston Churchill who promised his people nothing but blood, toil, tears and sweat? The twists and turns of words. But as the speech makers pause, the President, spreading his arms to engulf the two old enemies, presses them towards each other, to the historic handshake, the old General pumping the Chairman's hand as if a golden oil would flow from his glazed, grimacing and grizzled visage, the *kefiya* draped down his right khaki clad breast in the carefully arranged shape of Mandate Palestine. The fragile shape is disturbed, as the General pumps his hand, but the Chairman stands his ground, reluctant to let go, perhaps hoping that the milk of human kindness would soon ooze out of his enemy's neck, the uncomfortable chafe-line of the starched white shirt, but the General, having done his due, peels off, jerking his palm back, allowing the Chairman's hand to stretch further towards his partner, the Foreign Minister, architect of the deal hewn out in enviable secrecy in a log cabin deep in the Norwegian woods, with goodluck goblins peeking in the windows and blonde cooks plying the Levantine guests with dumplings until, stomachs distended and gorges rising, they agreed to sign upon the dotted line.

Now let's watch it all again, in slow motion. The hands reach out, clasp, the General pumping, the Chairman pumped, the slow withdrawal. The beefy smile from Arkansas. The little yellow trumpets, blaring the news of ancient prophecies fulfilled.

"If only Salim could be here to see this."

"Let's hope he's watching it, Benjamin, wherever he is."

The vanished Palestinian. Last seen floating in a canoe down the Black Creek River together with Ibn Battuta and Blue Mountain's mutinous maid. Swallowed up by the vastness of Lake Ontario, somewhere between Oswego and Oshawa. In Canada sanctuary now?

Meanwhile, in Cairo, Allan Darwish must be watching on Egyptian T.V.. Departed on a long home visit late in August, putting a distance of two continents between himself and the horror found on his bed when he unlocked his door, returned from his futile search Upstate for Salim. Three nightmare days of police interrogation. The fruitless search for the dead boy's real identity. A hastily arranged plot in Woodlawn Cemetery, way out in the Bronx, beyond all pain. Frances keeping to the two of us her paraphysical thoughts about Mo Smith's offshoots breaking free to walk the earth. Flesh Golems, all too human. "Letting my imagination run away with me," she decided. Our old convocation at the Gourmet Szechuan shrunk now to four: Frances, Caroline, myself and Aram, down for a few days from the University at Amherst, as the good tidings blew in from the East:

"So they signed the deal. Sealed with a Clinton smooch."

"Miracles do happen."

"Only in the sense that miracles are illusions. But there was no other political choice."

"Come on, Aram, there's always a choice."

"Between realpolitik and the leap into darkness? Sometimes the pressures are too great, and even the most stubborn and bone headed politicians have to give. O.K., I'll join the ranks of the hopeful, but only on a temporary basis. In the Middle East, everything can go wrong. But I'll have a steamed dumpling in honor of the moment. And for Caroline - to fight the good fight. Life."

A jasmine tea le'chayim. For once, the streets are full of happy people. The Jews of New York City, gearing up for the New Year, at one with the White House celebrants. For once the brave new world seems truly brave, an open door to that better future so fondly prattled about. The dissidents, the lumpy youth of the extremist *Kach* movement, venerating the assassinated Mad Rabbi Kahane, shout down the Israeli ambassador to Washington as he tries to explain the new Peace Policy, throwing bags of flour at him in a synagogue. Casting their bread.

I am really lifted up by these scenes, the turns of fortune and the new formal faces to replace me as the recipient of thrown flour, piss, ordure or whatever. Lolling on Frances' couch, watching the Palestinian flags, banned for the last twenty-five years, billowing out onto the dusty streets of still occupied towns, armed soldiers standing by while crowds hoist the forbidden colours, red, green, white and black, on their rooftops. Ah, Salim, Salim.

Not everyone, of course, is cheering, Popular Fronts (by name if not by nature) murmuring dark charges of betrayal, the warnings of exile academics that too much has been conceded, too soon, that the blithely assumed parity of oppressed with oppressor will not stand the test of time. What would you say, Salim? But you were long ago a convert to the cause, only to be rewarded by the brand of the "terrorist" and hunted like a wild beast. Are you a precursor, of the tides to come?

Frances viewing me with deep suspicion.

"You're always looking for the worm in the apple, Benjamin."

That's me. Never the satisfied customer. But the worm in the apple is wriggling in front of us, the cancer in Caroline's blood cells, immune to all external wonders. The irrevocable fact that cuts us off from each other. The insufficiency of the imagination.

More jubilation in the West Bank and Gaza as the first prisoners are freed. In Tunis, exile headquarters of the Palestine Liberation Organisation, Israeli T.V. crews mingle with men who were until two weeks ago the blood-stained terrorists of their nightmares. Commanders who sent armed guerrillas to kill and maim. *En la guerre comme a la guerre,* mutter the old grey haired generals, with a shrug of Armani shoulders. *Kalan zaman.* Once upon a time. And now the world has changed, old walls are coming down, watchtowers and barbed wire dismantled, borders melting in the heart.

So let the good times roll? Winding up another avante-garde summer at the 4th Street Film Co-Op: the "Tango twins" Javez and Ros's documentary on the street murals of Alphabet City won a prize in Colorado. An evening of tequila and weed at the painters' "commune" on East Houston, above Yonah Shimmel's Knish Bakery, with lion-maned Jacinta and her daubing acolytes. Roped in to search the streets for her missing assistant, Lincoln, who disappeared as suddenly as he had popped up, wrapped in frozen mud in a pile of garbage on Avenue D. Picked up, we assumed, in one of the periodic sweeps ordered by the Mayor to clear the homeless from the streets into their designated shelters. Like Mo Smith, slipping out of Caroline's door into the usual oblivion. Unable to call on Salim's yellow cab eye, I spent a week alone, combing the area, from Columbus to Riverside Drive, up to 125th Street, beyond which we of the lighter skins do not tread.

Goin home, Mama, goin home. Karim departed from the old brownstone at 93rd, returning to the bosom of the Reverend Farrakhan in Saint Louis Missouri, perhaps persuaded that his sojourn by his mother's side was not guiding her towards salvation. Caroline's mother Paula took up the slack, but at least I could now visit the house without the tension between the Evil Israeli and the Good Muslim setting the dog to howl in the dead of night in sympathy, like a true lost soul.

Being liked by animals is one of my better traits. The human race and I still have our problems. I wake at night and still wonder, as I did when a child, whether I'd just been dropped from a distant star. I understand it is a common phenomenon. Sometimes the search for the grey aliens just stops at my bathroom mirror. Perhaps I do exist only inside Mo Smith, visiting the outside world on an extended ticket of leave. Wherever the hell he is now, the poor ragged bastard. As winter closes in, he could be anywhere, in the caves below Riverside Drive, the old tunnels of the Con-Edison Railway, seven levels below Grand Central. But I am the above-ground type.

Planning to spend Christmas with Caroline, watching the Israeli army withdrawing from Gaza and Jericho on long distance live broadcast. The Birth of Freedom! But Caroline is whisked off by her mother and aunts to a house in furthest New Jersey, better heated, they claim, than the damp caverns of 93rd Street. Leaving me to fall back on Old Faithful Frances, and the stockpiles of the Learning Annexe, unread Jewish Sentinels Village Voices and New York Times Book Reviews. Hannukah 5754. The Maccabees Noel Noel. Packages of home made knish and pecan pie from Zaybars, the kaleidoscopes of Ex-Mass T.V...

"Switch it on, Frances. Let them throw the whole shmeer at us."

Fade in the drills breaching the Long Island Dome...

"WHAT THE FUCK IS THAT SMELL??"

Rotting food, lying all over the central dining room table, located in the very center of the geodesic golf ball, twenty feet below ground. Putrefying fruit, vegetables and unidentifiable congealed gunk on plates and bowls, uneaten, spoiled manna. Twenty-four empty chairs, and plastic cutlery, partly soiled, partly untouched. And no signs of human presence, no dead bodies, live bodies, skeletons, skin, bones, even discarded clothing. No Dwight Deeblethwaite, no Nehemiah Snead, no Patricia Windstrom, no Selina Hasek, Czech refugee, surrealiste and art gallery supplier in days of yore. The air thick, fetid, unventilated.

It was several hours before the Sheriff's deputies, swarming in, located the emergency hatch, at the lower end of the golf ball, leading to a narrow tunnel which opened at a manhole cover on Sycamore Avenue. The only problem being that the emergency hatch was locked, by three separate mechanisms, from inside. No other exit could be found, only a message, scrawled in black aerosol paint on the wall of the putrescent dining room -

- THEY'RE COMING TO TAKE US AWAY -

Ten days later, they found Pat Windstrom's diary, hidden in a futon, in the empty living quarters. But this was after New Year. The night before, having shunned the Times Square jamboree for an early screening yet again of Stan Brakhage's Dog Star Man at the film co-op under the influence of some old fashioned weed home grown by the Tango Twins, I spent quietly at Caroline's, having volunteered to look after the Black Beast during her New Jersey sojourn. While the crowds cheered the New Year downtown I fed the hound his chunky carnivore stew and settled down in what had been Karim's room, unable to contemplate Caroline's bed, with its aura of night sweats and chemically suppressed pain. Sinking in marijuana afterfumes below the Time Magazine cover of Muhammad Ali (alias Cassius Clay - does anyone remember?) and the inscription of the holy Islamic credo, with crossed swords Saudi style. *There is no God but God and Muhammad is His Prophet.* At least I am spared the Ayatollah Khomeini, whom Caroline banned from her walls. What was that famous religious ruling of his? The one about eating a camel which had been sodomized? Was it forbidden or sanctioned, and under which circumstances? With such thoughts, I went under, and dreamed -

THEY'RE COMING TO TAKE US AWAY!

- In my rags, staggering up Broadway. Night. The street glittering of fresh autumn rain. Only a few people about, figures, blurred, insubstantial, as if caught by stop-motion photography, pixilated. The shops along the way each offering some kind of occult service: DISCOUNT TAROT! EMPIRE SZECHUAN CRYSTALS! CITIBANK OF LOST SOULS! VIDEO SECRETS OF THE VOID! ACME CLEANERS - YOUR PAST LAUNDERED! PALMS READ BY AUTHORIZED SHAMANS! There was an eerie silence, which I realized was due to the absence of any vehicle on either side of the way.

Up ahead of me, I could see another ragged figure, like myself, moving painfully up the road. I knew it was Caroline, although her walk was far removed from her usual rugged stride. A great sense of melancholy and sadness overwhelmed me as I realized her decline. I hobbled forward, but was overtaken by a feeling of dread that, when I finally caught up with her, and she turned round, I would see the face of an old woman, wrinkled, white haired and drooped, with sagging rheumy eyes. Nevertheless I spurred myself forward, but every time I crossed a road she was half way over the crossing to the next block. I stopped, panting for breath at a doorway beside a glass window with a printed notice: "Job Applications Now Being Accepted for Career Minded Persons With Knowledge of Tropical Fish."

Behind the notice, on a shelf inside the shop, among packets of pet food and dog harnesses and empty hamster cages, with their tiny treadmills still lazily turning, were two bluish, glowing, metallic looking eggs, larger than ostrich eggs, like the product of the mythical Roc of the Thousand and One Nights. The right phrase echoed in my brain - Sinbad Spheres. In the shop window, a reflection alerted me to another figure that had glided up beside me, looking inside. A tall man in a shabby raincoat, hatless, with a cadaverous, skull-like face. He glanced at me with glowing, coal-black eyes.

"Pretty, aren't they?" His voice was cultured, with a kind of Brahmin burr. "You can't afford them. They're mine."

I felt a strong, visceral loathing, as if I'd been accused of desiring something repulsive, a sexual perversion so unimaginable that it had no name or designation, even by the American Psychiatric Association, of which I knew this person to be a prominent member, although I had never seen him before.

"Yes," he said, "I am He."

Looking past him, I could see Caroline toiling across the next street, 99th Street, having almost reached the safety of the other side. But I knew he could pull her back and crush her by one stretch of his long arm, which was folded into his coat. It was clear the thing in front of me was the same creature that had lured the Dome Pioneers out of the safety of their new-world womb to their deaths. Trapped and squeezed in the exit tunnel, they had emerged onto the verges of the outside Avenue as long wriggling white worms, to be scooped up in a jar, with the spaceship waiting to whisk them off across the galaxy parked on the avenue verge. Their eventual fate a complete Unknown.

"Do you love her?" the loathsome creature asked me. "Do you really love her?"

"Of course I love her." My voice sounded strangled, dribbling out against a suffocating, outside force.

"Will you take the worms?" He asked maliciously. "Will you take the worms from her blood?"

I could see, across the other side of Broadway, a Red Star of David ambulance parked. It was clearly marked in scarlet letters: "MOUNT SINAI RIGHTEOUS MERCY." A man in a dark coat standing by it gestured frantically to me, waving me over. I could see it was the former Mayor of New York, Ed Koch. I knew he had come to take me to the City shelter, uptown at Fort Washington. No one who had entered there had ever come out alive.

"Who did you vote for?" asked the skull man. I looked past him. Caroline had fallen in the road. I could see her as a crumpled pile of rags, arm outstretched, just short of the sanctuary of the 100th Street block, an amber on and off sign at the corner flickering with the legend "CHEESY PIZZA."

I looked back into the shop window. But the two blue eggs had broken open. They had hatched, and whatever had emerged was crawling, a quick shadow, into the unlit corner of the shop. I turned back, and the skull man had, to my immense relief, gone. Instead, Mayor Koch, in a plastic raincoat, beamed up at me, offering a cigar.

"You made the right choice," he told me. I looked again, desperately, up the road. But the pile of rags on 99th Street had vanished too.

"Oh no!" I cried out, grabbing the Mayor by his lapels, shaking him like a rat. "Where did he take her? You motherfucking bankrupt shit! Where did he take her?" The Mayor, smiling, shook his head.

"WHERE DID SHE GO?"

A camel, thin, scabby, bleeding from the rump, staggered by. It looked at me with pleading, terrified eyes.

"WHERE DID SHE GO?"

The camel laid its filthy head on my neck. Its smell was like a field of rotting offal. But I clasped its coarse forehead with my hand. It had no other friend.

"We're in this together." I murmured in its ear. Its terrible fetid nose nuzzled my chin. Above us, suddenly, and without any logical origin, an elevated train rushed by, its passing windows garishly lit, the number clear on its front carriage. Number One, heading for the South Ferry. I realised it had come from the Shelter. Rattling on, towards the Battery Park, Castle Clinton, the docks and embarkation points to Ellis Island, Liberty Island, the tall stone lady with the outstretched torch and beacon, indifferent to all the outstayed welcomes, then out the Upper Bay and the Verrazano Narrows to the Atlantic Ocean.

The homeless were all going home.

* * *

*

*

*

At this point, the main manuscript of THE COSMIC FOLLIES ends, although there are other fragments, scattered in several envelopes, which I have done my best to gather together. The work has not been easy, as the segments were left in a number of different places, gathering dust in lofts and damp blotches in cellars, mislaid behind the backs of filing cabinets, forgotten inside old suitcases, unopened crates of house-moved flotsam, even, in one instance, in the pocket of an old coat hung up in an abandoned closet. None of this should be surprising, given the status of the primary manuscript as an artefact preserved in a special glass case in Ervine Lazar's office.

The office, in any event, had to be cleared, due to the closure and abolition of Ervine's personal imprint, Lazar Books, as an inevitable result of the termination of the entire trade department of Richman & Cullings, due to the acquisition of the parent company, Globalread, by the German entrepeneur, Heinz Buchalter, and his company, Buchalter GMBH. A common corporate tale of our day.

For my own part, I can proclaim to the world, I am not a publisher, nor even an editor or "publishing assistant," as some folks are called these days, but only a lowly "reader", a figure much despised, I know, by authors, who expect their work to be evaluated by the top dog, or at least one of the pack team, and not by an impoverished ex-student living on climbing debts and borrowed hopes. Andy McCloud is the name. Not the McCloud of old T.V. fame, crimesolver with a moustache and large Texan hat, but the more hesitant, wavering type who thought the study of literature and history might be a gateway to - what?

I can't imagine what I was thinking about, seven years ago, when I began my quest for what I imagined might be a "career" in the publishing business, but it did lead me to Ervine Lazar and his slush pile. All your poor, your eager, hungry masses, yearning to be print.

The "Cosmic" manuscript was in Lazar's office the day I had my first interview. A jumbled pile of dogeared, smudged pages, covered with what seemed to be an unreadable handwritten scrawl. He took it out of its glass case the second time I came round, when he told me I was now on the payroll. "I keep this as a reminder," he said, "of the astonishing self-delusion of writers. Nobody has been able to decipher this manuscript, or more than a paragraph here and there. It's in English, but that's about the end of the story. We might have here a masterpiece or a great pile of incoherent nonsense. You never know. Jack Kerouack's manuscript of `On the Road' came in a kind of messed up roll. Friedrich Nietzsche's handwriting was so bad only his student, Gast, could understand it well enough to transcribe it."

"I can give it a try." I offered. But he put the pile back in its case. "Another time. I've got more urgent stuff for you. I want you to feel free to follow your instinct. Don't try and second guess my own taste. I can't figure it out myself sometimes. You know authors hate to be told I don't feel right about this, I don't feel right about that, but that's the way it goes."

Ervine Lazar had built a reputation for taking on other publishers' rejects. He never liked the obvious candidates. He would have loved to have discovered James Joyce, Samuel Beckett or Henry Miller. But he always regarded himself as an old fashioned throwback in the hegemonic world of Marketing. "I want to know if the writer has something to say. End of story. I don't need the money. I got stomach problems. All I can eat is bland. I have this house my father built upstate and the apartment my wife and I bought on the Upper East Side in 1956. My kids are out there making money in the law and medical rackets. All my authors are dirt poor. If they want rich they go to the big *macher* agents and move on to Viking or Putnam. Lazar loves romantic losers. I might publish this shmuck" - waving to the glass case - "if I could figure out what the fuck he's on about. If I could make out even one sentence! When it came in, I took it home, spent a month, late nights, poring over it. No dice. Gave it to my teenage daughter, who goes for something called `Thrash Head Acid.' It's supposed to be a kind of music. Go figure. She gave up after ten minutes. Take my advice, work with the legible only."

Which I did, for the next eight months, trying to sort the wheat from the chaff. Lazar took me on because he said he was amazed to find somebody of my age and generation who had read Flann O'Brien, George Orwell, Virginia Woolf, Andre Gide, Willa Cather, William

Gaddis, Roth, Bellow, Heller et al, as well as mavericks like "Fan Man" William Kotzwinkle, Gilbert Sorrentino and Carolyn Chute. The Beans of Egypt Maine, oh boy. "More people can read than ever before," he once said to me, sighing, "and less people can read than ever before, if you get my meaning." There are so many distractions. But reading suited my solitary nature. While my friends hooked themselves up to their personal computers and began talking to the world on the Internet, I became addicted to curling up by myself with paper. The banal fact is, it all comes from my father, who owned a bookshop in New Hope, Pennsylvania, at a time when bookshops were owned by people, not by conglomerates. Hasta la vista baby.

Unfortunately, during my eight months' reading through Lazar's slush pile, I could not find a new O'Brien, Orwell, Woolf or Bellow, though I did recommend a couple of possible Kotzwinkles or Chutes. We have to be grateful for small mercies, and I'm sure the authors I gave the thumbs down would have hated my guts, if they knew I was there. You might accept being turned down by the voice of experience, but not by the hired help. Since, of course, I was secretly tapping out my own sad efforts, very painfully and slowly, at the same time, there was always that shadow of guilt. But I needed the money, and the hours were better than shovelling shit for the city at dawn.

All the time though, from that first glimpse, I was intrigued by the glass case manuscript. During the two minutes I had to glance through the mound of pages the writing didn't seem to me so obscure. My mother suffered from arthritis for years before she died, but she insisted on writing long letters by hand to her various friends around the globe, which I took and transcribed. Even my Dad couldn't read her writing, which looked like a chicken with Parkinsons. But I could make it out, no problem. I was sure I could transcribe the "Cosmic" manuscript. The Gast for a new Nietzsche as it were. Or at any rate, I would be able to judge its merit pretty quick.

After eight months the slush pile had visibly shrunk. Perhaps Lazar's rejection letters, based on my poor judgement, were creating a great despair out there. Or perhaps the computer age was really kicking in. Or the U.S. Mail becoming even less efficient at delivering these packages to the right address, delete the inapplicable. At any rate, I volunteered to "read" the Glass Cage Book, as it was called in house, and type out at least some sections, to give a flavour of the impossible whole.

The first conundrum of the Glass Cage Book was of course the author's anonymity. There was no name on the ms., no covering letter, nothing but a greasy and filthy brown paper package, which Lazar's secretary Hilda Hurrick had thrown away, as there was no return address. The title page was a dire omen, a mass of scribbles of occult symbols and hieroglyph-like signs, with even the main title barely legible: The word "Cosmic" can just about be made out, but the next word seemed to be "Slies." Lazar's next thought was the word "Slips." Or "Flies"? But I could see the "o", which had fallen slightly, and been mistaken for a dot above a triangle. I knew it was "Follies" – the two "l"s running together.

As well as the illegibility of the script, the other turn-off was the dirty, stained and frankly smelly nature of the crumpled pages themselves. Most of the script was on standard quarto paper, which seemed to have been inscribed while in some kind of motion, or held against some slippery and filthy surface, though there were also notepapers and even segments on unused envelopes, tacked on to other pages with sellotape. "We would have thought it was a kind of joke," Lazar told me, "if it wasn't for the sheer size of the thing." Counted, seven hundred and eighty nine pages of the main script, tied with a frayed length of blackened string. "Something colossal, mad and slightly sinister," said Lazar, "because you can see the work that went in. I did have four sample pages analysed by an expert, who said the writer was either a paranoid schizophrenic or a foreign refugee who had been tortured, perhaps in an Albanian jail." Lazar had called in an Albanian translator, who reported no discernible trace of Albanian, but suggested the writer might be someone who originally wrote write in Greek script, possibly a Macedonian attempting the Latin.

"I can read it," I said, "I'll do it for you."

"I can't pay you for this," Lazar said. Already the rumbles of the coming demise of Richman & Cullings were being heard. Mergers, takeovers and "rationalisations." A strange robotic man, with a crew cut and the blank stare of an achetypal FBI agent, came and measured the offices, while Lazar was at lunch consoling an author whose Lazar Books opus had been reviewed by the Sunday Oregonian, the Toledo Bee, the Lompoc Picayune Intelligencer and no one else. When I met him later that afternoon, he looked old in spirit, rather than just physically old, for the first time.

"I can feel my blood turning to dust," he told me wearily, "it's all too dry, too fucking dry." He went home, and left Hilda H. to try and piece together how much or how little time was left.

I set to work, nevertheless, on the Glass Cage Book, which Lazar removed from its enclosure and gave into my hands as if he were handing me the fate of a wayward, junkie child. I took it home in my bag, rattling down in the D train from Seventh Avenue and 53rd Street across the bridge to Brooklyn's Seventh Avenue. I live in Park Slope, a rainbow district of refugees from Greenwich Village and SoHo's spiralling rents. A a kind of reservation of what remains of old style New York, with its individual coffee shops and stores, and small enough to be a real community, where you stop and chat to people on the street. As these neighborhoods in Brooklyn are, it's an enclave. Three blocks to the west, you cross Fourth Avenue and the harsh side of the Borough confronts you, with its depressed neighbourhoods stretching down to Red Hook and beyond, to Bay Ridge and Bensonhurst, where the forgotten people live. All the potential Mo Smiths.

Due to my disordered brain, I no longer sleep nights, which is why the "reading" job was a boon. Morning appointments are agony. The real joy is when everthing shuts down, everyone else except the night owls crawls between the sheets, the babies stop crying for a few hours at least, the weekend sound-system addicts are dormant too and I commune with my little night light in my kitchen, surrounded by last week's leftovers and unshelved crockery. It used to be very different, when Annie was with me, but that is a closed chapter. Or at least, that was her view of things. For myself, everything always stays open. My father always told me never to close the door to opportunities. But I'm more like a room with open doors at both sides – opportunities flow in, and then flow out again, without stopping.

The manuscript of the "Cosmic Follies" simply merged with all my unresolved mess. It didn't take me long, in fact, to unlock it. Once I could decipher one sentence, the next followed, and once the first page could be read, the next was easier. Pretty soon, I abandoned my original intention to alternate between the "Follies" and my own magnum opus, which normally advanced at about a page a day. Pulling up my battered Adler typewriter, my great act of rebellion against new technology, a massive thing which would have driven the downstairs neighbours to mutiny if I hadn't muffled it with a special foam bedding and they were not the world's heaviest sleepers - the yang to my yin - in all is balance, saith the Tao - I sailed off, into Mo's world.

Cue the old cinematic montage of calendar pages flipping past. August,

September,

October,

November,

December,

January. In February I sat, with the hand-written pile on one side, and my own Adlered mound on the other, not quite the whole shebang, as I had still not located all the seven separate envelopes that had dribbled in to Lazar Books over a period of six months following the main package, and which had become entangled with different piles of manuscripts Ervine had either taken home, or had been taken by Hilda H. and left in the safekeeping of various friends while she apartment-hunted on the Upper West Side. Eventually I would find them all, but in that freezing midwinter I had enough to bite on. Enough questions that had no clear answers. *

First the Big and Obvious One: Who was the author? Certainly not somebody looking for easy pickings. In this era of market mania, the multi-voiced, long drawn out saga was by definition one for the rejection pile. But from the start it was clear that the "presentation," the impenetrable scrawl, the stained, soiled, torn paper, pointed to the author as Mo Smith himself: The autobiographical voice of the homeless tramp, hunched in corners and doorways, bent over under the dim light of the shelters, leaning in the semi-dark against the stone roots of bridges, painstakingly scratching, scratching away with his ragbag of pencils and pens. An obviously attractive idea: The discovery by lowly reader Andy McCloud of an unexpected literary tour-de-force by an idiot-savant - the genuine article. Like Sartre's discovery of Genet - except that I was no Sartre, and Mo Smith, or whatever his name was, would never be the darling of the literary salons. Or would he? In this world of anything goes – might this be the next mangy lion of Showbiz TV and the Color Supplements - Oprah's Opal, everyman evangelized? If I could find him... This, too, was thought...

---

* see *My Search For Mo's Apocrypha*, The New Yorker, 13 April 1996, pp. 6-12.

But the other obvious option, in this age of the phony: the elaborate hoax. The fake. The writer desperate for a jaded gimmick. As I oozed further and further into the manuscript, I became more and more convinced of this, not only because of the writer's somewhat "highbrow" knowledge, the history and politics, not to speak of basic matters of grammar and spelling. Or might there have been a co-writer? A "ghost"? Or, to take a different tack, might not "Mo Smith" be some black scholar, a Professor of some sort fallen on hard times. But if so, why the impossible scrawl?

Might the forger have miscalculated, mistaking his own ability to read his own counterfeit for a more general savvy? Or might he be, like my mother, arthritic, or physically disabled some other way?

None of the theories fit the stubborn fact of the manuscript – its sheer, unwieldy length. But there were other questions, arising from the text. Apart from the ordinary locations, streets and shopfronts of the city, there were coincidences which began to bother me. I began to recognize names. I was sure I had come across Benjamin, who in the text runs the film co-op at East 4th Street. I remembered my sister had a close friend named Ros, who had made a documentary movie about the street murals of "Alphabet City" a few years back. I remembered vague talk of an Israeli who produced her movie, somewhere in the East Village. And yet another recognition: The palm-reader and occultist, Madame Cropfin, located in my own neighborhood, in Park Slope. In fact I probably had at least one of her leaflets, somewhere in my mound of old garbage. I remembered hearing that she died, and, in fact, glimpsing the tall, Middle Eastern man who took over, though I'd not seen him around for some time. Trading under the name... What was it now?

Brooklyn, snow, February. A good day for sifting long-piled garbage. But the leaflet turned up, pretty quickly, among the pile of local takeaway menus, the Lemongrass grill, the Szechuan Palace, the Hunan Taste - just waiting for me to pluck it out:

MERENPTAH THE MAGUS.
The Seeing Eye.
Thousands of people suffer daily:
Misery, domestic sorrows,
lack of love, failure of prosperity, financial disasters.

Merenptah the Magus Sees All:
Past, present and future are revealed by the Master of
the Ancient Mysteries. Tarot, divination, the Mystic Kabalah,
Birth numbers, arithmancy, mystic squares, cheiromancy,
tasseomancy, teacups, finger rings (dactylomancy),
geomancy, the hermetic creeds.
MERENPTAH taps the forces which inspired Ancient Egypt
and sustained the Pharaohs for three thousand years.
Your satisfaction GUARANTEED or MONEY BACK.
Call (718-xxx-xxxx). 148 Seventh Avenue. D train, Bklyn.

Staying up all night has this effect on me. I lose all sense of time and place. This is the essence of my own poor opus, the story of an unnamed young man for whom place and period have no real meaning. Musil wrote about "The Man Without Qualities." But my man goes the extra mile to become the "Man Without Consequences," the man whom life just washes over. Nevertheless, he is alive, in a time-space frame. So I have a paradox to deal with. I wanted to relate him in some way to the great clowns of the golden age of the movies - Chaplin, Keaton, W.C. Fields, Groucho, Keaton above all. It's not easy. In the current climate, I've not been in a hurry, particularly since Ervine Lazar gave me advance warning that he expected the chop. "Don't show me work in progress in any case, Andy," he had told me, at the earliest stage. "I'd like to see the end product. Over and out." Which gave me another potential title: "Ends and Meaning." But then again, mebbe not.

My sister, in Seattle, in the bowels of Microsoft, could not give me any current address or telephone number for Ros. 148 Seventh Avenue drew a blank. The house was now owned by an interior designer who had gutted the previous setup completely. No spooky, lowlit art deco lamps and dark curtains. Everything was light, open plan, with white walls and straight-lined, uncomfortable furniture. To balance it up, there was a Lichtenstein on the wall. You never know what's inside these houses. But he had bought the place empty from the real estate company and they had removed all the previous fittings. He wouldn't know Merenptah from a manicure. The real estate company were not releasing information on past or present clients, apart from telling me they had no present address for the previous owner. If they had it they wouldn't have given it out.

This left me to chase after other fictional characters, needles in the reality haystack. I trudged up in the snow to the corner of Bond and Lafayette, but no trace of the "Acme" art gallery. There was a gallery nearby, the Ralston, but no-one knew of a "Frances Stein" or an "Ada." The Acme Building and Acme Bar and Grill were across the road, but that didn't get me anywhere. I sat in the Time Cafe, glaring at its inverted clock, the hands going backwards instead of forwards. It was, in my own book, a favourite haunt. Thinking, as I often do, about Annie, and what she would invevitably say about my confusions of fact and fiction:

"There are real people out there, Andy."

In New York City, you must be kidding. My employer, Ervine Lazar, finally ran out of luck in early March. The axe fell during one of the worst snowstorms of the year, the seventeenth of the winter, burying the first storeys of the city's buildings right up to their windows. The temperatures at night were fearsome. In the pale light of morning, Lazar called me from the office:

"You know that glass case manuscript? You can keep it. And the rest of the stuff. The manuscripts you're reading, Hilda will collect those, or you can send them direct to her. Do we owe you any money?"

"A few dollars."

"Invoice me. I'll pay you out of my pocket. You don't want to wait till hell freezes over for the bastards to sign checks. They killed literature a long time ago, now they want to make sure it stays buried. But the human heart, Andy, it just keeps beating. The brains I am not so sure about."

"I can wait for the money, Mr Lazar."

"Don't be chivalrous, Andy. Chivarly died before Don Quixote. You know that. And that was the sixteenth century. It's all downhill from there. Except for medical science, I'll grant you that. There's real promise there. They're promising me some more years of misery."

"You fought the good fight."

"Fight shmight. I gave false hope to some people I should have advised to go into the schmutter trade. Come to think about it I did advise them to into the schmutter trade. But I'll be in touch with you, Andy. Take my advice, go into the schmutter trade."

"What about the `Cosmic Follies'?"

"Don't spend any more time on it, you'll go blind. What do you care about some shmuck who can't even bother to make himself readable, let alone understood? Forget your tramp-savant, Andy. Go back to your own work. I'll get you a good agent who's not yet died of heartbreak and congealed arteries. I'll give you the number for Hanna Gartree."

"You gave it me already."

"So get going. Forget your old pal Lazar. I am beyond help. Stranded in the ice, with my leg trapped under the tree trunk. Go on, save yourself."

Then silence at the other end of the line.

Having become unemployed, I had to find feeding money. It was back to the old Messenger job, couriering letters and packages across town on the battered scooter I had garaged free at Jose's Fix-Em-All down Bergen Street, across Jay. Once the snow had cleared, this work became non-lethal, and I could resume my private detective mission. I had listed the broad areas of inquiry to disentangle cosmic fact from fiction:

1. Verify or discard "true" characters: Benjamin, Frances, Allan Darwish, Caroline, Salim.
2. Salim involvment in the World Trade Center bombing? Check press reports, yellow cab drivers, records?
3. The Geodesic Dome: was this one I had missed, or fiction?
4. Merenptah and Ada, locate Acme gallery elsewhere?
5. Read up on MPD, Multiple Personality Syndrome, and
6. Track down the needle in the haystack, Mo Smith?
7. Track down, read and transcribe, examining for further clues, the scattered chapters following end of main manuscript.
8. Arnold Flint, Lincoln Korombane, Jaime, any basis in fact? Sources?
9. Orville Dullest and the CIA. Must be some data somewhere.
10. The Alchemist, Mephistopheles, Frank Ox and other "occult" matters, exegete, refute, exorcise?

The courier job is one step up from pizza delivery. At least the packages don't get cold, most occasions, though once I had to deliver a bowl of home made soup from Bleecker Street to Elmhurst, Queens. Most times though, I have no idea what's inside the packages. It could be the "Cosmic Eggs" for all I knew. My life became a succession of briefly unlocked doors, opaque faces eyeing the wrapped bounty, the rapidly scribbled signature and shut portals, mine not to reason why, or what. Just the abstraction of urgency. At least a plumber or a decorator gets invited inside, to see the contours of other people's lives. All I know is they want something fast. Sometimes I fantasize that these are just empty packages, filled with old newspapers or feathers, illusions of communication rushing to and fro in the grid...

One thing I could more easily do while delivering was to check the geography of Mo Smith's journey Uptown. The City seems at times so fixed and eternal, with its skyline unchanged since Pharaonic times, or at least since the 1960's. But of course the City has been renewing itself all the time, tearing itself down and building itself up, with new holes in the ground filled with new towers rising at three days per storey, the Mohawk workmen clambering up the webs of scaffolding and girders, impervious to vertigo, as if rushing ever upwards so that, as the last, highest of all floors is capped, a brief glimpse can be had, a starburst sample of the happy hunting grounds. We all know that man is not meant to leave the ground, and invade the sky, except at the very last moments. Now the busy traffic up there cuts it all off. The ancient Egyptians of course, got there long before us. When NASA's probe finally reaches the penultimate planet, Uranus, will it merely record the welcoming committee of the United Pharaohs of Memphis, sipping palm wine and cracking those Turkish pistachio nuts upon the sulphurous hills?

But down below, all is flux, change and bustle. Many of the shops Mo Smith passed by have changed hands. Forty-Second Street, once the model of glamour, is undergoing yet another of its periodic transformations. Gone are the peepshows and porno emporiums that fronted Frank Ox's spyholes, the low-priced fleapit theatres showing fifth rate trash along with repeat runs of mainstream sleepers, the Hot Hot Hot XXX universe, now exiled to a handful of regulated venues, even all the dead marquees which were livened for a while with their bizarre haikus - "BACK FROM THE MOUNTAINS A YELLOW

HANDRAIL GUIDES ME DOWN THE SUBWAY STAIRS" - no more, the marquees are all dead, awaiting their turn to be torn apart and reconstituted as 21st Century Entertainment Centers, shiny new garishly colored monuments to pre-censored showbiz, the shadows giving way to Disney, a mighty cardboard cartoon Hercules rising four storeys high.

We all have to worship something, and the more that can be persuaded to worship the same thing the better, for the flow of manna unchecked. A "cleaner" kind of money, with the filthier lucre shifted back into the shadow-lands where it belongs.

"INTO THE LAUNDROMAT SHE PEERS, INTO THE MACHINE AS THE SUN GOES DOWN..." MERENPTAH THE MAGUS, The Seeing Eye. What did you foresee, in your crystal ball, whoever you are or were? Did you foresee the aftermath of that brave handshake on the White House lawn which closes Benjamin's narrative - the cry for an end to blood and tears? And three years down the line, the high tide of hope, and then the ebb, the bullet fired in the peacemaker's back, the fall from grace, the casting out of the sincere but bumbling partner, the return of warrior drums, terrorist bombs, shattered corpses, the squandered possibilities, the zombie words of international platitudes, and the mystery waves, broken on our own shores, of the zealots' explosive outrage...

What does it all have to do with me? Of course the global village and so forth. But I have travelled enough, like almost everyone else, to see that close as the other parts of the world are to us, they are equally, or even more radically, distant. I walked through the streets of Cairo and there were no Pharaohs, no sinister Alchemists, no exotic medieval travellers. Even the Presidential palace merely houses, we know, an ordinary, rather frightened man, with a set of uniforms and expensive suits, an entourage, some – but far from all levers of power, armies and policemen to do his bidding, or pretend to while they dissimulate and plot and plan other ascendances. All around me the eternal poor, strewn on a thousand dusty streets and alleys. The merest mortgage holder in New Jersey was a grand mogul in comparison. Despite the instant, global live transmission, we are as far apart as ever. Despite Mo Smith's cosmic conceit. And despite Starbucks, Disney and McDonalds.

Thus endeth the day's sermon.

But back to foreseeing the future. George Orwell, in 1949, saw 1984 as the allegorical year of ultimate tyranny, when everyone would be subjected to the lies of the all-powerful Ministry of Truth. 1984 came and went and all we got was the whimpering end of Jimmy Carter and the geriatric dawn of Ronald Reagan. Orwell's triumph, nevertheless, was to define our deepest political anxieties and to prophesy the excesses of Newspeak, which babbles at us, in the spirit, if not the letter of Orwell, from every technological and meritological orifice. Doubleplus ungood indeed. Now that 1984 is long gone it's all just another facet of design. Been there, done that and got the t-shirt. Generation X thru Z, and start, at A, all over again.

I cut my teeth on Bellow, Roth, Mailer, Pynchon, Gaddis. Voices and scribbles of the middle century. America as chaos. Vietnam the demon in the machine, the great idea gone sour, twisted morals. The Great Society against the napalmed child. But dissent too grew warped and jaded. Arbiters of order, high and low, rebelled against the trashing of Optimism, and begat the Republican Right, the Christian backlash, but also the redemptive voice, the therapeutic novel: Alice Walker, Toni Morrison, Maya Angelou, the African-American earth mothers, cliches coming home to roost. Give me Beckett's Unnameable any day, with his whole body stuck in a jar in the dark, and only the mind rambling on, trying to make sense. But I am just an old throwback, not all that distant from Ervine Lazar. Delivering other people's thoughts on an old mo-bike is just the right thing for me now.

So here I am, left with two unusable manuscripts. My own indefinitely postponed work-in-progress, and the hulk of Mo Smith. As the spring thaw set in, I followed the trail of the missing envelopes, scootering around to Hilda's dumping places, then settling down again in my own chaos to fill the gaps and wrestle with the spider-scratch writing. Left, finally, with the "definitive" version, the most complete edition, to date, of Mo Smith's (or Benjamin's?) work, pending the re-appearance of the man himself, the shambling tramp or his inventor. For there was, I verified in mid-April, a real Benjamin, or Benny, who had worked for a few months at a video and film co-op in the East Village – not at East 4th, but on First Avenue, just up from Saint Marks Place.

A cavernous basement, it turned out to be in fact a kind of museum of something I had thought was long defunct - the American "Underground" film. There were shelves and shelves of 16mm prints of the films of Jonas and Adolphus Mekas, Stan Brakhage, Bruce Conner, Ed Emshwiller, Kenneth Anger, Stan VanDerBeek, Robert Nelson, Jack Smith. The avant-gardists, who looked for new and different ways to tell a story, or, in fact, to throw out the challenge that stories are not everything. It should have taken me back, except that I was never there, being only an unsuspecting new-born babe. I live vicariously in all eras, including, and especially, my own. But there was a living relic of the "swinging" sixties in the building, Fred Katskan, current director of the co-op, described in the leaflet of his own retrospective as "student, sculptor, alchemist and ex-heroin-addict." A gangling figure, all elbows and knees, with two bright blue eyes staring out of a mass of white hair. He wrinkled his eyebrows, or rather shifted the mid-section of his great tuft, as he conjured up the memory of "Benny, yes. He was Israeli, but an unusual one, they're usually pretty kinetic, aren't they? A noisy, jerky kind of people. But Benny was very quiet. Large fellow, but kind of pensive. Used to sit around in the cutting rooms and think. The members liked him. He was here about the time you're talking about. The Trade Center bombing. I remember the explosion rocked the whole area. I did consider the aesthetic angle of those two huge towers falling, but the Nazis kind of put us off that kind of mass surreal destruction, don't you think? It was more an Andy Warhol kind of project: You focus for twelve hours on the World Trade Center and then the film runs out just before the bang. We could have given it a Dalian title: 'Serenity of the Pre-Flaccid Age.'" He said all this with a straight face, his eyes focusing on some private distance, beyond the walls.

"What happened to this Benny?" I asked him, trying to revert to our own space-time.

"He left, I think. I mean I know he left, but I think he went back to Israel. After the peace agreement, the Oslo Thing. He left with his friend, beautiful black lady. Psychiatrist. I forget her name. She was very sick, the Big C. But they were going to visit the New Middle East. Always makes me think of Ohio, that phrase. The New World Order. That's another one. Make mine a malted sundae please."

All the answers lead to new questions. Someone, somewhere, has been infecting fictions with facts. I went back to my list of enquiries to try and update what I thought I knew:

1. Cannot verify Frances or Allan Darwish, but serious problems still with "Benny" and "Caroline."
2. Trawling through New York Times reports of the World Trade Center bombing reveal no "Salim Halimi" or "Battuta" involved. One Ramzi Ali Yussuf is on trial for masterminding the bombing. A mysterious exemplar of the general brand of "international terrorists", he has been arrested in Pakistan by U.S. agents and brought to book, even though grave doubts remain as to his actual original identity. Rumours abound that he is in fact an agent of Saddam Hussein of Iraq, who used the network of "Afghan" veterans, once supported by the CIA but then abandoned, to set up the Twin Tower bombing. The "Cosmic" character "Sheikh Jedid" seems to derive from the real-life Egyptian Sheikh Omar Abdel Rahman, also blind, who was convicted of the bombing plot in 1995 and is now serving time. No G.G. Gittlin can be found.
3. The Geodesic Dome - no trace in the news cuttings of the time. Another coverup, in these post-X-Files days?
4. Merenptah and Ada, still as elusive.
5. Still reading up on MPD.
6. Mo Smith, Mo Smith, where are you?
7. Chapters tracked, and being transcribed.
8. No sign of Flint, Korombane, Jaime. So many Jaimes out there.
9. No Orville Dullest known, another X-File?
10. Alchemy remaining alchemical...

Sitting, pen in mouth, chewing, I am diverted by an item in the morning's New York Times. The headlines hammer about death and disease in Zaire, massacres in Algeria, IRA bomb threats in England, and the killer-pyschiatrist still running his sideshow in the ruins of Serbian Bosnia. Allen Ginsberg has died, aged 70. The best minds of, etcetera. Howl, howl against the dying of the light. But further down the page, the science wonks have come up with a new discovery: "Extremophiles" - creatures that thrive in extremes: microbes that live in boiling vents on the deep-sea bed, or buried under thousands of feet of polar ice, or can swim in acid, eat sulphur, draw energy from barren rocks. Scientists around the globe are in a complete spate of excitement.

Together with the revelation of long dead microbes inside Martian meteorites, this points, they say, to the universality of life, a microbiological revolution. The impossible can be confounded: "`When I studied my biology in school, I was told the only reason we had life on earth is because we have this perfect set of conditions...' said Chris Fox of the National Oceanic and Atmospheric Administration's VENT program to study deep-sea volcanic activity. `What we're finding here is that you can grow bugs in magma, just about.'" The most intriguing part of the report comes several paragraphs on:

> **"The government is financing several new research programs based on the tantalising premise that, if these diverse groups all work together, they can comprehend the nature of life at its most fundamental level. Among other things, participants in in this multinational, multi-planetary, multidisciplinary quest are hoping to learn the nature of the cosmic Mother Cell, the universal ancestor of all life."**

Which brings us directly back, to the "Follies" -

The Apocrypha:

*   *

From the Diary of Patricia Windstrom -

Friday, April 6:

The Friday night meal, always an event in our little world, is made more poignant by Easter and the coming Jewish Passover, both celebrations of rebirth and freedom. Dwight's agitation seems to be peaking. He made a long rambling speech over dinner about the resurrection of Christ and the repression by Pharaoh of the Israelite prisoners of war in Goshen. The gist of his speech was that both events, rather than revealing the greatness of the human spirit, as the religious scriptures had it, were in fact recurring samples of man's endemic inhumanity to man. Both were tales of an excessive violence and brutality, against the man Christ, on the one hand, and an entire captive nation, on the other. When the Israelites were driven out, they ended up despoiling and dispossessing other nations, despite the supposedly purifying nature of their forty years of wandering with Moses in the desert. Christ, too, preached a doctrine of peace and love but his followers massacred each other, and others, in his name. The only honest religion, Dwight said, were the Muslims, who revered their founder but accepted that violence was part of our world.

Dwight then said that he had been thinking of this problem for many years, and had welcomed the opportunity provided by our Group to lead a life cut off from all these sources of evil. He then revealed that he had been keeping from us the real reason for his enthusiasm to enter the Dome. He said that Cruller had sworn him to secrecy until such time as he considered the other Pioneers ready, and he judged that this time had now come.

Cruller, Dwight said, had been in touch for some time with an Intelligence from another world, a world which could not be defined by the "science-fiction" mode of beings from outer space, or from another galaxy, but a force of "pure reason" which was beyond our normal spheres of space and time. Cruller had been in contact with this Intelligence since his college days, when It/He/She had revealed itself to him in a drive-in cinema in Indianapolis. It was this Intelligence which had advised Cruller to build the Dome, and to prepare a group of people who would be made ready to depart on the next stage of a "disconnection" with the human/material world.

The name of this Intelligence, said Dwight, was Ang. Ang was an "immanence", or an "emanation" of the rational principle of the cosmos. We anthropomorphized him because we had no other way, in our present state, of experiencing "him" in any other way. Ang was not God. He was not a Creator, but an aspect of Creation which humanity could not even aspire to, unless it departed from its "improper shell." Dwight hurried to assure us that he was not pronouncing some crackpot proposal of mass suicide like Jim Jones. We would be summoned and would physically depart the Dome, to a mode of transport - he avoided the word "spaceship" - which would take us to a "situation", not in our space-time, in which we could experience Ang. The time for this move would be in one month.

This was not, Dwight said, a choice with no return. Each could choose, after experiencing Ang, to return to our mode of life, on Earth, but not inside the Dome, which would have to be abandoned. We could resume our mundane and dangerous lives and experience humanity's wretched and melancholy attempts to come to terms with itself in the Millennium to come.

This speech by Dwight completely spoiled my dinner, despite the fact that it consisted of my own enhanced beetroot. The shock has not been Dwight's speech itself but the realization that half the Group had been prepared for it in advance. The main surprise was Ned Snead, our astronaut, whom I thought was the steadiest mind we had. He took me aside later and told me that since he had walked on the moon, he had felt some presence, outside ordinary experience, that couldn't be explained as a religious element. Other fellow astronauts had had similar feelings, but only spoke of them among themselves. He was convinced Dwight and Cruller were right on this.

Saturday, April 7:

I am very depressed, and have taken valium. This is the first time I've taken any chemicals since I came here. The revelation that almost half our number have cracked in some way is scaring me out of my wits. For eighteen months we've acted scientifically, monitoring our progress, discussing our findings, working out each other's problems. Now I discover twelve of us have been dissembling, maybe all along, like Dwight. Twelve, the ironic number. So am I to be cast as Judas? I feel I ought to be contacting the outside world about this, but I can't do this alone. The idea that we should all be open to each other is so deep. My idea. God knows what everyone else is thinking. Selina Hasek gave me a conspiratorial look at breakfast. But I decided to be alone all day, and night, till Sunday morning. Then I'll try to talk to her. Selina has been the one most in touch with the Outside, as she's still been working on her craft objects, decorating our rooms with her exquisite wood sculptures. But of course, she has been fucking Ned. So dare I talk to her after all?

Sunday, April 8:

Thank God, Selina agrees with me. We had a long talk in the toilet. The experiment has completely failed, Selina says. We've shown that isolation from the outside world creates a kind of social inbreeding. The people of the Israeli kibbutz, whose model we had technically adopted, were not cut off from their environment. And of course, they reared children, which we decided from the onset we would not do. Ned was, Selina said, totally insane, and in thrall to Dwight, whom he had adopted as a substitute father. She also thought Dwight and Ned were probably lovers, though Dwight presented himself as completely celibate, and homophobic to boot. Our whole world was a sham, most of us could not stand being cooped up here any longer, and the twelve had seized on Dwight's crazy idea as an excuse to get the hell out.

I asked Selina what she thought we could do about this, and she said she would try and devise a code to alert her friend, Frances, at the Art gallery in New York which had showcased her work. But we should be very cautious, because we couldn't know how Dwight and Ned might react to such a "rebellion" and we had to guard against a violent response. She said Ned used to mutter about "blood oceans," and other things, in his sleep.

I asked her what other things. She said he also mentioned "grasshoppers", "mandelbrot waves" and "earthquakes." She said that came after his "rosebud" period. (???)

Monday, April 9:

Dwight and Ned have cut all our communications to the outside world, and physically destroyed the equipment. They claim that the coming four weeks had to be a period of total contemplation, as we sought to prepare ourselves for the journey to the "other side" of the universe. This preparation would consist, Dwight declared, in a crash course in something called "the ultimate mathematics," which he and Snead have been developing. This new math, developed out of the work of Godel, has apparently cracked the paradoxes implicit in Godel's incompleteness theorem, solved the riddle of Fermat's Last Theorem, encompassed and surpassed Hawking's extrapo-lations on black holes, and provided the unified field theory that has eluded mathematical and physical science for decades. It was, Dwight said, the "kiddie version" of Ang's own basic principles, but had been simplified in accordance with the biological limitations of the normal human brain.

"They're quite mad," Selina whispered to me, in the toilet, "but we have to go along with it, till we can figure out what we can do. I think Nadine and Pancho can be trusted, but I'm not sure." She gave me a strange frightened glance, as if I too might be a Dwightee! I haven't cried since I was five years old, but I felt tears welling up in my eyes. We clasped hands, mutely.

Wednesday, April 11:

It's becoming quite difficult to keep this diary. Everybody is watching everybody else. Dwight now says that we have to exercise our intelligence in such a way that our individual brains get in synch. Our individual thoughts, emotions, predelictions, got in the way of achieving contact with even the weakest emanations of Ang. This did not mean we were not individuals, but that we had to construct a compartment in which we kept our individuality, while we concentrated on the new math and on progressing towards Ang. All other activities should be set aside, as we now had enough food to last us through until our "immanentation", and all other aspects of the Dome functioned automatically in any case.

The first two sessions of "ultimate math" lasted an exhausting sixteen hours each! Much talk of formal systems, multifurcation, refutations of Godel's incompleteness theory. Apparently completeness is possible, but only Ang (of course!) has achieved it.

Thursday, April 19:

Eight days since I last did diary! Dwight moved us all into the central quarters, setting up bunks in the classroom, so that we slept for two hour period and then were woken for another session of math. The idea is to tap into the brain's semi-waking state, when its normal inhibitors are weak. True rationality is only properly achieved in dreams. I am so dog tired. There is absolutely no time to sound out any potentially sane allies. Not a moment even with Selina. Rescued diary in ten minute break to salvage sanitary stuff from former room.

Friday April 20:

Hallucinations setting in. Can they see me writing. Today we lapped up each other's spit. Or did I dream it? Dwight dipped his finger in tomato juice and intoned the Jewish Passover malediction: BLOOD, FROGS, LICE, BEASTS, BLIGHT, BOILS, HAIL, LOCUSTS, DARKNESS, DEATH OF THE FIRST-BORN. *Detzach Adash Be'ahav.*

Saturday:

I see the Nile foaming with much blood. Dwight tells of earthquakes devastating New York City, and a cyclone which will topple all the remaining skyscrapers. Weird.

Monday (or Tuesday)?

Must keep track. Not easy. Dwight is definitely not human. I saw, for just a brief flash, his mask slip and something reptilian underneath. Or was that some old T.V. show? Ned says we're well advanced towards rationality. Ang Day less than three weeks away.

Thursday?

Big flurry. Selina Hasek has escaped. Or so Dwight says. Opened the emergency hatch and blew the coop. Dwight and Ned sealed it shut. Pancho looks at me with plaintive eyes. So tired. Enough.

Sunday?

Pancho leans against me in toilet (all pee and shit in one line now): "They killed Selina. Body in the septic tank. Help me kill Dwight." I shook my head. Impossible. All seem reptilian now. Myself? No mirrors anywhere.

The brain may be rational. The mind is not. Hofstaeder?

Sometime:

I think I got it: DwightNed poisoned the fodd. We've all been drugged to the I-balls. Pethidine? Semetidine? Demons coming thru the vents.

Evrybody totlly fatigued. Xcept Dwight and Ned, who sleep in relays. One asleep while the other teaches. But all still watching each other.

- if p implies q does q imply p? old mammaries... - please God somebody find this dairy after weave gone!!!

- Well, that was a self fulfilling prophecy! Woke up this morning to find Dwight leaning over me with a big smile. Everything looks and smells pristine. It's as if some antidote was administered in the night, or day, of course we stopped counting and all the clocks and calendars were removed. Dwight was holding my diary, flipping through it. "You didn't trust me, Pat," he said, "but it doesn't matter. It just shows the strength of your will, and there can be no Intelligence without willpower." He handed it back to me quite cheerfully. "Write what you like," he said, "Ang is coming. In about twelve hours." "Is it one month already?" I asked, innocently. "Time makes no difference," he said. "Ang can flip through time like I flipped through these pages. Backwards, forwards, skipping pages, back again. Write what you want, let the humans read it. We won't care, in the next stage."

I felt a cold fear. Was this the moment, like the last hours of Jonesville, when they bring round the poison in the Koolaid? He saw the fear in my face.

"You'll be happy," he said, "when you realize the truth."

"And what if I don't?" I asked, maybe too boldly.

"The doors will be open," he said, "and you can go where you wish."

Everyone around me was getting up, groggily, from the bunk beds. I really missed Selina. I looked at Pancho, but he too was wearing this beatific look. He was one of them. Everybody happy, except me. I'm sitting writing my diary and no-one is taking any notice, or asking me why, or asking to see it. It's as if they've already left.

Later:

I wandered through the Dome. Everything was neglected. The plants were growing wild, the allotments unharvested, the lockers full of unused jumble. Most the food was bad, but Harvey and Elena were picking out the unspoiled stuff for a "last banquet." I tried to make a joke, like "is there Szechuan where we're going?" but everybody just moves on, like automatons. I helped them lay out the table, looking for signs of some rebellion or questioning. But there was none. I've walked all around the Dome, looking for a way out, in full view of the others, who've taken no notice. But both the maingate and the emergency exit are sealed, and can't be manually opened. If I could get at the master controls, but Dwight has his section locked off. If I were in a movie I could perform some heroic trick to break out, but there are no weapons, except kitchen knives, or a hoe or spade, which are useless, and in any case I could never use violence. At least some principle must remain in this shambles.

Two hours later:

Even more unreal. Everybody is preparing to leave. After setting the table, they began packing, loading the blue Cruller rucksacks with folded overalls, spare shoes, underwear, socks. I even saw Janine and Pollock put in their driving licences! Are they going to rentacar, at the other side of the cosmos, Black-Hole Budget? You'd think everybody would be talking, discussing, if not arguing about, what is to come, the new life, the possible awesome journey that they believe lies ahead. But nothing, just small talk, such as, pass me that shoehorn. Maybe their shoes will shrink, or their feet swell, across the galaxy. Harvey's taking insect repellent. Maybe it's only me who's mad.

One hour to go! I threw caution to the winds, or the calm, as it is, by telling everybody I am not going. They all nodded, smiling. Poor Pat. Janine put her arm around me. "You'll come, honey, when it happens. Everybody feels like you." They do? Well it was news to me. Or are they all dissimulating? Is everybody just marking time, fearful of crossing Dwight and Ned, afraid of what they'd do if balked. "It's all nonsense," I told Janine, "it's a delusion. Something that went in the food. We need to get back in communication with the outside. Get some good advice." If I'd have said this just days ago I'm sure I would have been killed, like Selina. But now, as Dwight said, nobody cares. They all look at me encouragingly, like a three year old child.

Nearly time -

Have to find a place to hide this, just before... I can write what I like. Dwight is a madman. Nehemiah Snead is a jerk. Harvey Fassbinder is a fuckpig. Janine is a stupid cow. Pancho is a bastard, he knows it's crap, but wouldn't help. Which one of them killed Selina? Or did she really get away? If so she would have alerted the outside. We're only on Long Island for God's sake. The way things have gone you'd think we were marooned in the Gobi desert. Or on a space station orbiting

Saturn. Just a few hundred yards from here families are enjoying the Conetquot Park, birds are singing, kids are laughing, cars are passing, people are shopping at stores. If it's Sunday my Mum might be chairing another picnic brunch meeting of the Tenafly Grey Panthers in the Eleanor Roosevelt Park. Henry, Hooray Henry, God, that was a long time ago.

How will it happen? Will they pass the cup around, the Dwight Deeblethwaite hemlock? Will Ned be there with a concealed pistol, even a machine gun, to mow us all down? Or am I the fool? The bright light, descending, the softly spreading balm, the magical sphere - and will it be forever Sunday, blue sky and sunlight on the green, the kids playing little league baseball, sleek dogs, chasing their own tails, families round the picnic hamper, Dad, Grandad, Grandma, Uncle Julius, Aunt Mae, the Bisbee brothers... root beer - please God, not root beer! - or is another thing entirely, as Dwight says, a better way of being - rationality - intelligence - a balanced mind - sounds like a bank book - I don't want to be without my memories, good or bad - my self. Me.

Fuck Ang. We are not just the "thinking machine." We are the sum of our biology, our sack of flesh and bones and nails and hair and excretions, but also of the intangible mind. The brain is rational, the mind is not.

I'd quite like to meet Ang, and ask "him/her/it" just what this pure Intelligence is supposed to do for us all.

No more fear. I made my bed when I walked in to this tomb, marching jauntily, of my own free will. I embraced the experiment. So be it.

Let's go to Ang, and

The Alchemist Mordecai in the Underworld.

Down, down, down, level after level, below the platforms of the Canal Street Subway. This is the most confusing of Manhattan's stations, as the weary citizens trudge up and down stairs, along crumbling corridors, echoing to the drip of leaking liquids. They seek the J, or the M, the N, the R or the Q trains, following arrows pointing in strange directions. Take the wrong turning, which may be any turning, and you find yourself arriving on one of the abandoned platforms, with fallen girders and loose stones covering the rusted tracks, and great piles of rubble choking the ends of the tunnels, past which unidentified carriages roar.

The abode of the homeless, the "mole people," begins just behind these landfills, in holes dug out from the packed gravel, the niches carved by the twist and thrust of girders, the grottos manhandled out of old packing cases, construction planks, corrugated iron and wire mesh. These are the dwellers of the half dark, those not yet willing or able to cut themselves free of the outside, those still dependent on the flow and whiff of stale surface air, the glow of neon lights, the chinks of daylight visible from the nearby turnstiles, the clatter of feet and jabber of landlubber voices.

The weak kneed and the inadequate, the insecure and the inept of body and spirit, the impaired of resolve and purpose, unequipped for the true rigors of life without the hope of light. For what is light but that which washes out the shadows, and what is the dark but that that forces us to look inside ourselves, to find that which has been concealed.

I welcomed the dark because, in the first place, it hid the blood that had soaked at least part of my clothing when I had dismembered Frank Ox. The killing of the pimp Jaime had been stainless, except for the soul, which had been, for so long, impure. We are all born innocent, though the sages have said that our teeth are stained by the corruption of our fathers. But we emerge like the naked fire, which can either nurture or destroy, and only slowly learn how to inflict evil. Now the latest modernity of science returns to the worst calumniations of the Calvinists, and tells us that our stars are in our genes. After two hundred years of the Enlightenment, the burning zeal to knowledge of Galvani, and Faraday, and Watt, and Davy, and Morse, and Morton the anaesthetist, and Mendel with his cross-breeded peas, and Lister, and Laveran, and Louis Pasteur, and Koch, and Hendrik Antoon Lorentz, and Kitasako, exposer of the bubonic plague, and the Curies, and Freud, and Roentgen, and Wasserman, and Einstein, and Heisenberg, the king-makers of Uncertainty, and all the trailblazers of our individual free will to power, we are back with bad blood once again. Soon we shall be back with phlegm and the humours. Black, yellow, green and red bile. And they will remake us, in our own image. Are these the things I must see?

Down below the level of the tracks are the maintenance tunnels, and the sewers. And down below the sewers are the safety ducts, down which the effluence can pass without rising to clog up the works. And down below the safety tunnels are the tunnels which were dug by mistake, to false specifications, during the decades of drilling. And down below the mistaken tunnels are the shafts bored by those government agencies entrusted with the nuclear shelters which were all the rage thirty and forty years ago, when thought was given to the power elites who were to survive the holocaust while everyone up above ducked and covered. Like mineshafts, they sunk deep pits below the city, steel liftshafts, which opened up, over one kilometer below the surface, into a series of bunkers, some of which were equipped with all the modern conveniences of bubble baths, soft mattresses, telephone communications, libraries, pantries and gymnasiums, while others remained empty hollowed out shells, which nevertheless provide shelter for those who can climb down the rusted ladders hammered into the rock for the maintenance workers, some of whom simply dropped off out of sight, their skeletons still white in the absolute gloom of long failed light bulbs and tubes. A few of the shafts are still operational, humming to the sound of deep generators, buzzing with the smalltalk of selected Senators and Congressmen and Municipal grandees, Captains of Industry and chosen media personnel who can be relied upon to keep their mouths and minds zipped. Those in on the best kept secret, the fact that the Truth is not Out There, but In Here.

As it has always been. This is an old story. Frank Ox learned it from Mephistopheles. The horse's mouth, as it were. The fallen angel. Those who have seen it both from good and bad have seen a more rounded picture. Goodness is simply not enough, or we would have been out of this shebang a long time ago.

"A man calls me out of my beauty sleep," said Mephisto, "said his name was Faust and that his entire village was dying from the plague. He was a scientist but all his science was not good enough. The people were still dying. He would make a pact with me, and mortgage his soul, for a few years of my effective assistance. He would start from scratch, and be young again. And then, anything was possible.

"The only problem was, he didn't want to pay."

The oldest economic conundrum. Of course, Faust wasn't paying Frank Ox either, except with promises and i.o.u.s. In those days Frank Ox wasn't his name. It was Fleischig something. Conrad Fleischig. A common alchemist like myself. We met at the Alchemists Anonymous, in Hanover. We were both trying to kick the habit.

"Faust wanted me to find an angle," Conrad/Frank told me in Hiffenlooper's Tavern, in the Schneiders' alley. "Something on Mephisto, that would force him to release the old man from his contract. But what can you get on the devil? He can wriggle out of anything. But at least he could show you a good time, I'll say that for him."

What happened to Faust? In Goethe's long long screed, he is redeemed, at last, by the eternal power of love in its feminine entity, "Eternal Womanhood," an old story, and just the old kraut's own wishful thinking. Modern feminism embraces the same counterpart, the cracking of the patriarchal phallic tyranny. But what is more phallically tyrannical than God? Substitute the Goddess, it still cuts the same way. Power from above. But the tree is nourished by its roots, and all the vapour that comes down to enrich the soil is only that which rose up from below. Deep below the oceans, over four-fifths of the world's surface has never been seen, let alone explored, let alone tamed, and they are still talking of reaching for the stars. Ridiculous.

Here down below, one hears the clock ticking. But it is the very heartbeat of the earth. Not the long dead buzz of the generators which have been cut off, the thump of man made engines, long dormant, not even of the buried machines of long dead alien cultures which lived here for reasons beyond anyone's guess, now rotted away and porous with holes inhabited by blind insects which cannot be found in your entymologies, Horatio, but that tap tap tap of the core of the planet itself. The crick-crack of that molten magma that pumps at the hub, sometimes leaking out and blowing out of volcanos, the purifying and destroying fire. The Alchemical idea was that the thing to be redeemed was not Man, but the Divinity that is entrapped in Matter, in the Jewish lore - the Divine who was damaged by his own Creation, by the shrinking that the kabbalists called the *tsimtsum*. An interesting counterpoint to the modern scientists who are telling us that the Creation was a Big Bang. Something that any child could conjure, but which they say they can test with state of the art instruments that measure the expansion of the earliest fragments of the blast. And now they are just down to the very first milli-milliseconds, which they cannot yet elucidate. But the kabbalists said that what was Before the Creation was the Infinite, and the Creation is literally the construction of the Finite out of the boundless, which could not be measured, perceived, or even imagined. The Incredible Shrinking Universe. Eventually it will be like the head of a pin, then a zillionth smaller, and then simply be snuffed out. Put that in your pipe and smoke it, Hawking.

Science is bunk. Until it can bring back the dead, it is not a jot of use to anyone. Ask Frank Ox, if you can wield that ouija board. Of course modern man lives by science, whether he believes in it or not. He turns on a switch and expects the light to come on or he'll know the reason why. Even the most rabid religious zealots cry out for the doctor when the staggers hit them, rather than the old soothsayer. Oh, but they keep old Sooth's palm greased as well, just in case. Liars and hypocrites.

Only those who dwell down here have completely turned their back on everything. All the home comforts, physical and spiritual. Nothing down here but the wild ego.

Martian is a good example. He was called that way because, as a "sniffer" for the personnel of Bunker Squad Z-19, his special senses were quite out of this world. Blind from birth, he had the most hyperacute hearing that had ever been registered by NSA's boffins. He could sit one and a half miles underground and listen to every rustle and tremor on the surface for a ground radius of fifteen miles. His problem was that when actually on the surface the noise level was so excruciating for him that he had worn special ear plugs from childhood. Thus, when the bunker was closed down, and all its entrances dynamited and sealed by Executive Order of Jimmy Carter in his most do-gooding phase, he slipped away from his security minders and remained underground, secure in the knowledge that enough tinned food had been stockpiled to last one man six thousand years, give or take a decade or two. Furthermore, to confound the lovers of Twilight Zone allegories, there were at least three dozen manual can openers stored around the facility. When the mole people began tunnelling down, in the mid-eighties, to escape the attention of the Subway Patrol cops who had been ordered to round them up and scatter them to cosy overground shelters, Martian was the first to greet them and open up the great steel doors inscribed **"Government Zone - Extreme Danger - Radiation Leak Beyond This Level,"** though of course, they could not see this, as Martian was incapable of repairing the long blown generators which had provided heat, illumination and ventilation, becoming inured to the damp cold, the fetid atmosphere filtered through the porous rock, and in no need of the light.

There were, on the other hand, the tunnellers found, candles, amply supplied, which could be used, sparingly, as the fire voraciously licked up the meagre oxygen. Eventually, the bunker-people discovered they could survive with one candle per week, placed in a strategic position, just below the great screen which would have revealed the deployment of Soviet Intercontinental missiles, their trajectories and targets, but had long been a vast expanse of scratched and blackened plastic, and that the ineffable afterimages of that single light could last, to their increasingly sensitised retinas, for several days after its extinction, until the next wick was lit.

I have lied, therefore, in giving the impression that all below was total darkness, but, compared to the blazing lights of the city above, we are quite dim. Nothing is absolute, all is relative, as all revolves around the central hub.

Now I can lie on the bunk marked with the placque **"Reserved for the Vice President of the United States,"** (Martian has the top bunk) and Martian reels off for me all the movements and mutterings of my enemies above. The NYPD and their tame psychics, the X File team, the FBI, the CIA, the NSA, the IRS, the GSU, the DEA, the ASV or Alien Surveillance Verifiers, the DACs or Deportable Alien Control System, the BRND or Bank Robbery Nickname Department, the FIP or False Identity Patrol and divers other idiotic acronyms, as well as all the surviving personas of Mo Smith and his OOBWWs, or Out-of-Body Well-Wishers. Filtering the voices one from the other, the distinctive timbres of over fifteen million larynxes, has been the Martian's crowning glory. Once put to the service of the State, he now serves me, the humble scion of rabbis, goldsmiths, communal cobblers and half-blind Torah scribes.

But after a while I stopped caring about all the plots and conspiracies, all the cabals and schemes, the stratagems and intrigues. In the fading light of the flickering candle I could review my lives, my ordeals, my journeys and adventures. I could see, when the light finally flickered out, to usher in the six day darkness, all my errors, like tattered ghosts mingling with the floaters on my eyeballs. The lingering afterglow of hopes of that much younger, vital man...

So what happened to Faust? Mephisto, when found by Frank Ox, urged Conrad Fleischig to forget him. "That boy is burnt meat," he said, flicking the ash of his sixth finger into a convenient spitoon. "I have a policy of no refunds. It's a matter of hygiene. Once I have used a soul it cannot be readily recycled. Though one might consider vending them to missionaries for use among the Heathen and the Infidel. What do you think? You seem to be a smart fellow. I'll make you a business proposition."

It was at this point that Frank Ox/ Fleischig/ and many other aliases became a roving salesman for the Devil. It was a lucrative second string to his bow, and covered his ongoing expenses. There was no soul so tarnished or degraded that Frank Ox would not sell, vastly overpriced, to some poor peasant living in a remote hovel, barrio or favela who coughed up his life's savings for the inner accoutrements of a superior. Sometimes the lives of these recipients were so degraded and miserable that even the tarnished souls were an improvement on what they had before. But more often than not the diseased souls would eat away at their new owners and leave them in possession of a thing so ragged it could not be passed on for love nor money, nor even shake itself loose by sorcery, therapy or exorcism, and remain attached till death. These unsellable, bottom of the barrel souls can be sensed everywhere in the third world, scrabbling along the ground, shrivelling plants and animals, and causing droughts and famine. Thus was Frank Ox a scourge of which the world is finally well rid, loosing his own pathetic and moth eaten soul upon the spavined city.

So what became of Faust? Wandering, shriven and woebegone, singing his melancholy odes. Blinded by Care, who breathes her curses on him, the Old Kraut leaves him egging on his people to noble toils and labours, to drain the bogs of destitution and contagion and build a Paradise -

Raised by a bold and zealous people's skill... none is of freedom or of life deserving unless he conquers it anew. With dangers thus begirt, defying fears, Childhood, youth, age shall strive through strenuous years. Such busy, teeming throngs I long to see, Standing on Freedom's soil, a people free.

Like every good Liberal and Socialist, he spurred others on to build his vision, brick after strawless brick. And so he fell, exhausted by his own apocalypse, and by the disappointment meted out by all those recalcitrant proles.

The Skull's Quest (continued).

Balked by the events at the Deacon Hotel, The Skull watched helplessly as the morgue attendants and forensic experts of the New York Police Department loaded the body-bagged remnants of the murdered detective into a police ambulance and drove them away, sirens wailing. He watched with further frustration as policemen entered and exited the premises bearing with them sacks of crime-scene properties, blackened armchairs, tables and cabinets. Plying the NYNEX call booth on the corner of 85th Street and Broadway, he instructed his agent at the Mayor's office to have the materials held for his inspection, but held back from entering the hotel until nightfall, when he registered as Otis B. Underwood. Waiting until two a.m., just before the witching hour, he broke into the tape-sealed room, examining every inch of space in the charred walls, floorboards and ceiling. He had not expected to find the stolen Cosmic Egg, but a good tracker pursued every possible clue. Leaving the building at four a.m., the hour of the wolf, he took a yellow cab bucking over the city's potholes to the 53rd Precinct, where his Mayoral toadie, Carlos Yip, took him through directly to the evidence room, where he spent two hours combing through the charcoaled furnishings. No clues there. He returned to the hotel and slept through until two a.m. the next morning, waking to prowl through the hotel corridors, floor by floor. On the twelfth floor he was disturbed by one of the elderly ladies permanently resident at the Deacon since her retirement from the Ziegfeld Girls' chorus in 1932. She fell dead as his hand closed round her windpipe, without even attempting to assay her great moment of triumph of 1918, when she had replaced the star,

Lillian Lorraine, to sing the big solo, "When I'm Looking At You," accompanied by Marie Wallace, the Fairbanks sisters and full chorus, on the stage of the New Amsterdam Theatre. Dragging her back to his room, he broke the brittle boned body apart in the kitchenette sink, cooked and ate her brain, heart and entrails, and disposed of the leavings in the basement incinerator before the engineers came on duty.

The accumulated knowledge absorbed by The Skull from the old Ziegfeld Girl's vital organs provided him, however, with no further clues. In the morning the Times published the receptionist's photofit impression of the Mystery Man who had asked to see the victim, but its close resemblance to Robert De Niro, famous Hollywood star, caused only confusion and ridicule. The Skull considered cooking and eating the receptionist too, but prudence lead him to forego this option. He went out into the Broadway heat, humming the medley of 1920's tunes which he could not get out of his head.

Give My Regards to Broadway, I'm Just a Yankee Doodle Dandy, Hold Me In Your Loving Arms, I Was a Floradora Baby, Home Sweet Home, If You Were the Only Girl In the World, Raggedy Rag, and Yes We Have No Bananas were only the tip of the mound. The Skull knew these would eventually wither and drown in the quicksands of his memory sump. Stopping at Big Nick's, he sunk his yellowing teeth into an 8 oz Platter Texasburger ("topped with an egg for egg-stra energy") allowing the loose yolk to pour down over his grizzled chin. There are old, forgotten pleasures that even the most dedicated hangman desires. He cast his eye over the menu to see whether there were any new clues, signs or calls to action in the week's misprints or typos, but could find nothing significant apart from the usual recruiting code, this time pointing the careful interpreter towards a pretzel booth in Grand Central Station.

The Skull sat back, allowing the 100 percent charcoal grilled steerbeef pattie to serve as his madeleine to his recruitment to the Cosmic Inquiry Unit by J. Edgar Hoover, at McAnn's Bar at Rector and Trinity Place, just across the way from the Trinity Churchyard, way downtown, in 1950. It was a blizzarding cold January day, the same day Alger Hiss was found guilty of perjury for denying his Communist fink credentials and his role in passing State Department secrets to the Soviet Union and its master, Stalin. Within a week, President Harry Truman would give the go-ahead for the development of the first hydrogen bomb, and five months later, the United States would go into action in Korea. Senator Joseph McCarthy was doing his best to expose communist agents in every government department. It was an exciting time for a hangman to be alive, although Alger Hiss was merely imprisoned.

"Son," said Edgar Hoover, who did not eat beefburgers but whose head closely resembled a Big Mac (as it was later to be named), "I won't call you by your name, since I don't know what it is, and I have at least a dozen on file, I don't know how you've lasted this long but I'd like you to join me in a small elite group that we're putting together to deal, long term, with the greatest threat to the integrity of these United States, greater even than the curse of communism which has infiltrated right up our ass."

It was a proud day, despite all the service that The Skull had already rendered, in the trenches of war, and special ops far from home. Outside the wind howled with a keen desperation, while inside the director of the FBI ignored the juke box music emitting Duke Ellington's Big Band Sound. Here, in McAnn's, with men in thick coats munching the Best Burgers in Town, The Skull heard his first tales of the Eggs.

"The cuckoo lays eggs in its rival's nest," said Hoover, "but who's laying these in ours? Our best scientists have been unable to even dent the things, crack the surface or chip off even a flake for analysis. The best linguists have been stumped by the runes. Spectrum analysis shows up no material of earthly origin."

"The spaceships?" The Skull had heard of rumours of visitations from outer space, the later-to-be famous alien "crash" at Roswell, project Blue Book, and various UFO theories. He had even met a catholic priest from Plymouth, Massachusetts, who had been abducted to Venus, and subjected to unspeakable tactile abuse.

"Forget the spaceships and the abductees and the UFO-nuts," Hoover waved a dismissive hand. "This is the one and only real thing."

Whether Hoover was telling him the truth or not The Skull could not tell. He had to assume Hoover was lying. But the next day he was driven, blindfolded, to a facility somewhere deep underground below the city, where, in a bare steel-walled warehouse, he was shown an array of fourteen eggs, the only time in his life he was to see so many laid out at one time. He was allowed to touch them, and their touch caused his entire body to tingle, and his blood sing in his veins. Hoover pointed out each egg and its point of discovery: "Kaiyuh Mountains,

Alaska. Pocatello, Idaho. Moosehead Lake, Maine. Glacier Peak, Washington. Jimmy's Bar, Fresno. Elko Nevada. Greyhound bus restroom, Chicago, Illinois. Zanesville Ohio. Marsh Island, Louisiana. And five, repeat five, at the Staten Island Depository. Does that mean something to you?"

"People are throwing them away," said The Skull, "at least in New York City."

It was the last time he tried to joke with the Director of the Federal Bureau of Investigation. The comment went into his file, and was cited twelve years later, when his present tenure as Commander of the Staten Island "Hen House" commenced. Since then, three Eggs had been recovered in the Depository, and all three passed on to the unnamed agent at Justice who took over when Hoover finally relinquished his personal control of the Cosmic Project, one year before his death. This was the fourth, the one The Skull had promised himself he would, at last, with his own powers, hatch.

If only Frank Ox had not intervened. It was said that Hoover had died clutching the Fresno Egg, and that his grip upon it was so tight it was buried with him, with instructions to exhume the body after thirty years, which would mean the year 2002. But by 1980 the nation-wide Egg Search had been abandoned, and the project's partisans in the Senate Appropriations Committee were finding great difficulties in maintaining the budget even for the scaled down Hen House. The loss of an Egg, which had never occurred before, might kill off the entire mission.

I shall be on the scrap heap, The Skull thought, dully, as his happy Big Nick memory faded. Tipped myself onto the Staten Island Reclamation dump. Already the Eggs were considered small potatos. Attention had moved on, to Alien Incursions, and the three million Americans who claimed to have been abducted and abused like Father Craig Futtock of Plymouth, Mass. An entire, immense industry had grown around the alien presence on Earth, media and press empires, academic careers, countless reputations, and very soon a poor left-over Civil War hangman would be hardly a blip on the scale.

Perhaps I should kill a few more people and eat them, thought The Skull, glumly, and become an instant celebrity, feted and feared on global tee vee. But then my chance at hatching an Egg would be gone forever, for a mess of pottage, a sound bite of fame.

He paid nine dollars seventy-five for the burger and coffee, and left a dollar tip on the table. The hot blast of the mid-August day broke in as he opened the door, to mingle with the pungent heat and sizzle of the restaurant's grill. The spatula holding down the Butcher's Tenderloin Steak, served with grilled onions and mushroom gravy. Yum yum. The Skull walked out into the baking sunlight. The rays punching down from our own star. Sagging, hawking dry spit, perspiring, the citizens of the city drag by. He stepped forth, throwing his shoulders back, defiantly.

Yes, we have no bananas. We have no bananas today.

The Pharaoh's Return.

Everybody wants to be a U.S. citizen, thought Ada Em, but when they finally get those papers they often look back whence they came. Merenptah, for the first few months after he swore allegiance to the Constitution of the United States and was received into the ever growing fold, seemed happy to stay put in Park Slope, sending out his local urchins to advertise his home wares, and eke his meagre living from the five dollars flat fee required for his soothing gaze into the palms, retinas, finger and toe nails, souls and psyches of the supplicant anxious. Week by week his reputation grew. "He looked into my eyes, and it was as if I was looking into a deep black pool of water. Or not of water, but some very ancient liquid. Like mercury, or something. You know what I'm sayin'?" "That man is genuinely connected. You know he has seen great sorrow. He is a genuine magus." "He put his hand on my forehead, and I saw. You can't imagine, it, the things I saw! Long processions, of hundreds of thousands of people, all waving palm fronds and shit, just walking straight into the pyramid. And then the pyramid closed behind them. And I knew that I was also in there. Waiting, between one world and the next. It was worth even ten dollars."

For a while, Ada Em became his assistant, after the Acme Gallery closed in SoHo, when Frances' main backer, the art loving investor Klaus Von Hookspappen, lost his shirt in the junk bond market. He had gazed into his own pyramid of speculation and saw vast profit emanating from a scheme which had mutated from unknown sources onto the global insiders' web to move imaginary monies at lightning speed from one currency to another according to a prearranged code.

Thus billions would shoot at not far below the speed of light from yen to rials, from rials to won, from won to deutschmarks, francs, sterling, dollars, yuan and back again to yen. No one could lose, as the insider tips enabled the cabal to slip out of an endangered currency at the flicker of an eye. However, the eye could not flick fast enough. Mr Von Hookspappen's accumulated losses were seventy five million dollars.

And so Ada Em dressed up in a strange costume she had constructed some years earlier in a Learning Annexe course about "Recovering Cleopatra," bedecked with fake rhinestones and lapis luzuli (*notation: insert more jewels here*) and stood behind Merenptah as he massaged the foreheads and battered egos seated in the red light dimmed by the inherited shades of Madame Cropfin's art deco lamps.

"You are troubled," he told an extremely obese woman who sagged before him like a wobbling mound of rubber, "your disorders are caused by your impulses to devour the world before it devours you. All is chaos and pressure, because you cannot escape the Now. Loved ones have died and you are overwhelmed because they are not in the present. But the past is equally present, and the future is unshaped. You come to me expecting me to lie about what will be. But within you is all the knowledge of what was. I do not need to look into a glass ball and see your departed brother and mother. You have devoured them. Eat only fruit and nuts for six months."

The woman was carried off, by her coterie of bodybuilding sons, all six of them squeezing her through the door and bearing her down the stairs, scraping the walls on either side. Occasionally, Merenptah would accept the occult challenge of contacting the dead beyond the grave. But in this mode his mind would always wander, speaking to persons unrelated to the supplicant, often entering into long dialogues with long gone luminaries like Frederick Barbarossa, the Mamluk Sultan Baibars, Woodrow Wilson or Eleanor Roosevelt, about the technicalities of power. In these cases he would take no payment, waiving his fee and apologising profusely to the client, who would despite this invariably stagger off shaken and awed by this display of psychic prowess.

After these rare mediumistic events Merenptah invariably felt invigorated, and would demonstrate his heightened potency and vigor later that night in bed with Ada Em. These bouts would last for six hours, and would leave her sprawled, completely exhausted, in the four-poster, as he, ravenously hungry, would venture out for an early triple-egg with pancakes maple syrup and muffins breakfast at the New Purity Restaurant down 7th Avenue at Union Street. *(Notation: Street life, the blotched chicken skin of bare arms in summer, armpit odours, eggstains on unshaved chins, the rough proles, more?? – Andy McC.)*

Thus summer passed into autumn and autumn into winter, the leaves turning red and falling on the sidewalks of Park Slope and then drying out and turning yellow and swept away by the municipal refuse and then the rain, and snow. The winter depressed Merenptah, recalling the intense pain and fear of his ejection from the Body, just one year before. Despite the central heating and the donning of multiple sweaters and scarves to brave the freezing outside, his powers waned, and the visions in his mind began to blur and tarnish, and his potency decreased, so that the night bouts of valour reduced from six to four hours, then three, then two, then one, then dwindled to the national norm.

Ada hugged him in the night, whispering in his ear, biting his ear lobes, licking his cheeks and nostrils, assuring him that sex was only a part, though a delightful part, of life. If the winter ailed him, why they could travel, escape the frost and blizzards, and holiday abroad, now that, as a proper passport holder, the world was open to his gaze and touch. "We could go to Egypt," she said, embracing his wiry torso, "you've talked about it so much. It's off-peak, we could get bargains. The Red Sea, Gizah, Luxor."

Thebes!! Land of his birthright! The mighty pillars of his father's house... The great hypostile hall, the white robed priests, carrying their pestles and unguents, their gold vessels and alabaster canisters, mumbling the endless praises of Rameses: the Lord of Strength, the Valiant, the Victorious, the Conqueror of the World, the Lord of the Two Lands, the Embodiment of Re, the Light of the Day and the Night... How his father gazed down upon them, seeing and yet not seeing, appearing to look far beyond them, into vistas they could not perceive... Karnak, the world's greatest edifice, built to last for all eternity. And some of it was even still there, according to the guide books which Ada brought home, to tempt him, although the halls were in a pitiful state, the roof completely missing, the blazing colours terribly faded, the inscriptions blurred, the statues hacked and defaced. Even the Tombs appeared to be pathetic shadows, their innermost walls pitted and pockmarked, their glorious images scraped, the messages made incoherent by meddling archaeologists and thrill seekers. The sarcophagii long broken and empty, with the mummies, the bodies of the effervescent dead, removed to be displayed to the plebeian masses in glass cages in the Cairo museum.

"Is my father there?" he asked Ada, afraid to turn the pages of the books. She nodded, caressing the nape of his neck.

"And all may stand there, spit and gawp at him?"

She nodded.

"This I must see."

She did not show him the catalogue of the Cairo Museum, which showed a photograph of his own sarcophagus, with hands crossed in the manner of Osiris, holding the kingly crook and flail. Nor that of his bust, on the ground floor, Gallery 9, "an idealized portrait at a younger age," although it looked practically like every other bust of a Pharaoh on display. Seen one, you've seen them all, excepting Akhenaten, of course. Or Hatshepshut, the warrior queen. His eyes had flicked by the picture of his tomb in the Luxor guide book. After all, he had overseen its building for over fifteen years. Like a place in the best private schools, one began subscribing to it from birth.

"We must go." But it was early March before they could bring themselves to brave the blizzards, purchase the tickets and climb aboard the local American cab service for the frozen ride down the abysmal wilderness of Brooklyn to JFK. The driver, whose name was Hohe, played them cassettes of Ecuadorian *nostalgias*. By the time they reached the airport their faces were all streaming tears, which turned to ice as they got out the door. All about them, gigantic flying machines squatted sullenly on the icy tarmac, waiting for the word to scatter noisily to the four corners of the earth.

*

There is a green hill far away
Beyond the city walls,
Where Jesus Christ was crucified
Who died to save us all...

Benjamin sits in the car, drumming his finger on the steering wheel, as a group of Arab teenagers eye them from a fence across the road with a world weary indifference. Caroline leans out the window, drinking in the vista which brings back to her the ring of old hymns and raptures. Jerusalem, the City on the Hill, the prototype, the original, its domes, its spires, its battlements and TV aerials glistening in the winter sun.

Songs of Our Mother's House, before the worm of knowledge wriggled in the apple of innocence. *Though I walk through the valley of the shadow of death...* She conjured up those early images: a dark vale, with withered, drooping trees, decayed jungle foliage, thorny creepers, bushes that burned but were never consumed. Jagged mountains with caves like gouged out eyes, and a sky lowered down, heavy with grief, leaking tendrils of poisonous cloud. Like the disease that was now eating her blood. But there had been a light, within, that could keep her going.

Thy rod and thy staff. Benjamin waited behind the wheel of the hired car, patient but uninfatuated. Everybody wants to go home at some point, but this was not even home to Benjamin, who was born and bred in Givatayim, a suburb of Tel Aviv which he described as "New Jersey in prefab concrete." And in any case this is Occupied Territory, the Old City gouged out of the Hashemite Kingdom of Jordan by war in 1967, still overwhelmingly Palestinian Arab despite the incursions and reincursions of the Israelis far beyond the old Jewish Quarter. "I have no religious feeling in my bones," he told Caroline. "Of course, there is the DNA, but where's the DNA when you need it? It just sits there, with the grin of all your ancestors."

"Don't knock the DNA," she said, "it has its way of getting even." Pointing to the sweep down from the Mount of Olives and across the Valley of Jehoshaphat, the valley of the dry bones. "Doesn't do anything to you at all?"

"I'm a New Yorker," he said, "and a Tel Aviv one. Cafe Latte, the subway, yellow cabs, the beach at Allenby, financial markets, the stock exchange, people treading on your toes and cursing, smoke, exhaust fumes and noise, sitting in a busy coffee shop watching the world go by. What have I got to do with an open air museum of hustling bigots, bloodthirsty madmen and fanatics?"

The wriggling worms in the blood. At least one can remember. Benjamin's mother, on the other hand, remembered nothing, trapped in the spongiform decay of her brain in the geriatric ward of the Jerusalem hospice in which she had lived ever since Benjamin's father had moved to the capital from the Big City to give her access to dryer air. And perhaps he himself was being tugged back by the DNA of his rabbinical ancestors, a worrying thought, as Benjamin found him engrossed in a gold-embossed edition of the Jerusalem Talmud. "I've never read this stuff before," he asserted, peering at his son over the hard top of the heavy cover. "It has an aesthetic force. Nothing to do with the politics. Or the synagogues. I don't need to mumble in public. But what is the point of glorifying books if we can't pay attention to our own old graphomaniacs?"

"Whatever you want," Benjamin agreed warily. "As long as it helps you get through the day."

Benjamin's father beamed at his son, and at the son's frail black woman companion, who had captured his heart by entering into the spirit of his Talmudic musings. Whatever his misgivings and qualms, they were buried well under his joy at this reunion. He even convinced Caroline to accompany them to visit Benjamin's mother in the hospice. An attractive quarried stone building on the side of the hill overlooking the national cemetery in the lee of Mount Herzl. This was a new annexe to what had been in a previous incarnation the Jerusalem mental asylum, and before that, the Arab village of Dir Yassin. In the War of Independence in 1948, Jewish military forces committed a massacre there that had triggered the mass flight of Palestinian civilians which became the basis of all the woes, afflictions and sorrows that the handshakers of the White House lawn, back in September, were supposed to begin to heal.

But Benjamin's mother was beyond healing. She was on the brink of the vegetative state which is the final stage of her disease, when the brain's decay becomes so pronounced that movement is slowed almost to paralysis, and even reflexive actions such as swallowing food collapse, until death approaches. She could still walk a few steps, with the aid of an attendant, her scraggy legs scrambling along the floor, her head bobbing wildly with a vacant look as her hands trembled and her fingers twitched uncontrollably. Benjamin's father sat beside her caressing her like a big rag doll, a thing of wonderment that could actually move and quiver, though to no discernable purpose. "This is Benjamin, your son. Remember? He was always a big boy, but not as big as now. And this is his friend, Caroline, she's come all the way from New York City. Benjamin lives there now."

The eyes did move, towards Caroline, but without any hint of emotion, the brow furrowed, perhaps with a certain confusion, as one of the regular nurses on shift was an Ethiopian woman of similar age and build. Or perhaps neither color nor shape, features, accents, the individual buzz, count for anything any more, and the entire world manifests itself as just a slow blur. Or an endless succession of quick flashes, going by before the remnants of what was once rumination can establish what they were. Only music, in this state, seems to cause a response, as Benjamin's father demonstrated, singing an old Russian tune. *Ochichornya.* Her head bobs along to the rhythm, the slack mouth cracking in a slight smile. "She still responds to the radio," explained Benjamin's father. "Old homeland tunes. Sometimes Bach, Beethoven. It was incredible how she awoke to the Fifth. For a few moments, there were sparks of the real person. The vegetative rhythms. But that's all. Say goodbye to your son, now, Marta. Your son Benjamin. He has to go. I'll stay for another hour, Benny. I'm a fixture here. You don't have to be here. There's no difference. Last year a flash. But now nothing."

They travelled north, along the coast motorway, breaking off northeast of Tel Aviv to cross the invisible "green line" between the old Israel and the even older occupied "west bank" before the Palestinian town of Kalkiliya. Here, too, memory becoming ever more jaded. "This was where you were patrolling in the army, wasn't it?" Caroline trying a little archaeology, which he resisted firmly. "It was a hallucination," he replied. But they were looking for the turn off to the small Arab village of Kafr T—, which, unlike all the new Israeli settlements along the line, was not graced with a newly tarred approach road and an obtrusive sign, but had to be pointed out by two teenagers selling lettuce at the roadside, a bumpy dirt track winding round the curve of a hill fenced off by Israeli army signs, opening out to a sleepy conglomeration of stone houses around a freshly built mosque. Benjamin pointed out to Caroline the Palestinian flags, until so recently banned, sprouting from every roof. They stopped again to ask directions from a group of languid men who blocked the car's progress by ambling at snail's pace across the track.

"Rashed Halimi?" Benjamin addressed them in his most American English, though the DNA cannot, as ever, be denied. "We are friends of his brother Salim, from New York." Affecting a total lack of curiosity, the men pointed them towards an even narrower dirt track up a white painted wall, towards a small neat house in a courtyard of half a dozen fruit trees. A tangle of washing lines below the Palestine flag, and women standing mutely as a gang of small children surrounded the car.

"Rashed Halimi?" Both Benjamin and Caroline were astounded as the young man came out of the house. It was Salim, returned to life, if more traditionally dressed, but with the same shy, anxious smile. Only the halting English seemed to separate this double from the disappeared green-card cab driver.

"You have news from my brother?" They were already seated, on cushions and quilts, a younger brother bringing trays of coffee and bread with a goat's butter dip. Four elder adults having entered and sat around, and women hoovering in the doorway. (*I have kept this of this segment's many typos, I assume the author meant to say "hovering", but one can never be sure with these entries. A.McC.*)

"We have heard nothing, either good or bad," said Benjamin, "but it is possible he's hiding in Canada. The lawyers are still working on the case. But it's difficult to make a breakthrough when the accused has absconded. When he has escaped. But there are good people working for him. With the new situation, perhaps things will become easier, other possibilities might open up."

Rashed nodded, and the others grunted, but volunteered no information, comfort, absolution, accusations or complaints. Benjamin knew they had assessed him instantly, the bleeding heart Israeli on his goodwill mission. Get him out of here as soon as possible, as quickly as politeness allows. The black woman, she was an unknown factor. The unknown is always best left unknown. Here, knowledge is tragedy, not power.

In the claustrophobia of the quilted room, Caroline felt faint, and asked for a glass of water to take with her array of pills. Benjamin regarding her anxiously, dreading the relapse that would maroon her far from her backup team of doctors, the glittering machines of Mount Sinai Hospital, the familiarity of her cavernous home. The doctors had only weakly endorsed this trip, but Caroline had, as usual, made her own decisions.

As Caroline lay resting for a while on the quilts, surrounded by a clutch of women, the men chased away like sullen chickens, Rashed took Benjamin by the arm away from the house, up to the end of the dirt track, on a ridge overlooking the valley stretching down towards the green green swathe of the Israeli mainland, the coastal conurbations hidden by another fold of the hills. Speaking to Benjamin in Hebrew.

"This peace agreement, do you think it's real? Will they allow Arafat back into Palestine? Rabin made a good speech, but when he was a young officer he threw the Palestinians out of Lyd and Ramleh. He is the man who tried to break our bones."

"I don't know," Benjamin shrugged his shoulders. "Politicians never do the right thing until they've done all the wrong things and failed."

"If it has happened, it's what the Americans want," said Rashed. "So it can't be anything good for the Arabs. My brother went to live among them, and trusted them. And they accused him of this terrible thing. You knew my brother. He wrote to me about you. There are Israelis who are gold, he wrote, to compensate for all the others who are such shit. It is a question of balance. The Arabs are so low and weakened, any little glitter shines bright."

"I would do what I could for Salim," said Benjamin, "if I only knew where he was. But even if you know, I understand that you won't tell me. I understand the tangle we are in."

"I don't know where he is," said Rashed. "That woman, she is quite beautiful. Is she ill?"

"She has leukemia," said Benjamin. "The doctors take bets how long she'll live. But she is one of life's fighters."

"We have women like that," Rashed sighed, "but why do they always break your balls?"

Benjamin and Caroline departed, no wiser than when they had come, but shaken at the vanished friend's twin. Salim had mentioned no twin, Benjamin had the impression his brother was two or three years younger. But perhaps it was just a trick of hope. The new dispensation, the opening up on state television, viewed at his father's home, the sudden rush of Israeli TV crews to Tunis to interview the PLO leadership, and even seeking out the most bloodthirsty of the last generation's terrorists to talk, some in fluent Hebrew, about the "inevitable civilian casualties of war." Now it's Beace, Beace, Beace, and a new garden will bloom, and Yassir Arafat and Yitzhak Rabin will gambol together while the water sprinklers merrily turn, urging forth new shoots from the stones.

We are travelling with a ghost, Benjamin thought. If only Salim were with us now. This was his trip, not Caroline's. But in his heart, he felt Salim was not present, not among the living. Either perished, drowned in the expanse of Lake Ontario, or even liquidated by the swattest of SWAT teams, cleaning up the residue of unexplained conspiracies, all manner of murky unfinished business stretching from the Afghan war to New York City and the shaken towers of the World Trade Center. If Mo Smith is right, and we are all emanations of the Mo-head, we should all be present, one way or another, in the great, interconnected flux. But here the connections seem to end, cut short like a snapped electric wire, the point at which imagination ceases and the real world begins.

Chasing reality, north, to Galilee, Nazareth (Upper and Lower) and Tiberias. Capernaum. Where Jesus walked upon the water. Or was that on the other side of the lake? The places where reality dissolves again, leaving the smudge of scribbling scribes. The miracle at Cana. Water into wine. Loaves and fishes. E unum pluribus. What was the language that God spoke? Hebrew? Aramaic? Greek? Sumerian? Rap?

They took refuge in the Scottish Hospice, in Tiberias, a charmed house of small, spartan rooms, set among palm trees and rhododendrons, overlooking the lake, with cats snoozing on deck chairs, and a framed card in the wash-cubicle with the cosy homily:

My God, I thank thee who has made the earth so bright,
So full of splendor and of joy, beauty and light.
So many gentle thoughts and deeds, circling us round.
That in the darkest spot of earth, some love is found.

On the hard, narrow single bed, separated from Caroline by a bare table, Benjamin dreamed. He saw himself at Caroline's funeral, standing aghast, over the open grave, with the friends: Allan Darwish, Aram, Frances and Salim, a small knot among a great crowd of mourners, all the down and outs and outcasts of the City. Thousands of Mo Smiths, male and female, poured out of some invisible ark. Everyone standing around in silence, watching the gravediggers carrying the dead woman's shroud. It was not a coffin, but the cloth swaddlings of a Jewish burial, though the workmen had the unmistakeable features of Manhattan's Mohawk labourers, the vertigoless skyscrape scaffolders, toiling silently under steel grey sky. Salim reached out and held his hand and, glancing at him, Benjamin realized it was not Salim but Rashed, dressed in his Palestine jelabiya. Another, bearded man beside him was in a medieval costume, baggy tunic, turban and ornate pointed shoes, a man of about fifty, with a weatherbeaten face, as craggy as the Atlas Mountains, though Benjamin had never seen the Atlas Mountains. And there were other figures there he recognised, although he knew he had not clapped eyes on them before: A wiry, compact black man with a furrowed forehead and wary, heavy lidded eyes, a tall, paunchy, florid faced white man with a shock of unkempt white hair, dressed oddly in red striped pajamas, a Hispanic youth with a twisted neck, massaging it constantly with his right hand, an ageless, weasel-faced man in a trench coat and fedora, who seemed to be shifting places all the time, disappearing and reappearing in different places in the crowd, a dour, striking figure in an old navy surplus greatcoat, black bearded, with a permanent scowl. Blink and you missed them, then they were there again, at the corner of the eye.

Another pair of eyes regarded him accusingly. The pure Islamic gaze of Karim, offspring of the young love of Caroline and Allan Darwish, *kalan zaman,* a long time ago, in a country far away. America, of the middle nineteen sixties, America of ferment and romantic hope. Levitating the Pentagon. But no levitation here. (Famous levitators: Saint Bernard Ptolemai, Saint Albert of Sicily, and Saint Dominic, founder of the Dominican Order. It is said that Savonarola, the dark priest of Florence, levitated in his dungeon cell the day before he was due to be burnt at the stake. But he was burnt none the less. *[A hardly relevant interjection, which I have left in place; Andy McCloud.]*) The shrouded body of Caroline was slowly lowered in the pit, a low keening sound arising from the crowd. Benjamin craned to look into the abyss. He realized, as he leaned forward, that he would soon have to resume the journey he had begun with her on his own, to Egypt, to meet with Allan Darwish in Cairo and fly south to the Pharaonic tombs of Luxor, the ruins of the grand temple of Karnak, the Valley of the Kings. But he feared to follow on alone. Our ancestors made such a song and dance of getting out of Egypt, one should not be in such a hurry to return, even at bargain basement prices. Not with the unsettling news of recent attacks by fundamentalist Islamic fanatics on European tourists there.

I want to go home, he thought, in his dream. But he could not figure out what home meant. He looked into the pit, willing the corpse of Caroline to rise up, the blood to run clean in the living veins again. But there was just the firm, black hand of Karim, on the back of his neck, forcing him down to join her in the grave. And the familiar faces gathering to watch his fall. The echoing lines of the latterday poet of doom: We are the hollow men, leaning together... shape without form, shade without colour...

Is that you, Mo? Is anybody there?

Between the desire   and the spasm...
Between the essence   and the descent
falls the Shadow.

Allan Darwish beamed at them, from the top of the stairway. Looking like a medieval imp in his striped jelaba and slippers, untidy hair falling all over his forehead and ears, he beckoned them up.

"Mind the stairs! They've not been fixed since the sixteenth century!"

Going carefully up, hugging the walls of the pre-Ottoman mansion, with ornate window grilles looking into the empty rooms with their reconstructed floor tiles and the remnants of the even earlier Mamluk niches and arches, they climbed to Allan's third floor sanctuary, marvelling at the fact that only he, perhaps, could manage to live inside, rather than beside a museum. The rooms he inhabited, under the somewhat ramshackle roof, were a large, almost New York sized loft, which had clearly been serving as an artist's studio, as it was full of easels, pots of paint, workbenches and exemplars of the paintings themselves, life sized canvases of dots and whirls in the characteristic Cairo dust colors, as busy as the streets outside. In one corner was Allan's bed, Spartan and lean, with a blue quilt; in another, his working desk with laptop and printer, as strange as a spaceship in this ancient frame.

"This used to be a *madrassa*, or school," Allan gestured around, "it was founded by the Sultan Qaitbay in 1472. I'll give you the full historical tour later. First, is it coffee or tea?"

As if summoned by a wand, a middle aged woman in a faded yellow dress and headscarf glided up from across the narrow top of the stairway with a wooden chair in each hand. "This is Clara," said Darwish, introducing them to her in Arabic. They shook her hand each in turn before she glided back, on her mission of service. It was interesting to see how Darwish in Cairo appeared to be a totally different person from the befuddled Professor of Manhattan. At home, as if he had inherited this from father to son, in an unbroken chain, rather than renting the space from the artist, Ali Bakri, who was presently away vending his canvases in Austria, Germany and France. Benjamin noted that Allan seemed completely recovered from the summer trauma of his murdered lover, the three days of police interrogation, and the terror of the press, which dropped the story after three days due to a triple slaughter in Queens. Darwish's well-nurtured talent of subsuming personal pain in the enthusiasms of the moment. "So how was your trip to that Other Place?"

"You'll never guess what they served on the El Al flight from Tel Aviv," said Benjamin, "bagel and lox. They must have worked really hard to find the right menu."

"It's called cultural dissonance. Denial has to be complete." He looked at Caroline with questing eyes. "I'm all right," she said. "I get tired easily. But it's been good. It doesn't feel like borrowed time."

"That's good," he said, "I have the full program for you. This is the city for long walks. As long as you like dust, and people. Fifteen million of them, all crowding in the same place. Just like New York if it survives for fifteen hundred years. It'll be lucky to last out the century. I'm glad I came, and not just because of the family. I had to leave that apartment. I never want to see that place again."

"And the teaching?"

"I'll be back in the autumn. I'll live in Brooklyn. Anywhere across the bridge."

The history lesson: Redundant words, as Cairo reveals itself to the eyes: The great hodge podge of the ages, the Fatimid city, overlaid with the Mamluk metropolis, overlaid with the Ottoman oeuvre, with Muhammad Ali, and the Frenchifications of Ismail Pasha, the breezeblock clutter of colonial Egypt, spiked through by the motorways of Anwar Sadat. "Tonight," Darwish said, "I have the treat of treats for you." He took them out into the overflowing streets of the Khan al-Khalil, past the majestic minaret of the al-Husein mosque, past the bustling compound of al-Azhar, under the traffic-jammed flyover, down the Ghuriya's maze of alleyways, the shouting cloth and kitchenware sellers - once the silk merchants' bazaar, through the graceful twin minarets of the Bab el-Zuweila, and right, into the swirling jungle of vehicle glut and choking exhaust fumes, skirting the Museum of Islamic Art (*Here I have cut out a long digression into a description of the contents of the museum, culled from some moribund guide book, which*

I thought justified the "censor's" slash, Andy M.)... past the back of the Abdin Palace, through quiet residential streets, eerily sparse after the hubbub of the suk, down towards what appeared to be a festive crowd, a rumble of several thousand voices, a splurge of colored lights and Arabic banners, onto the square before a shining high white turret, lit by a cat's cradle of multicolored lightbulbs hung over an exquisite mosque. The mausoleum of Sayidna Zeinab, the prophet's granddaughter, sister of the Shi-ite saint Hussein - an ocean of people surrounding them on every side, sidestepping hooting buses, the sidewalks conquered by large groups of peasants up for the day from out of town, camped out with their cooking pots, sacks of grain, fruit and vegetables, looking as puzzled in the Big City as any foreign tourist, the sidewalk of the mosque itself covered with little tents, before which grizzled wizards appeared to be administering blessings to bemused small boys, blind men holding on to sighted heads, and further on, into the market streets behind the mosque, a maze of funfair booths with rifle ranges, coconut shies and grilled meats, side by side with tents of magicians, snake charmers and dervish dancers leaping, whirling and shimmying together and sparring with long staves and swords. The *moulid*, the birth day of Sayidna Zeinab, a sufi festival of devotion and delirium, or a simple excuse to swamp the streets and have fun, transforming this corner of Cairo into a magic circus, the old and the new colliding and colluding, merging and combining, fusing into a wedding of the ages, the bride indistinguishable from the groom, or from the guests. The chain of life, bubbling, babbling and dancing. Where nothing stands still, all is a perpetual movement, going nowhere, but still enjoying the ride –

*

"What do you think?" asked Ada Em.

Merenptah looked down, out of the window of the ninth floor of the Flamenco Hotel. It overlooked the Nile, from the reclaimed island of Zamalek and Gezira towards the working class sprawl of Imbaba, with the illuminated mosque dominating the dark swathe across the river like a lighthouse in a dangerous bay. The hectoring voice of the local Imam booming out the Friday night sermon over the minaret's loudspeaker, penetrating the double-glazing of the room. If it were not for this, it could be a Holiday Inn or Ramada anywhere.

What's home then, Nep?

Merenptah, walking the streets of the city, from Zamalek down the Avenue of 20th July, across the bridge and down the ugly Corniche past the recent Pharaoh, Anwar Sadat's own pyramids, the Ramses Hilton, the Nile Hilton, the Cleopatra and the Semiramis, on to the hub of the square of Midan al-Tahrir, past the coffee shops with young men puffing their *shishas*, ogling the wary western tourists, up along the shopping mecca of Shari Talat Harb, past the Carlton and Claridge on to Ezbekia, and through the side streets into the market of al-Muski, pressing with the throngs of the lower classes past constantly hooting dust caked vehicles, carts of onions and garlic and the donkey carts of the *Zabaleen*, the Coptic rubbish collectors, stripping the streets of old rags and plastic for their recycling plants in the south of the City, tasting and smelling the body odours of his old countrymen, without even a shudder, after the rehearsals of rush hour New York. He took to leaving Ada to sleep in the hotel and walking out early, to catch the morning hubbub, while she sprawled exhausted after the small hours' struggle to remain asleep through the staggered calls to prayer, echoing at frustratingly spaced intervals from every mosque within hailing distance at the first crack of dawn.

Here they are, all the multitudes of Egypt, the drones who once toiled in the Nile valley fields, donating their corvee labour to the real business of the Nation, the construction of the tombs which would act as a conduit for their rulers to pass over into the Next World. For it was only in the Next World that the Ruler could bargain with the Gods directly for the well being and benefit of the people. It was only when one sat down with Osiris on that velvet cushion, sucking golden mint jujubes, that one could look down, on the blue thread of the River, with the barren dust closing in on the green swards alongside it, and say to Osiris: Make well with the land.

But the Pharaohs were dead. This Ada had to show him, in the catalogues of the Cairo Museum. As he strode, with bowed head, through the portals towards the giant Atrium in the center of the bulding, with its gigantic black granite statues torn from their proper places and functions. Stepping in and out of the cubbyholed halls with their clutter of sculpted figures, busts, coffins, sarcophagi, funerary objects of every kind, cups, canopic jars, wrappings, jewellery, mummified animals, amulets, scepters, shawabti figurines, wooden boats and armies of wooden guards and soldiers, remnants of reliefs from the most ancient times, the so-called "Old Kingdom", the "Middle" and the "New", stopping short before the figures of Akhenaten, the heretic king, whom Rameses, Nep's father, did his best to wipe from living memory, obviously in vain. The ugly, potbellied hermaphrodite, who tried to abolish all the Gods but one. E pluribus unum. But multiplicity endures. And now my father, Rameses, too, is here, in this very building, so they tell me, although Ada, bless her heart, tried to keep this painful fact from me at the start. He is kept, at the moment, from the public, locked in a glass casket, along with Ahmose I, Amenophis, Tuthmosis I II and III, Seti I, Sekenen-Re and Ramses III, whoever he may be. It is said they were found deep in a cave at Thebes guarded by a Bedouin tribe which lived off their accumulation of funeraria, or as much as might have been left by the robbers who were already breaking into and despoiling the tombs hundreds of years before even I came on the scene. *[Andy's note: I have excised six pages on tomb robbing, including ancient legal documents denouncing various governors of the Middle Kingdom for alleged collusion with the thieves, a personal rant against the priestly bureaucracy and two pages of hieroglyphic script.]*

Gently, diffidently, Ada Em followed me as I climbed up the gloomy stairs of the museum towards the Upper Floor and the locked room, number 52. The space before it covered with royal coffins and sarcophagi like so much unwanted litter. One rules the world, and spends one's entire life safeguarding one's passage to the next, and where does it all end? In a peep show, at ten Egyptian pounds a throw, fifty piastres for an Egyptian citizen, which translates at about fifteen cents a pop.

Ada hung back, respecting my privacy as I edged my way around the coffins. Room 52 is hidden away at the end of the building, behind a pile of workmen's detritus, wheelbarrows, steel pipes and coils of cable. The door is bolted with a large steel padlock and barred with a heavy wood plank. But above the padlock I could see a round, frayed keyhole, the vestige of an abandoned lock. I knelt down, on the dusty floor of the museum, putting my eye to the hole. I have a long nose, the legacy of my royal ancestors, which frustrated my efforts to place my eyeball near enough to the aperture, but, managing to flatten it somewhat against the coarse wood and press my cheek to the door, I was able to find an angle by which I could gaze at least partially into the chamber beyond. I could see bare, piss coloured walls, and a row of caskets, which at first only allowed me a distorted glance at the lower extremities of what appeared to be the dried grey remnants of the funerary shroud. I could see the heel and big toe of the closest mummy, which may or may not have been my father, or any other of his unfortunate colleagues, untimely ripped from their eternal quest.

Was this the man who had stood tall over the universe and had imperiously dismissed the upstart Hebrew, Mo-Says, who came before him with the impudent ultimatum: Let My People Go? I could not tell, though I was familiar with the big toe of my father, like every sibling, issue, relation, servant or counsellor of the court, so often prostrate, kissing his right foot. That very right foot which I spy now, dessicated like a old dry fig. How my father loved to have people kiss his foot. I think today they would call it a fetish.

You fucking dead bastard. I hope that is your foot, and if I could break through this locked door, I would break it off and eat it, brittle dilapidated bones and all. Break it off at the ankle, grab this crowbar lying on the floor and pulverise the rest of you into the tiniest millennial dust. Destroy, finally, and forever, this fear which grabbed hold of my innards from the moment when I first began to comprehend the world, a baby in my nurses' arms, looking up into those heavy lidded eyes wondering whether I was still too small to pose a threat, right up until this moment, which, Ada tells me, encompasses three thousand and two hundred years.

Was it because of you that I was condemned to take the wrong turning in the Halls of the Dead, to emerge, not in the Elysian fields of the blessed, but in the fetid gut of a destitute, homeless New York bum? Is that your last laugh, to kill me even in my death, to take revenge at the very fact of my inheritance, that I outlasted you, unlike so many of my half-brothers and sisters, whom you despatched into unmarked graves?

And I paid ten Egyptian pounds, as a tourist, twenty, counting Ada Em's passage, to stare upon your big toe. Kneeling, once again, at your feet. No more. I rose, turning away from the locked chamber, brushing past the empty, grubby coffins, with their smudged inscriptions supplicating eternity to keep their vanished souls, went by Ada, who hurried after me as I rushed down the spiralling stairs, down to the ground floor, past the clutterbutt of history, past the souvenir sellers with their shabby postcards and brochures, out into the bright, stark daylight of the Mother of Cities, the buses rattling by with the people hanging onto their doors, windows and bumpers like clusters of human grapes. And I, the merest beggar in this multitude, sweating and panting, rushing across six lanes of traffic, leaping and bounding, twisting this way and that to keep from being mown down, irate taxi drivers and divers civilians cursing me and shaking their fists.

*

...between the desire and the spasm...

I keep turning to her, afraid she might run out of steam. But Caroline seems to thrive on the crisp clean air under the bluest of blue skies over the jagged mountain of the valley. Allan Darwish brings up the rear, short of breath himself after our steep climb from the gate. Here, one can't avoid the tourists. They come, even in these unsafe times, in hordes, bused up from the luxury hotels of Luxor, across the river, the Hiltons, Movenpick and Winter Palace. Pressing up, clucking like costumed chickens, fat pink legs thrust into straining blue shorts, checkered blouses and outrageous straw hats or the blue and white *tembel* caps with "Welcome to Jerusalem" emblazoned on them from their previous stop. The tombs! The tombs! Gotta see the tombs! Bearing little maps of the excavated complex. Each ticket of ten Egyptian pounds entitles you to enter three tombs, so take your pick. The five available Ramseses, the three Tuthmoses, Hatshepshut, the Sethis, Merenptah. Some of the best tombs are closed, their exquisite carvings and paintwork endangered by the breath of all the visitgoth hordes. Ramses II is off limits. Only Ramses III, IV and IX are open. Of course, there is Tutankhamun. The longest line, but Allan dismissed it. The tomb itself is small potatos, all the main stuff you already saw in the museum, in Cairo. Let's try the tomb of Horemheb. The last Pharaoh of the Eighteenth Dynasty, the end of the line of Rameses II and Merenptah. Descending down the long parapet, lower and lower, beyond the tablet stones placed to seal the tomb after the King had been interred. Here, beyond the reach of natural light, the dimmed electric bulbs reveal the brilliant colors of the artists' work. The twin cartouches of the Pharaoh, bird, plow, sceptre, sun, scarab, yellow, red and purple. The figures and faces of Hathor, Isis, Thoth, bright as if they had been done yesterday, you wanted to reach out and see if you touched wet paint. Caroline is enraptured. You have to admit, there is an awe here. Things reach out, from time immemorial. A story told in pictures, meant only for dead eyes. An aide memoire for the dead Pharaoh to help him on his way below the world. And here the Pharaoh himself, a lithe youth, brown armed and bright eyed, offers two jars to Osiris. His twin souls, for safekeeping. The lightness and the delicacy of his bearing. Resurrections are the norm down here.

Squinting back into daylight. And down the ramp again. Rameses IX. A poor impostor carrying the illustrious name in vain. His rule bedevilled by famine and disorder, the beginning of the dynastic end. Even the carvings are debased, the lines more ragged, the figures more coarse, the artwork slapdash and skittery. It's downhill all the way from here, towards the Ptolemies and the long Greek winter. Somehow one feels a deep, irrational sadness. For all are scoundrels, after all. The bandit kings, ravaging the world, spreading misery and destruction. The golden age is neither here nor there.

One tomb left on the ticket. Still a long line to the boy-king Tut. One cannot stand in the posterior of Belgian tourists for an hour. Up a way, the entrance to one tomb seems free of visitors. Look here, Benjamin, the tomb of Merenptah. Mo Smith's Pharaoh, remember, says Allan, the son of Rameses the Great. Some scholars believe it's him, not Rameses, who was the Pharaoh of the Hebrew Exile. The one who cocked a snook at Moses. Your old cultural nemesis, Benjamin. Who gives a fuck? But Caroline presses forward. Let's lay this ghost once and for all.

Well, if he's in New York City, he certainly ain't here. Isn't he one of the mummies in Cairo? No, Allan says, Merenptah's mummy was never found. But part of his sarcophagus, the lid, I think, is there. Looking at the brochure. This tomb sure doesn't seem to be on the A list. Even Pharaohs have a sliding celebrity scale...

Stepping on the top of the ramp, stretching down, into darkness. No lights in the shaft down below. Perhaps this one is off limits after all. No, it's definitely open, says Darwish, or we couldn't get in. Caroline steps forward. Clutching on to the rickety wooden rail, leading down.

The carvings at the top are, as always, faded. Are we game? says Allan, we might meet the boogie man. This I got to do, says Caroline. Stepping down the ramp. Allan shrugs and follows. Who am I to be scared of a Pharaoh? Whose entire armies and men and chariots were swallowed up in the Red Sea. Just go easy on the pillar of fire.

As we reach into the gloom, a row of lights does come on, a chain of lightbulbs along the walls below. The shaft extending down, steeper and deeper than the ones before. Or is it that we don't have the spurious comfort of the Belgian hordes joining us to the real world? This is fantastic, says Caroline, her voice echoing. Alone at last! Just watch your step, cautions Allan. Down, down, level after level. A twist in the tunnel shuts out the daylight behind us. Now we are like those explorers in the old movies, please not Indiana Jones. I still think we should have made sure the place is supposed to be open. But who am I to divert thrill seekers?

Merenptah! Caroline calls out suddenly. Merenptah! King of Egypt! Are you there? One has to understand, she has taken her cocktail of drugs in the morning, and out into the sun. You have to take the rough with the smooth.

Merenptah! Merenptah! Her voice echoes clearly, booming around off the walls. Mo Smith! Are you there, Mo? The lights are dimmer, blinking, intermittent current. Power outages are the norm in the Third World. Though which world this is is a moot point. Fifth, Sixth, Seventh, Eighth, whatever. Beyond counting. The underworld of the underworld. You can believe that this ramp can go on forever, deep down into the center of the earth.

Merenptah! Hallooo! Allan Darwish joins in. I am trapped in the semi dark with two lunatics. But your friends are your friends. What can you do? I stepped after them, following, down, as the lights continued to flicker, drawing us further on, into the tomb.

Hallooooooo !!!

...between the essence and the descent...

I heard them again, calling my name. I had left Ada behind, in the Old Winter Palace, to sleep late, as I rose with the dawn. Crossing the wide street in front of the hotel, the slumbering calash drivers and felucca boys shaking awake to surround me. Calash sir? Boat to banana island? I want to cross to the Valley, I told them. Find me a boat and a driver on the other side. Someone who speaks the old language. Excuse me sir? I spoke a few words to them in the ancient vernacular. They shook their heads. Finland? Albania? Call Farid, he speaks Swedish and Magyar. I cursed them as best as I remembered. A wiry little man wrapped in a blue jelaba, with a waxed pointed moustache, ambled over. He addressed me haltingly in the right tongue: I will take you. I know all the Professors in Cairo. But you are Egyptian and I haven't met you. What is your name?

That is not your concern. You are a boatman? I am boatman, driver, guide, whatever you want sir. I want to go to the Valley right away. I will pay you well over the going rate. I always take only a fair price, he said. His ancient language was halting, but not bad. His face reminded me of my brother Khamwassett. If he had had a moustache. But this was a barbarian outgrowth unacceptable then, in civilised times. The sun was about to rise over the crags of the mountain across the Nile. The sky was pure turquoise. The waters of the River were rippling velvet. There were no sounds of cars. All was silent, pierced with the sharp cry of a bird. A hawk, I saw. It soared away, southwards, towards the depths of Upper Egypt. Towards Nubia, where I had cut my teeth as a young officer. Subduing insurgents. The taste of the sand, the smell of freshly spilled blood. I took my companion by the arm. He led me down the grassy bank to his boat. It was a felucca, trim and shipshape. Plying his oar, he pushed it away from the shoreline. Soon we were in the center of the River. All was soft and exquisite. The turquoise shifted into tendrils of dark red, then gold. The sun, rising over the mountain. My mouth began forming words. Coming back to me, the whispered prayers of the priests. The invocations, verses and psalms that were to smooth my passage in the underworld. The rising and falling cadences as they poured the embalming fluid into my veins, filling every orifice. Preparing the souls of my ineffable being for my final, most perilous journey. Now it all came pouring forth from my lips. The boatman looked at me, at first wary, then, as the common people do, enfolding his feelings, whatever they may be, under the skin of indifference. The need to dissimulate, faced with the unknown, authority, or dangerous power. Without saying a word, he rowed me across, pulling up to an unmanned jetty. I climbed on shore, and he tied the boat and followed me up the dirt track. At the top of the track several vehicles stood parked. My companion rapped on the window of one of them. A sleepy figure within stirred and opened the door. My companion ushered me in, but I told him he had to drive me himself, with no other. I handed the sleepy owner a sheaf of notes, and my companion climbed in the driver's seat. I sat beside him, as he whisked the rattling car up the track, onto the paved main road. The sun had risen now, bathing the shores of the Nile with a deep, blood red glow. The lush fields alongside the River of life, giving way, abruptly, to the barren desert, with rude outgrowths of shrubs and stunted trees. The low shacks of small villages along the way, their outer walls garishly decorated with pretend heiroglyphs and ersatz ancient pictures. Within a few minutes, we passed the Colossi, two immense, seated, defaced figures covered with graffiti from Greek times on, three millennia of impertinent scribblers. My driver pointed them out but I was not interested. Ada had taken me, the day before, around the sites of the town, the Luxor Temple, the complex of Karnak. All was remnants, ruins and rubble, pathetic vestiges of what had once been solid, the pillars of the earth, the very foundations which held up the world and kept it bounteous. Now all were peep shows and laughing stocks. The peasants with their instamatics and camcorders.

Take me to my tomb, I told my companion. I have to buy the ticket, he explained to me, having to use Arabic or English terms, he told me the site was not yet open. But I fix it, he said. We go in. I expect nothing less, I told him, you hear and obey. He scuttled off, and returned after a short while, alone, though I thought he might denounce me. But even if I have been lost, and strayed, into the worlds of destitution and delirium, I am who I am. He led me onward. The site had been much altered, and quarried out, since my day, but there was no mistaking the mountain. The rocks and the sandstone, vigil eternal. The wind comes and whips them, but they resist. Very slowly, they give way a little, but only the bare minimum. For they endure. I found the mouth of my tomb. The carvings on the lintel were still there, though chipped and fractured. This is far enough, I told my companion. I paid him off, and told him to begone, and never remember this journey. For I am he for which this tomb was furnished, I told him, do you doubt it? He shook his head. But he was a serf, they lie by nature. Let him tell who he wished. Then I remembered. Waking a little from my reverie. I gave him more money, and told him to go to the hotel and tell the American girl, Ada Em, that I had departed. He could tell her all that transpired. She would understand. He swore to his God he would do this. But I did not believe him then either. Why should he endanger himself with the authorities for a foreigner and a dangerous madman? But I had done all I could. Ada was a good soul. But a commoner in the end. I dismissed her. I strode down the shaft, into the darkness, turning my back on the serf and his new day. My feet recognised every step of this ramp, reconstructed as it may be. I knew the direction. Downwards, ever downwards. Towards the start of my journey. The tunnel twisted and turned, but led me surely onward, down to the bottom hall, the place of my resting. The battle with the snake Sekher all around me. I did not need light to see. My sarcophagus was still there, in the center. But the lid had been removed. All the objects and aids that had been entombed with me had been long robbed. I did not need them. I bent under the sarcophagus, which had been raised off the floor on wooden planks. Below, the figure of Nut, Goddess of the sky, stretches, willowy and nude, her arms reaching out above her head, adorned with stars.

I lie down, beneath the stone, placing my body in position, my groin to her groin, my breast to her breasts, my face to her face, my arms outstretched, my fingertips touching hers. I close my eyes, and await her touch, the transforming, transporting tingle.

I hear voices calling out, calling my name. A woman, then a man, then two men and a woman. All together, calling loudly, raucously.

I ignore them. For I can feel the tingle, I can sense the trace of finger to finger. The warm softness of her caress. The balm, unembalmed. Take me, mummy. Her lips are on my lips. My penis stiffens.

Her arms enfold me. They are calling my name. But I have departed. I have felt the weight of the sarcophagus lift like a feather. I am surrounded by shafts of light, star bursts, the warmth of the sun. I see the scarab beetle, moving towards me, shifting in its great claws the vast, congealed, dunglike globe of the earth itself, with all its multitudes teeming and keening on its surface. They are all uttering the same prayer, the incantation that transports me, the grand narrative of my quest, my Odyssey, my closing circle.

For I am one with the world. So I can now leave it.

They are calling my name. But that part of me has gone.

A Tale of Mordecai:
(narrated during a blackout in the bunker)

Truth or consequences? All around us, on the television news, they speak of "stories." Instead of dealing with facts, they succumb to tales. But a story is still only a story. The Epic of Gilgamesh. The Hindu Vedas. The Bible. The Gospels. Koran. Arabian Nights...

Who speaks? Did God narrate in Hebrew? In Aramaic? Arabic? Or in that secret language of his own of which the Holy Texts are cyphers? So here is one tale among many which might or might not be told:

In the year of Their Lord 1634, I arrived in Venice, having amassed a sufficiency of gold coinage due to my success in the alchemical field. I had decided to abandon the world of pure research for commerce, which had previously appeared to me as vulgar and unbefitting a scholar of humanity. But one cannot sit by, while others prosper. In this period, Venice had put behind her the critical upheaval that had become known as the Spanish Conspiracy, and was yet to endure the renewed Turkish invasion of her island colony, Crete. As a Jew, I was compelled to reside within the Ghetto Nuovissimo, a new portion of the segregated quarter enjoined for the Jews since 1516. The Venetians had the distinction of introducing the concept and the word to describe this enclosed area, named after the *geto* or foundry, which had once been the quarter's landmark. After dark, the gates were closed, though there were passageways across the canal Del Battello which the guards could be induced to neglect. It was amusing for me to live in those cramped, leaning tenements amid the cries and hubbub of my fractious brethren, while knowing my wealth could gain me access at any hour of the day or night to the sumptuous halls of the mighty. Later, these enforcements would create, among our detractors, the notion that the Jews enjoyed living in squalor in order that they could hoard their ill-gotten treasures. Although all my cohabitants would have preferred the odd Palazzo or two, not to speak of those who lusted after their pound of flesh, an apocryphal, if diverting tale.

But I enjoyed the subterfuge, creeping out at night, with my servant, Daniel, and crossing the dank, arched stone bridges over the shimmering velvet waters. The waters shimmered, it must be said, due to the refuse and offal which were tossed out from ten thousand windows, as well as the swimming maggots feeding on the corpses which were so often cast off as well. It was one of the unique attributes of the city that arguments could be settled with a terminal satisfaction, as the bodies, weighted properly, could be lowered out the scene of the crime immediately without the necessity of dangerous journeys to find a final resting place elsewhere.

My servant Daniel was, in fact, a slave, whom I had bought, for sixty-five ducats, at a knock-down bargain sale in Valencia during the local harvest festival. I furnished him with letters of freedom and he followed me like a devoted dog for well over twenty-five years. At one point he was married with five bright eyed black children and my house (in Cordoba) at the time, was a veritable family hive, but my days as a vicarious grandfather were cut short by an epidemic of the cholera which carried off my servant's wife and all his issue.

This twist of fate hardened both our hearts. He followed me to Vienna, the apogee of my alchemical experiments, which were, as I have said, crowned with success. I had myself long ceased to desire the comforts of wife and offspring, having seen so many come and go, and I settled into the life of the solitary savant, with the faithful moor by my side.

When I bought him, he could speak Spanish, of a sort, but quickly learned to speak in German and Italian too. He had been captured, so he told me, when a boy of twelve, in the heartlands of Gabon, a place he called N'Yanga, which he remembered as a lush plain of low trees and tall grasses, upon which his people grazed cattle, and lived under the hot sun by day, gazing by night upon the infinite dazzle of the stars. But he was a city man now, permeated with the dusty muddle of the streets, the hustle of the markets, the sweaty rub of pressing, grazing flesh, the crowds, the grime veiled skies. Like myself, he delighted now in Venice, a city where no carts or horse manure spoiled the pleasure of walking the narrow cobblestoned streets. At night, we lay in bed, in our embrace, and listened to the lapping water chuckling over its many hidden secrets.

I became the confidant of the Doge, a wiry, restless thug called Lodovico Malvolio, who was under threat of impeachment by the city council for his misappropriation of municipal funds. The Doge's own business investments, which involved the Far Eastern spice trade, had been singular failures, but his desire for expansion knew no bounds. His solution was to increase his interests in the slave trade, which was developing due to the growing demand from the colonies of the New World. In this he was opposed by powerful opponents who claimed to espouse the Catholic dogma that baptized negroes had to be considered in possession of souls, and therefore should enjoy certain minimal rights, but were in fact motivated by their own established interests in the business. The Doge was therefore extremely keen to use outsiders as his placemen in his aspiring venture. The irony of employing a Jew to manage this enterprise, and thus shift even the merest hint of opprobrium, appealed to him. He offered me the job.

I lay awake at night, discussing the proposition with Daniel. We knew that many of his race were partners in the slaving trade. Slavery was a common practice throughout the Africas, and in many regions of the Muslim East. It was a social reality, too, in ancient times, recognised by all the Holy Texts, though subject to some moral and legal constraints. Why should not one man own another, if kings and emperors could own entire nations? It was merely a question of who was above, and who below.

I decided to offer Daniel a full partnership in the venture. Loyalty must and should be repaid. I would be in charge of a fleet of ships, owned by the Doge, which would ply the route between the West of Africa and the West Indies, docking as far as Boston and New Amsterdam. What I would require was a reliable agent to oversee the sale and proper payment at the other side.

I resolved to send Daniel. Now that he was virtually an equal I found it uneasy to have him at my side and in my bed. Above all, I have always suspected comfort, the seductions of apparent sanctuaries, the illusions of permanence and security. And in any case, he would be a liability in the new circles within which I now planned to cavort. I equipped him with suitable costume, bank credit and written authority, as well as a certificate which authenticated his free status, guaranteed by the Doge himself.

"You are now an entity unto yourself," I told him, "a free man, standing on his own two feet, with crew, underlings, minions and servants of your own."

He set sail, in the good ship "Nuovissima", in the spring of 1636. I remained in Venice, enjoying my new found status, sitting in upon the counsels of the city, luxuriating upon the soft upholstered sofas of the Palazzo Ducale, though every day, as it grew dark, I bade my farewells and climbed aboard my private gondola, thrust by the strong strokes of my personal gondolier, Marco, all the way around the Grand Canal - if time allowed - and along the back routes of the Rio del Barcaroli, if not - towards the jetty of San Marcuola and the short walk back through the Ghetto gate. In the dawn, I returned the same way, taking my place among the graces and nobles. I became, in these months, I must say, quite the womanizer, as few of those delicate Venetian beauties could resist the lure of the mysterious stranger. One, Marcella, even accompanied me a number of times, back to the Ghetto, and was driven to absolute paroxysms of lust by the keening of the seminary students up on the seventh floor of the tenement just across the canal from my bedroom. It was my first intimation that the Hebrew language could induce multiple orgasms, a discovery that convinced me that one could learn new things despite all odds.

In this pleasant mode the spring and summer passed, but by the autumn I was aware that I should have received dispatches from my Colonial representative. The Doge was pressing for the first installment of the proceeds from the shipments which Daniel had gone forth to realize. I implored him to have patience and continued fucking my brains out with Marcella and the gondoliers. If I have one defect, it is that I apply myself to one thing at a time, to the exclusion of all else. I am imbued with the demon of the Absolute.

Thus I was in bed with Marcella, assaying a new position that I recalled from a Hindu mystic I had met once in Hadramaut, thrusting away to the somewhat tuneless rendition of "Lord of the World, Who Created All As He Desired" from across the ditch, when my door was broken down by the halberds of the Ducal Guard, who hauled me off the lady and, without allowing me even the time to wipe off my member, dragged me down the steps, past wide-eyed children and petrified neighbours, slung me in a black draped penal gondola, with a hood over my head, and ferried me away.

When my hood was finally removed I found myself in the *sala del inquisitori,* which latterday tourists could see decorated by some dismal Tintorettos but which was then charmingly hung with a row of leering skulls. The grim faces that faced me over their white ruffs and black cloaks were as cadaverous. I recognised the Chief of Police, Pozzo, and the Torturer General, the German, Straub, among the assembled nonentities. One of them read out a long list of charges, beginning with treason against the State, continuing with embezzlement, forgery, leaving the Ghetto after curfew, buggery, fellatio and cunnilingus. The essential charge was I was a Spanish spy, sent to revive the old Spanish Conspiracy and deliver the city either to the King of Spain, or to the Turkish Sultan, or to a combination of both, absurd as that may seem.

Having read the charges, the inquisitors thrust the hood back on my head, fastened me with shackles, and I was lead down several sets of winding stairs to the basement, the infamous *pozzi*, or wells, of the city. There the hood was removed, for all the good that did me, as the gloom around was all-engulfing. I sat in the dark, listening to the only sound that could be heard, the soft slow trickle of water drops between the stones and, occasionally, the muffled cry of another prisoner's despair. It was nothing. I had survived worse. The Doge could not afford the uncertainty of not knowing whether my knowledge of his affairs was safely buried with me. I could rely on politics to extricate me, rather than the old soap opera ploy of my lover, Marcella, descending with a candle and the guard's bunch of keys at her loins. Or even my gondoliers, burrowing through ancient, dank tunnels. And, indeed, a mere two years passed before I was dragged forth once again, not even hooded this time, lifted up the steps and hustled across the Bridge of Sighs to a private room, where the Doge simmered, having grown fat and warty during his abstention from my counsel. He seemed particularly disgruntled to see me unchanged by my ordeal, save for the unavoidable weight-loss. My unchanging nature has always baffled the unschooled. His Swiss accountant, Rinaldo Schmidt, was at his side, and we went over the shipping books as if nothing had occurred between us.

Finally I learnt what had transpired that summer. The "Nuovissima" had sailed, as planned, to Ashanti, where it had taken on board its shipload of captives, and then set sail for Boston. The Captain, an Englishman called Curtis, was a brute, and mid-Atlantic, the crew's displeasure turned into open mutiny. Daniel, as befitted his managerial position, sided with the officers, some of whom were killed in the engagement. The Captain was made to walk the plank, and perished. Daniel was thrown in and chained with the other captives. When the ship docked at Boston, the mutineers, having dressed themselves as the officers, delivered the captives, including Daniel, to the auctioneers, who, faced with a sudden surge in market demand, sold them promptly, within twenty-four hours. The mutineers, however, were not blessed with the highest intelligence, and their subterfuge was soon discovered. They were tried and hanged, within the week. Daniel's documents of authentication were found, but by then he had been sold by job lot. His owner, a southern plantationeer named La Farge, claimed legal ownership, but, unimpressed by Daniel's insubordinate nature, as he found it, passed him on, to an unnamed buyer. There the trail ended, and the Doge's informants, uninterested in a slave's fortunes, turned away, to file their report.

The Doge, having lost his consignment, the proceeds from the sale of his slaves being impounded by the British Crown in recompense for the loss of their national, vented his frustration upon me, although his charges of treason and malfeasance were palpably unproven. After I had given him my best suggestions for the further cooking of his books, he returned me to the Wells, where I remained another ten years. I was released only upon his death, to find myself utterly destitute, my gold impounded, stripped of all property and civil rights in the city.

Today, as I lie on my Vice-Presidential bunk in the defunct nuclear shelter, deep below this other island city, I can chuckle at all those twists and turns of fate, the obsolescence of so much endeavour, the transitory nature of individual ambition and greed. And yet, these vaunting desires and compulsions have left their mark on our history, blighting entire continents, destroying nations, decimating peoples, while the perpetrators grew old, withered, and died, if they did not succumb to pestilence or violence on the way. Only I remain.

It was a long time, indeed, before I could undertake my search for my missing partner, Daniel. By the time I had raised myself, after many adventures, out of penury, and amassed a sufficient fortune to travel in a modicum of safety over the oceans, a further twenty years had passed, by which time I was embroiled in other matters, involving the outcome of the Thirty Years War, and the Peace of Westphalia, which enjoined me to transfer certain commercial activities in the armaments field towards the East, and become enmeshed in the byzantine affairs of the Ottoman Empire, under Mohammed IV. Having been defeated in 1656 by the Venetians off the Dardanelles he and his Grand Vizier, Ahmed Kiuprili, were badly in need of a counsellor well versed in Venetian affairs. There followed wars with Poland, Russia and Austria, and the siege of Vienna, during which I renewed my acquaintance with a number of minor alchemists who had, like myself, been users of the Elixir of Life. Unfortunately, several of them were killed in the siege, leaving me the sole possessor of the formula. But I retreated, with the Ottomans, to Belgrade.

The Turkish Wars continuing, in essence, through the next century, and in fact beyond, I crossed the Mediterranean, again, to Egypt and rebuilt my laboratory, not far from the Hassan Mosque. But my patron, Ibrahim Bey, was suddenly overthrown by the unexpected invasion of the French fleet led by Napoleon, and I had to court new masters once more.

It was in Paris, in 1811, that I was made aware of trans-oceanic issues once again, when talk was rife of war between the newly proclaimed United States and England. I had become involved, with an Irish-Frenchman named O'Hare, with a business to manufacture underwater naval warships, in which the American Admirals were expressing a keen interest. One of our warships was most effective in the successful battle of Lake Erie, in 1813, but the next year the British captured and burned Washington. O'Hare and I soon had our work cut out. We manufactured thirteen of our vessels, ten of which burst and sank, but the other three kept afloat, just under the surface of the waters, long enough to ensure victory at New Orleans.

At last I was free to re-open the vexing case of Daniel. Armed with a commission by President Madison, renewed by the next incumbent, James Monroe, I proceeded upon an investigation of the records of the slave trade as far as they could be gathered, for the preceding two hundred years. I traversed the Union, from Louisiana to Maine, through both the slave states and the free. For a while, I tired of the daily cruelty of man to man and joined the newly formed settlement of New Harmony in Indiana, formed by the social experimenter Robert Owen, but the placid life was not for me. I wrote a work of religious phantasy, entitled "The Book of Mormon," but lost interest and passed it on to a man called Joseph Smith, in Fayette, New York, who used it to set up his own creed.

I found no record of Daniel, until well after the Civil War. A man could not but watch those events with absolute horror, no matter how imbued with the elixir of indifference, long sightedness and pessimism about the nature of Mankind. And there was worse to come. By this time it was far too dangerous to be a participant in these gargantuan bloodlettings that stained, scarred and shook the world. From 1860 onwards I adopted the newspapers as my bridge of sighs to the outside. I rented an apartment, in New York City, by the Bowery, and ventured out on rare, irregular tours. One of these, in 1876, was to Washington, where an archive of slave state records, an item informed me, had just been opened to the public. (I had been looking through the pages of the Washington Post for the record of the patent I had filed for a new device called "barbed wire," which turned out to be a key implement for the taming of the great western plains, as well as a source of strife between farmers and cattlemen, as immortalised in many written and cinematographed tales, and a source of funds which sustained me well into this century.*)

At last I found traces of my Daniel. He appeared to have given my own name, to the trader who brokered his sale at Boston in 1636. The name on the bill of sale was Danel Ben Mordeca. I knew immediately this was my man. He had been sold on to the man whose name the Doge had given me, Oral La Farge, whose own subsequent bills of sale, in another tranche of old papers, revealed that he had sold one Danel Ben to a John B. Locke in Virginia the following year. John B.

---

* It has also been said of me that, rather than becoming an armchair observer, I was engaged the next ten years in securing the primacy of my investment, travelling through the frontier states and accompanying, and indeed employing, such famous figures as Wyatt and Morgan Earp, Doc Holliday, Bat Masterson, Pat Garrett, William Brady, Jesse James, Hopalong Cassidy, Wild Bill Hickock and others, to ensure the onward march of my wires. Some said I was the sniper behind the water-barrel at the gunfight at the O.K. Corrall. But there are so many stories...

Locke, a meticulous man, kept impeccable records of his property and livestock, in which he recorded the alliances, offspring and deaths. And so my Daniel passed away, in the Year of Their Lord, 1667, leaving four sons and two daughters, and sixteen grandchildren, who remained to enrich Locke and his heirs.

It is dark now, and the weekly candle has guttered out. Above me, in the bunk marked President of the United States, my blind comrade Martian lies, listening to all the myriad sounds, rustles and voices of the city. In the next chamber, monitors can be activated to watch every street and kerb corner. It is much easier for me now to watch over my ward, Moses, than if I were rushing about above ground. He has taken me long enough to track down. The last progeny of my Daniel, who went from freedom to slavery in pursuit of my ephemeral gains. It was a complex genealogical trawl, from the cottonfields of Virginia to the boondocks of Alabama and the barracks of the U.S. Airforce at Jacksonville and Guam. But I can see him now, my Moses, the lost child who was not found in the bullrushes, who was not adopted by Pharaoh's daughter nor taken to the palace to be brought up as a prince. My Moses who could not free his people, as he could not free himself from the burden of the ages, from the legacy of torment and pain. Neither upwardly, nor downwardly mobile, he trod along his path, putting one foot after another and dragging his sack of troubles. The squalling, sputtering, bickering, battering horde. I did what I could to make order. In extremis, I had to resort to lethal sanctions. We have always lived in dangerous times.

Everybody needs somebody to watch over them. If not a guardian angel, then at least a modestly effective demon. If I am his burden, he is mine. If he made me, in the distorted mirror of his image, then I have made him, in my fears. There is nothing new under the sun, but only variations on the oldest themes.

Did you enjoy this tale? Or did it merely serve to frustrate, confuse, and enrage you? Are you enlightened by it, or merely thrust back into your own primal darkness? Closing your eyes, the better to comprehend the chaos and creation that swirls endlessly within. The dots and dashes dancing upon the flipside of your eyelids. Making sense of the senseless. At some point, the light will click on again, to reveal –

The Awakening of Ann Hedonia.

Snort! Snurf! Shplttrr!!

Aargh! Cough! Ptah! Thneek!

Froth, phlegm and khneuk ahoy!

Thar she blows! The hwite hwale! Rising from the deeps of ocean, vast bloated belly breaking the surface of the squalid sheets, which ripped aside like gossamer, falling away into the muck and ooze around the bed. Rising, and then falling again, the massive arms flailing, the podgy hands seeking to find a purchase on the mattress to raise the torso higher, the great bloated head tossing on the worn pillows, throwing out clouds of feathers and fluff, which settle like a down upon the stomach.

Who wins the golden doubloon???

Prospective Ahabs, stirring with flaccid harpoons. Orville Dullest, in the arms of Beatrice, face down in her bosom, with a broomstick inserted up his ass. Jesse, swinging gently in his hammock, rudely jerked awake, grabbing for his robe. Sticking his legs into the neck, falling over, disrobing and enrobing right way up.

Thar she blows!

The call! The call! The foghorn blast of her long dormant voice, blaring out to warn all shipping:

"Ooooohhh! Aaaaargghhhh! Gaaaaaahhh!! Fnnrrrrr!!!"

"Coming, honey! Coming!"

Rushing round the anterior abdominal wall to the small omentum, squeezing through the foramen of Winslow into the lesser peritoneal sac, knocking on her door.

"Are you all right Ann?"

"Fnrrrff!! Khnaaggkk!! Ggkkhhhhh!!!"

He opens the door, gagging on the blizzard of fluff, seeing her rise like the Abominable Snowman of the Himalayas, shaking the bed until its legs finally collapse under their gargantuan burden in a great spray of muck and ooze. The occupant, freed by this sudden downfall, instead of crashing down to disaster, rises, somehow finding a solid purchase on the swamp covered surface, the two colossal columns of her legs, like the pillars of Hercules, firmly anchored, the great white balloon erect, the snow white pendant breasts flopping like the sails of an ocean crunching vessel, the huge moon face with its plum pudding eyes and open O of the mouth, the thin lank hair threshing like Medusa's snakes.

"Where is my son? Where is that wicked boy??"

Echoes here of the Great Dames of the City in days gone by, the grand fomenters of the witches' brew of the long levelled Hell's Kitchen, the midriff of the City before Forty Second Street was tamed and lost again, majestic brawlers like Sadie the Goat, and Euchre Kate, and Hell Cat Maggie, Gallus Mag and Battle Annie, the whisky valkyrie and Orange scourge, eye gouger extraordinaire. Those were the days. But the battlecry now catches Mo Smith not in the midriff of the City but on its shoulder, crossing over the cusp of 99th Street at Broadway from the Fishmarket and astrology bookstore to Unity prescriptions and Irving Pearlberg Income Tax Advice and Auto Insurance, opposite the uptown Metro Cinema, currently showing at Number 1: Where the Day Takes You and at Number Two: Out on A Limb. Battle Annie's sudden leap into awareness kicking at his guts and throwing him forward, propelling him up across 100th and 101st, Cheesy Pizza, La Tacita de Oro Restaurant, Jinnie Nails NEW OFFER - FACIALS $35, Sterling Optical, Roses by Dozens - WE WILL HELP YOU MAKE SOMEBODY HAPPY! Broadway Bagels, All Bright Trading Company, Bit of Bengal, Sol & Carmine Pizza, Broadway Deli and Food Market, Petland Discounts - JOB APPLICATIONS NOW BEING ACCEPTED FOR CAREER MINDED PERSONS WITH KNOWLEDGE OF TROPICAL FISH; Safety Ferret Lead & Harness, Exercise Fun Wheel, Scratchex Flea & Tick Spray for Dogs & Cats, and, hwooop! - she kicks him again, knocking him across the street to the Chemical Bank, Love Fragrances and Cosmetics, Mr Wong's Noodle Closed for Renovation, Radio Shack For Rent. Leaning against the shuttered bankrupt shops, gasping for breath, clutching his distended abdomen.

"Oh, no, ma! No, God help me!"

"Where is that whining dog?!"

No time for Jesse to escape as the Awakened Annie grabs him by the throat and begins slamming his head against the fallen headboard of the bed.

"WHERE - IS - MY- FUCKING - BASTARD - SON??"

Pulling his long hair back with the slabs of her left hand fingers and yanking his tongue through his mouth with the thumb and forefinger of her left. "Talk to me, you ratfuck jewmick wop, or I'll pull this out by the root and eat your fucking brains! You hear me?

"WHERE IS MY NIGGER SON?"

Clutching his throat, Mo staggers across 103rd Street, to El Jalapeno, Mexican Cuisine Autentico, Superette Deli, Broadway Pizza, Middle Eastern Food, Kim's Hardware - Discounts on Multi Purpose Vertical Bake'n' Roaster, Chicken Holders, Vertical Roasters, Oscillation Fans, also Patented Roach Prufe, Odorless non-staining Powder, Keys Cut Wile-U-Wait. And off again, dodging the hooting, skirling traffic rushing to turn into Broadway. SUBA Pharmacy, Tina Cleaners, Golden Eagle Mediterranean and Continental Cuisine, Calcutta Cafe, Champs Elysee de Broadway Restaurant, French Cuisine by Mama Sylvia.

"No, Mama, no!"

Jesse can't know what's worse, having his tongue held in the Herculean grip of the monstress, or having it let go so he can tell her that she is inside her son, having been virtually comatose apart from brief dozy intervals in his peritoneal sac, not far from the liver and kidneys and a tad above the colon and bowels. It's not that bad once you get used to it. In my old sect, the Proto-Essenes, we used to fast in the barren heat of the Judaean Desert for two weeks at a time without any discernable ill effects. Or perhaps, on the other hand, this purgatory was the inevitable, irrevocable result. I should have left in the winter, with Arnold, Nep and Lincoln, or even with Jaime, when the going was good. All would have been well, or reasonably stable, as long as the Alchemist had remained, or at least occasionally put in an appearance, as the Controller, rather than vanishing completely. Beatrice and Orville Dullest had proved to be a pretty shabby substitute, wrapped in themselves, devoid of all communal vim.

"I stayed behind, so you would not be abandoned!" he wants to cry out. "I couldn't bear to let you starve! Someone had to be here to get the groceries!" But it's a long time since he foraged for supplies, let alone stocked up the best from Zabars. The body's dry, decaying, weakening, despite the lingering autumn balm. Winter due again, and survival, despite the toughening years, can never be guaranteed. Diseases of the blood, the liver, the kidneys, the pancreas, the spleen, the heart and lungs, are always lurking in the wings. Even God could die, allowing all to wither, atrophy and shrink back to the primeval spark. The Big Bang or the manifold Small Sighs. And will the Galaxies continue to blink? The Gods, in Orion, watching all the supernovas whsitle and fade, cracking their celestial sunflower seeds and spitting the husks out to form new worlds? Is Merenptah one with Osiris? Or has he got lost again on the way?

Shaken and stirred, Mo staggers on, over 105th Street, past Augie's Birdland Cafe Pub, the deli, La Casita Restaurant, across 106th, Duke Ellington Boulevard, to the small fenced triangle of Straus Park, marking the convergence, finally, of West End Avenue and Broadway, which continues up north, in a welter of roadworks, trucks, drills, cranes and smokestacks venting white steam from underground. In Memory of Isidor & Ada Straus: 'Lovely and Pleasant Were They in Their Lives, and in Their Deaths They Were Not Divided. 1 Samuel, 23.' Of course this line, in the original source, referred to David and Jonathan, and was of an avowedly homosexual, if platonic, flavor. But a much clearer message, fixed to the fence, affirmed the City's credo: No Pigeon Feeding in This Area. But the pigeons, unable to read, or else concealing their knowledge for unknown reasons, cluster around, cooing and clucking, hoping for a few breadcrumbs as in the halcyon days of Isidor and Ada, but in vain.

Collapsing on the park bench, groaning. Luckily this prime site is, for the nonce, unoccupied, except for the ubiquitous birds. Arcing their grey grimy necks at the rolling of the head, the convulsing limbs.

"NO MAMA! LEAVE ME ALONE!"

Letting go of Jesse's tongue, but still shaking him by the neck like a chicken: "DO YOU KNOW WHAT IT'S LIKE TO BE A WHITE WOMAN BRINGING UP A NIGGER KID IN ALABAMA, WHEN HIS NIGGER POP HAS FUCKED OFF?"

"Ook!"

"DO YOU KNOW WHAT IT'S LIKE TO BE THE SHIT OF THE WORLD, THE CRAP THAT'S SCRAPED OFF THE BOTTOM OF

THE SHOE? DO YOU KNOW WHAT IT'S LIKE TO BE STEPPED ON FOR TWENTY FIVE YEARS? I WANT AN ANSWER RIGHT NOW!"

He takes advantage of a momentary relaxing of her grip to twist free, and collapse, clasping his throat and gasping, in the slime of muck and fluff. Shaking his head vigorously. She stands there, rasping and heaving, looking down on him with a new suspicion.

"Who else is here?"

She moves ponderously, elephantine, aside, to put her ear to the rippling membrane of the wall.

"We are not alone."

The mewling multitudes of the City. Above and below. All those who were past and are now present. The dead weight of the looming buildings, not scraping the sky but keeping it at bay. All those vertigoless Mohicans, shimmying up the web of girders, dragging the empire state up up towards the heavens, defying the midnight sun and the gloating moon, all our latter day Munchausens, raised by our daily bread. The wages of financial sins, and the crumbs of the leftovers of progress. Up up and away! But they are unable to stop the rain, tumbling out of an autumnal New York cloudburst, washing the streets, triggering a million windscreen wipers and a thousand and one umbrella urchins, whipped out of doorways, caterwauling. "One dollar! Only one dollar!" Who has a dollar, shitkickers? This year's stocks have not yet matured. He chokes to his feet. Onwards, onwards! This is not the time for a park bench siesta. Lurching over the road, past Martin Bros. Wine & Liquor, Dry Cleaners, Restaurant 107 West and the Indian Cafe, reeling through the blaring traffic to shelter under the flapping tarpaulin draped over the spattered, chugging roadworks. Leaning against the thrumming generator, breathing heavily. The vibrations jogging his insides. Everyone hurled about, slipping and sliding in the transverse mesocolon, Battle Annie tightening her hold of the end of the TV cable she has wrapped around Jesse's neck. Down in the small intestine, Orville Dullest, having freed himself from his chains and broomstick, with a classic Houdini trick learned at the CIA training academy at Waccamaw North Carolina, staggers about in the falling debris of Beatrice's ramshackle emporium, the blood red curtains tearing, the tables and stools sent rolling, lamps smashing, the dungeon paraphernalia, stocks, paddles, padlocks, whips, masks, penis restrainers slithering down suddenly expanding and contracting cavities. Gotta get out of here! For once he regrets the extraction, from his left top bicuspid, of the Agency's personal locator, the minute transmitter, powered by a cluster of plutonium atoms, which had been disclosing his exact position twenty-four hours a day until the quacks advised him it was probably the cause of the tumour which was mashing his brain. It saved his life in Korea, the Dominican Republic, Vietnam, Angola and Libya, but now, in the most hazardous circumstances of all, lost somewhere in the grid of New York City, possibly, for all he knows, in Brooklyn's Red Hook or the Bronx, he is rendered utterly helpless. Beatrice, unconscious, knocked cold by the striking of her head against the crossbar of the rack, upon which he spent such happy, if physically demanding hours, only a little time ago. Scooping her up in his arms, lunging to avoid more falling debris, he carries her out the splintered door.

The rain stops, as abruptly as it started. The umbrella vendors vanish into doorways, trashbins, smokestacks, manholes. Mo feels the discomfort of the jangling generator at his back. Tottering up, tumbling past the labourers lifting their tarpaulin to look warily at the miraculously lightening sky. Onwards. Up Broadway to 109th. Mike's Papaya, Sloans, Woolworths. Over 110th, Khan Video, Bagels, Famous Famiglia Pizza Spinach Broccolli, American Savings Bank and Citibank. 111th, Nacho Mama's Burritos, Cafe Pertutti and the Book Street College Bookstore, with its second hand bookstalls hastily uncanopied to face the drying of the sun. All the academic studies you could wish for, from Feminist Acrostics of the Fin De Siecle to Civilization of Islam. Over 112th, inside Tom's Restaurant, two straggle haired yuppie men and an intense dark haired woman seemed to be arguing about the shape of an egg. The swanky blocks downwind of Columbia University, the uptown valhallas, Bon French Cleaners, Cafe 112, Daigaku Japanese Restaurant, Carnegie Hill Cosmetics, Manhattan Sportin, Haagen Dazs, The West End Cafe, Mr Dee, Monde Home Made Chocolates and the evergreen Papyrus Bookstore. Cosmopolitan Restaurant, Tamarind Seed Health Food Store and of course Grandma's Restaurant and Ollie's Noodle Shop and Grill.

All the good things of life. In his prison cell, awaiting trial on multiple arson charges, Arnold Flint tucks in to the lunch menu of the Ryker's Island holding facility: Chicken cacciatore with organic brown rice, hard-baked potato and tinned peach segments, topped up with Dekaff

Latte and a small, indefinable savory. The walls around him are a typical 1960's metallic blue sheen, decorated with photographs of forest fires torn out of National Geographic magazines. The inmate has been allowed a typewriter, which he may use in the morning hours, between 8:30 and 11:00, exercise time for most of the other prisoners, and has begun composing his next best-seller, INSIDE JAB, a hard-boiled tale of degradation and violence, leavened with the argot he is being taught, for an hour a day, by the King of Block C, Edgar James Hueck, alias Bigg Dadi Kool Wakeem. Meanwhile, in a safe facility on Eastern Neck Island, Maryland, Lincoln Korombane nibbles nachos and looks out over a foggy Chesapeake Bay. Watching the daily moves of his minders with a deadpan, apathetic air, dreaming of the New South Africa, of Nelson Mandela, the Prisoner become President, the low raised to the high, the despised into the venerated, the lost found, the meek transformed into the mighty, the abandoned poised to bind up the wounds.

"There were more of us, in the beginning," Jesse explains to Ann, as she prods him forward, flicking the leash round his neck, "quite a merry band we were, at times. Light at heart and quick of repartee. But people don't like to be tied down."

"Tough tittie, baby."

"Personally I'm cut to the discipline. The holding in, the self restraint of body and spirit. Breathing exercises, very important, particularly when the air is like it is in here. Back in the desert, you filled your lungs with God's breath whenever you chose to inhale. But even then we tried to limit these reflexives, to slow down the lungs, the heart, the brain waves. To produce an atonal hum. We believed if we prepared ourselves, physically and spiritually, then the Master would come forth. Not the Christian Christ, you understand, they were not favoured, in Qumran, his followers. Galileeans, very common stock. Riff raff. Our people were of the nobility, it was that way we sapped their power. The seed of David. You can't be the seed of David in Nazareth. That has to be ludicrous."

"Keep talking, fenian jew scum," she spits out, "ye're talking yourself into your grave. My family were Orangemen, from Ulster. Descendants of King Billy. I had a family tree, a real document, but that nigger kid of mine set fire to it. Just to spite me, the little black bastard. I nearly tore the skin off his back."

"Children are innocents," insists Jesse, "one cannot hold them to account. They are born unpolluted by man."

"They have the devil in them, they have to be taught. Spare the rod and spoil the child. His father didn't care. Gave him sweets and walked off into the sunrise. If it wasn't for me, where would my boy be now?"

"Well..."

"I slaved my guts out to keep him in school. They said he could learn, had a mind that could be moulded. I knew. I read him the Good Book every day. *I* taught him to read, not the teachers. White trash. Fuck the lot of 'em. Then he repaid me by burning the house down, him and that brother of his, Charlie. Charlie could pass for white. Not Thomas. Black as his Pop, burnt chocolate. They took 'em both away, to the reformatory. Knock some sense into 'em. I signed the papers. Charlie could pass for white, but the kids wouldn't have it. Told him his ma was fucked by a nigger. They beat him to death, with a shovel, my little white angel. I signed the papers. The other bastard ran away. Never saw him again. But I know he's out there. Wrote me a letter once, from New York City. Married a white woman, he said. Just like his Dad. Guess what, he said, her name is Beatrice, just like our home town. Beatrice, Alabama. Can you beat that?"

"Ah, well, um..."

"God, I remember so much I just wish I could forget. The smell of the dew and the morning freshness and the green of the bougainvilleas. The eucaplyptus trees in the wind. The twister that came, when we were real young. All bunched together in the church basement. Blacks, whites, rubbing up close. Kids, don't know the fucking difference. Soon learn. Barefoot in the grass. Boys, girls, soon learn the difference. Guarding the fence. I was a looker. You won't believe it of me but I was the trim one of the family. I weighed one-oh-three pounds. Belle of the ball. Like Scarlett O'Hara. But she was a mick, was she not? The little bastard's father. Tall dark man. Army officer. Air Corps. Not a flyer, administration. Muscles like a velvet statue. Big cock. They have big cocks, don't let 'em fool you. And don't they know it. Smart son of a bitch. The army put him through college. Read books, brought 'em home all the time. History, politics, heavy stuff. Read 'em to the boy, when he was a baby. Had this fandangled theory. You read smart things to a kid, you make him smart, even if he don't seem to understand. Play him good music. But we had the tee vee, that was enough for me.

All that hifalutin talk. Then the second kid came along. Pass for white. Man begins to suspect me. Drinking by then. Smart fool. Air force passed him over for promotion. Look in the mirror, I told him, what do you see? One black motherfucking fool. Said he wasn't the second kid's father. Charlie. Pass for white anyday. Could have grown up and made his mark. Stupid white kids. Stupid bastards. He wouldn't have lit the match if his brother hadn't made him do it. Took after his Dad. Thomas. Bad blood. Who was your mother and your father, boy?"

She tugs on the leash, bringing Jesse up short, causing him to trip and stumble. "Merchants in the temple," he replied, "at Jerusalem. Sold unguents, perfumes, holy utensils."

"Bad blood. And Jesus went into the temple, and cast them out, that sold and bought there, and overthrew the tables and chairs."

"Jesus was an extremist and troublemaker."

"Don't trifle with the Name of the Lord thy God. I can snap your neck like a twig."

Pushing past the crowds entering and exiting the 116th Street subway. Numbers 1 & 9. Segregation point, the whites heading downtown, while the deeper of pigment may merrily troll up to 125th, 137th and even, dare we whisper it, 145th, notwithstanding the rainbow of City College. Up up toward the rapper's beat. But Mo, weakened by inner turmoil, leans against the gates of Barnard College - No Dogs Permitted on Premises - gazing across the street at the open portals of the House of Learning itself, Columbia University, the Temple of Teach, the Pedagogic Pirate. Youth, eternally hopeful, hurrying towards the mock Greek pediments inscribed with the noble names of history: Homer, Herodotus, Sophocles, Plato, Aristotle, Demosthenes, Cicero, Virgil. Are all these, too, my children? Your grandchildren, ma? Did I make these, too, in Trinity Churchyard, vomiting out the upshot of a bad Macburger (a Double Double Mac, no less) with the janitor O'Connell holding my shoulders, and bathing my frozen feet in hot water, were these giants, too, my issue? no wonder my insides were ripped. Demosthenes, was he the one who put stones in his mouth to help him speak? Perhaps I should put boulders. Did not Virgil take Dante through hell? holding the poor bedraggled wop by the hand, as he went down down through those circles - the lustful, the gluttonous, the hoarders, spendthrifts, the wrathful, down down down, the panderers and seducers, the flatterers, simoniacs, sorcerors, barrators, whatever they be, hypocrites, thieves, counselors of fraud, sowers of discord, falsifiers... hey, and he ain't even left New York City yet! hot diggety damn! and down below that, he meets the giants (and probably the yankees too), probably these same noble fuckups who meant so well, Sophocles, Plato, Aristotle, Paul Bunyan, Davy Crockett. Beware of geeks bearing gifts. Homer, well, at least he could spin a yarn.

Boy, you sure larnt them books, Tommy! Is that you, ma? Are you talkin to me? I know you're out there, son, somewhere. I can feel you close, so close to me. I'm here Ma, but I'm hurting real bad. I feel like my guts are in a grinder, I feel like I'm giving birth again, but there's nothing inside, do you understand me, ma? I don't have em in me any more. Just that weak sop Jesse and that bastard Orville Dullest who wormed into me while I was sleeping, and you know who. I know who what, Tommy? The other one, the other one, Ma. No, talk to me, son, talk to me, Tommy. You could have come back to see your dear old ma. Old battleaxe Annie. But you had to go away, and meet this bitch, this harpie, who took you away from me. No, Ma, but you see, that's just the point, I've always kept you together. You've always been with me, ma, then she came, and I had to keep her too. I couldn't run away, like Pop. She's here too. What you talkin about boy? maybe you need your head smashed in again. Maybe I do, Ma. But she's pretty groggy now, I think she hurt her head. Maybe that Orville, maybe he can take her away.

Up the thick thread of the ligamentum teres, or the obliterated umbilical vein, they stagger, bedraggled Orville and his rubber wrapped bride, shaking her head, trying to gain a foothold. Annie casts the sagging Jesse aside. Striding up, lifting up the Mistress's head.

"So you're Beatrice."

The ravaged cheeks, the drooping eyelids, the crow's feet tracked below the eyes, the dry chapped lips aquiver.

"The one my son married. His own white trophy. Geez fuck."

But she was beautiful then, Ma, and funny. A flower child. We met in the bus station. Port Authority. I got a job as a ticket seller for the Greyhound. People came up to me and bought tickets for all the destinations of the country - Winnemucca, Soda Springs, Laramie, North Platte, Okeechobee, Rapid City, Sioux Falls, Little Rock, Hope, Berlin, Jerusalem. I would muse about all those places, all those far off stops. But I stayed behind. Then I met her. She was buying a ticket to Vermont.

White River. I said, I would sure like to go there, it sounds nice. She said, why don't you come. Just like that. We went off together, I never did anything like it before. Except when I left you, Ma. But then I had the fear in my soul. This time I had the hope, and the joy. We lived up there, by the lake, for three months. What they called a "commune" in those days. Living together, all different people and races. Share and share alike. All for one and one for all. You remember those books, Ma? But it didn't last. The cops came and bust it all up. But we got away together. Beatrice and me. Although there was another girl... what was her name? Lilian? Lilith? But she was like the wind, Beatrice. She would change, just like that. Suddenly she wanted to get married. I said, O.K.. Why not. We got hitched, and came to live in the City. Then things started to go wrong. No money, company wouldn't take me back. Bad things. Bad things, ma. But I always loved her. Broke my heart when she left. Had us a place on East 10th Street. Came back one day and she was gone. Landlord threw out all my stuff. And then the streets, looking for her. Looking up her old friends. Chasing her all over the City. People told me she was still around. Bad things, Ma. But I found her again, in the great whirlpool. Set her up in the job she was most fitted for. After I'd spewed out the multitudes. Too many. Far too many. Couldn't hold em. Spewed em out. But I had to keep some. Even God gets lonely sometimes.

"So you're Beatrice." Ann lifts the head up by the hair, looking into the dull eyes. Shaking her head. "No, I cain't see it." Letting the head drop again. Orville Dullest regarding her warily. "It's Ann, isn't it. You're Ann. The sleeping one."

"Who the fuck are you?"

"I'm Orville Dullest. Director of Operations, C.I.A.. Retired. I can explain the whole thing. There is always a full picture, if only one finds the vantage point from which to see it. There is an outside to every inside, and an inside to every outside. Nothing is insurmountable, and every challenge can be met, if only you have the will to do it. If we two can work together on this, Madam, I'm sure we can find a way out."

"You're off your puff." Turning to Jesse, jerking him to his feet. Ruminating for a tick, then untying his leash. "Who is this guy? He's off his puff."

"He's new here," Jesse explains, getting his breath back. "He's a little impatient."

"I don't like his face. He looks like a rat's turd that's been preserved in a jar."

"I can help you. If we get out of here, I can pull a lot of strings. Whatever you want, I can arrange it. A house, a lawn, a garden, luxury bathrooms, a four poster bed. The best cars. Chauffeurs, servants. Satellite television. We can even rig the game shows. Make you millions. Write your own ticket."

"The only ticket you can write is to the cemetery."

"I'm not a well man, that's true. But I can hold on. I have grit. We're all Americans here after all. Except for this gentleman," nodding at Jesse, "but I can look after him too."

And what about Salim, my Salim? And Ibn Battuta? And Merenptah? And Arnold Flint? And Lincoln? All my lost children?

"Them too. I guarantee it. I can make it happen. Just get me out of here."

How about it, Tommy?

I don't know, Ma. I can't bear to be left alone again. And what about Mordecai? He won't like it. He's somewhere out here too. Keeping an eye, even without Frank Ox. There's so much I haven't told you, Ma. So many layers. So many cries of pain and anger...

Pick yourself up, move on. Maybe they'll all die down. Maybe Ma will go back to sleep. But it's still long before dark. The street's still buzzing. The young ones still striding in and out of the university campus. Move on, there's nothing for me here. Carry someone else through hell, old Virgil. Dante the wop will do. Off you go then. Up the road. 120th. Reinhold Neibuhr Place. Who he? Fuck him. Past the Union Theological Seminar. Does God exist, or should he? Pros and con. Answers on a postcard, in block letters. Skip 121st. 122nd. Manhattan School of Music. Block of residences. 3111 Broadway. No Loitering, No Peddling, No Ball Playing, No Sitting in Front of Building. On the avenue, the elevated train tracks emerge out of the ground, rising on a vast metal causeway across La Salle and towards the 125th Street station. On we go. The Pizza Dough Shop. Laundromat and Thrifty Supermarket. Karyoe Restaurant West African Cuisine. Chiropractor Se habla Espanol. Sobel Bros We Buy Cash in a Flash. Red Sea Ethiopian Restaurant. Rap thy staff, or in its absence, thy booted foot upon the shores. Open says me! Part the waters! Let my people go! Open the prison doors! Go forth, mama! Walk out, Jesse!

Go down, Orville and Beatrice! I can write whatever tickets I want. Fairbanks, Salt Lake, Wichita Falls. Bakersfield, San Luis Obispo, Montevideo, Paris, Firenze, Skopje, Beijing! Go forth into the wide wide world, I can snap you back whenever I want. Do you hear me out there, Salim, Battuta? Come forth, into the tall fields of freedom. Free at last! Slip past the guards, Lincoln, swim the lake, shake off all the bloodhounds! Melt through the walls, Arnold! You can do it. You can twist the world how you choose. Let my people go!

But will they come? Will they be awakened from their torpor, their cosy dreams of prosperity, their warm glow of security and obedience, their narratives of vicarious escape? Salim and Battuta, canoeing down Lake Ontario, or bucketing down the Niagara Falls into Lake Erie. Past all the industrial heartlands. The wharfs of enclosed, trapped oceans. New travellers for old. The open pathways of the imagination, where wonders never cease, where innocence can still be rediscovered in a gaze, in an unknown face, in experiences waiting to be recorded, dormant in neglected domains.

Worlds without ends! Mo paused, at the corner of 125th Street. The market stalls, the flow of shoppers. The great banner strung across the borderland of the divided city: Welcome to the West Harlem Coalition 6th Annual Anti-Gentrification Fair. Shine or Rain, It's Your Gain. And below: Gethsemane Holiness Revival Church. All Welcome.

One should take people at their word. Pausing to extract, from the folds of his overcoat, the somewhat wrinkled, crushed cup. Regulation styrofoam, purchased for twenty-five cents at Dunkin Donuts by 96th Street. Making the proper investment in one's poverty. And are there some generous souls about, among this bustling crowd ambling along Martin Luther King Avenue? A man can only try his best. The step, the droop, the proper flinch. Spare a quarter for a brother, down on his luck now? Help a good man rise out of the sump of misfortune? Set a soul on the way to redemption, in the name of whichever God you choose? Your soul or mine, it's all the same. Yesterday I was you, tomorrow you might be me. I'm only telling it like it is. We all have it in us to rise and to fall.

Rattle the cup. You always have to put the first coins in it, to show that someone already gave. Who will cast the first coin? Rattle rattle, shake shake shake shake. The shuffle of the battered shoes on the sidewalk. My rod and my staff! Rap three times. Part the waters -

I stretch out my hand over the sea. And the great avenue of 125th Street opens up, letting in the human flood. Here they come, the exiled multitudes, gasping and spluttering and moaning, waving their arms and hosaneighing down the canyon that splits the city at the shoulders like the executioner's sword. For they are all here, all my children, resurrected, for the children of the bountiful imagination of the creator cannot die, bobbing and juddering and joyriding upon the human torrent, the young and the old, the fit and the lame, the yin and the yang, Lincoln, Arnold, Beatrice, Ann, Jaime, Merenptah the Magus and Ada Em, and Jesse, even Mordecai, coasting down the waves with powerful, steady strokes, riding the tide, aiming straight at my abdomen. Salim and Battuta, shooting the rapids, paddles flailing, faces flushed, gentle Frances, guilt-strained Benjamin, whirling Darwish, Aram, even Frank Ox, ectoplasmically transmuting into his various disguises, all the abductees of geodesic domes, the legions of the disappeared, and the abandoned, and the lost, poor Faust, and The Skull, and Orville Dullest, and the President of the Music of Our Time, with his miraculous organ, and all the armed and disarmed forces, all those who have gleefully drunk each other's piss, and eaten the excrement of our upbringing, and trespassed on our forgiveness, and walked away as we breathed our fetid desperation in their faces, and turned deaf ears to our cries for help, and blind eyes to our rags. I embrace them all. Even Andy McCloud and Ervine Lazar and Hilda H. and all the encroachers, writers, publishers, narrators, the would be usurpers of my absolute progenity. All those too, flow free, at last.

And are you there, Lilith? I turn my head this way and that, bob and crane to catch sight of you. Can you be absent, when everyone else is ingathering? Is this your doing, Mordecai? Thwarting me now, even at the moment of fusion, your mooncalf eyes, as you swim on towards me, mocking the vision of the body and the spirit healed, the scattered sparks risen and recombined, the yid and the yank. But there can be no controller now, no prophet, oracle, alchemist, savant, directing the traffic: East, west, north, south, up and down, above and below, establishing your spurious order: the fundamental laws, and science, the constriction of my boundless creation.

For I will not obey the laws of the universe! The laws of life and death. Death in particular. It is not a question of love, but sheer contrariness. For I decree it is not so!

Time. That too, can be mastered. For if they all left me, spewed from my gut, nevertheless I can pass my hand over their fate. Alms for the love of Allah! Adonai! Sweet Jesus! Spare a little change for a poor sinner. A dime or a nickel will do. Just to show somebody gives a fuck.

Can she die? Can Lilith be snuffed out, against my full command that she live on? The decay in her blood, rotting her cells, as it rots mine in every sphere of existence, can I not command it to cease? Mosays: Part the waters of that Red Sea, and lead her towards the farther shore! To stagger up, hand over hand, to Castle Garden, amid the crying, newborn crowd.

I see her dragging herself up, by the torn skin of her emaciated, shriven body. Disconnecting the tubes, the drips, the breathing mask, gathering up her old caseload: The wretched of the streets, the lost, the wandering, skins and bones of mislaid souls. The Listening Ear, poised for all the City's cadences of delusion and despair. Those who thought they saw her lowered into the grave, and eulogised the life cut short, would stop, turn and stare in their amazement and disbelief. And she would come to me, with her clipboard of questions and queries, enigmas and riddles, offering me secure shelters, positive programs, keys of the doors to secret gardens.

And we will sit, under the zamzam tree, you and I, Lilith, and ponder, why you could not have stayed with me from the start. The snake will be locked in its gilded cage forever devouring its own tail. We will rewrite the rules.

It's a date, Lilith. What shall we discuss? All the conundrums of the known world. And the unknown. How, what, where, why? If I am healed, why do the voices still blab and splutter? If I can fuse with them all, why do I still feel so alone? Remember, when we sat in that Greek diner, dead of winter, on 14th Street? When you wanted to get me in the shelter? You told me you were ill. And I was sick too. You told me that I was imagining everything. You told me that the world was not my child. That all my children who had stayed in me were illusions of my sick mind. You wanted to know about my childhood. I told you there was nothing to tell. There is no childhood. There's only dark and light. The fear stays the same it was when you first peeked out round the edge of that void. In the beginning. And then you feel the Creator straining and pushing, and sweating blood. She pushes you out. My poor white mother. The trash of the world. He had long gone.

Took it on the lam. The descendant of slaves. Like all of us. Mordecai's slave, lover, and burden. The Middle Passage. Two hundred years to find me. A piddling two centuries. Nothing at all, Lilith, in the scheme of things. In the life of the wandering jewel. How long have I been tramping these streets? How long has the world lasted? Less than two thousand years, since Christ, five thousand seven hundred and fifty years or so, since Jehovah, thirteen hundred plus since The Prophet. But never is God unaware of the actions of sinners. He only gives them respite to the day when all eyes will stare with consternation. As the Book says: They shall stare, but they shall see nothing, on that Day of all Days.

Can you save me, Lilith? You who were by my side from the beginning. Watching over my sleep and my waking. Then one day I slept and you were gone. Was it in Vermont? I don't remember. I have lost all sense of time. All space has shrunk, to these shopfronts, these market stalls, selling colored ribbons and scarves, portraits of saints, stolen cigarette lighters, and profane t-shirts, marked with strange messages: 12 Reasons Why a Beer is Better Than a Black Woman. All these messages I don't understand.

There is nothing you need to know, Mordecai told me. Just walk on and I will do the thinking. I will watch over you. I will be the Keeper of the Words. But I had a ravenous hunger. I could never be sated with knowledge. But it all came to me like scattered rain, like a downpour that could never be foreseen. Many days I was soaked to the bone. Nights there was no one to protect me. Weeks I sat in the Public Library, until closing hour. Day by day my children grew within me. Until they outgrew me completely. I was their boundary, but I had no limits. Do you understand this, Lilith?

Under the zamzam tree we will look, you and I, into our crystal ball. Examining the fate of our offspring. Glowing like any proud parents, as we gaze upon Arnold Flint, freed from the penitentiary, to be a celebrity upon the network talk shows. The repentant sinner, living in a "community" in Massachusetts, resolved to remake his life in absolute piety, abstaining from meat, renouncing sexual intercourse, donating to his fellow acolytes the entire proceeds of his next but one bestseller, Fire Down Below, the saga of his arsonist days. No longer consumed by the green dragon of jealousy, he has made his peace with Mark Twain, with Ernest Hemingway, Marcel Proust, even with Saul

Bellow. He has a new wife, a sixty-five year old widow, Orvietta Sagebrush, of Waynesburg, Ohio. That too, I now decree.

And here, winging across the oceans, is Link Korombane, home at last, free in liberated South Africa, the rainbow nation. Running a bakery, in Guguletu, Cape Town. Supplying bread to the hungry, unlike, he waggishly if wickedly comments, the sainted leader, Nelson Mandela, whose pledges, too, can be ephemeral. His partner in the enterprise, a Boer named Willem Ventner, is, like Link himself, a former agent of the Central Intelligence Agency's Africa Bureau. Watch them perspire, black and white together, in the heat of the great steel ovens, as the morning buns crisp and brown in the pungent odours of a new future...

Here, too, as we shoot far north, to a log cabin in the meadowlands of Saskatchewan, north of Prince Albert, by the Candle Lake, we can find Salim, and the Art Colony maid, Anita, happy as racoons in their isolation, with two small children, Jose and Amina, running about the rustic yard, in a veritable zoo of dogs and farm animals, chickens, goats, pigs, horses. Uncle Bat often looks in, running up in his old Buick from Saskatoon, where he runs a flourishing Internet business, managing a Server named, appropriately, Babel Dot Com. Connecting the globe, at vast profit.

Jaime's tomb, alas, I see, grows weeds and flowers, in the Woodlawn cemetery. No one visits, not even Allan Darwish. In winter, snow buries the cheap stone entirely, but in summer, it looks quite lush and green. The thump and thud of the city resounds from afar, the steady hum of the machines.

Tourists still frequent the tomb of Merenptah, of those that brave the harsh sands of the Arab Republic and the rage of the Brotherhood of Zealots, standard bearers of a revived, imagined purity. The throat cutters of the New-Old Millennium, the rebels who uphold the Sacred Words. Those who kill for one Book, but burn others. Even Arnold Flint would flinch from them now. But, it is said, according to the Egyptian Gazette (News in Brief), that, as sunset glows red upon the jagged peaks of the Valley of the Kings, a low sound, a kind of melodious humming, clearly human in origin, wafts up from the depths of Merenptah's tomb, trickling in the engulfing darkness, and then fading, as the crisp desert evening ushers in the incumbent's ancient journey.

In the night, within the locked, abandoned tomb, who can tell what dance occurs?

As for the women, and Orville Dullest, Lilith, I cannot say when they will leave. Waking from sleep, casting off chains. Flesh of my flesh, blood of my blood. But there is always a tumor, somewhere, just waiting to grow and take over. Like the lymphocytes swarming all over your blood stream, Lilith. I learned about them too. The white cells that crowd everything else out. The ALL devouring colonisers. Prognosis is better in the young. Bone marrow transplantation can work wonders. The healthy tissue pushing out the bad. Order against brutal chaos. It has been ever thus, for me. Jesse, at least, is a better controller than Mordecai. Still awaiting, with infinite patience, the coming of his Messiah: always lingering but always at the threshold. Just beyond the horizon, peace and quiet...

And does your rebellion die so easily, Mo-says, in a crowd of dust, the growing clamour of the mass? The grand moment of fusion deferred? The hypochondriac's fear of the cure?

These are my sorry fates, Lilith. The baggage in my gut. Life will eventually kill us. Why should you or I be spared?

Talk to me, Mo-says, tell me you still hope.

Under the zamzam tree, Lilith, just don't forget me, I'll be there. Like Felix the Cat, I have to keep on walking. Tramp tramp tramp, down 125th Street. Just one foot after the other. The boots, I won't forget the boots, Lilith, the gift of the New York Welfare Department. The Office of Human Resources. Onwards, onwards. The seas closing up behind me. Past African Hair Braiding, Mama's Kitchen, Mandela Quick Stop, the Apollo. All the bright and sassy dreams. The crowds dwindling, as I reach the junction. Turning north, up Adam Clayton Powell. Past the State Office Building and the parking stalls, Fayva Shoes, Sylvia's Soul Food, the Mandingo Restaurant. The taste of our roots: Eating the earth, and drinking the sky. *Kalan zaman.* A long long time ago. Allah School in Mecca Academy: Purity in knowledge, clarity of mind. Christ Temple House of Prayer. Crossing over, against the blaring horns. Shiloh Baptist Church. Newkirk Funeral Home. The Jamaican Hot Pot Restaurant. Harlem Hospital. Small's Paradise Club. The waiters there used to do the Charleston while balancing trays of drinks on their fingertips. The crazy blues that set weary feet to tap dance. Around the corner, on 137th, the Mother A.M.E. Zion Church, founded two hundred years ago to help the slaves run to freedom. And they are still running.

Strivers Row. Ghosts of old elegance and desires. Past Cindy's Restaurant and Smiley's Kitchen, up the forlorn 140's. The Seventh Avenue Mennonite Church: Do You Believe This - The Resurrection? Up, past Thelma's Lounge, and the abandoned, ruined houses of 148th Street, the roofs blasted and open to the sky, the blown out window frames blackened, deepforest jungle weeds weaving over the garbage floor, drug-wide eyes peeping out the undergrowth. Hide, boys and girls, hide from the reaper. Unlike the NYPD, he'll stick his long nose in anywheres.

On, past the Esplanade Gardens, the Harlem River Houses, into Macombs Place and around 154th Street and up on to the Macombs Dam Bridge. Ahead, the Bronx, the High Bridge Houses, Yankee Stadium, Penn Central Freight Terminal. Never ending stations.

And if I look back, what shall I see?

I shall not turn, but will proceed, onwards, across the iron span over the Harlem River Drive, across the Harlem River. The glutinous waters flowing sluggishly. No boatman waiting to ferry me to the other shore.

An old woman, bent on a stick, hobbles towards me, half way across the bridge, under the rusted struts, amid the gasping vehicles and fumes. The cup rattles with its meagre contents. Spare a little change madam? Just a small gesture of help for a Man whose only sin, after all, is to be. Just the old flesh and blood. Nothing special, but a small speck of the divine. Any contribution gratefully received. A dime or a nickel will do.

A pause, a groan, the rustle of old clothes, an aged hand reaching into a dusty pocket, somewhere in a tattered grey coat. Thrusting, scrabbling, searching. A sigh. Chink, chink, chunk. The clearing of a clogged throat. Bleary eyes looking out of wrinkled flesh. Asking a question, but not expecting an answer.

Clink.

A quarter. Two bits.

Thank you very much, mam -

God will bless you now -

Have a nice day...

And as, by one and one, leaves drift away
In autumn, till the bough from which they fall,
Sees the earth strewn with all its brave array.
So from the bank there, one by one, drop all
Adam's ill seed, when signalled off the mark,
As drops the falcon to the falconer's call.
Away they're borne across the waters dark,
And ere they land that side the stream, anon,
Fresh troops this side come flocking to embark.

- Dante Allighieri.

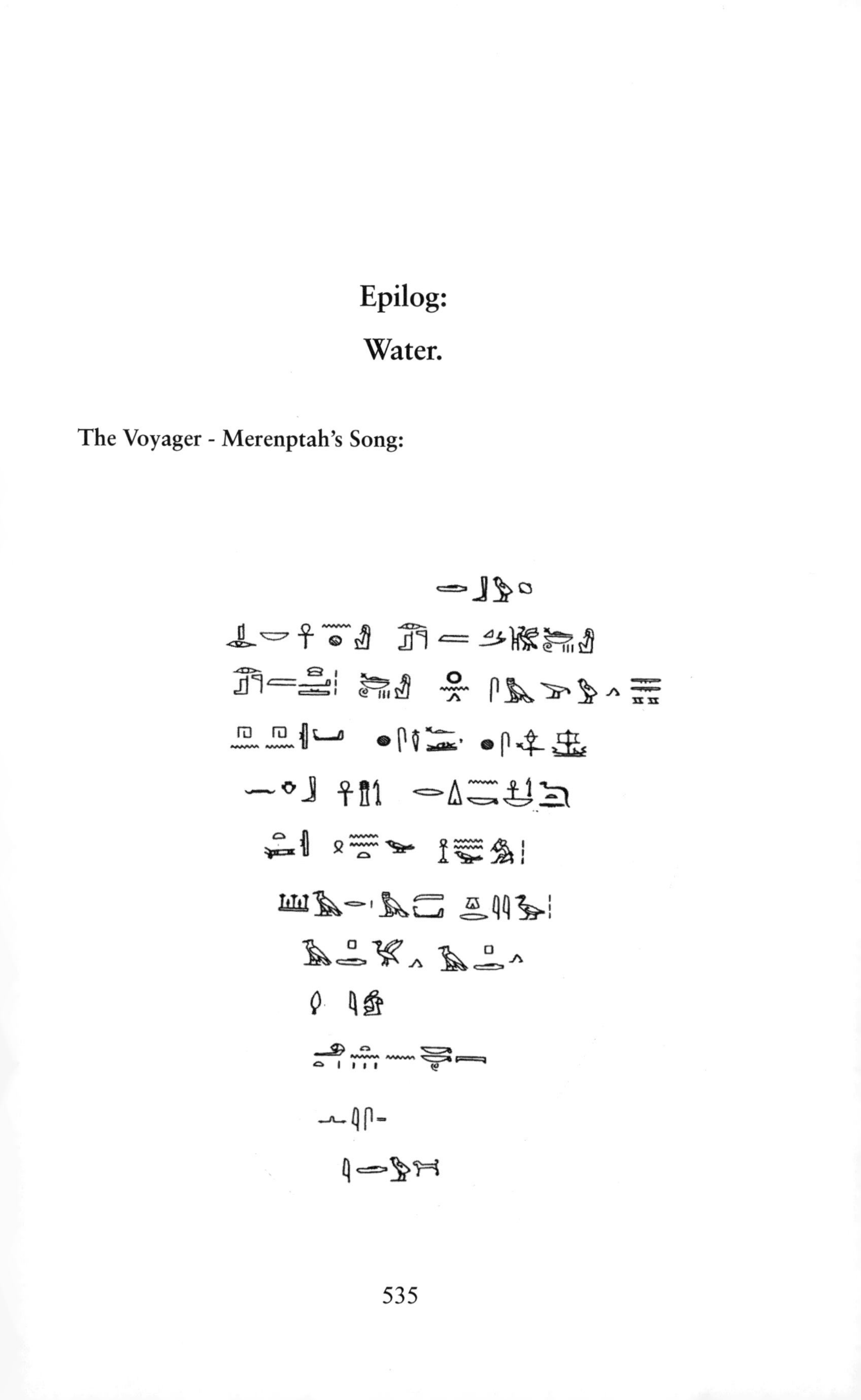

Epilog:

Water.

The Voyager - Merenptah's Song:

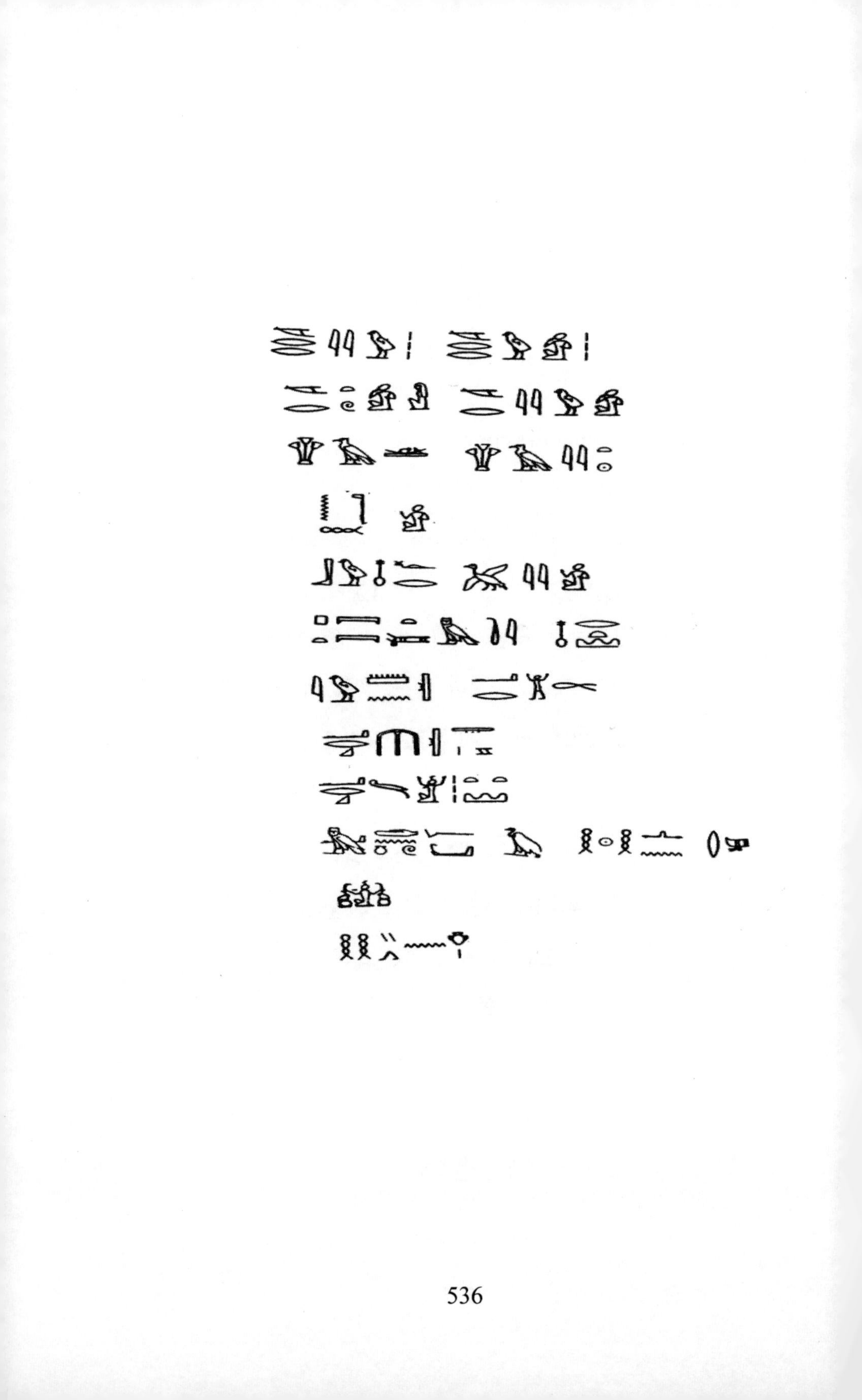

This book is dedicated to the memory of Dr. Saundra Shepherd, pediatrician, of New York City, who died well before her time of a rare lung disease, having moved like a tornado through the life of her friends.

New York - London, 1993-2001

The Author:

Simon Louvish was born in Glasgow, Scotland, in 1947, and lived in the state of Israel from 1949 to 1968. He attended the London School of Film Technique, made documentary films on South Africa, Greece and Israel between 1969 and 1974, and has published both fiction and non-fiction. He teaches part-time at the London Film School, and continues to scribe for a living. He is married and resides somewhere in London.